The Short Story

The Short Story
An Introductory Anthology

Second Edition

Robert A. Rees
University of California, Los Angeles

Barry Menikoff
University of Hawaii

Little, Brown and Company
Boston Toronto

LIBRARY OF CONGRESS CATALOG CARD NO. 74-15171

FIRST PRINTING

PUBLISHED SIMULTANEOUSLY IN CANADA
BY LITTLE, BROWN & COMPANY (CANADA) LIMITED

PRINTED IN THE UNITED STATES OF AMERICA

Acknowledgments

Sherwood Anderson. "I'm a Fool," from *The Triumph of the Egg*. Copyright © 1921 by B. W. Huebsch, renewed 1948 by Eleanor C. Anderson. Reprinted by permission of Harold Ober Associates Incorporated.

Jorge Luis Borges. "The Circular Ruins," from the book *The Aleph and Other Stories: 1939–1969* by Jorge Luis Borges. Ed. and trans. by Norman Thomas di Giovanni. Eng. trans. copyright © 1968, 1969, 1970 by Emece Editores, S. A., and Norman Thomas di Giovanni. Copyright © 1970 by Jorge Luis Borges, Adolfo Bioy-Casares, and Norman Thomas di Giovanni. Published by E. P. Dutton & Co, Inc., and used with their permission.

Hortense Calisher. "The Scream on 57th Street," in *Tale for the Mirror*. Copyright © 1952, 1953, 1954, 1955, 1956, 1957, 1960, 1962, by Hortense Calisher. Reprinted by permission of Candida Donadio Associates, Incorporated.

Dorothy Canfield. "Sex Education," copyright, 1945, by Dorothy Canfield Fisher. Reprinted from *Four Square* by Dorothy Canfield by permission of Harcourt Brace Jovanovich, Inc.

Truman Capote. "A Christmas Memory," copyright © 1956 by Truman Capote. Reprinted from *Selected Writings of Truman Capote*, by permission of Random House, Inc.

Anton Chekhov. "On the Road," reprinted with permission of Macmillan Publishing Co., Inc., and Chatto and Windus, Ltd., from *The Chorus Girl and Other Stories*, translated from the Russian by Constance Garnett. Copyright 1920 by Macmillan Publishing Co., Inc., renewed 1948 by David Garnett.

William Faulkner. "Pantaloon in Black," copyright 1940 and renewed 1968 by Estelle Faulkner and Jill Faulkner Summers. Copyright 1942 by William Faulkner. Reprinted from *Go Down, Moses*, by William Faulkner, by permission of Random House, Inc. "Spotted Horses," copyright 1931 and renewed 1959 by William Faulkner. Reprinted by permission of Random House, Inc. An expanded version of this story appears in *The Hamlet*, by William Faulkner.

F. Scott Fitzgerald. "Babylon Revisited," reprinted with the permission of Charles Scribner's Sons from *Taps at Reveille* by F. Scott Fitzgerald. Copyright 1931 The Curtis Publishing Company.

Ernest J. Gaines. "The Sky Is Gray," from *Bloodline* by Ernest J. Gaines. Copyright © 1963, 1964, 1968 by Ernest J. Gaines. Originally appeared in *Negro Digest*. Reprinted by permission of The Dial Press.

Nadine Gordimer. "The Defeated," reprinted from the author's collection *The Soft Voice of the Serpent and Other Stories*, © 1952 by Nadine Gordimer, by permission of the Shirley Collier Agency.

Graham Greene. "Cheap in August," from *May We Borrow Your Husband? and Other Comedies of the Sexual Life* by Graham Greene. Copyright © 1964 by Graham Greene. Reprinted by permission of The Viking Press Inc. and Lawrence Pollinger Limited.

Ernest Hemingway. "Hills Like White Elephants," reprinted with permission of Charles Scribner's Sons from *Men Without Women* by Ernest Hemingway. Copyright 1927 by Charles Scribner's Sons.

James Joyce. "Counterparts" and "Eveline," from *Dubliners* by James Joyce. Copyright © 1967 by The Estate of James Joyce. All rights reserved. Reprinted by permission of The Viking Press Inc.

Ervin D. Krause. "The Metal Sky," reprinted by permission from *Prairie Schooner*. Copyright © 1961 by the University of Nebraska Press.

D. H. Lawrence. "The Horse Dealer's Daughter," from *The Complete Short Stories of D. H. Lawrence*, Volume II, copyright 1922 by Thomas B. Seltzer, Inc., renewed 1950 by Frieda Lawrence. "The Rocking-Horse Winner," from *The Complete Short Stories of D. H. Lawrence*, Volume III, copyright 1933 by the Estate of D. H. Lawrence, © 1961 by Angelo Ravagli and C. Montague Weekley, Executors of the Estate of Frieda Lawrence Ravagli. Both stories reprinted by permission of The Viking Press Inc.

Gabriel García-Márquez. "The Handsomest Drowned Man in the World," from *Leaf Storm and Other Stories* by Gabriel García-Márquez, translated from the Spanish by Gregory Rabassa. English translation Copyright © 1971 by Harper & Row, Publishers, Inc. Reprinted by permission of the publishers.

Yukio Mishima. "Patriotism," from *Death in Midsummer and Other Stories*. Copyright © 1966 by New Directions Publishing Corporation. Reprinted by permission of New Directions Publishing Corporation.

Ezekiel Mphahlele. "Mrs. Plum" from *In Corner B* by Ezekiel Mphahlele. Copyright © 1967 by Ezekiel Mphahlele. Published by the East African Publishing House.

Vladimir Nabokov. "The Vane Sisters," from *Tyrants Destroyed and Other Stories* by Vladimir Nabokov, copyright © 1975 by Vladimir Nabokov, is reprinted by permission of the author and McGraw-Hill Book Company.

Abioseh Nicol. "The Truly Married Woman," reprinted by permission from *The Truly Married Woman and Other Stories* by Abioseh Nicol. © Oxford University Press 1965.

Joyce Carol Oates. "Where Are You Going, Where Have You Been?" reprinted from *The Wheel of Love* by Joyce Carol Oates by permission of the publisher, Vanguard Press, Inc. Copyright © 1970, 1969, 1968, 1967, 1966, 1965, by Joyce Carol Oates.

Flannery O'Connor. "Everything That Rises Must Converge" and "Revelation," reprinted with the permission of Farrar, Straus & Giroux, Inc., from *Everything That Rises Must Converge* by Flannery O'Connor, copyright © 1961, 1964, 1965 by the Estate of Mary Flannery O'Connor.

Grace Paley. "A Conversation with My Father," reprinted with permission of Farrar, Straus & Giroux from *Enormous Changes at the Last Minute* by Grace Paley, copyright © 1960, 1962, 1965, 1967, 1968, 1971, 1972, 1974 by Grace Paley.

Katherine Anne Porter. "Flowering Judas," copyright, 1930, 1958, by Katherine Anne Porter. Reprinted from her volume, *Flowering Judas and Other Stories* by permission of Harcourt Brace Jovanovich, Inc.

Jean-Paul Sartre. "The Room," from *The Wall*, translated by Lloyd Alexander. Copyright 1948 by New Directions Publishing Corporation. Reprinted by permission of New Directions Publishing Corporation.

Peter Taylor. "Dean of Men," reprinted with the permission of Farrar, Straus & Giroux, Inc., from *The Collected Stories of Peter Taylor*, copyright © 1969 by Peter Taylor.

Dylan Thomas. "One Warm Saturday," from *Portrait of the Artist as a Young Dog*. Copyright 1940 by New Directions Publishing Corporation. Reprinted by permission of New Directions Publishing Corporation, J. M. Dent & Sons Ltd., and the Trustees for the Copyrights of the late Dylan Thomas.

Eudora Welty. "A Visit of Charity," from *A Curtain of Green and Other Stories*, copyright, 1941, 1969, by Eudora Welty. Reprinted by permission of Harcourt Brace Jovanovich, Inc.

Richard Wright. "The Man Who Lived Underground," copyright © 1944 by L. B. Fischer Publishing Corporation. Reprinted by permission of Paul R. Reynolds, Inc., 599 Fifth Avenue, New York, N.Y. 10017.

PREFACE

Speaking about the manner in which an artist transforms his experience into fiction, Mark Schorer remarks that "technique is the only means he has of discovering, exploring, developing his subject, of conveying its meaning, and finally, of evaluating it." Technique means more than the dutiful observation of the customary elements of fiction — plot, setting, character, point of view, and tone. The term emphasizes the idea of method — the way in which a fictional element functions in the narrative. In "Flowering Judas," for example, the stiff and ascetic figure of Laura — her character — serves Katherine Anne Porter as a technique for revealing the unconscious betrayal of the self that springs from pride and vanity. The dismal streets of Dublin — the setting — provide James Joyce a means for discovering the despair and defeat that binds the soul of each Dubliner. The limited vision of the narrator — her point of view —

enables Flannery O'Connor to convey the terror that inheres in Mrs. Turpin's revelation. These details are merely indicative; through an understanding of technique we develop a sensitivity to an artist's themes, a heightened perception of his private vision of the world.

In order to explore the methods of fiction we have arranged the stories according to those techniques that they seem to emphasize. Hortense Calisher's "The Scream on 57th Street" would fit quite nicely under point of view, but the story provides such a vivid portrait of a modern faceless city—and the terror of that city—that we include it under setting. It ought to be obvious, however, that no story should be treated as if it were the exclusive property of a single dominant technique. The structure of any narrative depends on the seamless joining of all the elements to form an artistic unity, a composition in which plot appears indivisible from setting, setting from character, character from point of view—and in which all contribute to the composition's tone. For this reason our introduction to point of view draws on Nabokov's study of character in "The Vane Sisters," and our comment on setting makes use of Hemingway's masterpiece of tone, "Hills Like White Elephants." The appreciation of artistic unity comes after we have accustomed ourselves to the habit of analysis, a habit that sharpens and refines our perception and sensitivity. It enables us to penetrate the world of the artist and affords us the pleasures of the imagination.

NOTE TO THE SECOND EDITION

Each act of revision is an act of revaluation — and this major revision of *The Short Story* is no exception. For those who are familiar with the first edition, a glance at the present table of contents might seem startling. Rather than limiting ourselves to England and America, we have here drawn on writers from Africa (Abioseh Nicol, Nadine Gordimer), Europe (Anton Chekhov, Jean-Paul Sartre), Asia (Yukio Mishima), and South America (Gabriel García-Márquez, Jorge Luis Borges). Additionally, we have included a greater number of contemporary authors — those who are well known (Joyce Carol Oates, Hortense Calisher, Ernest Gaines, Peter Taylor) and some who are less well known (Ervin Krause, Ezekiel Mphahlele). We have also substituted a number of different stories by writers whom we have retained from the first edition, partly because one needs a respite from certain classic tales ("Young Goodman Brown" has been replaced by "My Kinsman, Major Molineux") and partly from the desire to draw attention to a little-known but equally brilliant tale by a major writer (Graham Greene's "Cheap in August" assumes the place earlier occupied by "The Destructors"). But the main purpose behind all these revisions is to provide students with a catholic and cosmopolitan range of literary experiences. We have not revised the text at the expense of our governing principle — that the quality of the stories is the basic criterion for their selection. Indeed, working with the text in the classroom, attending to the criticism and comments of our colleagues, we are more than ever convinced that highly wrought stories are durable products, that they are the surest introduction to the art of fiction.

We would be negligent if we did not thank Charles Christensen, Little, Brown's able editor, for his patience and his persistence throughout the preparation of this second edition.

CONTENTS

PLOT

POINT OF VIEW

TONE

STORIES FOR FURTHER STUDY 467

PLOT

The first question asked in relation to any story is usually not "Where does it take place?" "Who are the major characters?" "Who tells the story?" or "What kinds of images and symbols does the author use?" The first question invariably is "What's it about?" by which is meant "Tell me the plot." The answers to the other questions are important, but they are important only after we know what happens in a story. The plot is the frame of the story into which we place everything else. Only when the plot is clear to us can we move on to a consideration of other aspects of the story. As Eudora Welty says, "Plots are . . . indeed what we see with. What's seen is what we're interested in."

There have been a number of attempts to explain what plot is from Aristotle to the present, but perhaps none is simpler and more direct than E. M. Forster's:

We have defined a story as a narrative of events arranged in their time sequence. A plot is also a narrative of events, the emphasis falling on causality. "The king died and then the queen died," is a story. "The king died and then the queen died of grief," is a plot. The time-sequence is preserved, but the sense of causality overshadows it. Or again: "The queen died, no one knew why, until it was discovered that it was through grief at the death of the king." This is plot with a mystery in it.

Obviously we are more interested in a story in which causality exists. In Forster's first example we are not very curious about the king or the queen. Perhaps, we might speculate, they died of old age or the plague, but we know nothing about them except that they died. In the second narrative both the king and the queen begin to take on interest. The king must have been noble to have inspired such grief at his passing, and the queen must have loved him greatly to have died of grief. We might be drawn to speculate that they loved each other very much and wonder what will happen to their kingdom now that they are gone. It is thus that plot draws us into a story.

In the development of the short story during the past century and a half plot has undergone some significant changes. In the nineteenth century most stories followed a rather conventional formula with an *introduction* or *exposition*, wherein the dramatic situation is presented from which the action is to arise; a *complication* or *opposition*, in which the central character faces some significant trial, decision, or conflict; the *climax* or *crisis*, in which the character reaches the apex of his struggle; and the *conclusion* or *solution*, in which the opposing forces of the story are resolved.

Such a concept of plot often leads to a rather mechanical plotting of stories and to an emphasis on external action, dramatic turns, and trick endings. These can still be found in a good deal of popular fiction as well as in the majority of movies and television shows. Readers and viewers who wish simply to be entertained are usually content with stories of this nature.

Toward the end of the nineteenth century writers began experimenting with traditional forms of fiction and in so doing moved away from stories that had a definite beginning, middle, and end, and an excess of physical action, toward stories that attempted to present a more natural portrayal of life and which focused more on internal or psychological action.

This contrast is dramatized beautifully in Grace Paley's "A Conversation with My Father," in which the narrator and her father disagree as to what constitutes a good story. The father wants his daughter to write "a simple story just once more, the kind de Maupassant wrote, or Chekhov, the kind you used to write. Just recognizable people and then write down what happened to them next." The daughter, however, says she does not like to write stories that begin "'There was a woman . . . ' followed by plot, the absolute line between two points which I've always despised . . . because it takes all hope away. Everyone, real or invented, deserves the open destiny of life." The story she variously tells and the dialogue that ensues between her and her father clearly illuminate the difference between the conventional and the contemporary story.

The "open destiny of life" to which the daughter refers is another way of saying that an author is striving not so much to present a completed vision of life as a glimpse of a life in transition. All ends don't have to be tied up nicely at the story's close for the story to be believable or enjoyable. As W. H. Auden says about tragedy in "Musée des Beaux Arts":

> About suffering they were never wrong,
> The Old Masters: how well they understood
> Its human position; how it takes place
> While someone else is eating or opening a window or just
> walking dully along . . .

Or, as Flannery O'Connor has said, a good writer of fiction places us "in the middle of some human action and shows it as it is illuminated and outlined by mystery."

Whether it is traditional or modern, one way to understand plot is to see it as *movement*. No story ends where it begins. The setting may be the same, only a few minutes may have elapsed, but something has happened, and some change has taken place in the characters. Even Bartleby, in Herman Melville's story, who seems to be the same person at the end of the story that he is in the beginning—enigmatic, "motionless," "incurably forlorn"—has undergone a significant change. As the story opens he is willing to risk something by seeking employment, and at first he works vigorously. As the story progresses, however, he "prefers not to" read proof, go to the post office, carry messages, make copy, leave his employer's premises, and, finally, not to talk, to eat, or to live.

Following Forster we could say that Bartleby's withdrawal from life is the story, but to understand the plot we have to ask "Why?" What is it that motivates Bartleby, what causes his relinquishment of all hope? It is by such questions—even though we may not always find their answers or agree on what the answers are—that we explore beyond what happens in a story to how and why it happens and what it means.

The serious student, therefore, will seek for those subtleties that expand and deepen a story's meaning. To do this he must be willing to give himself completely to a story, to respond to it as fully as he can, both intellectually and emotionally. Emerson said that there is creative reading as well as creative writing. We might think of the plot as the bare bones of the story. As we give ourselves imaginatively to the artistry of the story it will come alive for us, or, as Lisel Mueller says in her poem "On Finding a Bird's Bones in the Wood":

> . . . we, who cannot escape
> imagination, swaddle
> this tiny world of bone
> in all that we have known
> of sound and motion.

Nathaniel Hawthorne *(1804–1864) was born in Salem, Massachusetts, in the home of his Puritan ancestors. After graduating from Bowdoin College in 1825, he retired to a quiet life in Salem for the next eleven years. Because his early publications*—Fanshawe *(1828),* Twice-Told Tales *(1837), and* Mosses from an Old Manse *(1846)—did not provide the financial independence he needed, from 1846 to 1849 he worked as surveyor at the Custom House in Salem. His next novels*—The Scarlet Letter *(1850),* The House of the Seven Gables *(1851), and* The Blithedale Romance *(1852)—firmly established his literary reputation. In 1853 Hawthorne was appointed United States Consul at Liverpool. His last complete novel,* The Marble Faun *(1860), was written during his stay in England and travels in Italy. From Europe he returned to Concord, Massachusetts, and died there four years later.*

My Kinsman, Major Molineux

NATHANIEL HAWTHORNE

After the kings of Great Britain had assumed the right of appointing the colonial governors, the measures of the latter seldom met with the ready and generous approbation which had been paid to those of their predecessors, under the original charters. The people looked with most jealous scrutiny to the exercise of power which did not emanate from themselves, and they usually rewarded their rulers with slender gratitude for the compliances by which, in softening their instructions from beyond the sea, they had incurred the reprehension of those who gave them. The annals of Massachusetts Bay will inform us, that of six governors in the space of about forty years from the surrender of the old charter, under James II, two imprisoned by a popular insurrection; a third, as Hutchinson inclines to believe, was driven from the province by the whizzing of a musket-ball; a fourth, in the opinion of the same historian, was hastened to his grave by continual bickerings with the House of Representatives; and the remaining two, as well as their successors, till the Revolution, were favored with few and brief intervals of peaceful sway. The inferior members of the court party, in times of high political excitement, led scarcely a more desirable life. These remarks may serve as a preface to the following adventures, which chanced upon a summer's night, not far from a hundred years ago. The reader, in order to avoid a long and dry detail of colonial affairs, is requested to dispense with an account of the train of circumstances that had caused much temporary inflammation of the popular mind.

It was near nine o'clock of a moonlight evening, when a boat crossed the ferry with a single passenger, who had obtained his conveyance at that unusual hour by the promise of an extra fare. While he stood on the landing-place, searching in either pocket for the means of fulfilling his agreement, the ferryman lifted a lantern, by the aid of which, and the newly risen moon, he took a very accurate survey of the stranger's figure. He was a youth of barely eighteen years, evidently country-bred, and now, as it should seem, upon his first visit to town. He was clad in a coarse gray coat, well worn, but in excellent repair; his under garments were durably constructed of leather, and fitted tight to a pair of serviceable and well-shaped limbs; his stockings of blue yarn were the incontrovertible work of a mother or a sister; and on his head was a three-cornered hat, which in its better days had perhaps sheltered the graver brow of the lad's father. Under his left arm was a heavy cudgel formed of an oak sapling, and retaining a part of the hardened root; and his equipment was completed by a wallet, not so abundantly stocked as to incommode the vigorous shoulders on which it hung. Brown, curly hair, well-shaped features, and bright, cheerful eyes were nature's gifts, and worth all that art could have done for his adornment.

The youth, one of whose names was Robin, finally drew from his pocket the half of a little province bill of five shillings, which, in the depreciation in that sort of currency, did but satisfy the ferryman's demand, with the surplus of a sexangular piece of parchment, valued at three pence. He then walked forward into the town, with as light a step as if his day's journey had not already exceeded thirty miles, and with as eager an eye as if he were entering London city, instead of the little metropolis of a New England colony. Before Robin had proceeded far, however, it occurred to him that he knew not whither to direct his steps; so he paused, and looked up and down the narrow street, scrutinizing the small and mean wooden buildings that were scattered on either side.

"This low hovel cannot be my kinsman's dwelling," thought he, "nor yonder old house, where the moonlight enters at the broken casement; and truly I see none hereabouts that might be worthy of him. It would have been wise to inquire my way of the ferryman, and doubtless he would have gone with me, and earned a shilling from the Major for his pains. But the next man I meet will do as well."

He resumed his walk, and was glad to perceive that the street now became wider, and the houses more respectable in their appearance. He soon discerned a figure moving on moderately in advance, and hastened his steps to overtake it. As Robin drew nigh, he saw that the passenger was a man in years, with a full periwig of gray hair, a wide-skirted coat of dark cloth, and silk stockings rolled above his knees. He carried a long and polished cane, which he struck down perpendicularly before him at every step: and at regular intervals he uttered two successive hems, of a peculiarly solemn and sepulchral intonation. Having made these observations, Robin laid hold of the skirt of the old man's coat, just when the light from the open door and windows of a barber's shop fell upon both their figures.

"Good evening to you, honored sir," said he, making a low bow, and still retaining his hold of the skirt. "I pray you tell me whereabouts is the dwelling of my kinsman, Major Molineux."

The youth's question was uttered very loudly; and one of the barbers, whose razor was descending on a well-soaped chin, and another who was dressing a Ramillies wig, left their occupations, and came to the door. The citizen, in the mean time, turned a long-favored countenance upon Robin, and answered him in a tone of excessive anger and annoyance. His two sepulchral hems, however, broke into the very center of his rebuke, with most singular effect, like a thought of the cold grave obtruding among wrathful passions.

"Let go my garment, fellow! I tell you, I know not the man you speak of. What! I have authority, I have—hem, hem—authority; and if this be the respect you show for your betters, your feet shall be brought acquainted with the stocks by daylight, tomorrow morning!"

Robin released the old man's skirt, and hastened away, pursued by an ill-mannered roar of laughter from the barber's shop. He was at first considerably surprised by the result of his question, but, being a shrewd youth, soon thought himself able to account for the mystery.

"This is some country representative," was his conclusion, "who has never seen the inside of my kinsman's door, and lacks the breeding to answer a stranger civilly. The man is old, or verily—I might be tempted to turn back and smite him on the nose. Ah, Robin, Robin! even the barber's boys laugh at you for choosing such a guide! You will be wiser in time, friend Robin."

He now became entangled in a succession of crooked and narrow streets, which crossed each other, and meandered at no great distance from the water-side. The smell of tar was obvious to his nostrils, the masts of vessels pierced the moonlight above the tops of the buildings, and the numerous signs, which Robin paused to read, informed him that he was near the center of business. But the streets were empty, the shops were closed, and lights were visible only in the second stories of a few dwelling-houses. At length, on the corner of a narrow lane, through which he was passing, he beheld the broad countenance of a British hero swinging before the door of an inn, whence proceeded the voices of many guests. The casement of one of the lower windows was thrown back, and a very thin curtain permitted Robin to distinguish a party at supper, round a well-furnished table. The fragrance of the good cheer steamed forth into the outer air, and the youth could not fail to recollect that the last remnant of his travelling stock of provision had yielded to his morning appetite, and that noon had found and left him dinnerless.

"Oh, that a parchment three-penny might give me a right to sit down at yonder table!" said Robin, with a sigh. "But the Major will make me welcome to the best of his victuals; so I will even step boldly in, and inquire my way to his dwelling."

He entered the tavern, and was guided by the murmur of voices and the fumes of tobacco to the public-room. It was a long and low apartment, with oaken walls, grown dark in the continual smoke, and a floor which was thickly sanded, but of no immaculate purity. A number of persons—the larger part of whom appeared to be mariners, or in some way connected with the sea—occupied the wooden benches, or leather-bottomed chairs, conversing on various matters, and occasionally lending their attention to some topic of general interest. Three or four little groups were draining as many bowls of punch, which the West India trade had long since made a familiar drink in the colony. Others, who had the appearance of men who lived by regular and laborious handicraft, preferred the insulated bliss of an unshared potation, and became more taciturn under its influence. Nearly all, in short, evinced a predilection for the Good Creature in some of its various shapes, for this is a vice to which, as Fast Day sermons of a hundred years ago will testify, we have a long hereditary claim. The only guests to whom Robin's sympathies inclined him were two or three sheepish countrymen, who were using the inn somewhat after the fashion of a Turkish caravansary; they had gotten themselves into the darkest corner of the room, and heedless of the Nicotian atmosphere, were supping on the bread of their own ovens, and the bacon cured in their own chimney-smoke. But though Robin felt a sort of brotherhood with these strangers, his eyes were attracted from them to a person who stood near the door, holding whispered conversation with a group of ill-dressed associates. His features were separately striking almost to grotesqueness, and the whole face left a deep impression on the memory. The forehead bulged out into a double prominence, with a vale between; the nose came boldly forth in an irregular curve, and its bridge was of more than a finger's breadth; the eyebrows were deep and shaggy, and the eyes glowed beneath them like fire in a cave.

While Robin deliberated of whom to inquire respecting his kinsman's dwelling, he was accosted by the innkeeper, a little man in a stained white apron, who had come to pay his professional welcome to the stranger. Being in the second generation from a French Protestant, he seemed to have inherited the courtesy of his parent nation; but no variety of circumstances was ever known to change his voice from the one shrill note in which he now addressed Robin.

"From the country, I presume, sir?" said he, with a profound bow. "Beg leave to congratulate you on your arrival, and trust you intend a long stay with us. Fine town here, sir, beautiful buildings, and much that may interest a stranger. May I hope for the honor of your commands in respect to supper?"

"The man sees a family likeness! the rogue has guessed that I am related to the Major!" thought Robin, who had hitherto experienced little superfluous civility.

All eyes were now turned on the country lad, standing at the door, in his worn three-cornered hat, gray coat, leather breeches, and blue yarn stockings, leaning on an oaken cudgel, and bearing a wallet on his back.

Robin replied to the courteous innkeeper, with such an assumption of confidence as befitted the Major's relative. "My honest friend," he said, "I shall make it a point to patronize your house on some occasion, when"—here he could not help lowering his voice—"when I may have more than a parchment three-pence in my pocket. My present business," continued he, speaking with lofty confidence, "is merely to inquire my way to the dwelling of my kinsman, Major Molineux."

There was a sudden and general movement in the room, which Robin interpreted as expressing the eagerness of each individual to become his guide. But the innkeeper turned his eyes to a written paper on the wall, which he read, or seemed to read, with occasional recurrences to the young man's figure.

"What have we here?" said he, breaking his speech into little dry fragments. " 'Left the house of the subscriber, bounden servant, Hezekiah Mudge,—had on, when he went away, gray coat, leather breeches, master's third-best hat. One pound currency reward to whosoever shall lodge him in any jail of the province.' Better trudge, boy; better trudge!"

Robin had begun to draw his hand towards the lighter end of the oak cudgel, but a strange hostility in every countenance induced him to relinquish his purpose of breaking the courteous innkeeper's head. As he turned to leave the room, he encountered a sneering glance from the bold-featured personage whom he had before noticed; and no sooner was he beyond the door, than he heard a general laugh, in which the innkeeper's voice might be distinguished, like the dropping of small stones into a kettle.

"Now, is it not strange," thought Robin, with his usual shrewdness,—"is it not strange that the confession of an empty pocket should outweigh the name of my kinsman, Major Molineux? Oh, if I had one of those grinning rascals in the woods, where I and my oak sapling grew up together, I would teach him that my arm is heavy though my purse be light!"

On turning the corner of the narrow lane, Robin found himself in a spacious street, with an unbroken line of lofty houses in each side, and a steepled building at the upper end, whence the ringing of a bell announced the hour of nine. The light of the moon, and the lamps from the numerous shop-windows, discovered people promenading on the pavement, and amongst them Robin had hoped to recognize his hitherto inscrutable relative. The result of his former inquiries made him unwilling to hazard another, in a scene of such publicity, and he determined to walk slowly and silently up the street, thrusting his face close to that of every elderly gentleman, in search of the Major's lineaments. In his progress, Robin encountered many gay and gallant figures. Embroidered garments of showy colors, enormous periwigs, gold-laced hats, and silver-hilted swords glided past him and dazzled his optics. Travelled youths, imitators of the European fine gentlemen of the period, trod jauntily along, half dancing to the fashionable tunes which they hummed, and making poor Robin ashamed of his quiet and natural gait. At length, after many pauses to examine the gorgeous display of goods in the shop-windows, and after suffering some rebukes for the impertinence of his scrutiny into people's faces, the Major's kinsman found himself near the steepled building, still unsuccessful in his search. As yet, however, he had seen only one side of the thronged street; so Robin crossed, and continued the same sort of inquisition down the opposite pavement, with stronger hopes than the philosopher seeking an honest man, but with no better fortune. He had arrived about midway towards the lower end, from which his course began, when he overheard the approach of some one who struck down a cane on the flag-stones at every step, uttering at regular intervals, two sepulchral hems.

"Mercy on us!" quoth Robin, recognizing the sound.

Turning a corner, which chanced to be close at his right hand, he hastened to pursue his researches in some other part of the town. His patience now was wearing low, and he seemed to feel more fatigue from his rambles since he crossed the ferry, than from his journey of several days on the other side. Hunger also pleaded loudly within him, and Robin began to balance the propriety of demanding, violently, and with lifted cudgel, the necessary guidance from the first solitary passenger whom he should meet. While a resolution to this effect was gaining strength, he entered a street of mean appearance, on either side of which a row of ill-built houses was straggling towards the harbor. The moonlight fell upon no passenger along the whole extent, but in the third domicile which Robin passed there was a half-opened door, and his keen glance detected a woman's garment within.

"My luck may be better here," said he to himself.

Accordingly, he approached the door, and beheld it shut closer as he did so; yet an open space remained, sufficing for the fair occupant to observe the stranger, without a corresponding display on her part. All that Robin could discern was a strip of scarlet petticoat, and the occasional sparkle of an eye, as if the moonbeams were trembling on some bright thing.

"Pretty mistress," for I may call her so with a good conscience, thought the shrewd youth, since I know nothing to the contrary,—"my sweet pretty mistress, will you be kind enough to tell me whereabouts I must seek the dwelling of my kinsman, Major Molineux?"

Robin's voice was plaintive and winning, and the female, seeing nothing to be shunned in the handsome country youth, thrust open the door, and came forth into the moonlight. She was a dainty little figure, with a white neck, round arms, and a slender waist, at the extremity of which her scarlet petticoat jutted out over a hoop, as if she were standing in a balloon. Moreover, her face was oval and pretty, her hair dark beneath the little cap, and her bright eyes possessed a sly freedom, which triumphed over those of Robin.

"Major Molineux dwells here," said this fair woman.

Now, her voice was the sweetest Robin had heard that night, yet he could not help doubting whether that sweet voice spoke Gospel truth. He looked up and down the mean street, and then surveyed the house before which they stood. It was a small, dark edifice of two stories, the second of which projected over the lower floor, and the front apartment had the aspect of a shop for petty commodities.

"Now, truly, I am in luck," replied Robin, cunningly, "and so indeed is my kinsman, the Major, in having so pretty a housekeeper. But I prithee trouble him to step to the door; I will deliver him a message from his friends in the country, and then go back to my lodgings at the inn."

"Nay, the Major has been abed this hour or more," said the lady of the scarlet petticoat; "and it would be to little purpose to disturb him to-night, seeing his evening draught was of the strongest. But he is a kind-hearted man, and it would be as much as my life's worth to let a kinsman of his turn away from the door. You are the good old gentleman's very picture, and I could swear that was his rainy-weather hat. Also he has garments very much resembling those leather small-clothes. But come in, I pray, for I bid you hearty welcome in his name."

So saying, the fair and hospitable dame took our hero by the hand; and the touch was light, and the force was gentleness, and though Robin read in her eyes what he did not hear in her words, yet the slender-waisted woman in the scarlet petticoat proved stronger than the athletic country youth. She had drawn his half-willing footsteps nearly to the threshold, when the opening of a door in the neighborhood startled the Major's housekeeper, and, leaving the Major's kinsman, she vanished speedily into her own domicile. A heavy yawn preceded the appearance of a man, who, like the Moonshine of Pyramus and Thisbe, carried a lantern, needlessly aiding his sister luminary in the heavens. As he walked sleepily up the street, he turned his broad, dull face on Robin, and displayed a long staff, spiked at the end.

"Home, vagabond, home!" said the watchman, in accents that seemed to fall asleep as soon as they were uttered. "Home, or we'll set you in the stocks by peep of day!"

"This is the second hint of the kind," thought Robin. "I wish they would end my difficulties, by setting me there to-night."

Nevertheless, the youth felt an instinctive antipathy towards the guardian of midnight order, which at first prevented him from asking his usual question. But just when the man was about to vanish behind the corner, Robin resolved not to lose the opportunity, and shouted lustily after him, —

"I say, friend! will you guide me to the house of my kinsman, Major Molineux?"

The watchman made no reply, but turned the corner and was gone; yet Robin seemed to hear the sound of drowsy laughter stealing along the solitary street. At that moment, also, a pleasant titter saluted him from the open window above his head; he looked up, and caught the sparkle of a saucy eye; a round arm beckoned to him, and next he heard light footsteps descending the staircase within. But Robin, being of the household of a New England clergyman, was a good youth, as well as a shrewd one; so he resisted temptation, and fled away.

He now roamed desperately, and at random, through the town, almost ready to believe that a spell was on him, like that by which a wizard of his country had once kept three pursuers wandering, a whole winter night, within twenty paces of the cottage which they sought. The streets lay before him, strange and desolate, and the lights were extinguished in almost every house. Twice, however, little parties of men, among whom Robin distinguished individuals in outlandish attire, came hurrying along; but, though on both occasions, they paused to address him, such intercourse did not at all enlighten his perplexity. They did but utter a few words in some language of which Robin knew nothing, and perceiving his inability to answer, bestowed a curse upon him in plain English and hastened away. Finally, the lad determined to knock at the door of every mansion that might appear worthy to be occupied by his kinsman, trusting that perseverance would overcome the fatality that had hitherto thwarted him. Firm in this resolve, he was passing beneath the walls of a church, which formed the corner of two streets, when, as he turned into the shade of its steeple, he encountered a bulky stranger, muffled in a cloak. The man was proceeding with the speed of earnest business, but Robin planted himself full before him, holding the oak cudgel with both hands across his body as a bar to further passage.

"Halt, honest man, and answer me a question," said he, very resolutely. "Tell me, this instant, whereabouts is the dwelling of my kinsman, Major Molineux!"

"Keep your tongue between your teeth, fool, and let me pass!" said a deep, gruff voice, which Robin partly remembered. "Let me pass, or I'll strike you to the earth!"

"No, no, neighbor!" cried Robin, flourishing his cudgel, and then thrusting its larger end close to the man's muffled face. "No, no, I'm not the fool you take me for, nor do you pass till I have an answer to my question. Whereabouts is the dwelling of my kinsman, Major Molineux?"

The stranger, instead of attempting to force his passage, stepped back into the moonlight, unmuffled his face, and stared full into that of Robin.

"Watch here an hour, and Major Molineux will pass by," said he.

Robin gazed with dismay and astonishment on the unprecedented physiognomy of the speaker. The forehead with its double prominence, the broad hooked nose, the shaggy eyebrows, and fiery eyes were those which he had noticed at the inn, but the man's complexion had undergone a singular, or, more properly, a twofold change. One side of the face blazed an intense red, while the other was black as midnight, the division line being in the broad bridge of the nose; and a mouth which seemed to extend from ear to ear was black or red, in contrast to the color of the cheek. The effect was as if two individual devils, a fiend of fire and a fiend of darkness, had united themselves to form this infernal visage. The stranger grinned in Robin's face, muffled his party-colored features, and was out of sight in a moment.

"Strange things we travellers see!" ejaculated Robin.

He seated himself, however, upon the steps of the churchdoor, resolving to wait the appointed time for his kinsman. A few moments were consumed in philosophical speculations upon the species of man who had just left him; but having settled this point shrewdly, rationally, and satisfactorily, he was compelled to look elsewhere for his amusement. And first he threw his eyes along the street. It was of more respectable appearance than most of those into which he had wandered; and the moon, creating, like the imaginative power, a beautiful strangeness in familiar objects, gave something of romance to a scene that might not have possessed it in the light of day. The irregular and often quaint architecture of the houses, some of whose roofs were broken into numerous little peaks, while others ascended, steep and narrow, into a single point, and others again were square; the pure snow-white of some of their complexions, the aged darkness of others, and the thousand sparklings, reflected from bright substances in the walls of many; these matters engaged Robin's attention for a while, and then began to grow wearisome. Next he endeavored to define the forms of distant objects, starting away, with almost ghostly indistinctness, just as his eye appeared to grasp them; and finally he took a minute survey of an edifice which stood on the opposite side of the street, directly in front of the church-door, where he was stationed. It was a large, square mansion, distinguished from its neighbors by a balcony, which rested on tall pillars, and by an elaborate Gothic window, communicating therewith.

"Perhaps this is the very house I have been seeking," thought Robin.

Then he strove to speed away the time, by listening to a murmur which swept continually along the street, yet was scarcely audible, except to an unaccustomed ear like his; it was a low, dull, dreamy sound, compounded of many noises, each of which was at too great a distance to be separately heard. Robin marvelled at this snore of a sleeping town, and marvelled more whenever its continuity was broken by now and then a distant shout, apparently loud where it originated. But altogether it was a sleep-inspiring sound, and, to shake off its drowsy influence, Robin arose, and climbed a window-frame, that he might view the interior of the church. There the moonbeams came trembling in, and fell down upon the deserted pews, and extended along the quiet aisles. A fainter yet more awful radiance was hovering around the pulpit, and one solitary ray had dared to rest upon the open page of the great Bible. Had nature, in that deep hour, become a worshipper in the house which man had builded? Or was that heavenly light the visible sanctity of the place,—visible because no earthly and impure feet were within the walls? The scene made Robin's heart shiver with a sensation of loneliness stronger than he had ever felt in the remotest depths of his native woods; so he turned away and sat down again before the door. There were graves around the church, and now an uneasy thought obtruded into Robin's breast. What if the object of his search, which had been so often and so strangely thwarted, were all the time mouldering in his shroud? What if his kinsman should glide through yonder gate, and nod and smile to him in dimly passing by?

"Oh that any breathing thing were here with me!" said Robin.

Recalling his thoughts from this uncomfortable track, he sent them over forest, hill, and stream, and attempted to imagine how that evening of ambiguity and weariness had been spent by his father's household. He pictured them assembled at the door, beneath the tree, the great old tree, which had been spared for its huge twisted trunk and venerable shade, when a thousand leafy brethren fell. There, at the going down of the summer sun, it was his father's custom to perform domestic worship, that the neighbors might come and join with him like brothers of the family, and that the wayfaring man might pause to drink at that fountain, and keep his heart pure by freshening the memory of home. Robin distinguished the seat of every individual of the little audience; he saw the good man in the midst, holding the Scriptures in the golden light that fell from the western clouds; he beheld him close the book and all rise up to pray. He heard the old thanksgivings for daily mercies, the old supplications for their continuance, to which he had so often listened in weariness, but which were now among his dear remembrances. He perceived the slight inequality of his father's voice when he came to speak of the absent one; he noted how his mother turned her face to the broad and knotted trunk; how his elder brother scorned, because the beard was rough upon his upper lip, to permit his features to be moved; how the younger sister drew down a low hanging branch before her eyes; and how the littlest one of all, whose sports had hitherto broken the decorum of the scene, understood the prayer for her playmate, and burst into clamorous grief. Then he saw them go in at the door; and when Robin would have entered also, the latch tinkled into its place, and he was excluded from his home.

"Am I here, or there?" cried Robin, starting; for all at once, when his thoughts had become visible and audible in a dream, the long, wide, solitary street shone out before him.

He aroused himself, and endeavored to fix his attention steadily upon the large edifice which he had surveyed before. But still his mind kept vibrating between fancy and reality; by turns, the pillars of the balcony lengthened into the tall, bare stems of pines, dwindled down to human figures, settled again into their true shape and size, and then commenced a new succession of changes. For a single moment, when he deemed himself awake, he could have sworn that a visage,—one which he seemed to remember, yet could not absolutely name as his kinsman's—was looking towards him from the Gothic window. A deeper sleep wrestled with and nearly overcame him, but fled at the sound of footsteps along the opposite pavement. Robin rubbed his eyes, discerned a man passing at the foot of the balcony, and addressed him in a loud, peevish, and lamentable cry.

"Hallo, friend! must I wait here all night for my kinsman, Major Molineux?"

The sleeping echoes awoke, and answered the voice; and the passenger, barely able to discern a figure sitting in the oblique shade of the steeple, traversed the street to obtain a nearer view. He was himself a gentleman in his prime, of open, intelligent, cheerful, and altogether prepossessing countenance. Perceiving a country youth, apparently homeless and without friends, he accosted him in a tone of real kindness, which had become strange to Robin's ears.

"Well, my good lad, why are you sitting here?" inquired he. "Can I be of service to you in any way?"

"I am afraid not, sir," replied Robin, despondingly; "yet I shall take it kindly, if you'll answer me a single question. I've been searching, half the night, for one Major Molineux; now, sir, is there really such a person in these parts, or am I dreaming?"

"Major Molineux! The name is not altogether strange to me," said the gentleman, smiling. "Have you any objection to telling me the nature of your business with him?"

Then Robin briefly related that his father was a clergyman, settled on a small salary, at a long distance back in the country, and that he and Major Molineux were brothers' children. The Major, having inherited riches, and acquired civil and military rank, had visited his cousin, in great pomp, a year or two before; had manifested much interest in Robin and an elder brother, and, being childless himself, had thrown out hints respecting the future establishment of one of them in life. The elder brother was destined to succeed to the farm which his father cultivated in the interval of sacred duties; it was therefore determined that Robin should profit by his kinsman's generous intentions, especially as he seemed to be rather the favorite, and was thought to possess other necessary endowments.

"For I have the name of being a shrewd youth," observed Robin, in this part of his story.

"I doubt not you deserve it," replied his new friend, good-naturedly; "but pray proceed."

"Well, sir, being nearly eighteen years old, and well grown, as you see," continued Robin, drawing himself up to his full height, "I thought it high time to begin in the world. So my mother and sister put me in handsome trim, and my father gave me half the remnant of his last year's salary, and five days ago I started for this place, to pay the Major a visit. But, would you believe it, sir! I crossed the ferry a little after dark, and have yet found nobody that would show me the way to his dwelling; only, an hour or two since, I was told to wait here, and Major Molineux would pass by."

"Can you describe the man who told you this?" inquired the gentleman.

"Oh, he was a very ill-favored fellow, sir," replied Robin, "with two great bumps on his forehead, a hook nose, fiery eyes; and, what struck me as the strangest, his face was of two different colors. Do you happen to know such a man, sir?"

"Not intimately," answered the stranger, "but I chanced to meet him a little time previous to your stopping me. I believe you may trust his word, and that the Major will very shortly pass through this street. In the mean time, as I have a singular curiosity to witness your meeting, I will sit down here upon the steps and bear you company."

He seated himself accordingly, and soon engaged his companion in animated discourse. It was but of brief continuance, however, for a noise of shouting, which had long been remotely audible, drew so much nearer that Robin inquired its cause.

"What may be the meaning of this uproar?" asked he. "Truly, if your town be always as noisy, I shall find little sleep while I am an inhabitant."

"Why, indeed, friend Robin, there do appear to be three or four riotous fellows abroad to-night," replied the gentleman. "You must not expect all the stillness of your native woods here in our streets. But the watch will shortly be at the heels of these lads and"—

"Ay, and set them in the stocks by peep of day," interrupted Robin, recollecting his own encounter with the drowsy lantern-bearer. "But, dear sir, if I may trust my ears, an army of watchmen would never make head against such a multitude of rioters. There were at least a thousand voices went up to make that one shout."

"May not a man have several voices, Robin, as well as two complexions?" said his friend.

"Perhaps a man may; but Heaven forbid that a woman should!" responded the shrewd youth, thinking of the seductive tones of the Major's housekeeper.

The sounds of a trumpet in some neighboring street now became so evident and continual, that Robin's curiosity was strongly excited. In addition to the shouts, he heard frequent bursts from many instruments of discord, and a wild and confused laughter filled up the intervals. Robin rose from the steps, and looked wistfully towards a point whither people seemed to be hastening.

"Surely some prodigious merry-making is going on," exclaimed he. "I have laughed very little since I left home, sir, and should be sorry to lose an opportunity. Shall we step round the corner by that darkish house, and take our share of the fun?"

"Sit down again, sit down, good Robin," replied the gentleman, laying his hand on the skirt of the gray coat. "You forget that we must wait here for your kinsman; and there is reason to believe that he will pass by, in the course of a very few moments."

The near approach of the uproar had now disturbed the neighborhood; windows flew open on all sides; and many heads, in the attire of the pillow, and confused by sleep suddenly broken, were protruded to the gaze of whoever had leisure to observe them. Eager voices hailed each other from house to house, all demanding the explanation, which not a soul could give. Half-dressed men hurried towards the unknown commotion, stumbling as they went over the stone steps that thrust themselves into the narrow footwalk. The shouts, the laughter, and the tuneless bray, the antipodes of music, came onwards with increasing din, till scattered individuals, and then denser bodies, began to appear round a corner at the distance of a hundred yards.

"Will you recognize your kinsman, if he passes in this crowd?" inquired the gentleman.

"Indeed, I can't warrant it, sir; but I'll take my stand here, and keep a bright lookout," answered Robin, descending to the outer edge of the pavement.

A mighty stream of people now emptied into the street, and came rolling slowly towards the church. A single horseman wheeled the corner in the midst of them, and close behind him came a band of fearful wind-instruments, sending forth a fresher discord now that no intervening buildings kept it from the ear. Then a redder light disturbed the moonbeams, and a dense multitude of torches shone along the street, concealing, by their glare, whatever object they illiuminated. The single horseman, clad in a military dress, and bearing a drawn sword, rode onward as the leader, and, by his fierce and variegated countenance, appeared like war personified; the red of one cheek was an emblem of fire and sword; the blackness of the other betokened the mourning that attends them. In his train were wild figures in the Indian dress, and many fantastic shapes without a model, giving the whole march a visionary air, as if a dream had broken forth from some feverish brain, and were sweeping visibly through the midnight streets. A mass of people, inactive, except as applauding spectators, hemmed the procession in; and several women ran along the sidewalk, piercing the confusion of heavier sounds with their shrill voices of mirth or terror.

"The double-faced fellow has his eye upon me," muttered Robin, with an indefinite but an uncomfortable idea that he was himself to bear a part in the pageantry.

The leader turned himself in the saddle, and fixed his glance full upon the country youth, as the steed went slowly by. When Robin had freed his eyes from those fiery ones, the musicians were passing before him, and the torches were close at hand; but the unsteady brightness of the latter formed a veil which he could not penetrate. The rattling of wheels over the stones sometimes found its way to his ear, and confused traces of a human form appeared at intervals, and then melted into the vivid light. A moment more, and the leader thundered a command to halt: the trumpets vomited a horrid breath, and then held their peace; the shouts and laughter of the people died away, and there remained only a universal hum, allied to silence. Right before Robin's eyes was an uncovered cart. There the torches blazed the brightest, there the moon shone out like day, and there, in tar-and-feathery dignity, sat his kinsman, Major Molineux!

He was an elderly man, of large and majestic person, and strong, square features, betokening a steady soul; but steady as it was, his enemies had found means to shake it. His face was pale as death, and far more ghastly; the broad forehead was contracted in his agony, so that his eyebrows formed one grizzled line; his eyes were red and wild, and the foam hung white upon his quivering lip. His whole frame was agitated by a quick and continual tremor, which his pride strove to quell, even in those circumstances of overwhelming humiliation. But perhaps the bitterest pang of all was when his eyes met those of Robin; for he evidently knew him on the instant, as the youth stood witnessing the foul disgrace of a head grown gray in honor. They stared at each other in silence, and Robin's knees shook, and his hair bristled, with a mixture of pity and terror. Soon, however, a bewildering excitement began to seize upon his mind; the preceding adventures of the night, the unexpected appearance of the crowd, the torches, the confused din and the hush that followed, the spectre of his kinsman reviled by that great multitude,—all this, and, more than all, a perception of tremendous ridicule in the whole scene, affected him with a sort of mental inebriety. At that moment a voice of sluggish merriment saluted Robin's ears; he turned instinctively, and just behind the corner of the church stood the lantern-bearer, rubbing his eyes, and drowsily enjoying the lad's amazement. Then he heard a peal of laughter like the ringing of silvery bells; a woman twitched his arm, a saucy eye met his, and he saw the lady of the scarlet petticoat. A sharp, dry cachinnation appealed to his memory, and standing on tiptoe in the crowd, with his white apron over his head, he beheld the courteous little innkeeper. And lastly, there sailed over the heads of the multitude a great, broad laugh, broken in the midst by two sepulchral hems; thus, "Haw, haw, haw,—hem, hem,—haw, haw, haw, haw!"

The sound proceeded from the balcony of the opposite edifice, and thither Robin turned his eyes. In front of the Gothic window stood the old citizen, wrapped in a wide gown, his gray periwig exchanged for a nightcap, which was thrust back from his forehead, and his silk stockings hanging about his legs. He supported himself on his polished cane in a fit of convulsive merriment, which manifested itself on his solemn old features like a funny inscription on a tombstone. Then Robin seemed to hear the voices of the barbers, of the guests of the inn, and of all who had made sport of him that night. The contagion was spreading among the multitude, when all at once, it seized upon Robin, and he sent forth a shout of laughter that echoed through the street,—every man shook his sides, every man emptied his lungs, but Robin's shout was the loudest there. The cloud-spirits peeped from their silvery islands, as the congregated mirth went roaring up the sky! The Man in the Moon heard the far bellow. "Oho," quoth he, "the old earth is frolicsome to-night!"

When there was a momentary calm in that tempestuous sea of sound, the leader gave the sign, the procession resumed its march. On they went, like fiends that throng in mockery around some dead potentate, mighty no more, but majestic still in his agony. On they went, in counterfeited pomp, in senseless uproar, in frenzied merriment, trampling all on an old man's heart. On swept the tumult, and left a silent street behind.

"Well, Robin, are you dreaming?" inquired the gentleman, laying his hand on the youth's shoulder.

Robin started, and withdrew his arm from the stone post to which he had instinctively clung, as the living stream rolled by him. His cheek was somewhat pale, and his eye not quite as lively as in the earlier part of the evening.

"Will you be kind enough to show me the way to the ferry?" said he, after a moment's pause.

"You have, then, adopted a new subject of inquiry?" observed his companion, with a smile.

"Why, yes, sir," replied Robin, rather dryly. "Thanks to you, and to my other friends, I have at last met my kinsman, and he will scarce desire to see my face again. I begin to grow weary of a town life, sir. Will you show me the way to the ferry?"

"No, my good friend Robin,—not to-night, at least," said the gentleman. "Some few days hence, if you wish it, I will speed you on your journey. Or, if you prefer to remain with us, perhaps, as you are a shrewd youth, you may rise in the world without the help of your kinsman, Major Molineux."

QUESTIONS

1. How does the historical introduction to the story illuminate our reading? If the story is an allegory of the American Revolution, as some have suggested, what elements in the story correspond to historical fact? What is Hawthorne's attitude toward the Revolution?
2. What does the "double-faced" figure who leads the procession at the end of the story symbolize? Why is his face half red and half black?
3. What is Robin's relation to his family? What do you make of his dream about his family?
4. It is common to read this story as an account of a young man's initiation into adulthood. Following such a reading, discuss the part that each of the characters in the story plays in Robin's initiation.
5. Why is Robin so interested in finding his kinsman? What explains Robin's treatment of his kinsman at the end of the story? How do we regard Major Molineux?

William Faulkner *(1897–1962) was born in New Albany, Mississippi. He served as a pilot in the British Royal Air Force and spent much of the 1920's in New Orleans—sharing an apartment with Sherwood Anderson, contributing poems and articles to a local magazine, and writing a newspaper column, "Mirrors of Chartres Street." Faulkner's novels of this period*—Sartoris *(1929),* The Sound and the Fury *(1929),* As I Lay Dying *(1930)—dramatically recreate the history of northern Mississippi. Faulkner settled in the university town of Oxford, Mississippi, and after the publication of the sensational* Sanctuary *(1931) he made several trips to Hollywood for script writing.* Light in August *(1932),* Absalom, Absalom! *(1936), and the volume of stories* Go Down, Moses *(1942) are among his major works of the 1930's and 1940's. He received the Nobel Prize in 1950 and died shortly after the publication of his popular comic novel,* The Reivers.

Spotted Horses

WILLIAM FAULKNER

I

Yes, sir. Flem Snopes has filled that whole country full of spotted horses. You can hear folks running them all day and all night, whooping and hollering, and the horses running back and forth across them little wooden bridges ever now and then kind of like thunder. Here I was this morning pretty near half way to town, with the team ambling along and me setting in the buckboard about half asleep, when all of a sudden something come swurging up outen the bushes and jumped the road clean, without touching hoof to it. It flew right over my team big as a billboard and flying through the air like a hawk. It taken me thirty minutes to stop my team and untangle the harness and the buckboard and hitch them up again.

That Flem Snopes. I be dog if he ain't a case, now. One morning about ten years ago the boys was just getting settled down on Varner's porch for a little talk and tobacco, when here come Flem out from behind the counter, with his coat off and his hair all parted, like he might have been clerking for Varner for ten years already. Folks all knowed him; it was a big family of them about five miles down the bottom. That year, at least. Share-cropping. They never stayed on any place over a year. Then they would move on to another place, with the chap or maybe the twins of that year's litter. It was a regular nest of them. But Flem. The rest of them stayed tenant farmers, moving ever year, but here come Flem one day, walking out from behind Jody Varner's counter like he owned it. And he wasn't there but a year or two before folks knowed that if him and Jody was both still in that store in ten years more it would be Jody clerking for Flem Snopes. Why, that fellow could make a nickel where it wasn't but four cents to begin with. He skun me in two trades myself, and the fellow that can do that, I just hope he'll get rich before I do; that's all.

All right. So here Flem was, clerking at Varner's, making a nickel here and there and not telling nobody about it. No, sir. Folks never knowed when Flem got the better of somebody lessen the fellow he beat told it. He'd just set there in the store chair, chewing his tobacco and keeping his own business to hisself, until about a week later we'd find out it was somebody else's business he was keeping to hisself —provided the fellow he trimmed was mad enough to tell it. That's Flem.

We give him ten years to own ever thing Jody Varner had. But he never waited no ten years. I reckon you-all know that gal of Uncle Billy Varner's, the youngest one; Eula. Jody's sister. Ever Sunday ever yellow-wheeled buggy and curried riding horse in that country would be hitched to Bill Varner's fence, and the young bucks setting on the porch, swarming around Eula like bees around a honey pot. One of these here kind of big, soft-looking gals that could giggle richer than plowed new-ground. Wouldn't none of them leave before the others, and so they would set there on the porch until time to go home, with some of them with nine and ten miles to ride and then get up tomorrow and go back to the field. So they would all leave together and they would ride in a clump down to the creek ford and hitch them curried horses and yellow-wheeled buggies and get out and fight one another. Then they would get in the buggies again and go on home.

Well, one day about a year ago, one of them yellow-wheeled buggies and one of them curried saddle-horses quit this country. We heard they was heading for Texas. The next day Uncle Billy and Eula and Flem come into town in Uncle Billy's surrey, and when they come back, Flem and Eula was married. And on the next day we heard that two more of them yellow-wheeled buggies had left the country. They mought have gone to Texas, too. It's a big place.

Anyway, about a month after the wedding, Flem and Eula went to Texas, too. They was gone pretty near a year. Then one day last month, Eula come back, with a baby. We figured up, and decided that it was as well-growed a three-months-old baby as we ever see. It can already pull up on a chair. I reckon Texas makes big men quick, being a big place. Anyway, if it keeps on like it started, it'll be chewing tobacco and voting time it's eight years old.

And so last Friday here come Flem himself. He was on a wagon with another fellow. The other fellow had one of these two-gallon hats and a ivory-handled pistol and a box of gingersnaps sticking out of his hind pocket, and tied to the tail-gate of the wagon was about two dozen of them Texas ponies, hitched to one another with barbed wire. They was colored like parrots and they was quiet as doves, and ere a one of them would kill you quick as a rattlesnake. Nere a one of them had two eyes the same color, and nere a one of them had ever seen a bridle, I reckon; and when that Texas man got down offen the wagon and walked up to them to show how gentle they was, one of them cut his vest clean offen him, same as with a razor.

Flem had done already disappeared; he had went on to see his wife, I reckon, and to see if that ere baby had done gone on to the field to help Uncle Billy plow, maybe. It was the Texas man that taken the horses on to Mrs. Littlejohn's lot. He had a little trouble at first, when they come to the gate, because they hadn't never see a fence before, and when he finally got them in and taken a pair of wire cutters and unhitched them and got them into the barn and poured some shell corn into the trough, they durn nigh tore down the barn. I reckon they thought that shell corn was bugs, maybe. So he left them in the lot and he announced that the auction would begin at sunup tomorrow.

That night we was setting on Mrs. Littlejohn's porch. You-all mind the moon was nigh full that night, and we could watch them spotted varmints swirling along the fence and back and forth across the lot same as minnows in a pond. And then now and then they would all kind of huddle up against the barn and rest themselves by biting and kicking one another. We would hear a squeal, and then a set of hoofs would go Bam! against the barn, like a pistol. It sounded just like a fellow with a pistol, in a nest of cattymounts, taking his time.

II

It wasn't ere a man knowed yet if Flem owned them things or not. They just knowed one thing: that they wasn't never going to know for sho if Flem did or not, or if maybe he didn't just get on that wagon at the edge of town, for the ride or not. Even Eck Snopes didn't know, Flem's own cousin. But wasn't nobody surprised at that. We knowed that Flem would skin Eck quick as he would ere a one of us.

They was there by sunup next morning, some of them come twelve and sixteen miles, with seed-money tied up in tobacco sacks in their overalls, standing along the fence, when the Texas man come out of Mrs. Littlejohn's after breakfast and clumb onto the gate post with that ere white pistol butt sticking outen his hind pocket. He taken a new box of gingersnaps outen his pocket and bit the end offen it like a cigar and spit out the paper, and said the auction was open. And still they was coming up in wagons and a horse- and mule-back and hitching the teams across the road and coming to the fence. Flem wasn't nowhere in sight.

But he couldn't get them started. He begun to work on Eck, because Eck holp him last night to get them into the barn and feed them that shell corn. Eck got out just in time. He come outen that barn like a chip on the crest of a busted dam of water, and clumb into the wagon just in time.

He was working on Eck when Henry Armstid come up in his wagon. Eck was saying he was skeered to bid on one of them, because he might get it, and the Texas man says, "Them ponies? Them little horses?" He clumb down offen the gate post and went toward the horses. They broke and run, and him following them, kind of chirping to them, with his hand out like he was fixing to catch a fly, until he got three or four of them cornered. Then he jumped into them, and then we couldn't see nothing for a while because of the dust. It was a big cloud of it, and them blare-eyed, spotted things swoaring outen it twenty foot to a jump, in forty directions without counting up. Then the dust settled and there they was, that Texas man and the horse. He had its head twisted clean around like a owl's head. Its legs was braced and it was trembling like a new bride and groaning like a saw mill, and him holding its head wrung clean around on its neck so it was snuffing sky. "Look it over," he says, with his heels dug too and that white pistol sticking outen his pocket and his neck swole up like a spreading adder's until you could just tell what he was saying, cussing the horse and talking to us all at once: "Look him over, the fiddle-headed son of fourteen fathers. Try him, buy him; you will get the best—" Then it was all dust again, and we couldn't see nothing but spotted hide and mane, and that ere Texas man's boot-heels like a couple of walnuts on two strings, and after a while that two-gallon hat come sailing out like a fat old hen crossing a fence.

When the dust settled again, he was just getting outen the far fence corner, brushing himself off. He come and got his hat and brushed it off and come and clumb onto the gate post again. He was breathing hard. The hammer-head horse was still running round and round the lot like a merry-go-round at a fair. That was when Henry Armstid come shoving up to the gate in them patched overalls and one of them dangle-armed shirts of hisn. Hadn't nobody noticed him until then. We was all watching the Texas man and the horse. Even Mrs. Littlejohn; she had done come out and built a fire under the washpot in her back yard, and she would stand at the fence a while and then go back into the house and come out again with a arm full of wash and stand at the fence again. Well, here come Henry shoving up, and then we see Mrs. Armstid right behind him, in that ere faded wrapper and sunbonnet and them tennis shoes. "Get on back to that wagon," Henry says.

"Henry," she says.

"Here, boys," the Texas man says; "make room for missus to get up and see. Come on Henry," he says; "here's your chance to buy that saddle-horse missus has been wanting. What about ten dollars, Henry?"

"Henry," Mrs. Armstid says. She put her hand on Henry's arm. Henry knocked her hand down.

"Git on back to that wagon, like I told you," he says.

Mrs. Armstid never moved. She stood behind Henry, with her hands rolled into her dress, not looking at nothing. "He hain't no more despair than to buy one of them things," she says. "And us not five dollars ahead of the pore house, he hain't no more despair." It was the truth, too. They ain't never made more than a bare living offen that place of theirs, and them with four chaps and the very clothes they wears she earns by weaving by the firelight at night when Henry's asleep.

"Shut your mouth and git on back to that wagon," Henry says. "Do you want I taken a wagon stake to you here in the big road?"

Well, that Texas man taken one look at her. Then he begun on Eck again; like Henry wasn't even there. But Eck was skeered. "I can git me a snapping turtle or a water moccasin for nothing. I ain't going to buy none."

So the Texas man said he would give Eck a horse. "To start the auction, and because you holp me last night. If you'll start the bidding on the next horse," he says, "I'll give you that fiddle-head horse."

I wish you could have seen them, standing there with their seed-money in their pockets, watching that Texas man give Eck Snopes a live horse, all fixed to call him a fool if he taken it or not. Finally Eck says he'll take it. "Only I just starts the bidding," he says. "I don't have the buy the next one lessen I ain't overtopped." The Texas man said all right, and Eck bid a dollar on the next one, with Henry Armstid standing there with his mouth already open, watching Eck and the Texas man like a mad-dog or something. "A dollar," Eck says.

The Texas man looked at Eck. His mouth was already open too, like he had started to say something and what he was going to say had up and died on him. "A dollar?" he says. "One dollar? You mean, *one* dollar, Eck?"

"Durn it," Eck says; "two dollars, then."

Well, sir, I wish you could a seen that Texas man. He taken out that gingersnap box and held it up and looked into it, careful, like it might have been a diamond ring in it, or a spider. Then he throwed it away and wiped his face with a bandana. "Well," he says. "Well. Two dollars. Two dollars. Is your pulse all right, Eck?" he says. "Do you have ager-sweats at night, maybe?" he says. "Well," he says, "I got to take it. But are you boys going to stand there and see Eck get two horses at a dollar a head?"

That done it. I be dog if he wasn't nigh as smart as Flem Snopes. He hadn't no more than got the words outen his mouth before here was Henry Armstid, waving his hand. "Three dollars," Henry says. Mrs. Armstid tried to hold him again. He knocked her hand off, shoving up to the gate post.

"Mister," Mrs. Armstid says, "we got chaps in the house and not corn to feed the stock. We got five dollars I earned my chaps a-weaving after dark, and him snoring in the bed. And he hain't no more despair."

"Henry bids three dollars," the Texas man says. "Raise him a dollar, Eck, and the horse is yours."

"Henry," Mrs. Armstid says.

"Raise him, Eck," the Texas man says.

"Four dollars," Eck says.

"Five dollars," Henry says, shaking his fist. He shoved up right under the gate post. Mrs. Armstid was looking at the Texas man too.

"Mister," she says, "if you take that five dollars I earned my chaps a-weaving for one of them things, it'll be a curse onto you and yourn during all the time of man."

But it wasn't no stopping Henry. He had shoved up, waving his fist at the Texas man. He opened it; the money was in nickels and quarters, and one dollar bill that looked like a cow's cud. "Five dollars," he says. "And the man that raises it'll have to beat my head off, or I'll beat his'n."

"All right," the Texas man says. "Five dollars is bid. But don't you shake your hand at me."

III

It taken till nigh sundown before the last one was sold. He got them hotted up once and the bidding got to seven dollars and a quarter, but most of them went around three or four dollars, him setting on the gate post and picking the horses out one at a time by mouth-word, and Mrs. Littlejohn pumping up and down at the tub and stopping and coming to the fence for a while and going back to the tub again. She had done got done too, and the wash was hung on the line in the back yard, and we could smell supper cooking. Finally they was all sold; he swapped the last two and the wagon for a buckboard.

We was all kind of tired, but Henry looked more like a mad-dog than ever. When he bought, Mrs. Armstid had went back to the wagon, setting in it behind them two rabbit-sized, bone-pore mules, and the wagon itself looking like it would fall all to pieces soon as the mules moved. Henry hadn't even waited to pull it outen the road; it was still in the middle of the road and her setting in it, not looking at nothing, ever since this morning.

Henry was right up against the gate. He went up to the Texas man. "I bought a horse and I paid cash," Henry says. "And yet you expect me to stand around here until they are all sold before I can get my horse. I'm going to take my horse outen that lot."

The Texas man looked at Henry. He talked like he might have been asking for a cup of coffee at the table. "Take your horse," he says.

Then Henry quit looking at the Texas man. He begun to swallow, holding onto the gate. "Ain't you going to help me?" he says.

"It ain't my horse," the Texas man says.

Henry never looked at the Texas man again, he never looked at nobody. "Who'll help me catch my horse?" he says. Never nobody said nothing. "Bring the plowline," Henry says. Mrs. Armstid got outen the wagon and brought the plowline. The Texas man got down offen the post. The woman made to pass him, carrying the rope.

"Don't you go in there, missus," the Texas man says.

Henry opened the gate. He didn't look back. "Come on here," he says.

"Don't go in there, missus," the Texas man says.

Mrs. Armstid wasn't looking at nobody, neither, with her hands across her middle, holding the rope. "I reckon I better," she says. Her and Henry went into the lot. The horses broke and run. Henry and Mrs. Armstid followed.

"Get him into the corner," Henry says. They got Henry's horse cornered finally, and Henry taken the rope, but Mrs. Armstid let the horse get out. They hemmed it up again, but Mrs. Armstid let it get out again, and Henry turned and hit her with the rope. "Why didn't you head him back?" Henry says. He hit her again. "Why didn't you?" It was about that time I looked around and see Flem Snopes standing there.

It was the Texas man that done something. He moved fast for a big man. He caught the rope before Henry could hit the third time, and Henry whirled and made like he would jump at the Texas man. But he never jumped. The Texas man went and taken Henry's arm and led him outen the lot. Mrs. Armstid come behind them and the Texas man taken some money outen his pocket and he give it into Mrs. Armstid's hand. "Get him into the wagon and take him on home," the Texas man says, like he might have been telling them he enjoyed his supper.

Then here come Flem. "What's that for Buck?" Flem says.

"Thinks he bought one of them ponies," the Texas man says. "Get him on away, missus."

But Henry wouldn't go. "Give him back that money," he says. "I bought that horse and I aim to have him if I have to shoot him."

And there was Flem, standing there with his hands in his pockets, chewing, like he had just happened to be passing.

"You take your money and I take my horse," Henry says. "Give it back to him," he says to Mrs. Armstid.

"You don't own no horse of mine," the Texas man says. "Get him home, missus."

Then Henry seen Flem. "You got something to do with these horses," he says. "I bought one. Here's the money for it." He taken the bill outen Mrs. Armstid's hand. He offered it to Flem. "I bought one. Ask him. Here. Here's the money," he says, giving the bill to Flem.

When Flem taken the money, the Texas man dropped the rope he had snatched outen Henry's hand. He had done sent Eck Snopes's boy up to the store for another box of gingersnaps, and he had taken the box outen his pocket and looked into it. It was empty and he dropped it on the ground. "Mr. Snopes will have your money for you tomorrow," he says to Mrs. Armstid. "You can get it from him tomorrow. He don't own no horse. You get him into the wagon and get him on home." Mrs. Armstid went back to the wagon and got in. "Where's that ere buckboard I bought?" the Texas man says. It was after sundown then. And then Mrs. Littlejohn come out on the porch and rung the supper bell.

IV

I come on in and et supper. Mrs. Littlejohn would bring in a pan of bread or something, then she would go out to the porch a minute and come back to tell us. The Texas man had hitched his team to the buckboard he had swapped them last two horses for, and him and Flem had gone, and then she told that the rest of them that never had ropes had went back to the store with I. O. Snopes to get some ropes, and wasn't nobody at the gate but Henry Armstid, and Mrs. Armstid setting in the wagon in the road, and Eck Snopes and that boy of hisn. "I don't care how many of them fool men gets killed by them things," Mrs. Littlejohn says, "but I ain't going to let Eck Snopes take that boy into that lot again." So she went down to the gate, but she come back without the boy or Eck neither.

"It ain't no need to worry about that boy," I says. "He's charmed." He was right behind Eck last night when Eck went to help feed them.

The whole drove of them jumped clean over that boy's head and never touched him. It was Eck that touched him. Eck snatched him into the wagon and taken a rope and frailed the tar outen him.

So I had done et and went to my room and was undressing, long as I had a long trip to make next day; I was trying to sell a machine to Mrs. Bundren up past Whiteleaf; when Henry Armstid opened that gate and went in by hisself. They couldn't make him wait for the balance of them to get back with their ropes. Eck Snopes said he tried to make Henry wait, but Henry wouldn't do it. Eck said Henry walked right up to them and that when they broke, then run clean over Henry like a haymow breaking down. Eck said he snatched that boy of hisn out of the way just in time and that them things went through that gate like a creek flood and into the wagons and teams hitched side the road, busting wagon tongues and snapping harness like it was fishing-line, with Mrs. Armstid still setting in their wagon in the middle of it like something carved outen wood. Then they scattered, wild horses and tame mules and pieces of harness and single trees dangling offen them, both ways up and down the road.

"There goes ourn, paw!" Eck says his boy said. "There it goes, into Mrs. Littlejohn's house." Eck says it run right up the steps and into the house like a boarder late for supper. I reckon so. Anyway, I was in my room, in my underclothes, with one sock on and one sock in my hand, leaning out the window when the commotion busted out, when I heard something run into the melodeon in the hall; it sounded like a railroad engine. Then the door to my room come sailing in like when you throw a tin bucket top into the wind and I looked over my shoulder and see something that looked like a fourteen-foot pinwheel a-blaring its eyes at me. It had to blare them fast, because I was already done jumped out the window.

I reckon it was anxious, too. I reckon it hadn't never seen barbed wire or shell corn before, but I know it hadn't never seen underclothes before, or maybe it was a sewing-machine agent it hadn't never seen. Anyway, it swirled and turned to run back up the hall and outen the house, when it met Eck Snopes and that boy just coming in, carrying a rope. It swirled again and run down the hall and out the back door just in time to meet Mrs. Littlejohn. She had just gathered up the clothes she had washed, and she was coming onto the back porch with an armful of washing in one hand and a scrubbing-board in the other, when the horse skidded up to her, trying to stop and swirl again. It never taken Mrs. Littlejohn no time a-tall.

"Git outen here, you son," she says. She hit it across the face with the scrubbing-board; that ere scrubbing-board split as neat as ere a axe could have done it, and when the horse swirled to run back up the hall, she hit it again with what was left of the scrubbing-board, not on the head this time. "And stay out," she says.

Eck and that boy was half-way down the hall by this time. I reckon that horse looked like a pinwheel to Eck too. "Git to hell outen here, Ad!" Eck says. Only there wasn't time. Eck dropped flat on his face, but the boy never moved. The boy was about a yard tall maybe, in overhalls just like Eck's; that horse swoared over his head without touching a hair. I saw that, because I was just coming back up the front step, still carrying that ere sock and still in my underclothes, when the horse come onto the porch again. It taken one look at me and swirled again and run to the end of the porch and jumped the banisters and the lot fence like a hen-hawk and lit in the lot running and went out the gate again and jumped eight or ten upsidedown wagons and went on down the road. It was a full moon then. Mrs. Armstid was still setting in the wagon like she had done been carved outen wood and left there and forgot.

That horse. It ain't never missed a lick. It was going about forty miles an hour when it come to the bridge over the creek. It would have had a clear road, but it so happened that Vernon Tull was already using the bridge when it got there. He was coming back from town; he hadn't heard about the auction; him and his wife and three daughters and Mrs. Tull's aunt, all setting in chairs in the wagon bed, and all asleep, including the mules. They waked up when the horse hit the bridge one time, but Tull said the first he knew was when the mules tried to turn the wagon around in the middle of the bridge and he seen that spotted varmint run right twixt the mules and run up the wagon tongue like a squirrel. He said he just had time to hit it across the face with his whip-stock because about that time the mules turned the wagon around on that ere one-way bridge and that horse clumb across onto the bridge again and went on, with Vernon standing up in the wagon and kicking at it.

Tull said the mules turned in the harness and clumb back into the wagon too, with Tull trying to beat them out again, with the reins wrapped around his wrist. After that he says all he seen was overturned chairs and women-folks' legs and white drawers shining in the moonlight, and his mules and that spotted horse going on up the road like a ghost.

The mules jerked Tull outen the wagon and drug him a spell on the bridge before the reins broke. They thought at first that he was dead, and while they was kneeling around him, picking the bridge splinters outen him, here come Eck and that boy, still carrying the rope. They was running and breathing a little hard. "Where'd he go?" Eck says.

V

I went back and got my pants and shirt and shoes on just in time to go and help get Henry Armstid outen the trash in the lot. I be dog if he didn't look like he was dead, with his head hanging back and his teeth showing in the moonlight, and a little rim of white under his eyelids. We could still hear them horses, here and there; hadn't none of them got more than four-five miles away yet, not knowing the country, I reckon. So we could hear them and folks yelling now and then: "Whooey. Head him!"

We toted Henry into Mrs. Littlejohn's. She was in the hall; she hadn't put down the armful of clothes. She taken one look at us, and she laid down the busted scrubbing-board and taken up the lamp and opened a empty door. "Bring him in here," she says.

We toted him in and laid him on the bed. Mrs. Littlejohn set the lamp on the dresser, still carrying the clothes. "I'll declare, you men," she says. Our shadows was way up the wall, tiptoeing too; we could hear ourselves breathing. "Better get his wife," Mrs. Littlejohn says. She went out, carrying the clothes.

"I reckon we had," Quick says. "Go get her, somebody."

"Whyn't you go?" Winterbottom says.

"Let Ernest git her," Durley says. "He lives neighbors with them."

Ernest went to fetch her. I be dog if Henry didn't look like he was dead. Mrs. Littlejohn come back, with a kettle and some towels. She went to work on Henry, and then Mrs. Armstid and Ernest come in. Mrs. Armstid come to the foot of the bed and stood there, with her hands rolled into her apron, watching what Mrs. Littlejohn was doing, I reckon.

"You men get outen the way," Mrs. Littlejohn says. "Git outside," she says. "See if you can't find something else to play with that will kill some more of you."

"Is he dead?" Winterbottom says.

"It ain't your fault if he ain't," Mrs. Littlejohn says. "Go tell Will Varner to come up here. I reckon a man ain't so different from a mule, come long come short. Except maybe a mule's got more sense."

We went to get Uncle Billy. It was a full moon. We could hear them, now and then, four miles away: "Whooey. Head him." The country was full of them, one on every wooden bridge in the land, running across it like thunder: "Whooey. There he goes. Head him."

We hadn't got far before Henry begun to scream. I reckon Mrs. Littlejohn's water had brung him to; anyway, he wasn't dead. We went on to Uncle Billy's. The house was dark. We called to him, and after a while the window opened and Uncle Billy put his head out, peart as a peckerwood, listening. "Are they still trying to catch them durn rabbits?" he says.

He come down, with his britches on over his nightshirt and his suspenders dangling, carrying his horse-doctoring grip. "Yes, sir," he says, cocking his head like a woodpecker; "they're still a-trying."

We could hear Henry before we reached Mrs. Littlejohn's. He was going Ah-Ah-Ah. We stopped in the yard. Uncle Billy went on in. We could hear Henry. We stood in the yard hearing them on the bridges, this-a-way and that: "Whooey. Whooey."

"Eck Snopes ought to caught hisn," Ernest says.

"Looks like he ought," Winterbottom said.

Henry was going Ah-Ah-Ah steady in the house; then he begun to scream. "Uncle Billy's started," Quick says. We looked into the hall. We could see the light where the door was. Then Mrs. Littlejohn come out.

"Will needs some help," she says. "You, Ernest, you'll do." Ernest went into the house.

"Hear them?" Quick said. "That one was on Four Mile bridge." We could hear them; it sounded like thunder a long way off; it didn't last long.

"Whooey."

We could hear Henry: "Ah-Ah-Ah-Ah-Ah."

"They are both started now," Winterbottom says. "Ernest too."

That was early in the night. Which was a good thing, because it taken a long night for folks to chase them things right and for Henry to lay there and holler, being as Uncle Billy never had none of this chloryfoam to set Henry's leg with. So it was considerate in Flem to get them started early. And what do you reckon Flem's comment was?

That's right. Nothing. Because he wasn't there. Hadn't nobody see him since that Texas man left.

VI

That was Saturday night. I reckon Mrs. Armstid got home about daylight, to see about the chaps. I don't know where they thought her and Henry was. But lucky the oldest one was a gal, about twelve, big enough to take care of the little ones. Which she did for the next two days. Mrs. Armstid would nurse Henry all night and work in the kitchen for hern and Henry's keep, and in the afternoon she would drive home (it was about four miles) to see to the chaps. She would cook up a pot of victuals and leave it on the stove, and the gal would bar the house and keep the little ones quiet. I would hear Mrs. Littlejohn and Mrs. Armstid talking in the kitchen. "How are the chaps making out?" Mrs. Littlejohn says.

"All right," Mrs. Armstid says.

"Don't they git skeered at night?" Mrs. Littlejohn says.

"Ina May bars the door when I leave," Mrs. Armstid says. "She's got the axe in bed with her. I reckon she can make out."

I reckon they did. And I reckon Mrs. Armstid was waiting for Flem to come back to town; hadn't nobody seen him until this morning; to get her money the Texas man said Flem was keeping for her. Sho. I reckon she was.

Anyway, I heard Mrs. Armstid and Mrs. Littlejohn talking in the kitchen this morning while I was eating breakfast. Mrs. Littlejohn had just told Mrs. Armstid that Flem was in town. "You can ask him for that five dollars," Mrs. Littlejohn says.

"You reckon he'll give it to me?" Mrs. Armstid says.

Mrs. Littlejohn was washing dishes, washing them like a man, like they was made out of iron. "No," she says. "But asking him won't do no hurt. It might shame him. I don't reckon it will, but it might."

"If he wouldn't give it back, it ain't no use to ask," Mrs. Armstid says.

"Suit yourself," Mrs. Littlejohn says. "It's your money."

I could hear the dishes.

"Do you reckon he might give it back to me?" Mrs. Armstid says. "That Texas man said he would. He said I could get it from Mr. Snopes later."

"Then go and ask him for it," Mrs. Littlejohn says.

I could hear the dishes.

"He won't give it back to me," Mrs. Armstid says.

"All right," Mrs. Littlejohn says. "Don't ask him for it, then."

I could hear the dishes; Mrs. Armstid was helping. "You don't reckon he would, do you?" she says. Mrs. Littlejohn never said nothing. It sounded like she was throwing the dishes at one another. "Maybe I better go and talk to Henry about it," Mrs. Armstid says.

"I would," Mrs. Littlejohn says. I be dog if it didn't sound like she had two plates in her hands, beating them together. "Then Henry can buy another five-dollar horse with it. Maybe he'll buy one next time that will out and out kill him. If I thought that, I'd give you back the money, myself."

"I reckon I better talk to him first," Mrs.Armstid said. Then it sounded like Mrs. Littlejohn taken up all the dishes and throwed them at the cook-stove, and I come away.

That was this morning. I had been up to Bundren's and back, and I thought that things would have kind of settled down. So after breakfast, I went up to the store. And there was Flem, setting in the store chair and whittling, like he might not have ever moved since he come to clerk for Jody Varner. I. O. was leaning in the door, in his shirt sleeves and with his hair parted too, same as Flem was before he turned the clerking job over to I. O. It's a funny thing about them Snopes: they all looks alike, yet there ain't ere a two of them that claims brothers. They're always just cousins, like Flem and Eck and Flem and I. O. Eck was there too, squatting against the wall, him and that boy, eating cheese and crackers outen a sack; they told me that Eck hadn't been home a-tall. And that Lon Quick hadn't got back to town, even. He followed his horse clean down to Samson's Bridge, with a wagon and a camp outfit. Eck finally caught one of hisn. It run into a blind lane at Freeman's and Eck and the boy taken and tied their rope across the end of the lane, about three foot high. The horse come to the end of the lane and whirled and run back without ever stopping. Eck says it never seen the rope a-tall. He says it looked just like one of these here Christmas pinwheels. "Didn't it try to run again?" I says.

"No," Eck says, eating a bite of cheese offen his knife blade. "Just kicked some."

"Kicked some?" I says.

"It broke its neck," Eck says.

Well, they was squatting there, about six of them, talking, talking at Flem; never nobody knowed yet if Flem had ere a interest in them horses or not. So finally I come right out and asked him. "Flem's done skun all of us so much," I says, "that we're proud of him. Come on, Flem," I says, "how much did you and that Texas man make offen them horses? You can tell us. Ain't nobody here but Eck that bought one of them; the others ain't got back to town yet, and Eck's your own cousin; he'll be proud to hear, too. How much did you-all make?"

They was all whittling, not looking at Flem, making like they was studying. But you could a heard a pin drop. And I. O. He had been rubbing his back up and down on the door, but he stopped now, watching Flem like a pointing dog. Flem finished cutting the sliver offen his stick. He spit across the porch, into the road. "Twarn't none of my horses," he says.

I. O. cackled, like a hen, slapping his legs with both hands. "You boys might just as well quit trying to get ahead of Flem," he said.

Well, about that time I see Mrs. Armstid come outen Mrs. Littlejohn's gate, coming up the road. I never said nothing. I says, "Well, if a man can't take care of himself in a trade, he can't blame the man that trims him."

Flem never said nothing, trimming at the stick. He hadn't seen Mrs. Armstid. "Yes, sir," I says, "a fellow like Henry Armstid ain't got nobody but hisself to blame."

"Course he ain't," I. O. says. He ain't seen her, neither. "Henry Armstid's a born fool. Always is been. If Flem hadn't a got his money, somebody else would."

We looked at Flem. He never moved. Mrs. Armstid come on up the road.

"That's right," I says. "But come to think of it, Henry never bought no horse." We looked at Flem; you could a heard a match drop. "That Texas man told her to get that five dollars back from Flem next day. I reckon Flem's done already taken that money to Mrs. Littlejohn's and give it to Mrs. Armstid."

We watched Flem. I. O. quit rubbing his back against the door again. After a while Flem raised his head and spit across the porch, into the dust. I. O. cackled, just like a hen. "Ain't he a beating fellow, now?" I. O. says.

Mrs. Armstid was getting closer, so I kept on talking, watching to see if Flem would look up and see her. But he never looked up. I went on talking about Tull, about how he was going to sue Flem, and Flem setting there, whittling his stick, not saying nothing else after he said they wasn't none of his horses.

Then I. O. happened to look around. He seen Mrs. Armstid. "Pssst!" he says. Flem looked up. "Here she comes!" I. O. says. "Go out the back. I'll tell her you done went in to town today."

But Flem never moved. He just set there, whittling, and we watched Mrs. Armstid come up onto the porch, in that ere faded sunbonnet and wrapper and them tennis shoes that made a kind of hissing noise on the porch. She come onto the porch and stopped, her hands rolled into her dress in front, not looking at nothing.

"He said Saturday," she says, "that he wouldn't sell Henry no horse. He said I could get the money from you."

Flem looked up. The knife never stopped. It went on trimming off a sliver same as if he was watching it. "He taken that money off with him when he left," Flem says.

Mrs. Armstid never looked at nothing. We never looked at her, neither, except that boy of Eck's. He had a half-et cracker in his hand, watching her, chewing.

"He said Henry hadn't bought no horse," Mrs. Armstid says. "He said for me to get the money from you today."

"I reckon he forgot about it," Flem said. "He taken that money off with him Saturday." He whittled again. I. O. kept on rubbing his back, slow. He licked his lips. After a while the woman looked up the road, where it went on up the hill, toward the graveyard. She looked up that way for a while, with that boy of Eck's watching her and I. O. rubbing his back slow against the door. Then she turned back toward the steps.

"I reckon it's time to get dinner started," she says.

"How's Henry this morning, Mrs. Armstid?" Winterbottom says.

She looked at Winterbottom; she almost stopped. "He's resting, I thank you kindly," she says.

Flem got up, outen the chair, putting his knife away. He spit across the porch. "Wait a minute, Mrs. Armstid," he says. She stopped again. She didn't look at him. Flem went on into the store, with I. O. done quit rubbing his back now, with his head craned after Flem, and Mrs. Armstid standing there with her hands rolled into her dress, not looking at nothing. A wagon come up the road and passed; it was Freeman, on the way to town. Then Flem come out again, with I. O. still watching him. Flem had one of these little striped sacks of Jody Varner's candy; I bet he still owes Jody that nickel, too. He put the sack into Mrs. Armstid's hand, like he would have put it into a hollow stump. He spit again across the porch. "A little sweetening for the chaps," he says.

"You're right kind," Mrs. Armstid says. She held the sack of candy in her hand, not looking at nothing. Eck's boy was watching the sack, the half-et cracker in his hand; he wasn't chewing now. He watched Mrs. Armstid roll the sack into her apron. "I reckon I better get on back and help with dinner," she says. She turned and went back across the porch. Flem set down in the chair again and opened his knife. He spit across the porch again, past Mrs. Armstid where she hadn't went down the steps yet. Then she went on, in that ere sunbonnet and wrapper all the same color, back down the road toward Mrs. Littlejohn's. You couldn't see her dress move, like a natural woman walking. She looked like a old snag still standing up and moving along on a high water. We watched her turn in at Mrs. Littlejohn's and go outen sight. Flem was whittling. I. O. begun to rub his back on the door. Then he begun to cackle, just like a durn hen.

"You boys might just as well quit trying," I. O. says. "You can't git ahead of Flem. You can't touch him. Ain't he a sight, now?"

I be dog if he ain't. If I had brung a herd of wild cattymounts into town and sold them to my neighbors and kinfolks, they would have lynched me. Yes, sir.

QUESTIONS

1. When asked what the spotted horses in this story symbolize, Faulkner remarked:

   As spotted horses, I don't know. They may be symbolical, but as horses, that was—they symbolized the hope, the aspiration of the masculine part of society that is capable of doing, of committing puerile folly for some geegaw that has drawn him, as juxtaposed to the cold practicality of the women whose spokesman Mrs. Littlejohn was when she said, "Them men!" or "What fools men are!" That the man even in a society where there's a constant pressure to conform can still be taken off by the chance to buy a horse for three dollars. Which to me is a good sign, I think. I hope that man can always be tolled off that way, to buy a horse for three dollars.

In light of how the story turns out and Flem's cheating of Mrs. Armstid, do you agree with Faulkner?

2. A different version of this story appears in Faulkner's novel *The Hamlet* (Book Four, "The Peasants"). Compare the two versions and discuss the differences between them. Are the plots different? Which version do you prefer?
3. What explains Flem's ability to sell horses to his fellow townsmen? They all know that Flem can't be trusted and they know the horses are essentially worthless, and yet they buy them—why?
4. The narrator uses a number of similes ("One of these here kind of big, soft-looking gals that could giggle richer than plowed new-ground"; "He had its head twisted clean around like a owl's head"; " . . . and that ere Texas man's boot-heels like a couple of walnuts on two strings"; "and one dollar bill that looked like a cow's cud"). How appropriate are these similes? How do they contribute to the sense of place? To the humor?
5. Faulkner writes in a tradition of American literature called Southwest humor. One of the conventions of Southwest humor is exaggeration. What examples of exaggeration do you find in the story?

Grace Paley (*1922-*) *was born in New York City and attended Hunter College and New York University. She has taught at Columbia and Syracuse Universities and now teaches at Sarah Lawrence, while writing wittily of contemporary problems in stories set among the varied ethnic groups and social classes of New York City. Her first collection of stories,* The Little Disturbances of Man *(1959), was reissued in 1968 and was followed by* Enormous Changes at the Last Minute *(1974). Miss Paley has received a Guggenheim fellowship and a National Council on the Arts grant.*

A Conversation with My Father

GRACE PALEY

My father is eighty-six years old and in bed. His heart, that bloody motor, is equally old and will not do certain jobs any more. It still floods his head with brainy light. But it won't let his legs carry the weight of his body around the house. Despite my metaphors, this muscle failure is not due to his old heart, he says, but to a potassium shortage. Sitting on one pillow, leaning on three, he offers last-minute advice and makes a request.

"I would like you to write a simple story just once more," he says, "the kind de Maupassant wrote, or Chekhov, the kind you used to write. Just recognizable people and then write down what happened to them next."

I say, "Yes, why not? That's possible." I want to please him, though

I don't remember writing that way. I *would* like to try to tell such a story, if he means the kind that begins: "There was a woman . . ." followed by plot, the absolute line between two points which I've always despised. Not for literary reasons, but because it takes all hope away. Everyone, real or invented, deserves the open destiny of life.

Finally I thought of a story that had been happening for a couple of years right across the street. I wrote it down, then read it aloud. "Pa," I said, "how about this? Do you mean something like this?"

Once in my time there was a woman and she had a son. They lived nicely, in a small apartment in Manhattan. This boy at about fifteen became a junkie, which is not unusual in our neighborhood. In order to maintain her close friendship with him, she became a junkie too. She said it was part of the youth culture, with which she felt very much at home. After a while, for a number of reasons, the boy gave it all up and left the city and his mother in disgust. Hopeless and alone, she grieved. We all visit her.

"O.K., Pa, that's it," I said, "an unadorned and miserable tale."

"But that's not what I mean," my father said. "You misunderstood me on purpose. You know there's a lot more to it. You know that. You left everything out. Turgenev wouldn't do that. Chekhov wouldn't do that. There are in fact Russian writers you never heard of, you don't have an inkling of, as good as anyone, who can write a plain ordinary story, who would not leave out what you have left out. I object not to facts but to people sitting in trees talking senselessly, voices from who knows where . . ."

"Forget that one, Pa, what have I left out now? In this one?"

"Her looks, for instance."

"Oh. Quite handsome, I think. Yes."

"Her hair?"

"Dark, with heavy braids, as though she were a girl or a foreigner."

"What were her parents like, her stock? That she became such a person. It's interesting, you know."

"From out of town. Professional people. The first to be divorced in their county. How's that? Enough?" I asked.

"With you, it's all a joke," he said. "What about the boy's father? Why didn't you mention him? Who was he? Or was the boy born out of wedlock?"

"Yes," I said. "He was born out of wedlock."

"For Godsakes, doesn't anyone in your stories get married? Doesn't anyone have the time to run down to City Hall before they jump into bed?"

"No," I said. "In real life, yes. But in my stories, no."

"Why do you answer me like that?"

"Oh, Pa, this is a simple story about a smart woman who came to N. Y .C. full of interest love trust excitement very up to date, and about her son, what a hard time she had in this world. Married or not, it's of small consequence."

"It is of great consequence," he said.

"O.K.," I said.

"O.K. O.K. yourself," he said, "but listen, I believe you that she's good-looking, but I don't think she was so smart."

"That's true," I said. "Actually that's the trouble with stories. People start out fantastic. You think they're extraordinary, but it turns out as the work goes along, they're just average with a good education. Sometimes the other way around, the person's kind of dumb innocent, but he outwits you and you can't even think of an ending good enough."

"What do you do then?" he asked. He had been a doctor for a couple of decades and then an artist for a couple of decades and he's still interested in details, craft, technique.

"Well, you just have to let the story lie around till some agreement can be reached between you and the stubborn hero."

"Aren't you talking silly, now?" he asked. "Start again," he said. "It so happens I'm not going out this evening. Tell the story again. See what you can do this time."

"O.K.," I said. "But it's not a five minute job." Second attempt:

Once, across the street from us, there was a fine handsome woman, our neighbor. She had a son whom she loved because she'd known him since birth (in helpless chubby infancy, and in the wrestling, hugging ages, seven to ten, as well as earlier and later). This boy, when he fell into the fist of adolescence, became a junkie. He was not a hopeless one. He was in fact hopeful, an ideologue and successful converter. With his busy brilliance, he wrote persuasive articles for his high-school newspaper. Seeking a wider audience, using important connections, he drummed into Lower Manhattan newsstand distribution a periodical called *Oh! Golden Horse!*

In order to keep him from feeling guilty (because guilt is the stony heart of nine-tenths of all clinically diagnosed cancers in America today, she said), and because she had always believed in giving bad habits room at home where one could keep an eye on them, she too became a junkie. Her kitchen was famous for a while—a center for intellectual addicts who knew what they were doing. A few felt artistic like Coleridge and others were scientific and revolutionary like Leary. Although she was often high herself, certain good mothering reflexes remained, and she saw to it that there was lots of orange juice around and honey and milk and vitamin pills. However, she never cooked anything but chili, and that no more than once a week. She explained, when we talked to her, seriously, with neighborly concern, that it was her part in the youth culture and she would rather be with the young, it was an honor, than with her own generation.

One week, while nodding through an Antonioni film, this boy was severely jabbed by the elbow of a stern and proselytizing girl, sitting beside him. She offered immediate apricots and nuts for his sugar level, spoke to him sharply, and took him home.

She had heard of him and his work and she herself published, edited, and wrote a competitive journal called *Man Does Live By Bread Alone*. In the organic heat of her continuous presence he could not help but become interested once more in his muscles, his arteries, and nerve connections. In fact he began to love them, treasure them, praise them with funny little songs in *Man Does Live . . .*

the fingers of my flesh transcend
my transcendental soul
the tightness in my shoulders end
my teeth have made me whole

To the mouth of his head (that glory of will and determination) he brought hard apples, nuts, wheat germ, and soybean oil. He said to his old friends, From now on, I guess I'll keep my wits around me. I'm going on the natch. He said he was about to begin a spiritual deep-breathing journey. How about you too, Mom? he asked kindly.

His conversion was so radiant, splendid, that neighborhood kids his age began to say that he had never been a real addict at all, only a journalist along for the smell of the story. The mother tried several times to give up what had become without her son and his friends a lonely habit. This effort only brought it to supportable levels. The boy and his girl took their electronic mimeograph and moved to the bushy edge of another borough. They were very strict. They said they would not see her again until she had been off drugs for sixty days.

At home alone in the evening, weeping, the mother read and reread the seven issues of *Oh! Golden Horse!* They seemed to her as truthful as ever. We often crossed the street to visit and console. But if we mentioned any of our children who were at college or in the hospital or dropouts at home, she would cry out, My baby! My baby! and burst into terrible, face-scarring, time-consuming tears. The End.

First my father was silent, then he said. "Number One: You have a nice sense of humor. Number Two: I see you can't tell a plain story. So don't waste time." Then he said sadly, "Number Three: I suppose that means she was alone, she was left like that, his mother. Alone. Probably sick?"

I said, "Yes."

"Poor woman. Poor girl, to be born in a time of fools, to live among fools. The end. The end. You were right to put that down. The end."

I didn't want to argue, but I had to say, "Well, it is not necessarily the end, Pa."

"Yes," he said, "what a tragedy. The end of a person."

"No, Pa," I begged him. "It doesn't have to be. She's only about forty. She could be a hundred different things in this world as time goes on. A teacher or a social worker. An ex-junkie! Sometimes it's better than having a master's in education."

"Jokes," he said. "As a writer that's your main trouble. You don't want to recognize it. Tragedy! Plain tragedy! Historical tragedy! No hope. The end."

"Oh, Pa," I said. "She could change."

"In your own life, too, you have to look it in the face." He took a couple of nitroglycerin. "Turn to five," he said, pointing to the dial on the oxygen tank. He inserted the tubes into his nostrils and breathed deep. He closed his eyes and said, "No."

I had promised the family to always let him have the last word when arguing, but in this case I had a different responsibility. That woman lives across the street. She's my knowledge and my invention. I'm sorry for her. I'm not going to leave her there in that house crying. (Actually neither would Life, which unlike me has no pity.)

Therefore: She did change. Of course her son never came home again. But right now, she's the receptionist in a storefront community clinic in the East Village. Most of the customers are young people, some old friends. The head doctor has said to her, "If we only had three people in this clinic with your experiences . . ."

"The doctor said that?" My father took the oxygen tubes out of his nostrils and said, "Jokes. Jokes again."

"No, Pa, it could really happen that way, it's a funny world nowadays."

"No," he said. "Truth first. She will slide back. A person must have character. She does not."

"No, Pa," I said. "That's it. She's got a job. Forget it. She's in that storefront working."

"How long will it be?" he asked. "Tragedy! You too. When will you look it in the face?"

QUESTIONS

1. How does the daughter define good and bad plots? What does the father require of a well-plotted story? Why? Does the frame story reflect the standards of the daughter, the father, or both in its plot?
2. How does the plot of the story of the daughter and father differ from that of the story of the mother and son? The father says he prefers stories by Chekhov, de Maupassant, and Turgenev to those of modern writers. Compare this story with Chekhov's "On the Road" in STORIES FOR FURTHER STUDY. Are the father's observations correct?
3. Compare the daughter's expanded version of the story she tells with the first version. What is significant about the details she adds? Why does she make the second version humorous with an exaggerated ending?
4. What does the end of the story tell us about fictional characters as opposed to real people who live "across the street"? Is there a clear line between them?
5. How does the conflict about storytelling develop into a second difference over personality and the changes possible in life? Why do the daughter and father insist on the respective endings they have chosen for the story of the mother and son?
6. The father and daughter have very different ideas about fiction. Does this affect their relationship with one another? How would you describe that relationship?

Joyce Carol Oates *(1938–) was born in Lockport, New York, a rural area represented ironically in her fiction as Eden County. She began writing stories in high school and continued at Syracuse University where she worked on the literary magazine. Following graduate work at the University of Wisconsin, she began teaching at the University of Detroit. She now teaches at the University of Windsor in Canada. Her stories, first collected in* By the North Gate *(1963), investigate arbitrary violence and the influence of money, themes which unify all her work. Miss Oates' first novel,* With Shuddering Fall *(1964) was followed by a trilogy:* A Garden of Earthly Delights *(1967),* Expensive People *(1968), and* Them *(1969. Her most recent work includes a play,* Sunday Dinner *(1970); poetry,* Love and Its Derangements *and* Angel Fire *(1973); a number of stories, collected in* Marriages and Infidelities *(1972) and* The Wheel of Love *(1972); and a novel,* Do With Me What You Will *(1974). Miss Oates, who considers herself as "really a romantic writer in the tradition of Stendhal and Flaubert," has won a number of awards and prizes for her work, including the O. Henry Prize, a Guggenheim Fellowship, and the National Book Award for Fiction (1970).*

Where Are You Going, Where Have You Been?

JOYCE CAROL OATES

for Bob Dylan

Her name was Connie. She was fifteen and she had a quick, nervous giggling habit of craning her neck to glance into mirrors or checking other people's faces to make sure her own was all right. Her mother, who noticed everything and knew everything and who hadn't much reason any longer to look at her own face, always scolded Connie about it. "Stop gawking at yourself. Who are you? You think you're so pretty?" she would say. Connie would raise her eyebrows at these familiar old complaints and look right through her mother, into a shadowy vision of herself as she was right at the moment: she knew she was pretty and that was everything. Her mother had been pretty once too, if you could believe those old snapshots in the album, but now her looks were gone and that was why she was always after Connie.

"Why don't you keep your room clean like your sister? How've you got your hair fixed—what the hell stinks? Hair spray? You don't see your sister using that junk."

Her sister June was twenty-four and still lived at home. She was a secretary in the high school Connie attended, and if that wasn't bad enough—with her in the same building—she was so plain and chunky and steady that Connie had to hear her praised all the time by her mother and her mother's sisters. June did this, June did that, she saved money and helped clean the house and cooked and Connie couldn't do a thing, her mind was all filled with trashy daydreams. Their father was away at work most of the time and when he came home he wanted supper and he read the newspaper at supper and after supper he went to bed. He didn't bother talking much to them, but around his bent head Connie's mother kept picking at her until Connie wished her mother was dead and she herself was dead and it was all over. "She makes me want to throw up sometimes," she complained to her friends. She had a high, breathless, amused voice that made everything she said sound a little forced, whether it was sincere or not.

There was one good thing: June went places with girl friends of hers, girls who were just as plain and steady as she, and so when Connie wanted to do that her mother had no objections. The father of Connie's best girl friend drove the girls the three miles to town and left them at a shopping plaza so they could walk through the stores or go to a movie, and when he came to pick them up again at eleven he never bothered to ask what they had done.

They must have been familiar sights, walking around the shopping plaza in their shorts and flat ballerina slippers that always scuffed on the sidewalk, with charm bracelets jingling on their thin wrists; they would lean together to whisper and laugh secretly if someone passed who amused or interested them. Connie had long dark blond hair that drew anyone's eye to it, and she wore part of it pulled up on her head and puffed out and the rest of it she let fall down her back. She wore a pull-over jersey blouse that looked one way when she was at home and another way when she was away from home. Everything about her had two sides to it, one for home and one for anywhere that was not home: her walk, which could be childlike and bobbing, or languid enough to make anyone think she was hearing music in her head; her mouth, which was pale and smirking most of the time, but bright and pink on these evenings out; her laugh, which was cynical and drawling at home—"Ha, ha, very funny,"— but highpitched and nervous anywhere else, like the jingling of the charms on her bracelet.

Sometimes they did go shopping or to a movie, but sometimes they went across the highway, ducking fast across the busy road, to a drive-in restaurant where older kids hung out. The restaurant was shaped like a big bottle, though squatter than a real bottle, and on its cap was a revolving figure of a grinning boy holding a hamburger aloft. One night in midsummer they ran across, breathless with daring, and right away someone leaned out a car window and invited them over, but it was just a boy from high school they didn't like. It made them feel good to be able to ignore him. They went up through the maze of parked and cruising cars to the bright-lit, fly-infested restaurant, their faces pleased and expectant as if they were entering a sacred building that loomed up out of the night to give them what haven and blessing they yearned for. They sat at the counter and crossed their legs at the ankles, their thin shoulders rigid with excitement, and listened to the music that made everything so good: the music was always in the background, like music at a church service; it was something to depend upon.

A boy named Eddie came in to talk with them. He sat backwards on his stool, turning himself jerkily around in semicircles and then stopping and turning back again, and after a while he asked Connie if she would like something to eat. She said she would and so she tapped her friend's arm on her way out—her friend pulled her face up into a brave, droll look—and Connie said she would meet her at eleven, across the way. "I just hate to leave her like that," Connie said earnestly, but the boy said that she wouldn't be alone for long. So they went out to his car, and on the way Connie couldn't help but let her eyes wander over the windshields and faces all around her, her face gleaming with a joy that had nothing to do with Eddie or even this place; it might have been the music. She drew her shoulder up and sucked in her breath with the pure pleasure of being alive, and just at that moment she happened to glance at a face just a few feet away from hers. It was a boy with shaggy black hair, in a convertible jalopy painted gold. He stared at her and then his lips widened into a grin. Connie slit her eyes at him and turned away, but she couldn't help glancing back and there he was, still watching her. He wagged a finger and laughed and said, "Gonna get you, baby," and Connie turned away again without Eddie noticing anything.

She spent three hours with him, at the restaurant where they ate hamburgers and drank Cokes in wax cups that were always sweating, and then down an alley a mile or so away, and when he left her off at five to eleven only the movie house was still open at the plaza. Her girl friend was there, talking with a boy. When Connie came up, the two girls smiled at each other and Connie said, "How was the movie?" and the girl said, "*You* should know." They rode off with the girl's father, sleepy and pleased, and Connie couldn't help but look back at the darkened shopping plaza with its big empty parking lot and its signs that were faded and ghostly now, and over at the drive-in restaurant where cars were still circling tirelessly. She couldn't hear the music at this distance.

Next morning June asked her how the movie was and Connie said, "So-so."

She and that girl and occasionally another girl went out several times a week, and the rest of the time Connie spent around the house—it was summer vacation—getting in her mother's way and thinking, dreaming about the boys she met. But all the boys fell back and dissolved into a single face that was not even a face but an idea, a feeling, mixed up with the urgent insistent pounding of the music and the humid night air of July. Connie's mother kept dragging her back to the daylight by finding things for her to do or saying suddenly, "What's this about the Pettinger girl?"

And Connie would say nervously, "Oh, her. That dope." She always drew thick clear lines between herself and such girls, and her mother was simple and kind enough to believe it. Her mother was so simple, Connie thought, that it was maybe cruel to fool her so much. Her mother went scuffling around the house in old bedroom slippers and complained over the telephone to one sister about the other, then the other called up and the two of them complained about the third one. If June's name was mentioned her mother's tone was approving, and if Connie's name was mentioned it was disapproving. This did not really mean she disliked Connie, and actually Connie thought that her mother preferred her to June just because she was prettier, but the two of them kept up a pretense of exasperation, a sense that they were tugging and struggling over something of little value to either of them. Sometimes, over coffee, they were almost friends, but something would come up—some vexation that was like a fly buzzing suddenly around their heads—and their faces went hard with contempt.

One Sunday Connie got up at eleven—none of them bothered with church—and washed her hair so that it could dry all day long in the sun. Her parents and sister were going to a barbecue at an aunt's house and Connie said no, she wasn't interested, rolling her eyes to let her mother know just what she thought of it. "Stay home alone then," her mother said sharply. Connie sat out back in a lawn chair and watched them drive away, her father quiet and bald, hunched around so that he could back the car out, her mother with a look that was still angry and not at all softened through the windshield, and in the back seat poor old June, all dressed up as if she didn't know what a barbecue was, with all the running yelling kids and the flies. Connie sat with her eyes closed in the sun, dreaming and dazed with the warmth about her as if this were a kind of love, the caresses of love, and her mind slipped over onto thoughts of the boy she had been with the night before and how nice he had been, how sweet it always was, not the way someone like June would suppose but sweet, gentle, the way it was in movies and promised in songs; and when she opened her eyes she hardly knew where she was, the back yard ran off into weeds and a fence-like line of trees and behind it the sky was perfectly blue and still. The asbestos "ranch house" that was now three years old startled her—it looked small. She shook her head as if to get awake.

It was too hot. She went inside the house and turned on the radio to drown out the quiet. She sat on the edge of her bed, barefoot, and listened for an hour and a half, to a program called XYZ Sunday Jamboree, record after record of hard, fast, shrieking songs she sang along with, interspersed by exclamations from "Bobby King": "An' look here, you girls at Napoleon's—Son and Charley want you to pay real close attention to this song coming up!"

And Connie paid close attention herself, bathed in a glow of slow-pulsed joy that seemed to rise mysteriously out of the music itself and lay languidly about the airless little room, breathed in and breathed out with each gentle rise and fall of her chest.

After a while she heard a car coming up the drive. She sat up at once, startled, because it couldn't be her father so soon. The gravel kept crunching all the way in from the road—the driveway was long—and Connie ran to the window. It was a car she didn't know. It was an open jalopy, painted a bright gold that caught the sunlight opaquely. Her heart began to pound and her fingers snatched at her hair, checking it, and she whispered, "Christ, Christ," wondering how she looked. The car came to a stop at the side door and the horn sounded four short taps, as if this were a signal Connie knew.

She went into the kitchen and approached the door slowly, then hung out the screen door, her bare toes curling down off the step. There were two boys in the car and now she recognized the driver: he had shaggy, shabby black hair that looked crazy as a wig and he was grinning at her.

"I ain't late, am I?" he said.

"Who the hell do you think you are?" Connie said.

"Toldja I'd be out, didn't I?"

"I don't even know who you are."

She spoke sullenly, careful to show no interest or pleasure, and he spoke in a fast, bright monotone. Connie looked past him to the other boy, taking her time. He had fair brown hair, with a lock that fell onto his forehead. His sideburns gave him a fierce, embarrassed look, but so far he hadn't even bothered to glance at her. Both boys wore sunglasses. The driver's glasses were metallic and mirrored everything in miniature.

"You wanta come for a ride?" he said.

Connie smirked and let her hair fall loose over one shoulder.

Don'tcha like my car? New paint job," he said. "Hey."

"What?"

"You're cute."

She pretended to fidget, chasing flies away from the door.

"Don'tcha believe me, or what?" he said.

"Look, I don't even know who you are," Connie said in disgust.

"Hey, Ellie's got a radio, see. Mine broke down." He lifted his friend's arm and showed her the little transistor radio the boy was holding, and now Connie began to hear the music. It was the same program that was playing inside the house.

"Bobby King?" she said.

"I listen to him all the time. I think he's great."

"He's kind of great," Connie said reluctantly.

"Listen, that guy's *great*. He knows where the action is."

Connie blushed a little, because the glasses made it impossible for her to see just what this boy was looking at. She couldn't decide if she liked him or if he was a jerk, and so she dawdled in the doorway and wouldn't come down or go back inside. She said, "What's all that stuff painted on your car?"

"Can'tcha read it?" He opened the door very carefully, as if he were afraid it might fall off. He slid out just as carefully, planting his feet firmly on the ground, the tiny metallic world in his glasses slowing down like gelatine hardening and in the midst of it Connie's bright green blouse. "This here is my name, to begin with," he said. ARNOLD FRIEND was written in tarlike black letters on the side, with a drawing of a round, grinning face that reminded Connie of a pumpkin, except it wore sunglasses. "I wanta introduce myself. I'm Arnold Friend and that's my real name and I'm gonna be your friend, honey, and inside the car's Ellie Oscar, he's kinda shy." Ellie brought his transistor radio up to his shoulder and balanced it there. "Now, these numbers are a secret code, honey," Arnold Friend explained. He read off the numbers 33, 19, 17 and raised his eyebrows at her to see what she thought of that, but she didn't think much of it. The left rear fender had been smashed and around it was written, on the gleaming gold background: DONE BY CRAZY WOMAN DRIVER. Connie had to laugh at that. Arnold Friend was pleased at her laughter and looked up at her. "Around the other side's a lot more—you wanta come and see them?"

"No."

"Why not?"

"Why should I?"

"Don'tcha wanta see what's on the car? Don'tcha wanta go for a ride?"

"I don't know."

"Why not?"

"I got things to do."

"Like what?"

"Things."

He laughed as if she had said something funny. He slapped his thighs. He was standing in a strange way, leaning back against the car as if he were balancing himself. He wasn't tall, only an inch or so taller than she would be if she came down to him. Connie liked the way he was dressed, which was the way all of them dressed: tight faded jeans stuffed into black, scuffed boots, a belt that pulled his waist in and showed how lean he was, and a white pull-over shirt that was a little soiled and showed the hard small muscles of his arms and shoulders. He looked as if he probably did hard work, lifting and carrying things. Even his neck looked muscular. And his face was a familiar face, somehow; the jaw and chin and cheeks slightly darkened because he hadn't shaved for a day or two, and the nose long and hawklike, sniffing as if she were a treat he was going to gobble up and it was all a joke.

"Connie, you ain't telling the truth. This is your day set aside for a ride with me and you know it," he said, still laughing. The way he straightened and recovered from his fit of laughing showed that it had been all fake.

"How do you know what my name is?" she said suspiciously.

"It's Connie."

"Maybe and maybe not."

"I know my Connie," he said, wagging his finger. Now she remembered him even better, back at the restaurant, and her cheeks warmed at the thought of how she had sucked in her breath just at the moment she passed him—how she must have looked to him. And he had remembered her. "Ellie and I come out here especially for you," he said. "Ellie can sit in back. How about it?"

"Where?"

"Where what?"

"Where're we going?"

He looked at her. He took off the sunglasses and she saw how pale the skin around his eyes was, like holes that were not in shadow but instead in light. His eyes were like chips of broken glass that catch the light in an amiable way. He smiled. It was as if the idea of going for a ride somewhere, to someplace, was a new idea to him.

"Just for a ride, Connie sweetheart."

"I never said my name was Connie,"she said.

"But I know what it is. I know your name and all about you, lots of things," Arnold Friend said. He had not moved yet but stood still leaning back against the side of his jalopy. "I took a special interest in you, such a pretty girl, and found out all about you—like I know your parents and sister are gone somewheres and I know where and how long they're going to be gone, and I know who you were with last night, and your best girl friend's name is Betty. Right?"

He spoke in a simple lilting voice, exactly as if he were reciting the words to a song. His smile assured her that everything was fine. In the car Ellie turned up the volume on his radio and did not bother to look around at them.

"Ellie can sit in the back seat," Arnold Friend said. He indicated his friend with a casual jerk of his chin, as if Ellie did not count and she should not bother with him.

"How'd you find out all that stuff?" Connie said.

"Listen: Betty Schultz and Tony Fitch and Jimmy Pettinger and Nancy Pettinger," he said in a chant. "Raymond Stanley and Bob Hutter—"

"Do you know all those kids?"

"I know everybody."

"Look, you're kidding. You're not from around here."

"Sure."

"But—how come we never saw you before?"

"Sure you saw me before," he said. He looked down at his boots, as if he were a little offended. "You just don't remember."

"I guess I'd remember you," Connie said.

"Yeah?" He looked up at this, beaming. He was pleased. He began to mark time with the music from Ellie's radio, tapping his fists lightly together. Connie looked away from his smile to the car, which was painted so bright it almost hurt her eyes to look at it. She looked at that name, ARNOLD FRIEND. And up at the front fender was an expression that was familiar—MAN THE FLYING SAUCERS. It was an expression kids had used the year before but didn't use this year. She looked at it for a while as if the words meant something to her that she did not yet know.

"What're you thinking about? Huh?" Arnold Friend demanded. "Not worried about your hair blowing around in the car, are you?"

"No."

"Think I maybe can't drive good?"

"How do I know?"

"You're a hard girl to handle. How come?" he said. "Don't you know I'm your friend? Didn't you see me put my sign in the air when you walked by?"

"What sign?"

"My sign." And he drew an X in the air, leaning out toward her. They were maybe ten feet apart. After his hand fell back to his side the X was still in the air, almost visible. Connie let the screen door close and stood perfectly still inside it, listening to the music from her radio and the boy's blend together. She stared at Arnold Friend. He stood there so stiffly relaxed, pretending to be relaxed, with one hand idly on the door handle as if he were keeping himself up that way and had no intention of ever moving again. She recognized most things about him, the tight jeans that showed his thighs and buttocks and the greasy leather boots and the tight shirt, and even that slippery friendly smile of his, that sleepy dreamy smile that all the boys used to get across ideas they didn't want to put into words. She recognized all this and also the sing-song way he talked, slightly mocking, kidding, but serious and a little melancholy, and she recognized the way he tapped one fist against the other in homage to the perpetual music behind him. But all these things did not come together.

She said suddenly, "Hey, how old are you?"

His smiled faded. She could see then that he wasn't a kid, he was much older—thirty, maybe more. At this knowledge her heart began to pound faster.

"That's a crazy thing to ask. Can'tcha see I'm your own age?"

"Like hell you are."

"Or maybe a coupla years older. I'm eighteen."

"Eighteen?" she said doubtfully.

He grinned to reassure her and lines appeared at the corners of his mouth. His teeth were big and white. He grinned so broadly his eyes became slits and she saw how thick the lashes were, thick and black as if painted with a black tarlike material. Then, abruptly, he seemed to become embarrassed and looked over his shoulder at Ellie. "*Him*, he's crazy," he said. "Ain't he a riot? He's a nut, a real character." Ellie was still listening to the music. His sunglasses told nothing about what he was thinking. He wore a bright orange shirt unbuttoned halfway to show his chest, which was a pale, bluish chest and not muscular like Arnold Friend's. His shirt collar was turned up all around and the very tips of the collar pointed out past his chin as if they were protecting him. He was pressing the transistor radio up against his ear and sat there in a kind of daze, right in the sun.

"He's kinda strange," Connie said.

"Hey, she says you're kinda strange! Kinda strange!" Arnold Friend cried. He pounded on the car to get Ellie's attention. Ellie turned for the first time and Connie saw with shock that he wasn't a kid either—he had a fair, hairless face, cheeks reddened slightly as if the veins grew too close to the surface of his skin, the face of a forty-year-old baby. Connie felt a wave of dizziness rise in her at this sight and she stared at him as if waiting for something to change the shock of the moment, make it all right again. Ellie's lips kept shaping words, mumbling along with the words blasting in his ear.

"Maybe you two better go away," Connie said faintly.

"What? How come?" Arnold Friend cried. "We come out here to take you for a ride. It's Sunday." He had the voice of the man on the radio now. It was the same voice, Connie thought. "Don'tcha know it's Sunday all day? And honey, no matter who you were with last night, today you're with Arnold Friend and don't you forget it! Maybe you better step out here," he said, and this last was in a different voice. It was a little flatter, as if the heat was finally getting to him.

"No. I got things to do."

"Hey."

"You two better leave."

"We ain't leaving until you come with us."

"Like hell I am—"

"Connie, don't fool around with me. I mean—I mean, don't fool *around*," he said, shaking his head. He laughed incredulously. He placed his sunglasses on top of his head, carefully, as if he were indeed wearing a wig, and brought the stems down behind his ears. Connie stared at him, another wave of dizziness and fear rising in her so that for a moment he wasn't even in focus but was just a blur standing there against his gold car, and she had the idea that he had driven up the driveway all right but had come from nowhere before that and belonged nowhere and that everything about him and even about the music that was so familiar to her was only half real.

"If my father comes and sees you—"

"He ain't coming. He's at a barbecue."

"How do you know that?"

"Aunt Tillie's. Right now they're—uh—they're drinking. Sitting around," he said vaguely, squinting as if he were staring all the way to town and over Aunt Tillie's back yard. Then the vision seemed to get clear and he nodded energetically. "Yeah. Sitting around. There's your sister in a blue dress, huh? And high heels, the poor sad bitch—

nothing like you, sweetheart! And your mother's helping some fat woman with the corn, they're cleaning the corn—husking the corn—"

"What fat woman?" Connie cried.

"How do I know what fat woman, I don't know every goddamn fat woman in the world!" Arnold Friend laughed.

"Oh, that's Mrs. Hornsby. . . . Who invited her?" Connie said. She felt a little lightheaded. Her breath was coming quickly.

"She's too fat. I don't like them fat. I like them the way you are, honey," he said, smiling sleepily at her. They stared at each other for a while through the screen door. He said softly, "Now, what you're going to do is this: you're going to come out that door. You're going to sit up front with me and Ellie's going to sit in the back, the hell with Ellie, right? This isn't Ellie's date. You're my date. I'm your lover, honey."

"What? You're crazy—"

"Yes. I'm your lover. You don't know what that is but you will," he said. "I know that too. I know all about you. But look: it's real nice and you couldn't ask for nobody better than me, or more polite. I always keep my word. I'll tell you how it is, I'm always nice at first, the first time. I'll hold you so tight you won't think you have to try to get away or pretend anything because you'll know you can't. And I'll come inside you where it's all secret and you'll give in to me and you'll love me—"

"Shut up! You're crazy!" Connie said. She backed away from the door. She put her hands up against her ears as if she'd heard something terrible, something not meant for her. "People don't talk like that, you're crazy," she muttered. Her heart was almost too big now for her chest and its pumping made sweat break out all over her. She looked out to see Arnold Friend pause and then take a step toward the porch, lurching. He almost fell. But, like a clever drunken man, he managed to catch his balance. He wobbled in his high boots and grabbed hold of one of the porch posts.

"Honey?" he said. "You still listening?"

"Get the hell out of here!"

"Be nice, honey. Listen."

"I'm going to call the police—"

He wobbled again and out of the side of his mouth came a fast spat curse, an aside not meant for her to hear. But even this

"Christ!" sounded forced. Then he began to smile again. She watched this smile come, awkward as if he were smiling from inside a mask. His whole face was a mask, she thought wildly, tanned down to his throat but then running out as if he had plastered makeup on his face but had forgotten about his throat.

"Honey—? Listen, here's how it is. I always tell the truth and I promise you this: I ain't coming in that house after you."

"You better not! I'm going to call the police if you—if you don't—"

"Honey," he said, talking right through her voice, "honey. I'm not coming in there but you are coming out here. You know why?"

She was panting. The kitchen looked like a place she had never seen before, some room she had run inside but that wasn't good enough, wasn't going to help her. The kitchen window had never had a curtain, after three years, and there were dishes in the sink for her to do—probably—and if you ran your hand across the table you'd probably feel something sticky there.

"You listening, honey? Hey?"

"—going to call the police—"

"Soon as you touch the phone I don't need to keep my promise and can come inside. You won't want that."

She rushed forward and tried to lock the door. Her fingers were shaking. "But why lock it," Arnold Friend said gently, talking right into her face. "It's just a screen door. It's just nothing." One of his boots was at a strange angle, as if his foot wasn't in it. It pointed out to the left, bent at the ankle. "I mean, anybody can break through a screen door and glass and wood and iron or anything else if he needs to, anybody at all, and specially Arnold Friend. If the place got lit up with a fire, honey, you'd come runnin' out into my arms, right into my arms an' safe at home—like you knew I was your lover and'd stopped fooling around. I don't mind a nice shy girl but I don't like no fooling around." Part of those words were spoken with a slight rhythmic lilt, and Connie somehow recognized them—the echo of a song from last year, about a girl rushing into her boy friend's arms and coming home again—

Connie stood barefoot on the linoleum floor, staring at him. "What do you want?" she whispered.

"I want you," he said.

"What?"

"Seen you that night and thought, that's the one, yes sir. I never needed to look anymore."

"But my father's coming back. He's coming to get me. I had to wash my hair first— " She spoke in a dry, rapid voice, hardly raising it for him to hear.

"No, your daddy is not coming and yes, you had to wash your hair and you washed it for me. It's nice and shining and all for me. I thank you sweetheart," he said with a mock bow, but again he almost lost his balance. He had to bend and adjust his boots. Evidently his feet did not go all the way down; the boots must have been stuffed with something so that he would seem taller. Connie stared out at him and behind him at Ellie in the car, who seemed to be looking off toward Connie's right, into nothing. This Ellie said, pulling the words out of the air one after another as if he were just discovering them, "You want me to pull out the phone?"

"Shut your mouth and keep it shut," Arnold Friend said, his face red from bending over or maybe from embarrassment because Connie had seen his boots. "This ain't none of your business."

"What—what are you doing? What do you want?" Connie said. "If I call the police they'll get you, they'll arrest you— "

"Promise was not to come in unless you touch that phone, and I'll keep that promise," he said. He resumed his erect position and tried to force his shoulders back. He sounded like a hero in a movie, declaring something important. But he spoke too loudly and it was as if he were speaking to someone behind Connie. "I ain't made plans for coming in that house where I don't belong but just for you to come out to me, the way you should. Don't you know who I am?"

"You're crazy," she whispered. She backed away from the door but did not want to go into another part of the house, as if this would give him permission to come through the door. "What do you . . . you're crazy, you. . . . "

"Huh? What're you saying, honey?"

Her eyes darted everywhere in the kitchen. She could not remember what it was, this room.

"This is how it is, honey: you come out and we'll drive away, have a nice ride. But if you don't come out we're gonna wait till your people come home and then they're all going to get it."

"You want that telephone pulled out?" Ellie said. He held the radio away from his ear and grimaced, as if without the radio the air was too much for him.

"I toldja shut up, Ellie," Arnold Friend said, "you're deaf, get a hearing aid, right? Fix yourself up. This little girl's no trouble and's gonna be nice to me, so Ellie keep to yourself, this ain't your date — right? Don't hem in on me, don't hog, don't crush, don't bird dog, don't trail me," he said in a rapid, meaningless voice, as if he were running through all the expressions he'd learned but was no longer sure which of them was in style, then rushing on to new ones, making them up with his eyes closed. "Don't crawl under my fence, don't squeeze in my chipmunk hole, don't sniff my glue, suck my popsicle, keep your own greasy fingers on yourself!" He shaded his eyes and peered in at Connie, who was backed against the kitchen table. "Don't mind him, honey, he's just a creep. He's a dope. Right? I'm the boy for you and like I said, you come out of here nice like a lady and give me your hand, and nobody else gets hurt, I mean, your nice old bald-headed daddy and your mummy and your sister in her high heels. Because listen: why bring them in this?"

"Leave me alone," Connie whispered.

"Hey, you know that old woman down the road, the one with the chickens and stuff—you know her?"

"She's dead!"

"Dead? What? You know her?" Arnold Friend said.

"She's dead—"

"Don't you like her?"

"She's dead—she's—she isn't here any more—"

"But don't you like her, I mean, you got something against her? Some grudge or something?" Then his voice dipped as if he were conscious of a rudeness. He touched the sunglasses perched up on top of his head as if to make sure they were still there. "Now, you be a good girl."

"What are you going to do?"

"Just two things, or maybe three," Arnold Friend said. "But I promise it won't last long and you'll like me the way you get to like people you're close to. You will. It's all over for you here, so come on out. You don't want your people in any trouble, do you?"

She turned and bumped against a chair or something, hurting her leg, but she ran into the back room and picked up the telephone. Something roared in her ear, a tiny roaring, and she was so sick with fear that she could do nothing but listen to it—the telephone was clammy and very heavy and her fingers groped down to the dial but were too weak to touch it. She began to scream into the phone, into the roaring. She cried out, she cried for her mother, she felt her breath start jerking back and forth in her lungs as if it were something Arnold Friend was stabbing her with again and again with no tenderness. A noisy sorrowful wailing rose all about her and she was locked inside it the way she was locked inside this house.

After a while she could hear again. She was sitting on the floor with her wet back against the wall.

Arnold Friend was saying from the door, "That's a good girl. Put the phone back."

She kicked the phone away from her.

"No, honey. Pick it up. Put it back right."

She picked it up and put it back. The dial tone stopped.

"That's a good girl. Now, you come outside."

She was hollow with what had been fear but what was now just an emptiness. All that screaming had blasted it out of her. She sat, one leg cramped under her, and deep inside her brain was something like a pinpoint of light that kept going and would not let her relax. She thought, I'm not going to see my mother again. She thought, I'm not going to sleep in my bed again. Her bright green blouse was all wet.

Arnold Friend said, in a gentle-loud voice that was like a stage voice, "The place where you came from ain't there any more, and where you had in mind to go is cancelled out. This place you are now—inside your daddy's house—is nothing but a cardboard box I can knock down any time. You know that and always did know it. You hear me?"

She thought, I have got to think. I have got to know what to do.

"We'll go out to a nice field, out in the country here where it smells so nice and it's sunny," Arnold Friend said. "I'll have my arms tight around you so you won't need to try to get away and I'll show you what love is like, what it does. The hell with this house! It looks solid all right," he said. He ran his fingernail down the screen and the noise did not make Connie shiver, as it would have the day before. "Now, put your hand on your heart, honey. Feel that? That feels solid too but we know better. Be nice to me, be sweet like you can because what else is there for a girl like you but to be sweet and pretty and give in?—and get away before her people get back?"

She felt her pounding heart. Her hand seemed to enclose it. She thought for the first time in her life that it was nothing that was hers, that belonged to her, but just a pounding, living thing inside this body that wasn't really hers either.

"You don't want them to get hurt," Arnold Friend went on. "Now, get up, honey. Get up all by yourself."

She stood.

"Now, turn this way. That's right. Come over here to me.—Ellie, put that away, didn't I tell you? You dope. You miserable creepy dope," Arnold Friend said. His words were not angry but only part of an incantation. The incantation was kindly. "Now, come out through the kitchen to me, honey, and let's see a smile, try it, you're a brave, sweet little girl and now they're eating corn and hot dogs cooked to bursting over an outdoor fire, and they don't know one thing about you and never did and honey, you're better than them because not a one of them would have done this for you."

Connie felt the linoleum under her feet; it was cool. She brushed her hair back out of her eyes. Arnold Friend let go of the post tentatively and opened his arms for her, his elbows pointing in toward each other and his wrists limp, to show that this was an embarrassed embrace and a little mocking, he didn't want to make her self-conscious.

She put out her hand against the screen. She watched herself push the door slowly open as if she were back safe somewhere in the other doorway, watching this body and this head of long hair moving out into the sunlight where Arnold Friend waited.

"My sweet little blue-eyed girl," he said, in a half-sung sigh that had nothing to do with her brown eyes but was taken up just the same by the vast sunlit reaches of the land behind him and on all sides of him—so much land that Connie had never seen before and did not recognize except to know that she was going to it.

QUESTIONS

1. This story ends on a very different note from the one it begins on. Where does it turn? To what extent is Connie responsible for what happens at the end of the story? Why does Miss Oates stop the story where she does? Can you imagine what will happen next?
2. How are we to regard Arnold Friend? How do you explain his seeming clairvoyance? How can he know everything he knows? What does he mean when he says to Connie, "Don't you know who I am?" Do the images and allusions associated with him give any clues as to his real character?
3. Compare the romanticized description of love that Connie dreams about with what Arnold Friend says about love.

4. The story is dedicated to Bob Dylan. Do you see any relation between the story and any of Dylan's songs?
5. Joyce Carol Oates said in a recent interview, "It seems that I write about things that are violent and extreme, but it is always against a background of something deep and imperishable. I feel I can wade in blood, I can endure the 10,000 evil visions because there is this absolutely imperishable reality behind it." How does this statement relate to "Where Are You Going, Where Have You Been?" Do you find such a background in the story?

Abioseh Nicol *(1924–) was born in Freetown, Sierra Leone, and educated in Nigeria and his own country before attending Cambridge University. A doctor, administrator, and diplomat as well as writer, Nicol represented his country as* Ambassador *to the United Nations (1968–1971) and still continues in the diplomatic service. He holds the Independence Medal of Sierra Leone (1961) and has lectured widely on medicine and literature. Nicol, encouraged in his writing by the American poet Langston Hughes, has focused his attention on Africa's colonial past. His stories have been collected in* The Truly Married Woman *(1965) and* Two African Tales *(1965). His essays include* Africa: A Subjective View *(1964) and* Black Nationalism in Africa, 1867 *(1969).*

The Truly Married Woman

ABIOSEH NICOL

Ajayi stirred for a while and then sat up. He looked at the cheap alarm clock on the chair by his bedside. It was six-fifteen, and light outside already; the African town was slowly waking to life. The night-watchmen roused from sleep by the angry crowing of cockerels were officiously banging the locks of stores and houses to assure themselves and their employers, if near, of their efficiency. Village women were tramping through the streets to the market place with their wares, arguing and gossiping.

Ajayi sipped his cup of morning tea. It was as he liked it, weak and sugary, without milk. With an effort of will, he got up and walked to the window, and standing there he took six deep breaths. This done daily, he firmly believed, would prevent tuberculosis. He walked through his ramshackle compound to an outhouse and took a quick bath, pouring the water over his head from a tin cup with which he scooped water from a bucket.

By then Ayo had laid out his breakfast. Ayo was his wife. Not really one, he would explain to close friends, but a mistress. A good one. She had borne him three children and was now three months gone with another. They had been together for twelve years. She was a patient, handsome woman. Very dark with very white teeth and open sincere eyes. Her hair was always carefully plaited. When she first came to him—to the exasperation of her parents—he had fully intended marrying her as soon as she had shown satisfactory evidence of fertility, but he had never quite got round to it. In the first year or so she would report to him in great detail the splendor of the marriage celebrations of her friends, looking at him with hopeful eyes. He would close the matter with a tirade on the sinfulness of ostentation. She gave up after some time. Her father never spoke to her again after she had left home. Her mother visited her secretly and attended the baptismal ceremonies of all her children. The Church charged extra for illegitimate children as a deterrent; two dollars instead of fifty cents. Apart from this, there was no other great objection. Occasionally, two or three times a year, the pastor would preach violently against adultery, polygamy, and unmarried couples living together. Ajayi and Ayo were good church-people and attended regularly, but sat in different pews. After such occasions, their friends would sympathize with them and other couples in similar positions. There would be a little grumbling and the male members of the congregation would say that the trouble with the Church was that it did not stick to its business of preaching the Gospel, but meddled in people's private lives. Ajayi would indignantly absent himself from Church for a few weeks but would go back eventually because he liked singing hymns and because he knew secretly that the pastor was right.

Ayo was a good mistress. Her father was convinced she could have married a high-school teacher at least, or a pharmacist, but instead she had attached herself to a junior Government clerk. But Ayo loved Ajayi, and was happy in her own slow, private way. She cooked his meals and bore him children. In what spare time she had she either did a little petty trading, visited friends, or gossiped with Omo, the woman next door.

With his towel round his waist, Ajayi strode back to the bedroom, dried himself, and dressed quickly but carefully in his pink tussore suit. He got down the new bottle of patent medicine which one of his friends who worked in a drug store had recommended to him. Ajayi believed that to keep healthy, a man must regularly take a dose of some medicine. He read the label of this one. It listed about twenty diseased conditions of widely differing pathology which the contents of the bottle were reputed to cure if the patient persevered in its daily intake. Ajayi underlined in his own mind at least six from which he believed he either suffered or was on the threshold of suffering: dizziness, muscle pain, impotence, fever, jaundice, and paralytic tremors. Intelligence and courage caused him to skip the obviously female maladies and others such as nervous debility or bladder pains. It said on the label too that a teaspoonful should be taken three times a day. But since he only remembered to take it in the morning and in any case believed in shock treatment, he took a swig and two large gulps. The medicine was bitter and astringent. He grimaced but was satisfied. It was obviously a good and strong medicine or else it would not have been so bitter.

He went in to breakfast. He soon finished his maize porridge, fried beans, and cocoa. He then severely flogged his eldest son, a ten-year-old boy, for wetting his sleeping-mat last night. Ayo came in after the boy had fled screaming to the backyard.

"Ajayi, you flog that boy too much," she said. "He should stop wetting the floor, he is a big boy," he replied. "In any case, no one is going to instruct me on how to bring up my son." "He is mine too," Ayo said. She seldom opposed him unless she felt strongly about something. "He has not stopped wetting, although you beat him every time he does. In fact, he is doing it more and more now. Perhaps if you stopped whipping him he might get better." "Did I whip him to begin doing it?" Ajayi asked. "No." "Well, how will stopping whipping him stop him doing it?" Ajayi asked triumphantly. "Nevertheless," Ayo said, "our own countrywoman Bimbola, who has just come back from England and America studying nursing, told us in a women's group meeting that it was wrong to punish children for such things." "All right, I'll see," he said, reaching for his sun-helmet.

All that day at the office he thought about this and other matters. So Ayo had been attending women's meetings. Well, what do you know. She would be running for the Town Council next. The sly woman. Always looking so quiet and meek and then quoting modern theories from overseas doctors at him. He smiled with pride. Indeed Ayo was an asset. Perhaps it was wrong to beat the boy. He decided he would not do so again.

Towards closing-time the chief clerk sent for him. Wondering what mistake he had made that day, or on what mission he was to be sent, he hurried along to the forward office. There were three white men sitting on chairs by the chief clerk, who was an aging African dressed with severe respectability. On seeing them, Ajayi's heart started thudding. The police, he thought; heavens, what have I done?

"Mr. Ajayi, these gentlemen have enquired for you," the chief clerk said formally. "Pleased to meet you, Mr. Ajayi," the tallest said, with a smile. "We represent the World Gospel Crusading Alliance from Minnesota. My name is Jonathan Olsen." Ajayi shook hands and the other two were introduced.

"You expressed an interest in our work a year ago and we have not forgotten. We are on our way to India and we thought we would look you up personally."

It transpired that the three Crusaders were *en route* and that their ship had stopped for refuelling off the African port for a few hours. The chief clerk looked at Ajayi with new respect. Ajayi tried desperately to remember any connection with W.G.C.A. (as Olsen by then had proceeded to call it) while he made conversation with them a little haltingly. Then suddenly he remembered. Some time ago he had got hold of a magazine from his sub-tenant who worked at the United States Information Service. He had cut a coupon from it and posted it to W.G.C.A. asking for information, but really hoping that they would send illustrated Bibles free which he might give away or sell. He hoped for at least large reproductions of religious paintings which, suitably framed, would decorate his parlor or which he might paste up on his bedroom wall. But nothing had come of it and he had forgotten. Now here was W.G.C.A. as large as life. Three lives. Instantly and recklessly he invited all three and the chief clerk to come to his house for a cold drink. They all agreed.

"Mine is a humble abode," he warned them. "No abode is humble that is illumined by Christian love," Olsen replied. "His is illumined all right, I can assure you," the chief clerk remarked drily.

Olsen suggested a taxi, but Ajayi neatly blocked that by saying that the roads were bad. He had hurriedly whispered to a fellow clerk to rush home on a bicycle and tell Ayo he was coming in half an hour with white men and that she should clean up and get fruit drinks. Ayo was puzzled by the message as she firmly imagined all white men drank only whiskey and iced beer. But the messenger had said that there was a mixture of friendliness and piety in the visitors' mien, which made him suspect that they might be missionaries. Another confirmatory point was that they were walking instead of being in a car. That cleared up the anomaly in Ayo's mind and she set to work at once. Oju, now recovered from his morning disgrace, was dispatched with a basket on his head to buy soft drinks. Ayo whisked off the wall all their commercial calendars with suggestive pictures. She propped up family photographs which had fallen face downwards on the table. She removed the Wild West novels and romance magazines from the parlor and put instead an old copy of Bunyan's *Pilgrim's Progress* and a prayer book which she believed would add culture and religious force to the decorations. She remembered the wine glasses and the beer-advertising table-mats in time and put those under the sofa. She just had time to change to her Sunday frock and borrow a wedding ring from her neighbor when Ajayi and the guests arrived. The chief clerk was rather surprised at the changes in the room—which he had visited before—and in Ayo's dress and ring. But he concealed his feelings. Ayo was introduced and made a little conversation in English. This pleased Ajayi a great deal. The children had been changed too into Sunday suits, faces washed and hair brushed. Olsen was delighted and insisted on taking photographs for the Crusade journal. Ayo served drinks and then modestly retired, leaving the men to discuss serious matters. Olsen by then was talking earnestly on the imminence of Christ's Second Coming and offering Ajayi ordination into deaconship.

The visit passed off well and soon the missionaries left to catch their boat. Ajayi had been saved from holy orders by the chief clerk's timely explanation that it was strictly against Government regulations for civil servants to indulge in nonofficial organizations. To help Ajayi out of his quandary, he had even gone further and said that contravention might result in a fine or imprisonment. "Talk about colonial oppression," the youngest of the missionaries had said, gloomily.

The next day Ajayi called at the clerk's office with a carefully wrapped bottle of beer as a present for his help generally on the occasion. They discussed happily the friendliness and interest the white men had shown.

This incident and Ayo's protest against flagellation as a specific against enuresis made Ajayi very thoughtful for a week. He decided to marry Ayo. Another consideration which added weight to the thought was the snapshot Olsen took for his magazine. In some peculiar way Ajayi felt he and Ayo should marry, as millions of Americans would see their picture—Olsen had assured him of this—as "one saved and happy African family." He announced his intention of marrying her to Ayo one evening, after a particularly good meal and a satisfactory bout of belching. Ayo at once became extremely solicitous and got up looking at him with some anxiety. Was he ill? she asked. Was there anything wrong at the office? Had anyone insulted him? No, he answered, there was nothing wrong with his wanting to get married, was there? Or had she anyone else in mind? Ayo laughed, "As you will," she said; "let us get married, but do not say I forced you into it."

They discussed the wedding that night. Ajayi wanted to have a white wedding with veil and orange blossom. But Ayo with regret decided it would not be quite right. They agreed on grey. Ayo particularly wanted a corset to strap down her obvious bulge; Ajayi gave way gallantly to this feminine whim, chucking her under the chin and saying, "You women with your vanity!" But he was firm about no honeymoon. He said he could not afford the expense and that one bed was as good as another. Ayo gave way on that. They agreed, however, on a church wedding and that their children could act as bridal pages to keep the cost of clothes within the family.

That evening Ajayi, inflamed by the idea and arrangements for the wedding, pulled Ayo excitedly to him as they lay in bed. "No," said Ayo, shyly, pushing him back gently, "you mustn't. Wait until after the marriage." "Why?" said Ajayi, rather surprised, but obedient. "Because it will not somehow be right," Ayo replied seriously and determinedly.

Ayo's father unbent somewhat when he heard of the proposed marriage. He insisted, however, that Ayo move herself and all her possessions back home to his house. The children were sent to Ayo's married sister. Most of Ajayi's family were in favor of the union, except his sister, who, moved by the threat implicit in Ayo's improved social position, had advised Ajayi to see a soothsayer first. As Ayo had got wind of this through friends met at market on Saturday, she saw the soothsayer first and fixed things. When Ajayi and his sister called at night to see him, he had, after consulting oracles, pronounced future happiness, avoiding the sister's eye. The latter had restrained herself from scratching the old man's face and had accepted defeat.

The only other flaw in a felicitous situation had been Ayo's neighbor Omo, who had always on urgent occasions at short notice loaned Ayo her wedding ring. She had suddenly turned cold. Especially after Ayo had shown her the wedding presents Ajayi intended to give her. The neighbor had handled the flimsy nylon articles with a mixture of envy and rage.

"Do you mean you are going to wear these?" she had asked. "Yes," Ayo had replied simply. "But, my sister," she had protested, "you will catch cold with these. Suppose you had an accident and all those doctors lifted your clothes in hospital. They will see everything through these," "I never have accidents," Ayo answered, and added, "Ajayi says all the 'Ollywood cinema women wear these. It says so there. Look—'Trademark Hollywood.' " "These are disgraceful; they hide nothing, it is extremely fast of you to wear them," the jealous girl said, pushing them back furiously over the fence to Ayo.

"Why should I want to hide anything from my husband when we are married?" Ayo said triumphantly, moving back to her own kitchen and feeling safe in the future from the patronizing way the wedding ring had always been lent her.

The arrangements had to be made swiftly, since time and the corset ribs were both against them; Ajayi's domestic routine was also sorely tried, especially his morning cup of tea which he badly missed. He borrowed heavily from a moneylender to pay the dowry and for the music, dancing, and feasting, and for dresses of the same pattern which Ayo and her female relations would wear after the ceremony on the wedding day.

The engagement took place quietly, Ajayi's uncle and other relations taking a Bible and a ring to Ayo's father and asking for her hand in marriage, the day before the wedding. They took with them two small girls carrying on their heads large hollow gourds. These contained articles like pins, farthings, fruit, kola nuts, and cloth. The articles were symbolic gifts to the bride from the bridegroom, so that she might be precluded in future marital disputes from saying, "Not a pin or a farthing has the blackguard given me since we got married."

On arrival at Ayo's father's house, the small procession passed it first as if uncertain, then returned to it. This gave warning to the occupants. Ajayi's uncle then knocked several times. Voices from within shouted back and ordered him to name himself, his ancestry, and his mission. He did this. Argument and some abuse followed on either side. After his family credentials had been seriously examined, questioned, doubted, and disparaged, Ajayi's uncle started wheedling and cajoling. This went on for about half an hour to the enjoyment and mock trepidation of Ajayi's relations. He himself had remained at home, waiting. Finally, Ayo's father opened the door. Honor was satisfied and it was now supposed to be clearly evident to Ajayi's relations, in case it had not been before, that they were entering a family and household which was distinguished, difficult, and jealous of their distinction.

"What is your mission here?" Ayo's father then asked sternly.

Ajayi's uncle answered humbly:

> "We have come to pluck a red, red, rose
> That in your beautiful garden grows.
> Which never has been plucked before,
> So lovelier than any other."

"Will you be able to nurture our lovely rose well?" another of Ayo's male relations asked.

Ajayi's family party replied:

> "So well shall we nurture your rose
> 'Twill bring forth many others."

They were finally admitted; drinks were served and prayers offered. The gifts were accepted and others given in exchange. Conversation went on for about thirty minutes on every conceivable subject but the one at hand. All through this, Ayo and her sisters and some young female relations were kept hidden in an adjoining bedroom. Finally with some delicacy, Ajayi's uncle broached the subject after Ayo's father had given him an opening by asking what, apart from the honor of being entertained by himself and his family, did Ajayi's relations seek. They had heard, the latter replied, that in this very household there was a maiden chaste, beautiful, and obedient, known to all by the name of Ayo. This maiden they sought as wife for their kinsman Ajayi. Ayo's father opened the bedroom door and brought forth Ayo's sister. Was this the one? he asked, testing them. They examined her. No it was not this one they replied, this one was too short to be Ayo. Then a cousin was brought out. Was this she? No, this one is too fat, the applicants said. About ten women in all were brought out. But none was the correct one. Each was too short or too fat or too fair, as the case was, to suit the description of the maiden they sought. At this point, Ajayi's uncle slapped his thigh, as if to show that his doubts were confirmed; turning to his party, he stated that it was a good thing they had insisted on seeing for themselves the bride demanded, or else the wrong woman would have been foisted on them. They agreed, nodding. All right, all right, Ayo's father had replied, there was no cause for impatience. He wanted to be sure they knew whom they wanted. Standing on guard at the bedroom door, he turned his back to the assembly, and with tears in his eyes beckoned to Ayo sitting on the bed inside. He kissed her lightly on the forehead to forgive the past years. Then he led her forth and turned fiercely to the audience. Was this then the girl they wanted, he asked them sternly?

"This *is* the very one," Ajayi's uncle replied with joy. "Hip, hip, hip, hooray," everybody shouted, encircling Ayo and waving white handkerchiefs over her head. The musicians smote their guitars instantly; someone beat an empty wine bottle rhythmically with a corkscrew; after a few preliminary trills the flutes rose high in melody; all danced round Ayo. And as she stood in the center, a woman in her mid-thirties, her hair slightly streaked grey, undergoing a ceremony of honor she had often witnessed and long put outside her fate, remembering the classic description of chastity, obedience, and beauty, she wept with joy and the unborn child stirred within her for the first time.

The next morning she was bathed by an old and respected female member of her family and her mother helped her to dress. Her father gave her away at the marriage service at church. It was a quiet wedding with only sixty guests or so. Ajayi looked stiff in dinner jacket with buttonhole, an ensemble which he wore only on special occasions. Afterwards they went to Ayo's family home for the wedding luncheon. At the door they were met by another of Ayo's numerous elderly aunts, who held a glass of water to their lips for them to sip in turn, Ajayi being first. The guests were all gathered outside behind the couple. The aunt made a conveniently long speech until all the guests had foregathered. She warned Ayo not to be too friendly with other women as they would inevitably steal her husband; that they should live peaceably and not let the sun go down on a quarrel between them. Turning to Ajayi, she told him with a twinkle in her eye that a wife could be quite as exciting as a mistress, and also not to use physical violence against their daughter, his wife.

After this they entered and the western part of the ceremony took place. The wedding cake (which Ayo had made) was cut and speeches made. Then Ajayi departed to his own family home where other celebrations went on. Later he changed into a lounge suit and called for Ayo. There was weeping in Ayo's household as if she were setting off on a long journey. Her mother in saying goodbye remarked between tears that although she would not have the honor next morning of showing the world evidence of Ayo's virginity, yet in the true feminine powers of procreation none except the blind and deaf could say Ayo had lacked zeal.

They called on various relations on both sides of the family and at last they were home. Ayo seemed different in Ajayi's eyes. He had never really looked at her carefully before. Now he observed her head held erectly and gracefully through years of balancing loads on it in childhood; her statuesque neck with its three natural horizontal ridges—to him, signs of beauty; her handsome shoulders. He clasped her with a new tenderness.

The next morning, as his alarm clock went off, he stirred and reached for his morning cup of tea. It was not there. He sprang up and looked. Nothing. He listened for Ayo's footsteps outside in the kitchen. Nothing. He turned to look beside him. Ayo was there and her bare ebony back was heaving gently. She must be ill, he thought; all that excitement yesterday.

"Ayo, Ayo," he cried, "are you ill?" She turned round slowly still lying down and faced him. She tweaked her toes luxuriously under the cotton coverlet and patted her breast slowly. There was a terrible calm about her. "No, Ajayi," she replied, "are you?" she asked him. "Are your legs paralyzed?" she continued. "No," he said. He was puzzled and alarmed, thinking that her mind had become unhinged under the strain.

"Ajayi, my husband," she said, "for twelve years I have got up every morning at five to make tea for you and breakfast. Now I am a truly married woman you must treat me with a little more respect. You are now a husband and not a lover. Get up and make yourself a cup of tea."

QUESTIONS

1. What evidence is there in this story of the influence of Western on African culture? Is this influence positive or negative?

2. Are we as surprised by Ayo's behavior at the end of the story as Ajayi is? In rereading the story can you find any clues that might prepare us for this behavior?
3. Are we to regard Ayo and Ajayi as hypocrites because they quickly change their house and pretend to be married and pious in the presence of the representatives of the World Gospel Crusading Alliance?
4. What is Nicol's attitude toward the convention of marriage? In what ways has marriage changed the relationship between Ayo and Ajayi?
5. The engagement ceremony that takes place at Ayo's father's home is a small dramatic piece within the story. Does it have a plot of its own? How are we to regard this ceremony?

SETTING

Setting can be defined as the place and period of a story, the canvas on which the dramatic events are drawn in detail. It should not be thought of, however, as mere atmosphere or mood but rather as an artistic technique that aids the writer in determining and developing a variety of individual themes. F. Scott Fitzgerald, for example, places the action of "Babylon Revisited" in Paris two years after the stock market crash of 1929. Before the debacle the international city was filled with Americans who lived casually and carelessly on the proceeds of a swollen economy. Now one of those Americans, Charlie Wales, whose wife died in that earlier Paris, has returned to reclaim custody of his little girl. He discovers that all his old friends are no longer in Paris—they are "gone."

He was not really disappointed to find Paris was so empty. But the stillness in the Ritz bar was strange and portentous. It was not an American bar anymore—he felt polite in it, and not as if he owned it. It had gone back into France. He felt the stillness from the moment he got out of the taxi and saw the doorman, usually in a frenzy of activity at this hour, gossiping with a *chasseur* by the servants' entrance.

The emptiness of Paris along with the chilling quiet of the bar conspire to make Charlie Wales feel like an intruder in the one city he believed he possessed. They serve to introduce the themes of loneliness and exile that come to dominate the story. In a series of flashbacks Charlie recalls Paris as it then was: "He remembered thousand-franc notes given to an orchestra for playing a single number, hundred-franc notes tossed to a doorman for calling a cab." Those memories are contrasted with Paris as it is now: "Zelli's was closed, the bleak and sinister cheap hotels surrounding it were dark; up in the Rue Blanche there was more light and a local, colloquial French crowd." Paris, the city of luxury and vice, as the title ironically indicates, has become a city of death—a bored, provincial, and alien capital. The setting conjures up for Charlie Wales the "nightmare" world of his past and also vividly drives home to him the bleak reality of his present existence—that he is alone and homeless.

While setting in "Babylon Revisited" lends credibility to the experience of the central character, in "Hills Like White Elephants" the brown dry Spanish countryside mirrors the barren life of a young couple. The physical details underline the action; they complete the meaning only partially revealed through the couple's conversation. The following paragraph opens "Hills Like White Elephants":

The hills across the valley of the Ebro were long and white. On this side there was no shade and no trees and the station was between two lines of rails in the sun. Close against the side of the station there was the warm shadow of the building and a curtain, made of strings of bamboo beads, hung across the open door into the bar, to keep out flies. The American and the girl with him sat at the table in the shade, outside the building. It was very hot and the express from Barcelona would come in forty minutes. It stopped at this junction for two minutes and went on to Madrid.

Hemingway's story concerns an impending abortion that controls the entire subject of the couple's dialogue. The American, a splendid characterization of harried calm, tries to persuade the girl that the abortion is in their best interests, that it will enable them to live intimately and preserve the freedom they enjoyed prior to her pregnancy. But the surroudings belie the man's frenetic hope. The isolated and imprisoned station, the debilitating heat, the parched and sterile earth—these images combine to form a portrait of death, a death that not only prefigures the destruction of the unborn child but also symbolizes the sterility of the couple's relations. Hemingway's setting develops and heightens our perception that emotional survival for this couple—like the growth of grass on the Spanish hills—is impossible.

In "Babylon Revisited," setting functions as an integral feature of the plot and contributes to the denouement of the tale; in "Hills Like White Elephants" it works symbolically to illuminate a dramatic incident. Both stories use setting as a technique for conveying and accenting their themes. Richard Wright, however, in "The Man Who Lived Underground," makes his setting the very theme of the story. By pulling his protagonist "freddaniels," a Black wrongly accused of murder, below the streets of Chicago, Wright draws us into the bowels of the earth in order to discover the soul of man. The black world of the sewer, with its rats and refuse, its sense of terror and imprisonment, must seem a fitting place for a black man to live. Wright converts this macabre joke into a terrible truth, for it is precisely underground, despite the stench, that the Black finds succor and spirit: "He had triumphed over the world aboveground! He was free!"

The black and white setting in "The Man Who Lived Underground" becomes a metaphor for the relations between black and white in America. Hunted like an animal aboveground, the narrator digs a "dirt cave" underground and becomes a sewer rat, enjoying the immunity and safety of darkness. True terror for the Negro exists above in the world of "dead sunshine," where the appearance of reason, sanity, and order proves a perpetual nightmare. Wright's setting informs us that vision is possible in darkness, while blindness exists in the light.

Often a writer will shift his setting within the story, as James Joyce does in "Counterparts." Although Dublin circumscribes the limits of the action, the scene shifts from the office where Farrington works, to the pubs he frequents, and to the home he inhabits. Each turn reveals to us a distinct side of Farrington's character, while the total movement augments Dublin's sordidness and squalor. Yukio Mishima's setting for "Patriotism," on the other hand, is largely restricted to the upstairs bedroom of the Lieutenant and his wife Reiko. Here the youthful lovers are insulated from the world outside and protected against the twin corruptions of politics and materialism. The room serves as a refuge for their erotic lovemaking and a sanctuary for their suicide. It becomes the embodiment of Japanese tradition—the only room in the house that receives the sun.

By detailing the moment and place of the dramatic action—a wasted Paris for Fitzgerald, a desolate and devastated Spain for Hemingway, a subterranean Chicago for Wright—the setting reveals and illuminates both character and event; it heightens the story's meaning. All our examples serve to support a single observation—that an author's setting helps us to discover his themes.

F. Scott Fitzgerald *(1896–1940) was born in St. Paul, Minnesota, and attended Princeton University, which he left in 1917 in order to join the army. He published his first novel,* This Side of Paradise *(1920), when he was twenty-four. During the 1920's —an era Fitzgerald christened "the Jazz Age" —he lived in New York, where his enormously popular stories appeared in* The Saturday Evening Post *and* Redbook; *Paris, where he met Ernest Hemingway; and the French Riviera, where he wrote* The Great Gatsby *(1925). Returning to America in the 1930's, Fitzgerald published* Tender Is the Night *(1934), a novel about expatriate life on the Riviera, and contributed essays and stories to* Esquire. *He settled in Hollywood as a script writer in 1937 and died there of a heart attack. His novel about the movie industry,* The Last Tycoon, *was never finished. Among his collections of stories are* All the Sad Young Men *(1926) and* Taps at Reveille *(1935). Fitzgerald's letters, notebooks, and remaining stories have appeared posthumously in* The Crack-up *(1956),* Afternoon of an Author *(1957),* The Pat Hobby Stories *(1962), and* Letters *(1963).*

Babylon Revisited

F. SCOTT FITZGERALD

I

"And where's Mr. Campbell?" Charlie asked.

"Gone to Switzerland. Mr. Campbell's a pretty sick man, Mr. Wales."

"I'm sorry to hear that. And George Hardt?" Charlie inquired.

"Back in America, gone to work."

"And where is the Snow Bird?"

"He was in here last week. Anyway, his friend, Mr. Schaeffer, is in Paris."

Two familiar names from the long list of a year and a half ago. Charlie scribbled an address in his notebook and tore out the page.

"If you see Mr. Schaeffer, give him this," he said. "It's my brother-in-law's address. I haven't settled on a hotel yet."

He was not really disappointed to find Paris was so empty. But the stillness in the Ritz bar was strange and portentous. It was not an American bar any more—he felt polite in it, and not as if he owned it. It had gone back into France. He felt the stillness from the moment he got out of the taxi and saw the doorman, usually in a frenzy of activity at this hour, gossiping with a *chasseur* by the servants' entrance.

Passing through the corridor, he heard only a single, bored voice in the once-clamorous women's room. When he turned into the bar he traveled the twenty feet of green carpet with his eyes fixed straight ahead by old habit; and then, with his foot firmly on the rail, he turned and surveyed the room, encountering only a single pair of eyes that fluttered up from a newspaper in the corner. Charlie asked for the head barman, Paul, who in the latter days of the bull market had come to work in his own custom-built car—disembarking, however, with due nicety at the nearest corner. But Paul was at his country house today and Alix giving him information.

"No, no more," Charlie said, "I'm going slow these days."

Alix congratulated him: "You were going pretty strong a couple of years ago."

"I'll stick to it all right," Charlie assured him. "I've stuck to it for over a year and a half now."

"How do you find conditions in America?"

"I haven't been to America for months. I'm in business in Prague, representing a couple of concerns there. They don't know about me down there."

Alix smiled.

"Remember the night of George Hardt's bachelor dinner here?" said Charlie. "By the way, what's become of Claude Fessenden?"

Alix lowered his voice confidentially: "He's in Paris, but he doesn't come here any more. Paul doesn't allow it. He ran up a bill of thirty thousand francs, charging all his drinks and his lunches, and usually his dinner, for more than a year. And when Paul finally told him he had to pay, he gave him a bad check."

Alix shook his head sadly.

"I don't understand it, such a dandy fellow. Now he's all bloated up—" He made a plump apple of his hands.

Charlie watched a group of strident queens installing themselves in a corner.

"Nothing affects them," he thought. "Stocks rise and fall, people loaf or work, but they go on forever." The place oppressed him. He called for the dice and shook with Alix for the drink.

"Here for long, Mr. Wales?"

"I'm here for four or five days to see my little girl."

"Oh-h! You have a little girl?"

Outside, the fire-red, gas-blue, ghost-green signs shone smokily through the tranquil rain. It was late afternoon and the streets were in movement; the *bistros* gleamed. At the corner of the Boulevard des Capucines he took a taxi. The Place de la Concorde moved by in pink majesty; they crossed the logical Seine, and Charlie felt the sudden provincial quality of the left bank.

Charlie directed his taxi to the Avenue de l'Opera, which was out of his way. But he wanted to see the blue hour spread over the magnificent facade, and imagine that the cab horns, playing endlessly the first few bars of *Le Plus que Lent*, were the trumpets of the Second Empire. They were closing the iron grill in front of Brentano's Bookstore, and people were already at dinner behind the trim little bourgeois hedge of Duval's. He had never eaten at a really cheap restaurant in Paris. Five-course dinner, four francs fifty, eighteen cents, wine included. For some odd reason he wished that he had.

As they rolled on to the Left Bank and he felt its sudden provincialism, he thought, "I spoiled this city for myself. I didn't realize it, but the days came along one after another, and then two years were gone, and everything was gone, and I was gone."

He was thirty-five, and good to look at. The Irish mobility of his face was sobered by a deep wrinkle between his eyes. As he rang his brother-in-law's bell in the Rue Palatine, the wrinkle deepened till it pulled down his brows; he felt a cramping sensation in his belly. From behind the maid who opened the door darted a lovely little girl of nine who shrieked "Daddy!" and flew up, struggling like a fish, into his arms. She pulled his head around by one ear and set her cheek against his.

"My old pie," he said.

"Oh, daddy, daddy, daddy, daddy, dads, dads, dads!"

She drew him into the salon, where the family waited, a boy and a girl his daughter's age, his sister-in-law and her husband. He greeted Marion with his voice pitched carefully to avoid either feigned enthusiasm or dislike, but her response was more frankly tepid, though she minimized her expression of unalterable distrust by directing her regard toward his child. The two men clasped hands in a friendly way and Lincoln Peters rested his for a moment on Charlie's shoulder.

The room was warm and comfortably American. The three children moved intimately about, playing through the yellow oblongs that led to other rooms; the cheer of six o'clock spoke in the eager smacks of the fire and the sounds of French activity in the kitchen. But Charlie did not relax; his heart sat up rigidly in his body and he drew confidence from his daughter, who from time to time came close to him, holding in her arms the doll he had brought.

"Really extremely well," he declared in answer to Lincoln's question. "There's a lot of business there that isn't moving at all, but we're doing even better than ever. In fact, damn well. I'm bringing my sister over from America next month to keep house for me. My income last year was bigger than it was when I had money. You see, the Czechs—"

His boasting was for a specific purpose; but after a moment, seeing a faint restiveness in Lincoln's eye, he changed the subject:

"Those are fine children of yours, well brought up, good manners."

"We think Honoria's a great little girl too."

Marion Peters came back from the kitchen. She was a tall woman with worried eyes, who had once possessed a fresh American loveliness. Charlie had never been sensitive to it and was always surprised when people spoke of how pretty she had been. From the first there had been an instinctive antipathy between them.

"Well, how do you find Honoria?" she asked.

"Wonderful. I was astonished how much she's grown in ten months. All the children are looking well."

"We haven't had a doctor for a year. How do you like being back in Paris?"

"It seems very funny to see so few Americans around."

"I'm delighted," Marion said vehemently. "Now at least you can go into a store without their assuming you're a millionaire. We've suffered like everybody, but on the whole it's a good deal pleasanter."

"But it was nice while it lasted," Charlie said. "We were a sort of royalty, almost infallible, with a sort of magic around us. In the bar this afternoon"—he stumbled, seeing his mistake—"there wasn't a man I knew."

She looked at him keenly. "I should think you'd have had enough of bars."

"I only stayed a minute. I take one drink every afternoon, and no more."

"Don't you want a cocktail before dinner?" Lincoln asked.

"I take only one drink every afternoon, and I've had that."

"I hope you keep to it," said Marion.

Her dislike was evident in the coldness with which she spoke, but Charlie only smiled; he had larger plans. Her very aggressiveness gave him an advantage, and he knew enough to wait. He wanted them to initiate the discussion of what they knew had brought him to Paris.

At dinner he couldn't decide whether Honoria was most like them or her mother. Fortunate if she didn't combine the traits of both that had brought them to disaster. A great wave of protectiveness went over him. He thought he knew what to do for her. He believed in character; he wanted to jump back a whole generation and trust in character again as the eternally valuable element. Everything else wore out.

He left soon after dinner, but not to go home. He was curious to see Paris by night with clearer and more judicious eyes than those of other days. He bought a *strapontin* for the Casino and watched Josephine Baker go through her chocolate arabesques.

After an hour he left and strolled toward Montmartre, up the Rue Pigalle into the Place Blanche. The rain had stopped and there were a few people in evening clothes disembarking from taxis in front of cabarets, and *cocottes* prowling singly or in pairs, and many Negroes. He passed a lighted door from which issued music, and stopped with the sense of familiarity; it was Bricktop's, where he had parted with so many hours and so much money. A few doors farther on he found another ancient rendezvous and incautiously put his head inside. Immediately an eager orchestra burst into sound, a pair of professional dancers leaped to their feet and a maître d'hôtel swooped toward him, crying, "Crowd just arriving, sir!" But he withdrew quickly.

"You have to be damn drunk," he thought.

Zelli's was closed, the bleak and sinister cheap hotels surrounding it were dark; up in the Rue Blanche there was more light and a local, colloquial French crowd. The Poet's Cave had disappeared, but the two great mouths of the Café of Heaven and the Café of Hell still yawned—even devoured, as he watched, the meager contents of a tourist bus—a German, a Japanese, and an American couple who glanced at him with frightened eyes.

So much for the effort and ingenuity of Montmartre. All the catering to vice and waste was on an utterly childish scale, and he suddenly realized the meaning of the word "dissipate"—to dissipate into thin air; to make nothing out of something. In the little hours of the night every move from place to place was an enormous human jump, an increase of paying for the privilege of slower and slower motion.

He remembered thousand-franc notes given to an orchestra for playing a single number, hundred-franc notes tossed to a doorman for calling a cab.

But it hadn't been given for nothing.

It had been given, even the most wildly squandered sum, as an offering to destiny that he might not remember the things most worth remembering, the things that now he would always remember—his child taken from his control, his wife escaped to a grave in Vermont.

In the glare of a *brasserie* a woman spoke to him. He bought her some eggs and coffee, and then, eluding her encouraging stare, gave her a twenty-franc note and took a taxi to his hotel.

II

He woke upon a fine fall day—football weather. The depression of yesterday was gone and he liked the people on the streets. At noon he sat opposite Honoria at Le Grand Vatel, the only restaurant he could think of not reminiscent of champagne dinners and long luncheons that began at two and ended in a blurred and vague twilight.

"Now, how about vegetables? Oughtn't you to have some vegetables?"

"Well, yes."

"Here's *épinards* and *chou-fleur* and carrots and *haricots*."

"I'd like *chou-fleur*."

"Wouldn't you like to have two vegetables?"

"I usually only have one at lunch."

The waiter was pretending to be inordinately fond of children. "*Qu'elle est mignonne la petite! Elle parle exactement comme une Francaise*."

"How about dessert? Shall we wait and see?"

The waiter disappeared. Honoria looked at her father expectantly.

"What are we going to do?"

"First, we're going to that toy store in the Rue Saint-Honoré and buy you anything you like. And then we're going to the vaudeville at the Empire."

She hesitated. "I like it about the vaudeville, but not the toy store."

"Why not?"

"Well, you brought me this doll." She had it with her. "And I've got lots of things. And we're not rich any more, are we?"

"We never were. But today you are to have anything you want."

"All right," she agreed resignedly.

When there had been her mother and a French nurse he had been inclined to be strict; now he extended himself, reached out for a new tolerance; he must be both parents to her and not shut any of her out of communication.

"I want to get to know you," he said gravely. "First let me introduce myself. My name is Charles J. Wales, of Prague."

"Oh, daddy!" her voice cracked with laughter.

"And who are you, please?" he persisted, and she accepted a rôle immediately: "Honoria Wales, Rue Palatine, Paris."

"Married or single?"

"No, not married. Single."

He indicated the doll. "But I see you have a child, madame."

Unwilling to disinherit it, she took it to her heart and thought quickly: "Yes, I've been married, but I'm not married now. My husband is dead."

He went on quickly, "And the child's name?"

"Simone. That's after my best friend at school."

"I'm very pleased that you're doing so well at school."

"I'm third this month," she boasted. "Elsie"—that was her cousin—"is only about eighteenth, and Richard is about at the bottom."

"You like Richard and Elsie, don't you?"

"Oh, yes. I like Richard quite well and I like her all right."

Cautiously and casually he asked: "And Aunt Marion and Uncle Lincoln—which do you like best?"

"Oh, Uncle Lincoln, I guess."

He was increasingly aware of her presence. As they came in, a murmur of ". . . adorable" followed them, and now the people at the next table bent all their silences upon her, staring as if she were something no more conscious than a flower.

"Why don't I live with you?" she asked suddenly. "Because mamma's dead?"

"You must stay here and learn more French. It would have been hard for daddy to take care of you so well."

"I don't really need much taking care of any more. I do everything for myself."

Going out of the restaurant, a man and a woman unexpectedly hailed him.

"Well, the old Wales!"

"Hello there, Lorraine . . . Dunc."

Sudden ghosts out of the past: Duncan Schaeffer, a friend from college. Lorraine Quarrles, a lovely, pale blonde of thirty; one of a crowd who had helped them make months into days in the lavish times of three years ago.

"My husband couldn't come this year," she said, in answer to his question. "We're poor as hell. So he gave me two hundred a month and told me I could do my worst on that. . . . This your little girl?"

"What about coming back and sitting down?" Duncan asked.

"Can't do it." He was glad for an excuse. As always, he felt Lorraine's passionate, provocative attraction, but his own rhythm was different now.

"Well, how about dinner?" she asked.

"I'm not free. Give me your address and let me call you."

"Charlie, I believe you're sober," she said judicially. "I honestly believe he's sober, Dunc. Pinch him and see if he's sober."

Charlie indicated Honoria with his head. They both laughed.

"What's your address?" said Duncan skeptically.

He hesitated, unwilling to give the name of his hotel.

"I'm not settled yet. I'd better call you. We're going to see the vaudeville at the Empire."

"There! That's what I want to do," Lorraine said. "I want to see some clowns and acrobats and jugglers. That's just what we'll do, Dunc."

"We've got to do an errand first," said Charlie. "Perhaps we'll see you there."

"All right, you snob. . . . Good-by, beautiful little girl."

"Good-by."

Honoria bobbed politely.

Somehow, an unwelcome encounter. They liked him because he was functioning, because he was serious, they wanted to see him, because he was stronger than they were now, because they wanted to draw a certain sustenance from his strength.

At the Empire, Honoria proudly refused to sit upon her father's folded coat. She was already an individual with a code of her own, and Charlie was more and more absorbed by the desire of putting a little of himself into her before she crystallized utterly. It was hopeless to try to know her in so short a time.

Between the acts they came upon Duncan and Lorraine in the lobby where the band was playing.

"Have a drink?"

"All right, but not up at the bar. We'll take a table."

"The perfect father."

Listening abstractedly to Lorraine, Charlie watched Honoria's eyes leave their table, and he followed them wistfully about the room, wondering what they saw. He met her glance and she smiled.

"I liked that lemonade," she said.

What had she said? What had he expected? Going home in a taxi afterward, he pulled her over until her head rested against his chest.

"Darling, do you ever think about your mother?"

"Yes, sometimes," she answered vaguely.

"I don't want you to forget her. Have you got a picture of her?"

"Yes, I think so. Anyhow, Aunt Marion has. Why don't you want me to forget her?"

"She loved you very much."

"I loved her too."

They were silent for a moment.

"Daddy, I want to come and live with you," she said suddenly.

His heart leaped; he had wanted it to come like this.

"Aren't you perfectly happy?"

"Yes, but I love you better than anybody. And you love me better than anybody, don't you, now that mummy's dead?"

"Of course I do. But you won't always like me best, honey. You'll grow up and meet somebody your own age and go marry him and forget you ever had a daddy."

"Yes, that's true," she agreed tranquilly.

He didn't go in. He was coming back at nine o'clock and he wanted to keep himself fresh and new for the thing he must say then.

"When you're safe inside, just show yourself in that window."

"All right. Good-by, dads, dads, dads, dads."

He waited in the dark street until she appeared, all warm and glowing, in the window above and kissed her fingers out into the night.

III

They were waiting. Marion sat behind the coffee service in a dignified black dinner dress that just faintly suggested mourning. Lincoln was walking up and down with the animation of one who had already been talking. They were as anxious as he was to get into the question. He opened it almost immediately:

"I suppose you know what I want to see you about—why I really came to Paris."

Marion played with the black stars on her necklace and frowned.

"I'm awfully anxious to have a home," he continued. "And I'm awfully anxious to have Honoria in it. I appreciate your taking in Honoria for her mother's sake, but things have changed now"—he hesitated and then continued more forcibly—"changed radically with me, and I want to ask you to reconsider the matter. It would be silly for me to deny that about three years ago I was acting badly—"

Marion looked up at him with hard eyes.

"—but all that's over. As I told you, I haven't had more than a drink a day for over a year, and I take that drink deliberately, so that the idea of alcohol won't get too big in my imagination. You see the idea?"

"No," said Marion succinctly.

"It's a sort of stunt I set myself. It keeps the matter in proportion."

"I get you," said Lincoln. "You don't want to admit it's got any attraction for you."

"Something like that. Sometimes I forget and don't take it. But I try to take it. Anyhow, I couldn't afford to drink in my position. The people I represent are more than satisfied with what I've done, and I'm bringing my sister over from Burlington to keep house for me, and I want awfully to have Honoria too. You know that even when her mother and I weren't getting along well we never let anything that happened touch Honoria. I know she's fond of me and I know I'm able to take care of her and—well, there you are. How do you feel about it?"

He knew that now he would have to take a beating. It would last an hour or two hours, and it would be difficult, but if he modulated his inevitable resentment to the chastened attitude of the reformed sinner, he might win his point in the end.

Keep your temper, he told himself. You don't want to be justified. You want Honoria.

Lincoln spoke first: "We've been talking it over ever since we got your letter last month. We're happy to have Honoria here. She's a dear little thing, and we're glad to be able to help her, but of course that isn't the question—"

Marion interrupted suddenly. "How long are you going to stay sober, Charlie?" she asked.

"Permanently, I hope."

"How can anybody count on that?"

"You know I never did drink heavily until I gave up business and came over here with nothing to do. Then Helen and I began to run around with—"

"Please leave Helen out of it. I can't bear to hear you talk about her like that."

He stared at her grimly; he had never been certain how fond of each other the sisters were in life.

"My drinking only lasted about a year and a half—from the time we came over until I—collapsed."

"It was time enough."

"It was time enough," he agreed.

"My duty is entirely to Helen," she said. "I try to think what she would have wanted me to do. Frankly, from the night you did that terrible thing you haven't really existed for me. I can't help that. She was my sister."

"Yes."

"When she was dying she asked me to look out for Honoria. If you hadn't been in a sanitarium then, it might have helped matters."

He had no answer.

"I'll never in my life be able to forget the morning when Helen knocked at my door, soaked to the skin and shivering, and said you'd locked her out."

Charlie gripped the sides of the chair. This was more difficult than he expected; he wanted to launch out into a long expostulation and explanation, but he only said: "The night I locked her out—" and she interrupted, "I don't feel up to going over that again."

After a moment's silence Lincoln said: "We're getting off the subject. You want Marion to set aside her legal guardianship and give you Honoria. I think the main point for her is whether she has confidence in you or not."

"I don't blame Marion," Charlie said slowly, "but I think she can have entire confidence in me. I had a good record up to three years ago. Of course, it's within human possibilities I might go wrong any time. But if we wait much longer I'll lose Honoria's childhood and my chance for a home." He shook his head. "I'll simply lose her, don't you see?"

"Yes, I see," said Lincoln.

"Why didn't you think of all this before?" Marion asked.

"I suppose I did, from time to time, but Helen and I were getting along badly. When I consented to the guardianship, I was flat on my back in a sanitarium and the market had cleaned me out. I knew I'd acted badly, and I thought if it would bring any peace to Helen, I'd agree to anything. But now it's different. I'm functioning, I'm behaving damn well, so far as—"

"Please don't swear at me," Marion said.

He looked at her, startled. With each remark the force of her dislike became more and more apparent. She had built up all her fear of life into one wall and faced it toward him. This trivial reproof was possibly the result of some trouble with the cook several hours before. Charlie became increasingly alarmed at leaving Honoria in this atmosphere of hostility against himself; sooner or later it would come out, in a word here, a shake of the head there, and some of that distrust would be irrevocably implanted in Honoria. But he pulled his temper down out of his face and shut it up inside him; he had won a point, for Lincoln realized the absurdity of Marion's remark and asked her lightly since when she had objected to the word "damn."

"Another thing," Charlie said: "I'm able to give her certain advantages now. I'm going to take a French governess to Prague with me. I've got a lease on a new apartment—"

He stopped, realizing that he was blundering. They couldn't be expected to accept with equanimity the fact that his income was again twice as large as their own.

"I suppose you can give her more luxuries than we can," said Marion. "When you were throwing away money we were living along watching every ten francs. . . . I suppose you'll start doing it again."

"Oh, no," he said. "I've learned. I worked hard for ten years, you know—until I got lucky in the market, like so many people. Terribly lucky. It didn't seem any use working any more, so I quit."

There was a long silence. All of them felt their nerves straining, and for the first time in a year Charlie wanted a drink. He was sure now that Lincoln Peters wanted him to have his child.

Marion shuddered suddenly; part of her saw that Charlie's feet were planted on the earth now, and her own maternal feeling recognized the naturalness of his desire; but she had lived for a long time with a prejudice—a prejudice founded on a curious disbelief in her sister's happiness, and which, in the shock of one terrible night, had turned to hatred for him. It had all happened at a point in her life where the discouragement of ill health and adverse circumstances made it necessary for her to believe in tangible villainy and a tangible villain.

"I can't help what I think!" she cried out suddenly. "How much you were responsible for Helen's death, I don't know. It's something you'll have to square with your own conscience."

An electric current of agony surged through him; for a moment he was almost on his feet, an unuttered sound echoing in his throat. He hung on to himself for a moment, another moment.

"Hold on there," said Lincoln uncomfortably. "I never thought you were responsible for that."

"Helen died of heart trouble," Charlie said dully.

"Yes, heart trouble." Marion spoke as if the phrase had another meaning for her.

Then, in the flatness that followed her outburst, she saw him plainly and she knew he had somehow arrived at control over the situation. Glancing at her husband, she found no help from him, and as abruptly as if it were a matter of no importance, she threw up the sponge.

"Do what you like!" she cried, springing up from her chair. "She's your child. I'm not the person to stand in your way. I think if it were my child I'd rather see her—" She managed to check herself. "You two decide it. I can't stand this. I'm sick. I'm going to bed."

She hurried from the room; after a moment Lincoln said:

"This has been a hard day for her. You know how strongly she feels—" His voice was almost apologetic: "Where a woman gets an idea in her head."

"Of course."

"It's going to be all right. I think she sees now that you—can provide for the child, and so we can't very well stand in your way or Honoria's way."

"Thank you, Lincoln."

"I'd better go along and see how she is."

"I'm going."

He was still trembling when he reached the street, but a walk down the Rue Bonaparte to the *quais* set him up, and as he crossed the Seine, fresh and new by the *quai* lamps, he felt exultant. But back in his room he couldn't sleep. The image of Helen haunted him. Helen whom he had loved so until they had senselessly begun to abuse each other's love, tear it into shreds. On that terrible February night that Marion remembered so vividly, a slow quarrel had gone on for hours. There was a scene at the Florida, and then he attempted to take her home, and then she kissed young Webb at a table; after that there was what she had hysterically said. When he arrived home alone he turned the key in the lock in wild anger. How could he know she would arrive an hour later alone, that there would be a snowstorm in which she wandered about in slippers, too confused to find a taxi? Then the aftermath, her escaping pneumonia by a miracle, and all the attendant horror. They were "reconciled," but that was the beginning of the end, and Marion, who had seen with her own eyes and who imagined it to be one of many scenes from her sister's martyrdom, never forgot.

Going over it again brought Helen nearer, and in the white, soft light that steals upon the half sleep near morning he found himself talking to her again. She said that he was perfectly right about Honoria and that she wanted Honoria to be with him. She said she was glad he was being good and doing better. She said a lot of other things—very friendly things—but she was in a swing in a white dress, and swinging faster and faster all the time, so that at the end he could not hear clearly all that she said.

IV

He woke up feeling happy. The door of the world was open again. He made plans, vistas, futures for Honoria and himself, but suddenly he grew sad, remembering all the plans he and Helen had made. She had not planned to die. The present was the thing—work to do and someone to love. But not to love too much, for he knew the injury that a father can do to a daughter or a mother to a son by attaching them too closely: afterward, out in the world, the child would seek in the marriage partner the same blind tenderness and, failing probably to find it, turn against love and life.

It was another bright, crisp day. He called Lincoln Peters at the bank where he worked and asked if he could count on taking Honoria when he left for Prague. Lincoln agreed that there was no reason for delay. One thing—the legal guardianship. Marion wanted to retain that a while longer. She was upset by the whole matter, and it would oil things if she felt that the situation was still in her control for another year. Charlie agreed, wanting only the tangible, visible child.

Then the question of a governess. Charles sat in a gloomy agency and talked to a cross Béarnaise and to a buxom Breton peasant, neither of whom he could have endured. There were others whom he would see tomorrow.

He lunched with Lincoln Peters at Griffons, trying to keep down his exultation.

"There's nothing quite like your own child," Lincoln said. "But you understand how Marion feels too."

"She's forgotten how hard I worked for seven years there," Charlie said. "She just remembers one night."

"There's another thing." Lincoln hesitated. "While you and Helen were tearing around Europe throwing money away, we were just getting along. I didn't touch any of the prosperity because I never got ahead enough to carry anything but my insurance. I think Marion felt there was some of kind of injustice in it—you not even working toward the end, and getting richer and richer."

"It went just as quick as it came," said Charlie.

"Yes, a lot of it stayed in the hands of *chasseurs* and saxophone players and maîtres d'hôtel—well, the big party's over now. I just said that to explain Marion's feeling about those crazy years. If you drop in about six o'clock tonight before Marion's too tired, we'll settle the details on the spot."

Back at his hotel, Charlie found a *pneumatique* that had been redirected from the Ritz bar where Charlie had left his address for the purpose of finding a certain man.

Dear Charlie: You were so strange when we saw you the other day that I wondered if I did something to offend you. If so, I'm not conscious of it. In fact, I have thought about you too much for the last year, and it's always been in the back of my mind that I might see you if I came over here. We *did* have such good times that crazy spring, like the night you and I stole the butcher's tricycle, and the time we tried to call on the president and you had the old derby rim and the wire cane. Everybody seems so old lately, but I don't feel old a bit. Couldn't we get together some time today for old time's sake? I've got a vile hang-over for the moment, but will be feeling better this afternoon and will look for you about five in the sweat-shop at the Ritz.

Always devotedly,
Lorraine.

His first feeling was one of awe that he had actually, in his mature years, stolen a tricycle and pedaled Lorraine all over the Etoile between the small hours and dawn. In retrospect it was a nightmare. Locking out Helen didn't fit in with any other act of his life, but the tricycle incident did—it was one of many. How many weeks or months of dissipation to arrive at that condition of utter irresponsibility?

He tried to picture how Lorraine had appeared to him then—very attractive; Helen was unhappy about it, though she said nothing. Yesterday, in the restaurant, Lorraine had seemed trite, blurred, worn away. He emphatically did not want to see her, and he was glad Alix had not given away his hotel address. It was a relief to think, instead, of Honoria, to think of Sundays spent with her and of saying good morning to her and of knowing she was there in his house at night, drawing her breath in the darkness.

At five he took a taxi and bought presents for all the Peters—a piquant cloth doll, a box of Roman soldiers, flowers for Marion, big linen handkerchiefs for Lincoln.

He saw, when he arrived in the apartment, that Marion had accepted the inevitable. She greeted him now as though he were a recalcitrant member of the family, rather than a menacing outsider. Honoria had been told she was going; Charlie was glad to see that her tact made her conceal her excessive happiness. Only on his lap did she whisper her delight and the question "When?" before she slipped away with the other children.

He and Marion were alone for a minute in the room, and on an impulse he spoke out boldly:

"Family quarrels are bitter things. They don't go according to any rules. They're not like aches or wounds; they're more like splits in the skin that won't heal because there's not enough material. I wish you and I could be on better terms."

"Some things are hard to forget," she answered. "It's a question of confidence." There was no answer to this and presently she asked, "When do you propose to take her?"

"As soon as I can get a governess. I hoped the day after tomorrow."

"That's impossible. I've got to get her things in shape. Not before Saturday."

He yielded. Coming back into the room, Lincoln offered him a drink.

"I'll take my daily whisky," he said.

It was warm here, it was a home, people together by a fire. The children felt very safe and important; the mother and father were serious, watchful. They had things to do for the children more important than his visit here. A spoonful of medicine was, after all, more important than the strained relations between Marion and himself. They were not dull people, but they were very much in the grip of life and circumstances. He wondered if he couldn't do something to get Lincoln out of his rut at the bank.

A long peal at the door-bell; the *bonne à tout faire* passed through and went down the corridor. The door opened upon another long ring, and then voices, and the three in the salon looked up expectantly; Richard moved to bring the corridor within his range of vision, and Marion rose. Then the maid came back along the corridor, closely followed by the voices, which developed under the light into Duncan Schaeffer and Lorraine Quarrles.

They were gay, they were hilarious, they were roaring with laughter. For a moment Charlie was astounded; unable to understand how they ferreted out the Peters' address.

"Ah-h-h!" Duncan wagged his finger roguishly at Charlie. "Ah-h-h!"

They both slid down another cascade of laughter. Anxious and at a loss, Charlie shook hands with them quickly and presented them to Lincoln and Marion. Marion nodded, scarcely speaking. She had drawn back a step toward the fire; her little girl stood beside her, and Marion put an arm about her shoulder.

With growing annoyance at the intrusion, Charlie waited for them to explain themselves. After some concentration Duncan said:

"We came to invite you out to dinner. Lorraine and I insist that all this chi-chi, cagy business 'bout your address got to stop."

Charlie came closer to them, as if to force them backward down the corridor.

"Sorry, but I can't. Tell me where you'll be and I'll phone you in half an hour."

This made no impression. Lorraine sat down suddenly on the side of a chair, and focusing her eyes on Richard, cried, "Oh, what a nice little boy! Come here, little boy." Richard glanced at his mother, but did not move. With a perceptible shrug of her shoulders, Lorraine turned back to Charlie:

"Come and dine. Sure your cousins won' mine. See you so sel'om. Or solemn."

"I can't," said Charlie sharply. "You two have dinner and I'll phone you."

Her voice became suddenly unpleasant. "All right, we'll go. But I remember once you hammered on my door at four A.M. I was enough of a good sport to give you a drink. Come on, Dunc."

Still in slow motion, with blurred, angry faces, with uncertain feet, they retired along the corridor.

"Good night," Charlie said.

"Good night!" responded Lorraine emphatically.

When he went back into the salon Marion had not moved, only now her son was standing in the circle of her other arm. Lincoln was still swinging Honoria back and forth like a pendulum from side to side.

"What an outrage!" Charlie broke out. "What an absolute outrage!"

Neither of them answered. Charlie dropped into an armchair, picked up his drink, set it down again and said:

"People I haven't seen for two years having the colossal nerve—"

He broke off. Marion had made the sound "Oh!" in one swift, furious breath, turned her body from him with a jerk, and left the room.

Lincoln set down Honoria carefully.

"You children go in and start your soup," he said, and when they obeyed, he said to Charlie:

"Marion's not well and she can't stand shocks. That kind of people make her really physically sick."

"I didn't tell them to come here. They wormed your name out of somebody. They deliberately—"

"Well, it's too bad. It doesn't help matters. Excuse me a minute."

Left alone, Charlie sat tense in his chair. In the next room he could hear the children eating, talking in monosyllables, already oblivious to the scene between their elders. He heard a murmur of conversation from a farther room and then the ticking bell of a telephone receiver picked up, and in a panic he moved to the other side of the room and out of earshot.

In a minute Lincoln came back. "Look here, Charlie, I think we'd better call off dinner for tonight. Marion's in bad shape."

"Is she angry with me?"

"Sort of," he said, almost roughly. "She's not strong and—"

"You mean she's changed her mind about Honoria?"

"She's pretty bitter right now. I don't know. You phone me at the bank tomorrow."

"I wish you'd explain to her I never dreamed these people would come here. I'm just as sore as you are."

"I couldn't explain anything to her now."

Charlie got up. He took his coat and hat and started down the corridor. Then he opened the door of the dining room and said in a strange voice, "Good night, children."

Honoria rose and ran around the table to hug him.

"Good night, sweetheart," he said vaguely, and then trying to make his voice more tender, trying to conciliate something, "Good night, dear children."

V

Charlie went directly to the Ritz bar with the furious idea of finding Lorraine and Duncan, but they were not there, and he realized that in any case there was nothing he could do. He had not touched his drink at the Peters', and now he ordered a whisky-and-soda. Paul came over to say hello.

"It's a great change," he said sadly. "We do about half the business we did. So many fellows I hear about back in the States lost everything, maybe not in the first crash, but then in the second. Your friend George Hardt lost every cent, I hear. Are you back in the States?"

"No, I'm in business in Prague."

"I heard that you lost a lot in the crash."

"I did," and he added grimly, "but I lost everything I wanted in the boom."

"Selling short."

"Something like that."

Again the memory of those days swept over him like a nightmare—the people they had met travelling; then people who couldn't add a row of figures or speak a coherent sentence. The little man Helen had consented to dance with at the ship's party, who had insulted her ten feet from the table; the women and girls carried screaming with drink or drugs out of public places—

—The men who locked their wives out in the snow, because the snow of twenty-nine wasn't real snow. If you didn't want it to be snow, you just paid some money.

He went to the phone and called the Peters' apartment; Lincoln answered.

"I called up because this thing is on my mind. Has Marion said anything definite?"

"Marion's sick," Lincoln answered shortly. "I know this thing isn't altogether your fault, but I can't have her go to pieces about it. I'm afraid we'll have to let it slide for six months; I can't take the chance of working her up to this state again."

"I see."

"I'm sorry, Charlie."

He went back to his table. His whisky glass was empty, but he shook his head when Alix looked at it questioningly. There wasn't much he could do now except send Honoria some things; he would send her a lot of things tomorrow. He thought rather angrily that this was just money—he had given so many people money. . . .

"No, no more," he said to another waiter. "What do I owe you?"

He would come back some day; they couldn't make him pay forever. But he wanted his child, and nothing was much good now, beside that fact. He wasn't young any more, with a lot of nice thoughts and dreams to have by himself. He was absolutely sure Helen wouldn't have wanted him to be so alone.

QUESTIONS

1. How are the themes of loneliness and expatriation developed through the setting? What major images contribute to their development?
2. What is the time scheme of the story? Does Fitzgerald use time dramatically? Does time serve any thematic function?
3. Naming is a favorite fictional device of Fitzgerald's. What function do names—proper names and place names—serve in the story? What is the significance of the title?
4. How would you characterize Charlie Wales—strong, weak, aggressive, passive, emotional, self-restrained? Is there any development in his character? How does he compare with other figures in the story?
5. Fitzgerald has often been accused of not understanding economics, or rather of not appreciating the social consequences of money. Does "Babylon Revisited" justify that criticism?

Graham Greene *(1904–) was born in Berkamstead, England, and was educated at the local boys' school where his father was headmaster. After an unhappy, introspective childhood and several suicide attempts, he attended Oxford and became interested in journalism. He traveled extensively, reporting on major international events and gathering factual material for his fiction. He covered the war in IndoChina as a newspaper reporter and later utilized his impressions for* The Quiet American *(1955). Many of his works, including his first novel,* The Man Within *(1929), are semi-mystery psychological thrillers. Although much of Greene's fiction has been considered religious in nature, it was not until* Brighton Rock *(1938) that Roman Catholicism became central in his works. In addition to twenty-six novels, Greene has written children's books, plays, and essays, published as* Collected Essays *(1969). His short stories have been collected in* A Sense of Reality *(1963),* May We Borrow Your Husband? and Other Comedies of Sexual Life *(1967), and, most recently,* Collected Stories *(1973). Mr. Greene holds The Chevalier of the Legion of Honor (1969).*

Cheap in August

GRAHAM GREENE

I

It was cheap in August: the essential sun, the coral reefs, the bamboo bar, and the calypsos—they were all of them at cut prices, like the slightly soiled slips in a bargain-sale. Groups arrived periodically from Philadelphia in the manner of school-treats and departed with less *bruit*, after an exact exhausting week, when the picnic was over. Perhaps for twenty-four hours the swimming pool and the bar were almost deserted, and then another school-treat would arrive, this time from St. Louis. Everyone knew everyone else; they had bussed together to an airport, they had flown together, together they had faced an alien customs; they would separate during the day and greet each other noisily and happily after dark, exchanging impressions of "shooting the rapids," the botanic gardens, the Spanish fort. "We are doing that tomorrow."

Mary Watson wrote to her husband in Europe, "I had to get away for a bit and it's so cheap in August." They had been married ten years and they had only been separated three times. He wrote to her every day and the letters arrived twice a week in little bundles. She arranged them like newspapers by the date and read them in the correct order. They were tender and precise; what with his research, with preparing lectures and writing letters, he had little time to *see* Europe—he insisted on calling it "your Europe" as though to assure her that he had not forgotten the sacrifice which she must have made by marrying an American professor from New England, but sometimes little criticisms of "her Europe" escaped him: the food was too rich, cigarettes too expensive, wine too often served and milk very difficult to obtain at lunchtime—which might indicate that, after all, she ought not to exaggerate her sacrifice. Perhaps it would have been a good thing if James Thomson, who was his special study at the moment, had written *The Seasons* in America—an American autumn, she had to admit, was more beautiful than an English one.

Mary Watson wrote to him every other day, but sometimes a postcard only, and she was apt to forget if she had repeated the postcard. She wrote in the shade of the bamboo bar where she could see everyone who passed on the way to the swimming pool. She wrote truthfully, "It's so cheap in August; the hotel is not half full, and the heat and the humidity are very tiring. But, of course, it's a change." She had no wish to appear extravagant; the salary, which to her European eyes had seemed astronomically large for a professor of literature, had long dwindled to its proper proportions, relative to the price of steaks and salads—she must justify with a little enthusiasm the money she was spending in his absence. So she wrote also about the flowers in the botanic gardens—she had ventured that far on one occasion—and with less truth of the beneficial changes wrought by the sun and the lazy life on her friend Margaret who from "her England" had written and demanded her company: a Margaret, she admitted frankly to herself, who was not visible to any eye but the eye of faith. But then Charlie had complete faith. Even good qualities become with the erosion of time a reproach. After ten years of being happily married, she thought, one undervalues security and tranquility.

She read Charlie's letters with great attention. She longed to find in them one ambiguity, one evasion, one time-gap which he had ill-explained. Even an unusually strong expression of love would have pleased her, for its strength might have been there to counterweigh a sense of guilt. But she couldn't deceive herself that there was any sense of guilt in Charlie's facile flowing informative script. She calculated that if he had been one of the poets he was now so closely studying, he would have completed already a standard-sized epic during his first two months in "her Europe," and the letters, after all, were only a spare-time occupation. They filled up the vacant hours, and certainly they could have left no room for any other occupation. "It is ten o'clock at night, it is raining outside and the temperature is rather cool for August, not above fifty-six degrees. When I have said good-night to you, dear one, I shall go happily to bed with the thought of you. I have a long day tomorrow at the museum and dinner in the evening with the Henry Wilkinsons who are passing through on their way from Athens—you remember the Henry Wilkinsons, don't you?" (Didn't she just?) She had wondered whether, when Charlie returned, she might perhaps detect some small unfamiliar note in his love-making which would indicate that a stranger had passed that way. Now she disbelieved in the possibility, and anyway the evidence would arrive too late—it was no good to her now that she might be justified later. She wanted her justification immediately, a justification not alas! for any act that she had committed but only for an intention, for the intention of betraying Charlie, of having, like so many of her friends, a holiday affair (the idea had come to her immediately the dean's wife had said, "It's so cheap in Jamaica in August").

The trouble was that, after three weeks of calypsos in the humid evenings, the rum punches (for which she could no longer disguise from herself a repugnance), the warm martinis, the interminable red snappers, and tomatoes with everything, there had been no affair, not even the hint of one. She had discovered with disappointment the essential morality of a holiday resort in the cheap season; there were no opportunities for infidelity, only for writing postcards—with great brilliant blue skies and seas—to Charlie. Once a woman from St. Louis had taken too obvious pity on her, when she sat alone in the bar writing postcards, and invited her to join their party which was about to visit the botanic gardens—"We are an awfully jolly bunch," she had said with a big turnip smile. Mary exaggerated her English accent to repel her better and said that she didn't much care for flowers. It had shocked the woman as deeply as if she had said she did not care for television. From the motion of the heads at the other end of the bar, the agitated clinking of the Coca-Cola glasses, she could tell that her words were being repeated from one to another. Afterwards, until the jolly bunch had taken the airport limousine on the way back to St. Louis, she was aware of averted heads. She was English, she had taken a superior attitude to flowers, and as she preferred even warm martinis to Coca-Cola, she was probably in their eyes an alcoholic.

It was a feature common to most of these jolly bunches that they contained no male attachment, and perhaps that was why the attempt to look attractive was completely abandoned. Huge buttocks were exposed in their full horror in tight large-patterned Bermuda shorts. Heads were bound in scarves to cover rollers which were not removed even by lunch-time—they stuck out like small mole-hills. Daily she watched the bums lurch by like hippos on the way to the water. Only in the evening would the women change from the monstrous shorts into monstrous cotton frocks, covered with mauve or scarlet flowers, in order to take dinner on the terrace where formality was demanded in the book of rules, and the few men who appeared were forced to wear jackets and ties though the thermometer stood at close on eighty degrees after sunset. The market in femininity being such, how could one hope to see any male foragers? Only old and broken husbands were sometimes to be seen towed towards an Issa store advertising free-port prices.

She had been encouraged during the first week by the sight of three men with crew-cuts who went past the bar towards the swimming pool wearing male bikinis. They were far too young for her, but in her present mood she would have welcomed altruistically the sight of another's romance. Romance is said to be contagious, and if in the candle-lit evenings the "informal" coffee-tavern had contained a few young amorous couples, who could say what men of maturer years might not eventually arrive to catch the infection? But her hopes dwindled. The young men came and went without a glance at the Bermuda shorts or the pinned hair. Why should they stay? They were certainly more beautiful than any girl there and they knew it.

By nine o'clock most evenings Mary Watson was on her way to bed. A few evenings of calypsos, of quaint false impromptus and the hideous jangle of rattles had been enough. Outside the closed windows of the hotel annex the boxes of the air conditioners made a continuous rumble in the starry palmy night like overfed hotel guests. Her room was full of dried air which bore no more resemblance to fresh air than the dried figs to the newly picked fruit. When she looked in the glass to brush her hair she often regretted her lack of charity to the jolly bunch from St. Louis. It was true she did not wear Bermuda shorts nor coil her hair in rollers, but her hair was streaky nonetheless with heat and the mirror reflected more plainly than it seemed to do at home her thirty-nine years. If she had not paid in advance for a four-weeks *pension* on her individual round-trip tour, with tickets exchangeable for a variety of excursions, she would have turned tail and returned to the campus. Next year, she thought, when I am forty, I must feel grateful that I have preserved the love of a good man.

She was a woman given to self-analysis, and perhaps because it is a great deal easier to direct questions to a particular face rather than to a void (one has the right to expect some kind of a response even from eyes one sees many times a day in a compact), she posed the questions to herself with a belligerent direct stare into the looking-glass. She was an honest woman, and for that reason the questions were all the cruder. She would say to herself, I have slept with no one other than Charlie (she wouldn't admit as sexual experiences the small exciting halfway points that she had reached before marriage); why am I now seeking to find a strange body, which will probably give me less pleasure than the body I already know? It had been more than a month before Charlie brought her real pleasure. Pleasure, she learned, grew with habit, so that if it were not really pleasure that she looked for, what was it? The answer could only be the unfamiliar. She had friends, even on the respectable campus, who had admitted to her, in the frank admirable American way, their adventures. These had usually been in Europe—a momentary marital absence had given the opportunity for a momentary excitement, and then with what a sigh of relief they had found themselves safely at home. All the same they felt afterwards that they had enlarged their experience; they understood something that their husbands did not really understand—the real character of a Frenchman, an Italian, even—there were such cases—of an Englishman.

Mary Watson was painfully aware, as an Englishwoman, that her experience was confined to one American. They all, on the campus, believed her to be European, but all she knew was confined to one man and he was a citizen of Boston who had no curiosity for the great Western regions. In a sense she was more American by choice than he was by birth. Perhaps she was less European even than the wife of the Professor of Romance Languages, who had confided to her that once—overwhelmingly—in Antibes . . . it had happened only once because the sabbatical year was over . . . her husband was up in Paris checking manuscripts before they flew home . . . .

Had she herself, Mary Watson sometimes wondered, been just such a European adventure which Charlie mistakenly had domesticated? (She couldn't pretend to be a tigress in a cage, but they kept smaller creatures in cages, white mice, love-birds.) And, to be fair, Charlie too was her adventure, her American adventure, the kind of man whom at twenty-seven she had not before encountered in frowsy London. Henry James had described the type, and at that moment in her history she had been reading a great deal of Henry James: "A man of intellect whose body was not much to him and its senses and appetites not importunate." All the same, for a while she had made the appetites importunate.

That was her private conquest of the American continent, and when the Professor's wife had spoken of the dancer of Antibes (no, that was a Roman inscription—the man had been a *marchand de vin*) she had thought, The lover I know and admire is American and I am proud of it. But afterwards came the thought: American or New England? Yet to know a country must one know every region sexually?

It was absurd at thirty-nine not to be content. She had her man. The book on James Thomson would be published by the University Press, and Charlie had the intention afterwards of making a revolutionary break from the romantic poetry of the eighteenth century into a study of the American image in European literature—it was to be called *The Double Reflection:* the effect of Fenimore Cooper on the European scene; the image of America presented by Mrs. Trollope—the details were not yet worked out. The study might possibly end with the first arrival of Dylan Thomas on the shores of America—at the Cunard quay or at Idlewild? That was a point for later research. She examined herself again closely in the glass—the new decade of the forties stared frankly back at her—an Englander who had become a New Englander. After all she hadn't traveled very far—Kent to Connecticut. This was not just the physical restlessness of middle age, she argued; it was the universal desire to see a little bit further, before one surrendered to old age and the blank certitude of death.

II

Next day she picked up her courage and went as far as the swimming pool. A strong wind blew and whipped up the waves in the almost land-girt harbor—the hurricane season would soon be here. All the world creaked around her: the wooden struts of the shabby harbor, the jalousies of the small hopeless houses which looked as though they had been knocked together from a make-it-yourself kit, the branches of the palms—a long, weary, worn-out creaking. Even the water of the swimming pool imitated in miniature the waves of the harbor.

She was glad that she was alone in the swimming pool, at least for all practical purposes alone, for the old man splashing water over himself, like an elephant, in the shallow end hardly counted. He was a solitary elephant and not one of the hippo band. They would have called her with merry cries to join them—and it's difficult to be standoffish in a swimming pool which is common to all as a table is not. They might even in their resentment have ducked her—pretending like schoolchildren that it was all a merry game; there was nothing she put beyond those thick thighs, whether they were encased in bikinis or Bermuda shorts. As she floated in the pool her ears were alert for their approach. At the first sound she would get well away from the water, but today they were probably making an excursion to Tower Isle on the other side of the island, or had they done that yesterday? Only the old man watched her, pouring water over his head to keep away sunstroke. She was safely alone, which was the next best thing to the adventure she had come here to find. All the same, as she sat on the rim of the pool, and let the sun and wind dry her, she realized the extent of her solitude. She had spoken to no one but black waiters and Syrian receptionists for more than two weeks. Soon, she thought, I shall even begin to miss Charlie—it would be an ignoble finish to what she had intended to be an adventure.

A voice from the water said to her, "My name's Hickslaughter—Henry Hickslaughter." She couldn't have sworn to the name in court, but that was how it had sounded at the time and he never repeated it.

She looked down at a polished mahogany crown surrounded by white hair; perhaps he resembled Neptune more than an elephant. Neptune was always outsize, and as he had pulled himself a little out of the water to speak, she could see the rolls of fat folding over the blue bathing-slip, with tough hair lying like weeds along the ditches. She replied with amusement, "My name is Watson. Mary Watson."

"You're English?"

"My husband's American," she said in extenuation.

"I haven't seen him around, have I?"

"He's in England," she said with a small sigh, for the geographical and national situation seemed too complicated for casual explanation.

"You like it here?" he asked and lifting a hand-cup of water he distributed it over his bald head.

"So-so."

"Got the time on you?"

She looked in her bag and told him, "Eleven-fifteen."

"I've had my half-hour," he said and trod heavily away towards the ladder at the shallow end.

An hour later, staring at her lukewarm martini with its great green unappetizing olive, she saw him looming down at her from the other end of the bamboo bar. He wore an ordinary shirt open at the neck and a brown leather belt; his type of shoes in her childhood had been known as co-respondent, but one seldom saw them today. She wondered what Charlie would think of her pick-up; unquestionably she had landed him, rather as an angler struggling with a heavy catch finds that he has hooked nothing better than an old boot. She was no angler; she didn't know whether a boot would put an ordinary hook out of action altogether, but she knew that *her* hook could be irremediably damaged. No one would approach her if she were in his company. She drained the martini in one gulp and even attacked the olive so as to have no excuse to linger in the bar.

"Would you do me the honor," Mr. Hickslaughter asked, "of having a drink with me?" His manner was completely changed; on dry land he seemed unsure of himself and spoke with an old-fashioned propriety.

"I'm afraid I've only just finished one. I have to be off." Inside the gross form she thought she saw a tousled child with disappointed eyes. "I'm having lunch early today." She got up and added rather stupidly, for the bar was quite empty, "You can have my table."

"I don't need a drink that much," he said solemnly. "I was just after company." She knew that he was watching her as she moved to the adjoining coffee tavern, and she thought with guilt, at least I've got the old boot off the hook. She refused the shrimp cocktail with tomato ketchup and fell back as was usual with her on a grapefruit, with grilled trout to follow. "Please no tomato with the trout," she implored, but the black waiter obviously didn't understand her. While she waited she began with amusement to picture a scene between Charlie and Mr. Hickslaughter, who happened for the purpose of her story to be crossing the campus. "This is Henry Hickslaughter, Charlie. We used to go bathing together when I was in Jamaica." Charlie, who always wore English clothes, was very tall, very thin, very concave. It was a satisfaction to know that he would never lose his figure—his nerves would see to that and his extreme sensibility. He hated anything gross; there was no grossness in *The Seasons*, not even in the lines on spring.

She heard slow footsteps coming up behind her and nearly panicked. "May I share your table?" Mr. Hickslaughter asked. He had recovered his terrestrial politeness, but only so far as speech was concerned, for he sat firmly down without waiting for her reply. The chair was too small for him; his thighs overlapped like a double mattress on a single bed. He began to study the menu.

"They copy American food; it's worse than the reality," Mary Watson said.

"You don't like American food?"

"Tomatoes even with the trout!"

"Tomatoes? Oh, you mean tomatoes," he said, correcting her accent. "I'm very fond of tomatoes myself."

"And fresh pineapple in the salad."

"There's a lot of vitamins in fresh pineapple." Almost as if he wished to emphasize their disagreement, he ordered shrimp cocktail, grilled trout, and a sweet salad. Of course, when her trout arrived, the tomatoes were there. "You can have mine if you want to," she said and he accepted with pleasure. "You are very kind. You are really very kind." He held out his plate like Oliver Twist.

She began to feel oddly at ease with the old man. She would have been less at ease, she was certain, with a possible adventure: she would have been wondering about her effect on him, while now she could be sure that she gave him pleasure—with the tomatoes. He was perhaps less the old anonymous boot than an old shoe comfortable to wear. And curiously enough, in spite of his first approach and in spite of his correcting her over the pronunciation of tomatoes, it was not really an old American shoe of which she was reminded. Charlie wore English clothes over his English figure, he studied English eighteenth-century literature, his book would be published in England by the Cambridge University Press who would buy sheets, but she had the impression that he was far more fashioned as an American shoe than Hickslaughter. Even Charlie, whose manners were perfect, if they had met for the first time today at the swimming pool, would have interrogated her more closely. Interrogation had always seemed to her a principal part of American social life—an inheritance perhaps from the Indian smoke-fires: "Where are you from? Do you know the so-and-so's? Have you been to the botanic gardens?" It came over her that Mr. Hickslaughter, if that were really his name, was perhaps an American reject—not necessarily more flawed than the pottery rejects of famous firms you find in bargain-basements.

She found herself questioning *him*, with circumlocutions, while he savored the tomatoes. "I was born in London. I couldn't have been born more than four hundred miles from there without drowning, could I? But you belong to a continent thousands of miles wide and long. Where were you born?" (She remembered a character in a Western movie directed by John Ford who asked, "Where do you hail from, stranger?" The question was more frankly put than hers.)

He said, "St. Louis."

"Oh, then there are lots of your people here—you are not alone." She felt a slight disappointment that he might belong to the jolly bunch.

"I'm alone," he said. "Room 63." It was in her own corridor on the third floor of the annex. He spoke firmly as though he were imparting information for future use. "Five doors down from you."

"Oh."

"I saw you come out your first day."

"I never noticed you."

"I keep to myself unless I see someone I like."

"Didn't you see anyone you liked from St. Louis?"

"I'm not all that fond of St. Louis, and St. Louis can do without me. I'm not a favorite son."

"Do you come here often?"

"In August. It's cheap in August." He kept on surprising her. First there was his lack of local patriotism, and now his frankness about money or rather about the lack of it, a frankness that could almost be classed as an un-American activity.

"Yes."

"I have to go where it's reasonable," he said, as though he were exposing his bad hand to a partner at gin.

"You've retired?"

"Well—I've been retired." He added, "You ought to take salad . . . It's good for you."

"I feel quite well without it."

"You could do with more weight." He added appraisingly, "A couple of pounds." She was tempted to tell him that he could do with less. They had both seen each other exposed.

"Were you in business?" She was being driven to interrogate. He hadn't asked her a personal question since his first at the pool.

"In a way," he said. She had a sense that he was supremely uninterested in his own doings; she was certainly discovering an America which she had not known existed.

She said, "Well, if you'll excuse me . . . "

"Aren't you taking any dessert?"

"No, I'm a light luncher."

"It's all included in the price. You ought to eat some fruit." He was looking at her under his white eyebrows with an air of disappointment which touched her.

"I don't care much for fruit and I want a nap. I always have a nap in the afternoon."

Perhaps, after all, she thought, as she moved away through the formal dining-room, he is disappointed only because I'm not taking full advantage of the cheap rate.

She passed his room going to her own: the door was open and a big white-haired mammy was making the bed. The room was exactly like her own; the same pair of double beds, the same wardrobe, the same dressing-table in the same position, the same heavy breathing of the air-conditioner. In her own room she looked in vain for the thermos of iced water; then she rang the bell and waited for several minutes. You couldn't expect good service in August. She went down the passage; Mr. Hickslaughter's door was still open and she went in to find the maid. The door of the bathroom was open too and a wet cloth lay on the tiles.

How bare the bedroom was. At least she had taken the trouble to add a few flowers, a photograph, and half a dozen books on a bedside table which gave her room a lived-in air. Beside his bed there was only a literary digest lying open and face down; she turned it over to see what he was reading—as she might have expected it was something to do with calories and proteins. He had begun writing a letter at his dressing-table and with the simple unscrupulousness of an intellectual she began to read it with her ears cocked for any sound in the passage.

"Dear Joe," she read, "the draft was two weeks late last month and I was in real difficulties. I had to borrow from a Syrian who runs a tourist junk-shop in Curaçao and pay him interest. You owe me a hundred dollars for the interest. It's your own fault. Mum never gave us lessons on how to live with an empty stomach. Please add it to the next draft and be sure to do that, you wouldn't want me coming back to collect. I'll be here till the end of August. It's cheap in August, and a man gets tired of nothing but Dutch, Dutch, Dutch. Give my love to Sis."

The letter broke off unfinished. Anyway she would have had no opportunity to read more because someone was approaching down the passage. She went to the door in time to see Mr. Hickslaughter on the threshold. He said, "You looking for me?"

"I was looking for the maid. She was in here a minute ago."

"Come in and sit down."

He looked through the bathroom door and then at the room in general. Perhaps it was only an uneasy conscience which made her think that his eyes strayed a moment to the unfinished letter.

"She's forgotten my iced water."

"You can have mine if it's filled." He shook his thermos and handed it to her.

"Thanks a lot."

"When you've had your sleep . . . " he began and looked away from her. Was he looking at the letter?

"Yes?"

"We might have a drink."

She was, in a sense, trapped. She said, "Yes."

"Give me a ring when you wake up."

"Yes." She said nervously, "Have a good sleep yourself."

"Oh, I don't sleep." He didn't wait for her to leave the room before turning away, swinging that great elephantine backside of his towards her. She had walked into a trap baited with a flask of iced water, and in her room she drank the water gingerly as though it might have a flavor different from hers.

III

She found it difficult to sleep: the old fat man had become an individual now that she had read his letter. She couldn't help comparing his style with Charlie's. "When I have said good-night to you, my dear one, I shall go happily to bed with the thought of you." In Mr. Hickslaughter's there was an ambiguity, a hint of menace. Was it possible that the old man could be dangerous?

At half past five she rang up room 63. It was not the kind of adventure she had planned, but it was an adventure nonetheless. "I'm awake," she said.

"You coming for a drink?" he asked.

"I'll meet you in the bar."

"Not the bar," he said. "Not at the prices they charge for bourbon. I've got all we need here." She felt as though she were being brought back to the scene of a crime, and she needed a little courage to knock on the door.

He had everything prepared: a bottle of Old Walker, a bucket of ice, two bottles of soda. Like books, drinks can make a room inhabited. She saw him as a man fighting in his own fashion against the sense of solitude.

"Siddown," he said, "make yourself comfortable," like a character in a movie. He began to pour out two highballs.

She said, "I've got an awful sense of guilt. I did come in here for iced water, but I was curious too. I read your letter."

"I knew someone had touched it," he said.

"I'm sorry."

"Who cares? It was only to my brother."

"I had no business . . . "

"Look," he said, "if I came into your room and found a letter open I'd read it, wouldn't I? Only your letter would be more interesting."

"Why?"

"I don't write love letters. Never did and I'm too old now." He sat down on a bed—she had the only easy chair. His belly hung in heavy folds under his sports-shirt, and his fly was a little open. Why was it always fat men who left them unbuttoned? He said, "This is good bourbon," taking a drain of it. "What does your husband do?" he asked—it was his first personal question since the pool, and it took her by surprise.

"He writes about literature. Eighteenth-century poetry," she added, rather inanely under the circumstances.

"Oh."

"What did you do? I mean when you worked?"

"This and that."

"And now?"

"I watch what goes on. Sometimes I talk to someone like you. Well, no, I don't suppose I've ever talked to anyone like you before." It might have seemed a compliment if he had not added, "A professor's wife."

"And you read the *Digest*?"

"Ye-eh. They make books too long—I haven't the patience. Eighteenth-century poetry. So they wrote poetry back in those days, did they?"

She said, "Yes," not sure whether or not he was mocking her.

"There was a poem I liked at school. The only one that ever stuck in my head. By Longfellow, I think. You ever read Longfellow?"

"Not really. They don't read him much in school any longer."

"Something about 'Spanish sailors with bearded lips and the something and mystery of the ships and the something of the sea.' It hasn't stuck all that well, after all, but I suppose I learned that sixty years ago and even more. Those were the days."

"The nineteen-hundreds?"

"No, no. I meant pirates, Kidd and Bluebeard and those fellows. This was their stamping ground, wasn't it? The Caribbean. It makes you kind of sick to see those women going around in their shorts here." His tongue had been tingled into activity by the bourbon.

It occurred to her that she had never really been curious about another human being; she had been in love with Charlie, but he hadn't aroused her curiosity except sexually, and she had satisfied that only too quickly. She asked him, "Do you love your sister?"

"Yes, of course, why? How do you know I've got a sister?"

"And Joe?"

"You certainly read my letter. Oh, he's O.K."

"O.K.?"

"Well, you know how it is with brothers. I'm the eldest in my family. There was one that died. My sister's twenty years younger than I am. Joe's got the means. He looks after her."

"You haven't got the means?"

"I had the means. I wasn't good at managing them though. We aren't here to talk about myself."

"I'm curious. That's why I read your letter."

"You? Curious about me?"

"It could be, couldn't it?"

She had confused him, and now that she had the upper hand, she felt that she was out of the trap; she was free, she could come and go as she pleased, and if she chose to stay a little longer, it was her own choice.

"Have another bourbon?" he said. "But you're English. Maybe you'd prefer Scotch?"

"Better not mix."

"No." He poured her another glass. He said, "I was wondering—sometimes I want to get away from this joint for a little. What about having dinner down the road?"

"It would be stupid," she said. "We've both paid our *pension* here, haven't we? And it would be the same dinner in the end. Red snapper. Tomatoes."

"I don't know what you have against tomatoes." But he did not deny the good sense of her economic reasoning: he was the first unsuccessful American she had ever had a drink with. One must have seen them in the street . . . But even the young men who came to the house were not yet unsuccessful. The Professor of Romance Languages had perhaps hoped to be head of a university—success is relative, but it remains success.

He poured out another glass. She said, "I'm drinking all your bourbon."

"It's in a good cause."

She was a little drunk by now and things—which only *seemed* relevant—came to her mind. She said, "That thing of Longfellow's. It went on—something about 'the thoughts of youth are long, long thoughts.' I must have read it somewhere. That was the refrain, wasn't it?"

"Maybe. I don't remember."

"Did you want to be a pirate when you were a boy?"

He gave an almost happy grin. He said, "I succeeded. That's what Joe called me once—'pirate.' "

"But you haven't any buried treasure?"

He said, "He knows me well enough not to send me a hundred dollars. But if he feels scared enough that I'll come back—he might send fifty. And the interest was only twenty-five. He's not mean, but he's stupid."

"How?"

"He ought to know I wouldn't go back. I wouldn't do one thing to hurt Sis."

"Would it be any good if I asked you to have dinner with me?"

"No. It wouldn't be right." In some ways he was obviously very conservative. "It's as you said—you don't want to go throwing money about." When the bottle of Old Walker was half empty, he said, "You'd better have some food even if it is red snapper and tomatoes."

"Is your name really Hickslaughter?"

"Something like that."

They went downstairs, following rather carefully in each other's footsteps like ducks. In the formal restaurant open to all the heat of the evening, the men sat and sweated in their jackets and ties. They passed, the two of them, through the bamboo bar into the coffee tavern, which was lit by candles that increased the heat. Two young men with crewcuts sat at the next table—they weren't the same young men she had seen before, but they came out of the same series. One of them said, "I'm not denying that he has a certain style, but even if you *adore* Tennessee Williams . . . "

"Why did he call you a pirate?"

"It was just one of those things."

When it came to the decision there seemed nothing to choose except red snapper and tomatoes, and again she offered him her tomatoes; perhaps he had grown to expect it and already she was chained by custom. He was an old man, he had made no pass which she could reasonably reject—how could a man of his age make a pass to a woman of hers?—and yet all the same she had a sense that she had landed on a conveyor belt . . . The future was not in her hands, and she was a little scared. She would have been more frightened if it had not been for her unusual consumption of bourbon.

"It was good bourbon," she commented for something to say, and immediately regretted it. It gave him an opening.

"We'll have another glass before bed."

"I think I've drunk enough."

"A good bourbon won't hurt you. You'll sleep well."

"I always sleep well." It was a lie—the kind of unimportant lie one tells a husband or a lover in order to keep some privacy. The young man who had been talking about Tennessee Williams rose from his table. He was very tall and thin and he wore a skin-tight black sweater; his small elegant buttocks were outlined in skin-tight trousers. It was easy to imagine him a degree more naked. Would he have looked at her, she wondered, with any interest if she had not been sitting there in the company of a fat old man so horribly clothed? It was unlikely; his body was not designed for a woman's caress.

"I don't."

"You don't what?"

"I don't sleep well." The unexpected self-disclosure after all his reticences came as a shock. It was as though he had put out one of his square bricklike hands and pulled her to him. He had been aloof, he had evaded her personal questions, he had lulled her into a sense of security, but now every time she opened her mouth, she seemed doomed to commit an error, to invite him nearer. Even her harmless remark about the bourbon . . . She said stupidly, "Perhaps it's the change of climate."

"What change of climate?"

"Between here and . . . and . . . "

"Curaçao? I guess there's no great difference. I don't sleep there either."

"I've got some very good pills . . . " she said rashly.

"I thought you said you slept well."

"Oh, there are always times. It's sometimes just a question of digestion."

"Yes, digestion. You're right there. A bourbon will be good for that. If you've finished dinner . . . "

She looked across the coffee tavern to the bamboo bar, where the young man stood *déhanché*, holding a glass of crème-de-menthe between his face and his companion's like an exotically colored monocle.

Mr. Hickslaughter said in a shocked voice, "You don't care for that type, do you?"

"They're often good conversationalists."

"Oh, conversation . . . If that's what you want." It was as though she had expressed an un-American liking for snails or frogs' legs.

"Shall we have our bourbon in the bar? It's a little cooler tonight."

"And listen to their chatter? No, we'll go upstairs."

He swung back again in the direction of old-fashioned courtesy and came behind her to pull her chair—even Charlie was not so polite, but was it politeness or the determination to block her way of escape to the bar?

They entered the lift together. The black attendant had a radio turned on, and from the small brown box came the voice of a preacher talking about the Blood of the Lamb. Perhaps it was a Sunday, and that would explain the temporary void around them—between one jolly bunch and another. They stepped out into the empty corridor like undesirables marooned. The boy followed them out and sat down upon a chair beside the elevator to wait for another signal, while the voice continued to talk about the Blood of the Lamb. What was she afraid of? Mr. Hickslaughter began to unlock his door. He was much older than her father would have been if he had been still alive; he could be her grandfather—the excuse, "What will the boy think?" was inadmissible—it was even shocking, for his manner had never ceased to be correct. He might be old, but what right had she to think of him as "dirty"?

"Damn the hotel key . . . " he said. "It won't open."

She turned the handle for him. "The door wasn't locked."

"I can sure do with a bourbon after those nancies . . . "

But now she had her excuse ready on the lips. "I've had one too many already, I'm afraid. I've got to sleep it off." She put her hand on his arm. "Thank you so much . . . It was a lovely evening." She was aware how insulting her English accent sounded as she walked quickly down the corridor leaving it behind her like a mocking presence, mocking all the things she liked best in him: his ambiguous character, his memory of Longfellow, his having to make ends meet.

She looked back when she reached her room: he was standing in the passage as though he couldn't make up his mind to go in. She was reminded of an old man whom she had passed one day on the campus leaning on his broom among the unswept autumn leaves.

IV

In her room she picked up a book and tried to read. It was Thomson's *Seasons*. She had carried it with her, so that she could understand any reference to his work that Charlie might make in a letter. This was the first time she had opened it, and she was not held:

> And now the mounting Sun dispels the Fog:
> The rigid Hoar-Frost melts before his Beam;
> And hung on every Spray, on every Blade
> Of Grass, the myriad Dew-Drops twinkle round.

If she could be so cowardly, she thought, with a harmless old man like that, how could she have faced the real decisiveness of an adventure? One was not, at her age, "swept off the feet." Charlie had been proved just as sadly right to trust her as she was right to trust Charlie. Now with the difference in time he would be leaving the Museum, or rather, if this were a Sunday as the Blood of the Lamb seemed to indicate, he would probably have just quit writing in his hotel room. After a successful day's work he always resembled an advertisement for a new shaving-cream: a kind of glow . . . She found it irritating, like living with a halo. Even his voice had a different timbre and he would call her "old girl" and pat her bottom patronizingly. She preferred him when he was touchy with failure: only temporary failure, of course, the failure of an idea which hadn't worked out, the touchiness of a child's disappointment at a party which has not come up to his expectations, not the failure of the old man—the rusted framework of a ship transfixed once and for all upon the rock where it had struck.

She felt ignoble. What earthly risk could the old man represent to justify refusing him half an hour's companionship? He could no more assault her than the boat could detach itself from the rock and steam out to sea for the Fortunate Islands. She pictured him sitting alone with his half-empty bottle of bourbon seeking unconsciousness. Or was he perhaps finishing the crude blackmailing letter to his brother? What a story she would make of it one day, she thought with self-disgust as she took off her dress, her evening with a blackmailer and "pirate."

There was one thing she could do for him: she could give him her bottle of pills. She put on her dressing gown and retrod the corridor, room by room, until she arrived at 63. His voice told her to come in. She opened the door and in the light of the bedside lamp saw him sitting on the edge of the bed wearing a crumpled pair of cotton pajamas with broad mauve stripes. She began, "I've brought you . . . " and then she saw to her amazement that he had been crying. His eyes were red and the evening darkness of his cheeks sparkled with points like dew. She had only once before seen a man cry—Charlie, when the University Press had decided against his first volume of literary essays.

"I thought you were the maid," he said. "I rang for her."

"What did you want?"

"I thought she might take a glass of bourbon," he said.

"Did you want so much . . . ? I'll take a glass." The bottle was still on the dressing-table where they had left it and the two glasses—she identified hers by the smear of lipstick. "Here you are," she said, "drink it up. It will make you sleep."

He said, "I'm not an alcoholic."

"Of course you aren't."

She sat on the bed beside him and took his left hand in hers. It was cracked and dry, and she wanted to clean back the cuticle until she remembered that was something she did for Charlie.

"I wanted company," he said.

"I'm here."

"You'd better turn off the bell-light or the maid will come."

"She'll never know what she missed in the way of Old Walker."

When she returned from the door he was lying back against the pillows in an odd twisted position, and she thought again of the ship broken-backed upon the rocks. She tried to pick up his feet to lay them on the bed, but they were like heavy stones at the bottom of a quarry.

"Lie down," she said, "you'll never be sleepy that way. What do you do for company in Curaçao?"

"I manage," he said.

"You've finished the bourbon. Let me put out the lights."

"It's no good pretending to you," he said.

"Pretending?"

"I'm afraid of the dark."

She thought, I'll smile later when I think of who it was I feared. She said, "Do the old pirates you fought come back to haunt you?"

"I've done some bad things," he said, "in my time."

"Haven't we all?"

"Nothing extraditable," he explained as though that were an extenuation.

"If you take one of my pills . . . "

"You won't go—not yet?"

"No, no. I'll stay till you're sleepy."

"I've been wanting to talk to you for days."

"I'm glad you did."

"Would you believe it—I didn't have the nerve." If she had shut her eyes it might have been a very young man speaking. "I don't know your sort."

"Don't you have my sort in Curaçao?"

"No."

"You haven't taken the pill yet."

"I'm afraid of not waking up."

"Have you so much to do tomorrow?"

"I mean ever." He put out his hand and touched her knee, searchingly, without sensuality, as if he needed support from the bone. "I'll tell you what's wrong. You're a stranger, so I can tell you. I'm afraid of dying, with nobody around, in the dark."

"Are you ill?"

"I wouldn't know. I don't see doctors. I don't like doctors."

"But why should you think. . . ?"

"I'm over seventy. The Bible age. It could happen any day now."

"You'll live to a hundred," she said with an odd conviction.

"Then I'll have to live with fear a hell of a long time."

"Was that why you were crying?"

"No. I thought you were going to stay awhile, and then suddenly you went. I guess I was disappointed."

"Are you never alone in Curaçao?"

"I pay not to bc alone."

"As you'd have paid the maid?"

"Ye-eh. Sort of."

It was as though she were discovering for the first time the interior of the enormous continent on which she had elected to live. America had been Charlie, it had been New England; through books and movies she had been aware of the wonders of nature like some great cineramic film with Lowell Thomas cheapening the Painted Desert and the Grand Canyon with his clichés. There had been no mystery anywhere from Miami to Niagara Falls, from Cape Cod to the Pacific Palisades; tomatoes were served on every plate and Coca-Cola in every glass. Nobody anywhere admitted failure or fear; they were like "sins hushed up"—worse perhaps than sins, for sins have glamour—

they were bad taste. But here stretched on the bed, dressed in striped pajamas which Brooks Brothers would have disowned, failure and fear talked to her without shame, and in an American accent. It was as though she were living in the remote future, after God knew what catastrophe.

She said, "I wasn't for sale? There was only the Old Walker to tempt *me*."

He raised his antique Neptune head a little way from the pillow and said, "I'm not afraid of death. Not sudden death. Believe me, I've looked for it here and there. It's this certain-sure business, closing in on you, like tax-inspectors . . . "

She said, "Sleep now."

"I can't."

"Yes, you can."

"If you'd stay with me awhile . . . "

"I'll stay with you. Relax." She lay down on the bed beside him on the outside of the sheet. In a few minutes he was deeply asleep and she turned off the light. He grunted several times and spoke only once, when he said, "You've got me wrong," and after that he became for a little while like a dead man in his immobility and his silence, so that during that period she fell asleep. When she woke she was aware from his breathing that he was awake too. He was lying away from her so that their bodies wouldn't touch. She put out her hand and felt no repulsion at all at his excitement. It was as though she had spent many nights beside him in the one bed, and when he made love to her, silently and abruptly in the darkness, she gave a sigh of satisfaction. There was no guilt; she would be going back in a few days, resigned and tender, to Charlie and Charlie's loving skill, and she wept a little, but not seriously, at the temporary nature of this meeting.

"What's wrong?" he asked.

"Nothing. Nothing. I wish I could stay."

"Stay a little longer. Stay till it's light." That would not be very long. Already they could distinguish the grey masses of the furniture standing around them like Caribbean tombs.

"Oh yes, I'll stay till it's light. That's wasn't what I meant." His body began to slip out of her, and it was as though he were carrying away her unknown child, away in the direction of Curaçao, and she tried to hold him back, the fat old frightened man whom she almost loved.

He said, "I never had this in mind."

"I know. Don't say it. I understand."

"I guess after all we've got a lot in common," he said, and she agreed in order to quieten him. He was fast asleep by the time the light came back, so she got off the bed without waking him and went to her room. She locked the door and began with resolution to pack her bag: it was time for her to leave, it was time for term to start again. She wondered afterwards, when she thought of him, what it was they could have had in common, except the fact, of course, that for both of them Jamaica was cheap in August.

QUESTIONS

1. How does Greene create the sensual and languid atmosphere that dominates the story? What images are used to develop the theme of youth and age? What do Mary Watson and Mr. Hickslaughter have in common?
2. Greene divides his story into four sections. Does this division reveal any structure in the narrative?
3. The title of the story is repeated, with variations, more than half-a-dozen times in the text. Does the repetition seem forced or amateurish? Does the title possess any symbolic significance?
4. The plot of the story turns upon an incident of sexual infidelity. Yet Greene has commonly been viewed as a religious artist. Is there a religious theme in the story?
5. "Cheap in August" is an international story—a European discovers America—in the tradition of Henry James. What elements does Greene use to develop the international theme? Read as a companion piece James' own tale, "The Jolly Corner."

Richard Wright *(1908–1960) was born on a plantation near Natchez, Mississippi, moved to Memphis at the age of six, and settled in Chicago at nineteen. He worked as a porter and street cleaner, joined the Communist Party, and contributed to The New Masses. The release of four short novels,* Uncle Tom's Children *(1938), led to a Guggenheim Fellowship and the enormously successful* Native Son *(1940), which Wright adapted into a play (1941). Wright also wrote the text for a photo essay,* Twelve Million Black Voices *(1941). Shortly after the publication of his autobiography,* Black Boy *(1945), Wright moved to Europe and there broke with the Communist Party, writing an essay for* The God That Failed *(1950). A collection of his stories,* Eight Men, *was published the year following his death in Paris.*

The Man Who Lived Underground

RICHARD WRIGHT

I've got to hide, he told himself. His chest heaved as he waited, crouching in a dark corner of the vestibule. He was tired of running and dodging. Either he had to find a place to hide, or he had to surrender. A police car swished by through the rain, its siren rising sharply. They're looking for me all over . . . He crept to the door and squinted through the fogged plate glass. He stiffened as the siren rose and died in the distance. Yes, he had to hide, but where? He gritted his teeth. Then a sudden movement in the street caught his attention. A throng of tiny columns of water snaked into the air from the perforations of a manhole cover. The columns stopped abruptly, as though the perforations had become clogged; a gray spout of sewer water jutted up from underground and lifted the circular metal cover, juggled it for a moment, then let it fall with a clang.

He hatched a tentative plan: he would wait until the siren sounded far off, then he would go out. He smoked and waited, tense. At last the siren gave him his signal; it wailed, dying, going away from him. He stepped to the sidewalk, then paused and looked curiously at the open manhole, half expecting the cover to leap up again. He went to the center of the street and stooped and peered into the hole, but could see nothing. Water rustled in the black depths.

He started with terror; the siren sounded so near that he had the idea that he had been dreaming and had awakened to find the car upon him. He dropped instinctively to his knees and his hands grasped the rim of the manhole. The siren seemed to hoot directly above him and with a wild gasp of exertion he snatched the cover far enough off to admit his body. He swung his legs over the opening and lowered himself into watery darkness. He hung for an eternal moment to the rim by his finger tips, then he felt rough metal prongs and at once he knew that sewer workmen used these ridges to lower themselves into manholes. Fist over fist, he let his body sink until he could feel no more prongs. He swayed in dank space; the siren seemed to howl at the very rim of the manhole. He dropped and was washed violently into an ocean of warm, leaping water. His head was battered against a wall and he wondered if this were death. Frenziedly his fingers clawed and sank into a crevice. He steadied himself and measured the strength of the current with his own muscular tension. He stood slowly in water that dashed past his knees with fearful velocity.

He heard a prolonged scream of brakes and the siren broke off. Oh, God! They had found him! Looming above his head in the rain a white face hovered over the hole. "How did this damn thing get off?" he heard a policeman ask. He saw the steel cover move slowly until the hole looked like a quarter moon turned black. "Give me a hand here," someone called. The cover clanged into place, muffling the sights and sounds of the upper world. Knee-deep in the pulsing current, he breathed with aching chest, filling his lungs with the hot stench of yeasty rot.

From the perforations of the manhole cover, delicate lances of hazy violet sifted down and wove a mottled pattern upon the surface of the streaking current. His lips parted as a car swept past along the wet pavement overhead, its heavy rumble soon dying out, like the hum of a plane speeding through a dense cloud. He had never thought that cars could sound like that; everything seemed strange and unreal under here. He stood in darkness for a long time, knee-deep in rustling water, musing.

The odor of rot had become so general that he no longer smelled it. He got his cigarettes, but discovered that his matches were wet. He searched and found a dry folder in the pocket of his shirt and managed to strike one; it flared weirdly in the wet gloom, glowing greenishly, turning red, orange, then yellow. He lit a crumpled cigarette; then, by the flickering light of the match, he looked for support so that he would not have to keep his muscles flexed against the pouring water. His pupils narrowed and he saw to either side of him two steaming walls that rose and curved inward some six feet above his head to form a dripping, mouse-colored dome. The bottom of the sewer was a sloping V-trough. To the left, the sewer vanished in ashen fog. To the right was a steep down-curve into which water plunged.

He saw now that had he not regained his feet in time, he would have been swept to death, or had he entered any other manhole he would have probably drowned. Above the rush of the current he heard sharper juttings of water; tiny streams were spewing into the sewer from smaller conduits. The match died; he struck another and saw a mass of debris sweep past him and clog the throat of the down-curve. At once the water began rising rapidly. Could he climb out before he drowned? A long hiss sounded and the debris was sucked from sight; the current lowered. He understood now what had made the water toss the manhole cover; the down-curve had become temporarily obstructed and the perforations had become clogged.

He was in danger; he might slide into a down-curve; he might wander with a lighted match into a pocket of gas and blow himself up; or he might contract some horrible disease . . . Though he wanted to leave, an irrational impulse held him rooted. To the left, the convex ceiling swooped to a height of less than five feet. With cigarette slanting from pursed lips, he waded with taut muscles, his feet sloshing over the slimy bottom, his shoes sinking into spongy slop, the slate-colored water cracking in creamy foam against his knees. Pressing his flat left palm against the lowered ceiling, he struck another match and saw a metal pole nestling in a niche of the wall. Yes, some sewer workman had left it. He reached for it, then jerked his head away as a whisper of scurrying life whisked past and was still. He held the match close and saw a huge rat, wet with slime, blinking beady eyes and baring tiny fangs. The light blinded the rat and the frizzled head moved aimlessly. He grabbed the pole and let it fly against the rat's soft body; there was shrill piping and the grizzly body splashed into the dun-colored water and was snatched out of sight, spinning in the scuttling stream.

He swallowed and pushed on, following the curve of the misty cavern, sounding the water with the pole. By the faint light of another manhole cover he saw, amid loose wet brick, a hole with walls of damp earth leading into blackness. Gingerly he poked the pole into it; it was hollow and went beyond the length of the pole. He shoved the pole before him, hoisted himself upward, got to his hands and knees, and crawled. After a few yards he paused, struck to wonderment by the silence; it seemed that he had traveled a million miles away from the world. As he inched forward again he could sense the bottom of the dirt tunnel becoming dry and lowering slightly. Slowly he rose and to his astonishment he stood erect. He could not hear the rustling of the water now and he felt confoundingly alone, yet lured by the darkness and silence.

He crept a long way, then stopped, curious, afraid. He put his right foot forward and it dangled in space; he drew back in fear. He thrust the pole outward and it swung in emptiness. He trembled, imagining the earth crumbling and burying him alive. He scratched a match and saw that the dirt floor sheered away steeply and widened into a sort of cave some five feet below him. An old sewer, he muttered. He cocked his head, hearing a feathery cadence which he could not identify. The match ceased to burn.

Using the pole as a kind of ladder, he slid down and stood in darkness. The air was a little fresher and he could still hear vague noises. Where was he? He felt suddenly that someone was standing near him and he turned sharply, but there was only darkness. He poked cautiously and felt a brick wall; he followed it and the strange sounds grew louder. He ought to get out of here. This was crazy. He could not remain here for any length of time; there was no food and no place to sleep. But the faint sounds tantalized him; they were strange but familiar. Was it a motor? A baby crying? Music? A siren? He groped on, and the sounds came so clearly that he could feel the pitch and timbre of human voices. Yes, singing! That was it! He listened with open mouth. It was a church service. Enchanted, he groped toward the waves of melody.

> *Jesus, take me to your home above*
> *And fold me in the bosom of Thy love . . .*

The singing was on the other side of a brick wall. Excited, he wanted to watch the service without being seen. Whose church was it? He knew most of the churches in this area above ground, but the singing sounded too strange and detached for him to guess. He looked to the left, to the right, down to the black dirt, then upward and was startled to see a bright sliver of light slicing the darkness like the blade of a razor. He struck one of his two remaining matches and saw rusty pipes running along an old concrete ceiling. Photographically he located the exact position of the pipes in his mind. The match flame sank and he sprang upward; his hands clutched a pipe. He swung his legs and tossed his body onto the bed of pipes and they creaked, swaying up and down; he thought that the tier was about to crash, but nothing happened. He edged to the crevice and saw a segment of black men and women, dressed in white robes, singing, holding tattered songbooks in their black palms. His first impulse was to laugh, but he checked himself.

What was he doing? He was crushed with a sense of guilt. Would God strike him dead for that? The singing swept on and he shook his head, disagreeing in spite of himself. They oughtn't to do that, he thought. But he could think of no reason *why* they should not do it. Just singing with the air of the sewer blowing in on them . . . He felt that he was gazing upon something abysmally obscene, yet he could not bring himself to leave.

After a long time he grew numb and dropped to the dirt. Pain throbbed in his legs and a deeper pain, induced by the sight of those black people groveling and begging for something they could never get, churned in him. A vague conviction made him feel that those people should stand unrepentant and yield no quarter in singing and praying, yet *he* had run away from the police, had pleaded with them to believe in *his* innocence. He shook his head, bewildered.

How long had he been down here? He did not know. This was a new kind of living for him; the intensity of feelings he had experienced when looking at the church people sing made him certain that he had been down here a long time, but his mind told him that the time must have been short. In this darkness the only notion he had of time was when a match flared and measured time by its fleeting light. He groped back through the hole toward the sewer and the waves of song subsided and finally he could not hear them at all. He came to where the earth hole ended and he heard the noise of the current and time lived again for him, measuring the moments by the wash of water.

The rain must have slackened, for the flow of water had lessened and came only to his ankles. Ought he to go up into the streets and take his chances on hiding somewhere else? But they would surely catch him. The mere thought of dodging and running again from the police made him tense. No, he would stay and plot how to elude them. But what could he do down here? He walked forward into the sewer and came to another manhole cover; he stood beneath it, debating. Fine pencils of gold spilled suddenly from the little circles in the manhole cover and trembled on the surface of the current. Yes, street lamps . . . It must be night . . .

He went forward for about a quarter of an hour, wading aimlessly, poking the pole carefully before him. Then he stopped, his eyes fixed and intent. What's that? A strangely familiar image attracted and repelled him. Lit by the yellow stems from another manhole cover was a tiny nude body of a baby snagged by debris and half-submerged in water. Thinking that the baby was alive, he moved impulsively to save it, but his roused feelings told him that it was dead, cold, nothing, the same nothingness he had felt while watching the men and women singing in the church. Water blossomed about the tiny legs, the tiny arms, the tiny head, and rushed onward. The eyes were closed, as though in sleep; the fists were clenched, as though in protest; and the mouth gaped black in a soundless cry.

He straightened and drew in his breath, feeling that he had been staring for all eternity at the ripples of veined water skimming impersonally over the shriveled limbs. He felt as condemned as when the policemen had accused him. Involuntarily he lifted his hand to brush the vision away, but his arm fell listlessly to his side. Then he acted; he closed his eyes and reached forward slowly with the soggy shoe of his right foot and shoved the dead baby from where it had been lodged. He kept his eyes closed, seeing the little body twisting in the current as it floated from sight. He opened his eyes, shivered, placed his knuckles in the sockets, hearing the water speed in the somber shadows.

He tramped on, sensing at times a sudden quickening in the current as he passed some conduit whose waters were swelling the stream that slid by his feet. A few minutes later he was standing under another manhole cover, listening to the faint rumble of noises above ground. Streetcars and trucks, he mused. He looked down and saw a stagnant pool of gray-green sludge; at intervals a balloon pocket rose from the scum, glistening a bluish-purple, and burst. Then another. He turned, shook his head, and tramped back to the dirt cave by the church, his lips quivering.

Back in the cave, he sat and leaned his back against a dirt wall. His body was trembling slightly. Finally his senses quieted and he slept. When he awakened he felt stiff and cold. He had to leave this foul place, but leaving meant facing those policemen who had wrongly accused him. No, he could not go back aboveground. He remembered the beating they had given him and how he had signed his name to a confession, a confession which he had not even read. He had been too tired when they had shouted at him, demanding that he sign his name; he had signed it to end his pain.

He stood and groped about in the darkness. The church singing had stopped. How long had he slept? He did not know. But he felt refreshed and hungry. He doubled his fist nervously, realizing that he could not make a decision. As he walked about he stumbled over an old rusty iron pipe. He picked it up and felt a jagged edge. Yes, there was a brick wall and he could dig into it. What would he find? Smiling, he groped to the brick wall, sat, and began digging idly into damp cement. I can't make any noise, he cautioned himself. As time passed he grew thirsty, but there was no water. He had to kill time or go aboveground. The cement came out of the wall easily; he extracted four bricks and felt a soft draft blowing into his face. He stopped, afraid. What was beyond? He waited a long time and nothing happened; then he began digging again, soundlessly, slowly; he enlarged the hole and crawled through into a dark room and collided with another wall. He felt his way to the right; the wall ended and his fingers toyed in space, like the antennae of an insect.

He fumbled on and his feet struck something hollow, like wood. What's this? He felt with his fingers. Steps . . . He stooped and pulled off his shoes and mounted the stairs and saw a yellow chink of light shining and heard a low voice speaking. He placed his eye to a keyhole and saw the nude waxen figure of a man stretched out upon a white table. The voice, low-pitched and vibrant, mumbled indistinguishable words, neither rising nor falling. He craned his neck and squinted to see the man who was talking, but he could not locate him. Above the naked figure was suspended a huge glass container filled with a blood-red liquid from which a white rubber tube dangled. He crouched closer to the door and saw the tip end of a black object lined with pink satin. A coffin, he breathed. This is an undertaker's establishment . . . A fine-spun lace of ice covered his body and he shuddered. A throaty chuckle sounded in the depths of the yellow room.

He turned to leave. Three steps down it occurred to him that a light switch should be nearby; he felt along the wall, found an electric button, pressed it, and a blinding glare smote his pupils so hard that he was sightless, defenseless. His pupils contracted and he wrinkled his nostrils at a peculiar odor. At once he knew that he had been dimly aware of this odor in the darkness, but the light had brought it sharply to his attention. Some kind of stuff they use to embalm, he thought. He went down the steps and saw piles of lumber, coffins, and a long workbench. In one corner was a tool chest. Yes, he could use tools, could tunnel through walls with them. He lifted the lid of the chest and saw nails, a hammer, a crowbar, a screwdriver, a light bulb, and a long length of electric wire. Good! He would lug these back to his cave.

He was about to hoist the chest to his shoulders when he discovered a door behind the furnace. Where did it lead? He tried to open it and found it securely bolted. Using the crowbar so as to make no sound, he pried the door open; it swung on creaking hinges, outward. Fresh air came to his face and he caught the faint roar of faraway sound. Easy now, he told himself. He widened the door and a lump of coal rattled toward him. A coalbin . . . Evidently the door led into another basement. The roaring noise was louder now, but he could not identify it. Where was he? He groped slowly over the coal pile, then ranged in darkness over a gritty floor. The roaring noise seemed to come from above him, then below. His fingers followed a wall until he touched a wooden ridge. A door, he breathed.

The noise died to a low pitch; he felt his skin prickle. It seemed that he was playing a game with an unseen person whose intelligence outstripped his. He put his ear to the flat surface of the door. Yes, voices . . . Was this a prize fight stadium? The sound of the voices came near and sharp, but he could not tell if they were joyous or despairing. He twisted the knob until he heard a soft click and felt the springy weight of the door swinging toward him. He was afraid to open it, yet captured by curiosity and wonder. He jerked the door wide and saw on the far side of the basement a furnace glowing red. Ten feet away was still another door, half ajar. He crossed and peered through the door into an empty, high-ceilinged corridor that terminated in a dark complex of shadow. The belling voices rolled about him and his eagerness mounted. He stepped into the corridor and the voices swelled louder. He crept on and came to a narrow stairway leading circularly upward; there was no question but that he was going to ascend those stairs.

Mounting the spiraled staircase, he heard the voices roll in a steady wave, then leap to crescendo, only to die away, but always remaining audible. Ahead of him glowed red letters: E—X—I—T. At the top of the steps he paused in front of a black curtain that fluttered uncertainly. He parted the folds and looked into a convex depth that gleamed with clusters of shimmering lights. Sprawling below him was a stretch of human faces, tilted upward, chanting, whistling, screaming, laughing. Dangling before the faces, high upon a screen of silver, were jerking shadows. A movie, he said with slow laughter breaking from his lips.

He stood in a box in the reserved section of a movie house and the impulse he had had to tell the people in the church to stop their singing seized him. These people were laughing at their lives, he thought with amazement. They were shouting and yelling at the animated shadows of themselves. His compassion fired his imagination and he stepped out of the box, walked out upon thin air, walked on down to the audience; and, hovering in the air just above them, he stretched out his hand to touch them . . . His tension snapped and he found himself back in the box, looking down into the sea of faces. No; it could not be done; he could not awaken them. He sighed. Yes, these people were children, sleeping in their living, awake in their dying.

He turned away, parted the black curtain, and looked out. He saw no one. He started down the white stone steps and when he reached the bottom he saw a man in trim blue uniform coming toward him. So used had he become to being underground that he thought that he could walk past the man, as though he were a ghost. But the man stopped. And he stopped.

"Looking for the men's room, sir?" the man asked, and, without waiting for an answer, he turned and pointed. "This way, sir. The first door to your right."

He watched the man turn and walk up the steps and go out of sight. Then he laughed. What a funny fellow! He went back to the basement and stood in the red darkness, watching the glowing embers in the furnace. He went to the sink and turned the faucet and the water flowed in smooth silent stream that looked like a spout of blood. He brushed the mad image from his mind and began to wash his hands leisurely, looking about for the usual bar of soap. He found one and rubbed it in his palms until a rich lather bloomed in his cupped fingers, like a scarlet sponge. He scrubbed and rinsed his hands meticulously, then hunted for a towel; there was none. He shut off the water, pulled off his shirt, dried his hands on it; when he put it on again he was grateful for the cool dampness that came to his skin.

Yes, he was thirsty; he turned on the faucet again, bowled his fingers and when the water bubbled over the brim of his cupped palms, he drank in long, slow swallows. His bladder grew tight; he shut off the water, faced the wall, bent his head, and watched a red stream strike the floor. His nostrils wrinkled against acrid wisps of vapor; though he had tramped in the waters of the sewer, he stepped back from the wall so that his shoes, wet with sewer slime, would not touch his urine.

He heard footsteps and crawled quickly into the coalbin. Lumps rattled noisily. The footsteps came into the basement and stopped. Who was it? Had someone heard him and come down to investigate? He waited, crouching, sweating. For a long time there was silence, then he heard the clang of metal and a brighter glow lit the room. Somebody's tending the furnace, he thought. Footsteps came closer and he stiffened. Looming before him was a white face lined with coal dust, the face of an old man with watery blue eyes. Highlights spotted his gaunt cheekbones, and he held a huge shovel. There was a screechy scrape of metal against stone, and the old man lifted a shovelful of coal and went from sight.

The room dimmed momentarily, then a yellow glare came as coal flared at the furnace door. Six times the old man came to the bin and went to the furnace with shovels of coal, but not once did he lift his eyes. Finally he dropped the shovel, mopped his face with a dirty handkerchief, and sighed: "Wheew!" He turned slowly and trudged out of the basement, his footsteps dying away.

He stood, and lumps of coal clattered down the pile. He stepped from the bin and was startled to see the shadowy outline of an electric bulb hanging above his head. Why had not the old man turned it on? Oh, yes . . . He understood. The old man had worked here for so long that he had no need for light; he had learned a way of seeing in his dark world, like those sightless worms that inch along underground by a sense of touch.

His eyes fell upon a lunch pail and he was afraid to hope that it was full. He picked it up; it was heavy. He opened it. *Sandwiches!* He looked guiltily around; he was alone. He searched farther and found a folder of matches and a half-empty tin of tobacco; he put them eagerly into his pocket and clicked off the light. With the lunch pail under his arm, he went through the door, groped over the pile of coal, and stood again in the lighted basement of the undertaking establishment. I've got to get those tools, he told himself. And turn off that light. He tiptoed back up the steps and switched off the light; the invisible voice still droned on behind the door. He crept down and, seeing with his fingers, opened the lunch pail and tore off a piece of paper bag and brought out the tin and spilled grains of tobacco into the makeshift concave. He rolled it and wet it with spittle, then inserted one end into his mouth and lit it; he sucked smoke that bit his lungs. The nicotine reached his brain, went out along his arms to his finger tips, down to his stomach, and over all the tired nerves of his body.

He carted the tools to the hole he had made in the wall. Would the noise of the falling chest betray him? But he would have to take a chance; he had to have those tools. He lifted the chest and shoved it; it hit the dirt on the other side of the wall with a loud clatter. He waited, listening; nothing happened. Head first, he slithered through and stood in the cave. He grinned, filled with a cunning idea. Yes, he would now go back into the basement of the undertaking establishment and crouch behind the coal pile and dig another hole. Sure! Fumbling, he opened the tool chest and extracted a crowbar, a screwdriver, and a hammer; he fastened them securely about his person.

With another lumpish cigarette in his flexed lips, he crawled back through the hole and over the coal pile and sat, facing the brick wall. He jabbed with the crowbar and the cement sheered away; quicker than he thought, a brick came loose. He worked an hour; the other bricks did not come easily. He sighed, weak from effort. I ought to rest a little, he thought. I'm hungry. He felt his way back to the cave and stumbled along the wall till he came to the tool chest. He sat upon it, opened the lunch pail, and took out two thick sandwiches. He smelled them. Pork chops . . . His mouth watered. He closed his eyes and devoured a sandwich, savoring the smooth rye bread and juicy meat. He ate rapidly, gulping down lumpy mouthfuls that made him long for water. He ate the other sandwich and found an apple and gobbled that up too, sucking the core till the last trace of flavor was drained from it. Then, like a dog, he ground the meat bones with his teeth, enjoying the salty, tangy marrow. He finished and stretched out full length on the ground and went to sleep. . . .

. . . His body was washed by cold water that gradually turned warm and he was buoyed upon a stream and swept out to sea where waves rolled gently and suddenly he found himself walking upon the water how strange and delightful to walk upon the water and he came upon a nude woman holding a nude baby in her arms and the woman was sinking into the water holding the baby above her head and screaming *help* and he ran over the water to the woman and he reached her just before she went down and he took the baby from her hands and stood watching the breaking bubbles where the woman sank and he called *lady* and still no answer yes dive down there and rescue that woman but he could not take this baby with him and he stooped and laid the baby tenderly upon the surface of the water expecting it to sink but it floated and he leaped into the water and held his breath and strained his eyes to see through the gloomy volume of water but there was no woman and he opened his mouth and called *lady* and the water bubbled and his chest ached and his arms were tired but he could not see the woman and he called again *lady lady* and his feet touched sand at the bottom of the sea and his chest felt as though it would burst and he bent his knees and propelled himself upward and water rushed past him and his head bobbed out and he breathed deeply and looked around where was the baby the baby was gone and he rushed over the water looking for the baby calling *where is it* and the empty sky and sea threw back his voice *where is it* and he began to doubt that he could stand upon the water and then he was sinking and as he struggled the water rushed him downward spinning dizzily and he opened his mouth to call for help and water surged into his lungs and he choked . . .

He groaned and leaped erect in the dark, his eyes wide. The images of terror that thronged his brain would not let him sleep. He rose, made sure that the tools were hitched to his belt, and groped his way to the coal pile and found the rectangular gap from which he had taken the bricks. He took out the crowbar and hacked. Then dread paralyzed him. How long had he slept? Was it day or night now? He had to be careful. Someone might hear him if it were day. He hewed softly for hours at the cement, working silently. Faintly quivering in the air above him was the dim sound of yelling voices. Crazy people, he muttered. They're still there in that movie . . .

Having rested, he found the digging much easier. He soon had a dozen bricks out. His spirits rose. He took out another brick and his fingers fluttered in space. Good! What lay ahead of him? Another basement? He made the hole larger, climbed through, walked over an uneven floor and felt a metal surface. He lighted a match and saw that he was standing behind a furnace in a basement; before him, on the far side of the room, was a door. He crossed and opened it; it was full of odds and ends. Daylight spilled from a window above his head.

Then he was aware of a soft, continuous tapping. What was it? A clock? No, it was louder than a clock and more irregular. He placed an old empty box beneath the window, stood upon it, and looked into an areaway. He eased the window up and crawled through; the sound of the tapping came clearly now. He glanced about; he was alone. Then he looked upward at a series of window ledges. The tapping identified itself. That's a typewriter, he said to himself. It seemed to be coming from just above. He grasped the ridges of a rain pipe and lifted himself upward; through a half-inch opening of window he saw a doorknob about three feet away. No, it was not a doorknob; it was a small circular disk made of stainless steel with many fine markings upon it. He held his breath; an eerie white hand, seemingly detached from its arm, touched the metal knob and whirled it, first to the left, then to the right. It's a safe! . . . Suddenly he could see the dial no more; a huge metal door swung slowly toward him and he was looking into a safe filled with green wads of paper money, rows of coins wrapped in brown paper, and glass jars and boxes of various sizes. His heart quickened. Good Lord! The white hand went in and out of the safe, taking wads of bills and cylinders of coins. The hand vanished and he heard the muffled click of the big door as it closed. Only the steel dial was visible now. The typewriter still tapped in his ears, but he could not see it. He blinked, wondering if what he had seen was real. There was more money in that safe than he had seen in all his life.

As he clung to the rain pipe, a daring idea came to him and he pulled the screwdriver from his belt. If the white hand twirled that dial again, he would be able to see how far to left and right it spun and he would have the combination! His blood tingled. I can scratch the numbers right here, he thought. Holding the pipe with one hand, he made the sharp edge of the screwdriver bite into the brick wall. Yes, he could do it. Now, he was set. Now, he had a reason for staying here in the underground. He waited for a long time, but the white hand did not return. Goddamn! Had he been more alert, he could have counted the twirls and he would have had the combination. He got down and stood in the areaway, sunk in reflection.

How could he get into that room? He climbed back into the basement and saw wooden steps leading upward. Was that the room where the safe stood? Fearing that the dial was now being twirled, he clambered through the window, hoisted himself up the rain pipe, and peered; he saw only the naked gleam of the steel dial. He got down and doubled his fists. Well, he would explore the basement. He returned to the basement room and mounted the steps to the door and squinted through the keyhole; all was dark, but the tapping was still somewhere near, still faint and directionless. He pushed the door in; along one wall of a room was a table piled with radios and electrical equipment. A radio shop, he muttered.

Well, he could rig up a radio in his cave. He found a sack, slid the radio into it, and slung it across his back. Closing the door, he went down the steps and stood again in the basement, disappointed. He had not solved the problem of the steel dial and he was irked. He set the radio on the floor and again hoisted himself through the window and up the rain pipe and squinted; the metal door was swinging shut. Goddamn! He's worked the combination again. If I had been patient, I'd have had it! How could he get into that room? He *had* to get into it. He could jimmy the window, but it would be much better if he could get in without any traces. To the right of him, he calculated, should be the basement of the building that held the safe; therefore, if he dug a hole right *here*, he ought to reach his goal.

He began a quiet scraping; it was hard work, for the bricks were not damp. He eventually got one out and lowered it softly to the floor. He had to be careful; perhaps people were beyond this wall. He extracted a second layer of brick and found still another. He gritted his teeth, ready to quit. I'll dig one more, he resolved. When the next brick came out he felt air blowing into his face. He waited to be challenged, but nothing happened.

He enlarged the hole and pulled himself through and stood in quiet darkness. He scratched a match to flame and saw steps; he mounted and peered through a keyhole: Darkness . . . He strained to hear the typewriter, but there was only silence. Maybe the office had closed? He twisted the knob and swung the door in; a frigid blast made him shiver. In the shadows before him were halves and quarters of hogs and lambs and steers hanging from metal hooks on the low ceiling, red meat encased in folds of cold white fat. Fronting him was frost-coated glass from behind which came indistinguishable sounds. The odor of fresh raw meat sickened him and he backed away. A meat market, he whispered.

He ducked his head, suddenly blinded by light. He narrowed his eyes; the red-white rows of meat were drenched in yellow glare. A man wearing a crimson-spotted jacket came in and took down a bloody meat cleaver. He eased the door to, holding it ajar just enough to watch the man, hoping that the darkness in which he stood would keep him from being seen. The man took down a hunk of steer and placed it upon a bloody wooden block and bent forward and whacked with the cleaver. The man's face was hard, square, grim; a jet of mustache smudged his upper lip and a glistening cowlick of hair fell over his left eye. Each time he lifted the cleaver and brought it down upon the meat, he let out a short, deep-chested grunt. After he had cut the meat, he wiped blood off the wooden block with a sticky wad of gunny sack and hung the cleaver upon a hook. His face was proud as he placed the chunk of meat in the crook of his elbow and left.

The door slammed and the light went off; once more he stood in shadow. His tension ebbed. From behind the frosted glass he heard the man's voice: "Forty-eight cents a pound, ma'am." He shuddered, feeling that there was something he had to do. But what? He stared fixedly at the cleaver, then he sneezed and was terrified for fear that the man had heard him. But the door did not open. He took down the cleaver and examined the sharp edge smeared with cold blood. Behind the ice-coated glass a cash register rang with a vibrating, musical tinkle.

Absentmindedly holding the meat cleaver, he rubbed the glass with his thumb and cleared the spot that enabled him to see the front of the store. The shop was empty, save for the man who was now putting on his hat and coat. Beyond the front window a wan sun shone in the streets; people passed and now and then a fragment of laughter or the whir of a speeding auto came to him. He peered closer and saw on the right counter of the shop a mosquito netting covering pears, grapes, lemons, oranges, bananas, peaches, and plums. His stomach contracted.

The man clicked out the light and he gritted his teeth, muttering, Don't lock the icebox door . . . The man went through the door of the shop and locked it from the outside. Thank God! Now, he would eat some more! He waited, trembling. The sun died and its rays lingered on in the sky, turning the streets to dusk. He opened the door and stepped inside the shop. In reverse letters across the front window was: NICK'S FRUITS AND MEATS. He laughed, picked up a soft ripe yellow pear and bit into it; juice squirted; his mouth ached as his saliva glands reacted to the acid of the fruit. He ate three pears, gobbled six bananas, and made away with several oranges, taking a bite out of their tops and holding them to his lips and squeezing them as he hungrily sucked the juice.

He found a faucet, turned it on, laid the cleaver aside, pursed his lips under the stream until his stomach felt about to burst. He straightened and belched, feeling satisfied for the first time since he had been underground. He sat upon the floor, rolled and lit a cigarette, his bloodshot eyes squinting against the film of drifting smoke. He watched a patch of sky turn red, then purple; night fell and he lit another cigarette, brooding. Some part of him was trying to remember the world he had left, and another part of him did not want to remember it. Sprawling before him in his mind was his wife, Mrs Wooten for whom he worked, the three policemen who had picked him up . . . He possessed them now more completely than he had ever possessed them when he had lived aboveground. How this had come about he could not say, but he had no desire to go back to them. He laughed, crushed the cigarette, and stood up.

He went to the front door and gazed out. Emotionally he hovered between the world aboveground and the world underground. He longed to go out, but sober judgment urged him to remain there. Then impulsively he pried the lock loose with one swift twist of the crowbar; the door swung outward. Through the twilight he saw a white man and a white woman coming toward him. He held himself tense, waiting for them to pass; but they came directly to the door and confronted him.

"I want to buy a pound of grapes," the woman said.

Terrified, he stepped back into the store. The white man stood to one side and the woman entered.

"Give me a pound of dark ones," the woman said.

The white man came slowly forward, blinking his eyes.

"Where's Nick?" the man asked.

"Were you just closing?" the woman asked.

"Yes, ma'am," he mumbled. For a second he did not breathe, then he mumbled again: "Yes, ma'am."

"I'm sorry," the woman said.

The street lamps came on, lighting the store somewhat. Ought he run? But that would raise an alarm. He moved slowly, dreamily, to a counter and lifted up a bunch of grapes and showed them to the woman.

"Fine," the woman said. "But isn't that more than a pound?"

He did not answer. The man was staring at him intently.

"Put them in a bag for me," the woman said, fumbling with her purse.

"Yes, ma'am."

He saw a pile of paper bags under a narrow ledge; he opened one and put the grapes in.

"Thanks," the woman said, taking the bag and placing a dime in his dark palm.

"Where's Nick?" the man asked again. "At supper?"

"Sir? Yes, sir," he breathed.

They left the store and he stood trembling in the doorway. When they were out of sight, he burst out laughing and crying. A trolley car rolled noisily past and he controlled himself quickly. He flung the dime to the pavement with a gesture of contempt and stepped into the warm night air. A few shy stars trembled above him. The look of things was beautiful, yet he felt a lurking threat. He went to an unattended newsstand and looked at a stack of papers. He saw a headline: HUNT NEGRO FOR MURDER.

He felt that someone had slipped up on him from behind and was stripping off his clothes; he looked about wildly, went quickly back into the store, picked up the meat cleaver where he had left it near the sink, then made his way through the icebox to the basement. He stood for a long time, breathing heavily. They know I didn't do anything, he muttered. But how could he prove it? He had signed a confession. Though innocent, he felt guilty, condemned. He struck a match and held it near the steel blade, fascinated and repelled by the dried blotches of blood. Then his fingers gripped the handle of the cleaver with all the strength of his body, he wanted to fling the cleaver from him, but he could not. The match flame wavered and fled; he struggled through the hole and put the cleaver in the sack with the radio. He was determined to keep it, for what purpose he did not know.

He was about to leave when he remembered the safe. Where was it? He wanted to give up, but he felt he ought to make one more try. Opposite the last hole he had dug, he tunneled again, plying the crowbar. Once he was so exhausted that he lay on the concrete floor and panted. Finally he made another hole. He wriggled through and his nostrils filled with the fresh smell of coal. He struck a match; yes, the usual steps led upward. He tiptoed to a door and eased it open. A fair-haired white girl stood in front of a steel cabinet, her blue eyes wide upon him. She turned chalky and gave a high-pitched scream. He bounded down the steps and raced to his hole and clambered through, replacing the bricks with nervous haste. He paused, hearing loud voices.

"What's the matter, Alice?"

"A man . . ."

"What man? Where?

"A man was at that door . . ."

"Oh, nonsense!"

"He was looking at me through the door!"

"Aw, you're dreaming."

"I *did* see a man!"

The girl was crying now.

"There's nobody here."

Another man's voice sounded.

"What is it, Bob?"

"Alice says she saw a man in here, in that door!"

"Let's take a look."

He waited, poised for flight. Footsteps descended the stairs.

"There's nobody down here."

"The window's locked."

"And there's no door."

"You ought to fire that dame."

"Oh, I don't know. Women are that way."

"She's too hysterical."

The men laughed. Footsteps sounded again on the stairs. A door slammed. He sighed, relieved that he had escaped. But he had not done what he had set out to do; his glimpse of the room had been too brief to determine if the safe was there. He had to know. Boldly he groped through the hole once more; he reached the steps and pulled off his shoes and tiptoed up and peered through the keyhole. His head accidentally touched the door and it swung silently in a fraction of an inch; he saw the girl bent over the cabinet, her back to him. Beyond her was the safe. He crept back down the steps, thinking exultingly: I found it!

Now he had to get the combination. Even if the window in the areaway was locked and bolted, he could gain entrance when the office closed. He scoured through the holes he had dug and stood again in the basement where he had left the radio and the cleaver. Again he crawled out of the window and lifted himself up the rain pipe and peered. The steel dial showed lonely and bright, reflecting the yellow glow of an unseen light. Resigned to a long wait, he sat and leaned against a wall. From far off came the faint sounds of life aboveground; once he looked with a baffled expression at the dark sky. Frequently he rose and climbed the pipe to see the white hand spin the dial, but nothing happened. He bit his lip with impatience. It was not the money that was luring him, but the mere fact that he could get it with impunity. Was the hand now twirling the dial? He rose and looked, but the white hand was not in sight.

Perhaps it would be better to watch continuously? Yes; he clung to the pipe and watched the dial until his eyes thickened with tears. Exhausted, he stood again in the areaway. He heard a door being shut and he clawed up the pipe and looked. He jerked tense as a vague figure passed in front of him. He stared unblinkingly, hugging the pipe with one hand and holding the screwdriver with the other, ready to etch the combination upon the wall. His ears caught: *Dong . . . Dong . . . Dong . . . Dong . . . Dong . . . Dong . . . Dong . . .* Seven o'clock, he whispered. Maybe they were closing now? What kind of a store would be open as late as this? he wondered. Did anyone live in the rear? Was there a night watchman? Perhaps the safe was *already* locked for the night! Goddamn! While he had been eating in that shop, they had locked up everything . . . Then, just as he was about to give up, the white hand touched the dial and turned it once to the right and stopped at six. With quivering fingers, he etched 1—R—6 upon the brick wall with the tip of the screwdriver. The hand twirled the dial twice to the left and stopped at two, and he engraved 2—L —2 upon the wall. The dial was spun four times to the right and stopped at six again; he wrote 4—R—6. The dial rotated three times to the left and was centered straight up and down; he wrote 3—L—O. The door swung open and again he saw the piles of green money and the rows of wrapped coins. I got it, he said grimly.

Then he was stone still, astonished. There were two hands now. A right hand lifted a wad of green bills and deftly slipped it up the sleeve of a left arm. The hands trembled; again the right hand slipped a packet of bills up the left sleeve. He's stealing, he said to himself. He grew indignant, as if the money belonged to him. Though *he* had planned to steal the money, he despised and pitied the man. He felt that his stealing the money and the man's stealing were two entirely different things. He wanted to steal the money merely for the sensation involved in getting it, and he had no intention whatever of spending a penny of it; but he knew that the man who was now stealing it was going to spend it, perhaps for pleasure. The huge steel door closed with a soft click.

Though angry, he was somewhat satisfied. The office would close soon. I'll clean the place out, he mused. He imagined the entire office staff cringing with fear; the police would question everyone for a crime they had not committed, just as they had questioned him. And they would have no idea of how the money had been stolen until they discovered the holes he had tunneled in the walls of the basements. He lowered himself and laughed mischievously, with the abandoned glee of an adolescent.

He flattened himself against the wall as the window above him closed with rasping sound. He looked; somebody was bolting the window securely with a metal screen. That won't help you, he snickered to himself. He clung to the rain pipe until the yellow light in the office went out. He went back into the basement, picked up the sack containing the radio and cleaver, and crawled through the two holes he had dug and groped his way into the basement of the building that held the safe. He moved in slow motion, breathing softly. Be careful now, he told himself. There might be a night watchman . . . In his memory was the combination written in bold white characters as upon a blackboard. Eel-like he squeezed through the last hole and crept up the steps and put his hands on the knob and pushed the door in about three inches. Then his courage ebbed; his imagination wove dangers for him.

Perhaps the night watchman was waiting in there, ready to shoot. He dangled his cap on a forefinger and poked it past the jamb of the door. If anyone fired, they would hit his cap; but nothing happened. He widened the door, holding the crowbar high above his head, ready to beat off an assailant. He stood like that for five minutes; the rumble of a streetcar brought him to himself. He entered the room. Moonlight floated in from a side window. He confronted the safe, then checked himself. Better take a look around first . . . He stepped about and found a closed door. Was the night watchman in there? He opened it and saw a washbowl, a faucet, and a commode. To the left was still another door that opened into a huge dark room that seemed empty; on the far side of that room he made out the shadow of still another door. Nobody's here, he told himself.

He turned back to the safe and fingered the dial; it spun with ease. He laughed and twirled it just for fun. Get to work, he told himself. He turned the dial to the figures he saw on the blackboard of his memory; it was so easy that he felt that the safe had not been locked at all. The heavy door eased loose and he caught hold of the handle and pulled hard, but the door swung open with a slow momentum of its own. Breathless, he gaped at wads of green bills, rows of wrapped coins, curious glass jars full of white pellets, and many oblong green metal boxes. He glanced guiltily over his shoulder; it seemed impossible that someone should not call to him to stop.

They'll be surprised in the morning, he thought. He opened the top of the sack and lifted a wad of compactly tied bills; the money was crisp and new. He admired the smooth, clean-cut edges. The fellows in Washington sure know how to make this stuff, he mused. He rubbed the money with his fingers, as though expecting it to reveal hidden qualities. He lifted the wad to his nose and smelled the fresh odor of ink. Just like any other paper, he mumbled. He dropped the wad into the sack and picked up another. Holding the bag, he thought and laughed.

There was in him no sense of possessiveness; he was intrigued with the form and color of the money, with the manifold reactions which he knew that men aboveground held toward it. The sack was one-third full when it occurred to him to examine the denominations of the bills; without realizing it, he had put many wads of one-dollar bills into the sack. Aw, nuts, he said in disgust. Take the big ones . . . He dumped the one-dollar bills onto the floor and swept all the hundred-dollar bills he could find into the sack, then he raked in rolls of coins with crooked fingers.

He walked to a desk upon which sat a typewriter, the same machine which the blond girl had used. He was fascinated by it; never in his life had he used one of them. It was a queer instrument of business, something beyond the rim of his life. Whenever he had been in an office where a girl was typing, he had almost always spoken in whispers. Remembering vaguely what he had seen others do, he inserted a sheet of paper into the machine; it went in lopsided and he did not know how to straighten it. Spelling in a soft diffident voice, he pecked out his name on the keys: *freddaniels*. He looked at it and laughed. He would learn to type correctly one of these days.

Yes, he would take the typewriter too. He lifted the machine and placed it atop the bulk of money in the sack. He did not feel that he was stealing, for the cleaver, the radio, the money, and the typewriter were all on the same level of value, all meant the same thing to him. They were the serious toys of the men who lived in the dead world of sunshine and rain he had left, the world that condemned him, branded him guilty.

But what kind of a place is this? He wondered. What was in that dark room to his rear? He felt for his matches and found that he had only one left. He leaned the sack against the safe and groped forward into the room, encountering smooth, metallic objects that felt like machines. Baffled, he touched a wall and tried vainly to locate an electric switch. Well, he *had* to strike his last match. He knelt and struck it, cupping the flame near the floor with his palms. The place seemed to be a factory, with benches and tables. There were bulbs with green shades spaced about the tables; he turned on a light and twisted it low so that the glare was limited. He saw a half-filled packet of cigarettes and appropriated it. There were stools at the benches and he concluded that men worked here at some trade. He wandered and found a few half-used folders of matches. If only he could find more cigarettes! But there were none.

But what kind of a place was this? On a bench he saw a pad of paper captioned: PEER'S—MANUFACTURING JEWELERS. His lips formed an "O," then he snapped off the light and ran back to the safe and lifted one of the glass jars and stared at the tiny white pellets. Gingerly he picked up one and found that it was wrapped in tissue paper. He peeled the paper and saw a glittering stone that looked like glass, glinting white and blue sparks. Diamonds, he breathed.

Roughly he tore the paper from the pellets and soon his palm quivered with precious fire. Trembling, he took all four glass jars from the safe and put them into the sack. He grabbed one of the metal boxes, shook it, and heard a tiny rattle.He pried off the lid with the screwdriver. Rings! Hundreds of them . . . Were they worth anything? He scooped up a handful and jets of fire shot fitfully from the stones. These are diamonds too, he said. He pried open another box. Watches! A chorus of soft, metallic ticking filled his ears. For a moment he could not move, then he dumped all the boxes into the sack.

He shut the safe door, then stood looking around, anxious not to overlook anything. Oh! He had seen a door in the room where the machines were. What was in there? More valuables? He re-entered the room, crossed the floor, and stood undecided before the door. He finally caught hold of the knob and pushed the door in; the room beyond was dark. He advanced cautiously inside and ran his fingers along the wall for the usual switch, then he was stark still. *Something had moved in the room!* What was it? Ought he to creep out, taking the rings and diamonds and money? Why risk what he already had? He waited and the ensuing silence gave him confidence to explore further. Dare he strike a match? Would not a match flame make him a good target? He tensed again as he heard a faint sigh; he was now convinced that there was something alive near him, something that lived and breathed. On tiptoe he felt slowly along the wall, hoping that he would not collide with anything. Luck was with him; he found the light switch.

No; don't turn the light on . . . Then suddenly he realized that he did not know in what direction the door was. Goddamn! He had to turn the light on or strike the match. He fingered the switch for a long time, then thought of an idea. He knelt upon the floor, reached his arm up to the switch and flicked the button, hoping that if anyone shot, the bullet would go above his head. The moment the light came on he narrowed his eyes to see quickly. He sucked in his breath and his body gave a violent twitch and was still. In front of him, so close that it made him want to bound up and scream, was a human face.

He was afraid to move lest he touch the man. If the man had opened his eyes at that moment, there was no telling what he might have done. The man—long and rawboned—was stretched out on his back upon a little cot, sleeping in his clothes, his head cushioned by a dirty pillow; his face, clouded by a dark stubble of beard, looked straight up to the ceiling. The man sighed, and he grew tense to defend himself; the man mumbled and turned his face away from the light. I've got to turn off that light, he thought. Just as he was about to rise, he saw a gun and cartridge belt on the floor at the man's side. Yes, he would take the gun and cartridge belt, not to use them, but just to keep them, as one takes a memento from a country fair. He picked them up and was about to click off the light when his eyes fell upon a photograph perched upon a chair near the man's head; it was the picture of a woman, smiling, shown against a background of open fields; at the woman's side were two young children, a boy and a girl. He smiled indulgently; he could send a bullet into that man's brain and time would be over for him . . .

He clicked off the light and crept silently back into the room where the safe stood; he fastened the cartridge belt about him and adjusted the holster at his right hip. He strutted about the room on tiptoe, lolling his head nonchalantly, then paused abruptly, pulled the gun, and pointed it with grim face toward an imaginary foe. "Boom!" he whispered fiercely. Then he bent forward with silent laughter. That's just like they do it in the movies, he said.

He contemplated his loot for a long time, then got a towel from the washroom and tied the sack securely. When he looked up he was momentarily frightened by his shadow looming on the wall before him. He lifted the sack, dragged it down the basement steps, lugged it across the basement, gasping for breath. After he had struggled through the hole, he clumsily replaced the bricks, then tussled with the sack until he got it to the cave. He stood in the dark, wet with sweat, brooding about the diamonds, the rings, the watches, the money; he remembered the singing in the church, the people yelling in the movie, the dead baby, the nude man stretched out upon the white table . . . He saw these items hovering before his eyes and felt that some dim meaning linked them together, that some magical relationship made them kin. He stared with vacant eyes, convinced that all of these images, with their tongueless reality, were striving to tell him something . . .

Later, seeing with his fingers, he untied the sack and sat each item neatly upon the dirt floor. Exploring, he took the bulb, the socket, and the wire out of the tool chest; he was elated to find a double socket at one end of the wire. He crammed the stuff into his pockets and hoisted himself upon the rusty pipes and squinted into the church; it was dim and empty. Somewhere in this wall were live electric wires; but where? He lowered himself, groped and tapped the wall with the butt of the screwdriver, listening vainly for hollow sounds. I'll just take a chance and dig, he said.

For an hour he tried to dislodge a brick, and when he struck a match, he found that he had dug a depth of only an inch! No use digging here, he sighed. By the flickering light of a match, he looked upward, then lowered his eyes only to glance up again, startled. Directly above his head, beyond the pipes, was a wealth of electric wiring. I'll be damned, he snickered.

He got an old dull knife from the chest and, seeing again with his fingers, separated the two strands of wire and cut away the insulation. Twice he received a slight shock. He scraped the wiring clean and managed to join the two twin ends, then screwed in the bulb. The sudden illumination blinded him and he shut his lids to kill the pain in his eyeballs. I've got that much done, he thought jubilantly.

He placed the bulb on the dirt floor and the light cast a blatant glare on the bleak clay walls. Next he plugged one end of the wire that dangled from the radio into the light socket and bent down and switched on the button; almost at once there was the harsh sound of static, but no words or music. Why won't it work? he wondered. Had he damaged the mechanism in any way? Maybe it needed grounding? Yes . . . He rummaged in the tool chest and found another length of wire, fastened it to the ground of the radio, and then tied the opposite end to a pipe. Rising and growing distinct, a slow strain of music entranced him with its measured sound. He sat upon the chest, deliriously happy.

Later he searched again in the chest and found a half-gallon can of glue; he opened it and smelled a sharp odor. Then he recalled that he had not even looked at the money. He took a wad of green bills and weighed it in his palm, then broke the seal and held one of the bills up to the light and studied it closely. *The United States of America will pay to the bearer on demand one hundred dollars*, he read in slow speech; then: *This note is legal tender for all debts, public and private*. . . . He broke into a musing laugh, feeling that he was reading of the doings of people who lived on some far-off planet. He turned the bill over and saw on the other side of it a delicately beautiful building gleaming with paint and set amidst green grass. He had no desire whatever to count the money; it was what it stood for—the various currents of life swirling aboveground—that captivated him. Next he opened the rolls of coins and let them slide from their paper wrapping to the ground; the bright, new gleaming pennies and nickels and dimes piled high at his feet, a glowing mound of shimmering copper and silver. He sifted them through his fingers, listening to their tinkle as they struck the conical heap.

Oh, yes! He had forgotten. He would now write his name on the typewriter. He inserted a piece of paper and poised his fingers to write. But what was his name? He stared, trying to remember. He stood and glared about the dirt cave, his name on the tip of his lips. But it would not come to him. Why was he here? Yes, he had been running away from the police. But why? His mind was blank. He bit his lips and sat again, feeling a vague terror. But why worry? He laughed, then pecked slowly: *itwasalonghotday*. He was determined to type the sentence without making any mistakes. How did one make capital letters? He experimented and luckily discovered how to lock the machine for capital letters and then shift it back to lower case. Next he discovered how to make spaces, then he wrote neatly and correctly: *It was a long hot day*. Just why he selected that sentence he did not know; it was merely the ritual of performing the thing that appealed to him. He took the sheet out of the machine and looked around with stiff neck and hard eyes and spoke to an imaginary person:

"Yes, I'll have the contracts ready tomorrow."

He laughed. That's just the way they talk, he said. He grew weary of the game and pushed the machine aside. His eyes fell upon the can of glue, and a mischievous idea bloomed in him, filling him with nervous eagerness. He leaped up and opened the can of glue, then broke the seals on all the wads of money. I'm going to have some wallpaper, he said with a luxurious, physical laugh that made him bend at the knees. He took the towel with which he had tied the sack and balled it into a swab and dipped it into the can of glue and dabbed glue onto the wall; then he pasted one green bill by the side of another. He stepped back and cocked his head. Jesus! That's funny . . . He slapped his thighs and guffawed. He had triumphed over the world aboveground! He was free! If only people could see this! He wanted to run from this cave and yell his discovery to the world.

He swabbed all the dirt walls of the cave and pasted them with green bills; when he had finished the walls blazed with a yellow-green fire. Yes, this room would be his hide-out; between him and the world that had branded him guilty would stand this mocking symbol. He had not stolen the money; he had simply picked it up, just as a man would pick up firewood in a forest. And that was how the world aboveground now seemed to him, a wild forest filled with death.

The walls of money finally palled on him and he looked about for new interests to feed his emotions. The cleaver! He drove a nail into the wall and hung the bloody cleaver upon it. Still another idea welled up. He pried open the metal boxes and lined them side by side on the dirt floor. He grinned at the gold and fire. From one box he lifted up a fistful of ticking gold watches and dangled them by their gleaming chains. He stared with an idle smile, then began to wind them up; he did not attempt to set them at any given hour, for there was no time for him now. He took a fistful of nails and drove them into the papered walls and hung the watches upon them, letting them swing down by their glittering chains, trembling and ticking busily against the backdrop of green with the lemon sheen of the electric light shining upon the metal watch casings, converting the golden disks into blobs of liquid yellow. Hardly had he hung up the last watch than the idea extended itself; he took more nails from the chest and drove them into the green paper and took the boxes of rings and went from nail to nail and hung up the golden bands. The blue and white sparks from the stones filled the cave with brittle laughter, as though enjoying his hilarious secret. People certainly can do some funny things, he said to himself.

He sat upon the tool chest, alternately laughing and shaking his head soberly. Hours later he became conscious of the gun sagging at his hip and he pulled it from the holster. He had seen men fire guns in movies, but somehow his life had never led him into contact with firearms. A desire to feel the sensation others felt in firing came over him. But someone might hear . . . Well, what if they did? They would not know where the shot had come from. Not in their wildest notions would they think that it had come from under the streets! He tightened his fingers on the trigger; there was a deafening report and it seemed that the entire underground had caved in upon his eardrums; and in the same instant there flashed an orange-blue spurt of flame that died quickly but lingered on as a vivid after-image. He smelled the acrid stench of burnt powder filling his lungs and he dropped the gun abruptly.

The intensity of his feelings died and he hung the gun and cartridge belt upon the wall. Next he lifted the jars of diamonds and turned them bottom upward, dumping the white pellets upon the ground. One by one he picked them up and peeled the tissue paper from them and piled them in a neat heap. He wiped his sweaty hands on his trousers, lit a cigarette, and commenced playing another game. He imagined that he was a rich man who lived aboveground in the obscene sunshine and he was strolling through a park of a summer morning, smiling, nodding to his neighbors, sucking an after-breakfast cigar. Many times he crossed the floor of the cave, avoiding the diamonds with his feet, yet subtly gauging his footsteps so that his shoes, wet with sewer slime, would strike the diamonds at some undetermined moment. After twenty minutes of sauntering, his right foot smashed into the heap and diamonds lay scattered in all directions, glinting with a million tiny chuckles of icy laughter. Oh, shucks, he mumbled in mock regret, intrigued by the damage he had wrought. He continued walking, ignoring the brittle fire. He felt that he had a glorious victory locked in his heart.

He stooped and flung the diamonds more evenly over the floor and they showered rich sparks, collaborating with him. He went over the floor and trampled the stones just deep enough for them to be faintly visible, as though they were set delicately in the prongs of a thousand rings. A ghostly light bathed the cave. He sat on the chest and frowned. Maybe *any*thing's right, he mumbled. Yes, if the world as men had made it was right, then anything else was right, any act a man took to satisfy himself, murder, theft, torture.

He straightened with a start. What was happening to him? He was drawn to these crazy thoughts, yet they made him feel vaguely guilty. He would stretch out upon the ground, then get up; he would want to crawl again through the holes he had dug, but would restrain himself; he would think of going again up into the streets, but fear would hold him still. He stood in the middle of the cave, surrounded by green walls and a laughing floor, trembling. He was going to do something, but what? Yes, he was afraid of himself, afraid of doing some nameless thing.

To control himself, he turned on the radio. A melancholy piece of music rose. Brooding over the diamonds on the floor was like looking up into a sky full of restless stars; then the illusion turned into its opposite: he was high up in the air looking down at the twinkling lights of a sprawling city. The music ended and a man recited news events. In the same attitude in which he had contemplated the city, so now, as he heard the cultivated tone, he looked down upon land and sea as men fought, as cities were razed, as planes scattered death upon open towns, as long lines of trenches wavered and broke. He heard the names of generals and the names of mountains and the names of countries and the names and numbers of divisions that were in action on different battle fronts. He saw black smoke billowing from the stacks of warships as they neared each other over wastes of water and he heard their huge guns thunder as red-hot shells screamed across the surface of night seas. He saw hundreds of planes wheeling and droning in the sky and heard the clatter of machine guns as they fought each other and he saw planes falling in plumes of smoke and blaze of fire. He saw steel tanks rumbling across fields of ripe wheat to meet other tanks and there was a loud clang of steel as numberless tanks collided. He saw troops with fixed bayonets charging in waves against other troops who held fixed bayonets and men groaned as steel ripped into their bodies and they went down to die . . . The voice of the radio faded and he was staring at the diamonds on the floor at his feet.

He shut off the radio, fighting an irrational compulsion to act. He walked aimlessly about the cave, touching the walls with his finger tips. Suddenly he stood still. *What was the matter with him?* Yes, he knew . . . It was these walls; these crazy walls were filling him with a wild urge to climb out into the dark sunshine aboveground. Quickly he doused the light to banish the shouting walls, then sat again upon the tool chest. Yes, he was trapped. His muscles were flexed taut and sweat ran down his face. He knew now that he could not stay here and he could not go out. He lit a cigarette with shaking fingers; the match flame revealed the green-papered walls with militant distinctness; the purple on the gun barrel glinted like a threat; the meat cleaver brooded with its eloquent splotches of blood; the mound of silver and copper smoldered angrily; the diamonds winked at him from the floor; and the gold watches ticked and trembled, crowning time the king of consciousness, defining the limits of living . . . The match blaze died and he bolted from where he stood and collided brutally with the nails upon the walls. The spell was broken. He shuddered, feeling that, in spite of his fear, sooner or later he would go up into that dead sunshine and somehow say something to somebody about all this.

He sat again upon the tool chest. Fatigue weighed upon his forehead and eyes. Minutes passed and he relaxed. He dozed, but his imagination was alert. He saw himself rising, wading again in the sweeping water of the sewer; he came to a manhole and climbed out and was amazed to discover that he had hoisted himself into a room filled with armed policemen who were watching him intently. He jumped awake in the dark; he had not moved. He sighed, closed his eyes, and slept again; this time his imagination designed a scheme of protection for him. His dreaming made him feel that he was standing in a room watching over his own nude body lying stiff and cold upon a white table. At the far end of the room he saw a crowd of people huddled in a corner, afraid of his body. Though lying dead upon the table, he was standing in some mysterious way at his side, warding off the people, guarding his body, and laughing to himself as he observed the situation. They're scared of me, he thought.

He awakened with a start, leaped to his feet, and stood in the center of the black cave. It was a full minute before he moved again. He hovered between sleeping and waking, unprotected, a prey of wild fears. He could neither see nor hear. One part of him was asleep; his blood coursed slowly and his flesh was numb. On the other hand he was roused to a strange, high pitch of tension. He lifted his fingers to his face, as though about to weep. Gradually his hands lowered and he struck a match, looking about, expecting to see a door through which he could walk to safety; but there was no door, only the green walls and the moving floor. The match flame died and it was dark again.

Five minutes later he was still standing when the thought came to him that he had been asleep. Yes . . . But he was not yet fully awake; he was still queerly blind and deaf. How long had he slept? Where was he? Then suddenly he recalled the green-papered walls of the cave and in the same instant he heard loud singing coming from the church beyond the wall. Yes, they woke me up, he muttered. He hoisted himself and lay atop the bed of pipes and brought his face to the narrow slit. Men and women stood here and there between pews. A song ended and a young black girl tossed back her head and closed her eyes and broke plaintively into another hymn:

Glad, glad, glad, oh, so glad
I got Jesus in my soul . . .

Those few words were all she sang, but what her words did not say, her emotions said as she repeated the lines, varying the mood and tempo, making her tone express meanings which her conscious mind did not know. Another woman melted her voice with the girl's, and then an old man's voice merged with that of the two women. Soon the entire congregation was singing:

Glad, glad, glad, oh, so glad
I got Jesus in my soul . . .

They're wrong, he whispered in the lyric darkness. He felt that their search for a happiness they could never find made them feel that they had committed some dreadful offense which they could not remember or understand. He was now in possession of the feeling that had gripped him when he had first come into the underground. It came to him in a series of questions: Why was this sense of guilt so seemingly innate, so easy to come by, to think, to feel, so verily physical? It seemed that when one felt this guilt one was retracing in one's feelings a faint pattern designed long before; it seemed that one was always trying to remember a gigantic shock that had left a haunting impression upon one's body which one could not forget or shake off, but which had been forgotten by the conscious mind, creating in one's life a state of eternal anxiety.

He had to tear himself away from this; he got down from the pipes. His nerves were so taut that he seemed to feel his brain pushing through his skull. He felt that he had to do something, but he could not figure out what it was. Yet he knew if he stood here until he made up his mind, he would never move. He crawled through the hole he had made in the brick wall and the exertion afforded him respite from tension. When he entered the basement of the radio store, he stopped in fear, hearing loud voices.

"Come on, boy! Tell us what you did with the radio!"

"Mister, I didn't steal the radio! I swear!"

He heard a dull thumping sound and he imagined a boy being struck violently.

"Please, mister!"

"Did you take it to a pawn shop?"

"No, sir! I didn't steal the radio! I got a radio at home," the boy's voice pleaded hysterically. "Go to my home and look!"

There came to his ears the sound of another blow. It was so funny that he had to clap his hand over his mouth to keep from laughing out loud. They're beating some poor boy, he whispered to himself, shaking his head. He felt a sort of distant pity for the boy and wondered if he ought to bring back the radio and leave it in the basement. No. Perhaps it was a good thing that they were beating the boy; perhaps the beating would bring to the boy's attention, for the first time in his life, the secret of his existence, the guilt that he could never get rid of.

Smiling, he scampered over a coal pile and stood again in the basement of the building where he had stolen the money and jewelry. He lifted himself into the areaway, climbed the rain pipe, and squinted through a two-inch opening of window. The guilty familiarity of what he saw made his muscles tighten. Framed before him in a bright tableau of daylight was the night watchman sitting upon the edge of a chair, stripped to the waist, his head sagging forward, his eyes red and puffy. The watchman's face and shoulders were stippled with red and black welts. Back of the watchman stood the safe, the steel door wide open showing the empty vault. Yes, they think he did it, he mused.

Footsteps sounded in the room and a man in a blue suit passed in front of him, then another, then still another. Policemen, he breathed. Yes, they were trying to make the watchman confess, just as they had once made him confess to a crime he had not done. He stared into the room, trying to recall something. Oh . . . Those were the same policemen who had beaten him, had made him sign that paper when he had been too tired and sick to care. Now, they were doing the same thing to the watchman. His heart pounded as he saw one of the policemen shake a finger into the watchman's face.

"Why don't you admit it's an inside job, Thompson?" the policeman said.

"I've told you all I know," the watchman mumbled through swollen lips.

"But nobody was here but you!" the policeman shouted.

"I was sleeping," the watchman said. "It was wrong, but I was sleeping all that night!"

"Stop telling us that lie!"

"It's the truth!"

"When did you get the combination?"

"I don't know how to open the safe," the watchman said.

He clung to the rain pipe, tense, he wanted to laugh, but he controlled himself. He felt a great sense of power; yes, he could go back to the cave, rip the money off the walls, pick up the diamonds and rings, and bring them here and write a note, telling them where to look for their foolish toys. No . . . What good would that do? It was not worth the effort. The watchman was guilty; although he was not guilty of the crime of which he had been accused, he was guilty, had always been guilty. The only thing that worried him was that the man who had been really stealing was not being accused. But he consoled himself: they'll catch him sometime during his life.

He saw one of the policemen slap the watchman across the mouth.

"Come clean, you bastard!"

"I've told you all I know," the watchman mumbled like a child.

One of the police went to the rear of the watchman's chair and jerked it from under him; the watchman pitched forward upon his face.

"Get up!" a policeman said.

Trembling, the watchman pulled himself up and sat limply again in the chair.

"Now, are you going to talk?"

"I've told you all I know," the watchman gasped.

"Where did you hide the stuff?"

"I didn't take it!"

"Thompson, your brains are in your feet," one of the policemen said. "We're going to string you up and get them back into your skull."

He watched the policemen clamp handcuffs on the watchman's wrists and ankles; then they lifted the watchman and swung him upside-down and hoisted his feet to the edge of a door. The watchman hung, head down, his eyes bulging. They're crazy, he whispered to himself as he clung to the ridges of the pipe.

"You going to talk?" a policeman shouted into the watchman's ear.

He heard the watchman groan.

"We'll let you hang there till you talk, see?"

He saw the watchman close his eyes.

"Let's take 'im down. He passed out," a policeman said.

He grinned as he watched them take the body down and dump it carelessly upon the floor. The policeman took off the handcuffs.

"Let 'im come to. Let's get a smoke," a policeman said.

The three policemen left the scope of his vision. A door slammed. He had an impulse to yell to the watchman that he could escape through the hole in the basement and live with him in the cave. But he wouldn't understand, he told himself. After a moment he saw the watchman rise and stand, swaying from weakness. He stumbled across the room to a desk, opened a drawer, and took out a gun. He's going to kill himself, he thought, intent, eager, detached, yearning to see the end of the man's actions. As the watchman stared vaguely about he lifted the gun to his temple; he stood like that for some minutes, biting his lips until a line of blood etched its way down a corner of his chin. No, he oughtn't do that, he said to himself in a mood of pity.

"Don't!" he half whispered and half yelled.

The watchman looked wildly about; he had heard him. But it did not help; there was a loud report and the watchman's head jerked violently and he fell like a log and lay prone, the gun clattering over the floor.

The three policemen came running into the room with drawn guns. One of the policemen knelt and rolled the watchman's body over and stared at a ragged, scarlet hole in the temple.

"Our hunch was right," the kneeling policeman said. "He was guilty, all right."

"Well, this ends the case," another policeman said.

"He knew he was licked," the third one said with grim satisfaction.

He eased down the rain pipe, crawled back through the holes he had made, and went back into his cave. A fever burned in his bones. He had to act, yet he was afraid. His eyes stared in the darkness as though propped open by invisible hands, as though they had become lidless. His muscles were rigid and he stood for what seemed to him a thousand years.

When he moved again his actions were informed with precision, his muscular system reinforced from a reservoir of energy. He crawled through the hole of earth, dropped into the gray sewer current, and sloshed ahead. When his right foot went forward at a street intersection, he fell backward and shot down into water. In a spasm of terror his right hand grabbed the concrete ledge of a down-curve and he felt the streaking water tugging violently at his body. The current reached his neck and for a moment he was still. He knew that if he moved clumsily he would be sucked under. He held onto the ledge with both hands and slowly pulled himself up. He sighed, standing once more in the sweeping water, thankful that he had missed death.

He waded on through sludge, moving with care, until he came to a web of light sifting down from a manhole cover. He saw steel hooks running up the side of the sewer wall; he caught hold and lifted himself and put his shoulder to the cover and moved it an inch. A crash of sound came to him as he looked into a hot glare of sunshine through which blurred shapes moved. Fear scalded him and he dropped back into the pallid current and stood paralyzed in the shadows. A heavy car rumbled past overhead, jarring the pavement, warning him to stay in his world of dark light, knocking the cover back into place with an imperious clang.

He did not know how much fear he felt, for fear claimed him completely; yet it was not a fear of the police or of people, but a cold dread at the thought of the actions he knew he would perform if he went out into that cruel sunshine. His mind said no; his body said yes; and his mind could not understand his feelings. A low whine broke from him and he was in the act of uncoiling. He climbed upward and heard the faint honking of auto horns. Like a frantic cat clutching a rag, he clung to the steel prongs and heaved his shoulder against the cover and pushed it off halfway. For a split second his eyes were drowned in the terror of yellow light and he was in a deeper darkness than he had ever known in the underground.

Partly out of the hole, he blinked, regaining enough sight to make out meaningful forms. An odd thing was happening: No one was rushing forward to challenge him. He had imagined the moment of his emergence as a desperate tussle with men who wanted to cart him off to be killed; instead, life froze about him as the traffic stopped. He pushed the cover aside, stood, swaying in a world so fragile that he expected it to collapse and drop him into some deep void. But nobody seemed to pay him heed. The cars were now swerving to shun him and the gaping hole.

"Why in hell don't you put up a red light, dummy?" a raucous voice yelled.

He understood; they thought that he was a sewer workman. He walked toward the sidewalk, weaving unsteadily through the moving traffic.

"Look where you're going, nigger!"

"That's right! Stay there and get killed!"

"You blind, you bastard?"

"Go home and sleep your drunk off!"

A policeman stood at the curb, looking in the opposite direction. When he passed the policeman, he feared that he would be grabbed, but nothing happened. Where was he? Was this real? He wanted to look about to get his bearings, but felt that something awful would happen to him if he did. He wandered into a spacious doorway of a store that sold men's clothing and saw his reflection in a long mirror: his cheekbones protruded from a hairy black face; his greasy cap was perched askew upon his head and his eyes were red and glassy. His shirt and trousers were caked with mud and hung loosely. His hands were gummed with a black stickiness. He threw back his head and laughed so loudly that passers-by stopped and stared.

He ambled on down the sidewalk, not having the merest notion of where he was going. Yet, sleeping within him, was the drive to go somewhere and say something to somebody. Half an hour later his ears caught the sound of spirited singing.

The Lamb, the Lamb, the Lamb
I hear thy voice a-calling
The Lamb, the Lamb, the Lamb
I feel thy grace a-falling

A church! he exclaimed. He broke into a run and came to brick steps leading downward to a sub-basement. This is it! The church into which he had peered. Yes, he was going in and tell them. What? He did not know; but, once face to face with them, he would think of what to say. Must be Sunday, he mused. He ran down the steps and jerked the door open; the church was crowded and a deluge of song swept over him.

The Lamb, the Lamb, the Lamb
Tell me again your story
The Lamb, the Lamb, the Lamb
Flood my soul with your glory

He stared at the singing faces with a trembling smile.

"Say!" he shouted.

Many turned to look at him, but the song rolled on. His arm was jerked violently.

"I'm sorry, Brother, but you can't do that in here," a man said.

"But, mister!"

"You can't act rowdy in God's house," the man said.

"He's filthy," another man said.

"But I want to tell 'em," he said loudly.

"He stinks," someone muttered.

The song had stopped, but at once another one began.

Oh, wondrous sight upon the cross
Vision sweet and divine
Oh, wondrous sight upon the cross
Full of such love sublime

He attempted to twist away, but other hands grabbed him and rushed him into the doorway.

"Let me alone!" he screamed, struggling.

"Get out!"

"He's drunk," somebody said. "He ought to be ashamed!"

"He acts crazy!"

He felt that he was failing and he grew frantic.

"But, mister, let me tell—"

"Get away from this door, or I'll call the police!"

He stared, his trembling smile fading in a sense of wonderment.

"The police," he repeated vacantly.

"Now, get!"

He was pushed toward the brick steps and the door banged shut. The waves of song came.

Oh, wondrous sight, wondrous sight
Lift my heavy heart above
Oh, wondrous sight, wondrous sight
Fill my weary soul with love

He was smiling again now. Yes, the police . . . That was it! Why had he not thought of it before? The idea had been deep down in him, and only now did it assume supreme importance. He looked up and saw a street sign: COURT STREET—HARTSDALE AVENUE. He turned and walked northward, his mind filled with the image of the police station. Yes, that was where they had beaten him, and had made him sign a confession of his guilt. He would go there and clear up everything, make a statement. What statement? He did not know. He was the statement, and since it was all so clear to him, surely he would be able to make it clear to others.

He came to the corner of Hartsdale Avenue and turned westward. Yeah, there's the station . . . A policeman came down the steps and walked past him without a glance. He mounted the stone steps and went through the door, paused; he was in a hallway where several policemen were standing, talking, smoking. One turned to him.

"What do you want, boy?"

He looked at the policeman and laughed.

"What in hell are you laughing about?" the policeman asked.

He stopped laughing and stared. His whole being was full of what he wanted to say to them, but he could not say it.

"Are you looking for the Desk Sergeant?"

"Yes, sir," he said quickly; then: "Oh, no, sir."

"Well, make up your mind, now."

Four policemen grouped themselves around him.

"I'm looking for the men," he said.

"What men?"

Peculiarly, at that moment he could not remember the names of the policemen; he recalled their beating him, the confession he had signed, and how he had run away from them. He saw the cave next to the church, the money on the walls, the gun, the rings, the cleaver, the watches, and the diamonds on the floor.

"They brought me here," he began.

"When?"

His mind flew back over the blur of the time lived in the underground blackness. He had no idea of how much time had elapsed, but the intensity of what had happened to him told him that it could not have transpired in a short space of time, yet his mind told him that time must have been brief.

"It was a long time ago." He spoke like a child relating a dimly remembered dream. "It was a long time," he repeated, following the promptings of his emotions. "They beat me . . . I was scared . . . I ran away."

A policeman raised a finger to his temple and made a derisive circle.

"Nuts," the policeman said.

"Do you know what place this is, boy?"

"Yes, sir. The police station," he answered sturdily, almost proudly.

"Well, who do you want to see?"

"The men," he said again, feeling that surely they knew the men. "You know the men," he said in a hurt tone.

"What's your name?"

He opened his lips to answer and no words came. He had forgotten. But what did it matter if he had? It was not important.

"Where do you live?"

Where did he live? It had been so long ago since he had lived up here in this strange world that he felt it was foolish even to try to remember. Then for a moment the old mood that had dominated him in the underground surged back. He leaned forward and spoke eagerly.

"They said I killed the woman."

"What woman?" a policeman asked.

"And I signed a paper that said I was guilty," he went on, ignoring their questions. "Then I ran off . . ."

"Did you run off from an institution?"

"No, sir," he said, blinking and shaking his head. "I came from under the ground. I pushed off the manhole cover and climbed out . . ."

"All right, now," a policeman said, placing an arm about his shoulder. "We'll send you to the psycho and you'll be taken care of."

"Maybe he's a Fifth Columnist!" a policeman shouted.

There was laughter and, despite his anxiety, he joined in. But the laughter lasted so long that it irked him.

"I got to find those men," he protested mildly.

"Say, boy, what have you been drinking?"

"Water," he said. "I got some water in a basement."

"Were the men you ran away from dressed in white, boy?"

"No, sir," he said brightly. "They were men like you."

An elderly policeman caught hold of his arm.

"Try and think hard. Where did they pick you up?"

He knitted his brows in an effort to remember, but he was blank inside. The policeman stood before him demanding logical answers and he could no longer think with his mind; he thought with his feelings and no words came.

"I was guilty," he said. "Oh, no, sir. I wasn't then, I mean, mister!"

"Aw, talk sense. Now, where did they pick you up?"

He felt challenged and his mind began reconstructing events in reverse; his feelings ranged back over the long hours and he saw the cave, the sewer, the bloody room where it was said that a woman had been killed.

"Oh, yes, sir," he said, smiling. "I was coming from Mrs. Wooten's."

"Who is she?"

"I work for her."

"Where does she live?"

"Next door to Mrs. Peabody, the woman who was killed."

The policemen were very quiet now, looking at him intently.

"What do you know about Mrs. Peabody's death, boy?"

"Nothing, sir. But they said I killed her. But it doesn't make any difference. I'm guilty!"

"What are you talking about, boy?"

His smile faded and he was possessed with memories of the underground; he saw the cave next to the church and his lips moved to speak. But how could he say it? The distance between what he felt and what these men meant was vast. Something told him, as he stood there looking into their faces, that he would never be able to tell them, that they would never believe him even if he told them.

"All the people I saw was guilty," he began slowly.

"Aw, nuts," a policeman muttered.

"Say," another policeman said, "that Peabody woman was killed over on Winewood. That's Number Ten's beat."

"Where's Number Ten?" a policeman asked.

"Upstairs in the swing room," someone answered.

"Take this boy up, Sam," a policeman ordered.

"O.K. Come along, boy."

An elderly policeman caught hold of his arm and led him up a flight of wooden stairs, down a long hall, and to a door.

"Squad Ten!" the policeman called through the door.

"What?" a gruff voice answered.

"Someone to see you!"

"About what?"

The old policeman pushed the door in and then shoved him into the room.

He stared, his lips open, his heart barely beating. Before him were the three policemen who had picked him up and had beaten him to extract the confession. They were seated about a small table, playing cards. The air was blue with smoke and sunshine poured through a high window, lighting up fantastic smoke shapes. He saw one of the policemen look up; the policeman's face was tired and a cigarette dropped limply from one corner of his mouth and both of his fat, puffy eyes were squinting and his hands gripped his cards.

"Lawson!" the man exclaimed.

The moment the man's name sounded he remembered the names of all of them: Lawson, Murphy, and Johnson. How simple it was. He waited, smiling, wondering how they would react when they knew that he had come back.

"Looking for me?" the man who had been called Lawson mumbled, sorting his cards. "For what?"

So far only Murphy, the red-headed one, had recognized him.

"Don't you-all remember me?" he blurted, running to the table.

All three of the policemen were looking at him now. Lawson, who seemed the leader, jumped to his feet.

"Where in hell have you been?"

"Do you know 'im, Lawson?" the old policeman asked.

"Huh?" Lawson frowned. "Oh, yes. I'll handle 'im." The old policeman left the room and Lawson crossed to the door and turned the key in the lock. "Come here, boy," he ordered in a cold tone.

He did not move; he looked from face to face. Yes, he would tell them about his cave.

"He looks batty to me," Johnson said, the one who had not spoken before.

"Why in hell did you come back here?" Lawson said.

"I—I just didn't want to run away no more," he said. "I'm all right, now." He paused; the men's attitude puzzled him.

"You've been hiding, huh?" Lawson asked in a tone that denoted that he had not heard his previous words. "You told us you were sick, and when we left you in the room, you jumped out of the window and ran away."

Panic filled him. Yes, they were indifferent to what he would say! They were waiting for him to speak and they would laugh at him. He had to rescue himself from this bog; he had to force the reality of himself upon them.

"Mister, I took a sackful of money and pasted it on the walls . . ." he began.

"I'll be damned," Lawson said.

"Listen," said Murphy, "let me tell you something for your own good. We don't want you, see? You're free, free as air. Now go home and forget it. It was all a mistake. We caught the guy who did the Peabody job. He wasn't colored at all. He was an Eyetalian."

"Shut up!" Lawson yelled. "Have you no sense!"

"But I want to tell 'im," Murphy said.

"We can't let this crazy fool go," Lawson exploded. "He acts nuts, but this may be a stunt . . ."

"I was down in the basement," he began in a childlike tone, as though repeating a lesson learned by heart; "and I went into a movie . . ." His voice failed. He was getting ahead of his story. First, he ought to tell them about the singing in the church, but what words could he use? He looked at them appealingly. "I went into a shop and took a sackful of money and diamonds and watches and rings . . . I didn't steal 'em; I'll give 'em all back. I just took 'em to play with . . ." He paused, stunned by their disbelieving eyes.

Lawson lit a cigarette and looked at him coldly.

"What did you do with the money?" he asked in a quiet, waiting voice.

"I pasted the hundred-dollar bills on the walls."

"What walls?" Lawson asked.

"The walls of the dirt room," he said, smiling, "the room next to the church. I hung up the rings and the watches and I stamped the diamonds into the dirt . . ." He saw that they were not understanding what he was saying. He grew frantic to make them believe, his voice tumbled on eagerly. "I saw a dead baby and a dead man . . ."

"Aw, you're nuts," Lawson snarled, shoving him into a chair.

"But, mister . . ."

"Johnson, where's the paper he signed?" Lawson asked.

"What paper?"

"The confession, fool!"

Johnson pulled out his billfold and extracted a crumpled piece of paper.

"Yes, sir, mister," he said, stretching forth his hand. "That's the paper I signed . . ."

Lawson slapped him and he would have toppled had his chair not struck a wall behind him. Lawson scratched a match and held the paper over the flame; the confession burned down to Lawson's fingertips.

He stared, thunderstruck; the sun of the underground was fleeing and the terrible darkness of the day stood before him. They did not believe him, but he *had* to make them believe him!

"But, mister . . ."

"It's going to be all right, boy," Lawson said with a quiet, soothing laugh. "I've burned your confession, see? You didn't sign anything." Lawson came close to him with the black ashes cupped in his palm. "You don't remember a thing about this, do you?"

"Don't you-all be scared of me," he pleaded, sensing their uneasiness. "I'll sign another paper, if you want me to. I'll show you the cave."

"What's your game, boy?" Lawson asked suddenly.

"What are you trying to find out?" Johnson asked.

"Who sent you here?" Murphy demanded.

"Nobody sent me, mister," he said. "I just want to show you the room . . ."

"Aw, he's plumb bats," Murphy said. "Let's ship 'im to the psycho."

"No," Lawson said. "He's playing a game and I wish to God I knew what it was."

There flashed through his mind a definite way to make them believe him; he rose from the chair with nervous excitement.

"Mister, I saw the night watchman blow his brains out because you accused him of stealing," he told them. "But he didn't steal the money and diamonds. I took 'em."

Tigerishly Lawson grabbed his collar and lifted him bodily.

"*Who told you about that?*"

"Don't get excited, Lawson," Johnson said. "He read about it in the papers."

Lawson flung him away.

"He couldn't have," Lawson said, pulling papers from his pocket. "I haven't turned in the reports yet."

"Then how *did* he find out?" Murphy asked.

"Let's get out of here," Lawson said with quick resolution. "Listen, boy, we're going to take you to a nice, quiet place, see?"

"Yes, sir," he said. "And I'll show you the underground."

"Goddamn," Lawson muttered, fastening the gun at his hip. He narrowed his eyes at Johnson and Murphy. "Listen," he spoke just above a whisper, "say nothing about this, you hear?"

"O.K.," Johnson said.

"Sure," Murphy said.

Lawson unlocked the door and Johnson and Murphy led him down the stairs. The hallway was crowded with policemen.

"What have you got there, Lawson?"

"What did he do, Lawson?"

"He's psycho, ain't he, Lawson?"

Lawson did not answer; Johnson and Murphy led him to the car parked at the curb, pushed him into the back seat. Lawson got behind the steering wheel and the car rolled forward.

"What's up, Lawson?" Murphy asked.

"Listen," Lawson began slowly, "we tell the papers that he spilled about the Peabody job, then he escapes. The Wop is caught and we tell the papers that we steered them wrong to trap the real guy, see? Now this dope shows up and acts nuts. If we let him go, he'll squeal that we framed him, see?"

"I'm all right, mister," he said, feeling Murphy's and Johnson's arm locked rigidly into his. "I'm guilty . . . I'll show you everything in the underground. I laughed and laughed . . ."

"Shut that fool up!" Lawson ordered.

Johnson tapped him across the head with a blackjack and he fell back against the seat cushion, dazed.

"Yes, sir," he mumbled. "I'm all right."

The car sped along Hartsdale Avenue, then swung onto Pine Street and rolled to State Street, then turned south. It slowed to a stop, turned in the middle of a block, and headed north again.

"You're going around in circles, Lawson," Murphy said.

Lawson did not answer; he was hunched over the steering wheel. Finally he pulled the car to a stop at a curb.

"Say, boy, tell us the truth," Lawson asked quietly. "Where did you hide?"

"I didn't hide, mister."

The three policemen were staring at him now; he felt that for the first time they were willing to understand him.

"Then what happened?"

"Mister, when I looked through all of those holes and saw how people were living, I loved 'em . . ."

"Cut out that crazy talk!" Lawson snapped. "Who sent you back here?"

"Nobody, mister."

"Maybe he's talking straight," Johnson ventured.

"All right," Lawson said. "Nobody hid you. Now, tell us *where* you hid."

"I went underground . . ."

"What goddamn underground do you keep talking about?"

"I just went . . ." He paused and looked into the street, then pointed to a manhole cover. "I went down in there and stayed."

"In the *sewer?*"

"Yes, sir."

The policemen burst into a sudden laugh and ended quickly. Lawson swung the car around and drove to Woodside Avenue; he brought the car to a stop in front of a tall apartment building.

"What're we going to do, Lawson?" Murphy asked.

"I'm taking him up to my place," Lawson said. "We've got to wait until night. There's nothing we can do now."

They took him out of the car and led him into a vestibule.

"Take the steps," Lawson muttered.

They led him up four flights of stairs and into the living room of a small apartment. Johnson and Murphy let go of his arms and he stood uncertainly in the middle of the room.

"Now, listen, boy," Lawson began, "forget those wild lies you've been telling us. Where did you hide?"

"I just went underground, like I told you."

The room rocked with laughter. Lawson went to a cabinet and got a bottle of whisky; he placed glasses for Johnson and Murphy. The three of them drank.

He felt that he could not explain himself to them. He tried to muster all the sprawling images that floated in him; the images stood out sharply in his mind, but he could not make them have the meaning for others that they had for him. He felt so helpless that he began to cry.

"He's nuts, all right," Johnson said. "All nuts cry like that."

Murphy crossed the room and slapped him.

"Stop that raving!"

A sense of excitement flooded him; he ran to Murphy and grabbed his arm.

"Let me show you the cave," he said. "Come on, and you'll see!"

Before he knew it a sharp blow had clipped him on the chin; darkness covered his eyes. He dimly felt himself being lifted and laid out on the sofa. He heard low voices and struggled to rise, but hard hands held him down. His brain was clearing now. He pulled to a sitting posture and stared with glazed eyes. It had grown dark. How long had he been out?

"Say, boy," Lawson said soothingly, "will you show us the underground?"

His eyes shone and his heart swelled with gratitude. Lawson believed him! He rose, glad; he grabbed Lawson's arm, making the policeman spill whisky from the glass to his shirt.

"Take it easy, goddammit," Lawson said.

"Yes, sir."

"O.K. We'll take you down. But you'd better be telling us the truth, you hear?"

He clapped his hands in wild joy.

"I'll show you everything!"

He had triumphed at last! He would now do what he had felt was compelling him all along. At last he would be free of his burden.

"Take 'im down," Lawson ordered.

They led him down to the vestibule; when he reached the sidewalk he saw that it was night and a fine rain was falling.

"It's just like when I went down," he told them.

"What?" Lawson asked.

"The rain," he said, sweeping his arm in a wide arc. "It was raining when I went down. The rain made the water rise and lift the cover off."

"Cut it out," Lawson snapped.

They did not believe him now, but they would. A mood of high selflessness throbbed in him. He could barely contain his rising spirits. They would see what he had seen; they would feel what he had felt. He would lead them through all the holes he had dug and . . . He wanted to make a hymn, prance about in physical ecstasy, throw his arm about the policemen in fellowship.

"Get in the car," Lawson ordered.

He climbed in and Johnson and Murphy sat at either side of him; Lawson slid behind the steering wheel and started the motor.

"Now, tell us where to go," Lawson said.

"It's right around the corner from where the lady was killed," he said.

The car rolled slowly and he closed his eyes, remembering the song he had heard in the church, the song that had wrought him to such a high pitch of terror and pity. He sang softly, lolling his head:

Glad, glad, glad, oh, so glad
I got Jesus in my soul . . .

"Mister," he said, stopping his song, "you ought to see how funny the rings look on the wall." He giggled. "I fired a pistol, too. Just once, to see how it felt."

"What do you suppose he's suffering from?" Johnson asked.

"Delusions of grandeur, maybe," Murphy said.

"Maybe it's because he lives in a white man's world," Lawson said.

"Say, boy, what did you eat down there?" Murphy asked, prodding Johnson anticipatorily with his elbow.

"Pears, oranges, bananas, and pork chops," he said.

The car filled with laughter.

"You didn't eat any watermelon?" Lawson asked, smiling.

"No, sir," he answered calmly. "I didn't see any."

The three policemen roared harder and louder.

"Boy, you're sure some case," Murphy said, shaking his head in wonder.

The car pulled to a curb.

"All right, boy," Lawson said. "Tell us where to go."

He peered through the rain and saw where he had gone down. The streets, save for a few dim lamps glowing softly through the rain, were dark and empty.

"Right there, mister," he said, pointing.

"Come on; let's take a look," Lawson said.

"Well, suppose he did hide down there," Johnson said, "what is that supposed to prove?"

"I don't believe he hid down there," Murphy said.

"It won't hurt to look," Lawson said. "Leave things to me."

Lawson got out of the car and looked up and down the street.

He was eager to show them the cave now. If he could show them what he had seen, then they would feel what he had felt and they in turn would show it to others and those others would feel as they had felt, and soon everybody would be governed by the same impulse of pity.

"Take 'im out," Lawson ordered.

Johnson and Murphy opened the door and pushed him out; he stood trembling in the rain, smiling. Again Lawson looked up and down the street; no one was in sight. The rain came down hard, slanting like black wires across the wind-swept air.

"All right," Lawson said. "Show us."

He walked to the center of the street, stopped and inserted a finger in one of the tiny holes of the cover and tugged, but he was too weak to budge it.

"Did you really go down in there, boy?" Lawson asked; there was a doubt in his voice.

"Yes, sir. Just a minute. I'll show you."

"Help 'im get that damn thing off," Lawson said.

Johnson stepped forward and lifted the cover; it clanged against the wet pavement. The hole gaped round and black.

"I went down in there," he announced with pride.

Lawson gazed at him for a long time without speaking, then he reached his right hand to his holster and drew his gun.

"Mister, I got a gun just like that down there," he said, laughing and looking into Lawson's face. "I fired it once then hung it on the wall. I'll show you."

"Show us how you went down," Lawson said quietly.

'I'll go down first, mister, and then you-all can come after me, hear?" He spoke like a little boy playing a game.

"Sure, sure," Lawson said soothingly. "Go ahead. We'll come."

He looked brightly at the policemen; he was bursting with happiness. He bent down and placed his hands on the rim of the hole and sat on the edge, his feet dangling into watery darkness. He heard the familiar drone of the gray current. He lowered his body and hung for a moment by his fingers, then he went downward on the steel prongs, hand over hand, until he reached the last rung. He dropped and his feet hit the water and he felt the stiff current trying to suck him away. He balanced himself quickly and looked back upward at the policemen.

"Come on, you-all!" he yelled, casting his voice above the rustling at his feet.

The vague forms that towered above him in the rain did not move. He laughed, feeling that they doubted him. But, once they saw the things he had done, they would never doubt again.

"Come on! The cave isn't far!" he yelled. "But be careful when your feet hit the water, because the current's pretty rough down here!"

Lawson still held the gun. Murphy and Johnson looked at Lawson quizzically.

"What are we going to do, Lawson?" Murphy asked.

"We are not going to follow that crazy nigger down into that sewer, are we?" Johnson asked.

"Come on, you-all!" he begged in a shout.

He saw Lawson raise the gun and point it directly at him. Lawson's face twitched, as though he were hesitating.

Then there was a thunderous report and a streak of fire ripped through his chest. He was hurled into the water, flat on his back. He looked in amazement at the blurred white faces looming above him. They shot me, he said to himself. The water flowed past him, blossoming in foam about his arms, his legs, and his head. His jaw sagged and his mouth gaped soundless. A vast pain gripped his head and gradually squeezed out consciousness. As from a great distance he heard hollow voices.

"What did you shoot him for, Lawson?"

"I had to."

"Why?"

"You've got to shoot his kind. They'd wreck things."

As though in a deep dream, he heard a metallic clank; they had replaced the manhole cover, shutting out forever the sound of wind and rain. From overhead came the muffled roar of a powerful motor and the swish of a speeding car. He felt the strong tide pushing him slowly into the middle of the sewer, turning him about. For a split second there hovered before his eyes the glittering cave, the shouting walls, and the laughing floor . . . Then his mouth was full of thick, bitter water. The current spun him around. He sighed and closed his eyes, a whirling object rushing alone in the darkness, veering, tossing, lost in the heart of the earth.

QUESTIONS

1. Describe the protagonist's feelings as he first enters the sewer. Does our attitude toward him change as he explores his world underground?

2. Wright makes conspicuous use of color and animal imagery. What function does this imagery serve in the story?
3 How does the setting contribute to the theme of freedom? To the theme of identity?
4. Describe the narrator's thoughts and feelings as he makes his forays aboveground. How valid are his observations upon incidents aboveground?
5. Negro spirituals or "slave songs" are used by modern black writers in a variety of ways. How do they function in this story?
6. Discuss the symbolic and psychological aspects of the underground. How does Wright use imagery to reinforce these aspects? What is the symbolic relation of the world aboveground to that underground?

Hortense Calisher *(1911–) was born in New York City. She attended Barnard College where she contributed prose and poetry to the college magazine. She has taught at a number of colleges and universities, including Sarah Lawrence, Brandeis, and Columbia. Her first collection of stories appeared in 1951,* In the Absence of Angels. *Her first novel,* False Entry *(1961), dealt with the South in journal form. More recent publications include a collection of stories,* Extreme Magic *(1964), and two novels,* Standard Dreaming *(1971) and* Eagle Eye *(1973). "The Scream on 57th Street" was an O. Henry prize story.*

The Scream on Fifty-Seventh Street

HORTENSE CALISHER

When the scream came, from downstairs in the street five flights below her bedroom window, Mrs. Hazlitt, who in her month's tenancy of the flat had become the lightest of sleepers, stumbled up, groped her way past the empty second twin bed that stood nearer the window, and looked out. There was nothing to be seen of course—the apartment house she was in, though smartly kept up to the standards of the neighborhood, dated from the era of front fire escapes, and the sound, if it had come at all, had come from directly beneath them. From other half-insomniac nights she knew that the hour must be somewhere between three and four in the morning. The "all-night" doorman who guarded the huge façade of the apartment house opposite had retired, per custom, to some region behind its canopy; the one down the block at the corner of First, who blew his taxi whistle so incessantly that she had for some nights mistaken it for a traffic policeman's, had been quiet for a long time. Even the white-shaded lamp that burned all day and most of the night on the top floor of the little gray town house sandwiched between the tall buildings across the way—an invalid's light perhaps—had been quenched. At this hour the wide expanse of the avenue, Fifty-Seventh Street at its easternmost end, looked calm, reassuring and amazingly silent for one of the main arteries of the city. The cross-town bus service had long since ceased; the truck traffic over on First made only an occasional dim rumble. If she went into the next room, where there was a French window opening like a double door, and leaned out, absurd idea, in her nightgown, she would see, far down to the right, the lamps of a portion of the Queensboro Bridge, quietly necklaced on the night. In the blur beneath them, out of range but comfortable to imagine, the beautiful cul-de-sac of Sutton Square must be musing, Edwardian in the starlight, its one antique bow-front jutting over the river shimmering below. And in the façades opposite her, lights were still spotted here and there, as was always the case, even in the small hours, in New York. Other consciousnesses were awake, a vigil of anonymous neighbors whom she would never know, that still gave one the hive-sense of never being utterly alone.

All was silent. No, she must have dreamed it, reinterpreted in her doze some routine sound, perhaps the siren of the police car that often keened through this street but never stopped, no doubt on its way to the more tumultuous West Side. Until the death of her husband, companion of twenty years, eight months ago, her ability to sleep had always been healthy and immediate; since then it had gradually, not unnaturally deteriorated, but this was the worst; she had never done this before. For she could still hear very clearly the character of the sound, or rather its lack of one—a long, oddly sustained note, then a shorter one, both perfectly even, not discernible as a man's or a woman's, and without—yes, without the color of any emotion—surely the sound that one heard in dreams. Never a woman of small midnight fears in either city or country, as a girl she had done settlement work on some of this city's blackest streets, as a mining engineer's wife had nestled peacefully within the shrieking velvet of an Andes night. Not to give herself special marks for this, it was still all the more reason why what she had heard, or thought she had heard, must have been hallucinatory. A harsh word, but she must be stern with herself at the very beginnings of any such, of what could presage the sort of disintegrating widowhood, full of the mouse-fears and softening self-indulgences of the manless, that she could not, would not abide. Scarcely a second or two could have elapsed between that long—yes, that was it, soulless—cry, and her arrival at the window. And look, down there on the street and upward, everything remained motionless. Not a soul, in answer, had erupted from a doorway. All the fanlights of the lobbies shone serenely. Up above, no one leaned, not a window had flapped wide. After twenty years of living outside of the city, she could still flatter herself that she knew New York down to the ground—she had been born here, and raised. Secretly mourning it, missing it through all the happiest suburban years, she had kept up with it like a scholar, building a red-book of it for herself even through all its savage, incontinent rebuilding. She still knew all its neighborhoods. She knew. And this was one in which such a sound would be policed at once, such a cry serviced at once, if only by doormen running. No, the fault, the disturbance, must be hers.

Reaching into the pretty, built-in wardrobe on her right—the flat, with so many features that made it more like a house, fireplace, high ceilings, had attracted her from the first for this reason—she took out a warm dressing gown and sat down on the bed to put on her slippers. The window was wide open and she meant to leave it that way; country living had made unbearable the steam heat of her youth. There was no point to winter otherwise, and she—she and Sam—had always been ones to enjoy the weather as it came. Perhaps she had been unwise to give up the dog, excuse for walks early and late, outlet for talking aloud—the city was full of them. Unwise too, in the self-denuding impulse of loss, to have made herself that solitary in readiness for a city where she would have to remake friends, and no longer had kin. And charming as this flat was, wooed as she increasingly was by the delicately winning personality of its unknown, absent owner, Mrs. Berry, by her bric-a-brac, her cookbooks, even by her widowhood, almost as recent as Mrs. Hazlitt's own—perhaps it would be best to do something about getting the empty second twin bed removed from this room. No doubt Mrs. Berry, fled to London, possibly even residing in the rooms of yet a third woman in search of recommended change, would understand. Mrs. Hazlitt stretched her arms, able to smile at this imagined procession of women inhabiting each other's rooms, fallen one against the other like a pack of playing cards. How could she have forgotten what anyone who had reached middle age through the normal amount of trouble should know, that the very horizontal position itself of sleep, when one could not, laid one open to every attack from within, on a couch with no psychiatrist to listen but oneself. The best way to meet the horrors was on two feet, vertical. What she meant to do now was to fix herself a sensible hot drink, not coffee, reminiscent of shared midnight snacks, not even tea, but a nursery drink, cocoa. In a lifetime, she thought, there are probably two eras of the sleep that is utterly sound: the nursery sleep (if one had the lucky kind of childhood I did) and the sleep next or near the heart and body of the one permanently loved and loving, if one has been lucky enough for that too. I must learn from within, as well as without, that both are over. She stood up, tying her sash more firmly. And at that moment the scream came again.

She listened, rigid. It came exactly as remembered, one shrilled long note, then the shorter second, like a cut-off Amen to the first and of the same timbre, dreadful in its cool, a madness expended almost with calm, near the edge of joy. No wonder she had thought of the siren; this had the same note of terror controlled. One could not tell whether it sped toward a victim or from one. As before, it seemed to come from directly below.

Shaking, she leaned out, could see nothing because of the high sill, ran into the next room, opened the French window and all but stood on the fire escape. As she did so, the sound, certainly human, had just ceased; at the same moment a cab, going slowly down the middle of the avenue, its toplight up, veered directly toward her, as if the driver too had heard, poised there beneath her with its nose pointed toward the curb, then veered sharply back to the center of the street, gathered speed, and drove on. Immediately behind it another cab, toplight off, slowed up, performed exactly the same orbit, then it too, with a hasty squeal of brakes, made for the center street and sped away. In the confusion of noises she thought she heard the grind of a window-sash coming down, then a slam—perhaps the downstairs door of the adjoining set of flats, or of this one. Dropping to her knees, she leaned both palms on the floor-level lintel of the window and peered down through the iron slats of her fire escape and the successive ones below. Crouched that way, she could see straight back to the building line. To the left, a streetlamp cast a pale, even glow on empty sidewalk and the free space of curb either side of a hydrant; to the right, the shadows were obscure, but motionless. She saw nothing to conjure into a half-expected human bundle lying still, heard no footfall staggering or slipping away. Not more than a minute could have elapsed since she had heard the cry. Tilting her head up at the façades opposite, she saw that their simple pattern of lit windows seemed the same. While she stared, one of the squares blotted out, then another, both on floors not too high to have heard. Would no one, having heard, attend? Would she?

Standing up, her hand on the hasp of the French window, she felt herself still shaking, not with fear, but with the effort to keep herself from in some way heeding that cry. Again she told herself that she had been born here, knew the city's ways, had not the *auslander's* incredulity about some of them. These ways had hardened since her day, people had warned her, to an indifference beyond that of any civilized city; there were no "good" neighborhoods now, none of any kind really, except the half-hostile enclosure that each family must build for itself. She had discounted this, knowing unsentimentally what city life was; even in the tender version of it that was her childhood there had been noises, human ones, that the most responsible people, the kindest, had shrugged away, saying, "Nothing, dear. Something outside." What she had not taken into account was her own twenty years of living elsewhere, where such a cry in the night would be succored at once if only for gossip's sake, if only because one gave up privacy—anonymity—forever, when one went to live in a house on a road. If only, she thought, holding herself rigid to stop her trembling, because it would be the cry of someone one knew. Nevertheless, it took all her strength not to rush downstairs, to hang on to the handle, while in her mind's eye she ran out of her apartment door, remembering to take the key, pressed the elevator button and waited, went down at the car's deliberate pace. After that there would be the inner, buzzer door to open, then at last the door to the outside. No, it would take too long, and it was already too late for the phone, by the time police could come or she could find the number of the superintendent in his back basement—and when either answered, what would she say? She looked at the fire escape. Not counting hers, there must be three others between herself and the street. Whether there was a ladder extending from the lowest one she could not remember; possibly one hung by one's hands and dropped to the ground. Years ago there had been more of them, even the better houses had had them in their rear areaways, but she had never in her life seen one used. And this one fronted direct on the avenue. It was this that brought her to her senses—the vision of herself in her blue robe creeping down the front of a building on Fifty-Seventh Street, hanging by her hands until she dropped to the ground. She shut the long window quickly, leaning her weight against it to help the slightly swollen frame into place, and turned the handle counterclockwise, shooting the long vertical bolt. The bolt fell into place with a thump she had never noticed before but already seemed familiar. Probably, she thought, sighing, it was the kind of sound—old hardware on old wood—that more often went with a house.

In the kitchen, over her cocoa, she shook herself with a reminiscent tremble, in the way one did after a narrow escape. It was a gesture made more often to a companion, an auditor. Easy enough to make the larger gestures involved in cutting down one's life to the pattern of the single; the selling of a house, the arranging of income or new occupation. Even the abnegation of sex had a drama that lent one strength, made one hold up one's head as one saw oneself traveling a clear, melancholy line. It was the small gestures for which there was no possible sublimation, the sudden phrase, posture—to no auditor, the constant clueing of identity in another's—its cessation. "Dear me," she would have said—they would have come to town for the winter months as they had often planned, and he would have just returned from an overnight business trip—"what do you suppose I'd have done, Sam, if I'd gone all the way, in my housecoat, really found myself outside? Funny how the distinction between outdoors and in breaks down in the country. I'd forgotten how absolute it is here—with so many barriers between." Of course, she thought, that's the simple reason why here, in the city, the sense of responsibility has to weaken. Who could maintain it, through a door, an elevator, a door and a door, toward everyone, anyone, who screamed? Perhaps that was the real reason she had come here, she thought, washing the cup under the faucet. Where the walls are soundproofed there are no more "people next door" with their ready "casserole" pity, at worst with the harbored glow of their own family life peering from their averted eyelids like the lamplight from under their eaves. Perhaps she had known all along that the best way to learn how to live alone was to come to the place where people really were.

She set the cup out for the morning and added a plate and a spoon. It was wiser not to let herself deteriorate to the utterly casual; besides, the sight of them always gave her a certain pleasure like a greeting if only from herself of the night before. Tomorrow she had a meeting, of one of the two hospital boards on which, luckily for now, she had served for years. There was plenty more of that kind of useful occupation available and no one would care a hoot whether what once she had done for conscience' sake she now did for her own. The meeting was not scheduled until two. Before that she would manage to inquire very discreetly, careful not to appear either eccentric or too friendly, both of which made city people uneasy, as to whether anyone else in the building had heard what she had. This too she would do for discipline's sake. There was no longer any doubt that the sound had been real.

The next morning at eight-thirty, dressed to go out except for her coat, she waited just inside her door for one or the other of the tenants on her floor to emerge. Her heart pounded at the very queerness of what she was doing, but she overruled it; if she did feel somewhat too interested, too much as if she were embarking on a chase, then let her get it out of her system at once, and have done. How to do so was precisely what she had considered while dressing. The problem was not to make too many inquiries, too earnest ones, and not to seem to be making any personal overture, from which people would naturally withdraw. One did not make inconvenient, hothouse friendships in the place one lived in, here. Therefore she had decided to limit her approaches to three—the first to the girl who lived in the adjacent apartment, who could usually be encountered at this hour and was the only tenant she knew for sure lived in the front of the building—back tenants were less likely to have heard. For the rest, she must trust to luck. And whatever the outcome, she would not let herself pursue the matter beyond today.

She opened the door a crack and listened. Still too early. Actually the place, being small—six floors of four or five flats each—had a more intimate feeling than most. According to the super's wife, Mrs. Stump, with whom she had had a chat or two in the hall, many of the tenants, clinging to ceiling rents in what had become a fancier district, had been here for years, a few for the thirty since the place had been built. This would account for so many middle-aged and elderly, seemingly either single or the remnants of families—besides various quiet, well-mannered women who, like herself, did not work, she had noticed at times two men who were obviously father and son, two others who, from their ages and nameplate, noticed at mailtime, might be brothers, and a mother with the only child in the place—a subdued little girl of about eight. As soon as a tenant of long standing vacated or died, Mrs. Stump had added, the larger units were converted to smaller, and this would account for the substratum of slightly showier or younger occupants: two modish blondes, a couple of homburged "decorator" types—all more in keeping with the newly sub-theatrical, antique-shop character of the neighborhood—as well as for the "career girl" on her floor. Mrs. Berry, who from evidences in the flat should be something past forty like herself, belonged to the first group, having been here, with her husband of course until recently, since just after the war. A pity that she, Mrs. Berry, who from her books, her one charming letter, her own situation, might have been just the person to understand, even share Mrs. Hazlitt's reaction to the event of last night, was not here. But this was nonsense; if she were, then she, Mrs. Hazlitt, would not be. She thought again of the chain of women, sighed, and immediately chid herself for this new habit of sighing, as well as for this alarming mound of gratuitous information she seemed to have acquired, in less than a month, about people with whom she was in no way concerned. At that moment she heard the door next hers creak open. Quickly she put on her coat, opened her door and bent to pick up the morning paper. The girl coming out stepped back, dropping one of a pile of boxes she was carrying. Mrs. Hazlitt returned it to her, pressed the button for the elevator, and when it came, held the door. It was the girl she had seen twice before; for the first time they had a nice exchange of smiles.

"Whoops, I'm late," said the girl, craning to look at her watch.

"Me too," said Mrs. Hazlitt, as the cage slid slowly down. She drew breath. "Overslept, once I did get to sleep. Rather a noisy night outside—did you hear all that fuss, must have been around three or four?" She waited hopefully for the answer: Why yes indeed, what on earth was it, did you?

"Uh-uh," said the girl, shaking her head serenely. " 'Fraid the three of us sleep like a log, that's the trouble. My roommates are still at it, lucky stiffs." She checked her watch again, was first out of the elevator, nodded her thanks when Mrs. Hazlitt hurried to hold the buzzer door for her because of the boxes, managed the outer door herself, and departed.

Mrs. Hazlitt walked briskly around the corner to the bakery, came back with her bag of two brioches, and reentered. Imagine, there are three of them, she thought, and I never knew. Well, I envy them their log. The inner door, usually locked, was propped open. Mrs. Stump was on her knees just behind it, washing the marble floor, as she did every day. It was certainly a tidy house, not luxurious but up to a firmly well-bred standard, just the sort a woman like Mrs. Berry would have, that she herself, when the sublease was over, would like to find. Nodding to Mrs. Stump, she went past her to the row of brass mail slots, pretending to search her own although she knew it was too early, weighing whether she ought to risk wasting one of her three chances on her.

"Mail don't come till ten," said Mrs. Stump from behind her.

"Yes, I know," said Mrs. Hazlitt, recalling suddenly that they had had this exchange before. "But I forgot to check yesterday."

"Yesterday vass holiday."

"Oh, so it was." Guiltily Mrs. Hazlitt entered the elevator and faced the door, relieved when it closed. The truth was that she had known yesterday was a holiday and had checked the mail anyway. The truth was that she often did this even on Sundays here, often even more than once. It made an errand in the long expanse of a day when she either flinched from the daily walk that was too dreary to do alone on Sunday, or had not provided herself with a ticket to something. One had to tidy one's hair, spruce a bit for the possible regard of someone in the hall, and when she did see someone, although of course they never spoke, she always returned feeling refreshed, reaffirmed.

Upstairs again, she felt that way now; her day had begun in the eyes of others, as a day should. She made a few phone calls to laundry and bank, and felt even better. Curious how, when one lived alone, one began to feel that only one's own consciousness held up the world, and at the very same time that only an incursion into the world, or a recognition from it, made one continue to exist at all. There was another phone call she might make, to a friend up in the country, who had broken an ankle, but she would save that for a time when she needed it more. This was yet another discipline—not to become a phone bore. The era when she herself had been a victim of such, had often thought of the phone as a nuisance, now seemed as distant as China. She looked at the clock—time enough to make another pot of coffee. With it she ate a brioche slowly, then with the pleasant sense of hurry she now had so seldom, another.

At ten sharp she went downstairs again, resolving to take her chance with whoever might be there. As she emerged from the elevator she saw that she was in luck; the owner of a big brown poodle—a tall, well-set-up man of sixty or so—was bent over his mail slot while the dog stood by. It was the simplest of matters to make an overture to the poodle, who was already politely nosing the palm she offered him, to expose her own love of the breed, remarking on this one's exceptional manners, to skip lightly on from the question of barking to noise in general, to a particular noise.

"Ah well, Coco's had stage training," said his owner, in answer to her compliments. She guessed that his owner might have had the same; he had that fine, bravura face which aging actors of another generation often had, a trifle shallow for its years perhaps but very fine, and he inclined toward her with the same majestic politeness as his dog, looking into her face very intently as she spoke, answering her in the slender, semi-British accent she recalled from matinee idols of her youth. She had to repeat her question on the noise. This time she firmly gave the sound its name—a scream, really rather an unusual scream.

"A scream?" The man straightened. She thought that for a moment he looked dismayed. Then he pursed his lips very judiciously, in almost an acting-out of that kind of response. "Come to think of it, ye-es, I may have heard something." He squared his shoulders. "But no doubt I just turned over. And Coco's a city dog, very blasé fellow. Rather imagine he did too." He tipped his excellent homburg. "Good morning," he added, with sudden reserve, and turned away, giving a flick to the dog's leash that started the animal off with his master behind him.

"Good morning," she called after them, "and thanks for the tip on where to get one like Coco." Coco looked back at her, but his master, back turned, disentangling the leash from the doorknob, did not, and went out without answering.

So I've done it after all, she thought. Too friendly. Especially too friendly since I'm a woman. Her face grew hot at this probable estimate of her—gushy woman chattering over-brightly, lingering in the hall. Bore of a woman who heard things at night, no doubt looked under the bed before she got into it. No, she thought, there was something—when I mentioned the scream. At the aural memory of that latter, still clear, she felt her resolve stiffen. Also—what a dunce she was being—there were the taxis. Taxis, one of them occupied, did not veer, one after the other, on an empty street, without reason. Emboldened, she bent to look at the man's mailbox. The name, Reginald Warwick, certainly fitted her imaginary dossier, but that was not what gave her pause. Apartment 3A. Hers was 5A. He lived in the front, two floors beneath her, where he must have heard.

As she inserted the key in her apartment door, she heard the telephone ringing, fumbled the key and dropped it, then had to open the double lock up above. All part of the city picture, she thought resentfully, remembering their four doors, never locked, in the country—utterly foolhardy, never to be dreamed of here. Even if she had, there were Mrs. Berry's possessions to be considered, nothing extraordinary, but rather like the modest, crotchety bits of treasure she had inherited or acquired herself—in the matter of bric-a-brac alone there was really quite a kinship between them. The phone was still ringing as she entered. She raced toward it eagerly. It was the secretary of the hospital board, telling her that this afternoon's meeting was put off.

"Oh . . . oh dear," said Mrs. Hazlitt. "I mean—I'm so sorry to hear about Mrs. Levin. Hope it's nothing serious."

"I really couldn't say," said the secretary. "But we've enough for a quorum the week after." She rang off.

Mrs. Hazlitt put down the phone, alarmed at the sudden sinking of her heart over such a minor reversal. She had looked forward to seeing people of course, but particularly to spending an afternoon in the brightly capable impersonality of the boardroom, among men and women who brought with them a sense of indefinable swathes of well-being extending behind them, of such a superfluity of it, from lives as full as their checkbooks, that they were met in that efficient room to dispense what overflowed. The meeting would have been an antidote to that dark, anarchic version of the city which had been obsessing her; it would have been a reminder that everywhere, on flight after flight of the city's high, brilliant floors, similar groups of the responsible were convening, could always be applied to, were in command. The phone gave a reminiscent tinkle as she pushed it aside, and she waited, but there was no further ring. She looked at her calendar, scribbled with domestic markings—the hairdresser on Tuesday, a fitting for her spring suit, the date when she must appear at the lawyer's for the closing on the sale of the house. Beyond that she had a dinner party with old acquaintances on the following Thursday, tickets with a woman friend for the Philharmonic on Saturday week. Certainly she was not destitute of either company or activity. But the facts were that within the next two weeks, she could look forward to only two occasions when she would be communicating on any terms of intimacy with people who, within limits, knew "who" she was. A default on either would be felt keenly—much more than the collapse of this afternoon's little—prop. Absently she twiddled the dial back and forth. Proportion was what went first "in solitary"; circling one's own small platform in space, the need for speech mute in one's own throat, one developed an abnormal concern over the night-cries of others. No, she thought, remembering the board meeting, those high convocations of the responsible, I've promised—Lord knows who, myself, somebody. She stood up and gave herself a smart slap on the buttock. "Come on, Millie," she said, using the nickname her husband always had. "Get on with it." She started to leave the room, then remained in its center, hand at her mouth, wondering. Talking aloud to oneself was more common than admitted; almost everyone did. It was merely that she could not decide whether or not she had.

Around eleven o'clock, making up a bundle of lingerie, she went down to the basement where there was a community washing machine, set the machine's cycle, and went back upstairs. Forty minutes later she went through the same routine, shifting the wet clothes to the dryer. At one o'clock she returned for the finished clothes and carried them up. This made six trips in all, but at no time had she met anyone en route; it was Saturday afternoon, perhaps a bad time. At two she went out to do her weekend shopping. The streets were buzzing, the women in the supermarket evidently laying in enough stores for a visitation of giants. Outside the market, a few kids from Third Avenue always waited in the hope of tips for carrying, and on impulse, although her load was small, she engaged a boy of about ten. On the way home, promising him extra for waiting, she stopped at the patisserie where she always lingered for the sheer gilt-and-chocolate gaiety of the place, bought her brioches for the morning, and again on impulse, an éclair for the boy. Going up in the elevator they encountered the mother and small girl, but she had never found any pretext for addressing that glum pair, the mother engaged as usual in a low, toneless tongue-lashing of the child. Divorcée, Mrs. Hazlitt fancied, and no man in the offing, an inconvenient child. In the kitchen, she tipped the boy and offered him the pastry. After an astonished glance, he wolfed it with a practical air, peering at her furtively between bites, and darted off at once, looking askance over his shoulder at her "See you next Saturday, maybe." Obviously he had been brought up to believe that only witches dispensed free gingerbread. In front of the bathroom mirror, Mrs. Hazlitt, tidying up before her walk, almost ritual now, to Sutton Square, regarded her image not yet a witch's but certainly a fool's, a country-cookie-jar fool's. "Oh well, you're company," she said, quite consciously aloud this time, and for some reason this cheered her. Before leaving, she went over face and costume with the laborious attention she always gave them nowadays before going anywhere outside.

Again, when she rode down, she met no one, but she walked with bracing step, making herself take a circuitous route for health's sake, all the way to Bloomingdale's, then on to Park and around again, along the Fifty-Eighth Street bridge pass, the dejectedly frivolous shops that lurked near it, before she let herself approach the house with the niche with the little statue of Dante in it, then the Square. Sitting in the Square, the air rapidly blueing now, lapping her like reverie, she wondered whether any of the residents of the windows surrounding her had noticed her almost daily presence, half hoped they had. Before it became too much of a habit, of course, she would stop coming. Meanwhile, if she took off her distance glasses, the scene before her, seen through the tender, Whistlerian blur of myopia—misted gray bridge, blue and green lights of a barge going at its tranced pace downriver—was the very likeness of a corner of the Chelsea embankment, glimpsed throughout a winter of happy teatime windows seven years ago, from a certain angle below Battersea Bridge. Surely it was blameless to remember past happiness if one did so without self-pity, better still, of course, to be able to speak of it to someone in an even, healing voice. Idly she wondered where Mrs. Berry was living in London. The flat in Cheyne Walk would have just suited her. "Just the thing for you," she would have said to her had she known her. "The Sebrings still let it every season. We always meant to go back." Her watch said five and the air was chilling. She walked rapidly home through the evening scurry, the hour of appointments, catching its excitement as she too hurried, half-persuaded of her own appointment, mythical but still possible, with someone as yet unknown. Outside her own building she paused. All day long she had been entering it from the westerly side. Now, approaching from the east, she saw that the fire escape on this side of the entrance did end in a ladder, about four feet above her. Anyone moderately tall, like herself, would have had an easy drop of it, as she would have done last night. Shaking her head at that crazy image, she looked up at the brilliant hives all around her. Lights were cramming in, crowding on, but she knew too much now about their nighttime progression, their gradual decline to a single indifferent string on that rising, insomniac silence in which she might lie until morning, dreading to hear again what no one else would appear to have heard. Scaring myself to death, she thought (or muttered?), and in the same instant resolved to drop all limits, go down to the basement and interrogate the Stumps, sit on the bench in the lobby and accost anyone who came in, ring doorbells if necessary, until she had confirmation—and not go upstairs until she had. "Excuse me," said someone. She turned. A small, frail, elderly woman, smiling timidly, waited to get past her through the outer door.

"Oh—sorry," said Mrs. Hazlitt. "Why—good evening!" she added with a rush, an enormous rush of relief. "Here—let me," she said more quietly, opening the door with a numb sense of gratitude for having been tugged back from the brink of what she saw now, at the touch of a voice, had been panic. For here was a tenant, unaccountably forgotten, with whom she was almost on speaking terms, a gentle old sort, badly crippled with arthritis, for whom Mrs. Hazlitt had once or twice unlocked the inner door. She did so now.

"Thank you, my dear—my hands are that knobbly." There was the trace of brogue that Mrs. Hazlitt had noticed before. The old woman, her gray hair sparse from the disease but freshly done in the artfully messy arrangements used to conceal the skulls of old ladies, her broadtail coat not new but excellently maintained, gave off the comfortable essence, pleasing as rosewater, of one who had been serenely protected all her life. Unmarried, for she had that strangely deducible aura about her even before one noted the lack of ring, she had also a certain simpleness, now almost bygone, of those household women who had never gone to business—Mrs. Hazlitt had put her down as perhaps the relict sister of a contractor, or of a school superintendent of the days when the system had been Irish from top to bottom, at the top, of Irish of just this class. The old lady fumbled now with the minute key to her mailbox.

"May I?"

"Ah, if you would now. Couldn't manage it when I came down. The fingers don't seem to warm up until evening. It's 2B."

Mrs. Hazlitt, inserting the key, barely noticed the name—Finan. 2B would be a front apartment also, in the line adjacent to the A's.

"And you would be the lady in Mrs. Berry's. Such a nicely spoken woman, she was."

"Oh, yes, isn't she," said Mrs. Hazlitt. "I mean . . . I just came through the agent. But when you live in a person's house—do you know her?"

"Just to speak. Half as long as me, they'd lived here. Fifteen years." The old lady took the one letter Mrs. Hazlitt passed her, the yellow-fronted rent bill whose duplicate she herself had received this morning. "Ah well, we're always sure of this one, aren't we?" Nodding her thanks, she shuffled toward the elevator on built-up shoes shaped like hods. "Still, it's a nice, quiet building, and lucky we are to be in it these days."

There was such a rickety bravery about her, of neat habit long overborne by the imprecisions of age, of dowager hat set slightly askew by fingers unable to deal with a key yet living alone, that Mrs. Hazlitt, reluctant to shake the poor, tottery dear further, had to remind herself of the moment before their encounter.

"Last night?" The old blue eyes looked blank, then brightened. "Ah no, I must have taken one of my Seconals. Otherwise I'd have heard it surely. 'Auntie,' my niece always says—'what if there should be a fire, and you there sleeping away?' Do what she says, I do sometimes, only to hear every pin drop till morning." She shook her head, entering the elevator. "Going up?"

"N-no," said Mrs. Hazlitt. "I—have to wait here for a minute." She sat down on the bench, the token bench that she had never seen anybody sitting on, and watched the car door close on the little figure still shaking its head, borne upward like a fairy godmother, willing but unable to oblige. The car's hum stopped, then its light glowed on again. Someone else was coming down. No, this is the nadir, Mrs. Hazlitt thought. Whether I heard it or not, I'm obviously no longer myself. Sleeping pills for me too, though I've never—and no more nonsense. And no more questioning, no matter who.

The car door opened. "Wssht!" said Miss Finan, scuttling out again. "I've just remembered. Not last night, but two weeks ago. And once before that. A scream, you said?"

Mrs. Hazlitt stood up. Almost unable to speak, for the tears that suddenly wrenched her throat, she described it.

"That's it, just what I told my niece on the phone next morning. Like nothing human, and yet it was. I'd taken my Seconal too early, so there I was wide awake again, lying there just thinking, when it came. 'Auntie,' she tried to tell me, 'it was just one of the sireens. Or hoodlums maybe.' " Miss Finan reached up very slowly and settled her hat. "The city's gone down, you know. Not what it was," she said in a reduced voice, casting a glance over her shoulder, as if whatever the city now was loomed behind her. "But I've laid awake on this street too many years, I said, not to know what I hear." She leaned forward. "But—she . . . they think I'm getting old, you know," she said, in the whisper used to confide the unimaginable. "So . . . well . . . when I heard it again I just didn't tell her."

Mrs. Hazlitt grubbed for her handkerchief, found it and blew her nose. Breaking down, she thought—I never knew what a literal phrase it is. For she felt as if all the muscles that usually held her up, knee to ankle, had slipped their knots and were melting her, unless she could stop them, to the floor. "I'm not normally such a nervous woman," she managed to say. "But it was just that no one else seemed to—why, there were people with lights on, but they just seemed to ignore."

The old lady nodded absently. "Well, thank God my hearing's as good as ever. Hmm. Wait till I tell Jennie that!" She began making her painful way back to the car.

Mrs. Hazlitt put out a hand to delay her. "In case it—I mean, in case somebody ought to be notified—do you have any idea what it was?"

"Oh, I don't know. And what could we—?" Miss Finan shrugged, eager to get along. Still, gossip was tempting. "I did think—" She paused, lowering her voice uneasily. "Like somebody in a fit, it was. We'd a sexton at church taken that way with epilepsy once. And it stopped short like that, just as if somebody'd clapped a hand over its mouth, poor devil. Then the next time I thought—no, more like a signal, like somebody calling. You know the things you'll think at night." She turned, clearly eager to get away.

"But, oughtn't we to inquire?" Mrs. Hazlitt thought of the taxis. "In case it came from this building?"

"This build—" For a moment Miss Finan looked scared, her chin trembling, eyes rounded in the misty, affronted stare that the old gave, not to physical danger, but to a new idea swum too late into their ken. Then she drew herself up, all five feet of her bowed backbone. "Not from here it wouldn't. Across from that big place, maybe. Lots of riffraff there, not used to their money. Or from Third Avenue, maybe. There's always been tenements there." She looked at Mrs. Hazlitt with an obtuse patronage that reminded her of an old nurse who had first instructed her on the social order, blandly mixing up all first causes—disease, money, poverty, snobbery—with a firm illogic that had still seemed somehow in possession—far more firmly so than her own good-hearted parents—of the crude facts. "New to the city, are you," she said, more kindly. "It takes a while."

This time they rode up together. "Now you remember," Miss Finan said, on leaving. "You've two locks on your door, one downstairs. Get a telephone put in by your bed. Snug as a bug in a rug you are then. Nothing to get at you but what's there already. That's what I always tell myself when I'm wakeful. Nothing to get at you then but the Old Nick."

The door closed on her. Watching her go, Mrs. Hazlitt envied her the simplicity, even the spinsterhood that had barred her from imagination as it had from experience. Even the narrowing-in of age would have its compensations, tenderly constricting the horizon as it cramped the fingers, adding the best of locks to Miss Finan's snugness, on her way by now to the triumphant phone call to Jennie.

But that was sinful, to wish for that too soon, what's more it was sentimental, in just the way she had vowed to avoid. Mrs. Hazlitt pushed the button for Down. Emerging from the building, she looked back at it from the corner, back at her day of contrived exits and entrances, abortive conversations. People were hurrying in and out now at a great rate. An invisible glass separated her from them; she was no longer in the fold.

Later that night, Mrs. Hazlitt, once more preparing for bed, peered down at the streets through the slats of the Venetian blind. Catching herself in the attitude of peering made her uneasy. Darkening the room behind her, she raised the blind. After dinner in one of the good French restaurants on Third Avenue and a Tati movie afterward—the French were such competent dispensers of gaiety—she could review her day more as a convalescent does his delirium—"Did I really say—do—that?" And even here she was addressing a vis-à-vis, so deeply was the habit ingrained. But she could see her self-imposed project now for what it was—only a hysterical seeking after conversation, the final breaking-point, like the old-fashioned "crisis" in pneumonia, of the long, low fever of loneliness unexpressed. Even the city, gazed at squarely, was really no anarchy, only a huge diffuseness that returned to the eye of the beholder, to the walker in its streets, even to the closed dream of its sleeper, his own mood, dark or light. Dozens of the solitary must be looking down at it with her, most of them with some *modus vivendi*, many of them booking themselves into life with the same painful intentness, the way the middle-aged sometimes set themselves to learning the tango. And a queer booking you gave yourself today, she told herself, the words lilting with Miss Finan's Irish, this being the last exchange of speech she had had. Testing the words aloud, she found her way with accents, always such a delight to Sam, as good as ever. Well, she had heard a scream, had discovered someone else who had heard it. And now to forget it as promised; the day was done. Prowling the room a bit, she took up her robe, draped it over her shoulders, still more providently put it on. "Oh Millie," she said, tossing the dark mirror a look of scorn as she passed it, "you're such a *sens*ible woman."

Wear out Mrs. Berry's carpet you will, Millie, she thought, twenty minutes later by the bedroom clock, but the accent, adulterated now by Sam's, had escaped her. Had the scream had an accent? The trouble was that the mind had its own discipline; one could remember, even with a smile, the story of the man promised all the gold in the world if he could but go for two minutes not thinking of the word "hippopotamus." She stopped in front of the mirror, seeking her smile, but it too had escaped. "Hippopotamus," she said, to her dark image. The knuckles of one hand rose, somnambulist, as she watched, and pressed against her teeth. She forced the hand, hers, down again. I will say it again, aloud, she thought, and while I am saying it I will be sure to say to myself that I am saying it aloud. She did so. "Hippopotamus." For a long moment she remained there, staring into the mirror. Then she turned and snapped on every light in the room.

Across from her, in another mirror, the full-length one, herself regarded her. She went forward to it, to that image so irritatingly familiar, so constant as life changed it, so necessarily dear. Fair hair, if maintained too late in life, too brightly, always made the most sensible of women look foolish. There was hers, allowed to gray gently, disordered no more than was natural in the boudoir, framing a face still rational, if strained. "Dear me," she said to it. "All you need is somebody to talk to, get it out of your system. Somebody like yourself." As if prodded, she turned and surveyed the room.

Even in the glare of the lights, the naked black projected from the window, the room sent out to her, in half a dozen pleasant little touches, the same sense of its compatible owner that she had had from the beginning. There, flung down, was Mrs. Berry's copy of *The Eustace Diamonds*, a book that she had always meant to read and had been delighted to find here, along with many others of its ilk and still others she herself owned. How many people knew good bisque and how cheaply it might still be collected, or could let it hobnob so amiably with grandmotherly bits of Tiffanyware, even with the chipped Quimper ashtrays that Mrs. Berry, like Mrs. Hazlitt at the time of her own marriage, must once have thought the cutest in the world. There were the white walls, with the silly, strawberry-mouthed Marie Laurencin just above the Beerbohm, the presence of good faded colors, the absence of the new or fauve. On the night table were the scissors, placed, like everything in the house, where Mrs. Hazlitt would have had them, near them a relic that winked of her own childhood—and kept on, she would wager, for the same reason—a magnifying glass exactly like her father's. Above them, the only floor lamp in the house, least offensive of its kind, towered above all the table ones, sign of a struggle between practicality and grace that she knew well, whose end she could applaud. Everywhere indeed there were the same signs of the struggles toward taste, the decline of taste into the prejudices of comfort, that went with a whole milieu and a generation—both hers. And over there was, even more personally, the second bed.

Mrs. Hazlitt sat down on it. If it were moved, into the study say, a few things out of storage with it, how sympathetically this flat might be shared. Nonsense, sheer fantasy to go on like this, to fancy herself embarking on the pitiable twin-life of leftover women, much less with a stranger. But was a woman a stranger if you happened to know that on her twelfth birthday she had received a copy of *Dr. Doolittle*, inscribed to Helena Nelson from her loving father, if you knew the secret, packrat place in the linen closet where she stuffed the neglected mending, of another, in a kitchen drawer, full of broken Mexican terrines and clipped recipes as shamefully grimy as your own cherished ones, if you knew that on 2/11/58 and on 7/25/57 a Dr. Burke had prescribed what looked to be sulfa pills, never used, that must have cured her at the point of purchase, as had embarrassingly happened time and again to yourself? If, in short, you knew almost every endearing thing about her, except her face?

Mrs. Hazlitt, blinking in the excessive light, looked sideways. She knew where there was a photograph album, tumbled once by accident from its shunted place in the bookshelf, and at once honorably replaced. She had seen enough to know that the snapshots, not pasted in separately, would have to be exhumed, one by one, from their packets. No, she told herself, she already knew more than enough of Mrs. Berry from all that had been so trustfully exposed here—enough to know that this was the sort of prying to which Mrs. Berry, like herself, would never stoop. Somehow this clinched it—their understanding. She could see them exchanging notes at some future meeting, Mrs. Berry saying, "Why, do you know—one night, when I was in London—"—herself, the vis-à-vis, nodding, their perfect rapprochement. Then what would be wrong in using, when so handily provided, so graciously awaiting her, such a comforting vis-à-vis, now?

Mrs. Hazlitt found herself standing, the room's glare pressing on her as if she were arraigned in a police line-up, as if, she reminded herself irritably, it were not self-imposed. She forced herself to make a circuit of the room, turning out each lamp with the crisp, no-nonsense flick of the wrist that nurses employed. At the one lamp still burning she hesitated, reluctant to cross over that last shadow-line. Then, with a shrug, she turned it out and sat down in the darkness, in one of the two opposing boudoir chairs. For long minutes she sat there. Once or twice she trembled on the verge of speech, covered it with a swallow. The conventions that guarded the mind in its strict relationship with the tongue were the hardest to flaunt. But this was the century of talk, of the long talk, in which all were healthily urged to confide. Even the children were encouraged toward, praised for, the imaginary companion. Why should the grown person, who for circumstance beyond his control had no other, be denied? As she watched the window, the light in the small gray house was extinguished. Some minutes later the doorman across the way disappeared. Without looking at the luminous dial of the clock, she could feel the silence aging, ripening. At last she bent forward to the opposite chair.

"Helena?" she said.

Her voice, clear-cut, surprised her. There was nothing so strange about it. The walls remained walls. No one could hear her, or cared to, and now, tucking her feet up, she could remember how cozy this could be, with someone opposite. "Helena," she said. "Wait till I tell you what happened while you were away."

She told her everything. At first she stumbled, went back, as if she were rehearsing in front of a mirror. Several times she froze, unsure whether a sentence had been spoken aloud entirely, or had begun, or terminated, unspoken, in the mind. But as she went on, this wavering borderline seemed only to resemble the clued conversation, meshed with silences, between two people who knew each other well. By the time she had finished her account she was almost at ease, settling back into the comfortably shared midnight post-mortem that always restored balance to the world—so nearly could she imagine the face, not unlike her own, in the chair opposite, smiling ruefully at her over the boy and his gingerbread fears, wondering mischievously with her as to in which of the shapes of temptation the Old Nick visited Miss Finan.

"That girl and her *log!*" said Mrs. Hazlitt. "You know how, when they're that young, you want to smash in the smugness. And yet, when you think of all they've got to go through, you feel so maternal. Even if—" Even if, came the nod, imperceptibly—you've never had children, like us.

For a while they were silent. "Warwick!" said Mrs. Hazlitt then. "Years ago there was an actor—Robert Warwick. I was in love with him—at about the age of eight." Then she smiled, bridling slightly, at the dark chair opposite, whose occupant would know her age. "Oh, all right then—twelve. But what is it, do you suppose, always makes old actors look seedy, even when they're not? Daylight maybe. Or all the pretenses." She ruminated. "Why . . . do you know," she said slowly, "I think I've got it. The way he looked in my face when I was speaking, and the way the dog turned back and he didn't. He was lip-reading. Why, the poor old boy is deaf!" She settled back, dropping her slippers one by one to the floor. "Of course, that's it. And he wouldn't want to admit that he couldn't have heard it. Probably doesn't dare wear an aid. Poor old boy, pretty dreary for him if he is an actor, and I'll bet he is." She sighed, a luxury permitted now. "Ah, well. Frail reed—Miss Finan. Lucky for me, though, that I stumbled on her." And on you.

A police siren sounded, muffled less and less by distance, approaching. She was at the window in time to see the car's red dome light streak by as it always did, its alarum dying behind it. Nothing else was on the road. "And there were the taxis," she said, looking down. "I don't know why I keep forgetting them. Veering to the side like that, one right after the other, and one had his light out, so it wasn't for a fare. Nothing on the curb either. Then they both shot away, almost as if they'd caught sight of something up here. And wanted no part of it—the way people do in this town. Wish you could've seen them—it was eerie." There was no response from behind her.

She sat down again. Yes, there was a response, for the first time faintly contrary.

"No," she said. "It certainly was *not* the siren. I was up in a flash. I'd have seen it." She found herself clenching the arms of the chair. "Besides," she said, in a quieter voice, "don't you remember? I heard it twice."

There was no answer. Glancing sideways, she saw the string of lights opposite, not quite of last night's pattern. But the silence was the same, opened to its perfect hour like a century plant, multiple-rooted, that came of age every night. The silence was in full bloom, and it had its own sound. Hark hark, no dogs do bark. And there is nobody in the chair.

Never was, never had been. It was sad to be up at this hour and sane. For now is the hour, now is the hour when all good men are asleep. Her hand smoothed the rim of the wastebasket, about the height from the floor of a dog's collar. Get one tomorrow. But how to manage until then, with all this silence speaking?

She made herself stretch out on the bed, close her eyes. "Sam," she said at last, as she had sworn never to do in thought or word, "I'm lonely." Listening vainly, she thought how wise her resolve had been. Too late, now she had tested his loss to the full, knew him for the void he was—far more of a one than Mrs. Berry, who, though unknown, was still somewhere. By using the name of love, when she had been ready to settle for anybody, she had sent him into the void forever. Opening her eyes, adjusted now to the sourceless city light that never ceased trickling on ceiling, lancing from mirrors, she turned her head right to left, left to right on the pillow, in a gesture to the one auditor who remained.

"No," she said, in the dry voice of correction. "I'm not lonely. I'm alone."

Almost at once she raised herself on her elbow, her head cocked. No, she had heard nothing from outside. But in her mind's ear she could hear the sound of the word she had just spoken, its final syllable twanging like a tuning fork, infinitely receding to octaves above itself, infinitely returning. In what seemed scarcely a stride, she was in the next room, at the French window, brought there by that thin, directional vibration which not necessarily even the blind would hear. For she had recognized it. She had identified the accent of the scream.

The long window frame, its swollen wood shoved tight by her the night before, at first would not budge; then, as she put both hands on the hasp and braced her knees, it gave slowly, grinding inward, the heavy man-high bolt thumping down. Both sounds, too, fell into their proper places. That's what I heard before, she thought, the noise of a window opening or closing, exactly like mine. Two lines of them, down the six floors of the building, made twelve possibles. But that was of no importance now. Stepping up on the lintel, she spread the casements wide.

Yes, there was the bridge, one small arc of it, sheering off into the mist, beautiful against the night, as all bridges were. Now that she was outside, past all barriers, she could hear, with her ordinary ear, faint nickings that marred the silence, but these were only the surface scratches on a record that still revolved one low, continuous tone. No dogs to bark. That was the key to it, that her own hand, smoothing a remembered dog-collar, had been trying to give her. There were certain dog-whistles, to be bought anywhere—one had hung, with the unused leash, on a hook near a door in the country—which blew a summons so high above the human range that only a dog could hear it. What had summoned her last night would have been that much higher, audible only to those tuned in by necessity—the thin, soaring decibel of those who were no longer in the fold. Alone-oh. Alone-oh. That would have been the shape of it, of silence expelled from the mouth in one long relieving note, cool, irrepressible, the second one clapped short by the hand. No dog would have heard it. No animal but one was ever that alone.

She stepped out onto the fire escape. There must be legions of them, of us, she thought, in the dim alleyways, the high, flashing terraces—each one of them come to the end of his bookings, circling his small platform in space. And who would hear such a person? Not the log-girls, not for years and years. None of any age who, body to body, bed to bed, either in love or in the mutual pluck-pluck of hate—like the little girl and her mother—were still nested down. Reginald Warwick, stoppered in his special quiet, might hear it, turn to his Coco for confirmation which did not come, and persuade himself once again that it was only his affliction. Others lying awake snug as a bug, listening for that Old Nick, death, would hear the thin, sororal signal and not know what they had heard. But an endless assemblage of others all over the city would be waiting for it—all those sitting in the dark void of the one lamp quenched, the one syllable spoken—who would start up, some from sleep, to their windows . . . or were already there.

A car passed below. Instinctively, she flattened against the casement, but the car traveled on. Last night someone, man or woman, would have been standing in one of the line of niches above and beneath hers—perhaps even a woman in a blue robe like her own. But literal distance or person would not matter; in that audience all would be the same. Looking up, she could see the tired, heated lavender of the midtown sky, behind which lay that real imperial into which some men were already hurling their exquisitely signaling spheres. But this sound would come from breast to breast, at an altitude higher than any of those. She brought her fist to her mouth, in savage pride at having heard it, at belonging to a race some of whom could never adapt to any range less than that. *Some of us*, she thought, *are still responsible*.

Stepping forward, she leaned on the iron railing. At that moment, another car, traveling slowly by, hesitated opposite, its red dome light blinking. Mrs. Hazlitt stood very still. She watched until the police car went on again, inching ahead slowly, as if somebody inside were looking back. The two men inside there would never understand what she was waiting for. Hand clapped to her mouth, she herself had just understood. She was waiting for it—for its company. She was waiting for a second chance—to answer it. She was waiting for the scream to come again.

QUESTIONS

1. The story—as the title and opening paragraph indicate—is set in New York City. What impression of the city is conveyed to the reader in the course of the narrative? How does the setting contribute to the theme of loneliness? To the theme of imprisonment?
2. Calisher skillfully employs a series of contrasting images: noise/silence, light/dark, upstairs/downstairs. How do these images function in the story?
3. The protagonist takes pride in the conviction that she is a well-mannered woman who truly knows herself. Is she justified in her belief? What signs do we have from the omniscient narrator that the protagonist is going mad?
4. Discuss in some detail the following assertion: Consciousness, and its contrary, unconsciousness, are both theme and technique in "The Scream on 57th Street."

CHARACTER

The most conspicuous thing that all stories have in common is that they deal with human beings. Even animal fables and fairy tales deal with human emotions. Stories are about people, and that is what attracts us to them, for we are as interested in well-drawn fictional characters as we are in real people. In fact, we know many fictional characters more completely than we do most of the people with whom we live and associate. Our world of literary acquaintances may include kings and heroes as well as paupers and fools.

An author uses many techniques to present and develop his characters, including point of view, plot, setting, and tone. A character may be revealed to us as he speaks through a stream-of-consciousness narration, moves toward some inevitable doom, lives in a particular house, or uses a special dialect. In any story the author uses whatever resources suit his purpose to create believable characters. And his characters exist ultimately to present some idea, philosophy or theme.

At times character may be subordinated or kept on a symbolic or allegorical plane. In Hawthorne's "My Kinsman, Major Molineux," for example, we were shown characters (the young woman, the old man, the man with a half red and half black face and Major Molineux himself) who function primarily on a symbolic level. The strange visage of the split-faced man is obviously of greater importance to Hawthorne's artistic purpose than is the man's individual character. And even Robin (whose name suggests youth and innocence) is more important as a type than an individual.

In "The Open Boat," Stephen Crane presents four characters who struggle toward the shore in a small boat. Crane identifies them generically as a cook, a captain, an oiler, and a correspondent, and he gives only one a name. None seems more important than the others until the end of the story, and most of the time we don't even know who is speaking. This is Crane's technique for showing how individuality is unimportant when men are struggling together toward a common goal. The story's emphasis is on the cooperation and kindness that this crisis has enkindled in the four characters.

Other characters may be real people on one level and symbolic figures on another. In Katherine Anne Porter's "Flowering Judas," we are shown two characters who represent opposite extremes: Braggioni, whose self-admiration and self-indulgence are evident in his rich clothing and "gluttonous bulk," represents the betrayal of the spirit; and Laura, who will not give herself to anyone, who hides her beautiful chaste body under heavy clothing, represents the betrayal of the flesh: "The very cells of her flesh reject knowledge and kinship in one monotonous word. No. No. No." Laura is further seen as a figure of death when her negation of the flesh leads to a negation of the spirit, as evidenced by her refusal to partake of the emblems of the Eucharist in her nightmare.

But Laura and Braggioni are not simply types or symbols; they exist primarily as real, that is, nonsymbolic characters. Porter has taken great care to prevent them from being one-dimensional. Thus, though Braggioni's vanity and gluttony are the focal point of his personality, they do not constitute its totality. The tenderness he displays for his wife and the devotion he inspires in her allow us to see him in a somewhat sympathetic light. And Laura's "private heresy" of wearing only handmade lace next to her body shows that she retains some remnant of her sensuality.

While it may be helpful to make distinctions between flat (simply depicted) and round (complex) characters and between static and developing characters, it is perhaps most helpful to discuss the approaches an author uses to reveal his characters. Most commonly we speak of *expository* and *dramatic* approaches. With the expository approach, either the author or one of his spokesmen describes or discusses the character in question. In "Counterparts" James Joyce begins his characterization of Farrington by giving us a brief description of him which emphasizes his facial features:

> The man muttered *Blast him!* under his breath and pushed back his chair to stand up. When he stood up he was tall and of great bulk. He had a hanging face, dark wine-colored, with fair eyebrows and mustache: his eyes bulged forward slightly and the whites of them were dirty. He lifted up the counter and, passing by the clients, went out of the office with a heavy step.
>
> He went heavily upstairs until he came to the second landing, where a door bore a brass plate with the inscription *Mr. Alleyne*. Here he halted, puffing with labor and vexation, and knocked.

With these sparse details Joyce tells us a great deal about Farrington. That he is of "great bulk" suggests that he is not simply large, but overweight (this is reinforced by the loose flesh on his "hanging face" and by his "puffing with labor and vexation" from climbing a few stairs). His fondness for alcohol is emphasized in his dark wine-colored skin and his bulging eyes with their muddied whites—telltale signs of the alcoholic. With fair eyebrows and mustache we might expect Farrington to have fair skin, but his continual escape through the bottle has left him with a darkened face as well as a darkened spirit.

But characters who are simply described or discussed by someone else are usually not as interesting as those who are presented to us dramatically. The dramatic approach reveals a character through his thoughts, his language, his actions, and his relations with other characters. Thus Joyce moves from such a brief but telling description to an unfolding of Farrington's character by placing him in conflict with his employer, Mr. Alleyne, by having the chief clerk remark that going to the pub "five times in one day is a little bit . . . ," by showing his stupor of thought and speech, by continually reminding us of the fury that rages inside him—in fact, every detail in the story seems calculated to serve Joyce's characterization of this pathetic Dubliner. This may have been what Henry James had in mind when he wrote in "The Art of Fiction":

> What is character but the determination of incident? What is incident but the illustration of character? . . . It is an incident for a woman to stand up with her hand resting on a table and look out at you in a certain way; or if it be not an incident I think it will be hard to say what it is. At the same time it is an expression of character.

It is certainly an expression of character for Joyce's Eveline to sit at the window at the opening of the story that bears her name, and to grasp the iron railing by the sea at the end of it. Both gestures, the one calm the other frantic, though seemingly insignificant, epitomize Eveline's physical and spiritual paralysis.

This is why it is important to pay attention to details in a story. The reader who quickly passes over Joyce's allusion to the "Blessed Margaret Mary Alacoque" without investigating Joyce's reason for including it will miss a subtle and significant step in Joyce's characterization of Eveline.

Perhaps the most subtle revelation of character comes when a fictive persona unknowingly reveals himself while attempting to tell us about another character. The narrator of "The Vane Sisters" sets out to tell us about Sybil and Cynthia Vane, concentrating on what he sees as their repulsive habits and strange behavior. Clearly he considers himself superior to them. He seems particularly interested in demeaning Cynthia's "ridiculous fondness for spiritualism." What he inadvertently reveals is that he is himself a serious student of psychical research. He also reveals without intending to that he is sexually attracted to Cynthia, something his snobbishness would never allow him to divulge openly, or perhaps even admit to himself.

All of the approaches or methods an author uses in delineating various aspects of human behavior allow us to know what motivates an individual character. One author focuses on the external actions of his character ("Pantaloon in Black"), another on his conversation ("Hills Like White Elephants"), and another on his thoughts ("I'm a Fool"). One author centers his narrative on a small moment in the life of a character ("A Visit of Charity"), while another moves across a lifetime ("Dean of Men"). One author concentrates on a character's conflict with himself ("One Warm Saturday"), and another on conflict between characters ("Spotted Horses"). Whatever an author does to present his character to us, his object is always to make that character believable and to convey some idea or meaning through him.

But it is also to provide esthetic and intellectual pleasure as we respond to characters in a variety of ways. Like the people we encounter in our everyday lives, fictional characters may evoke our love, anger, sympathy, pity, indifference, fear, or curiosity. But they may also expand the realm of our experience. After spending days in the Chicago underground with "freddaniels" ("The Man Who Lived Underground") or walking the streets of Bayonne, Louisiana, with the young black boy James ("The Sky is Gray"), we may have more insight into what it is like to be a black American than we could through any other way. Though we may never have been at sea in an open boat, or in Paris during the Twenties, or snowbound at a traveler's inn in Russia, we can have these experiences through fictional characters. We can live multiple lives, intimately and deeply, like Chekhov's Grigory Petrovitch Liharev, who declares, "I have been a Slavophile in my time, I used to pester Sksakov with letters, and I was a Ukrainophile, and an archeologist, and a collector of specimens of peasant art. . . . I was enthusiastic over ideas, people, events, places . . . my enthusiasm was endless!"

Our enthusiasm for fictional characters is undoubtedly related to the fact that we can know these characters more completely than we know any other beings and in ways that we perhaps don't even know ourselves. As will be seen in the discussion on POINT OF VIEW, an omniscient narrator tells us things about a character which no one in real life would tell us and which the character himself may not even know. The more we yield ourselves to an author's fictional world, the more his characters come alive in our imagination.

Katherine Anne Porter *(1894–) was born in Indian Creek, Texas, grew up in Texas and Louisiana, and received her education at small convent schools. She worked as a reporter in Denver, Colorado, during the First World War and spent much of the 1920's and 1930's in Paris—where she translated French songs—and in Mexico—where many of her stories are set.* Flowering Judas *(1930),* Pale Horse, Pale Rider *(1939), and* The Leaning Tower *(1944) have insured her reputation for impeccable craftsmanship.* Ship of Fools *(1961), her only novel and an immediate success, was the product of twenty years' work. The most recent collection of her stories appeared in 1968 and* The Collected Essays and Occasional Writings *in 1970. Miss Porter has received numerous awards, including a Pulitzer prize in 1966, and has lectured at American and European universities.*

Flowering Judas

KATHERINE ANNE PORTER

Braggioni sits heaped upon the edge of a straight-backed chair much too small for him, and sings to Laura in a furry, mournful voice. Laura has begun to find reasons for avoiding her own house until the latest possible moment, for Braggioni is there almost every night. No matter how late she is, he will be sitting there with a surly, waiting expression, pulling at his kinky yellow hair, thumbing the strings of his guitar, snarling a tune under his breath. Lupe the Indian maid meets Laura at the door, and says with a flicker of a glance towards the upper room, "He waits."

Laura wishes to lie down, she is tired of her hairpins and the feel of her long tight sleeves, but she says to him, "Have you a new song for me this evening?" If he says yes, she asks him to sing it. If he says no, she remembers his favorite one, and asks him to sing it again. Lupe brings her a cup of chocolate and a plate of rice, and Laura eats at the small table under the lamp, first inviting Braggioni, whose answer is always the same: "I have eaten, and besides, chocolate thickens the voice."

Laura says, "Sing, then," and Braggioni heaves himself into song. He scratches the guitar familiarly as though it were a pet animal, and sings passionately off key, taking the high notes in a prolonged painful squeal. Laura, who haunts the markets listening to the ballad singers, and stops every day to hear the blind boy playing his reed-flute in Sixteenth of September Street, listens to Braggioni with pitiless courtesy, because she dares not smile at his miserable performance. Nobody dares to smile at him. Braggioni is cruel to everyone, with a kind of specialized insolence, but he is so vain of his talents, and so sensitive to slights, it would require a cruelty and vanity greater than his own to lay a finger on the vast cureless wound of his self-esteem. It would require courage, too, for it is dangerous to offend him, and nobody has this courage.

Braggioni loves himself with such tenderness and amplitude and eternal charity that his followers—for he is a leader of men, a skilled revolutionist, and his skin has been punctured in honorable warfare—warm themselves in the reflected glow, and say to each other: "He has a real nobility, a love for humanity raised above mere personal affections." The excess of this self-love has flowed out, inconveniently for her, over Laura, who, with so many others, owes her comfortable situation and her salary to him. When he is in a very good humor, he tells her, "I am tempted to forgive you for being a *gringa. Gringita!*" and Laura, burning, imagines herself leaning forward suddenly, and with a sound back-handed slap wiping the suety smile from his face. If he notices her eyes at these moments he gives no sign.

She knows what Braggioni would offer her, and she must resist tenaciously without appearing to resist, and if she could avoid it she would not admit even to herself the slow drift of his intention. During these long evenings which have spoiled a long month for her, she sits in her deep chair with an open book on her knees, resting her eyes on the consoling rigidity of the printed page when the sight and sound of Braggioni singing threaten to identify themselves with all her remembered afflictions and to add their weight to her uneasy premonitions of the future. The gluttonous bulk of Braggioni has become a symbol of her many disillusions, for a revolutionist should be lean, animated by heroic faith, a vessel of abstract virtues. This is nonsense, she knows it now and is ashamed of it. Revolution must have leaders, and leadership is a career for energetic men. She is, her comrades tell her, full of romantic error, for what she defines as cynicism in them is merely "a developed sense of reality." She is almost too willing to say, "I am wrong, I suppose I don't really understand the principles," and afterward she makes a secret truce with herself, determined not to surrender her will to such expedient logic. But she cannot help feeling that she has been betrayed irreparably by the disunion between her way of living and her feeling of what life should be, and at times she is almost contented to rest in this sense of grievance as a private store of consolation. Sometimes she wishes to run away, but she stays. Now she longs to fly out of this room, down the narrow stairs, and into the street where the houses lean together like conspirators under a single mottled lamp, and leave Braggioni singing to himself.

Instead she looks at Braggioni, frankly and clearly, like a good child who understands the rules of behavior. Her knees cling together under sound blue serge, and her round white collar is not purposely nun-like. She wears the uniform of an idea, and has renounced vanities. She was born Roman Catholic, and in spite of her fear of being seen by someone who might make a scandal of it, she slips now and again into some crumbling little church, kneels on the chilly stone, and says a Hail Mary on the gold rosary she bought in Tehuantepec. It is no good and she ends by examining the altar with its tinsel flowers and ragged brocades, and feels tender about the battered doll-shape of some male saint whose white, lace-trimmed drawers hang limply around his ankles below the hieratic dignity of his velvet robe. She has encased herself in a set of principles derived from her early training, leaving no detail of gesture or of personal taste untouched, and for this reason she will not wear lace made on machines. This is her private heresy, for in her special group the machine is sacred, and will be the salvation of the workers. She loves fine lace, and there is a tiny edge of fluted cobweb on this collar, which is one of twenty precisely alike, folded in blue tissue paper in the upper drawer of her clothes chest.

Braggioni catches her glance solidly as if he had been waiting for it, leans forward, balancing his paunch between his spread knees, and sings with tremendous emphasis, weighing his words. He has, the song relates, no father and no mother, nor even a friend to console him; lonely as a wave of the sea he comes and goes, lonely as a wave. His mouth opens round and yearns sideways, his balloon cheeks grow oily with the labor of song. He bulges marvelously in his expensive garments. Over his lavender collar, crushed upon a purple necktie, held by a diamond hoop: over his ammunition belt of tooled leather worked in silver, buckled cruelly around his gasping middle: over the tops of his glossy yellow shoes Braggioni swells with ominous ripeness, his mauve silk hose stretched taut, his ankles bound with the stout leather thongs of his shoes.

When he stretches his eyelids at Laura she notes again that his eyes are the true tawny yellow cat's eyes. He is rich, not in money, he tells her, but in power, and this power brings with it the blameless ownership of things, and the right to indulge his love of small luxuries. "I have a taste for the elegant refinements," he said once, flourishing a yellow silk handkerchief before her nose. "Smell that? It is Jockey Club, imported from New York." Nonetheless he is wounded by life. He will say so presently. "It is true everything turns to dust in the hand, to gall on the tongue." He sighs and his leather belt creaks like a saddle girth. "I am disappointed in everything as it comes. Everything." He shakes his head. "You, poor thing, you will be disappointed too. You are born for it. We are more alike than you realize in some things. Wait and see. Some day you will remember what I have told you, you will know that Braggioni was your friend."

Laura feels a slow chill, a purely physical sense of danger, a warning in her blood that violence, mutilation, a shocking death, wait for her with lessening patience. She has translated this fear into something homely, immediate, and sometimes hesitates before crossing the street. "My personal fate is nothing, except as the testimony of a mental attitude," she reminds herself, quoting from some forgotten philosophic primer, and is sensible enough to add, "Anyhow, I shall not be killed by an automobile if I can help it."

"It may be true I am as corrupt, in another way, as Braggioni," she thinks in spite of herself, "as callous, as incomplete," and if this is so, any kind of death seems preferable. Still she sits quietly, she does not run. Where could she go? Uninvited she has promised herself to this place; she can no longer imagine herself as living in another country, and there is no pleasure in remembering her life before she came here.

Precisely what is the nature of this devotion, its true motives, and what are its obligations? Laura cannot say. She spends part of her days in Xochimilco, nearby, teaching Indian children to say in English, "The cat is on the mat." When she appears in the classroom they crowd about her with smiles on their wise, innocent, clay-colored faces, crying, "Good morning, my titcher!" in immaculate voices, and they make of her desk a fresh garden of flowers every day.

During her leisure she goes to union meetings and listens to busy important voices quarreling over tactics, methods, internal politics. She visits prisoners of her own political faith in their cells, where they entertain themselves with counting cockroaches, repenting of their indiscretions, composing their memoirs, writing out manifestoes and plans for their comrades who are still walking about free, hands in pockets, sniffing fresh air. Laura brings them food and cigarettes and a little money, and she brings messages disguised in equivocal phrases from the men outside who dare not set foot in the prison for fear of disappearing into the cells kept empty for them. If the prisoners confuse night and day, and complain, "Dear little Laura, time doesn't pass in this infernal hole, and I won't know when it is time to sleep unless I have a reminder," she brings them their favorite narcotics, and says in a tone that does not wound them with pity, "Tonight will really be night for you," and though her Spanish amuses them, they find her comforting, useful. If they lose patience and faith, and curse the slowness of their friends in coming to their rescue with money and influence, they trust her not to repeat everything, and if she inquires, "Where do you think we can find money, or influence?" they are certain to answer, "Well, there is Braggioni, why doesn't he do something?"

She smuggles letters from headquarters to men hiding from firing squads in back streets in mildewed houses, where they sit in tumbled beds and talk bitterly as if all Mexico were at their heels, when Laura knows positively they might appear at the band concert in the Alameda on Sunday morning, and no one would notice them. But Braggioni says, "Let them sweat a little. The next time they may be careful. It is very restful to have them out of the way for a while." She is not afraid to knock on any door in any street after midnight, and enter in the darkness, and say to one of these men who is really in danger: "They will be looking for you—seriously—tomorrow morning after six. Here is some money from Vicente. Go to Vera Cruz and wait."

She borrows money from the Roumanian agitator to give to his bitter enemy the Polish agitator. The favor of Braggioni is their disputed territory, and Braggioni holds the balance nicely, for he can use them both. The Polish agitator talks love to her over café tables, hoping to exploit what he believes is her secret sentimental preference for hm, and he gives her misinformation which he begs her to repeat as the solemn truth to certain persons. The Roumanian is more adroit. He is generous with his money in all good causes, and lies to her with an air of ingenuous candor, as if he were her good friend and confidant. She never repeats anything they may say. Braggioni never asks questions. He has other ways to discover all that he wishes to know about them.

Nobody touches her, but all praise her gray eyes, and the soft, round under lip which promises gayety, yet it is always grave, nearly always firmly closed: and they cannot understand why she is in Mexico. She walks back and forth on her errands, with puzzled eyebrows, carrying her little folder of drawings and music and school papers. No dancer dances more beautifully than Laura walks, and she inspires some amusing, unexpected ardors, which cause little gossip, because nothing comes of them. A young captain who had been a soldier in Zapata's army attempted, during a horseback ride near Cuernavaca, to express his desire for her with the noble simplicity befitting a rude folk-hero: but gently, because he was gentle. This gentleness was his defeat, for when he alighted, and removed her foot from the stirrup, and essayed to draw her down into his arms, her horse, ordinarily a tame one, shied fiercely, reared and plunged away. The young hero's horse careered blindly after his stable-mate, and the hero did not return to the hotel until rather late that evening. At breakfast he came to her table in full charro dress, gray buckskin jacket and trousers with strings of silver buttons down the leg, and he was in a humorous, careless mood. "May I sit with you?" and "You are a wonderful rider. I was terrified that you might be thrown and dragged. I should never have forgiven myself. But I cannot admire you enough for your riding!"

"I learned to ride in Arizona," said Laura.

"If you will ride with me again this morning, I promise you a horse that will not shy with you," he said. But Laura remembered that she must return to Mexico City at noon.

Next morning the children made a celebration and spent their playtime writing on the blackboard, "We lov ar ticher," and with tinted chalks they drew wreaths of flowers around the words. The young hero wrote her a letter: "I am a very foolish, wasteful, impulsive man. I should have first said I love you, and then you would not have run away. But you shall see me again." Laura thought, "I must send him a box of colored crayons," but she was trying to forgive herself for having spurred her horse at the wrong moment.

A brown, shock-haired youth came and stood in her patio one night and sang like a lost soul for two hours, but Laura could think of nothing to do about it. The moonlight spread a wash of gauzy silver over the clear spaces of the garden, and the shadows were cobalt blue. The scarlet blossoms of the Judas tree were dull purple, and the names of the colors repeated themselves automatically in her mind, while she watched not the boy, but his shadow, fallen like a dark garment across the fountain rim, trailing in the water. Lupe came silently and whispered expert counsel in her ear: "If you will throw him one little flower, he will sing another song or two and go away." Laura threw the flower, and he sang a last song and went away with the flower tucked in the band of his hat. Lupe said, "He is one of the organizers of the Typographers Union, and before that he sold corridos in the Merced market, and before that, he came from Guanajuato, where I was born. I would not trust any man, but I trust least those from Guanajuato."

She did not tell Laura that he would be back again the next night, and the next, nor that he would follow her at a certain fixed distance around the Merced market, through the Zócalo, up Francisco I, Madero Avenue, and so along the Paseo de la Reforma to Chapultepec Park, and into the Philosopher's Footpath, still with that flower withering in his hat, and an indivisible attention in his eyes.

Now Laura is accustomed to him, it means nothing except that he is nineteen years old and is observing a convention with all propriety, as though it were founded on a law of nature, which in the end it might well prove to be. He is beginning to write poems which he prints on a wooden press, and he leaves them stuck like handbills in her door. She is pleasantly disturbed by the abstract, unhurried watchfulness of his black eyes which will in time turn easily towards another object. She tells herself that throwing the flower was a mistake, for she is twenty-two years old and knows better; but she refuses to regret it, and persuades herself that her negation of all external events as they occur is a sign that she is gradually perfecting herself in the stoicism she strives to cultivate against that disaster she fears, though she cannot name it.

She is not at home in the world. Every day she teaches children who remain strangers to her, though she loves their tender round hands and their charming opportunist savagery. She knocks at unfamiliar doors not knowing whether a friend or a stranger shall answer, nd even if a known face emerges from the sour gloom of that unknown interior, still it is the face of a stranger. No matter what this stranger says to her, nor what her message to him, the very cells of her flesh reject knowledge and kinship in one monotonous word. No. No. No. She draws her strength from this one holy talismanic word which does not suffer her to be led into evil. Denying everything, she may walk anywhere in safety, she looks at everything without amazement.

No, repeats this firm unchanging voice of her blood; and she looks at Braggioni without amazement. He is a great man, he wishes to impress this simple girl who covers her great round breasts with thick dark cloth, and who hides long, invaluably beautiful legs under a heavy skirt. She is almost thin except for the incomprehensible fullness of her breasts, like a nursing mother's, and Braggioni, who considers himself a judge of women, speculates again on the puzzle of her notorious virginity, and takes the liberty of speech which she permits without a sign of modesty, indeed, without any sort of sign, which is disconcerting.

"You think you are so cold, *gringita!* Wait and see. You will surprise yourself some day! May I be there to advise you!" He stretches his eyelids at her, and his ill-humored cat's eyes waver in a separate glance for the two points of light marking the opposite ends of a smoothly drawn path between the swollen curve of her breasts. He is not put off by that blue serge, nor by her resolutely fixed gaze. There is all the time in the world. His cheeks are bellying with the wind of song. "O girl with the dark eyes," he sings, and reconsiders. "But yours are not dark. I can change all that. O girl with the green eyes, you have stolen my heart away!" Then his mind wanders to the song, and Laura feels the weight of his attention being shifted elsewhere. Singing thus, he seems harmless, he is quite harmless, there is nothing to do but sit patiently and say "No," when the moment comes. She draws a full breath, and her mind wanders also, but not far. She dares not wander too far.

Not for nothing has Braggioni taken pains to be a good revolutionist and a professional lover of humanity. He will never die of it. He has the malice, the cleverness, the wickedness, the sharpness of wit, the hardness of heart, stipulated for loving the world profitably. *He will never die of it*. He will live to see himself kicked out from his feeding trough by other hungry world-saviors. Traditionally he must sing in spite of his life which drives him to bloodshed, he tells Laura, for his father was a Tuscany peasant who drifted to Yucatan and married a Maya woman: a woman of race, an aristocrat. They gave him the love and knowledge of music, thus: and under the rip of his thumbnail, the strings of the instrument complain like exposed nerves.

Once he was called Delgadito by all the girls and married women who ran after him; he was so scrawny all his bones showed under his thin cotton clothing, and he could squeeze his emptiness to the very backbone with his two hands. He was a poet and the revolution was only a dream then; too many women loved him and sapped away his youth, and he could never find enough to eat anywhere, anywhere! Now he is a leader of men, crafty men who whisper in his ear, hungry men who wait for hours outside his office for a word with him, emaciated men with wild faces who waylay him at the street gate with a timid "Comrade, let me tell you . . ." and they blow the foul breath from their empty stomachs in his face.

He is always sympathetic. He gives them handfuls of small coins from his own pocket, he promises them work, there will be demonstrations, they must join the unions and attend the meetings, above all they must be on the watch for spies. They are closer to him than his own brothers, without them he can do nothing—until tomorrow, comrade!

Until tomorrow. "They are stupid, they are lazy, they are treacherous, they would cut my throat for nothing," he says to Laura. He has good food and abundant drink, he hires an automobile and drives in the Paseo on Sunday morning, and enjoys plenty of sleep in a soft bed beside a wife who dares not disturb him; and he sits pampering his bones in easy billows of fat, singing to Laura, who knows and thinks these things about him. When he was fifteen, he tried to drown himself because he loved a girl, his first love, and she laughed at him. "A thousand women have paid for that," and his tight little mouth turns down at the corners. Now he perfumes his hair with Jockey

Club, and confides to Laura: "One woman is really as good as another for me, in the dark. I prefer them all."

His wife organizes unions among the girls in the cigarette factories, and walks in picket lines, and even speaks at meetings in the evening. But she cannot be brought to acknowledge the benefits of true liberty. "I tell her I must have my freedom, net. She does not understand my point of view." Laura has heard this many times. Braggioni scratches the guitar and meditates. "She is an instinctively virtuous woman, pure gold, no doubt of that. If she were not, I should lock her up, and she knows it."

His wife, who works so hard for the good of the factory girls, employs part of her leisure lying on the floor weeping because there are so many women in the world, and only one husband for her, and she never knows where nor when to look for him. He told her: "Unless you can learn to cry when I am not here, I must go away for good." That day he went away and took a room at the Hotel Madrid.

It is this month of separation for the sake of higher principles that has been spoiled not only for Mrs. Braggioni, whose sense of reality is beyond criticism, but for Laura, who feels herself bogged in a nightmare. Tonight Laura envies Mrs. Braggioni, who is alone, and free to weep as much as she pleases about a concrete wrong. Laura has just come from a visit to the prison, and she is waiting for tomorrow with a bitter anxiety as if tomorrow may not come, but time may be caught immovably in this hour, with herself transfixed, Braggioni singing on forever, and Eugenio's body not yet discovered by the guard.

Braggioni says: "Are you going to sleep?" Almost before she can shake her head, he begins telling her about the May-day disturbances coming on in Morelia, for the Catholics hold a festival in honor of the Blessed Virgin, and the Socialists celebrate their martyrs on that day. "There will be two independent processions, starting from either end of town, and they will march until they meet, and the rest depends . . ." He asks her to oil and load his pistols. Standing up, he unbuckles his ammunition and spreads it laden across her knees. Laura sits with the shells slipping through the cleaning cloth dipped in oil, and he says again he cannot understand why she works so hard for the revolutionary idea unless she loves some man who is in it. "Are you not in love with someone?" "No," says Laura. "And no one is in love with you?" "No." "Then it is your own fault. No woman need go begging. Why, what is the matter with you? The legless beggar woman in the Alameda has a perfectly faithful lover. Did you know that?"

Laura peers down the pistol barrel and says nothing, but a long, slow faintness rises and subsides in her; Braggioni curves his swollen fingers around the throat of the guitar and softly smothers the music out of it, and when she hears him again he seems to have forgotten her, and is speaking in the hypnotic voice he uses when talking in small rooms to a listening, close-gathered crowd. Some day this world, now seemingly so composed and eternal, to the edges of every sea shall be merely a tangle of gaping trenches, or crashing walls and broken bodies. Everything must be torn from its accustomed place where it has rotted for centuries, hurled skyward and distributed, cast down again clean as rain, without separate identity. Nothing shall survive that the stiffened hands of poverty have created for the rich and no one shall be left alive except the elect spirits destined to procreate a new world cleansed of cruelty and injustice, ruled by benevolent anarchy: "Pistols are good, I love them, cannon are even better, but in the end I pin my faith to good dynamite," he concludes, and strokes the pistol lying in her hands. "Once I dreamed of destroying this city, in case it offered resistance to General Ortiz, but it fell into his hands like an overripe pear."

He is made restless by his own words, rises and stands waiting. Laura holds up the belt to him: "Put that on and go kill somebody in Morelia, and you will be happier," she says softly. The presence of death in the room makes her bold. "Today, I found Eugenio going into a stupor. He refused to allow me to call the prison doctor. He had taken all the tablets I had brought him yesterday. He said he took them because he was bored."

"He is a fool, and his death is his own business," says Braggioni, fastening his belt carefully.

"I told him if he had waited only a little while longer, you would have got him set free," says Laura. "He said he did not want to wait."

"He is a fool and we are well rid of him," says Braggioni, reaching for his hat.

He goes away. Laura knows his mood has changed,she will not see him any more for a while. He will send word when he needs her to go on errands into strange streets, to speak to the strange faces that will appear, like clay masks with the power of human speech, to mutter their thanks to Braggioni for his help. Now she is free, and she thinks, I must run while there is time. But she does not go.

Braggioni enters his own house where for a month his wife has spent many hours every night weeping and tangling her hair upon her pillow. She is weeping now, and she weeps more at the sight of him, the cause of all her sorrows. He looks about the room. Nothing is changed, the smells are good and familiar, he is well acquainted with the woman who comes toward him with no reproach except grief on her face. He says to her tenderly: "You are so good, please don't cry any more, you dear good creature." She says, "Are you tired, my angel? Sit here and I will wash your feet." She brings a bowl of water, and kneeling, unlaces his shoes, and when from her knees she raises her sad eyes under her blackened lids, he is sorry for everything, and bursts into tears. "Ah, yes, I am hungry, I am tired, let us eat something together," he says, between sobs. His wife leans her head on his arm and says, "Forgive me!" and this time he is refreshed by the solemn, endless rain of her tears.

Laura takes off her serge dress and puts on a white linen nightgown and goes to bed. She turns her head a little to one side, and lying still, reminds herself that it is time to sleep. Numbers tick in her brain like little clocks, soundless doors close of themselves around her. If you would sleep, you must not remember anything, the children will say tomorrow, good morning, my teacher, the poor prisoners who come every day bringing flowers to their jailor. 1-2-3-4-5—it is monstrous to confuse love with revolution, night with day, life with death—ah, Eugenio!

The tolling of the midnight bell is a signal, but what does it mean? Get up, Laura, and follow me: come out of your sleep, out of your bed, out of this strange house. What are you doing in this house? Without a word, without fear she rose and reached for Eugenio's hand, but he eluded her with a sharp, sly smile and drifted away. This is not all, you shall see—Murderer, he said, follow me, I will show you a new country, but it is far away and we must hurry. No, said Laura, not unless you take my hand, no; and she clung first to the stair rail, and then to the topmost branch of the Judas tree that bent down slowly and set her upon the earth, and then to the rocky ledge of a cliff, and then to the jagged wave of a sea that was not water but a desert of crumbling stone. Where are you taking me, she asked in wonder but without fear. To death, and it is a long way off, and we must hurry, said Eugenio. No, said Laura, not unless you take my hand. Then eat these flowers, poor prisoner, said Eugenio in a voice of pity, take and eat: and from the Judas tree he stripped the warm bleeding flowers, and held them to her lips. She saw that his hand was fleshless, a cluster of small white petrified branches, and his eye sockets were without light, but she ate the flowers greedily for they satisfied both hunger and thirst. Murderer! said Eugenio, and Cannibal! This is my body and my blood. Laura cried No! and at the sound of her own voice, she awoke trembling, and was afraid to sleep again.

QUESTIONS

1. Porter seems to adopt a scrupulously neutral attitude toward Laura—yet the tone actually conveys a feeling of emotional sterility. How does she convey this tone through diction and imagery? Through setting? Through point of view?
2. What devices are used to characterize Braggioni? Does the contrast between Braggioni and Laura illustrate distinct or simliar attitudes toward revolutionaries?
3. What dramatic effects are produced by compressing the action of many months into a few hours?
4. How are the themes of self-deception, duplicity, and cynicism developed through character and setting?
5. Betrayal appears as a major theme both in Laura's denial of herself and her denial of Eugenio. What is the function of the nightmare? Does the symbolism serve to heighten or rather diminish Laura's betrayal?

Flannery O'Connor *(1925–1964) was born in Savannah and raised on a small farm in Milledgeville, Georgia. She attended a Catholic high school, graduated from Georgia State College for Women in 1945, and studied creative writing under Paul Engle at the University of Iowa. She contributed regularly both to academic journals*—Kenyon Review, Sewanee Review—*and popular magazines*—Harper's Bazaar, Mademoiselle. *In 1950 Miss O'Connor began suffering from disseminated lupus, a disease that forced an invalid's life upon her at the family farm in Milledgeville. During these years she developed an art which joined a casual idiomatic style to a firm Catholic content. She produced two novels*—Wise Blood *(1952) and* The Violent Bear It Away *(1960)—and two collections of stories*—A Good Man Is Hard to Find *(1955) and* Everything That Rises Must Converge *(1965). Two additional volumes,* Mystery and Manners: Occasional Prose *(1969) and* The Complete Stories, *which won the National Book Award for 1972, have appeared since her death.*

Revelation

FLANNERY O'CONNOR

The doctor's waiting room, which was very small, was almost full when the Turpins entered and Mrs. Turpin, who was very large, made it look even smaller by her presence. She stood looming at the head of the magazine table set in the center of it, a living demonstration that the room was inadequate and ridiculous. Her little bright black eyes took in all the patients as she sized up the seating situation. There was one vacant chair and a place on the sofa occupied by a blond child in a dirty blue romper who should have been told to move over and make room for the lady. He was five or six, but Mrs. Turpin saw at once that no one was going to tell him to move over. He was slumped down in the seat, his arms idle at his sides and his eyes idle in his head; his nose ran unchecked.

Mrs. Turpin put a firm hand on Claud's shoulder and said in a voice that included everyone that wanted to listen, "Claud, you sit in that chair there," and gave him a push down into the vacant one. Claud was florid and bald and sturdy, somewhat shorter than Mrs. Turpin, but he sat down as if he were accustomed to doing what she told him to.

Mrs. Turpin remained standing. The only man in the room besides Claud was a lean stringy old fellow with a rusty hand spread out on each knee, whose eyes were closed as if he were asleep or dead or pretending to be so as not to get up and offer her his seat. Her gaze settled agreeably on a well-dressed grey-haired lady whose eyes met hers and whose expression said: If that child belonged to me, he would have some manners and move over—there's plenty of room there for you and him too.

Claud looked up with a sigh and made as if to rise.

"Sit down," Mrs. Turpin said. "You know you're not supposed to stand on that leg. He has an ulcer on his leg," she explained.

Claud lifted his foot onto the magazine table and rolled his trouser leg up to reveal a purple swelling on a plump marble-white calf.

"My!" the pleasant lady said. "How did you do that?"

"A cow kicked him," Mrs. Turpin said.

"Goodness!" said the lady.

Claud rolled his trouser leg down.

"Maybe the little boy would move over," the lady suggested, but the child did not stir.

"Somebody will be leaving in a minute," Mrs. Turpin said. She could not understand why a doctor—with as much money as they made charging five dollars a day just to stick their head in the hospital door and look at you—couldn't afford a decent-sized waiting room. This one was hardly bigger than a garage. The table was cluttered with limp-looking magazines and at one end of it there was a big green glass ash tray full of cigaret butts and cotton wads with little blood spots on them. If she had had anything to do with the running of the place, that would have been emptied every so often. There were no chairs against the wall at the head of the room. It had a rectangular-shaped panel in it that permitted a view of the office where the nurse came and went and the secretary listened to the radio. A plastic fern in a gold pot sat in the opening and trailed its fronds down almost to the floor. The radio was softly playing gospel music.

Just then the inner door opened and a nurse with the highest stack of yellow hair Mrs. Turpin had ever seen put her face in the crack and called for the next patient. The woman sitting beside Claud grasped the two arms of her chair and hoisted herself up; she pulled her dress free from her legs and lumbered through the door where the nurse had disappeared.

Mrs. Turpin eased into the vacant chair, which held her tight as a corset. "I wish I could reduce," she said, and rolled her eyes and gave a comic sigh.

"Oh, *you* aren't fat," the stylish lady said.

"Ooooo I am too," Mrs. Turpin said. "Claud he eats all he wants to and never weighs over one hundred and seventy-five pounds, but me I just look at something good to eat and I gain some weight," and her stomach and shoulders shook with laughter. "You can eat all you want to, can't you, Claud?" she asked turning to him.

Claud only grinned.

"Well, as long as you have such a good disposition," the stylish lady said, "I don't think it makes a bit of difference what size you are. You just can't beat a good disposition."

Next to her was a fat girl of eighteen or nineteen, scowling into a thick blue book which Mrs. Turpin saw was entitled *Human Development*. The girl raised her head and directed her scowl at Mrs. Turpin as if she did not like her looks. She appeared annoyed that anyone should speak while she tried to read. The poor girl's face was blue with acne and Mrs. Turpin thought how pitiful it was to have a face like that at that age. She gave the girl a friendly smile but the girl only scowled the harder. Mrs. Turpin herself was fat but she had always had good skin, and, though she was forty-seven years old, there was not a wrinkle in her face except around her eyes from laughing too much.

Next to the ugly girl was the child, still in exactly the same position, and next to him was a thin leathery old woman in a cotton print dress. She and Claud had three sacks of chicken feed in their pump house that was in the same print. She had seen from the first that the child belonged with the old woman. She could tell by the way they sat—kind of vacant and white-trashy, as if they would sit there until Doomsday if nobody called and told them to get up. And at right angles but next to the well-dressed pleasant lady was a lank-faced woman who was certainly the child's mother. She had on a yellow sweat shirt and wine-colored slacks, both gritty-looking, and the rims of her lips were stained with snuff. Her dirty yellow hair was tied behind with a little piece of red paper ribbon. Worse than niggers any day, Mrs. Turpin thought.

The gospel hymn playing was, "When I looked up and He looked down," and Mrs. Turpin, who knew it, supplied the last line mentally, "And wona these days I know I'll we-eara crown."

Without appearing to, Mrs. Turpin always noticed people's feet. The well-dressed lady had on red and grey suede shoes to match her dress. Mrs. Turpin had on her good black patent leather pumps. The ugly girl had on Girl Scout shoes and heavy socks. The old woman had on tennis shoes and the white-trashy mother had on what appeared to be bedroom slippers, black straw with gold braid threaded through them—exactly what you would have expected her to have on.

Sometimes at night when she couldn't go to sleep, Mrs. Turpin would occupy herself with the question of who she would have chosen to be if she couldn't have been herself. If Jesus had said to her before he made her, "There's only two places available for you. You can either be a nigger or white-trash," what would she have said? "Please, Jesus, please," she would have said, "just let me wait until there's another place available," and he would have said, "No, you have to go right now and I have only those two places so make up your mind." She would have wiggled and squirmed and begged and pleaded but it would have been no use and finally she would have said, "All right, make me a nigger then—but that don't mean a trashy one." And he would have made her a neat clean respectable Negro woman, herself but black.

Next to the child's mother was a red-headed youngish woman, reading one of the magazines and working a piece of chewing gum, hell for leather, as Claud would say. Mrs. Turpin could not see the woman's feet. She was not white-trash, just common. Sometimes Mrs. Turpin occupied herself at night naming the classes of people. On the bottom of the heap were most colored people, not the kind she would have been if she had been one, but most of them; then next to them—not above, just away from—were the white-trash; then above them were the home-owners, and above them the home-and-land owners, to which she and Claud belonged. Above she and Claud were people with a lot of money and much bigger houses and much more land. But here the complexity of it would begin to bear in on her, for some of the people with a lot of money were common and ought to be below she and Claud and some of the people who had good blood had lost their money and had to rent and then there were colored people who owned their homes and land as well. There was a colored dentist in town who had two red Lincolns and a swimming pool and a farm with registered white-face cattle on it. Usually by the time she had fallen asleep all the classes of people were moiling and roiling around in her head, and she would dream they were all crammed in together in a box car, being ridden off to be put in a gas oven.

"That's a beautiful clock," she said and nodded to her right. It was a big wall clock, the face encased in a brass sunburst.

"Yes, it's very pretty," the stylish lady said agreeably. "And right on the dot too," she added, glancing at her watch.

The ugly girl beside her cast an eye upward at the clock, smirked, then looked directly at Mrs. Turpin and smirked again. Then she returned her eyes to her book. She was obviously the lady's daughter because, although they didn't look anything alike as to disposition, they both had the same shape of face and the same blue eyes. On the lady they sparkled pleasantly but in the girl's seared face they appeared alternately to smolder and to blaze.

What if Jesus had said, "All right, you can be white-trash or a nigger or ugly"!

Mrs. Turpin felt an awful pity for the girl, though she thought it was one thing to be ugly and another to act ugly.

The woman with the snuff-stained lips turned around in her chair and looked up at the clock. Then she turned back and appeared to look a little to the side of Mrs. Turpin. There was a cast in one of her eyes. "You want to know wher you can get one of themther clocks?" she asked in a loud voice.

"No, I already have a nice clock," Mrs. Turpin said. Once somebody like her got a leg in the conversation, she would be all over it.

"You can get you one with green stamps," the woman said. "That's most likely wher he got hisn. Save you up enough, you can get you most anythang. I got me some joo'ry."

Ought to have got you a wash rag and some soap, Mrs. Turpin thought.

"I get contour sheets with mine," the pleasant lady said.

The daughter slammed her book shut. She looked straight in front of her, directly through Mrs. Turpin and on through the yellow curtain and the plate glass window which made the wall behind her. The girl's eyes seemed lit all of a sudden with a peculiar light, an unnatural light like night road signs give. Mrs. Turpin turned her head to see if there was anything going on outside that she should see, but she could not see anything. Figures passing cast only a pale shadow through the curtain. There was no reason the girl should single her out for her ugly looks.

"Miss Finley," the nurse said, cracking the door. The gum-chewing woman got up and passed in front of her and Claud and went into the office. She had on red high-heeled shoes.

Directly across the table, the ugly girl's eyes were fixed on Mrs. Turpin as if she had some very special reason for disliking her.

"This is wonderful weather, isn't it?" the girl's mother said.

"It's good weather for cotton if you can get the niggers to pick it," Mrs. Turpin said, "but niggers don't want to pick cotton any more. You can't get the white folks to pick it and now you can't get the niggers—because they got to be right up there with the white folks."

"They gonna *try* anyways," the white-trash woman said, leaning forward.

"Do you have one of those cotton-picking machines?" the pleasant lady asked.

"No," Mrs. Turpin said, "they leave half the cotton in the field. We don't have much cotton anyway. If you want to make it farming now, you have to have a little of everything. We got a couple of acres of cotton and a few hogs and chickens and just enough white-face that Claud can look after them himself."

"One thang I don't want," the white-trash woman said, wiping her mouth with the back of her hand. "Hogs. Nasty stinking things, a-gruntin and a-rootin all over the place."

Mrs. Turpin gave her the merest edge of her attention. "Our hogs are not dirty and they don't stink," she said. "They're cleaner than some children I've seen. Their feet never touch the ground. We have a pig-parlor—that's where you raise them on concrete," she explained to the pleasant lady, "and Claud scoots them down with the hose every afternoon and washes off the floor." Cleaner by far than that child right there, she thought. Poor nasty little thing. He had not moved except to put the thumb of his dirty hand into his mouth.

The woman turned her face away from Mrs. Turpin. "I know I wouldn't scoot down no hog with no hose," she said to the wall.

You wouldn't have no hog to scoot down, Mrs. Turpin said to herself.

"A-gruntin and a-rootin and a-groanin," the woman muttered.

"We got a little of everything," Mrs. Turpin said to the pleasant lady. "It's no use in having more than you can handle yourself with help like it is. We found enough niggers to pick our cotton this year but Claud he has to go after them and take them home again in the evening. They can't walk that half a mile. No they can't. I tell you," she said and laughed merrily, "I sure am tired of buttering up niggers, but you got to love em if you want em to work for you. When they come in the morning, I run out and I say, 'Hi yawl this morning?' and when Claud drives them off to the field I just wave to beat the band and they just wave back." And she waved her hand rapidly to illustrate.

"Like you read out of the same book," the lady said, showing she understood perfectly.

"Child, yes," Mrs. Turpin said. "And when they come in from the field, I run out with a bucket of icewater. That's the way it's going to be from now on," she said. "You may as well face it."

"One thang I know," the white-trash woman said. "Two thangs I ain't going to do: love no niggers or scoot down no hog with no hose." And she let out a bark of contempt.

The look that Mrs. Turpin and the pleasant lady exchanged indicated they both understood that you had to *have* certain things before you could *know* certain things. But every time Mrs. Turpin exchanged a look with the lady, she was aware that the ugly girl's peculiar eyes were still on her, and she had trouble bringing her attention back to the conversation.

"When you got something," she said, "you got to look after it." And when you ain't got a thing but breath and britches, she added to herself, you can afford to come to town every morning and just sit on the Court House coping and spit.

A grotesque revolving shadow passed across the curtain behind her and was thrown palely on the opposite wall. Then a bicycle clattered down against the outside of the building. The door opened and a colored boy glided in with a tray from the drug store. It had two large red and white paper cups on it with tops on them. He was a tall, very black boy in discolored white pants and a green nylon shirt. He was chewing gum slowly, as if to music. He set the tray down in the office opening next to the fern and stuck his head through to look for the secretary. She was not in there. He rested his arms on the ledge and waited, his narrow bottom stuck out, swaying slowly to the left and right. He raised a hand over his head and scratched the base of his skull.

"You see that button there, boy?" Mrs. Turpin said. "You can punch that and she'll come. She's probably in the back somewhere."

"Is thas right?" the boy said agreeably, as if he had never seen the button before. He leaned to the right and put his finger on it. "She sometime out," he said and twisted around to face his audience, his elbows behind him on the counter. The nurse appeared and he twisted back again. She handed him a dollar and he rooted in his pocket and made the change and counted it out to her. She gave him fifteen cents for a tip and he went out with the empty tray. The heavy door swung to slowly and closed at length with the sound of suction. For a moment no one spoke.

"They ought to send all them niggers back to Africa," the white-trash woman said. "That's wher they come from in the first place."

"Oh, I couldn't do without my good colored friends," the pleasant lady said.

"There's a heap of things worse than a nigger," Mrs. Turpin agreed. "It's all kinds of them just like it's all kinds of us."

"Yes, and it takes all kinds to make the world go round," the lady said in her musical voice.

As she said it, the raw-complexioned girl snapped her teeth together. Her lower lip turned downwards and inside out, revealing the pale pink inside of her mouth. After a second it rolled back up. It was the ugliest face Mrs. Turpin had ever seen anyone make and for a moment she was certain that the girl had made it at her. She was looking at her as if she had known and disliked her all her life—all of Mrs. Turpin's life, it seemed too, not just all the girl's life. Why, girl, I don't even know you, Mrs. Turpin said silently.

She forced her attention back to the discussion. "It wouldn't be practical to send them back to Africa," she said. "They wouldn't want to go. They got it too good here."

"Wouldn't be what they wanted—if I had anythang to do with it," the woman said.

"It wouldn't be a way in the world you could get all the niggers back over there," Mrs. Turpin said. "They'd be hiding out and lying down and turning sick on you and wailing and hollering and raring and pitching. It wouldn't be a way in the world to get them over there."

"They got over here," the trashy woman said. "Get back like they got over."

"It wasn't so many of them then," Mrs. Turpin explained.

The woman looked at Mrs. Turpin as if here was an idiot indeed but Mrs. Turpin was not bothered by the look, considering where it came from.

"Nooo," she said, "they're going to stay here where they can go to New York and marry white folks and improve their color. That's what they all want to do, every one of them, improve their color."

"You know what comes of that, don't you?" Claud asked.

"No, Claud, what?" Mrs. Turpin said.

Claud's eyes twinkled. "White-faced niggers," he said with never a smile.

Everybody in the office laughed except the white-trash and the ugly girl. The girl gripped the book in her lap with white fingers. The trashy woman looked around her from face to face as if she thought they were all idiots. The old woman in the feed sack dress continued to gaze expressionless across the floor at the high-top shoes of the man opposite her, the one who had been pretending to be asleep when the Turpins came in. He was laughing heartily, his hands still spread out on his knees. The child had fallen to the side and was lying now almost face down in the old woman's lap.

While they recovered from their laughter, the nasal chorus on the radio kept the room from silence.

You go to blank blank
And I'll go to mine
But we'll all blank along
To-geth-ther,
And all along the blank
We'll hep each other out
Smile-ling in any kind of
Weath-ther!

Mrs. Turpin didn't catch every word but she caught enough to agree with the spirit of the song and it turned her thoughts sober. To help anybody out that needed it was her philosophy of life. She never spared herself when she found somebody in need, whether they were white or black, trash or decent. And of all she had to be thankful for, she was most thankful that this was so. If Jesus had said, "You can be high society and have all the money you want and be thin and svelte-like, but you can't be a good woman with it," she would have had to say, "Well don't make me that then. Make me a good woman and it don't matter what else, how fat or how ugly or how poor!" Her heart rose. He had not made her a nigger or white-trash or ugly! He had made her herself and given her a little of everything. Jesus, thank you! she said. Thank you thank you thank you! Whenever she counted her blessings she felt as buoyant as if she weighed one hundred and twenty-five pounds instead of one hundred and eighty.

"What's wrong with your little boy?" the pleasant lady asked the white-trashy woman.

"He has a ulcer," the woman said proudly. "He ain't give me a minute's peace since he was born. Him and her are just alike," she said, nodding at the old woman, who was running her leathery fingers through the child's pale hair. "Look like I can't get nothing down them two but Co'Cola and candy."

That's all you try to get down em, Mrs. Turpin said to herself. Too lazy to light the fire. There was nothing you could tell her about people like them that she didn't know already. And it was not just that they didn't have anything. Because if you gave them everything, in two weeks it would all be broken or filthy or they would have chopped it up for lightwood. She knew all this from her own experience. Help them you must, but help them you couldn't.

All at once the ugly girl turned her lips inside out again. Her eyes were fixed like two drills on Mrs. Turpin. This time there was no mistaking that there was something urgent behind them.

Girl, Mrs. Turpin exclaimed silently, I haven't done a thing to you! The girl might be confusing her with somebody else. There was no need to sit by and let herself be intimidated. "You must be in college," she said boldly, looking directly at the girl. "I see you reading a book there."

The girl continued to stare and pointedly did not answer.

Her mother blushed at this rudeness. "The lady asked you a question, Mary Grace," she said under her breath.

"I have ears," Mary Grace said.

The poor mother blushed again. "Mary Grace goes to Wellesley College," she explained. She twisted one of the buttons on her dress. "In Massachusetts," she added with a grimace. "And in the summer she just keeps right on studying. Just reads all the time, a real book worm. She's done real well at Wellesley; she's taking English and

Math and History and Psychology and Social Studies," she rattled on, "and I think it's too much. I think she ought to get out and have fun."

The girl looked as if she would like to hurl them all through the plate glass window.

"Way up north," Mrs. Turpin murmured and thought, well, it hasn't done much for her manners.

"I'd almost rather to have him sick," the white-trash woman said, wrenching the attention back to herself. "He's so mean when he ain't. Look like some children just take natural to meanness. It's some gets bad when they get sick but he was the opposite. Took sick and turned good. He don't give me no trouble now. It's me waitin to see the doctor," she said.

If I was going to send anybody back to Africa, Mrs. Turpin thought, it would be your kind, woman. "Yes, indeed," she said aloud, but looking up at the ceiling, "it's a heap of things worse than a nigger." And dirtier than a hog, she added to herself.

"I think people with bad dispositions are more to be pitied than anyone on earth," the pleasant lady said in a voice that was decidedly thin.

"I thank the Lord he has blessed me with a good one," Mrs. Turpin said. "The day has never dawned that I couldn't find something to laugh at."

"Not since she married me anyways," Claud said with a comical straight face.

Everybody laughed except the girl and the white-trash.

Mrs. Turpin's stomach shook. "He's such a caution," she said, "that I can't help but laugh at him."

The girl made a loud ugly noise through her teeth.

Her mother's mouth grew thin and tight. "I think the worst thing in the world," she said, "is an ungrateful person. To have everything and not appreciate it. I know a girl," she said, "who has parents who would give her anything, a little brother who loves her dearly, who is getting a good education, who wears the best clothes, but who can never say a kind word to anyone, who never smiles, who just criticizes and complains all day long."

"Is she too old to paddle?" Claud asked.

The girl's face was almost purple.

"Yes," the lady said, "I'm afraid there's nothing to do but leave her to her folly. Some day she'll wake up and it'll be too late."

"It never hurt anyone to smile," Mrs. Turpin said. "It just makes you feel better all over."

"Of course," the lady said sadly, "but there are just some people you can't tell anything to. They can't take criticism."

"If it's one thing I am," Mrs. Turpin said with feeling, "it's grateful. When I think who all I could have been besides myself and what all I got, a little of everything, and a good disposition besides, I just feel like shouting, 'Thank you, Jesus, for making everything the way it is!' It could have been different!" For one thing, somebody else could have got Claud. At the thought of this, she was flooded with gratitude and a terrible pang of joy ran through her. "Oh thank you, Jesus, Jesus, thank you!" she cried aloud.

The book struck her directly over her left eye. It struck almost at the same instant that she realized the girl was about to hurl it. Before she could utter a sound, the raw face came crashing across the table toward her, howling. The girl's fingers sank like clamps into the soft flesh of her neck. She heard the mother cry out and Claud shout, "Whoa!" There was an instant when she was certain that she was about to be in an earthquake.

All at once her vision narrowed and she saw everything as if it were happening in a small room far away, or as if she were looking at it through the wrong end of a telescope. Claud's face crumpled and fell out of sight. The nurse ran in, then out, then in again. Then the gangling figure of the doctor rushed out of the inner door. Magazines flew this way and that as the table turned over. The girl fell with a thud and Mrs. Turpin's vision suddenly reversed itself and she saw everything large instead of small. The eyes of the white-trashy woman were staring hugely at the floor. There the girl, held down on one side by the nurse and on the other by her mother, was wrenching and turning in their grasp. The doctor was kneeling astride her, trying to hold her arm down. He managed after a second to sink a long needle into it.

Mrs. Turpin felt entirely hollow except for her heart which swung from side to side as if it were agitated in a great empty drum of flesh.

"Somebody that's not busy call for the ambulance," the doctor said in the off-hand voice young doctors adopt for terrible occasions.

Mrs. Turpin could not have moved a finger. The old man who had been sitting next to her skipped nimbly into the office and made the call, for the secretary still seemed to be gone.

"Claud!" Mrs. Turpin called.

He was not in his chair. She knew she must jump up and find him but she felt like some one trying to catch a train in a dream, when everything moves in slow motion and the faster you try to run the slower you go.

"Here I am," a suffocated voice, very unlike Claud's, said.

He was doubled up in the corner on the floor, pale as paper, holding his leg. She wanted to get up and go to him but she could not move. Instead, her gaze was drawn slowly downward to the churning face on the floor, which she could see over the doctor's shoulder.

The girl's eyes stopped rolling and focused on her. They seemed a much lighter blue than before, as if a door that had been tightly closed behind them was now open to admit light and air.

Mrs. Turpin's head cleared and her power of motion returned. She leaned forward until she was looking directly into the fierce brilliant eyes. There was no doubt in her mind that the girl did know her, knew her in some intense and personal way, beyond time and place and condition. "What you got to say to me?" she asked hoarsely and held her breath, waiting, as for a revelation.

The girl raised her head. Her gaze locked with Mrs. Turpin's. "Go back to hell where you came from, you old wart hog," she whispered. Her voice was low but clear. Her eyes burned for a moment as if she saw with pleasure that her message had struck its target.

Mrs. Turpin sank back in her chair.

After a moment the girl's eyes closed and she turned her head wearily to the side.

The doctor rose and handed the nurse the empty syringe. He leaned over and put both hands for a moment on the mother's shoulders, which were shaking. She was sitting on the floor, her lips pressed together, holding Mary Grace's hand in her lap. The girl's fingers were gripped like a baby's around her thumb. "Go on to the hospital," he said. "I'll call and make the arrangements."

"Now let's see that neck," he said in a jovial voice to Mrs. Turpin. He began to inspect her neck with his first two fingers. Two little moon-shaped lines like pink fish bones were indented over her windpipe. There was the beginning of an angry red swelling above her eye. His fingers passed over this also.

"Lea' me be," she said thickly and shook him off. "See about Claud. She kicked him."

"I'll see about him in a minute," he said and felt her pulse. He was a thin grey-haired man, given to pleasantries. "Go home and have yourself a vacation the rest of the day," he said and patted her on the shoulder.

Quit your pattin me, Mrs. Turpin growled to herself.

"And put an ice pack over that eye," he said. Then he went and squatted down beside Claud and looked at his leg. After a moment he pulled him up and Claud limped after him into the office.

Until the ambulance came, the only sounds in the room were the tremulous moans of the girl's mother, who continued to sit on the floor. The white-trash woman did not take her eyes off the girl. Mrs. Turpin looked straight ahead at nothing. Presently the ambulance drew up, a long dark shadow, behind the curtain. The attendants came in and set the stretcher down beside the girl and lifted her expertly onto it and carried her out. The nurse helped the mother gather up her things. The shadow of the ambulance moved silently away and the nurse came back in the office.

"That ther girl is going to be a lunatic, ain't she?" the white-trash woman asked the nurse, but the nurse kept on to the back and never answered her.

"Yes, she's going to be a lunatic," the white-trash woman said to the rest of them.

"Po' critter," the old woman murmured. The child's face was still in her lap. His eyes looked idly out over her knees. He had not moved during the disturbance except to draw one leg up under him.

"I thank Gawd," the white-trash woman said fervently, "I ain't a lunatic."

Claud came limping out and the Turpins went home.

As their pick-up truck turned into their own dirt road and made the crest of the hill, Mrs. Turpin gripped the window ledge and looked out suspiciously. The land sloped gracefully down through a field dotted with lavender weeds and at the start of the rise their small yellow frame house, with its little flower beds spread out around it like a fancy apron, sat primly in its accustomed place between two giant hickory trees. She would not have been startled to see a burnt wound between two blackened chimneys.

Neither of them felt like eating so they put on their house clothes and lowered the shade in the bedroom and lay down, Claud with his leg on a pillow and herself with a damp washcloth over her eye. The instant she was flat on her back, the image of a razor-backed hog with warts on its face and horns coming out behind its ears snorted into her head. She moaned, a low quiet moan.

"I am not," she said tearfully, "a wart hog. From hell." But the denial had no force. The girl's eyes and her words, even the tone of her voice, low but clear, directed only to her, brooked no repudiation. She had been singled out for the message, though there was trash in the room to whom it might justly have been applied. The full force of this fact struck her only now. There was a woman there who was neglecting her own child but she had been overlooked. The message had been given to Ruby Turpin, a respectable, hard-working, church-going woman. The tears dried. Her eyes began to burn instead with wrath.

She rose on her elbow and the washcloth fell into her hand. Claud was lying on his back, snoring. She wanted to tell him what the girl had said. At the same time, she did not wish to put the image of herself as a wart hog from hell into his mind.

"Hey, Claud," she muttered and pushed his shoulder.

Claud opened one pale baby blue eye.

She looked into it warily. He did not think about anything. He just went his way.

"Wha, whasit?" he said and closed the eye again.

"Nothing," she said. "Does your leg pain you?"

"Hurts like hell," Claud said.

"It'll quit terreckly," she said and lay back down. In a moment Claud was snoring again. For the rest of the afternoon they lay there. Claud slept. She scowled at the ceiling. Occasionally she raised her fist and made a small stabbing motion over her chest as if she was defending her innocence to invisible guests who were like the comforters of Job, reasonable-seeming but wrong.

About five-thirty Claud stirred. "Got to go after those niggers," he sighed, not moving.

She was looking straight up as if there were unintelligible handwriting on the ceiling. The protuberance over her eye had turned a greenish-blue. "Listen here," she said.

"What?"

"Kiss me."

Claud leaned over and kissed her loudly on the mouth. He pinched her side and their hands interlocked. Her expression of ferocious concentration did not change. Claud got up, groaning and growling, and limped off. She continued to study the ceiling.

She did not get up until she heard the pick-up truck coming back with the Negroes. Then she rose and thrust her feet in her brown oxfords, which she did not bother to lace, and stumped out onto the back porch and got her red plastic bucket. She emptied a tray of ice cubes into it and filled it half full of water and went out into the back yard. Every afternoon after Claud brought the hands in, one of the boys helped him put out hay and the rest waited in the back of the truck until he was ready to take them home. The truck was parked in the shade under one of the hickory trees.

"Hi yawl this evening?" Mrs. Turpin asked grimly, appearing with the bucket and the dipper. There were three women and a boy in the truck.

"Us doin nicely," the oldest woman said. "Hi you doin?" and her gaze stuck immediately on the dark lump on Mrs. Turpin's forehead. "You done fell down, ain't you?" she asked in a solicitous voice. The old woman was dark and almost toothless. She had on an old felt hat of Claud's set back on her head. The other two women were younger and lighter and they both had new bright green sun hats. One of them had hers on her head; the other had taken hers off and the boy was grinning beneath it.

Mrs. Turpin set the bucket down on the floor of the truck. "Yawl hep yourselves," she said. She looked around to make sure Claud had gone. "No. I didn't fall down," she said, folding her arms. "It was something worse than that."

"Ain't nothing bad happen to you!" the old woman said. She said it as if they all knew that Mrs. Turpin was protected in some special way by Divine Providence. "You just had you a little fall."

"We were in town at the doctor's office for where the cow kicked Mr. Turpin," Mrs. Turpin said in a flat tone that indicated they could leave off their foolishness. "And there was this girl there. A big fat girl with her face all broke out. I could look at that girl and tell she was peculiar but I couldn't tell how. And me and her mama were just talking and going along and all of a sudden WHAM! She throws this big book she was reading at me and . . ."

"Naw!" the old woman cried out.

"And then she jumps over the table and commences to choke me."

"Naw!" they all exclaimed, "naw!"

"Hi come she do that?" the old woman asked. "What ail her?"

Mrs. Turpin only glared in front of her.

"Somethin ail her," the old woman said.

"They carried her off in an ambulance," Mrs. Turpin continued, "but before she went she was rolling on the floor and they were trying to hold her down to give her a shot and she said something to me." She paused. "You know what she said to me?"

"What she say?" they asked.

"She said," Mrs. Turpin began, and stopped, her face very dark and heavy. The sun was getting whiter and whiter, blanching the sky overhead so that the leaves of the hickory tree were black in the face of it. She could not bring forth the words. "Something real ugly," she muttered.

"She sho shouldn't said nothin ugly to you," the old woman said. "You so sweet. You the sweetest lady I know."

"She pretty too," the one with the hat on said.

"And stout," the other one said. "I never knowed no sweeter white lady."

"That's the truth befo' Jesus," the old woman said. "Amen! You des as sweet and pretty as you can be."

Mrs. Turpin knew just exactly how much Negro flattery was worth and it added to her rage. "She said," she began again and finished this time with a fierce rush of breath, "that I was an old wart hog from hell."

There was an astounded silence.

"Where she at?" the youngest woman cried in a piercing voice.

"Lemme see her. I'll kill her!"

"I'll kill her with you!" the other one cried.

"She b'long in the sylum," the old woman said emphatically. "You the sweetest white lady I know."

"She pretty too," the other two said. "Stout as she can be and sweet. Jesus satisfied with her!"

"Deed he is," the old woman declared.

Idiots! Mrs. Turpin growled to herself. You could never say anything intelligent to a nigger. You could talk at them but not with them. "Yawl ain't drunk your water," she said shortly. "Leave the bucket in the truck when you're finished with it. I got more to do than just stand around and pass the time of day," and she moved off and into the house.

She stood for a moment in the middle of the kitchen. The dark protuberance over her eye looked like a miniature tornado cloud which might any moment sweep across the horizon of her brow. Her lower lip protruded dangerously. She squared her massive shoulders. Then she marched into the front of the house and out the side door and started down the road to the pig parlor. She had the look of a woman going single-handed, weaponless, into battle.

The sun was a deep yellow now like a harvest moon and was riding westward very fast over the far tree line as if it meant to reach the hogs before she did. The road was rutted and she kicked several good-sized stones out of her path as she strode along. The pig parlor was on a little knoll at the end of a lane that ran off from the side of the barn. It was a square of concrete as large as a small room, with a board fence about four feet high around it. The concrete floor sloped slightly so that the hog wash could drain off into a trench where it was carried to the field for fertilizer. Claud was standing on the outside, on the edge of the concrete, hanging onto the top board, hosing down the floor inside. The hose was connected to the faucet of a water trough nearby.

Mrs. Turpin climbed up beside him and glowered down at the hogs inside. There were seven long-snouted bristly shoats in it—tan with liver-colored spots—and an old sow a few weeks off from farrowing. She was lying on her side grunting. The shoats were running about shaking themselves like idiot children, their little slit pig eyes searching the floor for anything left. She had read that pigs were the most intelligent animal. She doubted it. They were supposed to be smarter than dogs. There had even been a pig astronaut. He had performed his assignment perfectly but died of a heart attack afterwards because they left him in his electric suit, sitting upright throughout his examination when naturally a hog should be on all fours.

A-gruntin and a-rootin and a-groanin.

"Gimme that hose," she said, yanking it away from Claud. "Go on and carry them niggers home and then get off that leg."

"You look like you might have swallowed a mad dog," Claud observed, but he got down and limped off. He paid no attention to her humors.

Until he was out of earshot, Mrs. Turpin stood on the side of the pen, holding the hose and pointing the stream of water at the hind quarter of any shoat that looked as if it might try to lie down. When he had had time to get over the hill, she turned her head slightly and her wrathful eyes scanned the path. He was nowhere in sight. She turned back again and seemed to gather herself up. Her shoulders rose and she drew in her breath.

"What do you send me a message like that for?" she said in a low fierce voice, barely above a whisper but with the force of a shout in its concentrated fury. "How am I a hog and me both? How am I saved and from hell too?" Her free fist was knotted and with the other she gripped the hose, blindly pointing the stream of water in and out of the eye of the old sow whose outraged squeal she did not hear.

The pig parlor commanded a view of the back pasture where their twenty beef cows were gathered around the hay-bales Claud and the boy had put out. The freshly cut pasture sloped down to the highway. Across it was their cotton field and beyond that a dark green dusty wood which they owned as well. The sun was behind the wood, very red, looking over the paling of trees like a farmer inspecting his own hogs.

"Why me?" she rumbled. "It's no trash around here, black or white, that I haven't given to. And break my back to the bone every day working. And do for the church."

She appeared to be the right size woman to command the arena before her. "How am I a hog?" she demanded. "Exactly how am I like them?" and she jabbed the stream of water at the shoats. "There was plenty of trash there. It didn't have to be me."

"If you like trash better, go get yourself some trash then," she railed. "You could have made me trash. Or a nigger. If trash is what you wanted why didn't you make me trash?" She shook her fist with the hose in it and a watery snake appeared momentarily in the air. "I could quit working and take it easy and be filthy," she growled. "Lounge about the sidewalks all day drinking root beer. Dip snuff and spit in every puddle and have it all over my face. I could be nasty."

"Or you could have made me a nigger. It's too late for me to be a nigger," she said with deep sarcasm, "but I could act like one. Lay down in the middle of the road and stop traffic. Roll on the ground."

In the deepening light everything was taking on a mysterious hue. The pasture was growing a peculiar glassy green and the streak of highway had turned lavender. She braced herself for a final assault and this time her voice rolled out over the pasture. "Go on," she yelled, "call me a hog! Call me a hog again. From hell. Call me a wart hog from hell. Put that bottom rail on top. There'll still be a top and bottom!"

A garbled echo returned to her.

A final surge of fury shook her and she roared, "Who do you think you are?"

The color of everything, field and crimson sky, burned for a moment with a transparent intensity. The question carried over the pasture and across the highway and the cotton field and returned to her clearly like an answer from beyond the wood.

She opened her mouth but no sound came out of it.

A tiny truck, Claud's, appeared on the highway, heading rapidly out of sight. Its gears scraped thinly. It looked like a child's toy. At any moment a bigger truck might smash into it and scatter Claud's and the niggers' brains all over the road.

Mrs. Turpin stood there, her gaze fixed on the highway, all her muscles rigid, until in five or six minutes the truck reappeared, returning. She waited until it had had time to turn into their own road. Then like a monumental statue coming to life, she bent her head slowly and gazed, as if through the very heart of the mystery, down into the pig parlor at the hogs. They had settled all in one corner around the old sow who was grunting softly. A red glow suffused them. They appeared to pant with a secret life.

Until the sun slipped finally behind the tree line, Mrs. Turpin remained there with her gaze bent to them as if she were absorbing some abysmal life-giving knowledge. At last she lifted her head. There was only a purple streak in the sky, cutting through a field of crimson and leading, like an extension of the highway, into the descending dusk. She raised her hands from the side of the pen in a gesture hieratic and profound. A visionary light settled in her eyes. She saw the streak as a vast swinging bridge extending upward from the earth through a field of living fire. Upon it a vast horde of souls were rumbling toward heaven. There were whole companies of white-trash, clean for the first time in their lives, and bands of black niggers in white robes, and battalions of freaks and lunatics shouting and clapping and leaping like frogs. And bringing up the end of the procession was a tribe of people whom she recognized at once as those who, like herself and Claud, had always had a little of everything and the God-given wit to use it right. She leaned forward to observe them closer. They were marching behind the others with great dignity, accountable as they had always been for good order and common sense and respectable behavior. They alone were on key. Yet she could see by their shocked and altered faces that even their virtues were being burned away. She lowered her hands and gripped the rail of the hog pen, her eyes small but fixed unblinkingly on what lay ahead. In a moment the vision faded but she remained where she was, immobile.

At length she got down and turned off the faucet and made her slow way on the darkening path to the house. In the woods around her the invisible cricket choruses had struck up, but what she heard were the voices of the souls climbing upward into the starry field and shouting hallelujah.

QUESTIONS

1. Mrs. Turpin has a habit of categorizing people. Do the individuals she encounters in the story fit her categories? Does she fit the category in which she places herself?
2. The "ugly girl" and the "white-trash woman" act as foils to the "pleasant woman" and Mrs. Turpin. Where do *they* place Mrs. Turpin on the story's continuum of characters?
3. What kinds of hierarchies do we find in this story? How does Mrs. Turpin's concluding vision fit in with these strata?
4. How do the gospel refrain and the radio song help characterize Mrs. Turpin? What do the adjectives and adverbs she uses in her unspoken judgments of other people tell us about her?
5. What is the meaning of the title? Does Mrs. Turpin have a revelation? If so, what is it? What is the meaning of the vision she has at the end of the story? Is her reaction to it consistent with what she has said about herself earlier in the story?

D. H. Lawrence *(1885–1930) was born in Eastwood, a coal-mining town in the English Midlands, was educated at nearby Nottingham, and taught at an elementary school south of London. His poetry appeared in The English Review, edited by Ford Madox Ford, and in 1911 he published his first novel,* The White Peacock. *The years following saw the publication of* Sons and Lovers *(1913), the suppression of* The Rainbow *(1915), and the delayed release of* Women in Love *(1920). After World War I Lawrence traveled from Italy to Australia to America, and settled briefly in the dry climate of New Mexico. He returned to Europe in 1925, completed* Lady Chatterley's Lover *in 1928, and—ever in ill-health—died of tuberculosis in southern France.*

The Horse Dealer's Daughter

D. H. LAWRENCE

"Well, Mabel, and what are you going to do with yourself?" asked Joe, with foolish flippancy. He felt quite safe himself. Without listening for an answer, he turned aside, worked a grain of tobacco to the tip of his tongue and spat it out. He did not care about anything, since he felt safe himself.

The three brothers and the sister sat round the desolate breakfast table, attempting some sort of desultory consultation. The morning's post had given the final tap to the family fortune, and all was over. The dreary dining-room itself, with its heavy mahogany furniture, looked as if it were waiting to be done away with.

But the consultation amounted to nothing. There was a strange air of ineffectuality about the three men, as they sprawled at table, smoking and reflecting vaguely on their own condition. The girl was alone, a rather short, sullen-looking young woman of twenty-seven. She did not share the same life as her brothers. She would have been good-looking, save for the impassive fixity of her face, "bull-dog," as her brothers called it.

There was a confused tramping of horses' feet outside. The three men all sprawled round in their chairs to watch. Beyond the dark holly-bushes that separated the strip of lawn from the highroad, they could see a cavalcade of shire horses swinging out of their own yard, being taken for exercise. This was the last time. These were the last horses that would go through their hands. The young men watched with critical, callous look. They were all frightened at the collapse of their lives, and the sense of disaster in which they were involved left them no inner freedom.

Yet they were three fine, well-set fellows enough. Joe, the eldest, was a man of thirty-three, broad and handsome in a hot, flushed way. His face was red, he twisted his black mustache over a thick finger, his eyes were shallow and restless. He had a sensual way of uncovering his teeth when he laughed, and his bearing was stupid. Now he watched the horses with a glazed look of helplessness in his eyes, a certain stupor of downfall.

The great draught-horses swung past. They were tied head to tail, four of them, and they heaved along to where a lane branched off from the highroad, planting their great hoofs floutingly in the fine black mud, swinging their great rounded haunches sumptuously, and trotting a few sudden steps as they were led into the lane, round the corner. Every movement showed a massive, slumbrous strength, and a stupidity which held them in subjection. The groom at the head looked back, jerking the leading rope. And the cavalcade moved out of sight up the lane, the tail of the last horse, bobbed up tight and stiff, held out taut from the swinging great haunches as they rocked behind the hedges in a motion-like sleep.

Joe watched with glazed hopeless eyes. The horses were almost like his own body to him. He felt he was done for now. Luckily he was engaged to a woman as old as himself, and therefore her father, who was steward of a neighboring estate, would provide him with a job. He would marry and go into harness. His life was over, he would be a subject animal now.

He turned uneasily aside, the retreating steps of the horses echoing in his ears. Then, with foolish restlessness, he reached for the scraps of bacon-rind from the plates, and making a faint whistling sound, flung them to the terrier that lay against the fender. He watched the dog swallow them, and waited till the creature looked into his eyes. Then a faint grin came on his face, and in a high, foolish voice he said:

"You won't get much more bacon, shall you, you little bitch?"

The dog faintly and dismally wagged its tail, then lowered its haunches, circled round, and lay down again.

There was another helpless silence at the table. Joe sprawled uneasily in his seat, not willing to go till the family conclave was dissolved. Fred Henry, the second brother, was erect, clean-limbed, alert. He had watched the passing of the horses with more *sang-froid*. If he was an animal, like Joe, he was an animal which controls, not one which is controlled. He was master of any horse, and he carried himself with a well-tempered air of mastery. But he was not master of the situations of life. He pushed his coarse brown mustache upwards, off his lip, and glanced irritably at his sister, who sat impassive and inscrutable.

"You'll go and stop with Lucy for a bit, shan't you?" he asked. The girl did not answer.

"I don't see what else you can do," persisted Fred Henry.

"Go as a skivvy," Joe interpolated laconically.

The girl did not move a muscle.

"If I was her, I should go in for training for a nurse," said Malcolm, the youngest of them all. He was the baby of the family, a young man of twenty-two, with a fresh, jaunty *museau*.

But Mabel did not take any notice of him. They had talked at her and round her for so many years, that she hardly heard them at all.

The marble clock on the mantelpiece softly chimed the half-hour, the dog rose uneasily from the hearthrug and looked at the party at the breakfast table. But still they sat on in ineffectual conclave.

"Oh, all right," said Joe suddenly, apropos of nothing. "I'll get a move on."

He pushed back his chair, straddled his knees with a downward jerk, to get them free, in horsey fashion, and went to the fire. Still he did not go out of the room; he was curious to know what the others would do or say. He began to charge his pipe, looking down at the dog and saying, in a high, affected voice:

"Going wi' me? Going wi' me are ter? Tha'rt goin' further than that counts on just now, dost hear?"

The dog faintly wagged its tail, the man stuck out his jaw and covered his pipe with his hands, and puffed intently, losing himself in the tobacco, looking down all the while at the dog with an absent brown eye. The dog looked at him in mournful distrust. Joe stood with his knees stuck out, in real horsey fashion.

"Have you had a letter from Lucy?" Fred Henry asked his sister.

"Last week," came the neutral reply.

"And what does she say?"

There was no answer.

"Does she *ask* you to go and stop there?" persisted Fred Henry.

"She says I can if I like."

"Well, then, you'd better. Tell her you'll come on Monday."

This was received in silence.

"That's what you'll do then, is it?" said Fred Henry, in some exasperation.

But she made no answer. There was a silence of futility and irritation in the room. Malcolm grinned fatuously.

"You'll have to make up your mind between now and next Wednesday," said Joe loudly, "or else find yourself lodgings on the curbstone."

The face of the young woman darkened, but she sat on immutable.

"Here's Jack Fergusson!" exclaimed Malcolm, who was looking aimlessly out of the window.

"Where?" exclaimed Joe, loudly.

"Just gone past."

"Coming in?"

Malcolm craned his neck to see the gate.

"Yes," he said.

There was a silence. Mabel sat on like one condemned, at the head of the table. Then a whistle was heard from the kitchen. The dog got up and barked sharply. Joe opened the door and shouted:

"Come on."

After a moment a young man entered. He was muffled up in overcoat and a purple woolen scarf, and his tweed cap, which he did not remove, was pulled down on his head. He was of medium height, his face was rather long and pale, his eyes looked tired.

"Hello, Jack! Well, Jack!" exclaimed Malcolm and Joe. Fred Henry merely said "Jack!"

"What's doing?" asked the newcomer, evidently addressing Fred Henry.

"Same. We've got to be out by Wednesday.—Got a cold?"

"I have—got it bad, too."

"Why don't you stop in?"

"*Me* stop in? When I can't stand on my legs, perhaps I shall have a chance." The young man spoke huskily. He had a slight Scotch accent.

"It's a knock-out, isn't it," said Joe boisterously, "if a doctor goes round croaking with a cold. Looks bad for the patients, doesn't it?"

The young doctor looked at him slowly.

"Anything the matter with *you*, then?" he asked sarcastically.

"Not as I know of. Damn your eyes, I hope not. Why?"

"I thought you were very concerned about the patients, wondered if you might be one yourself."

"Damn it, no, I've never been patient to no flaming doctor, and hope I never shall be," returned Joe.

At this point Mabel rose from the table, and they all seemed to become aware of her existence. She began putting the dishes together. The young doctor looked at her, but did not address her. He had not greeted her. She went out of the room with the tray, her face impassive and unchanged.

"When are you off then, all of you?" asked the doctor.

"I'm catching the eleven-forty," replied Malcolm. "Are you goin' down wi' th' trap, Joe?"

"Yes, I've told you I'm going down wi' th' trap, haven't I?"

"We'd better be getting her in then. So long, Jack, if I don't see you before I go," said Malcolm, shaking hands.

He went out, followed by Joe, who seemed to have his tail between his legs.

"Well, this is the devil's own," exclaimed the doctor, when he was left alone with Fred Henry. "Going before Wednesday, are you?"

"That's the orders," replied the other.

"Where, to Northampton?"

"That's it."

"The devil!" exclaimed Fergusson, with quiet chagrin.

And there was silence between the two.

"All settled up, are you?" asked Fergusson.

"About."

There was another pause.

"Well, I shall miss yer, Freddy boy," said the young doctor.

"And I shall miss thee, Jack," returned the other.

"Miss you like hell," mused the doctor.

Fred Henry turned aside. There was nothing to say. Mabel came in again, to finish clearing the table.

"What are *you* going to do, then, Miss Pervin?" asked Fergusson. "Going to your sister's, are you?"

Mabel looked at him with her steady, dangerous eyes, that always made him uncomfortable, unsettling his superficial ease.

"No," she said.

"Well, what in the name of fortune *are* you going to do? Say what you *mean* to do," cried Fred Henry, with futile intensity.

But she only averted her head, and continued her work. She folded the white table-cloth, and put on the chenille cloth.

"The sulkiest bitch that ever trod!" muttered her brother.

But she finished her task with perfectly impassive face, the young doctor watching her interestedly all the while. Then she went out.

Fred Henry stared after her, clenching his lips, his blue eyes fixing in sharp antagonism, as he made a grimace of sour exasperation.

"You could bray her into bits, and that's all you'd get out of her," he said in a small, narrowed tone.

The doctor smiled faintly.

"What's she *going* to do, then?" he asked.

"Strike me if *I* know!" returned the other.

There was a pause. Then the doctor stirred.

"I'll be seeing you to-night, shall I?" he said to his friend.

"Ay—where's it to be? Are we going over to Jessdale?"

"I don't know. I've got such a cold on me. I'll come round to the Moon and Stars, anyway."

"Let Lizzie and May miss their night for once, eh?"

"That's it—if I feel as I do now."

"All's one—"

The two young men went through the passage and down to the back door together. The house was large, but it was servantless now, and desolate. At the back was a small bricked house-yard, and beyond that a big square, graveled fine and red, and having stables on two sides. Sloping, dank, winter-dark fields stretched away on the open sides.

But the stables were empty. Joseph Pervin, the father of the family, had been a man of no education, who had become a fairly large horse dealer. The stables had been full of horses, there was a great turmoil and come-and-go of horses and of dealers and grooms. Then the kitchen was full of servants. But of late things had declined. The old man had married a second time, to retrieve his fortunes. Now he was dead and everything was gone to the dogs, there was nothing but debt and threatening.

For months, Mabel had been servantless in the big house, keeping the home together in penury for her ineffectual brothers. She had kept house for ten years. But previously, it was with unstinted means. Then, however brutal and coarse everything was, the sense of money had kept her proud, confident. The men might be foul-mouthed, the women in the kitchen might have bad reputations, her brothers might have illegitimate children. But so long as there was money, the girl felt herself established, and brutally proud, reserved.

No company came to the house, save dealers and coarse men. Mabel had no associates of her own sex, after her sister went away. But she did not mind. She went regularly to church, she attended to her father. And she lived in the memory of her mother, who had died when she was fourteen, and whom she had loved. She had loved her father, too, in a different way, depending upon him, and feeling secure in him, until at the age of fifty-four he married again. And then she had set hard against him. Now he had died and left them all hopelessly in debt.

She had suffered badly during the period of poverty. Nothing, however, could shake the curious sullen, animal pride that dominated each member of the family. Now, for Mabel, the end had come. Still she would not cast about her. She would follow her own way just the same. She would always hold the keys of her own situation. Mindless and persistent, she endured from day to day. Why should she think? Why should she answer anybody? It was enough that this was the end, and there was no way out. She need not pass any more darkly along the main street of the small town, avoiding every eye. She need not demean herself any more, going into the shops and buying the cheapest food. This was at an end. She thought of nobody, not even of herself. Mindless and persistent, she seemed in a sort of ecstasy to be coming nearer to her fulfillment, her own glorification, approaching her dead mother, who was glorified.

In the afternoon she took a little bag, with shears and sponge and a small scrubbing brush, and went out. It was a gray, wintry day, with saddened, dark-green fields and an atmosphere blackened by the smoke of foundries not far off. She went quickly, darkly along the causeway, heeding nobody, through the town to the churchyard.

There she always felt secure, as if no one could see her, although as a matter of fact she was exposed to the stare of everyone who passed along under the churchyard wall. Nevertheless, once under the shadow of the great looming church, among the graves, she felt immune from the world, reserved within the thick churchyard wall as in another country.

Carefully she clipped the grass from the grave, and arranged the pinky-white, small chrysanthemums in the tin cross. When this was done, she took an empty jar from a neighboring grave, brought water, and carefully, most scrupulously sponged the marble headstone and the coping-stone.

It gave her sincere satisfaction to do this. She felt in immediate contact with the world of her mother. She took minute pains, went through the park in a state bordering on pure happiness, as if in performing this task she came into a subtle, intimate connection with her mother. For the life she followed here in the world was far less real than the world of death she inherited from her mother.

The doctor's house was just by the church. Fergusson, being a mere hired assistant, was slave to the countryside. As he hurried now to attend to the outpatients in the surgery, glancing across the graveyard with his quick eye, he saw the girl at her task at the grave. She seemed so intent and remote, it was like looking into another world. Some mystical element was touched in him. He slowed down as he walked, watching her as if spellbound.

She lifted her eyes, feeling him looking. Their eyes met. And each looked away again at once, each feeling, in some way, found out by the other. He lifted his cap and passed on down the road. There remained distinct in his consciousness, like a vision, the memory of her face, lifted from the tombstone in the churchyard, and looking at him with slow, large, portentous eyes. It *was* portentous, her face. It seemed to mesmerize him. There was a heavy power in her eyes which laid hold of his whole being, as if he had drunk some powerful drug. He had been feeling weak and done before. Now the life came back into him, he felt delivered from his own fretted, daily self.

He finished his duties at the surgery as quickly as might be, hastily filling up the bottle of the waiting people with cheap drugs. Then, in perpetual haste, he set off again to visit several cases in another part of his round, before teatime. At all times he preferred to walk if he could, but particularly when he was not well. He fancied the motion restored him.

The afternoon was falling. It was gray, deadened, and wintry, with a slow, moist, heavy coldness sinking in and deadening all the faculties. But why should he think or notice? He hastily climbed the hill and turned across the dark-green fields, following the black cinder-track. In the distance, across a shallow dip in the country, the small town was clustered like smoldering ash, a tower, a spire, a heap of low, raw, extinct houses. And on the nearest fringe of the town, sloping into the dip, was Oldmeadow, the Pervins' house. He could see the stables and the outbuildings distinctly, as they lay towards him on the slope. Well, he would not go there many more times! Another resource would be lost to him, another place gone: the only company he cared for in the alien, ugly little town he was losing. Nothing but work, drudgery, constant hastening from dwelling to dwelling among the colliers and the iron-workers. It wore him out, but at the same time he had a craving for it. It was a stimulant to him to be in the homes of the working people, moving as it were through the innermost body of their life. His nerves were excited and gratified. He could come so near, into the very lives of the rough, inarticulate, powerfully emotional men and women. He grumbled, he said he hated the hellish hole. But as a matter of fact it excited him, the contact with the rough, strongly-feeling people was a stimulant applied direct to his nerves.

Below Oldmeadow, in the green, shallow, soddened hollow of fields, lay a square, deep pond. Roving across the landscape, the doctor's quick eye detected a figure in black passing through the gate of the field, down towards the pond. He looked again. It would be Mabel Pervin. His mind suddenly became alive and attentive.

Why was she going down there? He pulled up on the path on the slope above, and stood staring. He could just make sure of the small black figure moving in the hollow of the failing day. He seemed to see her in the midst of such obscurity, that he was like a clairvoyant, seeing rather with the mind's eye than with ordinary sight. Yet he could see her positively enough, while he kept his eye attentive. He felt, if he looked away from her, in the thick, ugly falling dusk, he would lose her altogether.

He followed her minutely as she moved, direct and intent, like something transmitted rather than stirring in voluntary activity, straight down the field towards the pond. There she stood on the bank for a moment. She never raised her head. Then she waded slowly into the water.

He stood motionless as the small black figure walked slowly and deliberately towards the center of the pond, very slowly, gradually moving deeper into the motionless water, and still moving forward as the water got up to her breast. Then he could see her no more in the dusk of the dead afternoon.

"There!" he exclaimed. "Would you believe it?"

And he hastened straight down, running over the wet, soddened fields, pushing through the hedges, down into the depression of callous wintry obscurity. It took him several minutes to come to the pond. He stood on the bank, breathing heavily. He could see nothing. His eyes seemed to penetrate the dead water. Yes, perhaps that was the dark shadow of her black clothing beneath the surface of the water.

He slowly ventured into the pond. The bottom was deep, soft clay, he sank in, and the water clasped dead cold round his legs. As he stirred he could smell the cold, rotten clay that fouled up into the water. It was objectionable in his lungs. Still, repelled and yet not heeding, he moved deeper into the pond. The cold water rose over his thighs, over his loins, upon his abdomen. The lower part of his body was all sunk in the hideous cold element. And the bottom was so deeply soft and uncertain, he was afraid of pitching with his mouth underneath. He could not swim, and was afraid.

He crouched a little, spreading his hands under the water and moving them round, trying to feel for her. The dead cold pond swayed upon his chest. He moved again, a little deeper, and again, with his hands underneath, he felt all around under the water. And he touched her clothing. But it evaded his fingers. He made a desperate effort to grasp it.

And so doing he lost his balance and went under, horribly, suffocating in the foul earthy water, struggling madly for a few moments. At last, after what seemed an eternity, he got his footing, rose again into the air and looked around. He gasped, and knew he was in the world. Then he looked at the water. She had risen near him. He grasped her clothing, and drawing her nearer, turned to take his way to land again.

He went very slowly, carefully, absorbed in the slow progress. He rose higher, climbing out of the pond. The water was now only about his legs; he was thankful, full of relief to be out of the clutches of the pond. He lifted her and staggered onto the bank, out of the horror of wet, gray clay.

He laid her down on the bank. She was quite unconscious and running with water. He made the water come from her mouth, he worked to restore her. He did not have to work very long before he could feel the breathing begin again in her; she was breathing naturally. He worked a little longer. He could feel her live beneath his hands; she was coming back. He wiped her face, wrapped her in his overcoat, looked round into the dim, dark-gray world, then lifted her and staggered down the bank and across the fields.

It seemed an unthinkably long way, and his burden so heavy he felt he would never get to the house. But at last he was in the stableyard, and then in the house-yard. He opened the door and went into the house. In the kitchen he laid her down on the hearthrug, and called. The house was empty. But the fire was burning in the grate.

Then again he kneeled to attend to her. She was breathing regularly, her eyes were wide open and as if conscious, but there seemed something missing in her look. She was conscious in herself, but unconscious of her surroundings.

He ran upstairs, took blankets from a bed, and put them before the fire to warm. Then he removed her saturated, earthy-smelling clothing, rubbed her dry with a towel, and wrapped her naked in the blankets. Then he went into the dining-room, to look for spirits. There was a little whisky. He drank a gulp himself, and put some into her mouth.

The effect was instantaneous. She looked full into his face, as if she had been seeing him for some time, and yet had only just become conscious of him.

"Dr. Fergusson?" she said.

"What?" he answered.

He was divesting himself of his coat, intending to find some dry clothing upstairs. He could not bear the smell of the dead, clayey water, and he was mortally afraid for his own health.

"What did I do?" she asked.

"Walked into the pond," he replied. He had begun to shudder like one sick, and could hardly attend to her. Her eyes remained full on him, he seemed to be going dark in his mind, looking back at her helplessly. The shuddering became quieter in him, his life came back in him, dark and unknowing, but strong again.

"Was I out of my mind?" she asked, while her eyes were fixed on him all the time.

"Maybe, for the moment," he replied. He felt quiet, because his strength had come back. The strange fretful strain had left him.

"Am I out of my mind now?" she asked.

"Are you?" he reflected a moment. "No," he answered truthfully, "I don't see that you are." He turned his face aside. He was afraid now, because he felt dazed, and felt dimly that her power was stronger than his, in this issue. And she continued to look at him fixedly all the time. "Can you tell me where I shall find some dry things to put on?" he asked.

"Did you dive into the pond for me?" she asked.

"No," he answered. "I walked in. But I went in overhead as well."

There was silence for a moment. He hesitated. He very much wanted to go upstairs to get into dry clothing. But there was another desire in him. And she seemed to hold him. His will seemed to have gone to sleep, and left him, standing there slack before her. But he felt warm inside himself. He did not shudder at all, though his clothes were sodden on him.

"Why did you?" she asked.

"Because I didn't want you to do such a foolish thing," he said.

"It wasn't foolish," she said, still gazing at him as she lay on the floor, with a sofa cushion under her head. "It was the right thing to do. *I* knew best, then."

"I'll go and shift these wet things," he said. But still he had not the power to move out of her presence, until she sent him. It was as if she had the life of his body in her hands, and he could not extricate himself. Or perhaps he did not want to.

Suddenly she sat up. Then she became aware of her own immediate condition. She felt the blankets about her, she knew her own limbs. For a moment it seemed as if her reason were going. She looked round, with wild eye, as if seeking something. He stood still with fear. She saw her clothing lying scattered.

"Who undressed me?" she asked, her eyes resting full and inevitable on his face.

"I did," he replied, "to bring you round."

For some moments she sat and gazed at him awfully, her lips parted.

"Do you love me, then?" she asked.

He only stood and stared at her, fascinated. His soul seemed to melt.

She shuffled forward on her knees, and put her arms round him, round his legs, as he stood there, pressing her breasts against his knees and thighs, clutching him with strange, convulsive certainty, pressing his thighs against her, drawing him to her face, her throat, as she looked up at him with flaring, humble eyes of transfiguration, triumphant in first possession.

"You love me," she murmured, in strange transport, yearning and triumphant and confident. "You love me. I know you love me, I know."

And she was passionately kissing his knees, through the wet clothing, passionately and indiscriminately kissing his knees, his legs, as if unaware of everything.

He looked down at the tangled wet hair, the wild, bare, animal shoulders. He was amazed, bewildered, and afraid. He had never thought of loving her. He had never wanted to love her. When he rescued her and restored her, he was a doctor, and she was a patient. He had had no single personal thought of her. Nay, this introduction of the personal element was very distasteful to him, a violation of his professional honor. It was horrible to have her there embracing his knees. It was horrible. He revolted from it, violently. And yet—and yet—he had not the power to break away.

She looked at him again, with the same supplication of powerful love, and that same transcendent, frightening light of triumph. In view of the delicate flame which seemed to come from her face like a light, he was powerless. And yet he had never intended to love her. He had never intended. And something stubborn in him could not give way.

"You love me," she repeated, in a murmur of deep, rhapsodic assurance. "You love me."

Her hands were drawing him, drawing him down to her. He was afraid, even a little horrified. For he had, really, no intention of loving her. Yet her hands were drawing him towards her. He put out his hand quickly to steady himself, and grasped her bare shoulder. A flame seemed to burn the hand that grasped her soft shoulder. He had no intention of loving her: his whole will was against his yielding. It was horrible. And yet wonderful was the touch of her shoulders, beautiful the shining of her face. Was she perhaps mad? He had a horror of yielding to her. Yet something in him ached also.

He had been staring away at the door, away from her. But his hand remained on her shoulder. She had gone suddenly very still. He looked down at her. Her eyes were now wide with fear, with doubt, the light was dying from her face, a shadow of terrible grayness was returning. He could not bear the touch of her eyes' question upon him, and the look of death behind the question.

With an inward groan he gave way, and let his heart yield towards her. A sudden gentle smile came on his face. And her eyes, which never left his face, slowly, slowly filled with tears. He watched the strange water rise in her eyes, like some slow fountain coming up. And his heart seemed to burn and melt away in his breast.

He could not bear to look at her any more. He dropped on his knees and caught her head with his arms and pressed her face against his throat. She was very still. His heart, which seemed to have broken, was burning with a kind of agony in his breast. And he felt her slow, hot tears wetting his throat. But he could not move.

He felt the hot tears wet his neck and the hollows of his neck, and he remained motionless, suspended through one of man's eternities. Only now it had become indispensable to him to have her face pressed close to him; he could never let her go again. He could never let her head go away from the close clutch of his arm. He wanted to remain like that forever, with his heart hurting him in a pain that was also life to him. Without knowing, he was looking down on her damp, soft brown hair.

Then, as it were suddenly, he smelt the horrid stagnant smell of that water. And at the same moment she drew away from him and looked at him. Her eyes were wistful and unfathomable. He was afraid of them, and he fell to kissing her, not knowing what he was doing. He wanted her eyes not to have that terrible, wistful, unfathomable look.

When she turned her face to him again, a faint delicate flush was glowing, and there was again dawning that terrible shining of joy in her eyes, which really terrified him, and yet which he now wanted to see, because he feared the look of doubt still more.

"You love me?" she said, rather faltering.

"Yes." The word cost him a painful effort. Not because it wasn't true. But because it was too newly true, the *saying* seemed to tear open again his newly-torn heart. And he hardly wanted it to be true, even now.

She lifted her face to him, and he bent forward and kissed her on the mouth, gently, with the one kiss that is an eternal pledge. And as he kissed her his heart strained again in his breast. He never intended to love her. But now it was over. He had crossed over the gulf to her, and all that he had left behind had shriveled and become void.

After the kiss, her eyes again slowly filled with tears. She sat still, away from him, with her face drooped aside, and her hands folded in her lap. The tears fell very slowly. There was complete silence. He too sat there motionless and silent on the hearthrug. The strange pain of his heart that was broken seemed to consume him. That he should love her? That this was love! That he should be ripped open in this way!—Him, a doctor!—How they would all jeer if they knew!—It was agony to him to think they might know.

In the curious naked pain of the thought he looked again to her. She was sitting there drooped into a muse. He saw a tear fall, and his heart flared hot. He saw for the first time that one of her shoulders was quite uncovered, one arm bare, he could see one of her small breasts; dimly, because it had become almost dark in the room.

"Why are you crying?" he asked, in an altered voice.

She looked up at him, and behind her tears the consciousness of her situation for the first time brought a dark look of shame to her eyes.

"I'm not crying, really," she said, watching him half frightened.

He reached his hand, and softly closed it on her bare arm.

"I love you! I love you!" he said in a soft, low, vibrating voice, unlike himself.

She shrank, and dropped her head. The soft, penetrating grip of his hand on her arm distressed her. She looked up at him.

"I want to go," she said. "I want to go and get you some dry things."

"Why?" he said. "I'm all right."

"But I want to go," she said. "And I want you to change your things."

He released her arm, and she wrapped herself in the blanket, looking at him rather frightened. And still she did not rise.

"Kiss me," she said wistfully.

He kissed her, but briefly, half in anger.

Then, after a second, she rose nervously, all mixed up in the blanket. He watched her in her confusion, as she tried to extricate herself and wrap herself up so that she could walk. He watched her relentlessly, as she knew. And as she went, the blanket trailing, and as he saw a glimpse of her feet and her white leg, he tried to remember her as she was when he had wrapped her in the blanket. But then he didn't want to remember, because she had been nothing to him then, and his nature revolted from remembering her as she was when she was nothing to him.

A tumbling, muffled noise from within the dark house startled him. Then he heard her voice:—"There are clothes." He rose and went to the foot of the stairs, and gathered up the garments she had thrown down. Then he came back to the fire, to rub himself down and dress. He grinned at his own appearance, when he had finished.

The fire was sinking, so he put on coal. The house was now quite dark, save for the light of a street-lamp that shone in faintly from beyond the holly trees. He lit the gas with matches he found on the mantelpiece. Then he emptied the pockets of his own clothes, and threw all his wet things in a heap into the scullery. After which he gathered up her sodden clothes, gently, and put them in a separate heap on the copper-top in the scullery.

It was six o'clock on the clock. His own watch had stopped. He ought to go back to the surgery. He waited, and still she did not come down. So he went to the foot of the stairs and called:

"I shall have to go."

Almost immediately he heard her coming down. She had on her best dress of black voile, and her hair was tidy, but still damp. She looked at him—and in spite of herself, smiled.

"I don't like you in those clothes," she said.

"Do I look a sight?" he answered.

They were shy of one another.

"I'll make you some tea," she said.

"No, I must go."

"Must you?" And she looked at him again with the wide, strained, doubtful eyes. And again, from the pain of his breast, he knew how he loved her. He went and bent to kiss her, gently, passionately, with his heart's painful kiss.

"And my hair smells so horrible," she murmured in distraction. "And I'm so awful, I'm so awful! Oh, no, I'm too awful." And she broke into bitter, heartbroken sobbing. "You can't want to love me, I'm horrible."

"Don't be silly, don't be silly," he said, trying to comfort her, kissing her, holding her in his arms. "I want you, I want to marry you, we're going to be married, quickly, quickly—tomorrow if I can."

But she only sobbed terribly, and cried:

"I feel awful. I feel awful. I feel I'm horrible to you."

"No, I want you, I want you," was all he answered, blindly, with that terrible intonation which frightened her almost more than her horror lest he should *not* want her.

QUESTIONS

1. To what extent is Lawrence interested in Mabel and Dr. Fergusson as individual characters? Are they in any way symbolic?
2. Briefly characterize each of Mabel's brothers. How is she different from them? Does her relation with them prepare us in any way for her attempted suicide?
3. Why does Lawrence repeat the question, "What are you going to do?" Does the question always have the same meaning? How does this persistent question convey the situation facing Mabel, later Dr. Fergusson, and at the end the two of them together?
4. In what ways does Mabel's relation with her mother and father explain her character? What do you make of Lawrence's statement: "For the life she followed here in the world was far less real than the world of death she inherited from her mother"?
5. What changes have taken place in Mabel's and Dr. Fergusson's characters after the experience in the pond? How do you explain these changes? Has the experience had the same effect for both of them? What is the nature of their relationship at the end of the story?

Vladimir Nabokov (1899–), the son of a wealthy and cosmopolitan Russian statesman, was born in St. Petersburg. He was educated locally and at Cambridge University. His family left Russia after the Revolution destroyed their fortune, and Nabokov spent the 1920's and 1930's in Berlin and Paris teaching English and composing under the pen name of V. Sirin. Since coming to America in 1940 Nabokov has written exclusively in English. His early novels received critical acclaim, but Lolita *(1955) established him as a popular writer and relieved him of the need to teach at American universities. Among his better-known books are* Pnin *(1957) and* Pale Fire *(1962). His most recent publications include a brief collection of short stories,* Nabokov's Quartet *(1966), and two novels,* Ada: or, Ardor: A Family Chronicle *(1969), and* Look at the Harlequin, *(1974). A recipient of the award of Merit from the American Academy of Arts and Letters (1969), the prolific Nabokov lives in Switzerland.*

The Vane Sisters

VLADIMIR NABOKOV

I might never have heard of Cynthia's death, had I not run, that night, into D., whom I had also lost track of for the last four years or so; and I might never have run into D., had I not got involved in a series of trivial investigations.

The day, a compunctious Sunday after a week of blizzards, had been part jewel, part mud. In the midst of my usual afternoon stroll through the small hilly town attached to the girls' college where I taught French literature, I had stopped to watch a family of brilliant icicles drip-dripping from the eaves of a frame house. So clear-cut were their pointed shadows on the white boards behind them that I was sure the shadows of the falling drops should be visible too. But they were not. The roof jutted too far out, perhaps, or the angle of vision was faulty, or, again, I did not chance to be watching the right icicle when the right drop fell. There was a rhythm, an alternation in the dripping that I found as teasing as a coin trick. It led me to inspect the corners of several house blocks, and this brought me to Kelly Road, and right to the house where D. used to live when he was instructor here. And as I looked up at the eaves of the adjacent garage with its full display of transparent stalactites backed by their blue silhouettes, I was rewarded at last, upon choosing one, by the sight of what might be described as the dot of an exclamation mark leaving its ordinary position to glide down very fast—a jot faster than the thaw-drop it raced. This twinned twinkle was delightful but not completely satisfying; or rather it only sharpened my appetite for other tidbits of light and shade, and I walked on in a state of raw awareness that seemed to transform the whole of my being into one big eyeball rolling in the world's socket.

Through peacocked lashes I saw the dazzling diamond reflection of the low sun on the round back of a parked automobile. To all kinds of things a vivid pictorial sense had been restored by the sponge of the thaw. Water in overlapping festoons flowed down one sloping street and turned gracefully into another. With ever so slight a note of meretricious appeal, narrow passages between buildings revealed treasures of brick and purple. I remarked for the first time the humble fluting—last echoes of grooves on the shafts of columns—ornamenting a garbage can, and I also saw the rippling upon its lid—circles diverging from a fantastically ancient center. Erect, dark-headed shapes of dead snow (left by the blades of a bulldozer last Friday) were lined up like rudimentary penguins along the curbs, above the brilliant vibration of live gutters.

I walked up, and I walked down, and I walked straight into a delicately dying sky, and finally the sequence of observed and observant things brought me, at my usual eating time, to a street so distant from my usual eating place that I decided to try a restaurant which stood on the fringe of the town. Night had fallen without sound or ceremony when I came out again. The lean ghost, the elongated umbra cast by a parking meter upon some damp snow, had a strange ruddy tinge; this I made out to be due to the tawny red light of the restaurant sign above the sidewalk; and it was then—as I loitered there, wondering rather wearily if in the course of my return tramp I might be lucky enough to find the same in neon blue—it was then that a car crunched to a standstill near me and D. got out of it with an exclamation of feigned pleasure.

He was passing, on his way from Albany to Boston, through the town he had dwelt in before, and more than once in my life have I felt that stab of vicarious emotion followed by a rush of personal irritation against travelers who seem to feel nothing at all upon revisiting spots that ought to harass them at every step with wailing and writhing memories. He ushered me back into the bar that I had just left, and after the usual exchange of buoyant platitudes came the inevitable vacuum which he filled with the random words: "Say, I never thought there was anything wrong with Cynthia Vane's heart. My lawyer tells me she died last week."

He was still young, still brash, still shifty, still married to the gentle, exquisitely pretty woman who had never learned or suspected anything about his disastrous affair with Cynthia's hysterical young sister, who in her turn had known nothing of the interview I had had with Cynthia when she suddenly summoned me to Boston to make me swear I would talk to D. and get him "kicked out" if he did not stop seeing Sybil at once—or did not divorce his wife (whom incidentlly she visualized through the prism of Sybil's wild talk as a termagant and a fright). I had cornered him immediately. He had said there was nothing to worry about—had made up his mind, anyway, to give up his college job and move with his wife to Albany where he would work in his father's firm; and the whole matter, which had threatened to become one of those hopelessly entangled situations that drag on for years, with peripheral sets of well-meaning friends endlessly discussing it in universal secrecy—and even founding, among themselves, new intimacies upon its alien woes—came to an abrupt end.

I remember sitting next day at my raised desk in the large classroom where a midyear examination in French Lit was being held on the eve of Sybil's suicide. She came in on high heels, with a suitcase, dumped it in a corner where several other bags were stacked, with a single shrug slipped her fur coat off her thin shoulders, folded it on her bag, and with two or three other girls stopped before my desk to ask when would I mail them their grades. It would take me a week, beginning from tomorrow, I said, to read the stuff. I also remember wondering whether D. had already informed her of his decision—and I felt acutely unhappy about my dutiful little student as during one hundred and fifty minutes my gaze kept reverting to her, so childishly slight in closefitting gray, and kept observing that carefully waved dark hair, that small, small-flowered hat with a little hyaline veil as worn that season and under it her small face broken into a cubist pattern by scars due to a skin disease, pathetically masked by a sunlamp tan that hardened her features whose charm was further impaired by her having painted everything that could be painted, so that the pale gums of her teeth between cherry-red chapped lips and the diluted blue ink of her eyes under darkened lids were the only visible openings into her beauty.

Next day, having arranged the ugly copybooks alphabetically, I plunged into their chaos of scripts and came prematurely to Valevsky and Vane whose books I had somehow misplaced. The first was dressed up for the occasion in a semblance of legibility, but Sybil's work displayed her usual combination of several demon hands. She had begun in very pale, very hard pencil which had conspicuously embossed the blank verso, but had produced little of permanent value on the upperside of the page. Happily the tip soon broke, and Sybil continued in another, darker, lead, gradually lapsing into the blurred thickness of what looked almost like charcoal, to which, by sucking the blunt point, she had contributed some traces of lipstick. Her work, although even poorer than I had expected, bore all the signs of a kind of desperate conscientiousness, with underscores, transposes, unnecessary footnotes, as if she were intent upon rounding up things in the most respectable manner possible. Then she had borrowed Mary Valevsky's fountain pen and added: "*Cette examain est finie ainsi que ma vie. Adieu, jeunes filles!* Please, *Monsieur le Professeur*, contact *ma soeur* and tell her that Death was not better than D minus, but definitely better than Life minus D."

I lost no time in ringing up Cynthia who told me it was all over—had been all over since eight in the morning—and asked me to bring her the note, and when I did, beamed through her tears with proud admiration for the whimsical use ("Just like her!") Sybil had made of an examination in French literature. In no time she "fixed" two highballs, while never parting with Sybil's notebook—by now splashed with soda water and tears—and went on studying the death message, whereupon I was impelled to point out to her the grammatical mistakes in it and to explain the way "girl" is translated in American colleges lest students innocently bandy around the French equivalent of "wench," or worse. These rather tasteless trivialities pleased Cynthia hugely as she rose, with gasps, above the heaving surface of her grief. And then, holding that limp notebook as if it were a kind of passport to a casual Elysium (where pencil points do not snap and a dreamy young beauty with an impeccable complexion winds a lock of her hair on a dreamy forefinger, as she meditates over some celestial test), Cynthia led me upstairs, to a chilly little bedroom just to show me, as if I were the police or a sympathetic Irish neighbor, two empty pill bottles and the tumbled bed from which a tender, inessential body, that D. must have known down to its last velvet detail, had been already removed.

It was four or five months after her sister's death that I began seeing Cynthia fairly often. By the time I had come to New York for some vocational research in the Public Library she had also moved to that city where for some odd reason (in vague connection, I presume, with artistic motives) she had taken what people, immune to gooseflesh, term a "cold water" flat, low down in the scale of the city's transverse streets. What attracted me were neither her ways, which I thought repulsively vivacious, nor her looks, which other men thought striking. She had wide-spaced eyes very much like her sister's, of a frank, frightened blue with dark points in a radial arrangement. The interval between her thick black eyebrows was always shiny, and shiny too were the fleshy volutes of her nostrils. The coarse texture of her epiderm looked almost masculine, and, in the stark lamplight of her studio, you could see the pores of her thirty-two-year-old face fairly gaping at you like something in an aquarium. She used cosmetics with as much zest as her little sister had, but with an additional slovenliness that would result in her big front teeth getting some of the rouge. She was handsomely dark, wore a not too tasteless mixture of fairly smart heterogeneous things, and had a so-called good figure; but all of her was curiously frowsy, after a way I obscurely associated with left-wing enthusiasms in politics and "advanced" banalities in art, although, actually, she cared for neither. Her coily hairdo, on a part-and-bun basis, might have looked feral and bizarre had it not been thoroughly domesticated by its own soft unkemptness at the vulnerable nape. Her fingernails were gaudily painted, but badly bitten and not clean. Her lovers were a silent young photographer with a sudden laugh and two older men, brothers, who owned a small printing establishment across the street. I wondered at their tastes whenever I glimpsed, with a secret shudder, the higgledy-piggledy striation of black hairs that showed all along her pale shins through the nylon of her stockings with the scientific distinctness of a preparation flattened under glass; or when I felt, at her every movement, the dullish, stalish, not particularly conspicuous but all-pervading and depressing emanation that her seldom-bathed flesh spread from under weary perfumes and creams.

Her father had gambled away the greater part of a comfortable fortune, and her mother's first husband had been of Slav origin, but otherwise Cynthia Vane belonged to a good, respectable family. For aught we know, it may have gone back to kings and soothsayers in the mists of ultimate islands. Transferred to a newer world, to a landscape of doomed, splendid deciduous trees, her ancestry presented, in one of its first phases, a white churchful of farmers against a black thunderhead, and then an imposing array of townsmen engaged in mercantile pursuits, as well as a number of learned men, such as Dr. Jonathan Vane, the gaunt bore (1780–1839), who perished in the conflagration of the steamer "Lexington" to become later an habitué of Cynthia's tilting table. I have always wished to stand genealogy on its head, and here I have an opportunity to do so, for it is the last scion, Cynthia, and Cynthia alone, who will remain of any importance in the Vane dynasty. I am alluding of course to her artistic gift, to her delightful, gay, but not very popular paintings which the friends of her friends bought at long intervals—and I dearly should like to know where they went after her death, those honest and poetical pictures that illuminated her living room—the wonderfully detailed images of metallic things, and my favorite "Seen Through a Windshield"—a windshield partly covered with rime, with a brilliant trickle (from an imaginary car roof) across its transparent part and, through it all, the sapphire flame of the sky and a green and white fir tree.

Cynthia had a feeling that her dead sister was not altogether pleased with her—had discovered by now that she and I had conspired to break her romance; and so, in order to disarm her shade, Cynthia reverted to a rather primitive type of sacrificial offering (tinged, however, with something of Sybil's humor), and began to send to D's business address, at deliberately unfixed dates, such trifles as snapshots of Sybil's tomb in a poor light; cuttings of her own hair which was indistinguishable from Sybil's; a New England sectional map with an inked-in cross, midway between two chaste towns, to mark the spot where D. and Sybil had stopped on October the twenty-third, in broad daylight, at a lenient motel, in a pink and brown forest; and, twice, a stuffed skunk.

Being as a conversationalist more voluble than explicit, she never could describe in full the theory of intervenient auras that she had somehow evolved. Fundamentally there was nothing particularly new about her private creed since it presupposed a fairly conventional hereafter, a silent solarium of immortal souls (spliced with mortal antecedents) whose main recreation consisted of periodical hoverings over the dear quick. The interesting point was a curious practical twist that Cynthia gave to her tame metaphysics. She was sure that her existence was influenced by all sorts of dead friends each of whom took turns in directing her fate much as if she were a stray kitten which a schoolgirl in passing gathers up, and presses to her cheek, and carefully puts down again, near some suburban hedge—to be stroked presently by another transient hand or carried off to a world of doors by some hospitable lady.

For a few hours, or for several days in a row, and sometimes recurrently, in an irregular series, for months or years, anything that happened to Cynthia, after a given person had died, would be, she said, in the manner and mood of that person. The event might be extraordinary, changing the course of one's life; or it might be a string of minute incidents just sufficiently clear to stand out in relief against one's usual day and then shading off into still vaguer trivia as the aura gradually faded. The influence might be good or bad; the main thing was that its source could be identified. It was like walking through a person's soul, she said. I tried to argue that she might not always be able to determine the exact source since not everybody has a recognizable soul; that there are anonymous letters and Christmas presents which anybody might send; that, in fact, what Cynthia called "a usual day" might be itself a weak solution of mixed auras or simply the routine shift of a humdrum guardian angel. And what about God? Did or did not people who would resent any omnipotent dictator on earth look forward to one in heaven? And wars? What a dreadful idea—dead soldiers still fighting with living ones, or phantom armies trying to get at each other through the lives of crippled old men.

But Cynthia was above generalities as she was beyond logic. "Ah, that's Paul," she would say when the soup spitefully boiled over, or: "I guess good Betty Brown is dead"—when she won a beautiful and very welcome vacuum cleaner in a charity lottery. And, with Jamesian meanderings that exasperated my French mind, she would go back to a time when Betty and Paul had not yet departed, and tell me of the showers of well-meant, but odd and quite unacceptable bounties—beginning with an old purse that contained a check for three dollars which she picked up in the street and, of course, returned (to the aforesaid Betty Brown—this is where she first comes in—a decrepit colored woman hardly able to walk), and ending with an insulting proposal from an old beau of hers (this is where Paul comes in) to paint "straight" pictures of his house and family for a reasonable remuneration—all of which followed upon the demise of a certain Mrs. Page, a kindly but petty old party who had pestered her with bits of matter-of-fact advice since Cynthia had been a child.

Sybil's personality, she said, had a rainbow edge as if a little out of focus. She said that had I known Sybil better I would have at once understood how Sybil-like was the aura of minor events which, in spells, had suffused her, Cynthia's, existence after Sybil's suicide. Ever since they had lost their mother they had intended to give up their Boston home and move to New York, where Cynthia's paintings, they thought, would have a chance to be more widely admired; but the old home had clung to them with all its plush tentacles. Dead Sybil, however, had proceeded to separate the house from its view—a thing that affects fatally the sense of home. Right across the narrow street a building project had come into loud, ugly, scaffolded life. A pair of familiar poplars died that spring, turning to blond skeletons. Workmen came and broke up the warm-colored lovely old sidewalk that had a special violet sheen on wet April days and had echoed so memorably to the morning footsteps of museum-bound Mr. Lever, who upon retiring from the business at sixty had devoted a full quarter of a century exclusively to the study of snails.

Speaking of old men, one should add that sometimes these posthumous auspices and interventions were in the nature of parody. Cynthia had been on friendly terms with an eccentric librarian called Porlock who in the last years of his dusty life had been engaged in examining old books for miraculous misprints such as the substitution of "l" for the second "h" in the word "hither." Contrary to Cynthia, he cared nothing for the thrill of obscure predictions; all he sought was the freak itself, the chance that mimics choice, the flaw that looks like a flower; and Cynthia, a much more perverse amateur of misshapen or illicitly connected words, puns, logogriphs, and so on, had helped the poor crank to pursue a quest that in the light of the example she cited struck me as statistically insane. Anyway, she said, on the third day after his death she was reading a magazine and had just come across a quotation from an imperishable poem (that she, with other gullible readers, believed to have been really composed in a dream) when it dawned upon her that "Alph" was a prophetic sequence of the initial letters of Anna Livia Plurabelle (another sacred river running through, or rather around, yet another fake dream), while the additional "h" modestly stood, as a private signpost, for the word that had so hypnotized Mr. Porlock. And I wish I could recollect that novel or short story (by some contemporary writer, I believe) in which, unknown to its author, the first letters of the words in its last paragraph formed, as deciphered by Cynthia, a message from his dead mother.

I am sorry to say that not content with these ingenious fancies Cynthia showed a ridiculous fondness for spiritualism. I refused to accompany her to sittings in which paid mediums took part: I knew too much about that from other sources. I did consent, however, to attend little farces rigged up by Cynthia and her two poker-faced gentlemen-friends of the printing shop. They were podgy, polite and rather eerie old fellows, but I satisfied myself that they possessed considerable wit and culture. We sat down at a light little table, and crackling tremors started almost as soon as we laid our fingertips upon it. I was treated to an assortment of ghosts who rapped out their reports most readily though refusing to elucidate anything that I did not quite catch. Oscar Wilde came and in rapid garbled French, with the usual anglicisms, obscurely accused Cynthia's dead parents of what appeared in my jottings as "*plagiatisme*." A brisk spirit contributed the unsolicited information that he, John Moore, and his brother Bill had been coal miners in Colorado and had perished in an avalanche at "Crested Beauty" in January 1883. Frederic Myers, an old hand at the game, hammered out a piece of verse (oddly resembling Cynthia's own fugitive productions) which in part reads in my notes:

What is this—a conjuror's rabbit,
Or a flawy but genuine gleam—
Which can check the perilous habit
And dispel the dolorous dream?

Finally, with a great crash and all kinds of shudderings and jig-like movements on the part of the table, Leo Tolstoy visited our little group and, when asked to identify himself by specific traits of terrene habitation, launched upon a complex description of what seemed to be some Russian type of architectural woodwork ("figures on boards—man, horse, cock, man, horse, cock"), all of which was difficult to take down, hard to understand and impossible to verify.

I attended two or three other sittings which were even sillier but I must confess that I preferred the childish entertainment they afforded and the cider we drank (Podgy and Pudgy were teetotalers) to Cynthia's awful house parties.

She gave them at the Wheelers' nice flat next door—the sort of arrangement dear to her centrifugal nature, but then, of course, her own living room always looked like a dirty old palette. Following a barbaric, unhygienic, and adulterous custom, the guests' coats, still warm on the inside, were carried by quiet baldish Bob Wheeler into the sanctity of a tidy bedroom and heaped on the conjugal bed. It was also he who poured out the drinks which were passed around by the young photographer while Cynthia and Mrs. Wheeler took care of the canapés.

A late arrival had the impression of lots of loud people unnecessarily grouped within a smoke-blue space between two mirrors gorged with reflections. Because, I suppose, Cynthia wished to be the youngest in the room, the women she used to invite, married or single, were, at the best, in their precarious forties; some of them would bring from their homes, in dark taxis, intact vestiges of good looks, which, however, they lost as the party progressed. It has always amazed me—the capacity sociable weekend revelers have of finding almost at once, by a purely empiric but very precise method, a common denominator of drunkenness, to which everybody loyally sticks before descending, all together, to the next level. The rich friendliness of the matrons was marked by tomboyish overtones, while the fixed inward look of amiably tight men was like a sacrilegious parody of pregnancy. Although some of the guests were connected in one way or another with the arts, there was no inspired talk, no wreathed, elbow-propped heads, and of course no flute girls. From some vantage point where she had been sitting in a stranded mermaid pose on the pale carpet with one or two younger fellows, Cynthia, her face yarnished with a film of beaming sweat, would creep up on her knees, a proffered plate of nuts in one hand, and crisply tap with the other the athletic leg of Cochran or Corcoran, an art dealer, ensconced, on a pearl-gray sofa, between two flushed, happily disintegrating ladies.

At a further stage there would come spurts of more riotous gaiety. Corcoran or Coransky would grab Cynthia or some other wandering woman by the shoulder and lead her into a corner to confort her with a grinning embroglio of private jokes and rumors, whereupon, with a laugh and a toss of her head, she would break away. And still later there would be flurries of intersexual chumminess, jocular reconciliations, a bare fleshy arm flung around another woman's husband (he standing very upright in the midst of a swaying room), or a sudden rush of flirtatious anger, of clumsy pursuit—and the quiet half smile of Bob Wheeler picking up glasses that grew like mushrooms in the shade of chairs.

After one last party of that sort, I wrote Cynthia a perfectly harmless and, on the whole, well-meant note, in which I poked a little Latin fun at some of her guests. I also apologized for not having touched her whiskey, saying that as a Frenchman I preferred the grape to the grain. A few days later I met her on the steps of the Public Library, in the broken sun, under a weak cloudburst, opening her amber umbrella, struggling with a couple of armpitted books (of which I relieved her for a moment), "Footfalls on the Boundary of Another World," by Robert Dale Owen, and something on "Spiritualism and Christianity"; when, suddenly, with no provocation on my part, she blazed out at me with vulgar vehemence, using poisonous words, saying—through pear-shaped drops of sparse rain—that I was a prig and a snob; that I only saw the gestures and disguises of people; that Corcoran had rescued from drowning, in two different oceans, two men—by an irrelevant coincidence both called Corcoran; that romping and screeching Joan Winter had a little girl doomed to grow completely blind in a few months; and that the woman in green with the freckled chest whom I had snubbed in some way or other had written a national best seller in 1932. Strange Cynthia! I had been told she could be thunderously rude to people whom she liked and respected; one had, however, to draw the line somewhere and since I had by then sufficiently studied her interesting auras and other odds and ids, I decided to stop seeing her altogether.

The night D. informed me of Cynthia's death I returned after eleven to the two-storied house I shared, in horizontal section, with an emeritus professor's widow. Upon reaching the porch I looked with the apprehension of solitude at the two kinds of darkness in the two rows of windows: the darkness of absence and the darkness of sleep.

I could do something about the first but could not duplicate the second. My bed gave me no sense of safety; its springs only made my nerves bounce. I plunged into Shakespeare's sonnets—and found myself idiotically checking the first letters of the lines to see what sacramental words they might form. I got FATE (LXX), ATOM (CXX) and, twice, TAFT (LXXXVIII, CXXXI). Every now and then I would glance around to see how the objects in my room were behaving. It was strange to think that if bombs began to fall I would feel little more than a gambler's excitement (and a great deal of earthy relief) whereas my heart would burst if a certain suspiciously tense-looking little bottle on yonder shelf moved a fraction of an inch to one side. The silence, too, was suspiciously compact as if deliberately forming a black backdrop for the nerve flash caused by any small sound of unknown origin. All traffic was dead. In vain did I pray for the groan of a truck up Perkins Street. The woman above who used to drive me crazy by the booming thuds occasioned by what seemed monstrous feet of stone (actually, in diurnal life, she was a small dumpy creature resembling a mummified guinea pig) would have earned my blessings had she now trudged to her bathroom. I put out my light and cleared my throat several times so as to be responsible for at least *that* sound. I thumbed a mental ride with a very remote automobile but it dropped me before I had a chance to doze off. Presently a crackle (due, I hoped, to a discarded and crushed sheet of paper opening like a mean, stubborn night flower)—started and stopped in the waste-paper basket, and my bed-table responded with a little click. It would have been just like Cynthia to put on right then a cheap poltergeist show.

I decided to fight Cynthia. I reviewed in thought the modern era of raps and apparitions, beginning with the knockings of 1848, at the hamlet of Hydesville, N.Y., and ending with grotesque phenomena at Cambridge, Mass.; I evoked the ankle-bones and other anatomical castanets of the Fox sisters (as described by the sages of the University of Buffalo); the mysteriously uniform type of delicate adolescent in bleak Epworth or Tedworth, radiating the same disturbances as in old Peru; solemn Victorian orgies with roses falling and accordions floating to the strains of sacred music; professional impostors regurgitating moist cheesecloth; Mr. Duncan, a lady medium's dignified husband, who, when asked if he would submit to a search, excused himself on the ground of soiled underwear; old Alfred Russel Wallace, the naïve naturalist, refusing to believe that the white form with bare feet and unperforated earlobes before him, at a private pandemonium in Boston, could be prim Miss Cook whom he had just seen asleep, in her curtained corner, all dressed in black, wearing laced-up boots and earrings; two other investigators, small, puny, but reasonably intelligent and active men, closely clinging with arms and legs about Eusapia, a large plump elderly female reeking of garlic, who still managed to fool them; and Dingwall, the sceptical and embarrassed magician, instructed by charming young Margery's "control" not to get lost in the bathrobe's lining but to follow up the left stocking until he reached the bare thigh—upon the warm skin of which he felt a "teleplastic" mass that appeared to the touch uncommonly like cold uncooked liver.

I was appealing to flesh, and the corruption of flesh, to refute and defeat the possible persistence of discarnate life. Alas, these conjurations only enhanced my fear of Cynthia's phantom. Atavistic peace came with dawn, and when I slipped into sleep, the sun through the tawny window shades penetrated a dream that somehow was full of Cynthia.

This was disappointing. Secure in the fortress of daylight, I said to myself that I had expected more. She, a painter of glass-bright minutiae—and now so vague! I lay in bed, thinking my dream over and listening to the sparrows outside: Who knows, if recorded and then run backward, those bird sounds might not become human speech, voiced words, just as the latter become a twitter when reversed? I set myself to reread my dream—backward, diagonally, up, down—trying hard to unravel something Cynthia-like in it, something strange and suggestive that must be there.

I could isolate, consciously, little. Everything seemed blurred, yellow-clouded, yielding nothing tangible. Her inept acrostics, maudlin evasions, theopathies—every recollection formed ripples of mysterious meaning. Everything seemed yellowly blurred, illusive, lost.

QUESTIONS

1. What kind of a person is the narrator? Does our attitude toward him change as the story progresses? Does he inadvertently reveal things about

himself that he may not wish us to know? Do you agree with Cynthia's statement that he is a "prig and a snob"?

2. If the narrator dislikes Cynthia's friends and her house parties, why does he continue to visit her? What is significant about his inability at the end of the story to bring his dream of her back into focus? Why should he want to?
3. Is there anything ironic about Sybil's and Cynthia's names? What multiple meanings do you find in the story for the word "Vane"?
4. Contrast the narrator's attitude toward the sèance at Cynthia's house and his behavior the night he learns of Cynthia's death. How seriously does he regard spiritualism? What is the function of the long list of "raps and apparitions" he gives toward the end of the story?
5. The title of the story would lead us to believe that the story is about Sybil and Cynthia. To what extent is it their story? What kinds of persons are they? How does Cynthia differ from Sybil?
6. Nabokov delights in playing little games with his readers, especially word games. In this story he refers to a "contemporary writer" whose story had an inadvertent acrostic message in its last paragraph. Can you find any acrostics in this story?

James Joyce *(1882–1941), the eldest son of a witty and improvident government officeholder, was born in Dublin. He was educated at Jesuit schools and graduated from University College in 1902. He left Ireland two years later—returning only for a brief visit in 1912—and settled in Trieste as a language teacher in a Berlitz school. During this period he produced a volume of verse,* Chamber Music *(1907), a collection of short stories,* Dubliners *(1915), and an autobiographical novel,* A Portrait of the Artist as a Young Man *(1916). Joyce moved to Zurich during World War I and there began the writing of* Ulysses. *The novel was published in Paris in 1922, two years after Joyce made that city his permanent home. The following years were devoted to the composition of* Finnegans Wake *(1939). Joyce returned to Zurich at the outbreak of World War II and died there of a perforated ulcer.*

Counterparts

JAMES JOYCE

The bell rang furiously and, when Miss Parker went to the tube, a furious voice called out in a piercing North of Ireland accent:

"Send Farrington here!"

Miss Parker returned to her machine, saying to a man who was writing at a desk:

"Mr. Alleyne wants you upstairs."

The man muttered *Blast him!* under his breath and pushed back his chair to stand up. When he stood up he was tall and of great bulk. He had a hanging face, dark wine-colored, with fair eyebrows and mustache: his eyes bulged forward slightly and the whites of them were dirty. He lifted up the counter and, passing by the clients, went out of the office with a heavy step.

He went heavily upstairs until he came to the second landing, where a door bore a brass plate with the inscription *Mr. Alleyne*. Here he halted, puffing with labor and vexation, and knocked. The shrill voice cried:

"Come in!"

The man entered Mr. Alleyne's room. Simultaneously Mr. Alleyne, a little man wearing gold-rimmed glasses on a clean-shaven face, shot his head up over a pile of documents. The head itself was so pink and hairless that it seemed like a large egg reposing on the papers. Mr. Alleyne did not lose a moment:

"Farrington? What is the meaning of this? Why have I always to complain of you? May I ask you why you haven't made a copy of that contract between Bodley and Kirwan? I told you it must be ready by four o'clock."

"But Mr. Shelley said, sir—"

"*Mr. Shelley said, sir*. . . . Kindly attend to what I say and not to what *Mr. Shelley says, sir*. You have always some excuse or another for shirking work. Let me tell you that if the contract is not copied before this evening I'll lay the matter before Mr. Crosbie. . . . Do you hear me now?"

"Yes, sir."

"Do you hear me now? . . . Ay and another little matter! I might as well be talking to the wall as talking to you. Understand once and for all that you get a half an hour for your lunch and not an hour and a half. How many courses do you want, I'd like to know. . . . Do you mind me, now?"

"Yes, sir."

Mr. Alleyne bent his head again upon his pile of papers. The man stared fixedly at the polished skull which directed the affairs of Crosbie & Alleyne, gauging its fragility. A spasm of rage gripped his throat for a few moments and then passed, leaving after it a sharp sensation of thirst. The man recognized the sensation and felt that he must have a good night's drinking. The middle of the month was passed and, if he could get the copy done in time, Mr. Alleyne might give him an order on the cashier. He stood still, gazing fixedly at the head upon the pile of papers. Suddenly Mr. Alleyne began to upset all the papers, searching for something. Then, as if he had been unaware of the man's presence till that moment, he shot up his head again, saying:

"Eh? Are you going to stand there all day? Upon my word, Farrington, you take things easy!"

"I was waiting to see . . ."

"Very good, you needn't wait to see. Go downstairs and do your work."

The man walked heavily towards the door and, as he went out of the room, he heard Mr. Alleyne cry after him that if the contract was not copied by evening Mr. Crosbie would hear of the matter.

He returned to his desk in the lower office and counted the sheets which remained to be copied. He took up his pen and dipped it in the ink but he continued to stare stupidly at the last words he had written: *In no case shall the said Bernard Bodley be* . . . The evening was falling and in a few minutes they would be lighting the gas: then he could write. He felt that he must slake the thirst in his throat. He stood up from his desk and, lifting the counter as before, passed out of the office. As he was passing out the chief clerk looked at him inquiringly.

"It's all right, Mr. Shelley," said the man, pointing with his finger to indicate the objective of his journey.

The chief clerk glanced at the hat-rack but, seeing the row complete, offered no remark. As soon as he was on the landing the man pulled a shepherd's plaid cap out of his pocket, put it on his head and ran quickly down the rickety stairs. From the street door he walked on furtively on the inner side of the path towards the corner and all at once dived into a doorway. He was now safe in the dark snug of O'Neill's shop, and, filling up the little window that looked into the bar with his inflamed face, the color of dark wine or dark meat, he called out:

"Here, Pat, give us a g.p., like a good fellow."

The curate brought him a glass of plain porter. The man drank it at a gulp and asked for a caraway seed. He put his penny on the counter and, leaving the curate to grope for it in the gloom, retreated out of the snug as furtively as he had entered it.

Darkness, accompanied by a thick fog, was gaining upon the dusk of February and the lamps in Eustace Street had been lit. The man went up by the houses until he reached the door of the office, wondering whether he could finish his copy in time. On the stairs a moist pungent odor of perfumes saluted his nose: evidently Miss Delacour had come while he was out in O'Neill's. He crammed his cap back again into his pocket and re-entered the office, assuming an air of absent-mindedness.

"Mr. Alleyne has been calling for you," said the chief clerk severely. "Where were you?"

The man glanced at the two clients who were standing at the counter as if to intimate that their presence prevented him from answering. As the clients were both male the chief clerk allowed himself a laugh.

"I know that game," he said. "Five times in one day is a little bit. . . . Well, you better look sharp and get a copy of our correspondence in the Delacour case for Mr. Alleyne."

This address in the presence of the public, his run upstairs and the porter he had gulped down so hastily confused the man and, as he sat down at his desk to get what was required, he realized how hopeless was the task of finishing his copy of the contract before half past five. The dark damp night was coming and he longed to spend it in the bars, drinking with his friends amid the glare of gas and the clatter of glasses. He got out the Delacour correspondence and passed out of the office. He hoped Mr. Alleyne would not discover that the last two letters were missing.

The moist pungent perfume lay all the way up to Mr. Alleyne's room. Miss Delacour was a middle-aged woman of Jewish appearance. Mr. Alleyne was said to be sweet on her or on her money. She came to the office often and stayed a long time when she came. She was sitting beside his desk now in an aroma of perfumes, smoothing the handle of her umbrella and nodding the great black feather in her hat. Mr. Alleyne had swivelled his chair round to face her and thrown his right foot jauntily upon his left knee. The man put the correspondence on the desk and bowed respectfully but neither Mr. Alleyne nor Miss Delacour took any notice of his bow. Mr. Alleyne tapped a finger on the correspondence and then flicked it towards him as if to say: *That's all right: you can go.*

The man returned to the lower office and sat down again at his desk. He stared intently at the incomplete phrase: *In no case shall the said Bernard Bodley be* . . . and thought how strange it was that the last three words began with the same letter. The chief clerk began to hurry Miss Parker, saying she would never have the letters typed in time for post. The man listened to the clicking of the machine for a few minutes and then set to work to finish his copy. But his head was not clear and his mind wandered away to the glare and rattle of the public-house. It was a night for hot punches. He struggled on with his copy, but when the clock struck five he had still fourteen pages to write. Blast it! He couldn't finish it in time. He longed to execrate aloud, to bring his fist down on something violently. He was so enraged that he wrote *Bernard Bernard* instead of *Bernard Bodley* and had to begin again on a clean sheet.

He felt strong enough to clear out the whole office single-handed. His body ached to do something, to rush out and revel in violence. All the indignities of his life enraged him. . . . Could he ask the cashier privately for an advance? No, the cashier was no good, no damn good: he wouldn't give an advance. . . . He knew where he would meet the boys; Leonard and O'Halloran and Nosey Flynn. The barometer of his emotional nature was set for a spell of riot.

His imagination had so abstracted him that his name was called twice before he answered. Mr. Alleyne and Miss Delacour were standing outside the counter and all the clerks had turned round in anticipation of something. The man got up from his desk. Mr. Alleyne began a tirade of abuse, saying that two letters were missing. The man answered that he knew nothing about them, that he had made a faithful copy. The tirade continued: it was so bitter and violent that the man could hardly restrain his fist from descending upon the head of the manikin before him.

"I know nothing about any other two letters," he said stupidly.

"*You—know—nothing*. Of course you know nothing," said Mr. Alleyne. "Tell me," he added, glancing first for approval to the lady beside him, "do you take me for a fool? Do you think me an utter fool?"

The man glanced from the lady's face to the little egg-shaped head and back again; and, almost before he was aware of it, his tongue had found a felicitous moment:

"I don't think, sir," he said, "that that's a fair question to put to me."

There was a pause in the very breathing of the clerks. Everyone was astounded (the author of the witticism no less than his neighbors) and Miss Delacour, who was a stout amiable person, began to smile broadly. Mr. Alleyne flushed to the hue of a wild rose and his mouth twitched with a dwarf's passion. He shook his fist in the man's face till it seemed to vibrate like the knob of some electric machine:

"You impertinent ruffian! You impertinent ruffian! I'll make short work of you! Wait till you see! You'll apologize to me for your impertinence or you'll quit the office instanter! You'll quit this, I'm telling you, or you'll apologize to me!"

He stood in a doorway opposite the office watching to see if the cashier would come out alone. All the clerks passed out and finally the cashier came out with the chief clerk. It was no use trying to say a word to him when he was with the chief clerk. The man felt that his position was bad enough. He had been obliged to offer an abject apology to Mr. Alleyne for his impertinence but he knew what a hornet's nest the office would be for him. He could remember the way in which Mr. Alleyne had hounded little Peake out of the office in order to make room for his own nephew. He felt savage and thirsty and revengeful, annoyed with himself and with everyone else. Mr. Alleyne would never give him an hour's rest; his life would be a hell to him. He had made a proper fool of himself this time. Could he not keep his tongue in his cheek? But they had never pulled together from the first, he and Mr. Alleyne, ever since the day Mr. Alleyne had overheard him mimicking his North of Ireland accent to amuse Higgins and Miss Parker: that had been the beginning of it. He might have tried Higgins for the money, but sure Higgins never had anything for himself. A man with two establishments to keep up, of course he couldn't. . . .

He felt his great body again aching for the comfort of the public-house. The fog had begun to chill him and he wondered could he touch Pat in O'Neill's. He could not touch him for more than a bob—and a bob was no use. Yet he must get money somewhere or other: he had spent his last penny for the g.p. and soon it would be too late for getting money anywhere. Suddenly, as he was fingering his watch-chain, he thought of Terry Kelly's pawn-office in Fleet Street. That was the dart! Why didn't he think of it sooner?

He went through the narrow alley of Temple Bar quickly, muttering to himself that they could all go to hell because he was going to have a good night of it. The clerk in Terry Kelly's said "A *crown!*" but the consignor held out for six shillings; and in the end the six shillings was allowed him literally. He came out of the pawn-office joyfully, making a little cylinder of the coins between his thumb and fingers. In Westmoreland Street the footpaths were crowded with young men and women returning from business and ragged urchins ran here and there yelling out the names of the evening editions. The man passed through the crowd, looking on the spectacle generally with proud satisfaction and staring masterfully at the office-girls. His head was full of the noises of tram-gongs and swishing trolleys and his nose already sniffed the curling fumes of punch. As he walked on he preconsidered the terms in which he would narrate the incident to the boys:

So, I just looked at him—coolly, you know, and looked at her. Then I looked back at him again—taking my time, you know. *I don't think that that's a fair question to put to me*, says I.

Nosey Flynn was sitting up in his usual corner of Davy Byrne's and, when he heard the story, he stood Farrington a half-one, saying it was as smart a thing as ever he heard. Farrington stood a drink in his turn. After a while O'Halloran and Paddy Leonard came in and the story was repeated to them. O'Halloran stood tailors of malt, hot, all round and told the story of the retort he had made to the chief clerk when he was in Callan's of Fownes's Street; but, as the retort was after the manner of the liberal shepherds in the eclogues, he had to admit that it was not so clever as Farrington's retort. At this Farrington told the boys to polish off that and have another.

Just as they were naming their poisons who should come in but Higgins! Of course he had to join in with the others. The men asked him to give his version of it, and he did so with great vivacity, for the sight of five small hot whiskies was very exhilarating. Everyone roared laughing when he showed the way in which Mr. Alleyne shook his fist in Farrington's face. Then he imitated Farrington, saying, "*And here was my nabs, as cool as you please*," while Farrington looked at the company out of his heavy dirty eyes, smiling and at times drawing forth stray drops of liquor from his mustache with the aid of his lower lip.

When that round was over there was a pause. O'Halloran had money but neither of the other two seemed to have any; so the whole party left the shop somewhat regretfully. At the corner of Duke Street Higgins and Nosey Flynn bevelled off to the left while the other three turned back towards the city. Rain was drizzling down on the cold streets and, when they reached the Ballast Office, Farrington suggested the Scotch House. The bar was full of men and loud with the noise of tongues and glasses. The three men pushed past the whining match-sellers at the door and formed a little party at the corner of the counter. They began to exchange stories. Leonard introduced them to a young fellow named Weathers who was performing at the Tivoli as an acrobat and knockabout *artiste*. Farrington stood a drink all round. Weathers said he would take a small Irish and Apollinaris. Farrington, who had definite notions of what was what, asked the boys would they have an Apollinaris too; but the boys told Tim to make theirs hot. The talk became theatrical. O'Halloran stood a round and then Farrington stood another round, Weathers protesting that the hospitality was too Irish. He promised to get them in behind the scenes and introduce them to some nice girls. O'Halloran said that he and Leonard would go but that Farrington wouldn't go because he was a married man; and Farrington's heavy dirty eyes leered at the company in token that he understood he was being chaffed. Weathers made them all have just one little tincture at his expense and promised to meet them later on at Mulligan's in Poolbeg Street.

When the Scotch House closed they went round to Mulligan's. They went into the parlor at the back and O'Halloran ordered small hot specials all round. They were all beginning to feel mellow. Farrington was just standing another round when Weathers came back. Much to Farrington's relief he drank a glass of bitter this time. Funds were running low but they had enough to keep them going. Presently two young women with big hats and a young man in a check suit came in and sat at a table close by. Weathers saluted them and told the company that they were out of the Tivoli. Farrington's eyes wandered at every moment in the direction of one of the young women. There was something striking in her appearance. An immense scarf of peacock-blue muslin was wound round her hat and knotted in a great bow under her chin; and she wore bright yellow gloves, reaching to the elbow. Farrington gazed admiringly at the plump arm which she moved very often and with much grace; and when, after a little time, she answered his gaze he admired still more her large dark brown eyes. The oblique staring expression in them fascinated him. She glanced at him once or twice and, when the party was leaving the room, she brushed against his chair and said "O, *pardon!*" in a London accent. He watched her leave the room in the hope that she would look back at him, but he was disappointed. He cursed his want of money and cursed all the rounds he had stood, particularly all the whiskies and Apollinaris which he had stood to Weathers. If there was one thing that he hated it was a sponge. He was so angry that he lost count of the conversation of his friends.

When Paddy Leonard called him he found that they were talking about feats of strength. Weathers was showing his biceps muscle to the company and boasting so much that the other two had called on Farrington to uphold the national honor. Farrington pulled up his sleeve accordingly and showed his biceps muscle to the company. The two arms were examined and compared and finally it was agreed to have a trial of strength. The table was cleared and the two men rested their elbows on it, clasping hands. When Paddy Leonard said "*Go!*" each was to try to bring down the other's hand onto the table. Farrington looked very serious and determined.

The trial began. After about thirty seconds Weathers brought his opponent's hand slowly down onto the table. Farrington's dark wine-colored face flushed darker still with anger and humiliation at having been defeated by such a stripling.

"You're not to put the weight of your body behind it. Play fair," he said.

"Who's not playing fair?" said the other.

"Come on again. The two best out of three."

The trial began again. The veins stood out on Farrington's forehead, and the pallor of Weathers' complexion changed to peony. Their hands and arms trembled under the stress. After a long struggle Weathers again brought his opponent's hand slowly onto the table. There was a murmur of applause from the spectators. The curate, who was standing beside the table, nodded his red head towards the victor and said with loutish familiarity:

"Ah! that's the knack!"

"What the hell do you know about it?" said Farrington fiercely, turning on the man. "What do you put in your gab for?"

"Sh, sh!" said O'Halloran, observing the violent expression of Farrington's face. "Pony up, boys. We'll have just one little smahan more and then we'll be off."

A very sullen-faced man stood at the corner of O'Connell Bridge waiting for the little Sandymount tram to take him home. He was full of smoldering anger and revengefulness. He felt humiliated and discontented; he did not even feel drunk; and he had only twopence in his pocket. He cursed everything. He had done for himself in the office, pawned his watch, spent all his money; and he had not even got drunk. He began to feel thirsty again and he longed to be back again in the hot reeking public-house. He had lost his reputation as a strong man, having been defeated twice by a mere boy. His heart swelled with fury and, when he thought of the woman in the big hat who had brushed against him and said "*Pardon!*" his fury nearly choked him.

His tram let him down at Shelbourne Road and he steered his great body along in the shadow of the wall of the barracks. He loathed returning to his home. When he went in by the side-door he found the kitchen empty and the kitchen fire nearly out. He bawled upstairs:

"Ada! Ada!"

His wife was a little sharp-faced woman who bullied her husband when he was sober and was bullied by him when he was drunk. They had five children. A little boy came running down the stairs.

"Who is that?" said the man, peering through the darkness.

"Me, pa."

"Who are you? Charlie?"

"No, pa. Tom."

"Where's your mother?"

"She's out at the chapel."

"That's right. . . . Did she think of leaving any dinner for me?"

"Yes, pa. I—"

"Light the lamp. What do you mean by having the place in darkness? Are the other children in bed?"

The man sat down heavily on one of the chairs while the little boy lit the lamp. He began to mimic his son's flat accent, saying half to himself: *At the chapel. At the chapel, if you please!* When the lamp was lit he banged his fist on the table and shouted:

"What's for my dinner?"

"I'm going . . . to cook it, pa," said the little boy.

The man jumped up furiously and pointed to the fire.

"On that fire! You let the fire out! By God, I'll teach you to do that again!"

He took a step to the door and seized the walking-stick which was standing behind it.

"I'll teach you to let the fire out!" he said, rolling up his sleeve in order to give his arm free play.

The little boy cried "O, *pa!*" and ran whimpering round the table, but the man followed him and caught him by the coat. The little boy looked about him wildly but, seeing no way of escape, fell upon his knees.

"Now, you'll let the fire out the next time!" said the man, striking at him viciously with the stick. "Take that, you little whelp!"

The boy uttered a squeal of pain as the stick cut his thigh. He clasped his hands together in the air and his voice shook with fright.

"O, pa!" he cried. "Don't beat me, pa! And I'll . . . I'll say a *Hail Mary* for you. . . . I'll say a *Hail Mary* for you, pa, if you don't beat me. . . . I'll say a *Hail Mary*. . . ."

QUESTIONS

1. In the story we see Farrington in relation to a number of different characters—Mr. Alleyne, Higgins, O'Halloran, Weathers, the woman from London, his wife, and, finally, his son. What part do each of these relations play in the unfolding of Farrington's character?
2. What is the meaning of the title? Who is counter to whom? Find other instances in which Joyce uses the word *counter*. What various meanings does he convey through this word?
3. In a letter to his brother Stanislaus, Joyce wrote that "If many husbands are brutal, the atmosphere in which they live (vide 'Counterparts') is brutal." This suggests that Joyce might see Farrington as a victim of his society. Does Joyce allow us to feel any sympathy for Farrington? How do we feel about him at the end?
4. Of *Dubliners*, the collection of stories from which "Counterparts" comes, Joyce remarks. "My intention was to write a chapter of the moral history of my country and I chose Dublin for the scene because that city seemed to me the center of paralysis." What evidence of paralysis do you find in the story?
5. Below is the original version of Farrington's encounter with the young woman in the pub. Compare it with the revised version in the text. What is the nature of the changes Joyce makes? How do they affect our understanding of the story?

   Farrington said he wouldn't mind having the far one and began to smile at her but when Weathers offered to introduce her he said "No," he was only chaffing because he knew he had not money enough. She continued to cast bold glances at him and changed the position of her legs often and when she was going out she brushed against his chair and said "Pardon!" in a Cockney accent.
6. Farrington and Bartleby are both legal copyists by trade. Do you see any similarities in the effects of their work on their lives?

POINT OF VIEW

Point of view describes the narrative technique an author uses to tell his story. Unlike the infinite variety of plots, settings, and characters that are at his disposal, the number of available narrative techniques are few. He may decide, as William Faulkner does in "Spotted Horses," to employ a narrator who will relate the events in his own person: this technique is called *first-person* narration.

Yes, sir. Flem Snopes has filled that whole country full of spotted horses. You can hear folks running them all day and all night, whooping and hollering, and the horses running back and forth across them little wooden bridges ever now and then kind of like thunder. Here I was this morning pretty near halfway to town, with the team ambling along and me setting in the buckboard about half asleep, when all of a sudden something come swurging up outen the bushes and jumped the road clean, without touching hoof to it.

It flew right over my team big as a billboard and flying through the air like a hawk. It taken me thirty minutes to stop my team and untangle the harness and the buckboard and hitch them up again.

What does Faulkner achieve by using as his point of view a narrator who is himself a part of the rural Mississippi landscape he describes? For one thing he introduces us to a broad colloquial idiom; for another he places us close to the events of the story. The overall effect is to contribute an air of realism to the fiction, persuading us that what the narrator reports actually happened. But Faulkner goes further than this: he insures the integrity of the narrator by putting him at some distance from the events he relates. "Yes, sir. Flem Snopes has filled that whole country full of spotted horses." The narrator—although he has been "skun" by Flem Snopes in the past—has not been taken in this time by Snopes' scheme to sell "a herd of wild cattymounts" to everyone in town. Therefore he can narrate the events without feeling any pain or hurt pride. Indeed, his detachment, his reflectiveness, his uncanny ability to recite the most hilarious episodes with a pokerface—all these details make him especially suited to convey the comedy and pathos of his small community's life. The point of view, furthermore, has the added virtue of giving unity to the story: we are exposed to a single and consistent view of the characters and events.

The narrator in "Spotted Horses" remains throughout the story a trustworthy commentator on the action. But the first-person point of view can also use a narrator who is directly involved in the events, often so deeply that the reader comes to question his judgment and reliability. Consider the narrator in "The Vane Sisters," an instructor of French literature who by his meddling action has indirectly brought about the suicide of young Sybil Vane. Here we see him describing the Vane family:

Her father had gambled away the greater part of a comfortable fortune, and her mother's first husband had been of Slav origin, but otherwise Cynthia Vane belonged to a good, respectable family.

Although the snobbery displayed in these observations is evident to the reader, the narrator himself is oblivious to it. He assumes the reader will applaud his distaste for wastrels and Eastern Europeans in general while sharing his solid admiration for families both "good" and "respectable"—terms which actually function as ironic comments on the narrator's personality. Near the end of the tale the reader suddenly sees just how mean and chilling the narrator's perceptions actually are. Confronted by Cynthia Vane (who was also indirectly involved in her sister's suicide and who has been suffering immeasurably for it ever since) the narrator reports that

> suddenly, with no provocation on my part, she blazed out at me with vulgar vehemence, using poisonous words, saying—through pear-shaped drops of sparse rain—that I was a prig and a snob; that I only saw the gestures and disguises of people; . . . Strange Cynthia! I had been told she could be thunderously rude to people whom she liked and respected; one had, however, to draw the line somewhere and since I had by then sufficiently studied her interesting auras and other odds and ids, I decided to stop seeing her altogether.

We must remember that in a first-person narrative the narrator remains the reader's sole source of information. Yet in this instance we realize how fundamentally unreliable the narrator is. The melodramatic language he uses ("vulgar vehemence," "poisonous words," "thunderously rude"), the elaborate metaphor ("pear-shaped drops of sparse rain"), the tasteless pun ("odds and ids")—all underline his priggishness, egotism, and self-deception. At this moment in the story Cynthia Vane's suffering becomes sharpened for us by our recognition of the narrator's brutal imperceptiveness.

Vladimir Nabokov achieves two ends through his use of an implicated first-person narrator: he tells a story about the Vane sisters—a tale of passion, remorse, and suffering—while simultaneously telling a story about the narrator—a tale of a meddling and cynical snob, a mean egotist whose crowning feature is his inability to see himself as he really is. Although not all implicated narrators are so unpleasant as Nabokov's (Sherwood Anderson's is sympathetic, and Melville's well-meaning), the method serves to remind us just how much our deepest personal convictions, our unexamined selves, affect our vision and judgment of the world.

Turning from the first-person point of view we encounter what seems the most casual or "natural" method of telling a story——*omniscient* narration. This technique employs a narrator (writing in the third person) who adopts a traditional stance of the storyteller—thoroughly knowledgeable about the characters and events, yet maintaining a discreet distance from the tale. The opening of D. H. Lawrence's "The Rocking-Horse Winner" provides an excellent illustration of the omniscient point of view.

> There was a woman who was beautiful, who started with all the advantages, yet she had no luck. She married for love, and the love turned to dust. She had bonny children, yet she felt they had been thrust upon her, and she could not love them. They looked at her coldly, as if they were finding fault with her. And hurriedly she felt she must cover up some fault in herself. Yet what it was that she must cover up she never knew. Nevertheless, when her children were present, she always felt the center of her heart go hard. This troubled her, and in her manner she was all the more gentle and anxious for her children, as if she loved them very much. Only she herself knew that at the center of her heart was a hard little place that could not feel love, no, not for anybody. Everybody else said of her: "She is such a good mother. She adores her children." Only she herself, and her children themselves, knew it was not so. They read it in each other's eyes.

The narrator begins by summarizing the details about the woman's person and fortune that are necessary for an understanding of the story. He compresses information covering some thirty- or forty-odd years of the woman's life—social background, marriage, love, disillusion, misfortune, children—into a few brief sentences and brings us immediately to the story proper, the events he will now proceed to describe in a more restricted chronological sequence. The most important feature of the passage, however, is the ability of the omniscient narrator to enter the minds of both the mother and children in order to convey to the reader their secret thoughts and feelings. He tells us not just of the woman's beauty and lack of good fortune but specifically of the hardness she felt always at "the center of her heart." By giving the reader an essential insight into the woman's character the narrator sharpens our judgment of her, illuminates for us her relationship with her children, and aids us in understanding the events of the story. Unlike a first-person narrator, who is limited in his report by what he has personally seen or heard and who can under no circumstances enter another character's mind, the omniscient narrator tells us *more* than we could ever possibly know through mere observation. Since we have the privilege of sharing the narrator's knowledge, we are obligated to judge carefully and objectively the characters and events. We should not believe, as everybody else said of her, that the woman in "The Rocking-Horse Winner" is "a good mother" who "adores her children."

When the omniscient narrator enters a character's mind, however, he does it only at a certain expense—the expense of placing the reader at some distance or remove from the character. If we look at the paragraph from Lawrence again we will notice that at no point are we made to feel any close connection with either the woman or the children—although our natural sympathies, as well as the narrator's, tend to be allied with the children and aligned against the mother. Instead we are persuaded to accept the narrator's statements about the woman's and the children's feelings. It should be emphasized that there is nothing improper about the author's not involving the reader intimately with his characters: Lawrence's artistic purpose in "The Rocking-Horse Winner" demands that he keep the reader at some distance from the characters. What is important to remember is that the narrative method in this particular case—the omniscient point of view—creates the distance that exists between the reader and the characters.

Omniscient narration depends upon a literary convention accepted both by the reader and author—that the author is an urbane and civilized man of affairs who interests us with his "stories" or "fictions." In nineteenth-century fiction this convention often led to the habit of authorial intrusion—stopping the action at some particularly heightened moment to comment upon the scene or to generalize upon social, moral, or philosophical matters. An example can be found in Stephen Crane's "The Open Boat." The newspaper corespondent in the story, stranded in an open boat with three other men, has the sudden thought that nature is not cruel to men—merely indifferent. The narrator proceeds to comment:

> It is, perhaps, plausible that a man in this situation, impressed with the unconcern of the universe, should see the innumerable flaws of his life and have them taste wickedly in his mind and wish for another chance. A distinction between right and wrong seems absurdly clear to him, then, in this new ignorance of the grave-edge, and he understands that if he were given another opportunity he would mend his conduct and his words, and be better and brighter during an introduction or at a tea.

As a comment upon the effects of fatigue and fear on the mind of an individual the statement surely seems commonplace enough. By personally appearing in the story and addressing the reader, however, the narrator may disrupt the plot, sacrifice unity, and diminish the illusion of reality which the story creates. Authorial intrusion, common enough in the nineteenth century, has lost favor in our own time. Nevertheless, it does remain a mannerism to which the omniscient point of view is particularly susceptible.

We have seen how the use of a first-person narrator establishes a realistic atmosphere by developing a close rapport between the narrator and the reader. We have also noticed how the narrator's limited knowledge, his inability to penetrate the minds of the other characters, hampers our ability to judge other characters and events—binds us in a sense to the narrator's report. The omniscient narrator, on the other hand, enjoys the luxury of complete knowledge, but because of this he may establish a distance between the reader and the characters.

A third narrative method works to combine the immediacy of the first-person point of view with the scope of omniscient narration. It is called *selective* or *limited omniscience*. Here the author, using the third person, limits himself to a single character's view of the events. In the following example of selective omniscience drawn from "The Scream on 57th Street" we see the action through the eyes of the protagonist, Mrs. Hazlitt.

Standing up, her hand on the hasp of the French window, she felt herself still shaking, not with fear, but with the effort to keep herself from in some way heeding that cry. Again she told herself that she had been born here, knew the city's ways, had not the *auslander's* incredulity about some of them. These ways had hardened since her day, people had warned her, to an indifference beyond that of any civilized city; there were no "good" neighborhoods now, none of any kind really, except the half-hostile enclosure that each family must build for itself. She had discounted this, knowing unsentimentally what city life was; even in the tender version of it that was her childhood there had been noises, human ones, that the most responsible people, the kindest, had shrugged away, saying, "Nothing, dear. Something outside." What she had not taken into account was her own twenty years of living elsewhere, where such a cry in the night would be succored at once if only for gossip's sake, if only because one gave up privacy—anonymity—forever, when one went to live in a house on a road. If only, she thought, holding herself rigid to stop her trembling, because it would be the cry of someone one knew.

Instead of an omniscient narrator telling the reader what Mrs. Hazlitt thought, the technique of selective omniscience draws us into her mind and enables us to witness the terror and loneliness that overcome her. The fear of madness, the panic at being enclosed within the prison of an apartment, the pitiless realization that there can be no escape from the anonymity of the city—all these feelings are heightened and intensified by the selective omniscient point of view. By pulling the reader into a character's mind, the technique shows us the very manner in which an individual apprehends his experience—it creates an extremely intimate psychological realism.

The realism of selective omniscience is so intense, the involvement between reader and character so personal, that we have always to remind ourselves that the character's interpretation of the events may be wrong. As a matter of fact, in our example from Calisher, Mrs. Hazlitt does indeed hear a scream—but as we discover in the story it is her own. A close adherence to the selective omniscient point of view obviously makes exacting demands on the reader's attention. But the artistic compensations surely justify the demands. Unity is achieved by focusing our attention on one character and not distracting us through constant shifts to other characters. Suspense is encouraged by forcing the reader to discover the action simultaneously with the character. And the entailing psychological realism insures the reader's intense involvement with both character and event.

An author chooses a point of view which will most effectively serve his artistic purpose. If his main interest is the compulsive quest for self-discovery that overtakes a basically good man in middle age, and if he wants the reader to share that experience, then the limited omniscient point of view might be best ("The Jolly Corner"). If, on the other hand, he strives to suggest the pathos and sadness that disillusionment can have for an adolescent, and he intends to convey the personal flavor of a young boy's idiom, then the first-person method appears to have a decided advantage ("I'm a Fool"). If the writer has a disposition for a story with a sharply introduced beginning, a carefully developed middle, and a climactic ending, then the omniscient point of view with its ability to give the reader a view of all the characters and events while minimally involving him in the action may be desirable ("My Kinsman, Major Molineux"). There is a single important question to ask when dealing with the problem of point of view: what function does the narrative method have in the story?

Dorothy Canfield Fisher *(1879–1958) was born in Lawrence, Kansas, and attended a girl's school in Paris. She then studied French literature at Ohio State University, the Sorbonne, and Columbia University. Before turning to fiction she established herself as a scholar with studies of Corneille and Racine. Her first novel,* Gunhild, *appeared in 1907. Many short stories followed, including those collected in* Home Fires in France *(1918),* Basque People *(1931), and* A Harvest of Stories *(1956). A supporter of women's suffrage, minority rights, and internationalism, Miss Canfield received a number of awards and distinctions during her lifetime, the most conspicuous being honorary doctorates from a number of colleges and universities, including her two alma maters, Ohio State and Columbia.*

Sex Education

DOROTHY CANFIELD

It was three times—but at intervals of many years—that I heard my Aunt Minnie tell about an experience of her girlhood that had made a never-to-be-forgotten impression on her. The first time was in her thirties, still young. But she had been married for ten years, so that to my group of friends, all in the early teens, she seemed quite of another generation.

The day she told us the story, we had been idling on one end of her porch as we made casual plans for a picnic supper in the woods. Darning stockings at the other end, she paid no attention to us until one of the girls said, "Let's take blankets and sleep out there. It'd be fun."

"No," Aunt Minnie broke in sharply, "you mustn't do that."

"Oh, for goodness' sakes, why not!" said one of the younger girls, rebelliously, "the boys are always doing it. Why can't we, just once."

Aunt Minnie laid down her sewing. "Come here, girls," she said, "I want you should hear something that happened to me when I was your age."

Her voice had a special quality which, perhaps, young people of today would not recognize. But we did. We knew from experience that it was the dark voice grownups used when they were going to say something about sex.

Yet at first what she had to say was like any dull family anecdote; she had been ill when she was fifteen; and afterwards she was run down, thin, with no appetite. Her folks thought a change of air would do her good, and sent her from Vermont out to Ohio—or was it Illinois? I don't remember. Anyway, one of those places where the corn grows high. Her mother's Cousin Ella lived there, keeping house for her son-in-law.

The son-in-law was the minister of the village church. His wife had died some years before, leaving him a young widower with two little girls and a baby boy. He had been a normally personable man then, but the next summer, on the Fourth of July when he was trying to set off some fireworks to amuse his children, an imperfectly manufactured rocket had burst in his face. The explosion had left one side of his face badly scarred. Aunt Minnie made us see it, as she still saw it, in horrid detail; the stiffened, scarlet scar tissue distorting one cheek, the lower lip turned so far out at one corner that the moist red mucous-membrane lining always showed, one lower eyelid hanging loose, and watering.

After the accident, his face had been a long time healing. It was then that his wife's elderly mother had gone to keep house and take care of the children. When he was well enough to be about again, he found his position as pastor of the little church waiting for him. The farmers and village people in his congregation, moved by his misfortune, by his faithful service and by his unblemished character, said they would rather have Mr. Fairchild, even with his scarred face, than any other minister. He was a good preacher, Aunt Minnie told us, "and the way he prayed was kind of exciting. I'd never known a preacher, not to live in the same house with him, before. And when he was in the pulpit, with everybody looking up at him, I felt the way his children did, kind of proud to think we had just eaten breakfast at the same table. I liked to call him 'Cousin Malcolm' before folks. One side of his face was all right, anyhow. You could see from that that he *had* been a good-looking man. In fact, probably one of those ministers that all the women—" Aunt Minnie paused, drew her lips together, and looked at us uncertainly.

Then she went back to the story as it happened—as it happened that first time I heard her tell it. "I thought he was a saint. Everybody out there did. That was all *they* knew. Of course, it made a person sick to look at that awful scar—the drooling corner of his mouth was the worst. He tried to keep that side of his face turned away from folks. But you always knew it was there. That was what kept him from marrying again, so Cousin Ella said. I heard her say lots of times that he knew no woman would touch any man who looked the way he did, not with a ten-foot pole.

"Well, the change of air did do me good. I got my appetite back, and ate a lot and played outdoors a lot with my cousins. They were younger than I (I had my sixteenth birthday there) but I still liked to play games. I got taller and laid on some weight. Cousin Ella used to say I grew as fast as the corn did. Their house stood at the edge of the village. Beyond it was one of those big cornfields they have out West. At the time when I first got there, the stalks were only up to a person's knee. You could see over their tops. But it grew like lightning, and before long, it was the way thick woods are here, way over your head, the stalks growing so close together it was dark under them.

"Cousin Ella told us youngsters that it was lots worse for getting lost in than woods, because there weren't any landmarks in it. One spot in a cornfield looked just like any other. 'You children keep out of it,' she used to tell us almost every day, '*especially you girls*. It's no place for a decent girl. You could easy get so far from the house nobody could hear you if you hollered. There are plenty of men in this town that wouldn't like anything better than—' she never said what.

"In spite of what she said, my little cousins and I had figured out that if we went across one corner of the field, it would be a short cut to the village, and sometimes, without letting on to Cousin Ella, we'd go that way. After the corn got really tall, the farmer stopped cultivating, and we soon beat down a path in the loose dirt. The minute you were inside the field it was dark. You felt it as if you were miles from anywhere. It sort of scared you. But in no time the path turned and brought you out on the far end of Main Street. Your breath was coming fast, maybe, but that was what made you like to do it.

"One day I missed the turn. Maybe I didn't keep my mind on it. Maybe it had rained and blurred the tramped-down look of the path. I don't know what. All of a sudden, I knew I was lost. And the minute

I knew that, I began to run, just as hard as I could run. I couldn't help it, any more than you can help snatching your hand off a hot stove. I didn't know what I was scared of, I didn't even know I *was* running, till my heart was pounding so hard I had to stop.

"The minute I stood still, I could hear Cousin Ella saying, 'There are plenty of men in this town that wouldn't like anything better than—' I didn't know, not really, what she meant. But I knew she meant something horrible. I opened my mouth to scream. But I put both hands over my mouth to keep the scream in. If I made any noise, one of those men would hear me. I thought I heard one just behind me, and whirled around. And then I thought another one had tiptoed up behind me, the other way, and I spun around so fast I almost fell over. I stuffed my hands hard up against my mouth. And then—I couldn't help it—I ran again—but my legs were shaking so I soon had to stop. There I stood, scared to move for fear of rustling the corn and letting the men know where I was. My hair had come down, all over my face. I kept pushing it back and looking around, quick, to make sure one of the men hadn't found out where I was. Then I thought I saw a man coming towards me, and I ran away from him—and fell down, and burst some of the buttons off my dress, and was sick to my stomach—and thought I heard a man close to me and got up and staggered around, knocking into the corn because I couldn't even see where I was going.

"And then, off to one side, I saw Cousin Malcolm. Not a man. The minister. He was standing still, one hand up to his face, thinking. He hadn't heard me.

"I was so *terrible* glad to see him, instead of one of those men, I ran as fast as I could and just flung myself on him, to make myself feel how safe I was."

Aunt Minnie had become strangely agitated. Her hands were shaking, her face was crimson. She frightened us. We could not look away from her. As we waited for her to go on, I felt spasms twitch at the muscles inside my body. "And what do you think that *saint*, that holy minister of the Gospel, did to an innocent child who clung to him for safety? The most terrible look came into his eyes—you girls are too young to know what he looked like. But once you're married, you'll find out. He grabbed hold of me—that dreadful face of his was *right on mine*—and began clawing the clothes off my back."

She stopped for a moment, panting. We were too frightened to speak. She went on, "He had torn my dress right down to the waist before I—then I *did* scream—all I could—and pulled away from him so hard I almost fell down, and ran and all of a sudden I came out of the corn, right in the back yard of the Fairchild house. The children were staring at the corn, and Cousin Ella ran out of the kitchen door. They had heard me screaming. Cousin Ella shrieked out, 'What is it? What happened? Did a man scare you?' And I said, 'Yes, yes, yes, a man—I ran—!' And then I fainted away. I must have. The next thing I knew I was on the sofa in the living room and Cousin Ella was slapping my face with a wet towel."

She had to wet her lips with her tongue before she could go on. Her face was gray now. "There! that's the kind of thing girls' folks ought to tell them about—so they'll know what men are like."

She finished her story as if she were dismissing us. We wanted to go away, but we were too horrified to stir. Finally one of the youngest girls asked in a low trembling voice, "Aunt Minnie, did you tell on him?"

"No, I was ashamed to," she said briefly. "They sent me home the next day anyhow. Nobody ever said a word to me about it. And I never did either. Till now."

By what gets printed in some of the modern child-psychology books, you would think that girls to whom such a story had been told would never develop normally. Yet, as far as I can remember what happened to the girls in that group, we all grew up about like anybody. Most of us married, some happily, some not so well. We kept house. We learned—more or less—how to live with our husbands, we had children and struggled to bring them up right—we went forward into life, just as if we had never been warned not to.

Perhaps, young as we were that day, we had already had enough experience of life so that we were not quite blank paper for Aunt Minnie's frightening story. Whether we thought of it then or not, we couldn't have failed to see that at this very time, Aunt Minnie had been married for ten years or more, comfortably and well married, too. Against what she tried by that story to brand into our minds stood the cheerful home life of that house, the good-natured, kind, hard-working husband, and the children—the three rough-and-tumble, nice little boys, so adored by their parents, and the sweet little girl baby who died, of whom they could never speak without tears. It was such actual contact with adult life that probably kept generation after generation of girls from being scared by tales like Aunt Minnie's into a neurotic horror of living.

Of course, since Aunt Minnie was so much older than we, her boys grew up to be adolescents and young men while our children were still little enough so that our worries over them were nothing more serious than whooping cough and trying to get them to make their own beds. Two of our aunt's three boys followed, without losing their footing, the narrow path which leads across adolescence into normal adult life. But the middle one, Jake, repeatedly fell off into the morass. "Girl trouble," as the succinct family phrase put it. He was one of those boys who have "charm," whatever we mean by that, and was always being snatched at by girls who would be "all wrong" for him to marry. And once, at nineteen, he ran away from home, whether with one of these girls or not we never heard, for through all her ups and downs with this son, Aunt Minnie tried fiercely to protect him from scandal that might cloud his later life.

Her husband had to stay on his job to earn the family living. She was the one who went to find Jake. When it was gossiped around that Jake was in "bad company" his mother drew some money from the family savings-bank account, and silent, white-cheeked, took the train to the city where rumor said he had gone.

Some weeks later he came back with her. With no girl. She had cleared him of that entanglement. As of others, which followed, later. Her troubles seemed over when, at a "suitable" age, he fell in love with a "suitable" girl, married her and took her to live in our shire town, sixteen miles away, where he had a good position. Jake was always bright enough.

Sometimes, idly, people speculated as to what Aunt Minnie had seen that time she went after her runaway son, wondering where her search for him had taken her—very queer places for Aunt Minnie to be in, we imagined. And how could such an ignorant, homekeeping woman ever have known what to say to an errant willful boy to set him straight?

Well, of course, we reflected, watching her later struggles with Jake's erratic ways, she certainly could not have remained ignorant, after seeing over and over what she probably had; after talking with Jake about the things which, a good many times, must have come up with desperate openness between them.

She kept her own counsel. We never knew anything definite about the facts of those experiences of hers. But one day she told a group of us—all then married women—something which gave us a notion about what she had learned from them.

We were hastily making a layette for a not-especially welcome baby in a poor family. In those days, our town had no such thing as a district-nursing service. Aunt Minnie, a vigorous woman of fifty-five, had come in to help. As we sewed, we talked, of course; and because our daughters were near or in their teens, we were comparing notes about the bewildering responsibility of bringing up girls.

After a while, Aunt Minnie remarked. "Well, I hope you teach your girls some *sense*. From what I read, I know you're great on telling them 'the facts,' facts we never heard of when we were girls. Like as not, some facts I don't know, now. But knowing the facts isn't going to do them any more good than *not* knowing the facts ever did, unless they have some sense taught them, too."

"What do you mean, Aunt Minnie?" one of us asked her uncertainly.

She reflected, threading a needle, "Well, I don't know but what the best way to tell you what I mean is to tell you about something that happened to me, forty years ago. I've never said anything about it before. But I've thought about it a good deal. Maybe—"

She had hardly begun when I recognized the story—her visit to her Cousin Ella's Midwestern home, the widower with his scarred face and saintly reputation and, very vividly, her getting lost in the great cornfield. I knew every word she was going to say—to the very end, I thought.

But no, I did not. Not at all.

She broke off, suddenly, to exclaim with impatience, "Wasn't I the big ninny? But not so big a ninny as that old cousin of mine. I could wring her neck for getting me in such a state. Only she didn't know any better, herself. That was the way they brought young people up in those days, scaring them out of their wits about the awfulness of getting lost, but not telling them a thing about how *not* to get lost. Or how to act, if they did.

"If I had had the sense I was born with, I'd have known that running my legs off in a zigzag was the worst thing I could do. I couldn't have been more than a few feet from the path when I noticed I wasn't on it. My tracks in the loose plow dirt must have been perfectly plain. If I'd h' stood still, and collected my wits, I could have looked down to see which way my footsteps went and just walked back over them to the path and gone on about my business.

"Now I ask you, if I'd been told how to do that, wouldn't it have been a lot better protection for me—if protection was what my aunt thought she wanted to give me—than to scare me so at the idea of being lost that I turned deef-dumb-and-blind when I thought I was?

"And anyhow that patch of corn wasn't as big as she let on. And she knew it wasn't. It was no more than a big field in a farming country. I was a well-grown girl of sixteen, as tall as I am now. If I couldn't have found the path, I could have just walked along one line of cornstalks—*straight*—and I'd have come out somewhere in ten minutes, fifteen at the most. Maybe not just where I wanted to go. But all right, safe, where decent folks were living."

She paused, as if she had finished. But at the inquiring blankness in our faces, she went on, "Well, now, why isn't teaching girls—and boys, too, for the Lord's sake don't forget they need it as much as the girls—about this man-and-woman business, something like that? If you give them the idea—no matter whether it's *as* you tell them the facts, or as you *don't* tell them the facts, that it is such a terribly scary thing that if they take a step into it, something's likely to happen to them so awful that you're ashamed to tell them what—well, they'll lose their heads and run around like crazy things, first time they take one step away from the path.

"For they'll be trying out the paths, all right. You can't keep them from it. And a good thing too. How else are they going to find out what it's like? Boys' and girls' going together is a path across one corner of growing up. And when they go together, they're likely to get off the path some. Seems to me, it's up to their folks to bring them up so when they do, they don't start screaming and running in circles, but stand still, right where they are, and get their breath and figure out how to get back.

"And anyhow, you don't tell 'em the truth about sex" (I was astonished to hear her use the actual word, taboo to women of her generation) "if they get the idea from you that it's all there is to living. It's not. If you don't get to where you want to go in it, well, there's a lot of landscape all around it a person can have a good time in.

"D'you know, I believe one thing that gives girls and boys the wrong idea is the way folks *look!* My old cousin's face, I can see her now, it was as red as a rooster's comb when she was telling me about men in that cornfield. I believe now she kind of *liked* to talk about it."

(Oh, Aunt Minnie—and yours! I thought.)

Someone asked, "But how *did* you get out, Aunt Minnie?"

She shook her head, laid down her sewing. "More foolishness. That minister my mother's cousin was keeping house for—her son-in-law—I caught sight of him, down along one of the aisles of cornstalks, looking down at the ground, thinking, the way he often did. And I was so glad to see him I rushed right up to him, and flung my arms around his neck and hugged him. He hadn't heard me coming. He gave a great start, put one arm around me and turned his face full towards me—I suppose for just a second he had forgotten how awful one side of it was. His expression, his eyes—well, you're all married women, you know how he looked, the way any able-bodied man thirty-six or -seven, who'd been married and begotten children, would look—for a minute anyhow, if a full-blooded girl of sixteen, who ought to have known better, flung herself at him without any warning, her hair tumbling down, her dress half unbuttoned, and hugged him with all her might.

"I was what they called innocent in those days. That is, I knew just as little about what men are like as my folks could manage I should. But I was old enough to know all right what that look meant. And it gave me a start. But of course the real thing of it was that dreadful scar of his, so close to my face—that wet corner of his mouth, his eye drawn down with the red inside of the lower eyelid showing—

"It turned me so sick, I pulled away with all my might, so fast that I ripped one sleeve nearly loose, and let out a screech like a wildcat. And ran. Did I run? And in a minute, I was through the corn and had come out in the back yard of the house. I hadn't been more than a few feet from it, probably, any of the time. And then I fainted away. Girls were always fainting away; it was the way our corset strings were pulled tight, I suppose, and then—oh, a lot of fuss.

"But anyhow," she finished, picking up her work and going on, setting neat, firm stitches with steady hands, "there's one thing, I never told anybody it was Cousin Malcolm I had met in the cornfield. I told my old cousin that 'a man had scared me.' And nobody said anything more about it to me, not ever. That was the way they did in those days. They thought if they didn't let on about something, maybe it wouldn't have happened. I was sent back to Vermont right away and Cousin Malcolm went on being minister of the church. I've always been," said Aunt Minnie moderately, "kind of proud that I didn't go and ruin a man's life for just one second's slip-up. If you could have called it that. For it *would* have ruined him. You know how hard as stone people are about other folks' let-downs. If I'd have told, not one person in that town would have had any charity. Not one would have tried to understand. One slip, *once*, and they'd have pushed him down in the mud. If I had told, I'd have felt pretty bad about it, later—when I came to have more sense. But I declare, I can't see how I came to have the decency, dumb as I was then, to know that it wouldn't be fair."

It was not long after this talk that Aunt Minnie's elderly husband died, mourned by her, by all of us. She lived alone then. It was peaceful October weather for her, in which she kept a firm roundness of face and figure, as quiet-living country-women often do, on into her sixties.

But then Jake, the boy who had had girl trouble, had wife trouble. We heard he had taken to running after a young girl, or was it that she was running after him? It was something serious. For his nice wife left him and came back with the children to live with her mother in our town. Poor Aunt Minnie used to go see her for long talks which made them both cry. And she went to keep house for Jake, for months at a time.

She grew old, during those years. When finally she (or something) managed to get the marriage mended so that Jake's wife relented and went back to live with him, there was no trace left of her pleasant brisk freshness. She was stooped and slow-footed and shrunken. We, her kins-people, although we would have given our lives for any one of our own children, wondered whether Jake was worth what it had cost his mother to—well, steady him, or reform him. Or perhaps just understand him. Whatever it took.

She came of a long-lived family and was able to go on keeping house for herself well into her eighties. Of course we and the other neighbors stepped in often to make sure she was all right. Mostly, during those brief calls, the talk turned on nothing more vital than her geraniums. But one midwinter afternoon, sitting with her in front of her cozy stove, I chanced to speak in rather hasty blame of someone who had, I thought, acted badly. To my surprise this brought from her the story about the cornfield which she had evidently quite forgotten telling me, twice before.

This time she told it almost dreamily, swaying to and fro in her rocking chair, her eyes fixed on the long slope of snow outside her window. When she came to the encounter with the minister she said, looking away from the distance and back into my eyes, "I know now that I had been, all along, kind of *interested* in him, the way any girl as old as I was would be, in any youngish man living in the same house with her. And a minister, too. They have to have the gift of gab so much more than most men, women get to thinking they are more alive than men who can't talk so well. I *thought* the reason I threw my arms around him was because I had been so scared. And I certainly had been scared, by my old cousin's horrible talk about the cornfield being full of men waiting to grab girls. But that wasn't all the reason I flung myself at Malcolm Fairchild and hugged him. I know that now. Why in the world shouldn't I have been taught *some* notion of it then? "Twould do girls good to know that they are just like everybody else—human nature *and* sex, all mixed up together. I didn't have to hug him. I wouldn't have, if he'd been dirty or fat and old, or chewed tobacco."

I stirred in my chair, ready to say, "But it's not so simple as all that to tell girls—" and she hastily answered my unspoken protest. "I know, I know, most of it can't be put into words. There just aren't any words to say something that's so both-ways-at-once all the time as this man-and-woman business. But look here, you know as well as I do that there are lots more ways than in words to teach young folks what you want 'em to know."

The old woman stopped her swaying rocker to peer far back into the past with honest eyes. "What was in my mind back there in the cornfield—partly anyhow—was what had been there all the time I was living in the same house with Cousin Malcolm—that he had long straight legs, and broad shoulders, and lots of curly brown hair, and was nice and flat in front, and that one side of his face was good-looking. But most of all, that he and I were really alone, for the first time, without anybody to see us.

"I suppose, if it hadn't been for that dreadful scar, he'd have drawn me up, tight, and—most any man would—kissed me. I know how I must have looked, all red and hot and my hair down and my dress torn open. And, used as he was to big cornfields, he probably never dreamed that the reason I looked that way was because I was scared to be by myself in one. He may have thought—you know what he may have thought.

"Well—if his face had been like anybody's—when he looked at me the way he did, the way a man does look at a woman he wants to have, it would have scared me—some. But I'd have cried, maybe. And probably he'd have kissed me again. You know how such things go. I might have come out of the cornfield halfway engaged to marry him. Why not? I was old enough, as people thought then. That would have been nature. That was probably what he thought of, in that first instant.

"But what did I do? I had one look at his poor, horrible face, and started back as though I'd stepped on a snake. And screamed and ran.

"What do you suppose *he* felt, left there in the corn? He must have been sure that I would tell everybody he had attacked me. He probably thought that when he came out and went back to the village he'd already be in disgrace and put out of the pulpit.

"But the worst must have been to find out, so rough, so plain from the way I acted—as if somebody had hit him with an ax—the way he would look to any woman he might try to get close to. That must have been—" she drew a long breath, "well, pretty hard on him."

After a silence, she murmured pityingly, "Poor man!"

QUESTIONS

1. What is distinctive about Canfield's use of point of view? Who is the principal narrator? What purpose is served by the use of dual narrators?
2. Describe the incident in the cornfield. What distinguishes each recollected account of the incident? How do the listeners react each time? What is significant about the different versions of the story?
3. Is Mr. Fairchild a symbolic character? What does his scarred face symbolize? What does the cornfield symbolize? What function does the color imagery serve in the story?
4. How is the theme of time affected by the point of view? By the setting? How much time elapses during the course of the narrative?
5. Have both major characters been educated by the end of the story? What does "sex education" mean?

Eudora Welty *(1909–) was born in Jackson, Mississippi, and still lives there. She attended Mississippi State College for Women, the University of Wisconsin—where she received a B.A. in English in 1929—and Columbia University. She worked for brief periods in advertising, radio, and journalism. After the appearance of* "Death of a Traveling Salesman" *in* manuscript *in 1936, Miss Welty became a frequent contributor to Albert Erskine's* Southern Review. *Her first volume of stories,* A Curtain of Green *(1941), was followed by* The Wide Net *(1943),* The Golden Apples *(1949), and, more recently,* Thirteen Stories *(1965). Among her novels are* The Ponder Heart *(1954),* The Bride of Innisfallen *(1955),* Losing Battles *(1970), and* The Optimist's Daughter *(1972).*

A Visit of Charity

EUDORA WELTY

It was mid-morning—a very cold, bright day. Holding a potted plant before her, a girl of fourteen jumped off the bus in front of the Old Ladies' Home, on the outskirts of town. She wore a red coat, and her straight yellow hair was hanging down loose from the pointed white cap all the little girls were wearing that year. She stopped for a moment beside one of the prickly dark shrubs with which the city had beautified the Home, and then proceeded slowly toward the building, which was of whitewashed brick and reflected the winter sunlight like a block of ice. As she walked vaguely up the steps she shifted the small pot from hand to hand; then she had to set it down and remove her mittens before she could open the heavy door.

"I'm a Campfire Girl. . . . I have to pay a visit to some old lady," she told the nurse at the desk. This was a woman in a white uniform who looked as if she were cold; she had close-cut hair which stood up on the very top of her head exactly like a sea wave. Marian, the little girl, did not tell her that this visit would give her a minimum of only three points in her score.

"Acquainted with any of our residents?" asked the nurse. She lifted one eyebrow and spoke like a man.

"With any old ladies? No—but—that is, any of them will do," Marian stammered. With her free hand she pushed her hair behind her ears, as she did when it was time to study Science.

The nurse shrugged and rose. "You have a nice *multiflora cineraria* there," she remarked as she walked ahead down the hall of closed doors to pick out an old lady.

There was loose, bulging linoleum on the floor. Marian felt as if she were walking on the waves, but the nurse paid no attention to it. There was a smell in the hall like the interior of a clock. Everything was silent until, behind one of the doors, an old lady of some kind cleared her throat like a sheep bleating. This decided the nurse. Stopping in her tracks, she first extended her arm, bent her elbow, and leaned forward from the hips—all to examine the watch strapped to her wrist; then she gave a loud double-rap on the door.

"There are two in each room," the nurse remarked over her shoulder.

"Two what?" asked Marian without thinking. The sound like a sheep's bleating almost made her turn around and run back.

One old woman was pulling the door open in short, gradual jerks, and when she saw the nurse a strange smile forced her old face dangerously awry. Marian, suddenly propelled by the strong, impatient arm of the nurse, saw next the side-face of another old woman, even older, who was lying flat in bed with a cap on and a counterpane drawn up to her chin.

"Visitor," said the nurse, and after one more shove she was off up the hall.

Marian stood tongue-tied; both hands held the potted plant. The old woman, still with that terrible, square smile (which was a smile of welcome) stamped on her bony face, was waiting. . . . Perhaps she said something. The old woman in bed said nothing at all, and she did not look around.

Suddenly Marian saw a hand, quick as a bird claw, reach up in the air and pluck the white cap off her head. At the same time, another claw to match drew her all the way into the room, and the next moment the door closed behind her.

"My, my, my," said the old lady at her side.

Marian stood enclosed by a bed, a washstand, and a chair; the tiny room had altogether too much furniture. Everything smelled wet—even the bare floor. She held onto the back of the chair, which was wicker and felt soft and damp. Her heart beat more and more slowly, her hands got colder and colder, and she could not hear whether the old women were saying anything or not. She could not see them very clearly. How dark it was! The window shade was down, and the only door was shut. Marian looked at the ceiling. . . . It was like being caught in a robbers' cave, just before one was murdered.

"Did you come to be our little girl for a while?" the first robber asked.

Then something was snatched from Marian's hand—the little potted plant.

"Flowers!" screamed the old woman. She stood holding the pot in an undecided way. "Pretty flowers," she added.

Then the old woman in bed cleared her throat and spoke. "They are not pretty," she said, still without looking around, but very distinctly.

Marian suddenly pitched against the chair and sat down in it.

"Pretty flowers," the first old woman insisted. "Pretty—pretty . . ."

Marian wished she had the little pot back for just a moment—she had forgotten to look at the plant herself before giving it away. What did it look like?

"Stinkweeds," said the other old woman sharply. She had a bunchy white forehead and red eyes like a sheep. Now she turned them toward Marian. The fogginess seemed to rise in her throat again, and she bleated, "Who—are—you?"

To her surprise, Marian could not remember her name. "I'm a Campfire Girl," she said finally.

"Watch out for the germs," said the old woman like a sheep, not addressing anyone.

"One came out last month to see us," said the first old woman.

A sheep or a germ? wondered Marian dreamily, holding onto the chair.

"Did not!" cried the other old woman.

"Did so! Read to us out of the Bible, and we enjoyed it!" screamed the first.

"Who enjoyed it!" said the woman in bed. Her mouth was unexpectedly small and sorrowful, like a pet's.

"We enjoyed it," insisted the other. "You enjoyed it—I enjoyed it."

"We all enjoyed it," said Marian, without realizing that she had said a word.

The first old woman had just finished putting the potted plant high, high on the top of the wardrobe, where it could hardly be seen from below. Marian wondered how she had ever succeeded in placing it there, how she could ever have reached so high.

"You mustn't pay any attention to old Addie," she now said to the little girl. "She's ailing today."

"Will you shut your mouth?" said the woman in bed. "I am not."

"You're a story."

"I can't stay but a minute—really, I can't," said Marian suddenly. She looked down at the wet floor and thought that if she were sick in here they would have to let her go.

With much to-do the first old woman sat down in a rocking chair—still another piece of furniture!—and began to rock. With the fingers of one hand she touched a very dirty cameo pin on her chest. "What do you do at school?" she asked.

"I don't know . . ." said Marian. She tried to think but she could not.

"Oh, but the flowers are beautiful," the old woman whispered. She seemed to rock faster and faster; Marian did not see how anyone could rock so fast.

"Ugly," said the woman in bed.

"If we bring flowers—" Marian began, and then fell silent. She had almost said that if Campfire Girls brought flowers to the Old Ladies' Home, the visit would count one extra point, and if they took a Bible with them on the bus and read it to the old ladies, it counted double. But the old woman had not listened, anyway; she was rocking and watching the other one, who watched back from the bed.

"Poor Addie is ailing. She has to take medicine—see?" she said, pointing a horny finger at a row of bottles on the table, and rocking so high that her black comfort shoes lifted off the floor like a little child's.

"I am no more sick than you are," said the woman in bed.

"Oh, yes you are!"

"I just got more sense than you have, that's all," said the other old woman, nodding her head.

"That's only the contrary way she talks when *you all* come," said the first old lady with sudden intimacy. She stopped the rocker with a neat pat of her feet and leaned toward Marian. Her hand reached over—it felt like a petunia leaf, clinging and just a little sticky.

"Will you hush! Will you hush!" cried the other one.

Marian leaned back rigidly in her chair.

"When I was a little girl like you, I went to school and all," said the old woman in the same intimate, menacing voice. "Not here—another town. . . ."

"Hush!" said the sick woman. "You never went to school. You never came and you never went. You never were anything—only here. You never were born! You don't know anything. Your head is empty, your heart and hands and your old black purse are all empty, even that little old box that you brought with you you brought empty—you showed it to me. And yet you talk, talk, talk, talk, talk all the time until I think I'm losing my mind! Who are you? You're a stranger—a perfect stranger! Don't you know you're a stranger? Is it possible that they have actually done a thing like this to anyone—sent them in a stranger to talk, and rock, and tell away her whole long rigmarole? Do they seriously suppose that I'll be able to keep it up, day in, day out, night in, night out, living in the same room with a terrible old woman—forever?"

Marian saw the old woman's eyes grow bright and turn toward her. This old woman was looking at her with despair and calculation in her face. Her small lips suddenly dropped apart, and exposed a half circle of false teeth with tan gums.

"Come here, I want to tell you something," she whispered. "Come here!"

Marian was trembling, and her heart nearly stopped beating altogether for a moment.

"Now, now, Addie," said the first old woman. "That's not polite. Do you know what's really the matter with old Addie today?" She, too, looked at Marian; one of her eyelids drooped low.

"The matter?" the child repeated stupidly. "What's the matter with her?"

"Why, she's mad because it's her birthday!" said the first old woman, beginning to rock again and giving a little crow as though she had answered her own riddle.

"It is not, it is not!" screamed the old woman in bed. "It is not my birthday, no one knows when that is but myself, and will you please be quiet and say nothing more, or I'll go straight out of my mind!" She turned her eyes toward Marian again, and presently she said in the soft, foggy voice, "When the worst comes to the worst, I ring this bell, and the nurse comes." One of her hands was drawn out from under the patched counterpane—a thin little hand with enormous black freckles. With a finger which would not hold still she pointed to a little bell on the table among the bottles.

"How old are you?" Marian breathed. Now she could see the old woman in bed very closely and plainly, and very abruptly, from all sides, as in dreams. She wondered about her—she wondered for a moment as though there was nothing else in the world to wonder about. It was the first time such a thing had happened to Marian.

"I won't tell!"

The old face on the pillow, where Marian was bending over it, slowly gathered and collapsed. Soft whimpers came out of the small open mouth. It was a sheep that she sounded like—a little lamb. Marian's face drew very close, the yellow hair hung forward.

"She's crying!" She turned a bright, burning face up to the first old woman.

"That's Addie for you," the old woman said spitefully.

Marian jumped up and moved toward the door. For the second time, the claw almost touched her hair, but it was not quick enough. The little girl put her cap on.

"Well, it was a real visit," said the old woman, following Marian through the doorway and all the way out into the hall. Then from behind she suddenly clutched the child with her sharp little fingers. In an affected, high-pitched whine she cried, "Oh, little girl, have you a penny to spare for a poor old woman that's not got anything of her own? We don't have a thing in the world—not a penny for candy—not a thing! Little girl, just a nickel—a penny—"

Marian pulled violently against the old hands for a moment before she was free. Then she ran down the hall, without looking behind her and without looking at the nurse, who was reading *Field & Stream* at her desk. The nurse, after another triple motion to consult her wrist watch, asked automatically the question put to visitors in all institutions: "Won't you stay and have dinner with *us*?"

Marian never replied. She pushed the heavy door open into the cold air and ran down the steps.

Under the prickly shrub she stooped and quickly, without being seen, retrieved a red apple she had hidden there.

Her yellow hair under the white cap, her scarlet coat, her bare knees all flashed in the sunlight as she ran to meet the big bus rocketing through the street.

"Wait for me!" she shouted. As though at an imperial command, the bus ground to a stop.

She jumped on and took a big bite out of the apple.

QUESTIONS

1. Describe the young girl's feelings toward her mission. How do these feelings affect her attitude toward the old ladies? What explains the change in her attitude during the course of the visit?
2. Welty makes conspicuous use of animal and flower imagery. What function does this imagery serve in the story? For example, what kind of a plant is a *multiflora cineraria?*
3. How does the point of view contribute to the theme of innocence? To the theme of charity?
4. How does Welty jar our conventional response to old people? Describe the relationship between the two old ladies.
5. Welty makes use of Christian myth in developing her narrative (the apple at the end is just one obvious clue). How does the use of myth affect the meanings of the story?

Ernest J. Gaines (1933–) was born in rural southern Louisiana and educated at San Francisco State College and Stanford University. The history of Louisiana with its legacy of miscegenation shapes his fiction and characters—poor blacks, creoles, cajuns, and whites of the past and present. His short stories are collected in Bloodline *(1968). Mr. Gaines has also written three novels:* Catherine Carmier *(1964),* Of Love and Dust *(1967), and* The Autobiography of Miss Jane Pittman *(1971), which was televised in 1974 and won an Emmy.*

The Sky Is Gray

ERNEST J. GAINES

1. Go'n be coming in a few minutes. Coming 'round that bend down there full speed. And I'm go'n get out my hankercher and I'm go'n wave it down, and us go'n get on it and go.

I keep on looking for it, but Mama don't look that way no more. She looking down the road where us jest come from. It's a long old road, and far's you can see you don't see nothing but gravel. You got dry weeds on both sides, and you got trees on both sides, and fences on both sides, too. And you got cows in the pastures and they standing close together. And when us was coming out yer to catch the bus I seen the smoke coming out o' the cow's nose.

I look at my mama and I know what she thinking. I been with Mama so much, jest me and her, I know what she thinking all the time. Right now it's home—Auntie and them. She thinking if they got 'nough wood—if she left 'nough there to keep 'em warm till us get back. She thinking if it go'n rain and if any of 'em go'n have to go out in the rain. She thinking 'bout the hog—if he go'n get out, and if Ty and Val be able to get him back in. She always worry like that when she leave the house. She don't worry too much if she leave me there with the smaller ones 'cause she know I'm go'n look after 'em and look after Auntie and everything else. I'm the oldest and she say I'm the man.

I look at my mama and I love my mama. She wearing that black coat and that black hat and she looking sad. I love my mama and I want put my arm 'round her and tell her. But I'm not s'pose to do that. She say that's weakness and that's cry-baby stuff, and she don't want no cry-baby 'round her. She don't want you to be scared neither. 'Cause Ty scared of ghosts and she always whipping him. I'm scared of the dark, too. But I make 'tend I ain't. I make 'tend I ain't 'cause I'm the oldest, and I got to set a good sample for the rest. I can't ever be scared and I can't ever cry. And that's the reason I didn't never say nothing 'bout my teef. It been hurting me and hurting me close to a month now. But I didn't say it. I didn't say it 'cause I didn't want act like no cry-baby, and 'cause I know us didn't have 'nough money to have it pulled. But, Lord, it been hurting me. And look like it won't start till at night when you trying to get little sleep. Then soon's you shet your eyes—umm-umm, Lord, look like it go right down to your heart string.

"Hurting, hanh?" Ty'd say.

I'd shake my head, but I wouldn't open my mouth for nothing. You open your mouth and let that wind in, and it almost kill you.

I'd just lay there and listen to 'em snore. Ty, there, right 'side me, and Auntie and Val over by the fireplace. Val younger 'an me and Ty, and he sleep with Auntie. Mama sleep 'round the other side with Louis and Walker.

I'd just lay there and listen to 'em, and listen to that wind out there, and listen to that fire in the fireplace. Sometimes it'd stop long enough to let me get little rest. Sometimes it just hurt, hurt, hurt. Lord, have mercy.

2. Auntie knowed it was hurting me. I didn't tell nobody but Ty, 'cause us buddies and he ain't go'n tell nobody. But some kind o'way Auntie found out. When she asked me, I told her no, nothing was wrong. But she knowed it all the time. She told me to mash up a piece o' aspirin and wrap it in some cotton and jugg it down in that hole. I did it, but it didn't do no good. It stopped for a little while, and started right back again. She wanted to tell Mama, but I told her Uh-uh. 'Cause I knowed she didn't have no money, and it jest was go'n make her mad again. So she told Monsieur Bayonne, and Monsieur Bayonne came to the house and told me to kneel down 'side him on the fireplace. He put his finger in his mouth and made the Sign of the Cross on my jaw. The tip of Monsieur Bayonne finger is some hard, 'cause he always playing on that guitar. If us sit outside at night us can always hear Monsieur Bayonne playing on his guitar. Sometime us leave him out there playing on the guitar.

He made the Sign of the Cross over and over on my jaw, but that didn't do no good. Even when he prayed and told me to pray some, too, that teef still hurt.

"How you feeling?" he say.

"Same," I say.

He kept on praying and making the Sign of the Cross and I kept on praying, too.

"Still hurting?" he say.

"Yes, sir."

Monsieur Bayonne mashed harder and harder on my jaw. He mashed so hard he almost pushed me on Ty. But then he stopped.

"What kind o' prayers you praying, boy?" he say.

"Baptist," I say.

"Well, I'll be—no wonder that teef still killing him. I'm going one way and he going the other. Boy, don't you know any Catholic prayers?"

"Hail Mary," I say.

"Then you better start saying it."

"Yes, sir."

He started mashing again, and I could hear him praying at the same time. And sure 'nough, afterwhile it stopped.

Me and Ty went outside where Monsieur Bayonne two hounds was, and us started playing with 'em. "Let's go hunting," Ty say. "All right," I say; and us went on back in the pasture. Soon the hounds got on a trail, and me and Ty followed 'em all 'cross the pasture and then back in the woods, too. And then they cornered this little old rabbit and killed him, and me and Ty made 'em get back, and us picked up the rabbit and started on back home. But it had started hurting me again. It was hurting me plenty now, but I wouldn't tell Monsieur Bayonne. That night I didn't sleep a bit, and first thing in the morning Auntie told me go back and let Monsieur Bayonne pray over me some more. Monsieur Bayonne was in his kitchen making coffee when I got there. Soon's he seen me, he knowed what was wrong.

"All right, kneel down there 'side that stove," he say. "And this time pray Catholic. I don't know nothing 'bout Baptist, and don't want know nothing 'bout him."

3. Last night Mama say: "Tomorrow us going to town."

"It ain't hurting me no more," I say. "I can eat anything on it."

"Tomorrow us going to town," she say.

And after she finished eating, she got up and went to bed. She always go to bed early now. 'Fore Daddy went in the Army, she used to stay up late. All o' us sitting out on the gallery or 'round the fire. But now, look like soon's she finish eating she go to bed.

This morning when I woke up, her and Auntie was standing 'fore the fireplace. She say: "'Nough to get there and back. Dollar and a half to have it pulled. Twenty-five for me to go, twenty-five for him. Twenty-five for me to come back, twenty-five for him. Fifty cents left. Guess I get a little piece o' salt meat with that."

"Sure can use it," Auntie say. "White beans and no salt meat ain't white beans."

"I do the best I can," Mama say.

They was quiet after that, and I made 'tend I was still asleep.

"James, hit the floor," Auntie say.

I still made 'tend I was asleep. I didn't want them to know I was listening.

"All right," Auntie say, shaking me by the shoulder. "Come on. Today's the day."

I pushed the cover down to get out, and Ty grabbed it and pulled it back.

"You, too, Ty," Auntie say.

"I ain't getting no teef pulled," Ty say.

"Don't mean it ain't time to get up," Auntie say. "Hit it, Ty."

Ty got up grumbling.

"James, you hurry up and get in your clothes and eat your food," Auntie say. "What time y'all coming back?" she say to Mama.

"That 'leven o'clock bus," Mama say. "Got to get back in that field this evening."

"Get a move on you, James," Auntie say.

I went in the kitchen and washed my face, then I ate my breakfast. I was having bread and syrup. The bread was warm and hard and tasted good. And I tried to make it last a long time.

Ty came back there grumbling and mad at me.

"Got to get up," he say. "I ain't having no teefes pulled. What I got to be getting up for?"

Ty poured some syrup in his pan and got a piece of bread. He didn't wash his hands, neither his face, and I could see that white stuff in his eyes.

"You the one getting your teef pulled," he say. "What I got to get up for. I bet if I was getting a teef pulled, you wouldn't be getting up. Shucks; syrup again. I'm getting tired of this old syrup. Syrup, syrup, syrup. I'm go'n take with the sugar diabetes. I want me some bacon sometime."

"Go out in the field and work and you can have your bacon," Auntie say. She stood in the middle door looking at Ty. "You better be glad you got syrup. Some people ain't got that—hard's time is."

"Shucks," Ty say. "How can I be strong."

"I don't know too much 'bout your strength," Auntie say; "but I know where you go'n be hot at, you keep that grumbling up. James, get a move on you; your mama waiting."

I ate my last piece of bread and went in the front room. Mama was standing 'fore the fireplace warming her hands. I put on my coat and my cap, and we left the house.

4. I look down there again, but it still ain't coming. I almost say, "It ain't coming yet," but I keep my mouth shet. 'Cause that's something else she don't like. She don't like for you to say something just for nothing. She can see it ain't coming, I can see it ain't coming, so why say it ain't coming. I don't say it, and I turn and look at the river that's back o' us. It so cold the smoke just raising up from the water. I see a bunch of pull-doos not too far out—jest on the other side the lilies. I'm wondering if you can eat pull-doos. I ain't too sure, 'cause I ain't never ate none. But I done ate owls and black birds, and I done ate red birds, too. I didn't want kill the red birds, but she made me kill 'em. They had two of 'em back there. One in my trap, one in Ty trap. Me and Ty was go'n play with 'em and let 'em go. But she made me

kill 'em 'cause us needed the food.

"I can't," I say. "I can't."

"Here," she say. "Take it."

"I can't," I say. "I can't. I can't kill him, Mama. Please."

"Here," she say. "Take this fork, James."

"Please, Mama, I can't kill him," I say.

I could tell she was go'n hit me. And I jecked back, but I didn't jeck back soon enough.

"Take it," she say.

I took it and reached in for him, but he kept hopping to the back.

"I can't, Mama," I say. The water just kept running down my face. "I can't."

"Get him out o' there," she say.

I reached in for him and he kept hopping to the back. Then I reached in farther, and he pecked me on the hand.

"I can't Mama," I say.

She slapped me again.

I reached in again, but he kept hopping out my way. Then he hopped to one side, and I reached there. The fork got him on the leg and I heard his leg pop. I pulled my hand out 'cause I had hurt him.

"Give it here," she say, and jecked the fork out of my hand.

She reached and got the little bird right in the neck. I heard the fork go in his neck, and I heard it go in the ground. She brought him out and helt him right in front o' me.

"That's one," she say. She shook him off and gived me the fork. "Get the other one."

"I can't, Mama. I do anything. But I can't do that."

She went to the corner o' the fence and broke the biggest switch over there. I knelt 'side the trap crying.

"Get him out o' there," she say.

"I can't, Mama."

She started hitting me cross the back. I went down on the ground crying.

"Get him," she say.

"Octavia," Auntie say.

'Cause she had come out o' the house and she was standing by the tree looking at us.

"Get him out o' there," Mama say.

"Octavia," Auntie say; "explain to him. Explain to him. Jest don't beat him. Explain to him."

But she hit me and hit me and hit me.

I'm still young. I ain't no more 'an eight. But I know now. I know why I had to. (They was so little, though. They was so little. I 'member how I picked the feathers off 'em and cleaned 'em and helt 'em over the fire. Then us all ate 'em. Ain't had but little bitty piece, but us all had little bitty piece, and ever'body jest looked at me, 'cause they was so proud.) S'pose she had to go away? That's why I had to do it. S'pose she had to go away like Daddy went away? Then who was go'n look after us? They had to be somebody left to carry on. I didn't know it then, but I know it now. Auntie and Monsieur Bayonne talked to me and made me see.

5. Time I see it, I get out my hankercher and start waving. It still 'way down there, but I keep waving anyhow. Then it come closer and stop and me and Mama get on. Mama tell me go sit in the back while she pay. I do like she say, and the people look at me. When I pass the little sign that say White and Colored, I start looking for a seat. I jest see one of 'em back there, but I don't take it, 'cause I want my mama to sit down herself. She come in the back and sit down, and I lean on the seat. They got seats in the front, but I know I can't sit there, 'cause I have to sit back o' the sign. Anyhow, I don't want sit there if my mama go'n sit back here.

They got a lady sitting 'side my mama and she look at me and grin little bit. I grin back, but I don't open my mouth, 'cause the wind'll get in and make that teef hurt. The lady take out a pack o' gum and reach me a slice, but I shake my head. She reach Mama a slice, and Mama shake her head. The lady jest can't understand why a little boy'll turn down gum and she reached me a slice again. This time I point to my jaw. The lady understand and grin little bit, and I grin little bit, but I don't open my mouth, though.

They got a girl sitting 'cross from me. She got on a red overcoat, and her hair plaited in one big plait. First, I make 'tend I don't even see her. But then I start looking at her little bit. She make 'tend she don't see me neither, but I catch her looking that way. She got a cold, and ever' now and then she hist that little hankercher to her nose. She ought to blow it, but she don't. Must think she too much a lady or something.

Ever' time she hist that little hankercher, the lady 'side her say something in her yer. She shake her head and lay her hands in her lap again. Then I catch her kind o' looking where I'm at. I grin at her. But think she'll grin back? No. She turn up her little old nose like I got some snot on my face or something. Well, I show her both o' us can turn us head. I turn mine, too, and look out at the river.

The river is gray. The sky is gray. They have pull-doos on the water. The water is wavey, and the pull-doos go up and down. The bus go 'round a turn, and you got plenty trees hiding the river. Then the bus go 'round another turn, and I can see the river again.

I look to the front where all the white people sitting. Then I look at that little old gal again. I don't look right at her, 'cause I don't want all them people to know I love her. I jest look at her little bit, like I'm looking out that window over there. But she know I'm looking that way, and she kind o' look at me, too. The lady sitting 'side her catch her this time, and she lean over and say something in her yer.

"I don't love him nothing," that little old gal say out loud.

Ever'body back there yer her mouth, and all of 'em look at us and laugh.

"I don't love you, neither," I say. "So you don't have to turn up your nose, Miss."

"You the one looking," she say.

"I wasn't looking at you," I say. "I was looking out that window, there."

"Out that window, my foot," she say. "I seen you. Ever' time I turn 'round you look at me."

"You must o' been looking yourself if you seen me all them times," I say.

"Shucks," she say. "I got me all kind o' boyfriends."

"I got girlfriends, too," I say.

"Well, I just don't want you to get your hopes up," she say.

I don't say no more to that little old gal, 'cause I don't want have to bust her in the mouth. I lean on the seat where Mama sitting, and I don't even look that way no more. When us get to Bayonne, she jugg her little old tongue out at me. I make 'tend I'm go'n hit her, and she duck down 'side her mama. And all the people laugh at us again.

6. Me and Mama get off and start walking in town.Bayonne is a little bitty town. Baton Rouge is a hundred times bigger 'an Bayonne. I went to Baton Rouge once—me, Ty, Mama, and Daddy. But that was 'way back yonder—'fore he went in the Army. I wonder when us go'n see him again. I wonder when. Look like he ain't ever coming home. . . . Even the pavement all cracked in Bayonne. Got grass shooting right out the sidewalk. Got weeds in the ditch, too; jest like they got home.

It some cold in Bayonne. Look like it colder 'an it is home. The wind blow in my face, and I feel that stuff running down my nose. I sniff. Mama say use that hankercher. I blow my nose and put it back.

Us pass a school and I see them white children playing in the yard. Big old red school, and them children jest running and playing. Then us pass a café, and I see a bunch of 'em in there eating. I wish I was in there 'cause I'm cold. Mama tell me keep my eyes in front where they blonks.

Us pass stores that got dummies, and us pass another café, and then us pass a shoe shop, and that baldhead man in there fixing on a shoe. I look at him and I butt into that white lady, and Mama jeck me in front and tell me stay there.

Us come to the courthouse, and I see the flag waving there. This one yer ain't like the one us got at school. This one yer ain't got but a handful of stars. One at school got a big pile of stars—one for ever' state. Us pass it and us turn and there it is—the dentist office. Me and Mama go in, and they got people sitting ever'where you look. They even got a little boy in there younger 'an me.

Me and Mama sit on that bench, and a white lady come in there and ask me what my name. Mama tell her, and the white lady go back. Then I yer somebody hollering in there. And soon's that little boy hear him hollering, he start hollering, too. His mama pat him and pat him, trying to make him hush up, but he ain't thinking 'bout her.

The man that was hollering in there come out holding his jaw.

"Got it, hanh?" another man say.

The man shake his head.

"Man, I thought they was killing you in there," the other man say. "Hollering like a pig under a gate."

The man don't say nothing. He jest head for the door, and the other man follow him.

"John Lee," the white lady say. "John Lee Williams."

The little boy jugg his head down in his mama lap and holler more now. His mama tell him go with the nurse, but he ain't thinking 'bout her. His mama tell him again, but he don't even yer. His mama pick him up and take him in there, and even when the white lady shet the door I can still hear him hollering.

"I often wonder why the Lord let a child like that suffer," a lady say to my mama. The lady's sitting right in front o' us on another bench. She got on a white dress and a black sweater. She must be a nurse or something herself, I reckoned.

"Not us to question," a man say.

"Sometimes I don't know if we shouldn't," the lady say.

"I know definitely we shouldn't," the man say. The man look like a preacher. He big and fat and he got on a black suit. He got a gold chain, too.

"Why?" the lady say.

"Why anything?" the preacher say.

"Yes," the lady say. "Why anything?"

"Not us to question," the preacher say.

The lady look at the preacher a little while and look at Mama again.

"And look like it's the poor who do most the suffering," she say. "I don't understand it."

"Best not to even try," the preacher say. "He works in mysterious ways. Wonders to perform."

Right then Little John Lee bust out hollering, and ever'body turn they head.

"He's not a good dentist," the lady say. "Dr. Robillard is much better. But more expensive. That's why most of the colored people come here. The white people go to Dr. Robillard. Y'all from Bayonne?"

"Down the river," my mama say. And that's all she go'n say, 'cause she don't talk much. But the lady keep on looking at her, and so she say: "Near Morgan."

"I see," the lady say.

7. "That's the trouble with the black people in this country today," somebody else say. This one yer sitting on the same side me and Mama sitting, and he kind o' sitting in front of that preacher. He look like a teacher or somebody that go to college. He got on a suit, and he got a book that he been reading. "We don't question is exactly the trouble," he say. "We should question and question and question. Question everything."

The preacher jest look at him a long time. He done put a toothpick or something in his mouth, and he jest keep turning it and turning it. You can see he don't like that boy with that book.

"Maybe you can explain what you mean," he say.

"I said what I meant," the boy say. "Question everything. Every stripe, every star, every word spoken. Everything."

"It 'pears to me this young lady and I was talking 'bout God, young man," the preacher say.

"Question Him, too," the boy say.

"Wait," the preacher say. "Wait now."

"You heard me right," the boy say. "His existence as well as everything else. Everything."

The preacher jest look 'cross the room at the boy. You can see he getting madder and madder. But mad or no mad, the boy ain't thinking 'bout him. He look at the preacher jest's hard's the preacher look at him.

"Is this what they coming to?" the preacher say. "Is this what we educating them for?"

"You're not educating me," the boy say. "I wash dishes at night to go to school in the day. So even the words you spoke need questioning."

The preacher jest look at him and shake his head.

"When I come in this room and seen you there with your book, I said to myself, There's an intelligent man. How wrong a person can be."

"Show me one reason to believe in the existence of a God," the boy say.

"My heart tell me," the preacher say.

"My heart tells me," the boy say. "My heart tells me. Sure, my heart tells me. And as long as you listen to what your heart tells you, you will have only what the white man gives you and nothing more. Me, I don't listen to my heart. The purpose of the heart is to pump blood throughout the body, and nothing else."

"Who's your paw, boy?" the preacher say.

"Why?"

"Who is he?"

"He's dead."

"And your mom?"

"She's in Charity Hospital with pneumonia. Half killed herself working for nothing."

"And 'cause he's dead and she sick, you mad at the world?"

"I'm not mad at the world. I'm questioning the world. I'm questioning it with cold logic, sir. What do words like Freedom, Liberty, God, White, Colored mean? I want to know. That's why *you* are sending us to school, to read and to ask questions. And because we ask these questions, you call us mad. No, sir, it is not us who are mad."

"You keep saying 'us'?"

" 'Us' . . . why not? I'm not alone."

The preacher jest shake his head. Then he look at ever'body in the room—ever'body. Some of the people look down at the floor, keep from looking at him. I kind o' look 'way myself, but soon's I know he done turn his head, I look that way again.

"I'm sorry for you," he say.

"Why?" the boy say. "Why not be sorry for yourself? Why are you so much better off than I am? Why aren't you sorry for these other people in here? Why not be sorry for the lady who had to drag her child into the dentist office? Why not be sorry for the lady sitting on that bench over there? Be sorry for them. Not for me. Some way or other I'm going to make it."

"No, I'm sorry for you," the preacher say.

"Of course. Of course," the boy say, shaking his head. "You're sorry for me because I rock that pillar you're leaning on."

"You can't ever rock the pillar I'm leaning on, young man. It's stronger than anything man can ever do."

"You believe in God because a man told you to believe in God. A white man told you to believe in God. And why? To keep you ignorant, so he can keep you under his feet."

"So now, we the ignorant?"

"Yes," the boy say. "Yes." And he open his book again.

The preacher jest look at him there. The boy done forgot all about him. Ever'body else make 'tend they done forgot 'bout the squabble, too.

Then I see that preacher getting up real slow. Preacher a great big old man, and he got to brace hisself to get up. He come 'cross the room where the boy is. He jest stand there looking at him, but the boy don't raise his head.

"Stand up, boy," preacher say.

The boy look up at him, then he shet his book real slow and stand up. Preacher jest draw back and hit him in the face. The boy fall 'gainst the wall, but he straighten hisself up and look right back at that preacher.

"You forgot the other cheek," he say.

The preacher hit him again on the other side. But this time the boy don't fall.

"That hasn't changed a thing," he say.

The preacher jest look at the boy. The preacher breathing real hard like he jest run up a hill. The boy sit down and open his book again.

"I feel sorry for you," the preacher say. "I never felt so sorry for a man before."

The boy make 'tend he don't even hear that preacher. He keep on reading his book. The preacher go back and get his hat off the chair.

"Excuse me," he say to us. "I'll come back some other time. Y'all, please excuse me."

And he look at the boy and go out the room. The boy hist his hand up to his mouth one time, to wipe 'way some blood. All the rest o' the time he keep on reading.

8. The lady and her little boy come out the dentist, and the nurse call somebody else in. Then little bit later they come out, and the nurse call another name. But fast's she call somebody in there, somebody else come in the place where we at, and the room stay full.

The people coming in now, all of 'em wearing big coats. One of 'em say something 'bout sleeting, and another one say he hope not. Another one say he think it ain't nothing but rain. 'Cause, he say, rain can get awful cold this time o' year.

All 'cross the room they talking. Some of 'em talking to people right by 'em, some of'em talking to people clare 'cross the room, some of 'em talking to anybody'll listen. It's a little bitty room, no bigger 'an us kitchen, and I can see ever'body in there. The little old room's full of smoke, 'cause you got two old men smoking pipes. I think I feel my teef thumping me some, and I hold my breath and wait. I wait and wait, but it don't thump me no more. Thank God for that.

I feel like going to sleep, and I lean back 'gainst the wall. But I'm scared to go to sleep: Scared 'cause the nurse might call my name and I won't hear her. And Mama might go to sleep, too, and she be mad if neither us heard the nurse.

I look up at Mama. I love my mama. I love my mama. And when cotton come I'm go'n get her a newer coat. And I ain't go'n get a black one neither. I think I'm go'n get her a red one.

"They got some books over there," I say. "Want read one of 'em?"

Mama look at the books, but she don't answer me.

"You got yourself a little man there," the lady say.

Mama don't say nothing to the lady, but she must 'a' grin a little bit, 'cause I seen the lady grinning back. The lady look at me a little while, like she feeling sorry for me.

"You sure got that preacher out here in a hurry," she say to that other boy.

The boy look up at her and look in his book again. When I grow up I want be jest like him. I want clothes like that and I want keep a book with me, too.

"You really don't believe in God?" the lady say.

"No," he say.

"But why?" the lady say.

"Because the wind is pink," he say.

"What?" the lady say.

The boy don't answer her no more. He jest read in his book.

"Talking 'bout the wind is pink," that old lady say. She sitting on the same bench with the boy, and she trying to look in his face. The boy make 'tend the old lady ain't even there. He jest keep reading. "Wind is pink," she say again. "Eh, Lord, what children go'n be saying next?"

The lady 'cross from us bust out laughing.

"That's a good one," she say. "The wind is pink. Yes, sir, that's a good one."

"Don't you believe the wind is pink?" the boy say. He keep his head down in the book.

"Course I believe it, Honey," the lady say. "Course I do." She look at us and wink her eye. "And what color is grass, Honey?"

"Grass? Grass is black."

She bust out laughing again. The boy look at her.

"Don't you believe grass is black?" he say.

The lady quit laughing and look at him. Ever'body else look at him now. The place quiet, quiet.

"Grass is green, Honey," the lady say. "It was green yesterday, it's green today, and it's go'n be green tomorrow."

"How do you know it's green?"

"I know because I know."

"You don't know it's green. You believe it's green because someone told you it was green. If someone had told you it was black you'd believe it was black."

"It's green," the lady say. "I know green when I see green."

"Prove it's green."

"Surely, now," the lady say. "Don't tell me it's coming to that?"

"It's coming to just that," the boy say. "Words mean nothing. One means no more than the other."

"That's what it all coming to?" that old lady say. That old lady got on a turban and she got on two sweaters. She got a green sweater under a black sweater. I can see the green sweater 'cause some of the buttons on the other sweater missing.

"Yes, ma'am," the boy say. "Words mean nothing. Action is the only thing. Doing. That's the only thing."

"Other words, you want the Lord to come down here and show

Hisself to you?" she say.

"Exactly, ma'am."

"You don't mean that, I'm sure?"

"I do, ma'am."

"Done, Jesus," the old lady say, shaking her head.

"I didn't go 'long with that preacher at first," the other lady say; "but now—I don't know. When a person say the grass is black, he's either a lunatic or something wrong."

"Prove to me that it's green."

"It's green because the people say it's green."

"Those same people say we're citizens of the United States."

"I think I'm a citizen."

"Citizens have certain rights. Name me one right that you have. One right, granted by the Constitution, that you can exercise in Bayonne."

The lady don't answer him. She jest look at him like she don't know what he talking 'bout. I know I don't.

"Things changing," she say.

"Things are changing because some black men have begun to follow their brains instead of their hearts."

"You trying to say these people don't believe in God?"

"I'm sure some of them do. Maybe most of them do. But they don't believe that God is going to touch these white people's hearts and change them tomorrow. Things change through action. By no other way."

Ever'body sit quiet and look at the boy. Nobody say a thing. Then the lady 'cross from me and Mama jest shake her head.

"Let's hope that not all your generation feel the same way you do," she say.

"Think what you please, it doesn't matter," the boy say. "But it will be men who listen to their heads and not their hearts who will see that your children have a better chance than you had."

"Let's hope they ain't all like you, though," the old lady say. "Done forgot the heart absolutely."

"Yes, ma'am, I hope they aren't all like me," the boy say. "Unfortunately I was born too late to believe in your God. Let's hope that the ones who come after will have your faith—if not in your God, then in something else, something definitely that they can lean on. I haven't anything. For me, the wind is pink; the grass is black."

9. The nurse come in the room where us all sitting and waiting and

say the doctor won't take no more patients till one o'clock this evening. My mama jump up off the bench and go up to the white lady.

"Nurse, I have to go back in the field this evening," she say.

"The doctor is treating his last patient now," the nurse say. "One o'clock this evening."

"Can I at least speak to the doctor?" my mama say.

"I'm his nurse," the lady say.

"My little boy sick," my mama say. "Right now his teef almost killing him."

The nurse look at me. She trying to make up her mind if to let me come in. I look at her real pitiful. The teef ain't hurting me a tall, but Mama say it is, so I make 'tend for her sake.

"This evening," the nurse say, and go back in the office.

"Don't feel 'jected, Honey," the lady say to Mama. "I been 'round 'em a long time—they take you when they want to. If you was white, that's something else; but you the wrong shade."

Mama don't say nothing to the lady, and me and her go outside and stand 'gainst the wall. It's cold out there. I can feel that wind going through my coat. Some of the other people come out of the room and go up the street. Me and Mama stand there a little while and start to walking. I don't know where us going. When us come to the other street us jest stand there.

"You don't have to make water, do you?" Mama say.

"No, ma'am," I say.

Us go up the street. Walking real slow. I can tell Mama don't know where she going. When us come to a store us stand there and look at the dummies. I look at a little boy with a brown overcoat. He got on brown shoes, too. I look at my old shoes and look at his'n again. You wait till summer, I say.

Me and Mama walk away. Us come up to another store and us stop and look at them dummies, too. Then us go again. Us pass a café where the white people in there eating. Mama tell me keep my eyes in front where they blonks, but I can't help from seeing them people eat. My stomach start to growling 'cause I'm hungry. When I see people eating, I get hungry; when I see a coat, I get cold.

A man whistle at my mama when us go by a filling station. She make 'tend she don't even see him. I look back and I feel like hitting him in the mouth. If I was bigger, I say. If I was bigger, you see.

Us keep on going. I'm getting colder and colder, but I don't say nothing. I feel that stuff running down my nose and I sniff.

"That rag," she say.

I git it out and wipe my nose. I'm getting cold all over now—my face, my hands, my feet, ever'thing. Us pass another little café, but this'n for white people, too, and us can't go in there neither. So us jest walk. I'm so cold now, I'm 'bout ready to say it. If I knowed where us was going, I wouldn't be so cold, but I don't know where us going. Us go, us go, us go. Us walk clean out o' Bayonne. Then us cross the street and us come back. Same thing I seen when I got off the bus. Same old trees, same old walk, same old weeds, same old cracked pave—same old ever'thing.

I sniff again.

"That rag," she say.

I wipe my nose real fast and jugg that hankercher back in my pocket 'fore my hand get too cold. I raise my head and I can see David hardware store. When us come up to it, us go in. I don't know why, but I'm glad.

It warm in there. It so warm in there you don't want ever leave. I look for the heater, and I see it over by them ba'ls. Three white men standing 'round the heater talking in Creole. One of 'em come to see what Mama want.

"Got any ax handle?" she say.

Me, Mama, and the white man start to the back, but Mama stop me when us come to the heater. Her and the white man go on. I hold my hand over the heater and look at 'em. They go all the way in the back, and I see the white man point to the ax handle 'gainst the wall. Mama take one of 'em and shake it like she trying to figure how much it weigh. Then she rub her hand over it from one end to the other. She turn it over and look at the other side, then she shake it again, and shake her head and put it back. She get another one and she do it jest like she did the first one, then she shake her head. Then she get a brown one and do it that, too. But she don't like this one neither. Then she get another one, but 'fore she shake it or anything, she look at me. Look like she trying to say something to me, but I don't know what it is. All I know is I done got warm now and I'm feeling right smart better. Mama shake this ax handle jest like she done the others, and shake her head and say something to the white man. The white man jest look at his pile of ax handle, and when Mama pass by him to come to the front, the white man jest scratch his head and follow her. She tell me come on, and us go on out and start walking again.

Us walk and walk, and no time at all I'm cold again. Look like I'm colder now 'cause I can still remember how good it was back there. My stomach growl and I suck it in to keep Mama from yering it. She walking right 'side me, and it growl so loud you can yer it a mile. But Mama don't say a word.

10. When us come to the courthouse. I look at the clock. It got quarter to twelve. Mean us got another hour and a quarter to be out yer in the cold. Us go and stand 'side a building. Something hit my cap and I look up at the sky. Sleet falling.

I look at Mama standing there. I want stand close 'side her, but she don't like that. She say that's cry-baby stuff. She say you got to stand for yourself, by yourself.

"Let's go back to that office," she say.

Us cross the street. When us get to the dentist I try to open the door, but I can't. Mama push me on the side and she twist the knob. But she can't open it neither. She twist it some more, harder, but she can't open it. She turn 'way from the door. I look at her, but I don't move and I don't say nothing. I done seen her like this before and I'm scared.

"You hungry?" she say. She say it like she mad at me, like I'm the one cause of ever'thing.

"No, ma'am," I say.

"You want eat and walk back, or you rather don't eat and ride?"

"I ain't hungry," I say.

I ain't jest hungry, but I'm cold, too. I'm so hungry and I'm so cold I want cry. And look like I'm getting colder and colder. My feet done got numb. I try to work my toes, but I can't. Look like I'm go'n die. Look like I'm go'n stand right here and freeze to death. I think about home. I think about Val and Auntie and Ty and Louis and Walker. It 'bout twelve o'clock and I know they eating dinner. I can hear Ty making jokes. That's Ty. Always trying to make some kind o' joke. I wish I was right there listening to him. Give anything in the world if I was home 'round the fire.

"Come on," Mama say.

Us start walking again. My feet so numb I can't hardly feel 'em. Us turn the corner and go back up the street. The clock start hitting for twelve.

The sleet's coming down plenty now. They hit the pave and bounce like rice. Oh, Lord; oh, Lord, I pray. Don't let me die. Don't let me die. Don't let me die, Lord.

11. Now I know where us going. Us going back o' town where the colored people eat. I don't care if I don't eat. I been hungry before. I can stand it. But I can't stand the cold.

I can see us go'n have a long walk. It 'bout a mile down there. But I don't mind. I know when I get there I'm go'n warm myself. I think I can hold out. My hands numb in my pockets and my feet numb, too, but if I keep moving I can hold out. Jest don't stop no more, that's all.

The sky's gray. The sleet keep falling. Falling like rain now—plenty, plenty. You can hear it hitting the pave. You can see it bouncing. Sometimes it bounce two times 'fore it settle.

Us keep going. Us don't say nothing. Us jest keep going, keep going.

I wonder what Mama thinking. I hope she ain't mad with me. When summer come I'm go'n pick plenty cotton and get her a coat. I'm go'n get her a red one.

I hope they make it summer all the time. I be glad if it was summer all the time—but it ain't. Us got to have winter, too. Lord, I hate the winter. I guess ever'body hate the winter.

I don't sniff this time. I get out my hankercher and wipe my nose. My hand so cold I can hardly hold the hankercher.

I think us getting close, but us ain't there yet. I wonder where ever'body is. Can't see nobody but us. Look like us the only two people moving 'round today. Must be too cold for the rest of the people to move 'round.

I can hear my teefes. I hope they don't knock together too hard and make that bad one hurt. Lord, that's all I need, for that bad one to start off.

I hear a church bell somewhere. But today ain't Sunday. They must be ringing for a funeral or something.

I wonder what they doing at home. They must be eating. Monsieur Bayonne might be there with his guitar. One day Ty played with Monsieur Bayonne guitar and broke one o' the string. Monsieur Bayonne got some mad with Ty. He say Ty ain't go'n never 'mount to nothing. Ty can go jest like him when he ain't there. Ty can make ever'body laugh mocking Monsieur Bayonne.

I used to like to be with Mama and Daddy. Us used to be happy. But they took him in the Army. Now, nobody happy no more. . . . I be glad when he come back.

Monsieur Bayonne say it wasn't fair for 'em to take Daddy and give Mama nothing and give us nothing. Auntie say, Shhh, Etienne.

Don't let 'em yer you talk like that. Monsieur Bayonne say, It's God truth. What they giving his children? They have to walk three and a half mile to school hot or cold. That's anything to give for a paw? She's got to work in the field rain or shine jest to make ends meet. That's anything to give for a husband? Auntie say, Shhh, Etienne, shhh. Yes, you right, Monsieur Bayonne say. Best don't say it in front of 'em now. But one day they go'n find out. One day. Yes, s'pose so, Auntie say. Then what, Rose Mary? Monsieur Bayonne say. I don't know, Etienne, Auntie say. All us can do is us job, and leave ever'-thing else in His hand. . . .

Us getting closer, now. Us getting closer. I can see the railroad tracks.

Us cross the tracks, and now I see the café. Jest to get in there, I say. Jest to get in there. Already I'm starting to feel little better.

12. Us go in. Ahh, it good. I look for the heater; there 'gainst the wall. One of them little brown ones. I jest stand there and hold my hand over it. I can't open my hands too wide 'cause they almost froze.

Mama standing right 'side me. She done unbuttoned her coat. Smoke rise out the coat, and the coat smell like a wet dog.

I move to the side so Mama can have more room. She open out her hands and rub 'em from hurting. If you let 'em warm too fast, they hurt you sure. But if you let 'em warm jest little bit at a time, and you keep rubbin 'em, they be all right ever' time.

They got jest two more people in the café. A lady back o' the counter, and a man on this side the counter. They been watching us ever since us come in.

Mama get out the hankercher and count the money. Both o' us know how much money she got there. Three dollars. No, she ain't got three dollars. 'Cause she had to pay us way up here. She ain't got but two dollars and a half left. Dollar and a half to get my teef pulled, and fifty cents for us to go back on, and fifty cents worse o' salt meat.

She stir the money 'round with her finger. Most o' the money is change 'cause I can hear it rubbing together. She stir it and stir it. Then she look at the door. It still sleeting. I can yer it hitting 'gainst the wall like rice.

"I ain't hungry, Mama," I say.

"Got to pay 'em something for they heat," she say.

She take a quarter out the hankercher and tie the hankercher up again. She look over her shoulder at the people, but she still don't move. I hope she don't spend the money. I don't want her spend it on me. I'm hungry. I'm almost starving I'm so hungry, but I don't want her spending the money on me.

She flip the quarter over like she thinking. She must be thinking 'bout us walking back home. Lord, I sure don't want walk home. If I thought it done any good to say something, I say it. But my mama make up her own mind.

She turn 'way from the heater right fast, like she better hurry up and do it 'fore she change her mind. I turn to look at her go to the counter. The man and the lady look at her, too. She tell the lady something and the lady walk away. The man keep on looking at her. Her back turn to the man, and Mama don't even know he standing there.

The lady put some cakes and a glass o' milk on the counter. Then she pour up a cup o' coffee and set it 'side the other stuff. Mama pay her for the things and come back where I'm at. She tell me sit down at that table 'gainst the wall.

The milk and the cakes for me. The coffee for my mama. I eat slow, and I look at her. She looking outside at the sleet. She looking real sad. I say to myself, I'm go'n make all this up one day. You see, one day, I'm go'n make all this up. I want to say it now. I want to tell her how I feel right now. But Mama don't like for us to talk like that.

"I can't eat all this," I say.

They got just three little cakes there. And I'm so hungry right now, the Lord know I can eat a hundred times three. But I want her to have one.

She don't even look my way. She know I'm hungry. She know I want it. I let it stay there a while, then I get it and eat it. I eat jest on my front teefes, 'cause if it tech that back teef I know what'll happen. Thank God it ain't hurt me a tall today.

After I finish eating I see the man go to the juke box. He drop a nickel in it, then he jest stand there looking at the record. Mama tell me keep my eyes in front where they blonks. I turn my head like she say, but then I yer the man coming towards us.

"Dance, Pretty?" he say.

Mama get up to dance with him. But 'fore you know it, she done grabbed the little man and done throwed him 'side the wall. He hit the wall so hard he stop the juke box from playing.

"Some pimp," the lady back o' the counter say. "Some pimp."

The little man jump off the floor and start towards my mama. 'Fore you know it, Mama done sprung open her knife and she waiting for him.

"Come on," she say. "Come on. I'll cut you from your neighbo to your throat. Come on."

I go up to the little man to hit him, but Mama make me come and stand 'side her. The little man look at me and Mama and go back to the counter.

"Some pimp," the lady back o' the counter say. "Some pimp." She start laughing and pointing at the little man. "Yes, sir, you a pimp, all right. Yes, sir."

13. "Fasten that coat. Let's go," Mama say.

"You don't have to leave," the lady say.

Mama don't answer the lady, and us right out in the cold again. I'm warm right now—my hands, my yers, my feet—but I know this ain't go'n last too long. It done sleet so much now you got ice ever'where.

Us cross the railroad tracks, and soon's us do, I get cold. That wind go through this little old coat like it ain't nothing. I got a shirt and a sweater under it, but that wind don't pay 'em no mind. I look up and I can see us got a long way to go. I wonder if us go'n make it 'fore I get too cold.

Us cross over to walk on the sidewalk. They got jest one sidewalk back here. It's over there.

After us go jest a little piece, I smell bread cooking. I look, then I see a baker shop. When us get closer, I can smell it more better. I shet my eyes and make 'tend I'm eating. But I keep 'em shet too long and I butt up 'gainst a telephone post. Mama grab me and see if I'm hurt. I ain't bleeding or nothing and she turn me loose.

I can feel I'm getting colder and colder, and I look up to see how far us still got to go. Uptown is 'way up yonder. A half mile, I reckoned. I try to think of something. They say think and you won't get cold. I think of that poem, *Annabel Lee*. I ain't been to school in so long—this bad weather—I reckoned they done passed *Annabel Lee*. But passed it or not, I'm sure Miss Walker go'n make me recite it when I get there. That woman don't never forget nothing. I ain't never seen nobody like that.

I'm still getting cold. *Annabel Lee* or no *Annabel Lee*, I'm still getting cold. But I can see us getting closer. Us getting there gradually.

Soon's us turn the corner, I see a little old white lady up in front o' us. She the only lady on the street. She all in black and she got a long black rag over her head.

"Stop," she say.

Me and Mama stop and look at her. She must be crazy to be out in all this sleet. Ain't got but a few other people out there, and all of 'em men.

"Yall done ate?" she say.

"Jest finished," Mama say.

"Yall must be cold then?" she say.

"Us headed for the dentist," Mama say. "Us'll warm up when us get there."

"What dentist?" the old lady say. "Mr. Bassett?"

"Yes ma'am," Mama say.

"Come on in," the old lady say. "I'll telephone him and tell him yall coming."

Me and Mama follow the old lady in the store. It's a little bitty store, and it don't have much in there. The old lady take off her head piece and fold it up.

"Helena?" somebody call from the back.

"Yes, Alnest?" the old lady say.

"Did you see them?"

"They're here. Standing beside me."

"Good. Now you can stay inside."

The old lady look at Mama. Mama waiting to hear what she brought us in here for. I'm waiting for that, too.

"I saw yall each time you went by," she say. "I came out to catch you, but you were gone."

"Us went back o' town," Mama say.

"Did you eat?"

"Yes, ma'am."

The old lady look at Mama a long time, like she thinking Mama might be jest saying that. Mama look right back at her. The old lady look at me to see what I got to say. I don't say nothing. I sure ain't going 'gainst my mama.

"There's food in the kitchen," she say to Mama. "I've been keeping it warm."

Mama turn right around and start for the door.

"Just a minute," the old lady say. Mama stop. "The boy'll have to work for it. It isn't free."

"Us don't take no handout," Mama say.

"I'm not handing out anything," the old lady say. "I need my garbage moved to the front. Ernest has a bad cold and can't go out there."

"James'll move it for you," Mama say.

"Not unless you eat," the old lady say. "I'm old, but I have my pride, too, you know."

Mama can see she ain't go'n beat this old lady down, so she jest shake her head.

"All right," the old lady say. "Come into the kitchen."

She lead the way with that rag in her hand. The kitchen is a little bitty thing, too. The table and the stove jest about fill it up. They got a little room to the side. Somebody in there laying 'cross the bed. Must be the person she was talking with: Alnest or Ernest—I forget what she call him.

"Sit down," the old lady say to Mama. "Not you," she say to me. "You have to move the cans."

"Helena?" somebody say in the other room.

"Yes, Alnest?" the old lady say.

"Are you going out there again?"

"I must show the boy where the garbage is," the old lady say.

"Keep that shawl over your head," the old man say.

"You don't have to remind me. Come boy," the old lady say.

Us go out in the yard. Little old back yard ain't no bigger 'an the store or the kitchen. But it can sleet here jest like it can sleet in any big back yard. And 'fore you know it I'm trembling.

"There," the old lady say, pointing to the cans. I pick up one of the cans. The can so light I put it back down to look inside o' it.

"Here," the old lady say. "Leave that cap alone."

I look at her in the door. She got that black rag wrapped 'round her shoulders, and she pointing one of her fingers at me.

"Pick it up and carry it to the front," she say. I go by her with the can. I'm sure the thing's empty. She could 'a' carried the thing by herself, I'm sure. "Set it on the sidewalk by the door and come back for the other one," she say.

I go and come back, Mama look at me when I pass her. I get the other can and take it to the front. It don't feel no heavier 'an the other one. I tell myself to look inside and see jest what I been hauling. First, I look up and down the street. Nobody coming. Then I look over my shoulder. Little old lady done slipped there jest 's quiet 's mouse, watching me. Look like she knowed I was go'n try that.

"Ehh, Lord," she say. "Children, children. Come in here, boy, and go wash your hands."

I follow her into the kitchen, and she point, and I go to the bathroom. When I come out, the old lady done dished up the food. Rice, gravy, meat and she even got some lettuce and tomato in a saucer. She even got a glass o' milk and a piece o' cake there, too. It look so good. I almost start eating 'fore I say my blessing.

"Helena?" the old man say.

"Yes, Alnest?" she say.

"Are they eating?"

"Yes," she say.

"Good," he say. "Now you'll stay inside."

The old lady go in there where he is and I can hear 'em talking. I look at Mama. She eating slow like she thinking. I wonder what's the matter now. I reckoned she think 'bout home.

The old lady come back in the kitchen.

"I talked to Dr. Bassett's nurse," she say. "Dr. Bassett will take you as soon as you get there."

"Thank you, ma'am," Mama say.

"Perfectly all right," the old lady say. "Which one is it?"

Mama nod towards me. The old lady look at me real sad. I look sad, too.

"You're not afraid, are you?" she say.

"No'm," I say.

"That's a good boy," the old lady say. "Nothing to be afraid of."

When me and Mama get through eating, us thank the old lady again.

"Helena, are they leaving?" the old man say.

"Yes, Alnest."

"Tell them I say good-by."

"They can hear you, Alnest."

"Good-by both mother and son," the old man say. "And may God be with you."

Me and Mama tell the old man good-by, and us follow the old lady in the front. Mama open the door to go out, but she stop and come back in the store.

"You sell salt meat?" she say.

"Yes."

"Give me two bits worse."

"That isn't very much salt meat," the old lady say.

"That's all I have," Mama say.

The old lady go back o' the counter and cut a big piece off the chunk. Then she wrap it and put it in a paper bag.

"Two bits," she say.

"That look like awful lot of meat for a quarter," Mama say.

"Two bits," the old lady say. "I've been selling salt meat behind this counter twenty-five years. I think I know what I'm doing."

"You got a scale there," Mama say.

"What?" the old lady say.

"Weigh it," Mama say.

"What?" the old lady say. "Are you telling me how to run my business?"

"Thanks very much for the food," Mama say.

"Just a minute," the old lady say.

"James," Mama say to me. I move towards the door.

"Just one minute, I said," the old lady say.

Me and Mama stop again and look at her. The old lady take the meat out the bag and unwrap it and cut 'bout half o' it off. Then she wrap it up again and jugg it back in the bag and give it to Mama. Mama lay the quarter on the counter.

"Your kindness will never be forgotten," she say. "James," she say to me.

Us go out, and the old lady come to the door to look at us. After us go a little piece I look back, and she still there watching us.

The sleet's coming down heavy, heavy now, and I turn up my collar to keep my neck warm. My mama tell me turn it right back down.

"You not a bum," she say. "You a man."

QUESTIONS

1. How does the point of view contribute to the theme of childhood? Is there any discrepancy between the narrator's knowledge and the reader's?
2. Poverty and illness are among the physical conditions that James' family have to contend with. How are these conditions revealed through the setting? What effect do these conditions have on Ty? On Auntie Rosa? On James?
3. Forceful, mean, loving, violent, protective, kind—would any or all of these terms characterize James' mother? What motivates her? Describe her relationship with James.
4. What is the function of the scene between James and the little girl in Section V? Between the preacher and the young man in Section VII? Between the old white lady and James and his mother in Section XIII?
5. What does James' toothache symbolize? The red bird? The title of the story?

Jean-Paul Sartre [*Charles Aymard*] *(1905–) was born in Paris and studied philosophy at the University of Paris. He taught languages in Germany and France while publishing philosophical essays on consciousness. A prisoner of war and member of the Parisian resistance in World War II, Sartre founded the radical political journal* Les Temps Modernes *in 1945.His autobiographical first novel* Nausea *(1938) was followed by a collection of stories,* The Wall *(1939). Sartre acts on his own critical demand for socially engaged literature in such works as the wartime plays* The Flies *(1943) and* No Exit *(1944). In his basic philosophical work* Being and Nothingness *(1943), which established him as one of the most significant philosophers of contemporary society, Sartre asserts the existential position that man must constantly define his essence through action. He has been awarded the Legion of Honor and the Nobel Prize, both of which he refused.*

The Room

JEAN-PAUL SARTRE

Mme. Darbedat held a *rahat-loukoum* between her fingers. She brought it carefully to her lips and held her breath, afraid that the fine dust of sugar that powdered it would blow away. "Just right," she told herself. She bit quickly into its glassy flesh and a scent of stagnation filled her mouth. "Odd how illness sharpens the sensations." She began to think of mosques, of obsequious Orientals (she had been to Algeria for her honeymoon), and her pale lips started in a smile; the *rahat-loukoum* was obsequious too.

Several times she had to pass the palm of her hand over the pages of her book, for in spite of the precaution she had taken they were covered with a thin coat of white powder. Her hand made the little grains of sugar slide and roll, grating on the smooth paper: "That makes me think of Arcachon, when I used to read on the beach." She had spent the summer of 1907 at the seashore. Then she wore a big straw hat with a green ribbon; she sat close to the jetty, with a novel by Gyp or Colette Yver. The wind made swirls of sand rain down upon her knees, and from time to time she had to shake the book, holding it by the corners. It was the same sensation: only the grains of sand were dry while the small bits of sugar stuck a little to the ends of her fingers. Again she saw a band of pearl grey sky above a black sea. "Eve wasn't born yet." She felt herself all weighted down with memories and precious as a coffer of sandalwood. The name of the book she used to read suddenly came back to mind: it was called *Petite Madame*, not at all boring. But ever since an unknown illness had confined her to her room she preferred memories and historical works.

She hoped that suffering, heavy readings, a vigilant attention to her memories and the most exquisite sensations would ripen her as a lovely hothouse fruit.

She thought, with some annoyance, that her husband would soon be knocking at her door. On other days of the week he came only in the evening, kissed her brow in silence, and read *Le Temps*, sitting in the armchair across from her. But Thursday was M. Darbedat's *day:* he spent an hour with his daughter, generally from three to four. Before going he stopped in to see his wife and both discussed their son-in-law with bitterness. These Thursday conversations, predictable to their slightest detail, exhausted Mme. Darbedat. M. Darbedat filled the quiet room with his presence. He never sat, but walked in circles about the quiet room. Each of his outbursts wounded Mme. Darbedat like a glass splintering. This particular Thursday was worse than usual: at the thought that it would soon be necessary to repeat Eve's confessions to her husband, and to see his great terrifying body convulse with fury, Mme. Darbedat broke out in a sweat. She picked up a *loukoum* from the saucer, studied it for a while with hesitation, then sadly set it down: she did not like her husband to see her eating *loukoums*.

She heard a knock and started up. "Come in," she said weakly.

M. Darbedat entered on tiptoe. "I'm going to see Eve," he said, as he did every Thursday. Mme. Darbedat smiled at him. "Give her a kiss for me."

M. Darbedat did not answer and his forehead wrinkled worriedly: every Thursday at the same time, a muffled irritation mingled with the load of his digestion. "I'll stop in and see Franchot after leaving her, I wish he'd talk to her seriously and try to convince her."

He made frequent visits to Dr. Franchot. But in vain. Mme. Darbedat raised her eyebrows. Before, when she was well, she shrugged her shoulders. But since sickness had weighted down her body, she replaced the gestures which would have tired her by plays of emotion in the face: she said *yes* with her eyes, *no* with the corners of her mouth: she raised her eyebrows instead of her shoulders.

"There should be some way to take him away from her by force."

"I told you already it was impossible. And besides, the law is very poorly drawn up. Only the other day Franchot was telling me that they have a tremendous amount of trouble with the families: people who can't make up their mind, who want to keep the patient at home; the doctors' hands are tied. They can give their dvice, period. That's all. He would," he went on, "have to make a public scandal or else she would have to ask to have him put away herself."

"And that," said Mme. Darbedat, "isn't going to happen tomorrow."

"No." He turned to the mirror and began to comb his fingers through his beard. Mme. Darbedat looked at the powerful red neck of her husband without affection.

"If she keeps on," said M. Darbedat, "she'll be crazier than he is. It's terribly unhealthy. She doesn't leave his side, she only goes out to see you. She has no visitors. The air in their room is simply unbreathable. She never opens the window because Pierre doesn't want it open. As if you should ask a sick man. I believe they burn incense, some rubbish in a little pan, you'd think it was a church. Really, sometimes I wonder . . . she's got a funny look in her eyes, you know."

"I haven't noticed," Mme. Darbedat said. "I find her quite normal. She looks sad, obviously."

"She has a face like an unburied corpse. Does she sleep? Does she eat? but we aren't supposed to ask her about those things. But I should think that with a fellow like Pierre next to her, she wouldn't sleep a wink all night." He shrugged his shoulders. "What I find amazing is that we,, her parents, don't have the right to protect her against herself. Understand that Pierre would be much better cared for by Franchot. There's a big park. And besides, I think," he added, smiling a little, "he'd get along much better with people of his own type.

People like that are children, you have to leave them alone with each other; they form a sort of freemasonry. That's where he should have been put the first day and for his own good, I'd say. Of course it's in his own best interest."

After a moment, he added, "I tell you I don't like to know she's alone with Pierre, especially at night. Suppose something happened. Pierre has a very sly way about him."

"I don't know," Mme. Darbedat said, "if there's any reason to worry. He always looked like that. He always seemed to be making fun of the world. Poor boy," she sighed, "to have had his pride and then come to that. He thought he was cleverer than all of us. He had a way of saying 'You're right' simply to end the argument. . . . It's a blessing for him that he can't see the state he's in."

She recalled with displeasure the long, ironic face, always turned a little to the side. During the first days of Eve's marriage, Mme. Darbedat asked nothing more than a little intimacy with her son-in-law. But he had discouraged her: he almost never spoke, he always agreed quickly and absent-mindedly.

M. Darbedat pursued his idea. "Franchot let me visit his place," he said. "It was magnificent. The patients have private rooms with leather armchairs, if you please, and day-beds. You know, they have a tennis court and they're going to build a swimming pool."

He was planted before the window, looking out, rocking a little on his bent legs. Suddenly he turned lithely on his heel, shoulders lowered, hands in his pockets. Mme. Darbedat felt she was going to start perspiring. It was the same thing every time. Now he was pacing back and forth like a bear in a cage and his shoes squeaked at every step.

"Please, please, won't you sit down. You're tiring me." Hesitating, she added, "I have something important to tell you."

M. Darbedat sat in the armchair and put his hands on his knees; a slight chill ran up Mme. Darbedat's spine: the time had come, she had to speak.

"You know," she said with an embarrassed cough, "I saw Eve on Tuesday."

"Yes."

"We talked about a lot of things, she was very nice, she hasn't been so confiding for a long time. Then I questioned her a little. I got her to talk about Pierre. Well, I found out," she added, again embarrassed, "that she is *very* attached to him."

"I know that too damned well," said M. Darbedat.

He irritated Mme. Darbedat a little; she always had to explain things in such detail. Mme. Darbedat dreamed of living in the company of fine and sensitive people who would understand her slightest word.

"But I mean," she went on, "that she is attached to him *differently* than we imagined."

M. Darbedat rolled furious, anxious eyes, as he always did when he never completely grasped the sense of an allusion or something new.

"What does that all mean?"

"Charles," said Mme. Darbedat, "don't tire me. You should understand a mother has difficulty in telling certain things."

"I don't understand a damned word of anything you say," M. Darbedat said with irritation. "You can't mean . . . ?"

"Yes," she said.

"They're still . . . now, still . . . ?"

"Yes! Yes! Yes!" she said, in three annoyed and dry little jolts.

M. Darbedat spread his arms, lowered his head and was silent.

"Charles," his wife said, worriedly, "I shouldn't have told you. But I couldn't keep it to myself."

"Our child," he said slowly. "With that madman! He doesn't even recognize her any more. He calls her Agatha. She must have lost all sense of her own dignity."

He raised his head and looked at his wife severely. "You're sure you aren't mistaken?"

"No possible doubt. Like you," she added quickly, "I couldn't believe her and I still can't. The mere idea of being touched by that wretch . . . So . . . ," she sighed, "I suppose that's how he holds on to her."

"Do you remember what I told you," M. Darbedat said, "when he came to ask for her hand? I told you I thought he pleased Eve *too much*. You wouldn't believe me." He struck the table suddenly, blushing violently. "It's perversity! He takes her in his arms, kisses her and calls her Agatha, selling her on a lot of nonsense about flying statues and God knows what else! Without a word from her! But what in heaven's name's between those two? Let her be sorry for him, let her put him in a sanitorium and see him every day—fine. But I never thought . . . I considered her a widow. Listen, Jeannette," he said gravely, "I'm going to speak frankly to you; if she had any sense, I'd rather see her take a lover!"

"Be quiet, Charles!" Mme. Darbadat cried.

M. Darbedat wearily took his hat and the cane he had left on the stool. "After what you've just told me," he concluded, "I don't have much hope left. In any case, I'll have a talk with her because it's my duty."

Mme. Darbedat wished he would go quickly.

"You know," she said to encourage him, "I think Eve is more headstrong than . . . than anything. She knows he's incurable but she's obstinate, she doesn't want to be in the wrong."

M. Darbedat stroked his beard absently.

"Headstrong? Maybe so. If you're right, she'll finally get tired of it. He's not always pleasant and he doesn't have much to say. When I say hello to him he gives me a flabby handshake and doesn't say a word. As soon as they're alone, I think they go back to his obsessions: she tells me sometimes he screams as though his throat were being cut because of his hallucinations. He sees statues. They frighten him because they buzz. He says they fly around and make fishy eyes at him."

He put on his gloves and continued, "She'll get tired of it, I'm not saying she won't. But suppose she goes crazy before that? I wish she'd go out a little, see the world: she'd meet some nice young man—well, someone like Schroeder, an engineer with Simplon, somebody with a future, she could see him a little here and there and she'd get used to the idea of making a new life for herself."

Mme. Darbedat did not answer, afraid of starting the conversation up again. Her husband bent over her.

"So," he said, "I've got to be on my way."

"Goodbye, Papa," Mme. Darbedat said, lifting her forehead up to him. "Kiss her for me and tell her for me she's a poor dear."

Once her husband had gone, Mme. Darbedat let herself drift to the bottom of her armchair and closed her eyes, exhausted. "What vitality," she thought reproachfully. As soon as she got a little strength back, she quietly stretched out her pale hand and took a *loukoum* from the saucer, groping for it without opening her eyes.

Eve lived with her husband on the sixth floor of an old building on the Rue du Bac. M. Darbedat slowly climbed the 112 steps of the stairway. He was not even out of breath when he pushed the bell. He remembered with satisfaction the words of Mlle. Dormoy: "Charles, for your age, you're simply marvelous." Never did he feel himself stronger and healthier than on Thursday, especially after these invigorating climbs.

Eve opened the door: that's right, she doesn't have a maid. No girls *can* stay with her. I can put myself in their place. He kissed her. "Hello, poor darling."

Eve greeted him with a certain coldness.

"You look a little pale," M. Darbedat said, touching her cheek. "You don't get enough exercise."

There was a moment of silence.

"Is Mama well?" Eve asked.

"Not good, not too bad. You saw her Tuesday? Well, she's just the same. Your Aunt Louise came to see her yesterday, that pleased her. She likes to have visitors, but they can't stay too long. Aunt Louise came to Paris for that mortgage business. I think I told you about it, a very odd sort of affair. She stopped in at the office to ask my advice. I told her there was only one thing to do: sell. She found a taker, by the way: Bretonnel. You remember Bretonnel. He's retired from business now."

He stopped suddenly: Eve was hardly listening. He thought sadly that nothing interested her any more. It's like the books. Before you had to tear them away from her. Now she doesn't even read any more.

"How is Pierre?"

"Well," Eve said. "Do you want to see him?"

"Of course," M. Darbedat said gaily. "I'd like to pay him a little call."

He was full of compassion for this poor young man, but he could not see him without repugnance. *I detest unhealthy people*. Obviously, it was not Pierre's fault: his heredity was terribly loaded down. M. Darbedat sighed: *All the precautions are taken in vain, you find out these things too late*. No, Pierre was not responsible. But still he had always carried that fault in him; it formed the base of his character; it wasn't like cancer or tuberculosis, something you could always put aside when you wanted to judge a man as he is. His nervous grace, the subtlety which pleased Eve so much when he was courting her were the flowers of madness. He was already mad when he married her, only you couldn't tell.

It makes you wonder, thought M. Derbedat, *where responsibility begins, or rather, where it ends*. In any case, he was always analyzing himself too much, always turned in on himself. But was it the cause or effect of his sickness? He followed his daughter through a long, dim corridor.

"This apartment is too big for you," he said. "You ought to move out."

"You say that every time, Papa," Eve answered, "but I've already told you Pierre doesn't want to leave his room."

Eve was amazing. Enough to make you wonder if she realized her husband's state. He was insane enough to be in a strait-jacket and she respected his decisions and advice as if he still had good sense.

"What I'm saying is for your own good." M. Darbedat went on, somewhat annoyed, "It seems to me that if I were a woman I'd be afraid of these badly lighted old rooms. I'd like to see you in a bright apartment, the kind they're putting up near Auteuil, three airy little rooms. They lowered the rents because they couldn't find tenants; this would be just the time."

Eve quietly turned the doorknob and they entered the room. M. Darbedat's throat tightened at the heavy odor of incense. The curtains were drawn. In the shadows he made out a thin neck above the back of an armchair: Pierre's back was turned. He was eating.

"Hello, Pierre," M. Darbedat said, raising his voice. "How are we today?" He drew near him. The sick man was seated in front of a small table; he looked sly.

"I see we had soft-boiled eggs," M. Darbedat said, raising his voice higher. "That's good!"

"I'm not deaf," Pierre said quietly.

Irritated, M. Darbedat turned his eyes toward Eve as his witness. But Eve gave him a hard glance and was silent. M. Darbedat realized he had hurt her. Too bad for her. It was impossible to find just the right tone for this boy. He had less sense than a child of four and Eve wanted him treated like a man. M. Darbedat could not keep himself from waiting with impatience for the moment when all this ridiculous business would be finished. Sick people always annoyed him a little—especially madmen because they were wrong. Poor Pierre, for example, was wrong all along the line, he couldn't speak a reasonable word and yet it would be useless to expect the least humility from him, or even temporary recognition of his errors.

Eve cleared away the eggshells and the cup. She put a knife and fork in front of Pierre.

"What's he going to eat now?" M. Darbedat said jovially.

"A steak."

Pierre had taken the fork and held it in the ends of his long, pale fingers. He inspected it minutely and then gave a slight laugh.

"I can't use it this time," he murmured, setting it down, "I was warned."

Eve came in and looked at the fork with passionate interest.

"Agatha," Pierre said, "give me another one."

Eve obeyed and Pierre began to eat. She had taken the suspect fork and held it tightly in her hands, her eyes never leaving it; she seemed to make a violent effort. How suspicious all their gestures and relationships are! thought M. Darbedat.

He was uneasy.

"Be careful, Pierre, take it by the middle because of the prongs."

Eve sighed and laid the fork on the serving table. M. Darbedat felt his gall rising. He did not think it well to give in to all this poor man's whims—even from Pierre's viewpoint it was pernicious. Franchot had said, "One must never enter the delirium of a madman." Instead of giving him another fork, it would have been better to have reasoned quietly and made him understand that the first was like all the others.

He went to the serving table, took the fork ostentatiously and tested the prongs with a light finger. Then he turned to Pierre. But the latter was cutting his meat peacefully: he gave his father-in-law a gentle, inexpressive glance.

"I'd like to have a little talk with you," M. Darbedat said to Eve.

She followed him docilely into the salon. Sitting on the couch, M. Darbedat realized he had kept the fork in his hand. He threw it on the table.

"It's much better here," he said.

"I never come here."

"All right to smoke?"

"Of course, Papa," Eve said hurriedly. "Do you want a cigar?"

M. Darbedat preferred to roll a cigarette. He thought eagerly of the discussion he was about to begin. Speaking to Pierre he felt as embarrassed about his reason as a giant about his strength when playing with a child. All his qualities of clarity, sharpness, precision, turned against him; *I must confess it's somewhat the same with my poor Jeannette*. Certainly Mme. Darbedat was not insane, but this illness had . . . stultified her. Eve, on the other hand, took after her father . . . a straight, logical nature; discussion with her was a pleasure. *That's why I don't want them to ruin her.* M. Darbedat raised his eyes. Once again he wanted to see the fine intelligent features of his daughter. He was disappointed with this face; once so reasonable and transparent, there was now something clouded and opaque in it. Eve had always been beautiful. M. Darbedat noticed she was made up with great care, almost with pomp. She had blued her eyelids and put mascara on her long lashes. This violent and perfect make-up made a painful impression on her father.

"You're green beneath your rouge," he told her. "I'm afraid you're getting sick. And the way you make yourself up now! You used to be so discreet."

Eve did not answer and for an embarrassed moment M. Darbedat considered this brilliant, worn-out face beneath the heavy mass of black hair. He thought she looked like a tragedian. *I even know who she looks like. That woman . . . the Roumanian who played Phèdre in French at the Mur d'Orange.* He regretted having made so disagreeable a remark. *It escaped me! Better not worry her with little things.*

"Excuse me," he said smiling, "you know I'm an old purist. I don't like all these creams and paints women stick on their face today. But I'm in the wrong. You must live in your time."

Eve smiled amiably at him. M. Darbedat lit a cigarette and drew several puffs.

"My child," he began, "I wanted to talk with you; the two of us are going to talk the way we used to. Come, sit down and listen to me nicely; you must have confidence in your old Papa."

"I'd rather stand," Eve said. "What did you want to tell me?"

"I am going to ask you a single question," M. Darbedat said a little more dryly. "Where will all this lead you?"

"All this?" Eve asked astonished.

"Yes . . . all this whole life you've made for yourself. Listen," he went on, "don't think I don't understand you (he had a sudden illumination)" but what you want to do is beyond human strength. You want to live solely by imagination, isn't that it? You don't want to admit he's sick. You don't want to see the Pierre of today, do you? You have eyes only for the Pierre of before. My dear, my darling little girl, it's an impossible bet to win," M. Darbedat continued. "Now I'm going to tell you a story which perhaps you don't know. When we were at Sables-d'Olonne—you were three years old—your mother made the acquaintance of a charming young woman with a superb little boy. You played on the beach with this little boy, you were thick as thieves, you were engaged to marry him. A while later, in Paris, your mother wanted to see this young woman again; she was told she had had a terrible accident. That fine little boy's head was cut off by a car. They told your mother, 'Go and see her, but above all don't talk to her about the death of her child, she *will not* believe he is dead.' Your mother went, she found a half-mad creature: she lived as though her boy was still alive; she spoke to him, she set his place at the table. She lived in such a state of nervous tension that after six months they had to take her away by force to a sanitorium where she was obliged to stay three years. No, my child," M. Darbedat said, shaking his head, "these things are impossible. It would have been better if she had recognized the truth courageously. She would have suffered once, then time would have erased with its sponge. There is nothing like looking things in the face, believe me."

"You're wrong," Eve said with effort. "I know very well that Pierre is . . ."

The word did not escape. She held herself very straight and put her hands on the back of the armchair: there was something dry and ugly in the lower part of her face.

"So . . . ?" asked M. Darbedat, astonished.

"So . . . ?"

"You . . . ?"

"I love him as he is," said Eve rapidly and with an irritated look.

"Not true," M. Darbedat said forcefully. "It isn't true: you don't love him, you can't love him. You can only feel that way about a healthy, normal person. You pity Pierre, I don't doubt it, and surely you have the memory of three years of happiness he gave you. But don't tell me you love him. I won't believe you."

Eve remained wordless, staring at the carpet absently.

"You could at least answer me," M. Darbedat said coldly. "Don't think this conversation has been any less painful for me than it has for you."

"More than you think."

"Well then, if you love him," he cried, exasperated, "it is a great misfortune for you, for me, and for your poor mother because I'm going to tell you something I would rather have hidden from you.

Before three years Pierre will be sunk in complete dementia, he'll be like a beast."

He watched his daughter with hard eyes; he was angry at her for having compelled him, by stubbornness, to make this painful revelation.

Eve was motionless; she did not so much as raise her eyes.

"I knew."

"Who told you?" he asked stupefied.

"Franchot. I knew six months ago."

"And I told him to be careful with you," said M. Darbedat with bitterness. "Maybe it's better. But under those circumstances you must understand that it would be unpardonable to keep Pierre with you. The struggle you have undertaken is doomed to failure, his illness won't spare him. If there were something to be done, if we could save him by care, I'd say yes. But look: you're pretty, intelligent, gay, you're destroying yourself willingly and without profit. I know you've been admirable, but now it's over . . . done, you've done your duty and more; now it would be immoral to continue. We also have duties to ourselves, child. And then you aren't thinking about us. You must," he repeated, hammering the words, "send Pierre to Franchot's clinic. Leave this apartment where you've had nothing but sorrow and come home to us. If you want to be useful and ease the sufferings of someone else, you have your mother. The poor woman is cared for by nurses, she needs someone closer to her, and *she*," he added, "can appreciate what you do for her and be grateful."

There was a long silence. M. Darbedat heard Pierre singing in the next room. It was hardly a song, rather a sort of sharp, hasty recitative. M. Darbedat raised his eyes to his daughter.

"It's no, then?"

"Pierre will stay with me," she said quietly. "I get along well with him."

"By living like an animal all day long?"

Eve smiled and shot a glance at her father, strange, mocking and almost gay. *It's true*, Mr. Darbedat thought furiously, *that's not all they do; they sleep together*.

"You are completely mad," he said, rising.

Eve smiled sadly and murmured, as if to herself, "Not enough so."

"Not enough? I can only tell you one thing, my child. You frighten me."

He kissed her hastily and left. Going down the stairs he thought, *we should send out two strong-arm men who'd take the poor imbecile away and stick him under a shower without asking his advice on the matter.*

It was a fine autumn day, calm and without mystery; the sunlight gilded the faces of the passers-by. M. Darbedat was struck with the simplicity of the faces; some weather-beaten, others smooth, but they reflected all the happiness and care with which he was so familiar.

I know exactly what I resent in Eve, he told himself, entering the Boulevard St. Germain. *I resent her living outside the limits of human nature. Pierre is no longer a human being: in all the care and all the love she gives him she deprives human beings of a little. We don't have the right to refuse ourselves to the world; no matter what, we live in society.*

He watched the faces of the passers-by with sympathy; he loved their clear, serious looks. In these sunlit streets, in the midst of mankind, one felt secure, as in the midst of a large family.

A woman stopped in front of an open-air display counter. She was holding a little girl by the hand.

"What's that?" the little girl asked, pointing to a radio set.

"Mustn't touch," her mother said. "It's a radio; it plays music."

They stood for a moment without speaking, in ecstasy. Touched, M. Darbedat bent down to the little girl and smiled.

II

"He's gone." The door closed with a dry snap. Eve was alone in the salon. *I wish he'd die.*

She twisted her hands around the back of the armchair: she had just remembered her father's eyes. M. Darbedat was bent over Pierre with a competent air; he had said "That's good!" the way someone says when they speak to invalids. He had looked and Pierre's face had been painted in the depths of his sharp, bulging eyes. *I hate him when he looks at him because I think he sees him.*

Eve's hands slid along the armchair and she turned to the window. She was dazzled. The room was filled with sunlight, it was everywhere, in pale splotches on the rug, in the air like a blinding dust. Eve was not accustomed to this diligent, indiscreet light which darted from everywhere, scouring all the corners, rubbing the furniture like a busy housewife and making it glisten. However, she went to the window and raised the muslin curtain which hung against the pane. Just at that moment M. Darbedat left the building; Eve suddenly caught sight of his broad shoulders. He raised his head and looked at the sky, blinking, then with the stride of a young man he walked away. *He's straining himself*, thought Eve, *soon he'll have a stitch in the side*. She hardly hated him any longer: there was so little in that head; only the tiny worry of appearing young. Yet rage took her again when she saw him turn the corner of the Boulevard St. Germain and disappear. *He's thinking about Pierre*. A little of their life had escaped from the closed room and was being dragged through the streets, in the sun, among the people. *Can they never forget about us?*

The Rue du Bac was almost deserted. An old lady crossed the street with mincing steps; three girls passed, laughing. Then men, strong, serious men carrying briefcases and talking among themselves. *Normal people*, thought Eve, astonished at finding such a powerful hatred in herself. A handsome, fleshy woman ran heavily toward an elegant gentleman. He took her in his arms and kissed her on the mouth. Eve gave a hard laugh and let the curtain fall.

Pierre sang no more but the woman on the fourth floor was playing the piano; she played a Chopin Etude. Eve felt calmer; she took a step toward Pierre's room but stopped almost immediately and leaned against the wall in anguish; each time she left the room, she was panic-stricken at the thought of going back. Yet she knew she could live nowhere else: she loved the room. She looked around it with cold curiosity as if to gain a little time—this shadowless, odorless room where she waited for her courage to return. *You'd think it was a dentist's waiting room*. Armchairs of pink silk, the divan, the tabourets were somber and discreet, a little fatherly; man's best friends. Eve imagined these grave gentlemen dressed in light suits, all like the ones she saw at the window, entering the room, continuing a conversation already begun. They did not even take time to reconnoiter, but advanced with firm step to the middle of the room; one of them, letting his hand drag behind him like a wake, in passing knocked over cushions, objects on the table, and was never disturbed by their contact. And when a piece of furniture was in their way, these poised men, far from making a detour to avoid it, quietly changed its place. Finally they sat down, still plunged in their conversation, without even glancing behind them. A *living-room for normal people*, thought Eve. She stared at the knob of the closed door and anguish clutched her throat: *I must go back. I never leave him alone so long.* She would have to open the door, then stand for a moment on the threshold, trying to accustom her eyes to the shadow, and the room would push her back with all its strength. Eve would have to triumph over this resistance and enter all the way into the heart of the room. Suddenly she wanted violently to see Pierre; she would have liked to make fun of M. Darbedat with him. But Pierre had no need of her; Eve could not foresee the welcome he had in store for her. Suddenly she thought with a sort of pride that she had no place anywhere. *Normal people think I belong with them. But I couldn't stay an hour among them. I need to live out there, on the other side of the wall. But they don't want me out there.*

A profound change was taking place around her. The light had grown old and greying: it was heavy, like the water in a vase of flowers that hasn't been changed since the day before. In this aged light Eve found a melancholy she had long forgotten—the melancholy of an autumn afternoon that was ending. She looked around her, hesitant, almost timid: all that was so far away. There was neither day nor night nor season nor melancholy in the room. She vaguely recalled autumns long past, autumns of her childhood, then suddenly she stiffened: she was afraid of memories.

She heard Pierre's voice. "Agatha! Where are you?"

"Coming!" she cried.

She opened the door and entered the room.

The heavy odor of incense filled her mouth and nostrils as she opened her eyes and stretched out her hands—for a long time the perfume and the gloom had meant nothing more to her than a single element, acrid and heavy, as simple, as familiar as water, air, or fire—and she prudently advanced toward a pale stain which seemed to float in the fog. It was Pierre's face. Pierre's clothing (he dressed in black ever since he had been sick) melted in obscurity. Pierre had thrown back his head and closed his eyes. He was handsome. Eve looked at his long, curved lashes, then sat close to him on the low chair. *He seems to be suffering*, she thought. Little by little her eyes grew used to the darkness. The bureau emerged first, then the bed, then Pierre's personal things: scissors, the pot of glue, books, the herbarium which shed its leaves onto the rug near the armchair.

"Agatha?"

Pierre had opened his eyes. He was watching her, smiling. "You know, that fork?" he said. "I did it to frighten that fellow. There was *almost* nothing the matter with it."

Eve's apprehensions faded and she gave a light laugh. "You succeeded," she said. "You drove him completely out of his mind."

Pierre smiled. "Did you see? He played with it a long time, he held it right in his hands. The trouble is," he said, "they don't know how to take hold of things; they grab them."

"That's right," Eve said.

Pierre tapped the palm of his left hand lightly with the index of his right.

"They take with that. They reach out their fingers and when they catch hold of something they crack down on it to knock it out."

He spoke rapidly and hardly moving his lips; he looked puzzled.

"I wonder what they want," he said at last. "That fellow has already been here. Why did they send him to me? If they want to know what I'm doing all they have to do is read it on the screen, they don't even need to leave the house. They make mistakes. They have the power but they make mistakes. I never make any, that's my trump card. *Hoffka*!" he said. He shook his long hands before his forehead. "The bitch Hoffka! Paffka! Suffka! Do you want any more?"

"Is it the bell?" asked Eve.

"Yes. It's gone." He went on severely. "This fellow, he's just a subordinate. You know him, you went into the living-room with him."

Eve did not answer.

"What did he want?" asked Pierre. "He must have told you."

She hesitated an instant, then answered brutally. "He wanted you locked up."

When the truth was told quietly to Pierre he distrusted it. He had to be dealt with violently in order to daze and paralyze his suspicions. Eve preferred to brutalize him rather than lie: when she lied and he acted as if he believed it she could not avoid a very slight feeling of superiority which made her horrified at herself.

"Lock me up!" Pierre repeated ironically. "They're crazy. What can walls do to me. Maybe they think that's going to stop me. I sometimes wonder if there aren't two groups. The real one, the Negro—and then a bunch of fools trying to stick their noses in and making mistake after mistake."

He made his hand jump up from the arm of the chair and looked at it happily.

"I can get through walls. What did you tell them?" he asked, turning to Eve with curiosity.

"Not to lock you up."

He shrugged. "You shouldn't have said that. You made a mistake too . . . unless you did it on purpose. You've got to call their bluff."

He was silent. Eve lowered her head sadly. *"They grab things!" How scornfully he said that—and he was right. Do I grab things too? It doesn't do any good to watch myself, I think most of my movements annoy him. But he doesn't say anything.* Suddenly she felt as miserable as when she was fourteen and Mme. Darbedat told her, "You don't know what to do with your hands." She didn't dare make a move and just at that time she had an irresistible desire to change her position. Quietly she put her feet under the chair, barely touching the rug. She watched the lamp on the table—the lamp whose base Pierre had painted black—and the chess set. Pierre had left only the black pawns on the board. Sometimes he would get up, go to the table and take the pawns in his hands one by one. He spoke to them, called them Robots and they seemed to stir with a mute life under his fingers. When he set them down, Eve went and touched them in her turn (she always felt somewhat ridiculous about it). They had become little bits of dead wood again but something vague and incomprehensible stayed in them, something like understanding. *These are* his *things*, she thought. *There is nothing of mine in the room.* She had had a few pieces of furniture before; the mirror and the little inlaid dresser handed down from her grandmother and which Pierre jokingly called "*your* dresser." Pierre had carried them away with him; things showed their true face to Pierre alone. Eve could watch them for hours: they were unflaggingly stubborn and determined to deceive her, offering her nothing but their appearance—as they did to Dr. Franchot and M. Darbedat. *Yet*, she told herself with anguish, *I don't see them quite like my father. It isn't possible for me to see them exactly like him.*

She moved her knees a little: her legs felt as though they were crawling with ants. Her body was stiff and taut and hurt her; she felt it too alive, too demanding. *I would like to be invisible and stay here seeing him without his seeing me. He doesn't need me; I am useless in this room.* She turned her head slightly and looked at the wall above Pierre. Threats were written on the wall. Eve knew it but she could not read them. She often watched the big red roses on the wallpaper until they began to dance before her eyes. The roses flamed in shadow. Most of the time the threat was written near the ceiling, a little to the left of the bed; but sometimes it moved. *I must get up. I can't . . . I can't sit down any longer.* There were also white discs on the wall that looked like slices of onion. The discs spun and Eve's hands began to tremble: *Sometimes I think I'm going mad. But no,* she thought, *I* can't *go mad. I get nervous, that's all.*

Suddenly she felt Pierre's hand on hers.

"Agatha," Pierre said tenderly.

He smiled at her but he held her hand by the ends of his fingers with a sort of revulsion, as though he had picked up a crab by the back and wanted to avoid its claws.

"Agatha," he said, "I would so much like to have confidence in you."

She closed her eyes and her breast heaved. *I mustn't answer anything, if I do he'll get angry, he won't say anything more.*

Pierre had dropped her hand. "I like you, Agatha," he said, "but I can't understand you. Why do you stay in the room all the time?"

Eve did not answer.

"Tell me why."

"You know I love you," she said dryly.

"I don't believe you," Pierre said. "Why should you love me? I must frighten you: I'm haunted." He smiled but suddenly became serious. "There is a wall between you and me. I see you, I speak to you, but you're on the other side. What keeps us from loving? I think it was easier before. In Hamburg."

"Yes," Eve said sadly. Always Hamburg. He never spoke of their real past. Neither Eve nor he had ever been to Hamburg.

"We used to walk along the canal. There was a barge, remember? The barge was black; there was a dog on the deck."

He made it up as he went along; it sounded false.

"I held your hand. You had another skin. I believed all you told me. Be quiet!" he shouted.

He listened for a moment. "They're coming," he said mournfully.

Eve jumped up. "They're coming? I thought they wouldn't ever come again."

Pierre had been calmer for the past three days; the statues did not come. Pierre was terribly afraid of the statues even though he would never admit it. Eve was not afraid: but when they began to fly, buzzing, around the room, she was afraid of Pierre.

"Give me the ziuthre," Pierre said.

Eve got up and took the ziuthre: it was a collection of pieces of cardboard Pierre had glued together; he used it to conjure the statues. The ziuthre looked like a spider. On one of the cardboards Pierre had written, "Power over ambush," and on the other, "Black." On a third he had drawn a laughing face with wrinkled eyes: it was Voltaire.

Pierre seized the ziuthre by one end and looked at it darkly.

"I can't use it any more," he said.

"Why?"

"They turned it upside down."

"Will you make another?"

He looked at her for a long while. "You'd like me to, wouldn't you," he said between his teeth.

Eve was angry at Pierre. *He's warned every time they come: how does he do it? He's never wrong.*

The ziuthre dangled pitifully from the ends of Pierre's fingers. *He always finds a good reason not to use it. Sunday when they came he pretended he'd lost it but I saw it behind the paste pot and he couldn't fail to see it. I wonder if he isn't the one who brings them.* One could never tell if he were completely sincere. Sometimes Eve had the impression that despite himself Pierre was surrounded by a swarm of unhealthy thoughts and visions. But at other times Pierre seemed to invent them. *He suffers. But how much does he* believe *in the statues and the Negro. Anyhow, I know he doesn't see the statues, he only hears them: when they pass he turns his head away; but he still says he sees them; he describes them.* She remembered the red face of Dr. Franchot: "But my dear madame, all mentally unbalanced persons are liars; you're wasting your time if you're trying to distinguish between what they really feel and what they pretend to feel." She gave a start. *What is Franchot doing here? I don't want to start thinking like him.*

Pierre had gotten up. He went to throw the ziuthre into the wastebasket: *I want to think like you,* she murmured. He walked with tiny steps, on tiptoe, pressing his elbows against his hips so as to take up the least possible space. He came back and sat down and looked at Eve with a closed expression.

"We'll have to put black wallpaper," he said. "There isn't enough black in this room."

He was crouched in the armchair. Sadly Eve watched his meager body, always ready to withdraw, to shrink—the arms, legs, and head looked like retractable organs. The clock struck six. The piano downstairs was silent. Eve sighed: the statues would not come right away; they had to wait for them.

"Do you want me to turn on the light?"

She would rather not wait for them in darkness.

"Do as you please," Pierre said.

Eve lit the small lamp on the bureau and a red mist filled the room. Pierre was waiting too.

He did not speak but his lips were moving, making two dark stains in the red mist. Eve loved Pierre's lips. Before, they had been moving and sensual; but they had lost their sensuality. They were wide apart, trembling a little, coming together incessantly, crushing against each other only to separate again. They were the only living things in this blank face; they looked like two frightened animals. Pierre could mutter like that for hours without a sound leaving his mouth and Eve often let herself be fascinated by this tiny, obstinate movement. *I love his mouth.* He never kissed her any more; he was horrified at contacts: at night they touched him—the hands of men, hard and dry, pinched him all over; the long-nailed hands of women caressed him. Often he went to bed with his clothes on but the hands slipped under the clothes and tugged at his shirt. Once he heard laughter and puffy lips were placed on his mouth. He never kissed Eve after that night.

"Agatha," Pierre said, "don't look at my mouth."

Eve lowered her eyes.

"I am not unaware that people can learn to read lips," he went on insolently.

His hand trembled on the arm of the chair. The index finger stretched out, tapped three times on the thumb and the other fingers curled: this was a spell. *It's going to start*, she thought. She wanted to take Pierre in her arms.

Pierre began to speak at the top of his voice in a very sophisticated tone.

"Do you remember São Paulo?"

No answer. Perhaps it was a trap.

"I met you there," he said, satisfied. "I took you away from a

Danish sailor. We almost fought but I paid for a round of drinks and he let me take you away. All that was only a joke."

He's lying, he doesn't believe a word of what he says. He knows my name isn't Agatha. I hate him when he lies. But she saw his staring eyes and her rage melted. *He isn't lying*, she thought, *he can't stand it any more. He feels them coming; he's talking to keep from hearing them.* Pierre dug both hands into the arm of the chair. His face was pale; he was smiling.

"These meetings are often strange," he said, "but I don't believe it's by chance. I'm not asking who sent you. I know you wouldn't answer. Anyhow, you've been smart enough to bluff me."

He spoke with great difficulty, in a sharp, hurried voice. There were words he could not pronounce and which left his mouth like some soft and shapeless substance.

"You dragged me away right in the middle of the party, between the rows of black automobiles, but behind the cars there was an army with red eyes which glowed as soon as I turned my back. I think you made signs to them, all the time hanging on my arm, but I didn't see a thing. I was too absorbed by the great ceremonies of the Coronation."

He looked straight ahead, his eyes wide open. He passed his hand over his forehead very rapidly, in one spare gesture, without stopping his talking. He did not want to stop talking.

"It was the Coronation of the Republic," he said stridently, "an impressive spectacle of its kind because of all the species of animals that the colonies sent for the ceremony. You were afraid to get lost among the monkeys. I said among the monkeys," he repeated arrogantly, looking around him. "I could say *among the Negroes!* The abortions sliding under the tables, trying to pass unseen, are discovered and nailed to the spot by my Look. The password is silence. To be silent. Everything in place and attention for the entrance of the statues, that's the countersign. Tralala . . . ," he shrieked and cupped his hands to his mouth. "Tralalala, tralalalala!"

He was silent and Eve knew that the statues had come into the room. He was stiff, pale and distrustful. Eve stiffened too and both waited in silence. Someone was walking in the corridor: it was Marie the housecleaner, she had undoubtedly just arrived. Eve thought, *I have to give her money for the gas.* And then the statues began to fly; they passed between Eve and Pierre.

Pierre went "Ah!" and sank down in the armchair, folding his legs beneath him. He turned his face away; sometimes he grinned, but drops of sweat pearled his forehead. Eve could stand the sight no longer, this pale cheek, this mouth deformed by a trembling grimace; she closed her eyes. Gold threads began to dance on the red background of her eyelids; she felt old and heavy. Not far from her Pierre was breathing violently. *They're flying, they're buzzing, they're bending over him*. She felt a slight tickling, a pain in the shoulder and right side. Instinctively her body bent to the left as if to avoid some disagreeable contact, as if to let a heavy, awkward object pass. Suddenly the floor creaked and she had an insane desire to open her eyes, to look to her right, sweeping the air with her hand.

She did nothing; she kept her eyes closed and a bitter joy made her tremble: *I am afraid too*, she thought. Her entire life had taken refuge in her right side. She leaned towards Pierre without opening her eyes. The slightest effort would be enough and she would enter this tragic world for the first time. *I'm afraid of the statues*, she thought. It was a violent, blind affirmation, an incantation. She wanted to believe in their presence with all her strength. She tried to make a new sense, a sense of touch out of the anguish which paralyzed her right side. She *felt* their passage in her arm, in her side and shoulder.

The statues flew low and gently; they buzzed. Eve knew that they had an evil look and that eyelashes stuck out from the stone around their eyes; but she pictured them badly. She knew, too, that they were not quite alive but that slabs of flesh, warm scales appeared on their great bodies; the stone peeled from the ends of their fingers and their palms were eaten away. Eve could not *see* all that: she simply thought of enormous women sliding against her, solemn and grotesque, with a human look and compact heads of stone. *They are bending over Pierre*—Eve made such a violent effort that her hands began trembling—*they are bending over me*. A horrible cry suddenly chilled her. They had touched him. She opened her eyes. Pierre's head was in his hands, he was breathing heavily. Eve felt exhausted: *a game*, she thought with remorse; *it was only a game. I didn't sincerely believe it for an instant. And all that time he suffered as if it were real*.

Pierre relaxed and breathed freely. But his pupils were strangely dilated and he was perspiring.

"Did you see them?" he asked.

"I can't see them."

"Better for you. They'd frighten you," he said. "I am used to them."

Eve's hands were still shaking and the blood had rushed to her head. Pierre took a cigarette from his pocket and brought it up to his mouth. But he did not light it.

"I don't care whether I see them or not," he said, "but I don't want them to touch me. I'm afraid they'll give me pimples."

He thought for an instant, then asked, "Did you hear them?"

"Yes," Eve said, "it's like an airplane engine." (Pierre had told her this the previous Sunday.)

Pierre smiled with condescension. "You exaggerate," he said. But he was still pale. He looked at Eve's hands. "Your hands are trembling. That made quite an impression on you, my poor Agatha. But don't worry. They won't come back again before tomorrow." Eve could not speak. Her teeth were chattering and she was afraid Pierre would notice it. Pierre watched her for a long time.

"You're tremendously beautiful," he said, nodding his head. "It's too bad, too bad."

He put out his hand quickly and toyed with her ear. "My lovely devil-woman. You disturb me a little, you are too beautiful. That distracts me. If it weren't a question of recapitulation . . ."

He stopped and looked at Eve with surprise.

"That's not the word . . . it came . . . it came," he said, smiling vaguely. "I had another on the tip of my tongue . . . but this one . . . came in its place. I forget what I was telling you."

He thought for a moment, then shook his head.

"Come," he said, "I want to sleep." He added in a childish voice, "You know, Agatha, I'm tired. I can't collect my thoughts any more."

He threw away his cigarette and looked at the rug anxiously. Eve slipped a pillow under his head.

"You can sleep too," he told her, "they won't be back."

. . . *Recapitulation* . . .

Pierre was asleep, a candid half-smile on his face; his head was turned to one side. One might have thought he wanted to caress his cheek with his shoulder. Eve was not sleepy, she was thoughtful. *Recapitulation*. Pierre had suddenly looked stupid and the word had slipped out of his mouth, long and whitish. Pierre had stared ahead of him in astonishment, as if he had seen the word and didn't recognize it; his mouth was open, soft; something seemed broken in it. He stammered. *That's the first time it ever happened to him; he noticed it, too. He said he couldn't collect his thoughts any more*. Pierre gave a voluptuous little whimper and his hand made a vague movement. Eve watched him harshly: *how is he going to wake up?* It gnawed at her. As soon as Pierre was asleep she had to think about it. She was afraid he would wake up wild-eyed and stammering. *I'm stupid*, she thought. *It can't start before a year; Franchot said so*. But the anguish did not leave her—a year: a winter, a springtime, a summer, the beginning of another autumn. One day his features would grow confused, his jaw would hang loose, he would half open his weeping eyes. Eve bent over Pierre's hand and pressed her lips against it: *I'll kill you before that*.

QUESTIONS

1. How does the setting contribute to the theme of physical and spiritual decay? How does character contribute to the theme?
2. Sartre manipulates a number of contrasting images: ripeness/decay, light/dark, violence/peacefulness. How do these images function in the story?
3. What is the symbolic significance of the scene with the fork? Of the statues? Of the room?
4. How does the point of view contribute to the theme of reason and madness? Or consciousness and unconsciousness? What is the meaning of the word *anguish?* Of the word *imagination?*
5. What is "The Room" about? Love? Madness? Sex? Marriage? Art? Mind?

Peter Hillsman Taylor *(1919–   ) was born in Trenton, Tennessee, and was educated at Vanderbilt and Kenyon College. He taught for a number of years at the University of North Carolina and currently teaches at the University of Virginia. The historic traditions and social manners of Tennessee play an important role in his ironic and elegiac stories, first collected in* A Long Fourth and Other Stories *(1948). Later collections include* Happy Families Are All Alike *(1959),* Miss Leonora When Last Seen *(1963), and* The Collected Stories *(1969). A recipient of the O. Henry Award (1959), Mr. Taylor has also written two plays and a novel,* A Woman of Means *(1950).*

Dean of Men

PETER TAYLOR

I am not unsympathetic, Jack, to your views on the war. I am not unsympathetic to your views on the state of the world in general. From the way you wear your hair and from the way you dress I do find it difficult to decide whether you or that young girl you say you are about to marry is going to play the male role in your marriage—or the female role. But even that I don't find offensive. And I am not trying to make crude jokes at your expense. You must pardon me, though, if my remarks seem too personal. I confess I don't know you as well as a father *ought* to know his son, and I may seem to take liberties.

However, Jack, I do believe that I understand the direction in which you—all of you—think you are going. I have not observed college students during the past thirty years for nothing. And I must try to warn you that I don't think even your wonderful generation will succeed in going very far along the road you are on. In this connection, Jack, I want to tell you a story. I can tell you this story because even its most recent chapters took place a very long time ago and because the events of the story don't matter to anybody any more—neither to me nor even to your mother. When you see your mother next, and if you repeat what I am about to tell you, she may give you a somewhat different version. But that doesn't matter. It is not really a story about your mother and me or about our divorce. Perhaps it is a story about you and me—about men.

I think I know the very moment to begin: I was fitting the key into the lock of my office door on a Sunday morning. I was in such a temper I could hardly get the key into the keyhole or turn the lock after it was in. There had been a scene at our breakfast table at home; I had left the house. It was a strangely upsetting scene for me, though commonplace enough on the surface. Your sister Susie, who was no more than nine or ten then—she couldn't have been more, since *you* were still in a high chair, Jack—Susie had interrupted what I was saying across my Sunday morning grapefruit to your mother. And I had fired away at her, "Don't interrupt grown-up talk, Susie!"

That sounds commonplace enough, I know. But Susie persisted. "Why don't you go up to the trustees, Daddy," said she, advising me on how to behave in the professional crisis I was then in, which I had been discoursing upon across my grapefruit. "Why don't you go up to them and tell them how the president of the college is being unfair to you?"

Somehow I found her little remark enraging. I fairly shouted across the table, "For God's sake, Susie, shut up. Don't try to talk about things you don't understand or know a damned thing about!"

I blush now to think that I ever spoke so to a child, but I remember it too well to try to deny it. You see, Jack, I had actually already resigned my appointment at that college where I was then teaching, which was the very college where, a dozen years before, I had been an undergraduate. I had resigned just three weeks before, in protest against an injustice done me, and I had not yet received a definite commitment from the place where I was going next year. (I did receive the commitment the following day, as I recall, but that is not really significant.) Anyhow, I was feeling like a fool, I suppose, to have brought into the world three children for whom I might not be able to provide—only two children, actually, though little Maisie was on the way by then. And I was feeling like a fool, I suppose, to have risked their welfare—*your* welfare, if you please—over a principle of honest administration in a small Midwestern college. I was a very unhappy man, Jack, and there before me was my little ten-year-old daughter seeming to reproach me for my foolishness . . . At any rate, after my second blast at her, Susie had burst into tears and had run from the dining room and out into the yard. Your mother got up from her chair at the end of the table and said to me, "I would be ashamed of myself if I were you."

I made no reply except to say through my teeth: "This is too much."

Your mother's words were still in my ears when I shoved open the door to my office at the college. (Marie's words have a way of lingering in your ears for a very long time, Jack.) Anyhow, I had left the table without finishing breakfast, and left the dining room without any idea of where I was going. And then suddenly I had known. What drove me from the table, of course, were those words of Marie's that were still in my ears. For, Jack, those were the very words I had once heard my mother speak to my father, and, moreover, had heard her speak to Father at a Sunday breakfast table when *he* had teased my own sister Margaret till she cried and left the room. "I would be ashamed of myself if I were you," my mother had said, rising from the table in just the same way that my own wife was destined to do twenty years later. My father bolted from the table, left the house, and went downtown to his office, where he spent the whole of that Sunday. It seemed almost impossible that the incident should be repeating itself in my life. And yet to a remarkable degree it was so, and the memory of where it was my father had taken himself off to told me to what place I must take myself that Sunday morning.

It struck me, just as the door to my office came open, that I had never before seen my office at that early hour on Sunday. I had never, in fact, been in that building where my office was on a Sunday morning—or on the college campus itself, for that matter. It was a lovely campus, on a hill and with trees and with a little river at the foot of the hill, and it was a quite handsome neo-Gothic building I was in. I altogether liked that place, I can assure you. And in addition to my liking the other people on the faculty there, I had my old associations with the place from my undergraduate days. The truth is, I had thought I would settle down there for life, to do my teaching and my writing. It was the third teaching appointment I had had, but in my profession many people have to move around even more than I before they find a congenial spot, Jack. I was not yet thirty-five. I had considered myself lucky to find an agreeable place so early in my career, a small college where I had memories of my youth and where I would be allowed to do my mature work in peace . . .

But I knew by that Sunday morning that I was going to move on. I knew that by the next fall I would be in some other, almost identical office on some other campus and that your mother and I, with our three children, would be established in another house in another college town somewhere. But when I shoved open my office door, somehow it was not as though it were the door to just any little cubbyhole of an office. It was as if it were the door to my ancestral keep—my castle, so to speak; and I burst in upon my papers, my books, my pictures that morning as if expecting to catch them, my kinsmen—my cousins germane—in some conspiratorial act against me—yes, as though it were my books, my papers, my pictures who had betrayed me. But of course the room was just as I had left it. It was the same, and yet at that hour on Sunday morning it did seem different, too.

I can see myself there now, especially as I was during the first quarter hour of that long day. I didn't knock things about or tear up the place as it was my first impulse to do. Instead, after I had slammed the door and latched it, the first thing I did was to go quickly to my desk and turn down the photographs of your mother and Susie and even the one of yourself, Jack. I took the pages of my manuscript and of my typescript which had been in little stacks all over my desk top and quietly stuffed them inside the desk drawers. The books I had been reading recently—my own and those from the library—I removed from the table by my leather chair, putting them out of sight or at least placing them where they would not catch my eye, on the lowest shelf of my bookcase. Then I took down from the walls the four or five prints that hung there, reproductions I had brought back from my Fulbright in Italy, and I set them on the floor with their faces against the wall. If I handled these familiar objects gently, I believe it was just because I had not, after all, found them in active conspiracy against me.

There was no conspiracy among my books and papers and pictures; but what was perhaps worse, I seemingly had found them all dead—murdered. I felt they were strewn about the room like corpses in the last scene of an Elizabethan tragedy. Dead and murdered, that is, so far as I was concerned. Dead and wanting burial. And so, bending over them, I tenderly tucked them away as if to their last rest. Then I went and half sat, half leaned against the sill of the room's only window. The venetian blind there was lowered and the louvers were only half open. I leaned against the sill with my arms folded on my chest and observed the crepuscular light in the room, and I was aware of the Sunday morning stillness. Once again I heard Marie's voice, and after a moment once again heard my mother's voice. Presently I recalled my father's voice too, speaking not through his teeth as I had done that morning, but growling out of one corner of his mouth. I remembered how, as a younger man, I would sometimes wonder about that outburst of Father's temper on that other Sunday morning. It had seemed to me so unlike him. I used to speculate even, in the most literal-minded way, on how he had managed to occupy himself during the long hours he had spent alone in *his* office on that Sunday. The scene he had made at his breakfast table—or that my sister Margaret, or my mother had made—suddenly now became very easy for me to understand. Everything fell so easily into place that I felt I had always understood it. My father was a lawyer and a businessman who had lost most of what he had as a consequence of the '29 Crash. My sister Margaret was already a young lady at the time. She was no little girl like Susie when she sat down to breakfast with Father that other Sunday. She was a good-looking blond girl with wide green eyes, and she had a lovely disposition. She was always cheerful, always saying something clever or making you feel that you had said something clever. Margaret was the oldest child in the family, and I the youngest. But we were very close to each other, and I believe she confided her most serious thoughts to me more often than to anyone else, though surely it was Father she loved best. There was frequently a great deal of banter between her and Father at the table. She was such a well-behaved girl, so puritanical really, that Father would tease her sometimes about leading a wild life and keeping late hours. Mother would say she thought it in bad taste for Father to tease his own daughter about such things and that perhaps he would be putting ideas into her head. But Margaret would laugh at Mother and say that Father's evil mind made it all the more fun to deceive him. Then she and Father would laugh together in a sort of duet of laughter.

Margaret was popular with boys and always had a number of serious admirers. But the more serious the admirers were, the more she and Father seemed to delight in making fun of them. I don't believe Margaret ever imagined she was in love with any of those young men, until the time when Paul Kirkpatrick came along. Paul's family was one that nearly everybody knew about. They were such very rich people that even the Crash and the Depression hardly affected them at all. But it worried Margaret how rich the Kirkpatrick family was. It worried her, that is, that Paul would some day be rich, that she knew he would be rich, and that he was the only young man she found herself able to love. "I know I really love him for himself," she would say to me when we were walking in the park together or if we were in her room with the door shut, "but sometimes there seems to be an ugly, suspicious side of me—another person (old-nasty-minded Mag, I call her)—who laughs and cackles at me like a witch and says, 'I know why you love him so, dear Miss Margaret! You don't deceive me!' " Then Margaret and I would laugh together, rather the way she and Father did. But she was serious, and was worried.

Perhaps Father worried about it, too—more than I guessed, more than Margaret guessed. Naturally, he would have liked for her to marry a rich man, but there had been so much talk at our house about how hard times were for us that Father may have been afraid Margaret was going to marry into a rich family for *his* sake. At any rate, he was harder on Paul Kirkpatrick in his fun-making than he had been on any of the other young men. And Margaret went right along with him. They made fun of Paul's teeth—Margaret called them stalactites and stalagmites; made fun of his too lofty way of speaking, of the way he walked—they said he waddled; even made fun of his baby-smooth complexion.

Yet, after one of those sessions with Father, when she and I were alone, Margaret smiled at me and said, "You know something? I really think Paul's very good-looking, don't you?"

I told her that yes, I did think so. And it was true. Paul Kirkpatrick was quite handsome. He was an attractive and intelligent young man. But Margaret and Father kept on telling each other how ridiculous he was. It was the summer of 1930. Father was under great tension that summer. It was a year when he suffered one financial blow after another. And he never seemed more tense than when he and Margaret got on the subject of Paul. Sometimes it was very clear that he was prodding and trying to make her come to Paul's defense. But she never gave an inch. I was certain sometimes, however, from the way she sat smiling at Father that she was on the verge of blurting out that she loved Paul and was going to marry him. For I think my sister Margaret intended to marry Paul Kirkpatrick and would have done so had it not been for the family scene that Sunday morning. I had witnessed Paul's and Margaret's embraces and kisses at the side door more than once that summer. And once I saw—or just possibly imagined I saw—a ring with a large stone in Margaret's purse. Anyway, I remember she came down to breakfast later than the rest of us on that Sunday, and she was fully dressed, which was unusual for anyone at our breakfast table on Sunday. It seems to me that Father had not spoken at the table—he was often silent and abstracted then, though it was not in his nature to be so—he had not spoken until he looked up and saw Margaret sitting, fully dressed, at her place. "Well, you must have a church date with our toothy young friend," he said to her.

"He's coming over this morning," Margaret said with a smile. "I don't know about church." I am quite sure now that she was trying to prepare Father and that Paul was going to "speak" to him that day.

I saw Mother look at Father, and it seems to me that I heard him swallow, though his mouth and throat were empty. Then, lifting a fork heaped with scrambled eggs, he said, "Why not? It's just as easy to love a rich one as a poor one, isn't it, Margaret?"

I saw the first patches of red appear under Margaret's ears and then the same red suffuse her entire face. And I saw the tears fill her eyes before the first sob came. When she pushed herself back from the table, Father was still holding the fork with the eggs on it. He put his fork down on his plate without spilling a morsel. But he was as white as the big napkin which his left hand then drew from his lap and threw out upon the table. "My God. My God," he growled from the corner of his mouth as Margaret ran, weeping aloud, through the living room and then through the hall and on upstairs. And my mother rose at her place and said, "I would be ashamed of myself if I were you."

How Father occupied himself and what he thought about when he reached his office that Sunday were questions that occurred to me during the very hours he was there, occurred to me even though I was just a boy of twelve at the time. My father was known as "a devoted family man," he almost never went to his office at night, and if some piece of business called him there on a Saturday afternoon or a Sunday, he groaned and complained endlessly. We knew he had gone to his office that morning, however, because Mother telephoned him after about an hour, to make sure he was all right. She knew about the money worries he had then, of course, and so she was quick to blame his behavior on that. In fact she went to Margaret's room and reminded her of "the tensions Father was under" and told her that *she* must forgive him, too. I suspect that Margaret had already forgiven him. I know that she had telephoned Paul Kirkpatrick and told him not to come that day. Her romance with Paul did not last long after that. The next year she married a "struggling young lawyer" and with him, as my mother would have said, "she has had a good life."

No doubt my father wrote a few letters at his office desk, as I did during the course of my Sunday at my office. But probably it wasn't easy for him to concentrate on letters. I recall that even while I remained leaning against the sill of my office window it came to me that what my father might have thought about in his office, twenty years before, was his own father. For yes, there *was* a story in the family about a scene that my grandfather had made at *his* breakfast table, too. I cannot give so many details about it, though possibly my father could have. There are many obscurities about the old story that I can't possibly clear up and won't try to. In fact, I don't know anything definite about the immediate circumstances that led to the scene. Perhaps I never knew them. People in my grandfather's day disliked admitting they did wretched things to each other at home or that there *were* family scenes in their families. All of the incident that has come down is that my grandfather, no longer a young man—a man past middle age, standing in the doorway to his dining room with his broad-brimmed felt hat on, hurled a silver dollar at my grandmother, who was still seated at the breakfast table, and that the silver dollar landed in the sugar bowl. There is just the additional detail that my grandmother would allow no one to remove the coin and that that sugar bowl, with the silver dollar buried in the sugar, remained on her pantry shelf as long as the old lady lived.

I have always imagined that there had been a quarrel between my grandparents about housekeeping money; perhaps my grandfather, who was not much of a family man in the beginning and who lived a big part of his life away from home, among men, and who was known by all men for his quick temper, perhaps he lost his head momentarily. He forgot he was not among men and he hurled the piece of money at his wife as he would have at some man to whom he had lost a bet. He and my grandmother may have had other difficulties between them over money or over other matters. Perhaps it was really a symbolic gesture on his part, as refusing to remove the coin was on hers. He was not a rich man, but then he was certainly not a poor man either, and actually in his day he was quite a well-known public figure. He was in politics, as his father and his father's father before him were . . . I must tell you something about their politics. They were not exactly small-time politicians. Each one of them, at one time or another during his lifetime, represented our district in Congress. For nearly a hundred years, "we" more or less occupied that seat in Congress. But my grandfather was the most successful and best known of the line and in middle age was elected to the U.S. Senate to complete the unexpired term of an incumbent who had died in office.

Probably my grandfather brought the special type of politician they all three were to its highest possible point of development, a kind of frontiersman-gentleman politician with just the right mixture of realism and idealism to appeal to their constituents. Today people would no doubt call him a pragmatist. He was known for his elegant oratory on the platform and in public debate and known also for the coarseness of his speech in private debate or in private confrontation with his opponents. (My grandfather's grandfather had once horsewhipped an opponent on the public square, and his own father had fought a duel.) It was Grandfather's beautiful oratory and his beautiful voice that got him elected to the Senate. People didn't care what his stand on tariff or on the silver or gold issue was. They believed he was an honest man and they knew he was a spellbinder. He too believed he was an honest man and he didn't understand the new kind of urban politician who was coming to power in our state at the time. It may be he was actually betrayed and ruined by the new politicians simply because they were "low-born rascals." Or it may be he was inevitably betrayed and ruined by them because once a human type is perfected—or almost perfected—it immediately becomes an anachronism and has no place in society. Who can say? He was, at any rate, betrayed and ruined by a low-born man named Lon Lucas, and he never held political office again after that brief term in the Senate.

And now, Jack, I come to the part of the story that I believe it is essential for you to hear. If you have not understood why I have told you all that went before, you will, anyhow, understand why I wish to recount the three episodes that follow.

What happened to my grandfather's political career can be briefly summarized. The unexpired term in the Senate, which he was filling out, lasted but two years. When the time came for him to make his race for a full term, he was persuaded by Lon Lucas and others that instead of making that race it was his duty to his party to come home and run for governor of the state. The Lucas faction comprised a group of young men whom my grandfather considered more or less his protégés. In earlier days they had asked countless small favors of him, and no doubt they had done so in order to create that relationship to him. Now they pointed out to him that from another faction in the party there was a man who, though loathsome to them all, was a strong candidate for the party's nomination for governor, and pointed out that only he, my grandfather, could block the nomination and election of that man. It would be a disgrace to the state and to the party to have such a man in the governor's chair, they said. Yet the senator could easily come home and win the nomination and the election for himself and could just as easily regain his seat in the Senate at a later time.

You may well wonder that an experienced politician could be so naïve as to accept that line of reasoning or to entrust his fate to the hands of those ambitious younger men. Neither his father nor his grandfather would surely, under any circumstances, have relinquished that prize of prizes for a politician, a seat in the U.S. Senate. I cannot pretend to explain it. I knew my grandfather only as an embittered old man who didn't care to have children crawling all over him. But I have to tell you that, within a few weeks after he came home and began his campaign for governor, Lon Lucas and his faction turned on him. Some sort of deal was made with the other faction. No doubt the deal was made long beforehand. Lucas came out in support of the "loathsome man" for governor, and one of the Lucas faction was put up for the seat in the Senate. Very likely there were other considerations also, remunerative to Lon Lucas and company if not to the candidates themselves. Such details are not important here, and I never knew them anyway. But my grandfather was defeated, and he retired from public life to the bosom of his family, where, alas, I cannot say he was greatly loved and cherished.

He withdrew almost entirely from all male company, seeing men only as his rather limited law practice required him to do. He lived out his life in a household of women and children, a household consisting for many years of his wife, his wife's mother and maiden aunt, his own mother, who lived to be ninety-seven, five daughters, and three sons. He never allowed himself to be addressed as senator and forbade all political talk in his presence. The members of his household were destined to retain in their minds and to hand down to future generations their picture of him not as a statesman of high principle or even as a silver-tongued orator but as the coarse-tongued old tyrant of their little world. His three sons always feared him mightily and took from his life only the one lesson: an anathema on politics. My father was the only son who would consent to study law and become a member of the old gentleman's firm, but even he made it clear from the outset that he would not let his profession lead him astray, made it clear to everyone that his interest was not in government but solely in corporation law.

My father's guiding principle in life was that he must at all costs avoid the terrible pitfall of politics. He gave himself to making money and to becoming the family man his father had never been. What finally happened to him I must present in a more dramatic form than the summary I have given of Grandfather's affairs. It would be as difficult for me to summarize the story of Father's betrayal as it would have been for me to imagine and re-create the precise circumstances under which Grandfather first learned of Lon Lucas's double-dealing.

When I had opened the venetian blind at my office window that Sunday morning, I stared out at May's fresh green grass on the campus for a while and down at the small river, swollen by spring rains, at the bottom of the hill. Then I went to my desk and managed to write two letters to men who had published books on the subject—in "the field"—I was doing my work in. They were perfunctory, polite letters, requesting permission to quote from the work of those men in my own book. When I had sealed and stamped those two letters, I took out another sheet of departmental paper; but it lay on my desk untouched for I don't know how long, a blinding white sheet that I sat staring at impatiently as one does at a movie screen before the film begins. Finally, I put away my pen but left the piece of paper lying there as if meaning to project upon it the images taking shape in my mind. I saw my father stepping out of the family limousine in front of the Union Station in bright winter sunlight. My mother and I were already out of the car and waiting under the canopy. The Negro chauffeur stood holding the car door open and listening to some piece of instruction Father gave him in passing. Since this was in the earliest days of the Depression, we still lived in the world of limousines and chauffeurs, a world that my father's business career had lifted us into. A number of years before this he had ceased altogether to practice law, in order to accept the presidency of a large, "nationally known" insurance company for which he had formerly been the chief attorney and which maintained its head office locally. The insurance company was now in serious difficulties, however. The company's investments were under question. It began to appear that funds had been invested in various business enterprises that seemed hardly to have existed except on paper. Many of these investments had been made before my father's incumbency, but not all of them. Anyway, the man who had most influenced the company's investment of funds was a stockholder in the company and a member of the board of directors, Mr. Lewis Barksdale. He was an old school friend of my father's and had of course been instrumental in electing my father president of the company. It was he alone who would be able to explain the seemingly fraudulent use of moneys—explain it, that is, to the other members of the board—and he alone who could straighten out the snarl that the company's affairs seemed to be in. And it was this Lewis Barksdale whom we had come to the Union Station to meet at four o'clock on a remarkably bright winter afternoon.

The Negro chauffeur threw back his head and laughed at something my father said to him, and then Father advanced toward us, wearing a pleased smile. I remember remarking to Mother at just that moment what a fine day it was and reproaching her for having made me wear my heavy coat, in which I was uncomfortably warm. The truth was, I was still irked by Father's having made me leave a game with a group of boys to come with them to meet Mr. Barksdale's train, and I was taking out my resentment on Mother. Without looking at me, she replied that it was due to turn colder very shortly and, squeezing my hand, she said, "Why can't you have an agreeable disposition like your father's? Don't be an old sourpuss like me." Father was still smiling when he came up to us, and Mother asked him, "What is it that's so funny?"

"Oh," he explained, taking Mother's elbow and escorting us into the lobby of the station, "when I just now told Irwin not to come inside and fetch Lewis's bag but to wait right there with the car, he said he couldn't keep the car in that spot but fifteen minutes and that he was afraid the train might be late. I said to him that if he knew Lewis Barksdale as well as I do, he'd know that the engineer and the fireman would somehow understand that they *had* to get Lewis's train out here on time."

In the lobby, Father read the track number off the board and then marched us confidently down the concourse to the great iron gate at Track No. 6. Just as he predicted, the train rolled in on time. Father spoke to the uniformed gatekeeper, who let us go through the gateway along with the redcaps, so we could see Mr. Barksdale when he stepped off the train. Father trotted along ahead of us, peering up into the windows of the observation car and then into the windows of the next Pullman. Mother called after him that he had better wait there beside the first Pullman or we might miss Mr. Barksdale. And Father did stop there. But he told me to run on ahead and see if I could get a glimpse of him in the entry of any of the other cars. I said I was not certain I would recognize Mr. Barksdale, but Father said, "You can know him by his derby. Besides, *he*'ll recognize *you*."

I did run on ahead, looking up into the cars, watching the people who came down the steps from each car to the metal stool that the porter had set out for them. Mr. Barksdale, being a man who had no children of his own, was said to be extremely fond of all his friends' children. That was why, as the youngest child in the family—and the only boy—I was taken along to meet the train that day. I could vaguely recall earlier visits he had made to us and seemed to remember a sense of his paying special attention to me. Momentarily, I was persuaded that I *would* remember him if we came face to face. But no man wearing a derby got off the train, and I made out no remotely familiar face in the cars or in the crowded entry ways. Moreover, no passenger climbing down off that train showed any sign of recognizing me.

When I followed the crowd of passengers and redcaps back toward the iron gate, I found Mother still standing beside the observation car. She said that Father had climbed aboard and was going through all the cars in search of Mr. Barksdale. At last we saw Father step off the first of the day coaches, away down the track. He looked very small down there, and when he waved to us and climbed back on the train I felt a sudden ache in the pit of my stomach. "Mr. Barksdale's not on the train," I said to Mother.

"No, I guess not," she said. "I was afraid he mightn't be."

Finally, Father reappeared in the entry between the observation car and the next Pullman. "Lewis must have missed the train somehow," he said as he came down the steps and swung out onto the platform. "Let's go inside the station. I'm going to telephone New York and see if he's still there."

We found a telephone booth on the concourse just beyond Gate No. 6, but Father had to go inside the station lobby to get enough change to make the call. Mother and I stood beside the booth a long time. "He ought to have waited till we got home to make the call," she said at last. "I suppose, though, he couldn't bear to wait." She and I had just agreed to go into the lobby and look for him when we saw him coming toward us. He was all smiles and was holding up two fistfuls of coins.

"I got enough quarters to call China," he said, and seemed to be elated by the feel of the coins in his hands. When he stepped into the booth to make his call, Mother and I moved away some twenty or thirty feet. He must have talked for ten minutes or more. When he came out again, his smile was bigger than before, and he began calling out as he hurried toward us, "Lewis *did* miss the train! And it was so busy in New York today he couldn't get a line to call me. He's coming on an earlier train tonight and will be here by noon tomorrow!"

By noon of the next day, which was Saturday, it was very much colder, and so I didn't complain about having to wear my coat. I did complain somewhat, however, about having to give up several hours of a Saturday to meeting Mr. Barksdale's train. Father seemed to understand and was not so insistent upon my going, but in private Mother was insistent and said it was little enough for me to do if it was what my father wished. As we were leaving the house, Father stopped a moment to telephone the station and ask if the train was going to be on time. He had heard a report on the radio that the weather up East had turned bad. But the dispatcher's office reported that the train was scheduled to arrive exactly on time. In the car, Father said he hoped the dispatcher's office knew what it was talking about. "Trains on the weekend are often late," he said suspiciously. When we got to the station, he told Irwin that since the train might, after all, be late, he had better take the car to the parking lot, and that we would come and find him there.

As we were passing through the lobby, we all three read the gate number aloud from the blackboard, and we laughed at ourselves for it—rather nervously, I suppose. Father had kept silent most of the way down to the station in the car and had left the talking mostly to Mother and me. He began to look more cheerful once we were in the big lobby, and as we passed out onto the concourse he said to Mother under his breath, "Keep your fingers crossed." As soon as we came out onto the concourse, we could see that the train was already backing up to the gate. "Thar she be!" Father exclaimed with sudden gaiety, and he put an arm around each of us to hurry us along. But at the gate he didn't ask the gatekeeper to let us go beyond. We waited outside, and through the bars of the grating we watched the passengers stepping down onto the platform. After a few minutes Father said, "I won't be surprised if Lewis is the last to get off. He hates crowds." We kept watching until it was obvious that no more passengers were going to leave the train and come through the gate. In what was almost a whisper, Father said to Mother, "He didn't come. What do you suppose could have happened?" And as we were passing the telephone booth on the way out, he said, "I'll call him from home."

We had been at home about half an hour when I heard him speaking to Mother from the foot of the stairs. She was leaning over the banisters in the upstairs hall. "There have been a lot of complications. Lewis has been getting together papers to bring with him. He says he can clear everything up. He's coming in on the same train tomorrow."

"Wonderful," Mother said.

"But I'm not going to ask you all to traipse down to the depot again."

"Nonsense. The third time's the charm," said my mother.

At about eleven the next morning Father telephoned the station to ask if the train was scheduled to come in on time. He was told that it would be three hours late. There were heavy snowstorms all over the East now. When Mother came into the big sun room where my sister Margaret and my two other sisters and I were all reading the Sunday paper and told us that snow had delayed Mr. Barksdale's train for three hours, she glanced out the sunroom windows at the darkly overcast sky and said, "There will be snow here before night, I think." None of my sisters even looked up from the paper. I imagine I looked up from the funny paper only because I wished to know whether or not I was going to be taken to the station again. Mother saw me look up and said, "Father says you needn't go with us today, and I suppose he's right."

"I'll go," I said. It had occurred to me suddenly that the snow might be falling by that time and that I would like to see how the old gray stone Union Station looked with snow on all of its turrets and crenelations and how the train would look backing into Gate No. 6 with snow it brought in from the East piled all over its top.

"Well, we'll see," Mother said.

Sometime after two, Mother and Father were in the front hall getting into their coats. I was there too, still undecided as to whether or not I would go along. No snow had begun to fall yet. Father seemed unconcerned about my going or not going. When Mother asked him if he thought he might call the station again, he replied casually that he already had, that the train would arrive as predicted, at three o'clock. He had already buttoned up his heavy, double-breasted overcoat when he added suddenly, "But there's another call I believe I'll make before we set out. It might take a few minutes . . . You had better take off your coat," he said to Mother.

When he was gone, I asked, "Who do you think he's calling?"

"I imagine he's calling Mr. Barksdale in New York," Mother said. She didn't remove her coat, though. She and I said nothing more. We went and looked out at the sky through the sidelights at the front door. After a few minutes we heard Father's footsteps. When we turned around he was standing there in the hall, smiling wearily and beginning to unbutton his coat.

"Lewis is still in New York," he said.

"Why in the world?" Mother exclaimed. "What in the world did he say this time?" she asked.

"He didn't say anything. I didn't give him a chance to. As soon as I definitely heard his voice on the wire, I put down the receiver."

"What are you going to do?" Mother asked him.

"There's nothing I can do. He's not coming, that's all. I'll just have to take it however it turns out now."

We didn't go to the station, of course. And Father didn't go off to his room to be by himself, either, as one might have expected. He spent the rest of the afternoon with the family in the sun room, reading the paper, listening to the radio, and playing cards. The way he was with us that afternoon, you wouldn't have suspected anything was wrong. At just about twilight it began to snow outside. And we all went about from window to window with a certain relief, I suppose, watching the big flakes come down and, from the snug safety of our sun room, watching the outside world change.

Father didn't telephone Mr. Barksdale again. They had been close friends since boyhood, but I believe they didn't communicate again for more than twenty-five years. When they were very old men and most of their other contemporaries were dead, Mr. Barksdale took to calling Father over long-distance and they would sometimes talk for an hour at a time about their boyhood friends or about business friends they had had when they were starting out in business. We were glad whenever Mr. Barksdale called Father, because it cheered him and made him seem livelier than anything else did during those last years. He often seemed very lonely during those years, though he continued to have a reasonably cheerful disposition. After the legal difficulties and the embarrassing publicity that followed his being abandoned by his trusted friend, Father led a quiet, uneventful life. He returned to his law practice, and he was a respected member of his firm. But he made no real life for himself in his practice—that is, he seldom saw other members of the firm away from the office, and I don't remember his ever mentioning the name of a client at home. His real life was all at home, where, as he would point out, it had always been. He and Mother sometimes played bridge with neighbors, and whatever other social life they had was there in the neighborhood where we lived after we lost the old house and could no longer afford a staff of servants. He was an affectionate father, and I rarely saw him in what I would call depressed spirits. Yet how often one had the feeling that he was lonely and bored. I remember sometimes, even when the family was on a vacation together—when we had taken a cottage at the shore or were camping and fishing in the mountains—the look would come in his eye. And one was tempted to ask oneself, What's wrong? What's missing?

I don't honestly know when I decided to go into college teaching, Jack. I considered doing other things—a career in the army or the navy. Yes, I might have gone to Annapolis or West Point. Those appointments were much to be desired in the Depression years, and my family did still have a few political connections. One thing was certain, though. Business was just as much out of the question for me as politics had been for my father. An honest man, I was to understand, had too much to suffer there. Yes, considering our family history, an ivory tower didn't sound like a bad thing at all for an honest man and a serious man . . . A dozen years after graduation I found myself back teaching in that college where I had been an undergraduate. Physically, it was a beautiful spot and, as I have already said, I thought I would settle down there for life, to do my teaching and my writing.

After my second year of teaching there I was awarded a research Fulbright to Italy, and so was on leave for a year. You were a babe in arms that year, Jack. I saw the ancient world for the first time with you on my shoulder, and with your mother usually following behind, leading Susie by the hand. Well, while we were in Italy, the old president of the college died of a stroke. He had been president of the college when I was an undergraduate, and I suppose it was he, most of all, who made me feel that my talents were appreciated there. By the time I returned to the campus from Italy, the following fall, the dean of men had been made acting president. Your mother and I smiled over the appointment but made no comment on it to anyone—not even to each other. You see, Jack, although Marie and I still thought of ourselves as being ideally suited to each other then, and still believed ourselves to be very happy together, there were already subjects she and I had had to agree to keep off. One of these—and by far the most important—was my professional career itself, including how I conducted my classes, my role in the department, my stand on various academic questions, and even my possible advancement in rank. We had been in graduate school together—your mother and I—and during the first years of our marriage, before Susie was born, we both had taught at the same institution. It was understandably difficult for her to refrain from advising and criticizing me in matters she considered she knew as much about as I did. When I first began ruling out that subject as a topic for discussion, she became emotional about it. She had wanted to have a career herself, and she had had to give it up temporarily. I had not realized how much her plans for a career had meant to her. But now she accused me of being an antifeminist, accused me of trying to isolate her in the kitchen, even of trying to cut her off from all intellectual life. In time, however, she came to see the matter differently—or seemed to. I think perhaps she tired of hearing other faculty wives talk about their husbands' professional problems and didn't want to be like them. At any rate, she and I merely smiled over the news of the dean's promotion to acting president. His qualifications for such a high place seemed hardly to exist. He was formerly the chairman of the Department of Athletics—that is, the college's head coach.

But since I knew that certain trustees and certain senior members of the faculty were on a committee to select a permanent president, I was careful to mention my amusement to no one. When a group of younger members of the faculty came to me, however, and told me that it was generally understood that the committee was going to recommend that the dean be made permanent president, I could not keep myself from bursting into laughter.

It was on an evening in the middle of the week that that group of young professors came to my house for the very purpose of reporting the information to me. How well I can see them on my front porch, in the bright porch light I had switched on. They were a very attractive and intelligent-looking bunch of men. With their bright, intelligent eyes, with their pipes and tweed jackets, and with a neatly trimmed mustache or two among them, they gave one a feeling that here were men one would gladly and proudly be associated with, the feeling that one had found the right niche in life, that one had made the right choice of career. I remember that, before they came inside, two of them—there were six in the party—stepped back and knocked the ashes out of their pipes on the porch banisters, and that they looked with interest at the porch banisters and then looked up and noticed what the porch pillars were like. As a matter of fact, as they trooped into the hallway and then over into my study, they all of them were making comments of one kind or another on the house . . . This was not so rude of them as it might seem, or I thought it wasn't. You see, they had telephoned me in advance that they wished to come over and talk to me about a matter. And I understood, of course, that they were too polite and too civilized to come to my house and dive right into a matter of business without making some small talk first. That was not their style, not their tone. Moreover, talk about people's houses used to be a fair and favorite topic at such a college as that one was, because there one didn't really own—or even rent—one's house. All houses occupied by the faculty belonged to the college. The good thing about the system was that the house was provided in addition to your salary, and so one didn't have to pay income tax on that portion of one's income. But by and large it was an invidious arrangement. The elderly professors, when they retired, often had no place to go. Further, since the senior professors and the administrators naturally occupied the best houses and one's rank could generally be deduced from the quality of one's house, the younger men (and their wives) eyed the houses of their seniors and thought of the circumstances that would make them available. When someone near the top died or retired, practically the entire faculty would move up a house.

My house was not of course one of the best houses. I was still an assistant professor, whereas most of those young professors who had come to see me were a grade above me in rank. My house, when we moved into it, had in fact been one of the most ramshackle-looking places in the village—one that nobody else would have. I had spent a lot of time and work putting it into the reasonably good condition it was now in. It was upon this fact that my guests were commenting as they came in from the porch that night. And when we had seated ourselves in my study and I had started the coffee brewing, they went on to say that it had been a real advantage to me to have been an undergraduate there, that I had joined the faculty with a knowledge of which houses were basically good houses, that I *knew* (what no one else could have guessed) how recently the run-down-looking house I moved into had been in relatively good condition. There was some truth in what they said, but they were not of course really serious about it. And I saw of course that they were teasing. I replied that my disadvantage was that the old president knew me and knew I was the only person on the staff who was fool enough to accept such a house.

They went on from that to speak of how I had known the late president longer and better than they had, and to ask if it was not true that the newest and youngest member of the board of trustees had once been a classmate and a rather good friend of mine. They were speaking of Morgan Heartwell, who had during the brief years since our graduation gone on to add several million to the millions he inherited. Though I had seen him only two or three times since college, we had become rather good friends during the last term of our senior year and we still exchanged Christmas cards and even brief letters now and then when there was special occasion. Morgan had been elected to the board during the previous year, when I was in Italy. I had written him one of those brief letters, from Florence, saying that I wished to congratulate the other members of the board on the wisdom of their choice. And Morgan had replied briefly that he looked forward to our spending some time together whenever the trustees met at the college.

The young professors who came to see me were overjoyed when I confirmed the rumor that Morgan Heartwell and I were friends. They immediately revealed the purport of their visit. There was a certain amount of caution in the way they brought forth the information about the dean's candidacy, but after my explosive fit of laughter they had thrown caution to the wind. Morgan Heartwell was on the committee. They wanted me to speak to him. They wanted me to let him know that only the handful of aging senior professors on the committee thought the dean a possible candidate; that those men thought so primarily because they were conservative men getting along in years and because the dean represented to them a known quantity; that, except for them, the entire faculty regarded his proposed candidacy as a piece of lunacy. They insisted at once that I was the only feasible channel they had to the trustees, that if I could let Morgan Heartwell know unofficially how the overwhelming majority of the faculty felt, then the trustees would come to see for themselves what the situation was. As a result, there would be no ugly rift and contest between the older and the younger members of the faculty. They were thinking of the good of the college. They did not believe that under such a man as the former head coach the college could maintain its academic excellence. They were taking the only course that their collective conscience and professional ethics permitted them to take.

Here was precisely the sort of meddling, the sort of involvement I had long since determined to avoid. I had even managed to keep out of most committee work, on the grounds that it interfered with the more serious work I had to do and on the very legitimate grounds that there were people aplenty who liked nothing better than committee work. I used to say that when I received more than one notice of committee meetings in the morning mail, I had heard the sound of my neighbor's ax, and that it was time for me to move on. My first impulse was to laugh as heartily at the role they were now asking me to play as I had at the notion of the dean's being a college president. And yet, with their talk of academic excellence and professional ethics, they really left me no choice. I agreed on the spot to perform the mission.

And it turned out just as they predicted. Morgan Heartwell had entertained doubts even before I came to him, and so had the other trustees he subsequently spoke to. The night that the group of young professors came to my house was in November. By March, another man had been chosen for the presidency. The acting president would serve till the end of the current academic year, and then the new president would take office.

But by March of that year there had been other developments. One of the senior professors in the college had died. The faculty was once again playing a game of musical chairs with houses. There were days when the community held its breath, waiting to know whether or not Professor So-and-So was going to take such-and-such a house. By March also, Marie had learned definitely that she was pregnant once again. (Maisie was born the following November.) Marie began to think that with the new baby the inconveniences of the old house we were in would become quite intolerable. Moreover, I had come to realize that upon the arrival of the baby my study would have to be converted into a nursery. And so we began to take an interest in the houses which, one after another, became available.

The rule was that each house, as it became available, was offered first to the senior member of the faculty—no matter if he had moved the month before, no matter if the house had five bedrooms and he was childless or even wifeless—and then, if it were refused, the house was offered down through the ranks till it found a taker. We could hardly believe our luck—Marie and I—when no full professor and no associate professor spoke for the Dodson house, which was offered around during the first two weeks of March. It was a charming house with four bedrooms, a modern kitchen, a study. We knew that I stood first on the list of assistant professors. We waited for the customary mimeographed notice to appear in my mailbox at the college.

Days passed. Two weeks passed. Still no notice. On the first of

April, I went to the office of the acting president and made inquiry. I was told by the acting president's secretary, Mrs. Eason, that the acting president had decided that since no full or associate professor had taken the Dodson house it would be removed from the list and offered to the new chaplain, who was scheduled to be appointed within the next two years. Meanwhile, the house would stand empty. Meanwhile, Marie would continue to scrub our splintery old floors and would wash diapers in a tub in the cellar. Meanwhile, I would give up my study to the new baby . . . I lost my temper. I went to my office and wrote a letter to the acting president, saying that I wished my present house to be put on the available list and that I expected to be offered the Dodson house. I received no reply to my letter. But two days later my house was offered to another assistant professor and was accepted. After a further two days, I did receive a reply to my letter. The acting president had consulted the members of his committee on houses (whose membership coincided precisely with that of the now defunct Faculty Committee for Selecting a President) and they agreed with him that the Dodson house should not at this time be offered to anyone below the rank of associate professor.

Fortunately—or so I thought of it at the time—I had in my possession a letter from the late president, written to me in Italy only a few days before his stroke, promising that I would be promoted to the rank of associate professor on my return. Marie had urged me to present that letter to the administration as soon as we got home, but I felt certain that a copy of the letter was in the president's files and that some action would be taken on it in due time. It seemed unbecoming of me to go at once on my return and demand that action be taken on my dead benefactor's promise. And after I had waited six months, I felt that I hardly knew how best to introduce the subject. But now I did bring forth the letter from my file. If I was entitled to promotion, then we were entitled to the Dodson house. And only by presenting my just claims to the faculty would I be able to determine for certain whether or not the dean, having heard of my role in checking his ambitions, had taken his personal revenge upon me.

With my letter in my pocket, I went to call on all six of the young professors who had sent me on my mission to Morgan Heartwell. I pointed out to them, one by one, just how the business of the house had developed, and I received the impression from each of them that he was already well aware of the developments. With each of them, I then brought out my letter from the late president and insisted upon his reading it. And finally I asked each one of them if he would be willing to present my case, in its entirety, at the next faculty meeting. There was not one of them who did not indicate that he was convinced the acting president knew of the part I had played in blocking his permanent appointment. There was not one of them who expressed any doubt that the removal of the Dodson house from the list had been an act of reprisal against me. But they were a very responsible, discreet, and judicious group of young men. Each of them asserted that he was thoroughly sympathetic to my claim, but asked to be allowed to give the matter more thought before deciding what action ought to be taken. My supposition was that there would be a general consultation among the six of them and that some sort of presentation would be made at the April meeting.

I shall never forget walking alone from my house to the administration building for that April meeting—at four o'clock in the afternoon, on the first Monday in the month. I arrived earlier than I usually did at those meetings, and so was able to choose a seat at the back of the president's assembly room. Faculty meetings there, as in most places, usually filled the room from the rear forward, in just the same way that students ordinarily fill a college classroom. I sat in the next-to-last row and watched my colleagues strolling in from their afternoon classes, some in earnest conversation, others making jokes and tapping each other firmly on the forearm or even patting each other on the back, and some few peering into notes on reports they would give that afternoon. I kept my eye out, of course, for the arrival of my six friends. Unconsciously, I had invented an image of their arriving as a group, perhaps still consulting among themselves in whispers, and taking their places together on the first row squarely in front of the president's lectern. Instead, I saw them arrive one by one, seemingly unaware of my presence and certainly unaware of one another's. Before the meeting began, all six had arrived, but they were scattered over the room. I watched them in their tweed jackets and blue or striped shirts chatting casually and amiably with various black-suited, bow-tied senior members of the faculty. At the moment when the meeting was called to order, I was struck suddenly by the notion that I had not taken these men's character and style into account. They would never be so obvious as my fantasy had suggested. They *would* enter the room separately, having decided earlier on the strategy. One of them would rise at the proper time and bring up the question of the Dodson house. And then, with seeming spontaneity and from all corners of the room, the others would join in the attack, one of them finally—if the chair adamantly refused to offer the Dodson house to the lower rank—one of them finally making direct reference to the promise of promotion made me by the revered late president.

Following the minutes from the last meeting, pieces of old business occupied the first half hour of the meeting. I sat through the minutes and through the old business with patience, anticipating what I believed was to follow. When the question, "Any new business?" came, I closed my eyes and listened for the familiar voice. Unless my ears deceived me, it was the young biologist in my group who was speaking. He was one of those with a neat little mustache on his upper lip. With my eyes closed, I could see him, could see him self-consciously patting the bowl of his pipe on the palm of his left hand as he began to speak. "Mr. President—" I opened my eyes, and then for a moment I was convinced my ears did deceive me. It was the young biologist all right, standing near the front of the room and patting the bowl of his dark pipe on the palm of his left hand, but the piece of new business he was introducing was a matter of next year's curriculum. I sat through his remarks and through other remarks that followed on the subject. In fact, I sat through two other new pieces of business, even through a count of hands on one piece that came to a motion and a vote. But when a fourth piece, relating to the awarding of honorary degrees was introduced, I rose from my chair, moved down the row I was sitting in, saying, "Excuse me. Excuse me. Excuse me," marched down the center aisle and out of the meeting.

I went home, and behind the closed door of my study I began composing my letter of resignation. Marie, who was in the kitchen, had heard me come in. But she waited fifteen minutes or so before she came and knocked on my door.

When I opened the door, she looked at me questioningly. She was white with anger. "He refused to offer us the house?" she said.

"Not exactly." I replied. "The subject was not introduced. The six of them came to the meeting and spoke at length—about other things."

Her face turned from white to crimson. Her eyes, still on me, melted. She burst into tears and threw herself into my arms. Or, rather, she drew me into her arms, for as she wept I felt her two arms go around me and felt her hands patting me consolingly high on the back between the shoulder blades. As she held me there, it was all I could do to keep from weeping myself. And somehow, for all her tenderness at that moment and despite all the need I had of it, it came over me that this was the beginning of the end for us, that our marriage would not survive it. Perhaps that was nonsense. The thoughts that cross one's mind at such times cannot always be accounted for. But the life we had lived since graduate school—beginning in graduate school—was the life most couples live who take refuge in the Groves of Academe. We had lived with each other, had lived *together* in the most literal sense. We had shared intellectual interests, had shared domestic duties, had breakfasted together, lunched together, dined together. We had slept together, too, but that had come to seem only one, not too significant facet of our—our "togetherness." I had no right to complain against this life, because this life was the life I had chosen. But I could see that the future would mean a narrowing of my activities among my colleagues wherever I might go, and that things relating to my profession, which had for some time been ruled out of our talk at home, must now inevitably become the very center of it.

When, after dinner that night, I received a telephone call from my friend the biologist, saying that he and one other of the group would like to come by and talk to me, Marie, who was sitting close by my side with her arm about my waist, indicated with a shake of her head that I should not let them come. But I was not yet ready for that. I told them to come ahead, and then I went and switched on the front-porch light.

When they arrived, I led them to my study, and we sat down on three straight chairs in a triangle, facing each other. They told me that, before that afternoon's meeting, there *had* been a general consultation among the six men I went to see and that they had decided that to bring up my "problem" at this meeting would not be a wise move, could, in fact, create a very bad situation. "It would be most impolitic," one of them said. "Strategically speaking, it would be a very bad move," said the other. "It would be a bad business." And they proceeded to explain to me that though the dean would no longer be acting president, he would continue to be a very important part of the college's administration. A head-on collision with him just before the arrival of the new president might be a very disruptive thing for the college. After all, we were all going to have to continue to live with the dean. "Even you are," they said to me. And all of this was said with the same voice that had said we must avoid any ugly rift and contest with the senior members of the faculty. Before they finished speaking, I saw once and for all what a foolish man I had been. But I did not make myself a bigger fool by losing my temper and telling them that I saw what a fool they had made of me. As we went to the door, I agreed with them that probably my house could be reassigned to me—as no doubt it could have been—especially if one of them went to the dean and explained that I had written my letter to him in a moment of anger and that I now wished to remain where I was. But when they were gone, I put out the porch light, went back to my study, and typed up the final version of my letter of resignation.

Marie and I were in perfect agreement about the resignation. During the months that followed, which was naturally a very trying period, her understanding, her sympathy, her tenderness—her indulgence, really—were my great support. When I returned from my office late that Sunday afternoon, depressed and with a crick in my neck after a long sleep in my leather chair (I have since decided that that was most probably the way my father had spent *his* Sunday in *his* office), Marie greeted me cheerfully, and little Susie almost smothered me with kisses. But somehow the vision I had had of our future, after the fateful faculty meeting, stuck with me. I never for a moment believed our marriage could weather this new turn my life had taken. I don't know why. As my mother would have said, the Old Nick himself seemed to have got in me. I *wouldn't* be consoled, I *wouldn't* be comforted, though I consistently made an effort to seem so. I had never before been so much help in a move as I was in packing up our possessions and unpacking them again when we arrived at our new place. My new appointment was at an enormous state university, situated in a middle-sized Midwestern city. I felt it would be possible to pass unnoticed for years, in the university and in the city. I met my classes, I attended department meetings, I made revisions on the galley proofs of my book. It seems to me I spent a large part of every day taking Susie back and forth to school on the bus. And I spent hours in the park with you, Jack. I don't suppose you remember the little boy there who kept purposely interfering with your play on the jungle gym until one day I caught him and spanked him. His mother threatened to call the police. I'll never forget the satisfaction I took in laughing in her face and threatening to give her the same spanking I had given her little boy. And little Maisie, of course, was born in November after we arrived there. I never changed so many diapers for you and Susie put together as I did for Maisie, or gave so many bottles at predawn hours . . . No, I did not become the tyrant of my household, and I did not, like my father, disturb my wife with long looks and long silences. But I began to feel that with my talk about my book and my talk about the courses I was teaching I was almost intentionally boring Marie to death, boring my students to death, boring myself to death. Before the first semester was half over, Marie was helping me grade my papers and was reading all the books I had to read for my courses. By the time the second semester came round, she had made application to the department and was taken on as a part-time instructor.

It was almost a year to the day after my difficulties about the Dodson house began that two letters, which would altogether change everything for me, were put into my mailbox at the university. One letter came from my predecessor at the college where I have since made my most important contribution to the education of American youth. This letter stated that they were looking for a new dean of men at that college, and asked if I would be willing to come and be interviewed for the appointment. The other letter was from Morgan Heartwell. It was he who had recommended me for the appointment, and he wrote me that he had been able to do so because he had observed that I behaved with such discretion in my altercation with the acting president, putting the welfare of that institution above my personal interests. He also urged me to accept the new appointment, saying that this was a college that had recently been given a handsome endowment, a college with a growing academic reputation. He was not, himself, on the board of trustees there, but close associates of his were and they had happened to mention the opening there.

When Marie read the first letter, she broke into laughter. Then, giving me a serious glance, she read through Morgan's letter. "How dare Morgan Heartwell write you such a letter!" she said. "How dare he suggest such an appointment for you!" She and I were facing each other across the little carrel that we shared in the university library. When I remained silent, she put the letters down on the table and asked, "You are not seriously thinking of going for that interview?"

"I am going to take the job," I said, "if it's offered me."

Folding the letters and replacing them in their envelopes, she said, "Well, you may take it. But I'm staying on here."

"It has already occurred to me that you might say that," I told her directly. "I am not entirely surprised." She sat with her eyes lowered and she blushed so deeply that a new thought now occurred to me. "Is there someone else?" I asked.

"No, I don't think so," she said, looking up at me. "Is there for you?"

"I don't think so," I said.

Of course, the fact is we were both married again within two years to persons we did already know at that state university. But still, it is true that neither of us had been having a real love affair. Perhaps the persons we married, the persons we very soon afterward allowed ourselves to fall in love with, represented for us the only possibilities of happiness either of us had been able to imagine during that bleak year. I suppose it's significant that we both married people who shared none of our professional interests.

After I had been dean of men for two years, I was made academic dean of the college. In two more years, I was president of the college. Even with as little time as you have spent with me through the years, Jack, you have seen what a successful marriage my second marriage has been, and what a happy, active life I have had. One sacrifices the love, even the acquaintance of one's children. One loses something of one's self even. But at least I am not tyrannizing over old women and small children. At least I don't sit gazing into space while my wife or perhaps some kindly neighbor woman waits patiently to see whether or not I will risk a two-heart bid. A man must somehow go on living among men, Jack. A part of him must. It is important to broaden one's humanity, but it is important to remain a mere man, too. But it is a strange world, Jack, in which an old man must tell a young man this.

QUESTIONS

1. How would you describe the prose style of this story? Smooth? Mannered? Lucid? Opaque? Restrained? What does the style reveal about the character of the narrator?
2. What is distinctive about each of the three breakfast table scenes? About

each of the three episodes involving only men? Do these scenes and episodes reveal anything about the story's structure?

3. Social relations, family relations, and sexual relations are major themes in this story. How are these themes expressed through the point of view? Through the imagery of violence? Of money? Of color?
4. What is the time scheme of the story? Does it have any historic significance? What does it reveal about the theme of youth and age? Of innocence and experience?
5. Taylor's story is dominated by a single idea—betrayal. Interpret the story on a symbolic level. What is the significance of the title? As a contrast to "Dean of Men," or as a companion piece, read Katherine Anne Porter's story, "Flowering Judas."

TONE

Tone describes the writer's attitude toward his subject and his audience, the attitudes he encourages and develops in the reader through the dramatic action. The slightest shift in tone may alter the cumulative effect of a story; it may modify our perception of a character or color our sense of an incident's meaning. Is our attitude toward Bartleby hostile or sympathetic? Do we find the narrator in "Dean of Men" sensible and understanding or merely a fool? Does the setting in "Revelation" encourage our admiration for Mrs. Turpin or rather confirm us in our suspicion of her? In each case the author determines the reader's reaction to the narrative. As I. A. Richards remarks in *Practical Criticism*, "many of the secrets of 'style' could . . . be shown to be matters of tone, of the perfect recognition of the writer's relation to the reader in view of what is being said and their joint feelings about it."

One of an author's commonest devices for the manipulation of tone is diction. The following passage is drawn from Graham Greene's "Cheap in August."

> It was cheap in August: the essential sun, the coral reefs, the bamboo bar, and the calypsos—they were all of them at cut prices, like the slightly soiled slips in a bargain sale. Groups arrived periodically from Philadelphia in the manner of school-treats and departed with less *bruit*, after an exact exhausting week, when the picnic was over. Perhaps for twenty-four hours the swimming-pool and the bar were almost deserted, and then another school-treat would arrive, this time from St. Louis. Everyone knew everyone else; they had bussed together to an airport, they had flown together, together they had faced an alien customs; they would separate during the day and greet each other noisily and happily after dark, exchanging impressions of "shooting the rapids," the botanic gardens, the Spanish fort. "We are doing that tomorrow."

Although the paragraph seems on the surface a "neutral" or matter-of-fact description of a Caribbean resort in late summer, the tone is actually languid and enervating. Greene wants us to sense the fatigue that has overcome an otherwise beautiful place. To accomplish this he uses the language of exchange: "cheap in August," "cut prices," "bargain sale." These phrases do more than hint that Jamaica is a good buy in August—they convey an intimation of the sordid ("the slightly soiled slips") as if the "essential sun" and the "coral reefs" were themselves tainted by the slow season's prices. Even the tour groups are made to seem cheaper than they probably are. Philadelphia and St. Louis become interior cities where mindless and passionless people join together for economical fun: "they had bussed together," "they had flown together," "together they had faced an alien customs." Greene's diction, through repetition and variation, creates a portrait of a place dominated by physical exhaustion. The tone encourages us to see the reflection of that exhaustion later on in the heroine's moral lassitude—for, as it turns out, spiritual collapse is a central theme in the story.

Another device available to an author for the management of tone is imagery. Dylan Thomas provides us an example in his story of a young man's fond and foolish passion for Lou, a pretty tart he meets in a pub during one warm and lonely Saturday. The following selection finds the young man, drunk, headed with a boisterous group for Lou's apartment.

The young man, on Lou's knee, saw the town in a daze spin by them, the funnelled and masted smoke-blue outline of the still, droning docks, the lightning lines of the poor streets growing longer, and the winking shops that were snapped out one by one. The car smelt of scent and powder and flesh. He struck with his elbow, by accident, Mrs. Franklin's upholstered breast. Her thighs, like cushions, bore the drunk man's rolling weight. He was bumped and tossed on a lump of women. Breasts, legs, bellies, hands, touched, warmed, and smothered him. On through the night, towards Lou's bed, towards the unbelievable end of the dying holiday, they tore past black houses and bridges, a station in a smoke cloud, and drove up a steep side street with one weak lamp in a circle of railings at the top, and swerved into a space where a tall tenement house stood surrounded by cranes, standing ladders, poles and girders, barrows, brickheaps.

What first strikes us about the passage is the tumultuous use of imagery—the rapid proliferation of details in order to instill a sense of speed in the paragraph, a speed that reflects both the movement of the car and the spinning in the young man's mind. The turmoil, however proves upon closer inspection a skillful patterning of images which convey to us Thomas's vision of a modern nightmare. All the action occurs in the car, and the car becomes indistinguishable from the smell of "scent and powder and flesh." And Mrs. Franklin, with her "upholstered breast" and her thighs "like cushions," silently melds into the car. Both Mrs. Franklin and the car are manufactured products, artificial, sharing between them an absence of spirit. By joining the image of the machine to that of woman (traditionally the source of all renewal), Thomas drives home to us his own peculiar vision of death in the modern wasteland.

To control and enforce his vision Thomas relies on the images of light and dark. Although the action of the paragraph moves in an upward direction, the ascent is into the darkness rather than the light, From the barely perceptible "smoke-blue outline" of the docks to the deepening blackness of the sparsely lighted streets, the young man's journey toward Lou's bed and sexual release becomes a drive toward a final darkness, the death of the spirit. The tone of desolation, the grotesque comedy conveyed through the images and heightened by the fervent, almost compulsive, movement of the prose, reveals to us Thomas's perception of modern love and modern life. Our pilgrimage, he suggests, leads to its own special shrine, "a tall tenement house . . . surrounded by cranes, standing ladders, poles and girders, barrows, brickheaps."

We have seen how diction in "Cheap in August" and imagery in "One Warm Saturday" can contribute to the tone—a tone that in one case provides a background for Greene's view of sexual infidelity, and in another draws us to apprehend Thomas's terror-ridden vision of modern love. A selection from Flannery O'Connor's "Revelation" illustrates the role of irony in developing tone. The scene is a doctor's waiting room in a rural, Southern town. The narrator, Mrs. Turpin, has been observing the various occupants of the small room, silently commenting upon their person and station.

> Next to the child's mother was a red-headed youngish woman, reading one of the magazines and working a piece of chewing gum, hell for leather, as Claud would say. Mrs. Turpin could not see the woman's feet. She was not white-trash, just common. Sometimes Mrs. Turpin occupied herself at night naming the classes of people. On the bottom of the heap were most colored people, not the kind she would have been if she had been one, but most of them; then next to them—not above, just away from—were the white-trash; then above them were the home-owners, and above them the home-and-land owners, to which she and Claud belonged. Above she and Claud were people with a lot of money and much bigger houses and much more land. But here the complexity of it would begin to bear in on her, for some of the people with a lot of money were common and ought to be below she and Claud and some of the people who had good blood had lost their money and had to rent and then there were colored people who owned their homes and land as well. There was a colored dentist in town who had two red Lincolns and a swimming pool and a farm with registered white-face cattle on it. Usually by the time she had fallen asleep all the classes of people were moiling and roiling around in her head, and she would dream they were all crammed in together in a box car, being ridden off to be put in a gas oven.

Flannery O'Connor's method for stripping the narrator's decency depends upon revealing the chaos at the center of Mrs. Turpin's most cherished convictions. She accomplishes this by moving the prose from the assurance and order of calm judgment ("She was not white-trash, just common") through hesitancy ("next to them—not above, just away from") into confusion ("some of the people who had good blood has lost their money") and a final apocalypse. The prose charts the breakdown of Mrs. Turpin's dangerous illusion of her superiority and descends into a horrifying irony as we recognize the dream for the reality. The tone informs us that respectability is the obverse of indifference—and indifference remains our shared sin.

Flannery O'Connor couples an unobtrusive realism with an apparently absurd thought to produce a hilarious comic sequence. The sheer comedy might persuade us to read the passage with amusement; and the point of view might even elicit a note of sympathy for the narrator. But the tone belies the levity of the prose. "Revelation" probes the enormous exterior of Mrs. Turpin, an amiable and decent bourgeoise, uncovering self-deception, indifference, and a common nightmare.

Tone expresses an artist's intimate response to his subject and invites the reader to share that response. It can be developed through language ("Counterparts" dramatizes James Joyce's recognition that there is a thin line between frustration and fury), through imagery ("The Metal Sky" conveys Ervin Krause's view of the terrifying indifference of nature to man's survival), and through irony (the protagonist of "One Warm Saturday" loses the world while he gains his soul). Our sensitivity to tone might indeed prove the measure of our appreciation of the art of fiction.

Ernest Hemingway *(1899–1961) was born in Oak Park, Illinois, spent his summers in the northern Michigan woods, and entered World War I as a volunteer Red Cross ambulance driver on the Italian front. He was seriously wounded in combat, convalesced in Michigan, and returned to Europe as a newspaper correspondent. During the 1920's Hemingway lived in Paris.* In Our Time *(1924) introduced the lean and ironic manner he cultivated both in fiction*—The Sun Also Rises *(1926)*, A Farewell to Arms *(1929)—and non-fiction*—Death in the Afternoon *(1932)*, Green Hills of Africa *(1935)*, A Moveable Feast *(1964). The Spanish Civil War provided the experience dramatized in* For Whom the Bell Tolls *(1940) while the Caribbean served as setting for* The Old Man and the Sea *(1952). Hemingway received the Nobel Prize in 1954, moved to Idaho in 1958, and—in ill-health—there took his own life.* Islands in the Stream, *a novel, appeared posthumously in 1970.*

Hills Like White Elephants

ERNEST HEMINGWAY

The hills across the valley of the Ebro were long and white. On this side there was no shade and no trees and the station was between two lines of rails in the sun. Close against the side of the station there was the warm shadow of the building and a curtain, made of strings of bamboo beads, hung across the open door into the bar, to keep out flies. The American and the girl with him sat at a table in the shade, outside the building. It was very hot and the express from Barcelona would come in forty minutes. It stopped at this junction for two minutes and went on to Madrid.

"What should we drink?" the girl asked. She had taken off her hat and put it on the table.

"It's pretty hot," the man said.

"Let's drink beer."

"Dos cervezas," the man said into the curtain.

"Big ones?" a woman asked from the doorway.

"Yes. Two big ones."

The woman brought two glasses of beer and two felt pads. She put the felt pads and the beer glasses on the table and looked at the man and the girl. The girl was looking off at the line of hills. They were white in the sun and the country was brown and dry.

"They look like white elephants," she said.

"I've never seen one," the man drank his beer.

"No, you wouldn't have."

"I might have," the man said. "Just because you say I wouldn't have doesn't prove anything."

The girl looked at the bead curtain. "They've painted something on it," she said. "What does it say?"

"Anis del Toro. It's a drink."

"Could we try it?"

The man called "Listen" through the curtain. The woman came out from the bar.

"Four reales."

"We want two Anis del Toro."

"With water?"

"Do you want it with water?"

"I don't know," the girl said. "Is it good with water?"

"It's all right."

"You want them with water?" asked the woman.

"Yes, with water."

"It tastes like licorice," the girl said and put the glass down.

"That's the way with everything."

"Yes," said the girl. "Everything tastes of licorice. Especially all the things you've waited so long for, like absinthe."

"Oh, cut it out."

"You started it," the girl said. "I was being amused. I was having a fine time."

"Well, let's try and have a fine time."

"All right. I was trying. I said the mountains looked like white elephants. Wasn't that bright?"

"That was bright."

"I wanted to try this new drink. That's all we do, isn't it—look at things and try new drinks?"

"I guess so."

The girl looked across at the hills.

"They're lovely hills," she said. "They don't really look like white elephants. I just meant the coloring of their skin through the trees."

"Should we have another drink?"

"All right."

The warm wind blew the bead curtain against the table.

"The beer's nice and cool," the man said.

"It's lovely," the girl said.

"It's really an awfully simple operation, Jig," the man said. "It's not really an operation at all."

The girl looked at the ground the table legs rested on.

"I know you wouldn't mind it, Jig. It's really not anything. It's just to let the air in."

The girl did not say anything.

"I'll go with you and I'll stay with you all the time. They just let the air in and then it's all perfectly natural."

"Then what will we do afterward?"

"We'll be fine afterward. Just like we were before."

"What makes you think so?"

"That's the only thing that bothers us. It's the only thing that's made us unhappy."

The girl looked at the bead curtain, put her hand out and took hold of two of the strings of beads.

"And you think then we'll be all right and be happy."

"I know we will. You don't have to be afraid. I've known lots of people that have done it."

"So have I," said the girl. "And afterward they were all so happy."

"Well," the man said, "if you don't want to you don't have to. I wouldn't have you do it if you didn't want to. But I know it's perfectly simple."

"And you really want to?"

"I think it's the best thing to do. But I don't want you to do it if you don't really want to."

"And if I do it you'll be happy and things will be like they were and you'll love me?"

"I love you now. You know I love you."

"I know. But if I do it, then it will be nice again if I say things are like white elephants, and you'll like it?"

"I'll love it. I love it now but I just can't think about it. You know how I get when I worry."

"If I do it you won't ever worry?"

"I won't worry about that because it's perfectly simple."

"Then I'll do it. Because I don't care about me."

"What do you mean?"

"I don't care about me."

"Well, I care about you."

"Oh, yes. But I don't care about me. And I'll do it and then everything will be fine."

"I don't want you to do it if you feel that way."

The girl stood up and walked to the end of the station. Across, on the other side, were fields of grain and trees along the banks of the Ebro. Far away, beyond the river, were mountains. The shadow of a cloud moved across the field of grain and she saw the river through the trees.

"And we could have all this," she said. "And we could have everything and every day we make it more impossible."

"What did you say?"

"I said we could have everything."

"We can have everything."

"No, we can't."

"We can have the whole world."

"No, we can't."

"We can go everywhere."

"No, we can't. It isn't ours any more."

"It's ours."

"No, it isn't. And once they take it away, you never get it back."

"But they haven't taken it away."

"We'll wait and see."

"Come on back in the shade," he said. "You mustn't feel that way."

"I don't feel any way," the girl said. "I just know things."

"I don't want you to do anything that you don't want to do—"

"Nor that isn't good for me," she said. "I know. Could we have another beer?"

"All right. But you've got to realize—"

"I realize," the girl said. "Can't we maybe stop talking?"

They sat down at the table and the girl looked across at the hills on the dry side of the valley and the man looked at her and at the table.

"You've got to realize," he said, "that I don't want you to do it if you don't want to. I'm perfectly willing to go through with it if it means anything to you."

"Doesn't it mean anything to you? We could get along."

"Of course it does. But I don't want anybody but you. I don't want anyone else. And I know it's perfectly simple."

"Yes, you know it's perfectly simple."

"It's all right for you to say that, but I do know it."

"Would you do something for me now?"

"I'd do anything for you."

"Would you please please please please please please please stop talking?"

He did not say anything but looked at the bags against the wall of the station. There were labels on them from all the hotels where they had spent nights.

"But I don't want you to," he said. "I don't care anything about it."

"I'll scream," the girl said.

The woman came out through the curtains with two glasses of beer and put them down on the damp felt pads. "The train comes in five minutes," she said.

"What did she say?" asked the girl.

"That the train is coming in five minutes."

The girl smiled brightly at the woman, to thank her.

"I'd better take the bags over to the other side of the station," the man said. She smiled at him.

"All right. Then come back and we'll finish the beer."

He picked up the two heavy bags and carried them around the station to the other tracks. He looked up the tracks but could not see the train. Coming back, he walked through the barroom, where people waiting for the train were drinking. He drank an Anis at the bar and looked at the people. They were all waiting reasonably for the train. He went out through the bead curtain. She was sitting at the table and smiled at him.

"Do you feel better?" he asked.

"I feel fine," she said. "There's nothing wrong with me. I feel fine."

QUESTIONS

1. What is the immediate subject of the couple's quarrel? What means does Hemingway use for distinguishing his portraits of the man and the woman?

2. Hemingway's prose conveys both blandness and antagonism. How does the dialogue aid in adjusting the tone? What does irony contribute to the tone?
3. The time covered in this story is measured in minutes. What effect does the time sequence have on the tone of the story?
4. The emotional devastation of "Hills Like White Elephants" parallels the physical devastation of the landscape. How does Hemingway reinforce the one with the other? How is the setting used symbolically? Describe the two sides of the valley. What side are they on when the story opens? What is significant about the man taking their bags "to the other side" at the end of the story?

Ervin D. Krause *(1931–1970) was born in Nebraska, grew up on small farms in neighboring Iowa, and graduated from Iowa State University in 1953 with a degree in physics and mathematics. After a brief period in the Air Force and an even shorter stint as a technical writer for an aircraft manufacturer in St. Louis, he entered the University of Nebraska in 1957 and earned a Master's degree in English.* The Prairie Schooner *published his early stories, with their powerful evocation of the lonely and sparsely populated countryside along the Nebraska/Iowa border. "The Right Hand" (1960) won the Mari Sandoz Writing Award while "The Quick and the Dead" (1960) and "The Snake" (1961) were reprinted in the O. Henry award volumes for 1961 and 1963, respectively. Krause published his stories exclusively in journals and magazines, including* College English *and* Northwest Review. *His fiction has never been colleeted. In 1961 Krause joined the faculty at the University of Hawaii where he taught creative writing. Before his death from Hodgkin's disease at his home in Honolulu, Krause completed a large number of unpublished novels and stories.*

The Metal Sky

ERVIN D. KRAUSE

It was early when he brought the tractor down the hill from the farmstead to cultivate the corn. The cultivator hung on the tractor like a spider, moving and jerking and groaning with the movements of the tractor. It was cool in the hollow by the ditch, and the heavy dew hung in silent and plastic rainbow-colored droplets from the willows and from the bayonet-shaped cornleaves, and when the tractor raced through, the droplets shattered and rained on the tractor and on the blue denim legs of the man who was driving. The tractor went fast and the black earth curled up and turned like something alive before the cultivator shovels.

The ditch was broad and steep. It had been part of a pasture, but the man had plowed the fertile hill and put it in crops and then he had cut a few of the willows that grew in thicket-like profusion along the bank and had planted corn there too. There were still willows growing in the ditch and struggling along the edges of the bank. There was no water there except with heavy rains, and sometimes a puddle stood for days, hidden in weeds at the bottom of the ditch and hovered over by yellow butterflies.

The noise of the tractor was very loud in the hollow and the birds in the willows scattered when the tractor came by. The man turned at the end of the field and swung back into the corn and the shovels spun the earth up, loosening the earth and shaking it, and he worked near the edge of the bank, the large hind wheel of the tractor skirting the weed cover there.

The bank gave way almost soundlessly and leisurely far behind the tractor and the earth slid quietly down into the ditch, and the moving crust of bank ate away and pursued the tractor. The man was looking forward and he did not see it eating away behind him, and he felt it finally, the escaping earth tugging at the wheel.He looked and saw the almost casual destruction below him and he swung the wheel of the tractor hard, away from the bank, but this gesture only assisted the moving earth, for it threw the weight on the outer wheel. The front of the tractor rose and the spider arms of the cultivator sprang into the air above the corn, and the bright steel shovels glittered, and then with the sigh of the escaping earth the tractor slid and rolled and fell. The man held the wheel and he tried to move with the roll of the tractor but the steel bars caught him and pulled him in and he was held there, vised in between the wheel and the earth in the ditch.

The sun was looking at him when he recovered consciousness. It was all he could see at first, the hard and insistent yellow eye probing him. And around the sun the sky was a polished and bright metal blue. It occurred to him that he was yet in bed and the sun was already up and he strove suddenly to move, and it was then he felt that other insistent scalpel touch in his legs, and he remembered. He lay on his side, and his right arm was twisted under him and his face was burrowed partially into the hard dry earth; his face had struck the pebbly wash of the ditch. His legs were beneath the wheel of the silent tractor; he felt a great numbness there, broken by flashing and gritty sharpness at intervals. He tried to fix the moments of sharpness and he discovered that they came whenever he breathed. When he held his breath the pain did not come at all, there was only the rather satisfying numbness.

He was aware of a gurgling sound nearby and he lifted his head with great effort and looked about him. The sound was from the gasoline tank slowly leaking the fuel. The gasoline dribbled out around the closed cap and streaked down the painted metal and made a little pool in the ditch at the man's elbow. The tank had been full, he thought, it would take a little while to empty, and he tried to think how long he had been there by the way the tank was emptying. There would be help soon, he thought, as soon as he was missed there would be help. He felt his overall bib for the pocket watch and he labored with the fob, dragging the watch out but it was smashed. The hands had even been driven off, and the hand pointed nowhere from the bottom of the crushed crystal. The man looked dumbly at the watch, and he felt the smashed, still creased-together crystal as if it were impossible that the watch could not run. The man squinted at the sun, and it too looked like a watch dial. The sun hung over his head, but it could not be noon, he thought, and he looked again and the sun was directly over him. If it is noon, they will surely miss him, he thought, and they will come searching for him, and this knowledge made him feel a little better. It was hot and the sweat streaked into his eyes and smarted, blinding him at moments and then all he could see was the blurred yellowness of the sun. There was great heat and the sun seemed to focus on him, the heat and the light white and hot and blinding, and he knew it was just his imagination, the sun was the sun and it was always hot and it did not choose to focus on anyone or anything. He would have loved that heat before, he thought, the sunlight that pulled the growing corn and fattened the growing animals, and warmly rubbed his shoulders when he was on the tractor. The sun did not choose him to burn, he thought, and yet it was too hot.

The sharpness in his legs was coming more quickly now, and it was rising, too, feeling up to his thighs, and he tried to recall the connection he had worked out before and he remembered his breathing. He was breathing very quickly and each time there was the sharp hurt, climbing from his legs to his hip, and he tried to slow his breathing, but he could not. The sun, it is too hot, he thought, and he remembered his hat, but the hat had fallen somewhere. He lifted his head and looked carefully and slowly about him. To lift his head caused him great pain. The straw hat rested against the foxtail beyond the wash, perhaps two yards from him. One end of it was tipped up and the hat swayed from time to time as little breezes eddied down the gulley. The man looked at the hat and he watched, straining his head and eyes to see it. The man did not feel any of the breezes that moved the hat, and it was as if the foxtail swayed of their own accord and thus swayed the hat with them. The man reached for the hat but it was far far beyond him.

The exertion wore upon him and he turned his head down again. The sun poured down. He felt the heat and he closed his eyes to rest. But there was another yellowness and he squinted and saw the sun very close to him and very bright and hot. It glittered and it moved and swayed delicately. The sun had moved, he thought, and he looked where the sun was supposed to be and it was still there. The other light was the sun reflected clearly from the shiny metal that the pouring gasoline had cleansed and he could not look anywhere now without the sun being there.

Perhaps he could dig, he thought, perhaps there was loose dirt beneath his legs and he could pull himself away to the shade. He reached along his body and touched the area where the pain was growing to and he felt the earth beneath his legs. It was hard and dry and pebbly there in the wash of the gulley. He dug there and even his hard, calloused hands could do nothing; he scratched at the ground and made a little hole that he could just put his hand into, after great exertion, but his hand was bleeding then and exhaustion came on him. He cursed to himself, he cursed the hard dry ground and he cursed the tractor with its weight upon him and he cursed the pain and the land and the hard yellow sun. He let his head drop upon the pebbly earth and the sun lavished its yellow heat upon him.

The low strange sound awoke him; it was a heavy sound, like a groan or a sigh and he heard it dimly and listened and it was close to him. He thought of men coming in search for him, with shovels and strength to free him, but the sound was too strange and too heavy and he knew then it was himself, breathing, and he could listen to himself as from a distance. He moved his body slightly and the instant pain shot through him and seemed to burst in fire through his skull. He was truly awake then, and the heat was very heavy upon his face. He knew he was badly burned and he tried to pull his shirt up to cover his face, but he could not pull it far enough and if he moved too much the pain from his legs came driving up so that he could not do anything. Breathing was beginning to be hard for him now. The sun had moved slightly, he thought, for the reflection from the tractor was dull, and yet the sun was there, still above him. He looked across the sky for clouds, for the floating cotton clumps that collected on summer afternoons and sometimes glowered together to cause rain. But there were no clouds. The sky was hot and blue, shaped like a metal plate and with the color of the flame of a gasoline burner, and the blue became pale and brittled and yellow around the watch-dial sun.

He thought there were sounds and he listened. It was mid-afternoon and they would surely be looking for him, he thought. He pictured them coming through the corn rows and following the tractor tracks and noticing the cave-off beside the ditch. And he remembered he had told no one that he would be cultivating the corn in the hollow; the day before he had worked in the upper fields, and if he were missed, the children and the wife would go there first. And here, he thought, the ground dried quickly and the tractor tracks were obliterated by the harrow teeth that followed the wheels of the tractor, and there were the protective, hiding clumps of willows. Because of the trees it was difficult to see far along that winding ditch. There the clusters of willows and the tall weeds and cave-offs were frequent; the rains often undermined the banks and pulled the earth in and perhaps they would not detect this place where the fallen earth was already dried and where it looked like an ancient wound in the bank. The man turned his head to scan the bank and there were trees up there, protecting the slide, and only a very observant one would even notice. But they will have to come soon now, he thought.

He listened above the growing concentration of distractions that he knew was pain that grew in his brain. The birds were chattering and flitting among the willows and they were singing. The birds had been silent for a long time after the accident, or perhaps he did not hear before, the man thought. The birds were there in groups and they were singing, as they sang on any afternoon. And the breeze moved through the willows delicately, sinuously, moving the light green leaves into tentacles, but the breeze did not reach the gulley bed, did not even touch the cattails and the Indian tobacco and the foxtail where the hat still rested.

The mid-afternoon sun tortured the earth around him and wilted the weeds and grass. And yet they did not come. He would shout, he thought, perhaps they would hear. He opened his mouth, but the tongue, foreign and huge, filled up the cavern, and he tried to shout, but his voice escaped drily and he could only croak something he could not understand. He tried to swallow, but the alkali dryness of his mouth prevented it. He croaked the sound again and was satisfied when the chattering birds hesitated in their noise. Perhaps they will yet hear, he thought, and he tried again with all his energy, and a few of the birds flew away this time. He tried again and again to make a sound, but he knew they were not shouts anymore. The birds came back and he could not even hear his voice above the raucous and cheerful noise they made.

His thirst was violent. The man moved himself on his elbow and he looked at the bed of the ditch. Near him the pool of gasoline glittered rainbow-colored in the sun, and as the gasoline evaporated it caused the light to shimmer and the colors to diffuse. A distance away there was a puddle of water, perhaps the size of a man's head, and a cluster of yellow butterflies moved above the muddy, tiny pool. The butterflies surged in and out, restlessly, and without any sound. They fluttered and turned and milled in the brilliant light of their own coloring so that it was impossible to distinguish them one from another. The butterflies arose suddenly and hovered in a mass above the bank, and the man raised his head to look at the water, only three arm's lengths away. Now that he saw the water clearly, the thirst grew worse, and even the evil pain in his legs was insignificant.

The butterflies returned. One felt the man's motion and came to flutter in his face. He felt the faint elastic brush upon his burning skin. He knew the butterflies did this to drive other moving creatures away; it was the season of their breeding. The legs walked coolly on his cheek and rested, and the gorgeous yellow wings moved ever so slightly to give it balance.

The man felt the butterfly there, and it was unconcerned, as if he were already dead. The man lifted his free hand slowly and he brought his fingers up and then very carefully and quickly snapped the fingers shut on the arched yellow wings. The butterfly struggled, but its wings were caught and its fragile black body vibrated in its writhings. The yellow dust on the wings rubbed off and filtered down, lightly.

It will know I am not dead, the man thought. It alone, if nothing else, will know. He held the fragile wings of yellow light, with the wings so delicate he could not even feel them between his hardened hands. The butterfly tried to move and could not and the claws of its legs clasped the air. Perhaps it thinks it is near death, the man thought, it has not been in this position before and it knows it is strange and terrible to be near death with nothing else around. How easy it is to give death, the man thought, how easy to crush out something, to say, "I give thee death." But how impossible it is to say, "I give thee life." What was once something, something perhaps delicate and beautiful, becomes nothing in that terrible and decisive moment of death, and there was nothing dead that was ever beautiful. And there is nothing anyone can ever do to change it. How little it took sometimes, and he thought of the usual afternoons in the field, and where he would be, cultivating the tall corn on the hills now, where there was a breeze and coolness, where the sun was warmly light on his shoulders, and where the crops grew, and the wind was caressing, and he remembered the waterjugs and how he turned his face up and the cool water splashed over his face and down his shirt, and he remembered his son riding on the tractor with him, and it had been pleasant, for he took pride in that powerful machine, and in the good, rich soil, and in his son. But something had said, or they had conspired and said. "I give thee death," and in one moment of a usual morning, he lay half-crushed and enfeebled in the ditch.

He moved his fingers and he crushed the brittle butterfly. In one instant, now, the man thought, I give thee death, and the moment was gone, the instant, the now, already past, was irretrievable. He let the fragility fall, and there was still the light yellow smudge of the wing coloring covering the blood on the man's fingertips.

The sun was like a white hot hammer on his skull. The pain of his legs had settled to a heavy and throbbing sharpness. His mouth was arid and his lips were beginning to crack. He was aware of a labored, groaning sound when he worked to take a breath. And the worst was the sun and the metal sky.

It was as if he could feel his brain shrinking and drying out and beginning to flake off in little feathers of nothingness. It was then he thought that he would die. He knew no one would come. If it would only rain, he thought, if there would only be water.

He began to go under for moments and he did not want to lose consciousness, and he fought it, but gradually it overcame him and he would start into consciousness again and nothing would be changed. The sun hung in the same place, and the birds chattered and the breezes moved the top branches of the willows.

Two sparrows dropped from the trees and hung upon the hemp weeds, and their bright black eyes noted the man and forgot him, and the birds hit the pebbly wash of the ditch in a tangle of grayness and feathers, breeding. The female fled, but the male hopped with insolence almost to the man's face before it too flew away. A while later the goldfinches came to the ditch and they pecked at the foxtail seeds. They clawed at the weeds and they ate and left.

The man prayed. He tried to remember some of the prayers he'd learned long before, but even the common prayer that began with "Our Father" did not come back to him, and he said to himself, dear God, dear God, bring me water, let it rain. He heard himself murmuring, high-pitched and laboring, and he said, let the others find me. Let me have water, God.

When he looked again, the sun had visibly lowered, but it was no cooler. He thought perhaps he might have slept, for his head was clearer and he remembered many things. His legs did not pain so badly and he could actually raise himself on his elbow without the pain in his chest preventing it. The puddle of gasoline was still there beside him, and it was widening, and he noticed a different coloration, that the liquid was redder and thicker, and it came to him that he was bleeding, that he had been losing that steady trickle of blood all day and his blood and the gasoline were collecting there in front of him.

He was enraged suddenly, and he wanted to weep in his terrible anger. He pressed with all his strength against the hot wheel of the tractor, but nothing moved. He struck at the red steel of the tractor, and the metal was too hot to touch. The metal was foreign and alien there, burning and glistening, and there he was, he thought in his fury, caught beneath the machine, pinned by the hot, unwholesome metal into the earth, and he could not do anything at all. He beat at the metal until his hands began to bleed again, and it was no use. The hot steel of the tractor was shiny and undented.

The man cursed the machine. The tractor was an enemy to him, he thought, it had thrown him and trapped him, and it would not help him. It had been the tool to say, I give thee death. It had conspired to crush him, it and the sun.

And yet, he thought, when the ineffectual struggle was finished, when he lay back again, and yet, the machine was only part of it, for the hostile earth, the sliding bank and the hard, pebbly wash, pinned him there, too, and there was the hostile sun, and the blue-burner sky. He was a fool, he thought, there was nothing hostile there, nothing had conspired against him, the world was unchanged. There was really no concern with these things around him, with these things that led him to death, there was only disconcern and utter detachment. He was the alien, the hostile one, there. The land and the things that grew from the land, and the metal sky and the hot sun, and even the machine, fashioned by hands not unlike his, none of them had any concern, and even though he was wedded to that soil, pinned by the earth and the machine, and his blood mixed with the blood of the tractor, he had no connection with anything there. The units were detached; he was alien; he was alone. And he would die as he had lived. It was a terrible realization.

He felt the warm rubber tire, the same tire that pinned him there. The tractor will be all right again, he thought, they will lift the machine and drain it and clean it thoroughly and fill it with fuel and it will run as well as ever; life is not a part of it, it cannot be crushed. He remembered the pride he had had with it, and how he had loved to run this tractor and how he had talked of the work it could do, and how things were better because of this machine. And now only the machine would ever be good again, even if they now lay dead like this together, and the blood ran out of them both and mixed in the gravel beside them.

He turned his face away from the tractor. The sun beat down. The butterflies swarmed, the birds fought and screamed, the breeze touched the languid treetops.

The sun had set itself on the rim of the ditch when the deerflies struck him. They came buzzing suddenly and they tangled in his hair and found his ears to burrow into and they struggled into his nostrils and bit sharply and angrily. The man moved his hands feebly against the flies. He had lost all of his strength, he thought, and then he remembered the bloating, fly-infested bodies of animals he had seen dead in fields, and how the maggots were working almost before the carcass was cool. He thought how it would be to find him like that, green and with the worms lacerating his face, and he fought against the flies, but they were inexorable and angry. The man became furious too, and he struck at them, and then he dug at the dirt and he covered his skin and his head with the dust and crumbs of dirt. The flies persisted, but the man covered himself finally, and he lay beneath the gentle and cool layer of dust, with his hand over his nostrils, and the flies left gradually, and he was alone again.

The sun watched him lingeringly and moved with slowness beyond the edge of the bank. It was cool then, suddenly. The evening clouds came up, with the color of wine. The birds shrilled and worked high after mosquitoes. The butterflies were gone; they had gone with the sun. And there was the scurry of small animals in the weeds.

The flakes in his skull were falling rapidly now, he thought, there was no feeling in him any more, it was as if the weight of the tractor was already off him, as if there was no machine, no life, no light, nothing, around him; the world was settling in his flaking-off brain.

There was a padding sound near him and he saw the lean coyote slip along the bed of the ditch, and the coyote sniffed at the straw hat and it turned the hat, and the light wind rolled the hat very near the man, almost to his head. The coyote saw the man then and it came up, sniffing gingerly. The coyote had eyes that were yellow-green and the eyes burned in the darkness like oil, and the animal came to sniff at the dust-covered and swollen strangeness, and it brought its wet nostrils to within an inch of the man's. The coyote backed away and it began to pant lightly, and it scratched itself, leisurely, and then its head came up, alert, and the animal turned and slipped away, without sound.

The man thought he heard voices and shouts and footsteps and he looked up. No, he had been dreaming, he thought, and he turned his body quite easily. He recalled the yellow-green eyes, like fire, and he wondered if he had dreamed that too. His hand flung out and he touched moisture, and his mouth gagged after water, and it took him a thrilling instant to realize it was the gasoline puddle beside him. It was thick now, and coarse with blood.

The night came on blackly, the stars were out, and the locusts and crickets buzzed with violence near beside him. The moon rose above the ditch, and it was enormous and flattened and gold. The eyes and the mouth of it were agonized and lamenting. The man was glad when he saw the moon. The moon is my sister, he thought. The flakes within his skull were falling upon his eyes, and he thought of someone or something bringing him water. Overhead, the wind-swayed willows made scratches against the terrible moon.

QUESTIONS

1. How would you characterize the view of nature that the story reveals? Brutal? Passive? Malevolent? Indifferent? Does the narrator discover anything about nature? About himself?
2. Describe the structure of the story? Does the point of view contribute anything to the structure?
3. What does the scene between the man and the yellow butterfly symbolize? What does the coyote symbolize? What is the significance of the title?
4. Words like "evil," "pride," "cursed," and "fallen" seem out of place in a strictly naturalistic story of death. Could you offer a symbolic reading of the story?
5. A contemporary critic offers the following observation on Krause's style: "Faulkner, Hemingway, Stephen Crane, and especially Lawrence are active in his style without ever taking control of it. He is a writer with great meditative dignity of address." Comment on this observation.

Yukio Mishima (1925–1970), the internationally popular Japanese writer, wrote some eighty short stories, three dozen plays, and a score of novels before his death by suicide in protest against changes in post-World War Japan. His interest in the traditional samurai spirit contributed to the violence and blood symbolism that permeates his work. His works available in English include Death in Midsummer and Other Stories *(1966) and* Five Modern Noh Plays *(1957).*

Patriotism

YUKIO MISHIMA

1

On the twenty-eighth of February, 1936 (on the third day, that is, of the February 26 Incident). Lieutenant Shinji Takeyama of the Konoe Transport Battalion—profoundly disturbed by the knowledge that his closest colleagues had been with the mutineers from the beginning, and indignant at the imminent prospect of Imperial troops attacking Imperial troops—took his officer's sword and ceremonially disemboweled himself in the eight-mat room of his private residence in the sixth block of Aoba-cho, in Yotsuya Ward. His wife, Reiko, followed him, stabbing herself to death. The lieutenant's farewell note consisted of one sentence: "Long live the Imperial Forces." His

*Translated by Geoffrey W. Sargent.

wife's, after apologies for her unfilial conduct in thus preceding her parents to the grave, concluded: "The day which, for a soldier's wife, had to come, has come. . . ." The last moments of this heroic and dedicated couple were such as to make the gods themselves weep. The lieutenant's age, it should be noted, was thirty-one, his wife's twenty-three; and it was not half a year since the celebration of their marriage.

2

Those who saw the bride and bridegroom in the commemorative photograph—perhaps no less than those actually present at the lieutenant's wedding—had exclaimed in wonder at the bearing of this handsome couple. The lieutenant, majestic in military uniform, stood protectively beside his bride, his right hand resting upon his sword, his officer's cap held at his left side. His expression was severe, and his dark brows and wide-gazing eyes well conveyed the clear integrity of youth. For the beauty of the bride in her white over-robe no comparisons were adequate. In the eyes, round beneath soft brows, in the slender, finely shaped nose, and in the full lips, there was both sensuousness and refinement. One hand, emerging shyly from a sleeve of the over-robe, held a fan, and the tips of the fingers, clustering delicately, were like the bud of a moonflower.

After the suicide, people would take out this photograph and examine it, and sadly reflect that too often there was a curse on these seemingly flawless unions. Perhaps it was no more than imagination, but looking at the picture after the tragedy it almost seemed as if the two young people before the gold-lacquered screen were gazing, each with equal clarity, at the deaths which lay before them.

Thanks to the good offices of their go-between, Lieutenant General Ozeki, they had been able to set themselves up in a new home at Aoba-chō in Yotsuya. "New home" is perhaps misleading. It was an old three-room rented house backing onto a small garden. As neither the six- nor the four-and-a-half-mat room downstairs was favored by the sun, they used the upstairs eight-mat room as both bedroom and guest room. There was no maid, so Reiko was left alone to guard the house in her husband's absence.

The honeymoon trip was dispensed with on the grounds that these were times of national emergency. The two of them had spent the first night of their marriage at this house. Before going to bed, Shinji, sitting erect on the floor with his sword laid before him, had bestowed upon his wife a soldierly lecture. A woman who had become the wife of a soldier should know and resolutely accept that her husband's death might come at any moment. It could be tomorrow. It could be the day after. But, no matter when it came—he asked—was she steadfast in her resolve to accept it? Reiko rose to her feet, pulled open a drawer of the cabinet, and took out what was the most prized of her new possessions, the dagger her mother had given her. Returning to her place, she laid the dagger without a word on the mat before her, just as her husband had laid his sword. A silent understanding was achieved at once, and the lieutenant never again sought to test his wife's resolve.

In the first few months of her marriage Reiko's beauty grew daily more radiant, shining serene like the moon after rain.

As both were possessed of young, vigorous bodies, their relationship was passionate. Nor was this merely a matter of the night. On more than one occasion, returning home straight from maneuvers, and begrudging even the time it took to remove his mud-splashed uniform, the lieutenant had pushed his wife to the floor almost as soon as he had entered the house. Reiko was equally ardent in her response. For a little more or a little less than a month, from the first night of their marriage Reiko knew happiness, and the lieutenant, seeing this, was happy too.

Reiko's body was white and pure, and her swelling breasts conveyed a firm and chaste refusal; but, upon consent, those breasts were lavish with their intimate, welcoming warmth. Even in bed these two were frighteningly and awesomely serious. In the very midst of wild, intoxicating passions, their hearts were sober and serious.

By day the lieutenant would think of his wife in the brief rest periods between training; and all day long, at home, Reiko would recall the image of her husband. Even when apart, however, they had only to look at the wedding photograph for their happiness to be once more confirmed. Reiko felt not the slightest surprise that a man who had been a complete stranger until a few months ago should now have become the sun about which her whole world revolved.

All these things had a moral basis, and were in accordance with the Education Rescript's injunction that "husband and wife should be harmonious." Not once did Reiko contradict her husband, nor did the lieutenant ever find reason to scold his wife. On the god shelf below the stairway, alongside the tablet from the Great Ise Shrine, were set photographs of their Imperial Majesties, and regularly every morning, before leaving for duty, the lieutenant would stand with his wife at this hallowed place and together they would bow their heads low. The offering water was renewed each morning, and the sacred sprig of *sasaki* was always green and fresh. Their lives were lived beneath the solemn protection of the gods and were filled with an intense happiness which set every fiber in their bodies trembling.

3

Although Lord Privy Seal Saitō's house was in their neighborhood, neither of them heard any noise of gunfire on the morning of February 26. It was a bugle, sounding muster in the dim, snowy dawn, when the ten-minute tragedy had already ended, which first disrupted the lieutenant's slumbers. Leaping at once from his bed, and without speaking a word, the lieutenant donned his uniform, buckled on the sword held ready for him by his wife, and hurried swiftly out into the snow-covered streets of the still darkened morning. He did not return until the evening of the twenty-eighth.

Later, from the radio news, Reiko learned the full extent of this sudden eruption of violence. Her life throughout the subsequent two days was lived alone, in complete tranquility, and behind locked doors.

In the lieutenant's face, as he hurried silently out into the snowy morning, Reiko had read the determination to die. If her husband did not return, her own decision was made: she too would die. Quietly she attended to the disposition of her personal possessions. She chose her sets of visiting kimonos as keepsakes for friends of her schooldays, and she wrote a name and address on the stiff paper wrapping in which each was folded. Constantly admonished by her husband never to think of the morrow, Reiko had not even kept a diary and was now denied the pleasure of assiduously rereading her record of the happiness of the past few months and consigning each page to the fire as she did so. Ranged across the top of the radio were a small china dog, a rabbit, a squirrel, a bear, and a fox. There were also a small vase and a water pitcher. These comprised Reiko's one and only collection. But it would hardly do, she imagined, to give such things as keepsakes. Nor again would it be quite proper to ask specifically for them to be included in the coffin. It seemed to Reiko, as these thoughts passed through her mind, that the expressions on the small animals' faces grew even more lost and forlorn.

Reiko took the squirrel in her hand and looked at it. And then, her thoughts turning to a realm far beyond these childlike affections, she gazed up into the distance at the great sunlike principle which her husband embodied. She was ready, and happy, to be hurtled along to her destruction in that gleaming sun chariot—but now, for these few moments of solitude, she allowed herself to luxuriate in this innocent attachment to trifles. The time when she had genuinely loved these things, however, was long past. Now she merely loved the memory of having once loved them, and their place in her heart had been filled by more intense passions, by a more frenzied happiness. . . . For Reiko had never, even to herself, thought of those soaring joys of the flesh as a mere pleasure. The February cold, and the icy touch of the china squirrel, had numbed Reiko's slender fingers; yet, even so, in her lower limbs, beneath the ordered repetition of the pattern which crossed the skirt of her trim *meisen* kimono, she could feel now, as she thought of the lieutenant's powerful arms reaching out toward her, a hot moistness of the flesh which defied the snows.

She was not in the least afraid of the death hovering in her mind. Waiting alone at home, Reiko firmly believed that everything her husband was feeling or thinking now, his anguish and distress, was leading her—just as surely as the power in his flesh—to a welcome death. She felt as if her body could melt away with ease and be transformed to the merest fraction of her husband's thought.

Listening to the frequent announcements on the radio, she heard the names of several of her husband's colleagues mentioned among those of the insurgents. This was news of death. She followed the developments closely, wondering anxiously, as the situation became daily more irrevocable, why no Imperial ordinance was sent down, and watching what had at first been taken as a movement to restore the nation's honor come gradually to be branded with the infamous name of mutiny. There was no communication from the regiment. At any moment, it seemed, fighting might commence in the city streets, where the remains of the snow still lay.

Toward sundown on the twenty-eighth Reiko was startled by a furious pounding on the front door. She hurried downstairs. As she pulled with fumbling fingers at the bolt, the shape dimly outlined beyond the frosted-glass panel made no sound, but she knew it was her husband. Reiko had never known the bolt on the sliding door to be so stiff. Still it resisted. The door just would not open.

In a moment, almost before she knew she had succeeded, the lieutenant was standing before her on the cement floor inside the porch, muffled in a khaki greatcoat, his top boots heavy with slush from the street. Closing the door behind him, he returned the bolt once more to its socket. With what significance, Reiko did not understand.

"Welcome home."

Reiko bowed deeply, but her husband made no response. As he had already unfastened his sword and was about to remove his greatcoat, Reiko moved around behind to assist. The coat, which was cold and damp and had lost the odor of horse dung it normally exuded when exposed to the sun, weighed heavily upon her arm. Draping it across a hanger, and cradling the sword and leather belt in her sleeves, she waited while her husband removed his top boots and then followed behind him into the "living room." This was the six-mat room downstairs.

Seen in the clear light from the lamp, her husband's face, covered with a heavy growth of bristle, was almost unrecognizably wasted and thin. The cheeks were hollow, their luster and resilience gone. In his normal good spirits he would have changed into old clothes as soon as he was home and have pressed her to get supper at once, but now he sat before the table still in his uniform, his head drooping dejectedly. Reiko refrained from asking whether she should prepare the supper.

After an interval the lieutenant spoke.

"I knew nothing. They hadn't asked me to join. Perhaps out of consideration, because I was newly married. Kanō, and Homma too, and Yamaguchi."

Reiko recalled momentarily the faces of high-spirited young officers, friends of her husband, who had come to the house occasionally as guests.

"There may be an Imperial ordinance sent down tomorrow. They'll be posted as rebels, I imagine. I shall be in command of a unit with orders to attack them. . . . I can't do it. It's impossible to do a thing like that."

He spoke again.

"They've taken me off guard duty, and I have permission to return home for one night. Tomorrow morning, without question, I must leave to join the attack. I can't do it, Reiko."

Reiko sat erect with lowered eyes. She understood clearly that her husband had spoken of his death. The lieutenant was resolved. Each word, being rooted in death, emerged sharply and with powerful significance against this dark, unmovable background. Although the lieutenant was speaking of his dilemma, already there was no room in his mind for vacillation.

However, there was a clarity, like the clarity of a stream fed from melting snows, in the silence which rested between them. Sitting in his own home after the long two-day ordeal, and looking across at the face of his beautiful wife, the lieutenant was for the first time experiencing true peace of mind. For he had at once known, though she said nothing, that his wife divined the resolve which lay beneath his words.

"Well, then . . ." The lieutenant's eyes opened wide. Despite his exhaustion they were strong, and clear, and now for the first time they looked straight into the eyes of his wife. "Tonight I shall cut my stomach."

Reiko did not flinch.

Her round eyes showed tension as taut as the clang of a bell.

"I am ready," she said. "I ask permission to accompany you."

The lieutenant felt almost mesmerized by the strength in those eyes. His words flowed swiftly and easily, like the utterances of a man in delirium, and it was beyond his understanding how permission in a matter of such weight could be expressed so casually.

"Good. We'll go together. But I want you as a witness, first, for my own suicide. Agreed?"

When this was said a sudden release of abundant happiness welled up in both their hearts. Reiko was deeply affected by the greatness of her husband's trust in her. It was vital for the lieutenant, whatever else might happen, that there should be no irregularity in his death. For that reason there had to be a witness. The fact that he had chosen his wife for this was the first mark of his trust. The second, and even greater mark, was that though he had pledged that they should die together he did not intend to kill his wife first—he had deferred her death to a time when he would no longer be there to verify it. If the lieutenant had been a suspicious husband, he would doubtless, as in the usual suicide pact, have chosen to kill his wife first.

When Reiko said, "I ask permission to accompany you," the lieutenant felt these words to be the final fruit of the education which he had himself given his wife, starting on the first night of their marriage, and which had schooled her, when the moment came, to say what had to be said without a shadow of hesitation. This flattered the lieutenant's opinion of himself as a self-reliant man. He was not so romantic or conceited as to imagine that the words were spoken spontaneously, out of love for her husband.

With happiness welling almost too abundantly in their hearts, they could not help smiling at each other. Reiko felt as if she had returned to her wedding night.

Before her eyes was neither pain nor death. She seemed to see only a free and limitless expanse opening out into vast distances.

"The water is hot. Will you take your bath now?"

"Ah yes, of course."

"And supper . . .?"

The words were delivered in such level, domestic tones that the lieutenant came near to thinking, for the fraction of a second, that everything had been a hallucination.

"I don't think we'll need supper. But perhaps you could warm some sake?"

As Reiko rose and took a *tanzen* gown from the cabinet for after the bath, she purposely directed her husband's attention to the opened drawer. The lieutenant rose, crossed to the cabinet, and looked inside. From the ordered array of paper wrappings he read, one by one, the addresses of the keepsakes. There was no grief in the lieutenant's response to this demonstration of heroic resolve. His heart was filled with tenderness. Like a husband who is proudly shown the childish purchases of a young wife, the lieutenant, overwhelmed by affection, lovingly embraced his wife from behind and implanted a kiss upon her neck.

Reiko felt the roughness of the lieutenant's unshaven skin against her neck. This sensation, more than being just a thing of this world, was for Reiko almost the world itself, but now—with the feeling that it was soon to be lost forever—it had freshness beyond all her experience. Each moment had its own vital strength, and the senses in every corner of her body were reawakened. Accepting her husband's caresses from behind, Reiko raised herself on the tips of her toes, letting the vitality seep through her entire body.

"First the bath, and then, after some sake . . . lay out the bedding upstairs, will you?"

The lieutenant whispered the words into his wife's ear. Reiko silently nodded.

Flinging off his uniform, the lieutenant went to the bath. To faint background noises of slopping water Reiko tended the charcoal brazier in the living room and began the preparations for warming the sake.

Taking the *tanzen*, a sash, and some underclothes, she went to the bathroom to ask how the water was. In the midst of a coiling cloud of steam the lieutenant was sitting cross-legged on the floor, shaving, and she could dimly discern the rippling movements of the muscles on his damp, powerful back as they responded to the movement of his arms.

There was nothing to suggest a time of any special significance. Reiko, going busily about her tasks, was preparing side dishes from odds and ends in stock. Her hands did not tremble. If anything, she managed even more efficiently and smoothly than usual. From time to time, it is true, there was a strange throbbing deep within her breast. Like distant lightning, it had a moment of sharp intensity and then vanished without trace. Apart from that, nothing was in any way out of the ordinary.

The lieutenant, shaving in the bathroom, felt his warmed body miraculously healed at last of the desperate tiredness of the days of indecision and filled—in spite of the death which lay ahead—with pleasurable anticipation. The sound of his wife going about her work came to him faintly. A healthy physical craving, submerged for two days, reasserted itself.

The lieutenant was confident there had been no impurity in that joy they had experienced when resolving upon death. They had both sensed at that moment—though not, of course, in any clear and conscious way—that those permissible pleasures which they had shared in private were once more beneath the protection of Righteousness and Divine Power, and of a complete and unassailable morality. On looking into each other's eyes and discovering there an honorable death, they had felt themselves safe once more behind steel walls which none could destroy, encased in an impenetrable armor of Beauty and Truth. Thus, so far from seeing any inconsistency or conflict between the urges of his flesh and the sincerity of his patriotism, the lieutenant was even able to regard the two as parts of the same thing.

Thrusting his face close to the dark, cracked, misted wall mirror, the lieutenant shaved himself with great care. This would be his death face. There must be no unsightly blemishes. The clean-shaven face gleamed once more with a youthful luster, seeming to brighten the darkness of the mirror. There was a certain elegance, he even felt, in the association of death with this radiantly healthy face.

Just as it looked now, this would become his death face! Already, in fact, it had half departed from the lieutenant's personal possession and had become the bust above a dead soldier's memorial. As an experiment he closed his eyes tight. Everything was wrapped in blackness, and he was no longer a living, seeing creature.

Returning from the bath, the traces of the shave glowing faintly blue beneath his smooth cheeks, he seated himself beside the now well-kindled charcoal brazier. Busy though Reiko was, he noticed, she had found time lightly to touch up her face. Her cheeks were gay and her lips moist. There was no shadow of sadness to be seen. Truly, the lieutenant felt, as he saw this mark of his young wife's passionate nature, he had chosen the wife he ought to have chosen.

As soon as the lieutenant had drained his sake cup he offered it to Reiko. Reiko had never before tasted sake, but she accepted without hesitation and sipped timidly.

"Come here," the lieutenant said.

Reiko moved to her husband's side and was embraced as she leaned backward across his lap. Her breast was in violent commotion, as if sadness, joy, and the potent sake were mingling and reacting within her. The lieutenant looked down into his wife's face. It was the last face he would see in this world, the last face he would see of his wife. The lieutenant scrutinized the face minutely, with the eyes of a traveler bidding farewell to splendid vistas which he will never revisit. It was a face he could not tire of looking at—the features regular yet not cold, the lips lightly closed with a soft strength. The lieutenant kissed those lips, unthinkingly. And suddenly, though there was not the slightest distortion of the face into the unsightliness of sobbing, he noticed that tears were welling slowly from beneath the long lashes of the closed eyes and brimming over into a glistening stream.

When, a little later, the lieutenant urged that they should move to the upstairs bedroom, his wife replied that she would follow after taking a bath. Climbing the stairs alone to the bedroom, where the air was already warmed by the gas heater, the lieutenant lay down on the bedding with arms outstretched and legs apart. Even the time at which he lay waiting for his wife to join him was no later and no earlier than usual.

He folded his hands beneath his head and gazed at the dark boards of the ceiling in the dimness beyond the range of the standard lamp. Was it death he was now waiting for? Or a wild ecstasy of the senses? The two seemed to overlap, almost as if the object of this bodily desire was death itself. But however that might be, it was certain that never before had the lieutenant tasted such total freedom.

There was the sound of a car outside the window. He could hear the screech of its tires skidding in the snow piled at the side of the street. The sound of its horn re-echoed from near-by walls. . . . Listening to these noises he had the feeling that this house rose like a solitary island in the ocean of a society going as restlessly about its business as ever. All around, vastly and untidily, stretched the country for which he grieved. He was to give his life for it. But would that great country, with which he was prepared to remonstrate to the extent of destroying himself, take the slightest heed of his death? He did not know; and it did not matter. His was a battlefield without glory, a battlfield where none could display deeds of valor: it was the front line of the spirit.

Reiko's footsteps sounded on the stairway. The steep stairs in this old house creaked badly. There were fond memories in that creaking, and many a time, while waiting in bed, the lieutenant had listened to its welcome sound. At the thought that he would hear it no more he listened with intense concentration, striving for every corner of every moment of this precious time to be filled with the sound of those soft footfalls on the creaking stairway. The moments seemed transformed to jewels, sparkling with inner light.

Reiko wore a Nagoya sash about the waist of her *yukata*, but as the lieutenant reached toward it, its redness sobered by the dimness of the light, Reiko's hand moved to his assistance and the sash fell away, slithering swiftly to the floor. As she stood before him, still in her *yukata*, the lieutenant inserted his hands through the side slits beneath each sleeve, intending to embrace her as she was; but at the touch of his finger tips upon the warm naked flesh, and as the armpits closed gently about his hands, his whole body was suddenly aflame.

In a few moments the two lay naked before the glowing gas heater.

Neither spoke the thought, but their hearts, their bodies, and their pounding breasts blazed with the knowledge that this was the very last time. It was as if the words "The Last Time" were spelled out, in invisible brushstrokes, across every inch of their bodies.

The lieutenant drew his wife close and kissed her vehemently. As their tongues explored each other's mouths, reaching out into the smooth, moist interior, they felt as if the still-unknown agonies of death had tempered their senses to the keenness of red-hot steel. The agonies they could not yet feel, the distant pains of death, had refined their awareness of pleasure.

"This is the last time I shall see your body," said the lieutenant. "Let me look at it closely." And, tilting the shade on the lampstand to one side, he directed the rays along the full length of Reiko's outstretched form.

Reiko lay still with her eyes closed. The light from the low lamp clearly revealed the majestic sweep of her white flesh. The lieutenant, not without a touch of egocentricity, rejoiced that he would never see this beauty crumble in death.

At his leisure, the lieutenant allowed the unforgettable spectacle to engrave itself upon his mind. With one hand he fondled the hair, with the other he softly stroked the magnificent face, implanting kisses here and there where his eyes lingered. The quiet coldness of the high, tapering forehead, the closed eyes with their long lashes beneath faintly etched brows, the set of the finely shaped nose, the gleam of teeth glimpsed between full, regular lips, the soft cheeks and the small, wise chin . . . these things conjured up in the lieutenant's mind the vision of a truly radiant death face, and again and again he pressed his lips tight against the white throat—where Reiko's own hand was soon to strike—and the throat reddened faintly beneath his kisses. Returning to the mouth he laid his lips against it with the gentlest of pressures, and moved them rhythmically over Reiko's with the light rolling motion of a small boat. If he closed his eyes, the world became a rocking cradle.

Wherever the lieutenant's eyes moved his lips faithfully followed. The high, swelling breasts, surmounted by nipples like the buds of a wild cherry, hardened as the lieutenant's lips closed about them. The arms flowed smoothly downward from each side of the breast, tapering toward the wrists, yet losing nothing of their roundness or symmetry, and at their tips were those delicate fingers which had held the fan at the wedding ceremony. One by one, as the lieutenant kissed them, the fingers withdrew behind their neighbor as if in shame. . . . The natural hollow curving between the bosom and the stomach carried in its lines a suggestion not only of softness but of resilient strength, and while it gave forewarning of the rich curves spreading outward from here to the hips it had, in itself, an appearance only of restraint and proper discipline. The whiteness and richness of the stomach and hips was like milk brimming in a great bowl, and the sharply shadowed dip of the navel could have been the fresh impress of a raindrop, fallen there that very moment. Where the shadows gathered more thickly, hair clustered, gentle and sensitive, and as the agitation mounted in the now no longer passive body there hung over this region a scent like the smoldering of fragrant blossoms, growing steadily more pervasive.

At length, in a tremulous voice, Reiko spoke.

"Show me. . . . Let me look too, for the last time."

Never before had he heard from his wife's lips so strong and unequivocal a request. It was as if something which her modesty had wished to keep hidden to the end had suddenly burst its bonds of constraint. The lieutenant obediently lay back and surrendered himself to his wife. Lithely she raised her white, trembling body, and—burning with an innocent desire to return to her husband what he had done for her—placed two white fingers on the lieutenant's eyes, which gazed fixedly up at her, and gently stroked them shut.

Suddenly overwhelmed by tenderness, her cheeks flushed by a dizzying uprush of emotion. Reiko threw her arms about the lieutenant's close-cropped head. The bristly hairs rubbed painfully against her breast, the prominent nose was cold as it dug into her flesh, and his breath was hot. Relaxing her embrace, she gazed down at her husband's masculine face. The severe brows, the closed eyes, the splendid bridge of the nose, the shapely lips drawn firmly together . . . the blue, clean-shaven cheeks reflecting the light and gleaming smoothly. Reiko kissed each of these. She kissed the broad nape of the neck, the strong, erect shoulders, the powerful chest with its twin circles like shields and its russet nipples. In the armpits, deeply shadowed by the ample flesh of the shoulders and chest, a sweet and melancholy odor emanated from the growth of hair, and in the sweetness of this odor was contained, somehow, the essence of young death. The lieutenant's naked skin glowed like a field of barley, and everywhere the muscles showed in sharp relief, converging on the lower abdomen about the small, unassuming navel. Gazing at the youthful, firm stomach, modestly covered by a vigorous growth of hair, Reiko thought of it as it was soon to be, cruelly cut by the sword, and she laid her hand upon it, sobbing in pity, and bathed it with kisses.

At the touch of his wife's tears upon his stomach, the lieutenant felt ready to endure with courage the cruelest agonies of his suicide.

What ecstasies they experienced after these tender exchanges may well be imagined. The lieutenant raised himself and enfolded his wife in a powerful embrace, her body now limp with exhaustion after her grief and tears. Passionately they held their faces close, rubbing cheek against cheek. Reiko's body was trembling. Their breasts, moist with sweat, were tightly joined, and every inch of the young and beautiful bodies had become so much one with the other that it seemed impossible there should ever again be a separation. Reiko cried out. From the heights they plunged into the abyss, and from the abyss they took wing and soared once more to dizzying heights. The lieutenant panted like the regimental standard-bearer on a route march. . . . As one cycle ended, almost immediately a new wave of passion would be generated, and together—with no trace of fatigue—they would climb again in a single breathless movement to the very summit.

4

When the lieutenant at last turned away, it was not from weariness. For one thing, he was anxious not to undermine the considerable strength he would need in carrying out his suicide. For another, he would have been sorry to mar the sweetness of these last memories by overindulgence.

Since the lieutenant had clearly desisted, Reiko too, with her usual compliance, followed his example. The two lay naked on their backs, with fingers interlaced, staring fixedly at the dark ceiling. The room was warm from the heater, and even when the sweat had ceased to pour from their bodies they felt no cold. Outside, in the hushed night, the sounds of passing traffic had ceased. Even the noises of the trains and streetcars around Yotsuya station did not penetrate this far. After echoing through the region bounded by the moat, they were lost in the heavily wooded park fronting the broad driveway before Akasaka Palace. It was hard to believe in the tension gripping this whole quarter, where the two factions of the bitterly divided Imperial Army now confronted each other, poised for battle.

Savoring the warmth glowing within themselves, they lay still and recalled the ecstasies they had just known. Each moment of the experience was relived. They remembered the taste of kisses which had never wearied, the touch of naked flesh, episode after episode of dizzying bliss. But already, from the dark boards of the ceiling, the face of death was peering down. These joys had been final, and their bodies would never know them again. Not that joy of this intensity—and the same thought had occurred to them both—was ever likely to be reexperienced, even if they should live on to old age.

The feel of their fingers intertwined—this too would soon be lost. Even the wood-grain patterns they now gazed at on the dark ceiling boards would be taken from them. They could feel death edging in, nearer and nearer. There could be no hesitation now. They must have the courage to reach out to death themselves, and to seize it.

"Well, let's make our preparations," said the lieutenant. The note of determination in the words was unmistakable, but at the same time Reiko had never heard her husband's voice so warm and tender.

After they had risen, a variety of tasks awaited them.

The lieutenant, who had never once before helped with the bedding, now cheerfully slid back the door of the closet, lifted the mattress across the room by himself, and stowed it away inside.

Reiko turned off the gas heater and put away the lamp standard. During the lieutenant's absence she had arranged this room carefully, sweeping and dusting it to a fresh cleanness, and now—if one overlooked the rosewood table drawn into one corner—the eight-mat room gave all the appearance of a reception room ready to welcome an important guest.

"We've seen some drinking here, haven't we? With Kanō and Homma and Noguchi . . ."

"Yes, they were great drinkers, all of them."

"We'll be meeting them before long, in the other world. They'll tease us, I imagine, when they find I've brought you with me."

Descending the stairs, the lieutenant turned to look back into this calm, clean room, now brightly illuminated by the ceiling lamp. There floated across his mind the faces of the young officers who had drunk there, and laughed, and innocently bragged. He had never dreamed then that he would one day cut open his stomach in this room.

In the two rooms downstairs husband and wife busied themselves smoothly and serenely with their respective preparations. The lieutenant went to the toilet, and then to the bathroom to wash. Meanwhile Reiko folded away her husband's padded robe, placed his uniform tunic, his trousers, and a newly cut bleached loincloth in the bathroom, and set out sheets of paper on the living-room table for the farewell notes. Then she removed the lid from the writing box and began rubbing ink from the ink tablet. She had already decided upon the wording of her own note.

Reiko's fingers pressed hard upon the cold gilt letters of the ink tablet, and the water in the shallow well at once darkened, as if a black cloud had spread across it. She stopped thinking that this repeated action, this pressure from her fingers, this rise and fall of faint sound, was all and solely for death. It was a routine domestic task, a simple paring away of time until death should finally stand before her. But somehow, in the increasingly smooth motion of the tablet rubbing on the stone, and in the scent from the thickening ink, there was unspeakable darkness.

Neat in his uniform, which he now wore next to his skin, the lieutenant emerged from the bathroom. Without a word he seated himself at the table, bolt upright, took a brush in his hand, and stared undecidedly at the paper before him.

Reiko took a white silk kimono with her and entered the bathroom. When she reappeared in the living room, clad in the white kimono with her face lightly made up, the farewell note lay completed on the table beneath the lamp. The thick black brushstrokes said simply:

"Long Live the Imperial Forces—Army Lieutenant Takeyama Shinji."

While Reiko sat opposite him writing her own note, the lieutenant gazed in silence, intensely serious, at the controlled movement of his wife's pale fingers as they manipulated the brush.

With their respective notes in their hands—the lieutenant's sword strapped to his side, Reiko's small dagger thust into the sash of her white kimono—the two of them stood before the god shelf and silently prayed. Then they put out all the downstairs lights. As he mounted the stairs the lieutenant turned his head and gazed back at the striking, white-clad figure of his wife, climbing behind him, with lowered eyes, from the darkness beneath.

The farewell notes were laid side by side in the alcove of the upstairs room. They wondered whether they ought not to remove the hanging scroll, but since it had been written by their go-between,

Lieutenant General Ozeki, and consisted, moreover, of two Chinese characters signifying "Sincerity," they left it where it was. Even if it were to become stained with splashes of blood, they felt that the lieutenant general would understand.

The lieutenant, sitting erect with his back to the alcove, laid his sword on the floor before him.

Reiko sat facing him, a mat's width away. With the rest of her so severely white the touch of rouge on her lips seemed remarkably seductive.

Across the dividing mat they gazed intently into each other's eyes. The lieutenant's sword lay before his knees. Seeing it, Reiko recalled their first night and was overwhelmed with sadness. The lieutenant spoke, in a hoarse voice:

"As I have no second to help me I shall cut deep. It may look unpleasant, but please do not panic. Death of any sort is a fearful thing to watch. You must not be discouraged by what you see. Is that all right?"

"Yes."

Reiko nodded deeply.

Looking at the slender white figure of his wife the lieutenant experienced a bizarre excitement. What he was about to perform was an act in his public capacity as a soldier, something he had never previously shown his wife. It called for a resolution equal to the courage to enter battle; it was a death of no less degree and quality than death in the front line. It was his conduct on the battlefield that he was now to display.

Momentarily the thought led the lieutenant to a strange fantasy. A lonely death on the battlefield, a death beneath the eyes of his beautiful wife . . . in the sensation that he was now to die in these two dimensions, realizing an impossible union of them both, there was sweetness beyond words. This must be the very pinnacle of good fortune, he thought. To have every moment of his death observed by those beautiful eyes—it was like being borne to death on a gentle, fragrant breeze. There was some special favor here. He did not understand precisely what it was, but it was a domain unknown to others: a dispensation granted to no one else had been permitted to himself. In the radiant, bridelike figure of his white-robed wife the lieutenant seemed to see a vision of all those things he had loved and for which he was to lay down his life—the Imperial Household, the

Nation, the Army Flag. All these, no less than the wife who sat before him, were presences observing him closely with clear and never-faltering eyes.

Reiko too was gazing intently at her husband, so soon to die, and she thought that never in this world had she seen anything so beautiful. The lieutenant always looked well in uniform but now, as he contemplated death with severe brows and firmly closed lips, he revealed what was perhaps masculine beauty at its most superb.

"It's time to go," the lieutenant said at last.

Reiko bent her body low to the mat in a deep bow. She could not raise her face. She did not wish to spoil her make-up with tears, but the tears could not be held back.

When at length she looked up she saw hazily through the tears that her husband had wound a white bandage around the blade of his now unsheathed sword, leaving five or six inches of naked steel showing at the point.

Resting the sword in its cloth wrapping on the mat before him, the lieutenant rose from his knees, resettled himself cross-legged, and unfastened the hooks of his uniform collar. His eyes no longer saw his wife. Slowly, one by one, he undid the flat brass buttons. The dusky brown chest was revealed, and then the stomach. He unclasped his belt and undid the buttons of his trousers. The pure whiteness of the thickly coiled loincloth showed itself. The lieutenant pushed the cloth down with both hands, further to ease his stomach, and then reached for the white-bandaged blade of his sword. With his left hand he massaged his abdomen, glancing downward as he did so.

To reassure himself of the sharpness of his sword's cutting edge the lieutenant folded back the left trouser flap, exposing a little of his thigh, and lightly drew the blade across the skin. Blood welled up in the wound at once, and several streaks of red trickled downward, glistening in the strong light.

It was the first time Reiko had ever seen her husband's blood, and she felt a violent throbbing in her chest. She looked at her husband's face. The lieutenant was looking at the blood with calm appraisal. For a moment—though thinking at the same time that it was hollow comfort—Reiko experienced a sense of relief.

The lieutenant's eyes fixed his wife with an intense, hawklike stare. Moving the sword around to his front, he raised himself slightly on his hips and let the upper half of his body lean over the sword point.

That he was mustering his whole strength was apparent from the angry tension of the uniform at his shoulders. The lieutenant aimed to strike deep into the left of his stomach. His sharp cry pierced the silence of the room.

Despite the effort he had himself put into the blow, the lieutenant had the impression that someone else had struck the side of his stomach agonizingly with a thick rod of iron. For a second or so his head reeled and he had no idea what had happened. The five or six inches of naked point had vanished completely into his flesh, and the white bandage, gripped in his clenched fist, pressed directly against his stomach.

He returned to consciousness. The blade had certainly pierced the wall of the stomach, he thought. His breathing was difficult, his chest thumped violently, and in some far deep region, which he could hardly believe was a part of himself, a fearful and excruciating pain came welling up as if the ground had split open to disgorge a boiling stream of molten rock. The pain came suddenly nearer, with terrifying speed. The lieutenant bit his lower lip and stifled an instinctive moan.

Was this *seppuku?*—he was thinking. It was a sensation of utter chaos, as if the sky had fallen on his head and the world was reeling drunkenly. His will power and courage, which had seemed so robust before he had made the incision, had now dwindled to something like a single hairlike thread of steel, and he was assailed by the uneasy feeling that he must advance along this thread, clinging to it with desperation. His clenched fist had grown moist. Looking down, he saw that both his hand and cloth about the blade were drenched in blood. His loincloth too was dyed a deep red. It struck him as incredible that, amidst this terrible agony, things which could be seen could still be seen, and existing things existed still.

The moment the lieutenant thrust the sword into his left side and she saw the deathly pallor fall across his face, like an abruptly lowered curtain, Reiko had to struggle to prevent herself from rushing to his side. Whatever happened, she must watch. She must be a witness. That was the duty her husband had laid upon her. Opposite her, a mat's space away, she could clearly see her husband biting his lip to stifle the pain. The pain was there, with absolute certainty, before her eyes. And Reiko had no means of rescuing him from it.

The sweat glistened on her husband's forehead. The lieutenant closed his eyes, and then opened them again, as if experimenting. The eyes had lost their luster, and seemed innocent and empty like the eyes of a small animal.

The agony before Reiko's eyes burned as strong as the summer sun, utterly remote from the grief which seemed to be tearing herself apart within. The pain grew steadily in stature, stretching upward. Reiko felt that her husband had already become a man in a separate world, a man whose whole being had been resolved into pain, a prisoner in a cage of pain where no hand could reach out to him. But Reiko felt no pain at all. Her grief was not pain. As she thought about this, Reiko began to feel as if someone had raised a cruel wall of glass high between herself and her husband.

Ever since her marriage her husband's existence had been her own existence, and every breath of his had been a breath drawn by herself. But now, while her husband's existence in pain was a vivid reality, Reiko could find in this grief of hers no certain proof at all of her own existence.

With only his right hand on the sword the lieutenant began to cut sideways across his stomach. But as the blade became entangled with the entrails it was pushed constantly outward by their soft resilience; and the lieutenant realized that it would be necessary, as he cut, to use both hands to keep the point pressed deep into his stomach. He pulled the blade across. It did not cut as easily as he had expected. He directed the strength of his whole body into his right hand and pulled again. There was a cut of three or four inches.

The pain spread slowly outward from the inner depths until the whole stomach reverberated. It was like the wild clanging of a bell. Or like a thousand bells which jangled simultaneously at every breath he breathed and every throb of his pulse, rocking his whole being. The lieutenant could no longer stop himself from moaning. But by now the blade had cut its way through to below the navel, and when he noticed this he felt a sense of satisfaction, and a renewal of courage.

The volume of blood had steadily increased, and now it spurted from the wound as if propelled by the beat of the pulse. The mat before the lieutenant was drenched red with splattered blood, and more blood overflowed onto it from pools which gathered in the folds of the lieutenant's khaki trousers. A spot, like a bird, came flying across to Reiko and settled on the lap of her white silk kimono.

By the time the lieutenant had at last drawn the sword across to the right side of his stomach, the blade was already cutting shallow and had revealed its naked tip, slippery with blood and grease. But suddenly stricken by a fit of vomiting, the lieutenant cried out hoarsely. The vomiting made the fierce pain fiercer still, and the stomach, which had thus far remained firm and compact, now abruptly heaved, opening wide its wound, and the entrails burst through, as if the wound too were vomiting. Seemingly ignorant of their master's suffering, the entrails gave an impression of robust health and almost disagreeable vitality as they slipped smoothly out and spilled over into the crotch. The lieutenant's head drooped, his shoulders heaved, his eyes opened to narrow slits, and a thin trickle of saliva dribbled from his mouth. The gold markings on his epaulettes caught the light and glinted.

Blood was scattered everywhere. The lieutenant was soaked in it to his knees, and he sat now in a crumpled and listless posture, one hand on the floor. A raw smell filled the room. The lieutenant, his head drooping, retched repeatedly, and the movement showed vividly in his shoulders. The blade of the sword, now pushed back by the entrails and exposed to its tip, was still in the lieutenant's right hand.

It would be difficult to imagine a more heroic sight than that of the lieutenant at this moment, as he mustered his strength and flung back his head. The movement was performed with sudden violence, and the back of his head struck with a sharp crack against the alcove pillar. Reiko had been sitting until now with her face lowered, gazing with fascination at the tide of blood advancing toward her knees, but the sound took her by surprise and she looked up.

The lieutenant's face was not the face of a living man. The eyes were hollow, the skin parched, the once so lustrous cheeks and lips the color of dried mud. The right hand alone was moving. Laboriously gripping the sword, it hovered shakily in the air like the hand of a marionette and strove to direct the point at the base of the lieutenant's throat. Reiko watched her husband make this last, most heart-rending, futile exertion. Glistening with blood and grease, the point was thrust at the throat again and again. And each time it missed its aim. The strength to guide it was no longer there. The straying point struck the collar and the collar badges. Although its hooks had been unfastened, the stiff military collar had closed together again and was protecting the throat.

Reiko could bear the sight no longer. She tried to go to her husband's help, but she could not stand. She moved through the blood on her knees, and her white skirts grew deep red. Moving to the rear of her husband, she helped no more than by loosening the collar. The quivering blade at last contacted the naked flesh of the throat. At that moment Reiko's impression was that she herself had propelled her husband forward; but that was not the case. It was a movement planned by the lieutenant himself, his last exertion of strength. Abruptly he threw his body at the blade, and the blade pierced his neck, emerging at the nape. There was a tremendous spurt of blood and the lieutenant lay still, cold blue-tinged steel protruding from his neck at the back.

5

Slowly, her socks slippery with blood, Reiko descended the stairway. The upstairs room was now completely still.

Switching on the ground-floor lights, she checked the gas jet and the main gas plug and poured water over the smoldering, half-buried charcoal in the brazier. She stood before the upright mirror in the four-and-a-half-mat room and held up her skirts. The bloodstains made it seem as if a bold, vivid pattern was printed across the lower half of her white kimono. When she sat down before the mirror, she was conscious of the dampness and coldness of her husband's blood in the region of her thighs, and she shivered. Then, for a long while, she lingered over her toilet preparations. She applied the rouge generously to her cheeks, and her lips too she painted heavily. This was no longer make-up to please her husband. It was make-up for the world which she would leave behind, and there was a touch of the magnificent and the spectacular in her brushwork. When she rose, the mat before the mirror was wet with blood. Reiko was not concerned about this.

Returning from the toilet, Reiko stood finally on the cement floor of the porchway. When her husband had bolted the door here last night it had been in preparation for death. For a while she stood immersed in the consideration of a simple problem. Should she now leave the bolt drawn? If she were to lock the door, it could be that the neighbors might not notice their suicide for several days. Reiko did not relish the thought of their two corpses putrefying before discovery. After all, it seemed, it would be best to leave it open. . . . She released the bolt, and also drew open the frosted-glass door a fraction. . . . At once a chill wind blew in. There was no sign of anyone in the midnight streets, and stars glittered ice-cold through the trees in the large house opposite.

Leaving the door as it was, Reiko mounted the stairs. She had walked here and there for some time and her socks were no longer slippery. About halfway up, her nostrils were already assailed by a peculiar smell.

The lieutenant was lying on his face in a sea of blood. The point protruding from his neck seemed to have grown even more prominent than before. Reiko walked heedlessly across the blood. Sitting beside the lieutenant's corpse, she stared intently at the face, which lay on one cheek on the mat. The eyes were opened wide, as if the lieutenant's attention had been attracted by something. She raised the head, folding it in her sleeve, wiped the blood from the lips, and bestowed a last kiss.

Then she rose and took from the closet a new white blanket and a waist cord. To prevent any derangement of her skirts, she wrapped the blanket about her waist and bound it there firmly with the cord.

Reiko sat herself on a spot about one foot distant from the lieutenant's body. Drawing the dagger from her sash, she examined its dully gleaming blade intently, and held it to her tongue. The taste of the polished steel was slightly sweet.

Reiko did not linger. When she thought how the pain which had previously opened such a gulf between herself and her dying husband was now to become a part of her own experience, she saw before her only the joy of herself entering a realm her husband had already made his own. In her husband's agonized face there had been something inexplicable which she was seeing for the first time. Now she would solve that riddle. Reiko sensed that at last she too would be able to taste the true bitterness and sweetness of that great moral principle in which her husband believed. What had until now been tasted only faintly through her husband's example she was about to savor directly with her own tongue.

Reiko rested the point of the blade against the base of her throat. She thrust hard. The wound was only shallow. Her head blazed, and her hands shook uncontrollably. She gave the blade a strong pull sideways. A warm substance flooded into her mouth, and everything before her eyes reddened, in a vision of spouting blood. She gathered her strength and plunged the point of the blade deep into her throat.

QUESTIONS

1. What impels the lieutenant and his wife to commit suicide? Why is the act described in such meticulous detail? What is the symbolic significance of the sword? What is the meaning of *seppuku?*
2. Mishima divides his story into five sections. Does this division reveal any structure in the narrative?
3. Is there a contradiction in the story between the public need for honor and the private passion for pleasure? Is there a union of the two themes?
4. Mishima uses a number of contrasting images: cold/warmth, light/dark, rigidity/abandonment. How do these images function in the story?
5. Mishima, having been compared with a writer like Oscar Wilde, has been called a modern decadent. Is there any truth to the charge? Are there any similarities between "Patriotism" and Sartre's "The Room"?

Dylan Thomas *(1914–1953) was born in Swansea near the coast of South Wales and was educated at the Swansea Grammar School. He practiced journalism for a year, worked briefly at free-lance writing, and published his first volume of verse,* Eighteen Poems, *when he was twenty. During World War II he wrote radio scripts and film scenarios for the British Broadcasting Corporation. In 1950 Thomas made the first of three tours of America to read his poetry before huge college audiences. He died of a cerebral ailment in New York City. Apart from his poetry he wrote a play,* Under Milk Wood *(1954), and a volume of stories,* Portrait of the Artist as a Young Dog *(1940). Collections of other of his stories were published posthumously as* Adventures in the Skin Trade *(1955),* A Prospect of the Sea *(1955) and* Two Tales *(1968).*

One Warm Saturday

DYLAN THOMAS

The young man in a sailor's jersey, sitting near the summer huts to see the brown and white women coming out and the groups of pretty-faced girls with pale vees and scorched backs who picked their way delicately on ugly, red-toed feet over the sharp stones to the sea, drew on the sand a large, indented woman's figure; and a naked child, just out of the sea, ran over it and shook water, marking on the figure two wide wet eyes and a hole in the foot-printed middle. He rubbed the woman away and drew a paunched man; the child ran over it, tossing her hair, and shook a row of buttons down its belly and a line of drops, like piddle in a child's drawing, between the long legs stuck with shells.

In a huddle of picnicking women and their children, stretched out limp and damp in the sweltering sun or fussing over paper carriers or building castles that were at once destroyed by the tattered march of other picnickers to different pieces of the beach, among the ice-cream cries, the angrily happy shouts of boys playing ball, and the screams of girls as the sea rose to their waists, the young man sat alone with the shadows of his failure at his side. Some silent husbands, with rolled-up trousers and suspenders dangling, paddled slowly on the border of the sea, paddling women, in thick, black picnic dresses, laughed at their own legs, dogs chased stones, and one proud boy rode the water on a rubber seal. The young man, in his wilderness, saw the holiday Saturday set down before him, false and pretty, as a flat picture under the vulgar sun; the disporting families with paper bags, buckets and spades, parasols and bottles, the happy, hot, and aching girls with sunburn liniments in their bags, the bronzed young men with chests, and the envious, white young men in waistcoats, the thin, pale, hairy, pathetic legs of the husbands silently walking through the water, the plump and curly, shaven-headed and bowed-backed children up to no sense with unrepeatable delight in the dirty sand, moved him, he thought dramatically in his isolation, to an old shame and pity; outside all holiday, like a young man doomed forever to the company of his maggots, beyond the high and ordinary, sweating, sun-awakened power and stupidity of the summer flesh on a day and a world out, he caught the ball that a small boy had whacked into the air with a tin tray, and rose to throw it back.

The boy invited him to play. A friendly family stood waiting some way off, the tousled women with their dresses tucked in their knickers, the bare-footed men in shirt-sleeves, a number of children in slips and cut-down underwear. He bowled bitterly to a father standing with a tray before a wicket of hats. "The lone wolf playing ball," he said to himself as the tray whirled. Chasing the ball towards the sea, passing undressing women with a rush and a wink, tripping over a castle into a coil of wet girls lying like snakes, soaking his shoes as he grabbed the ball off a wave, he felt his happiness return in a boast of the body, and, "Look out, Duckworth, here's a fast one coming!" he cried to the mother behind the hats. The ball bounced on a boy's head. In and out of the scattered families, among the sandwiches and clothes, uncles and mothers fielded the bouncing ball. A bald man, with his shirt hanging out, returned it in the wrong direction, and a collie carried it into the sea. Now it was her mother's turn with the tray. Tray and ball together flew over her head. An uncle in a panama smacked the ball to the dog, who swam with it out of reach. They offered the young man egg-and-cress sandwiches and warm stout, and he and an uncle and a father sat down on the *Evening Post* until the sea touched their feet.

Alone again, hot and unhappy, for the boasting minute when he ran among the unknown people lying and running loudly at peace was struck away, like a ball, he said, into the sea, he walked to a space on the beach where a hell-fire preacher on a box marked "Mr. Matthews" was talking to a congregation of expressionless women. Boys with peashooters sat quietly near him. A ragged man collected nothing in a cap. Mr. Matthews shook his cold hands, stormed at the holiday, and cursed the summer from his shivering box. He cried for a new warmth. The strong sun shone into his bones, and he buttoned his coat collar. Valley children, with sunken, impudent eyes, quick tongues and singing voices, chests thin as shells, gathered round the Punch and Judy and the Stop Me tricycles, and he denied them all. He contradicted the girls in their underclothes combing and powdering, and the modest girls cleverly dressing under tents of towels.

As Mr. Matthews cast down the scarlet town, drove out the bare-bellied boys who danced around the ice-cream man, and wound the girls' sunburnt thighs about with his black overcoat—"Down! down!" he cried, "the night is upon us"—the young man in dejection stood, with a shadow at his shoulder, and thought of Porthcawl's Coney Beach, where his friends were rocking with girls on the Giant Racer or tearing in the Ghost Train down the skeletons' tunnel. Leslie Bird would have his arms full of coco-nuts. Brenda was with Herbert at the rifle-range. Gil Morris was buying Molly a cocktail with a cherry at the "Esplanade." Here he stood, listening to Mr. Matthews, the retired drinker, crying darkness on the evening sands, with money hot in his pocket and Saturday burning away.

In his loneliness he had refused their invitations. Herbert, in his low, red sports-car, G.B. at the back, a sea-blown nymph on the radiator, called at his father's house, but he said: "I'm not in the mood, old man. I'm going to spend a quiet day. Enjoy yourselves. Don't take too much pop." Only waiting for the sun to set, he stood in the sad circle with the pleasureless women who were staring at a point in the sky behind their prophet, and wished the morning back. Oh boy! to be wasting his money now on the rings and ranges of the fair, to be sitting in the chromium lounge with a short worth one and six and a Turkish cigarette, telling the latest one to the girls, seeing the sun, through the palms in the lounge window, sink over the promenade, over the bath-chairs, the cripples and widows, the beach-trousered, kerchiefed, weekend wives, the smart, kiss-curled girls with plain and spectacled girl friends, the innocent, swaggering, loud bad boys, and the poms at the ankles, and the cycling sweet-men. Ronald had sailed to Ilfracomb on the *Lady Moira*, and in the thick saloon, with a party from Brynhyfryd, he'd be knocking back nips without a thought that on the sands at home his friend was alone and pussyfoot at six o'clock, and the evening dull as a chapel. All his friends had vanished into their pleasures.

He thought: Poets live and walk with their poems; a man with visions needs no other company; Saturday is a crude day; I must go home and sit in my bedroom by the boiler. But he was not a poet living and walking, he was a young man in a sea-town on a warm bank holiday, with two pounds to spend; he had no visions; only two pounds and a small body with its feet on the littered sand; serenity was for old men; and he moved away, over the railway points, on to the tram-lined road.

He snarled at the flower clock in Victoria Gardens.

"And what shall a prig do now?" he said aloud, causing a young woman on the bench opposite the white-tiled urinal to smile and put her novel down.

She had chestnut hair arranged high on her head in an old-fashioned way, in loose coils and a bun, and a Woolworth's white rose grew out of it and drooped to touch her ear. She wore a white frock with a red paper flower pinned on the breast, and rings and bracelets that came from a fun-fair stall. Her eyes were small and quite green.

He marked, carefully and coldly in one glance, all the unusual details of her appearance; it was the calm, unstartled certainty of her bearing before his glance from head to foot, the innocent knowledge, in her smile and the set of her head, that she was defended by her gentleness and accessible strangeness against all rude encounters and picking looks, that made his fingers tremble. Though her frock was long and the collar high, she could as well be naked there on the blistered bench. Her smile confessed her body bare and spotless and willing and warm under the cotton, and she waited without guilt.

How beautiful she is, he thought, with his mind on words and his eyes on her hair and red and white skin, how beautifully she waits for me, though she does not know she is waiting and I can never tell her.

He had stopped and was staring. Like a confident girl before a camera, she sat smiling, her hands folded, her head slightly to one side so that the rose brushed her neck. She accepted his admiration. The girl in a million took his long look to herself, and cherished his stupid love.

Midges flew into his mouth. He hurried on shamefully. At the gates of the Gardens he turned to see her for the last time on earth. She had lost her calm with his abrupt and awkward going, and stared in confusion after him. One hand was raised as though to beckon him back. If he waited, she would call him. He walked round the corner and heard her voice, a hundred voices, and all hers, calling his name, and a hundred names that were all his, over the bushy walls.

And what shall the terrified prig of a love-made young man do next? he asked his reflection silently in the distorting mirror of the empty "Victoria" saloon. His ape-like, hanging face, with Bass across the forehead, gave back a cracked sneer.

If Venus came in on a plate, said the two red, melon-slice lips, I would ask for vinegar to put on her.

She could drive my guilt out; she could smooth away my shame; why didn't I stop to talk to her? he asked.

You saw a queer tart in a park, his reflection answered, she was a child of Nature, oh my! oh my! Did you see the dewdrops in her hair? Stop talking to the mirror like a man in a magazine, I know you too well.

A new head, swollen and lop-jawed, wagged behind his shoulder. He spun round, to hear the barman say:

"Has the one and only let you down? You look like death warmed up. Have this one on the house. Free beer today. Free X's." He pulled the beer handle. "Only the best served here. Straight from the rust. You do look queer," he said, "the only one saved from the wreck and the only wreck saved. Here's looking at you!" He drank the beer he had drawn.

"May I have a glass of beer, please?"

"What do you think this is, a public house?"

On the polished table in the middle of the saloon the young man drew, with a finger dipped in strong, the round head of a girl and piled a yellow froth of hair upon it.

"Ah! dirty, dirty!" said the barman, running round from behind the counter and rubbing the head away with a dry cloth.

Shielding the dirtiness with his hat, the young man wrote his name on the edge of the table and watched the letters dry and fade.

Through the open bay-window, across the useless railway covered with sand, he saw the black dots of bathers, the stunted huts, the jumping dwarfs round the Punch and Judy, and the tiny religious circle. Since he had walked and played down there in the crowded wilderness, excusing his despair, searching for company though he refused it, he had found his own true happiness and lost her all in one bewildering and clumsy half a minute by the "Gentlemen" and the flower clock. Older and wiser and no better, he would have looked in the mirror to see if his discovery and loss had marked themselves upon his face in shadows under the eyes or lines about the mouth, were it not for the answer he knew he would receive from the distorted reflection.

The barman came to sit near him, and said in a false voice: "Now you tell me all about it, I'm a regular storehouse of secrets."

"There isn't anything to tell. I saw a girl in Victoria Gardens and I was too shy to speak to her. She was a piece of God help us! alright."

Ashamed of his wish to be companionable, even in the depth of love and distress, with her calm face before his eyes and her smile reproving and forgiving him as he spoke, the young man defiled his girl on the bench, dragged her down into the spit and sawdust and dolled her up to make the barman say:

"I like them big myself. Once round Bessy, once round the gas-works. I missed the chance of a lifetime, too. Fifty lovelies in the rude and I'd left my Bunsen-burner at home."

"Give me the same, please."

"You mean similar."

The barman drew a glass of beer, drank it, and drew another.

"I always have one with the customers," he said, "it puts us on even terms. Now we're just two heartbroken bachelors together." He sat down again.

"You can't tell me anything I don't know," he said. "I've seen over twenty chorines from the Empire in this bar, drunk as printers. Oh, les girls! les limbs!"

"Will they be in tonight?"

"There's only a fellow sawing a woman in half this week."

"Keep a half for me."

A drunk man walked in on an invisible white line, and the barman, reeling in sympathy across the room, served him with a pint. "Free beer today," he said. "Free X's. You've been out in the sun."

"I've been out in the sun all day," said the man.

"I thought you looked sunburnt."

"That's drink," said the man. "I've been drinking."

"The holiday is drawing to an end," the young man whispered into his glass. Bye-bye blackbird, the moment is lost, he thought, examining, with an interest he could not forgive, the comic colored postcards of mountain-buttocked women on the beach and hen-pecked, pin-legged men with telescopes, pasted on the wall beneath the picture of a terrier drinking stout; and now, with a jolly barman and a drunk in a crushed cap, he was mopping the failing day down. He tipped his hat over his forehead, and a lock of hair that fell below the hat tickled his eyelid. He saw, with a stranger's darting eye that missed no single subtlety of the wry grin or the faintest gesture drawing the shape of his death on the air, an unruly-haired young man who coughed into his hand in the corner of the rotting room and puffed the smoke of his doped Weight.

But as the drunk man weaved towards him on wilful feet, carrying his dignity as a man might carry a full glass around a quaking ship, as the barman behind the counter clattered and whistled and dipped to drink, he shook off the truthless, secret tragedy with a sneer and a blush, straightened his melancholy hat into a hard-brimmed trilby, dismissed the affected stranger. In the safe center of his own identity, the familiar world about him like another flesh, he sat sad and content in the plain room of the undistinguished hotel at the sea-end of the shabby, spreading town where everything was happening. He had no need of the dark interior world when Tawe pressed in upon him and the eccentric ordinary people came bursting and crawling, with noise and colors, out of their houses, out of the graceless buildings, the factories and avenues, the shining shops and blaspheming chapels, the terminuses and the meeting halls, the falling alleys and brick lanes, from the arches and shelters and holes behind the hoardings, out of the common, wild intelligence of the town.

At last the drunk man had reached him. "Put your hand here," he said, and turned about and tapped himself on the bottom.

The barman whistled and rose from his drink to see the young man touch the drunk man on the seat of the trousers.

"What can you feel there?"

"Nothing."

"That's right. Nothing. Nothing. There's nothing there to feel."

"How can you sit down then?" asked the barman.

"I just sit down on what the doctor left," the man said angrily. "I had as good a bottom as you've got once. I was working underground in Dowlais, and the end of the world came down on me. Do you know what I got for losing my bottom? Four and three! Two and three ha'pence a cheek. That's cheaper than a pig!"

The girl from Victoria Gardens came into the bar with two friends: a blonde young girl almost as beautiful as she was, and a middle-aged woman dressed and made up to look young. The three of them sat at the table. The girl he loved ordered three ports and gins.

"Isn't it delicious weather?" said the middle-aged woman.

The barman said: "Plenty of sky about." With many bows and smiles he placed their drinks in front of them. "I thought the princesses had gone to a better pub," he said.

"What's a better pub without you, handsome?" said the blonde girl.

"This is the 'Ritz' and the 'Savoy,' isn't it, *garçon* darling?" the girl from the Gardens said, and kissed her hand to him.

The young man in the window seat, still bewildered by the first sudden sight of her entering the darkening room, caught the kiss to himself and blushed. He thought to run out of the room and through the miracle-making Gardens, to rush into his house and hide his head in the bed-clothes and lie all night there, dressed and trembling, her voice in his ears, her green eyes wide awake under his closed eyelids. But only a sick boy with tossed blood would run from his proper love into a dream, lie down in a bedroom that was full of his shames, and sob against the feathery, fat breast and face of the damp pillow. He remembered his age and poems, and would not move.

"Thanks a million, Lou," said the barman.

Her name was Lou, Louise, Louisa. She must be Spanish or French or a gypsy, but he could tell the street that her voice came from; he knew where her friends lived by the rise and fall of their sharp voices, and the name of the middle-aged woman was Mrs. Emerald Franklin. She was to be seen every night in the "Jew's Harp," sipping and spying and watching the clock.

"We've been listening to Matthews Hellfire on the sands. Down with this and down with that, and he used to drink a pint of biddy before his breakfast," Mrs. Franklin said. "Oh, there's a nerve!"

"And his eye on the fluff all the time," said the blonde girl. "I wouldn't trust him any further than Ramon Novarro behind the counter."

"Whoops! I've gone up in the world. Last week I was Charley Chase," said the barman.

Mrs. Franklin raised her empty glass in a gloved hand and shook it like a bell. "Men are deceivers ever," she said. "And a drop of mother's ruin right around."

"Especially Mr. Franklin," said the barman.

"But there's a lot in what the preacher says, mind," Mrs. Franklin said, "about the carrying on. If you go for a constitutional after stop-tap along the sands you might as well be in Sodom and Gomorrah."

The blonde girl laughed. "Hark to Mrs. Grundy! I see her with a black man last Wednesday, round by the museum."

"He was an Indian," said Mrs. Franklin, "from the university college, and I'd thank you to remember it. Every one's brothers under the skin, but there's no tarbrush in my family."

"Oh, dear! oh, dear!" said Lou. "Lay off it, there's loves. This is my birthday. It's a holiday. Put a bit of fun in it. Miaow! miaow! Marjorie, kiss Emerald and be friends." She smiled and laughed at them both. She winked at the barman, who was filling their glasses to the top. "Here's to your blue eyes, *garçon!*" She had not noticed the young man in the corner. "And one for grand-dad there," she said, smiling at the swaying, drunk man. "He's twenty-one today. There! I've made him smile."

The drunk man made a deep, dangerous bow, lifted his hat, stumbled against the mantelpiece, and his full pint in his free hand was steady as a rock. "The prettiest girl in Carmarthenshire," he said.

"This is Glamorganshire, dad," she said, "where's your geography? Look at him waltzing! mind your glasses! He's got that Kruschen feeling. Come on, faster! give us the Charleston."

The drunk man, with his pint held high, danced until he fell, and all the time he never spilt a drop. He lay at Lou's feet on the dusty floor and grinned up at her in confidence and affection. "I fell," he said. "I could dance like a trooper when I had a beatyem."

"He lost his bottom at the last trump," the barman explained.

"When did he lose his bottom?" said Mrs. Franklin.

"When Gabriel blew his whistle down in Dowlais."

"You're pulling my leg."

"It's a pleasure, Mrs. Em. Hoi! you, get up from the vomitorium."

The man wagged his end like a tail, and growled at Lou's feet.

"Put your head on my foot. Be comfy. Let him lie there," she said.

He went to sleep at once.

"I can't have drunks on the premises."

"You know where to go then."

"Cru-el Mrs. Franklin!"

"Go on, attend to your business. Serve the young man in the corner, his tongue's hanging out."

"Cru-el lady."

As Mrs. Franklin called attention to the young man, Lou peered shortsightedly across the saloon and saw him sitting with his back to the window.

"I'll have to get glasses," she said.

"You'll have plenty of glasses before the night's out."

"No, honest, Marjorie, I didn't know anyone was there. I do beg your pardon, you in the corner," she said.

The barman switched on the light. "A bit of *lux in Tenebris*."

"Oh," said Lou.

The young man dared not move for fear that he might break the long light of her scrutiny, the enchantment shining like a single line of light between them, or startle her into speaking; and he did not conceal the love in his eyes, for she could pierce through to it as easily as she could turn his heart in his chest and make it beat above the noises of the two friends' hurried conversation, the rattle of glasses behind the counter where the barman spat and polished and missed nothing, and the snores of the comfortable sleeper. Nothing can hurt me. Let the barman jeer. Giggle in your glass, our Em. I'm telling the world, I'm walking in clover, I'm staring at Lou like a fool, she's my girl, she's my lily. O love! O love! She's no lady, with her sing-song Tontine voice, she drinks like a deep-sea diver; but Lou, I'm yours, and Lou, you're mine. He refused to meditate on her calmness now and twist her beauty into words. She was nothing under the sun or moon but his. Unashamed and certain, he smiled at her, and, though he was prepared for all, her answering smile made his fingers tremble again, as they had trembled in the Gardens, and reddened his cheeks and drove his heart to a gallop.

"Harold, fill the young man's glass up," Mrs. Franklin said.

The barman stood still, a duster in one hand and a dripping glass in the other.

"Have you got water in your ears? Fill the young man's glass!"

The barman put the duster to his eyes. He sobbed. He wiped away the mock tears.

"I thought I was attending a *première* and this was the royal box," he said.

"He's got water on the brain, not in his earhole," said Marjorie.

"I dreamt it was a beautiful tragi-comedy entitled 'Love at First Sight, or Another Good Man Gone Wrong.' Act one in a boozer by the sea."

The two women tapped their foreheads.

Lou said, still smiling: "Where was the second act?"

Her voice was as gentle as he had imagined it to be before her gay and nervous playing with the over-familiar barman and the inferior women. He saw her as a wise, soft girl whom no hard company could spoil, for her soft self, bare to the heart, broke through every defense of her sensual falsifiers. As he thought this, phrasing her gentleness, faithlessly running to words away from the real room and his love in the middle, he woke with a start and saw her lively body six steps from him, no calm heart dressed in a sentence, but a pretty girl, to be got and kept. He must catch hold of her fast. He got up to cross to her.

"I woke before the second act came on," said the barman. "I'd sell my dear old mother to see that. Dim lights. Purple couches. Ecstatic bliss. La, la cherie!"

The young man sat down at the table, next to her.

Harold, the barman, leaned over the counter and cupped his hand to his ear.

The man on the floor rolled in his sleep, and his head lay in the spittoon.

"You should have come and sat here a long time ago," Lou whispered. "You should have stopped to talk to me in the Gardens. Were you shy?"

"I was too shy," the young man whispered.

"Whispering isn't manners. I can't hear a word," said the barman.

At a sign from the young man, a flick of the fingers that sent the waiters in evening dress bustling with oysters about the immense room, the barman filled the glasses with port, gin, and Nutbrown.

"We never drink with strangers," Mrs. Franklin said, laughing.

"He isn't a stranger," said Lou, "are you, Jack?"

He threw a pound note on the table: "Take the damage."

The evening that had been over before it began raced along among the laughter of the charming women sharp as knives, and the stories of the barman, who should be on the stage, and Lou's delighted smiles and silences at his side. Now she is safe and sure, he thought, after her walking, like my doubtful walking, around the lonely distances of the holiday. In the warm, spinning middle they were close and alike. The town and the sea and the last pleasure-makers drifted into the dark that had nothing to do with them, and left this one room burning.

One by one, some lost men from the dark shuffled into the bar, drank sadly, and went out. Mrs. Franklin, flushed and dribbling, waved her glass at their departures. Harold winked behind their backs. Marjorie showed them her long, white legs.

"Nobody loves us except ourselves," said Harold. "Shall I shut the bar and keep the riff-raff out?"

"Lou is expecting Mr. O'Brien, but don't let that stop you," Marjorie said. "He's her sugar daddy from old Ireland."

"Do you love Mr. O'Brien?" the young man whispered.

"How could I, Jack?"

He could see Mr. O'Brien as a witty, tall fellow of middle-age, with waved greying hair and a clipped bit of dirt on his upper lip, a flash ring on his marriage finger, a pouched, knowing eye, dummy dressed with a whale-boned waist, a broth of a man-about-Cardiff, Lou's horrible lover tearing towards her now down the airless streets in the firm's car. The young man clenched his hand on the table covered with dead, and sheltered her in the warmth of his fist. "My round, my round," he said, "up again, plenty! Doubles, trebles, Mrs. Franklin is a jibber!"

"My mother never had a jibber."

"Oh, Lou!" he said, "I am more than happy with you."

"Coo! coo! hear the turtle doves."

"Let them coo," said Marjorie. "I would coo, too."

The barman looked around him in surprise. He raised his hands, palms up, and cocked his head.

"The bar is full of birds," he said.

"Emerald's laying an egg," he said, as Mrs. Franklin rocked in her chair.

Soon the bar was full of customers. The drunk man woke up and ran out, leaving his cap in a brown pool. Sawdust dropped from his hair. A small, old, round, red-faced, cheery man sat facing the young man and Lou, who held hands under the table and rubbed their legs against each other.

"What a night for love!" said the old man. "On such a night as this did Jessica steal from the wealthy Jew. Do you know where that comes from?"

"*The Merchant of Venice*," Lou said. "But you're an Irishman, Mr. O'Brien."

"I could have sworn you were a tall man with a little tish," said the young man gravely.

"What's the weapons, Mr. O'Brien?"

"Brandies at dawn, I should think, Mrs. Franklin."

"I never described Mr. O'Brien to you at all. You're dreaming!" Lou whispered. "I wish this night could go on for ever."

"But not here. Not in the bar. In a room with a big bed."

"A bed in a bar," said the old man, "if you'll pardon me hearing you, that's what I've always wanted. Think of it, Mrs. Franklin."

The barman bobbed up from behind the counter.

"Time, gentlemen and others!"

The sober strangers departed to Mrs. Franklin's laughter.

The lights went out.

"Lou, don't you lose me."

"I've got your hand."

"Press it hard, hurt it."

"Break his bloody neck," Mrs. Franklin said in the dark. "No offense meant."

"Marjorie smack hand," said Marjorie. "Let's get out of the dark. Harold's a rover in the dark."

"And the girl guides."

"Let's take a bottle each and go down to Lou's," she said.

"I'll buy the bottles," said Mr. O'Brien.

"It's you don't lose me now," Lou whispered. "Hold on to me, Jack. The others won't stay long. Oh, Mr. Christ, I wish it was just you and me!"

"Will it be just you and me?"

"You and me and Mr. Moon."

Mr. O'Brien opened the saloon door. "Pile into the Rolls, you ladies. The gentlemen are going to see to the medicine."

The young man felt Lou's quick kiss on his mouth before she followed Marjorie and Mrs. Franklin out.

"What do you say we split the drinks?" said Mr. O'Brien.

"Look what I found in the lavatory," said the barman, "he was singing on the seat." He appeared behind the counter with the drunk man leaning on his arm.

They all climbed into the car.

"First stop, Lou's."

The young man, on Lou's knee, saw the town in a daze spin by them, the funnelled and masted smoke-blue outline of the still, droning docks, the lightning lines of the poor streets growing longer, and the winking shops that were snapped out one by one. The car smelt of scent and powder and flesh. He struck with his elbow, by accident, Mrs. Franklin's upholstered breast. Her thighs, like cushions, bore the drunk man's rolling weight. He was bumped and tossed on a lump of women. Breasts, legs, bellies, hands, touched, warmed, and smothered him. On through the night, towards Lou's bed, towards the unbelievable end of the dying holiday, they tore past black houses and bridges, a station in a smoke cloud, and drove up a steep side street with one weak lamp in a circle of railings at the top, and swerved into a space where a tall tenement house stood surrounded by cranes, standing ladders, poles and girders, barrows, brickheaps.

They climbed to Lou's room up many flights of dark, perilous stairs. Washing hung on the rails outside closed doors. Mrs. Franklin, fumbling along with the drunk man behind the others, trod in a bucket, and a lucky black cat ran over her foot. Lou led the young man by the hand through a passage marked with names and doors, lit a match, and whispered: "It won't be very long. Be good and patient with Mr. O'Brien. Here it is. Come in first. Welcome to you, Jack!" She kissed him again at the door of her home. "That kiss is my promise."

She turned on the light, and he walked with her proudly into her own room, into the room that he would come to know, and saw a wide bed, a gramophone on a chair, a wash-basin half-hidden in a corner, a gas-fire and a cooking ring, a closed cupboard, and her photograph in a cardboard frame on the chest of drawers with no handles. Here she slept and ate. In the double bed she lay all night, pale and curled, sleeping on her left side. When he lived with her always, he would not allow her to dream. No other men must lie and love in her head. He spread his fingers on her pillow.

"Why do you live at the top of the Eiffel Tower?" said the barman, coming in.

"What a climb!" said Mr. O'Brien. "But it's very nice and private when you get here."

"If you get here!" said Mrs. Franklin. "I'm dead beat. This old nuisance weighs a ton. Lie down, lie down on the floor and go to sleep. The old nuisance!" she said fondly. "What's your name?"

"Ernie," the drunk man said, raising his arm to shield his face.

"Nobody's going to bite you, Ernie. Here, give him a nip of whisky. Careful! Don't pour it on your waistcoat; you'll be squeezing your waistcoat in the morning. Pull the curtains, Lou, I can see the wicked old moon," she said.

"Does it put ideas in your head?"

"I love the moon," said Lou.

"There never was a young lover who didn't love the moon." Mr. O'Brien gave the young man a cheery smile, and patted his hand. His own hand was red and hairy. "I could see at the flash of a glance that Lou and this nice young fellow were made for each other. I could see it in their eyes. Dear me, no! I'm not so old and blind I can't see love in front of my nose. Couldn't you see it, Mrs. Franklin? Couldn't you see it, Marjorie?"

In the long silence, Lou collected glasses from the cupboard as though she had not heard Mr. O'Brien speak. She drew the curtains, shut out the moon, sat on the edge of her bed with her feet tucked under her, looked at her photograph as a stranger, folded her hands as she folded them, on the first meeting, before the young man's worship in the Gardens.

"A host of angels must be passing by," said Mr. O'Brien. "What a silence there is! Have I said anything out of place? Drink and be merry, tomorrow we die. What do you think I bought these lovely shining bottles for?"

The bottles were opened. The dead were lined on the mantelpiece. The whisky went down. Harold the barman and Marjorie, her dress lifted, sat in the one armchair together. Mrs. Franklin, with Ernie's head on her lap, sang in a sweet, trained contralto voice *The Shepherd's Lass*. Mr. O'Brien kept rhythm with his foot.

I want Lou in my arms, the young man said to himself, watching Mr. O'Brien tap and smile and the barman draw Marjorie down deep. Mrs. Franklin's voice sang sweetly in the small bedroom where he and Lou should be lying in the white bed without any smiling company to see them drown. He and Lou could go down together, one cool body weighted with a boiling stone, on to the falling, blank white, entirely empty sea, and never rise. Sitting on their bridal bed, near enough to hear his breath, she was farther from him than before they met. Then he had everything but her body; now she had given him two kisses, and everything had vanished but that beginning. He must be good and patient with Mr. O'Brien. He could wipe away the embracing old smile with the iron back of his hand. Sink lower, lower, Harold and Marjorie, tumble like whales at Mr. O'Brien's feet.

He wished that the light would fail. In the darkness he and Lou could creep beneath the clothes and imitate the dead. Who would look for them there, if they were dead still and soundless?

The others would shout to them down the dizzy stairs or rummage in the silence about the narrow, obstacled corridors or stumble out into the night to search for them among the cranes and ladders in the desolation of the destroyed houses. He could hear, in the made-up dark, Mr. O'Brien's voice cry, "Lou, where are you? Answer! answer!" the hollow answer of the echo, "answer!" and hear her lips in the cool pit of the bed secretly move around another name and feel them move.

"A fine piece of singing, Emerald, and very naughty words. That was a shepherd, that was," Mr. O'Brien said.

Ernie, on the floor, began to sing in a thick, sulking voice, but Mrs. Franklin placed her hand over his mouth and he sucked and nuzzled it.

"What about this young shepherd?" said Mr. O'Brien, pointing his glass at the young man. "Can he sing as well as make love? You ask him kindly, girlie," he said to Lou, "and he'll give up a song like a nightingale."

"Can you sing, Jack?"

"Like a crow, Lou."

"Can't he even talk poetry? What a young man to have who can't spout the poets to his lady!" Mr. O'Brien said.

From the cupboard Lou brought out a red-bound book and gave it to the young man, saying: "Can you read us a piece out of here? The second volume's in the hatbox. Read us a dreamy piece, Jack. It's nearly midnight."

"Only a love poem, no other kind," said Mr. O'Brien. "I won't hear anything but a love poem."

"Soft and sweet," Mrs. Franklin said. She took her hand away from Ernie's mouth and looked at the ceiling.

The young man read, but not aloud, lingering on her name, the inscription on the flyleaf of the first volume of the collected poems of

Tennyson: "To Louisa, from her Sunday School teacher, Miss Gwyneth Forbes. God's in His Heaven, all's right with the world."

"Make it a love poem, don't forget."

The young man read aloud, closing one eye to steady the dancing print, *Come into the Garden, Maud*. And when he reached the beginning of the fourth verse his voice grew louder:

"I said to the lily, 'There is but one
With whom she has heart to be gay.
When will the dancers leave her alone?
She is weary of dance and play.'
Now half to the setting moon are gone,
And half to the rising day;
Low on the sand and loud on the stone
The last wheel echoes away.

"I said to the rose, 'The brief night goes
In babble and revel and wine.
O young lord-lover, what sighs are those,
For one that will never be thine?
But mine, but mine,' so I sware to the rose,
'For ever and ever, mine.' "

At the end of the poem, Harold said, suddenly, his head hanging over the arm of the chair, his hair made wild, and his mouth red with lipstick: "My grandfather remembers seeing Lord Tennyson, he was a little man with a hump."

"No," said the young man, "he was tall and he had long hair and a beard."

"Did you ever see him?"

"I wasn't born then."

"My grandfather saw him. He had a hump."

"It couldn't have been the same Tennyson."

"You've got the wrong Tennyson, this was the famous poet with a hump."

Lou, on the wonderful bed, waiting for him alone of all the men, ugly or handsome, old or young, in the wide town and the small world that would be bound to fall, lowered her head and kissed her hand to him and held her hand in the river of light on the counterpane. The hand, to him, became transparent, and the light on the counterpane glowed up steadily through it in the thin shape of her palm and fingers.

"Ask Mr. O'Brien what Lord Tennyson was like," said Mrs. Franklin. "We appeal to you, Mr. O'Brien, did he have a hump or not?"

Nobody but the young man, for whom she lived and waited now, noticed Lou's little loving movements. She put her glowing hand to her left breast. She made a sign of secrecy on her lips.

"It depends," Mr. O'Brien said.

The young man closed one eye again, for the bed was pitching like a ship; a sickening, hot storm out of a cigarette cloud unsettled cupboard and chest. The motions of the sea-going bedroom were calmed with the cunning closing of his eye, but he longed for night air. On sailor's legs he walked to the door.

"You'll find the House of Commons on the second floor at the end of the passage," said Mr. O'Brien.

At the door, he turned to Lou and smiled with all his love, declaring it to the faces of the company and making her, before Mr. O'Brien's envious regard, smile back and say: "Don't be long, Jack. Please! You mustn't be long."

Now everyone knew. Love had grown up in an evening.

"One minute, my darling," he said. "I'll be here."

The door closed behind him. He walked into the wall of the passage. He lit a match. He had three left. Down the stairs, clinging to the sticky, shaking rails, rocking on see-saw floorboards, bruising his shin on a bucket, past the noises of secret lives behind doors he slid and stumbled and swore and heard Lou's voice in a fresh fever drive him on, call him to return, speak to him with such passion and abandonment that even in the darkness and the pain of his haste he was dazzled and struck still. She spoke, there on the rotting stairs in the middle of the poor house, a frightening rush of love words; from her mouth, at his ear, endearments were burned out. Hurry! hurry! Every moment is being killed. Love, adored, dear, run back and whistle to me, open the door, shout my name, lay me down. Mr. O'Brien has his hands on my side.

He ran into a cavern. A draught blew out his matches. He lurched into a room where two figures on a black heap on the floor lay whispering, and ran from there in panic. He made water at the dead end of the passage and hurried back towards Lou's room, finding himself at last on a silent patch of stairway at the top of the house; he put out his hand, but the rail was broken and nothing there prevented a long drop to the ground down a twisted shaft that would echo and double his cry, bring out from their holes in the wall the sleeping or stirring families, the whispering figures, the blind startled turners of night into day. Lost in a tunnel near the roof, he fingered the damp walls for a door; he found a handle and gripped it hard, but it came off in his hand. Lou had led him down a longer passage than this. He remembered the number of doors: there were three on each side. He ran down the broken-railed flight into another passage and dragged his hand along the wall. Three doors, he counted. He opened the third door, walked into darkness, and groped for the switch on the left. He saw, in the sudden light, a bed and a cupboard and a chest of drawers with no handles, a gas-fire, a wash-basin in the corner. No bottles. No glasses. No photograph of Lou. The red counterpane on the bed was smooth. He could not remember the color of Lou's counterpane.

He left the light burning and opened the second door, but a strange woman's voice cried, half-asleep: "Who is there? Is it you, Tom? Tom, put the light on." He looked for a line of light at the foot of the next door, and stopped to listen for voices. The woman was still calling in the second room.

"Lou, where are you?" he cried. "Answer! answer!"

"Lou, what Lou? There's no Lou here," said a man's voice through the open door of the first dark room at the entrance to the passage.

He scampered down another flight and counted four doors with his scratched hand. One door opened and a woman in a nightdress put out her head. A child's head appeared below her.

"Where does Lou live? Do you know where Lou lives?"

The woman and the child stared without speaking.

"Lou! Lou! her name is Lou!" he heard himself shout. "She lives here, in this house! Do you know where she lives?"

The woman caught the child by the hair and pulled her into the room. He clung to the edge of her door. The woman thrust her arm round the edge and brought down a bunch of keys sharply on his hands. The door slammed.

A young woman with a baby in a shawl stood at an open door on the opposite side of the passage, and caught his sleeve as he ran by. "Lou who? You woke my baby."

"I don't know her other name. She's with Mrs. Franklin and Mr. O'Brien."

"You woke my baby."

"Come in and find her in the bed," a voice said from the darkness behind the young woman.

"He's woken up the baby."

He ran down the passage, holding his wet hand to his mouth. He fell against the rails of the last flight of stairs. He heard Lou's voice in his head once more whisper to him to return as the ground floor rose, like a lift full of dead, towards the rails. Hurry! hurry! I can't, I won't wait, the bridal night is being killed.

Up the rotten, bruising, mountainous stairs he climbed, in his sickness, to the passage where he had left the one light burning in an end room. The light was out. He tapped all the doors and whispered her name. He beat on the doors and shouted, and a woman, dressed in a vest and a hat, drove him out of the passage with a walking-stick.

For a long time he waited on the stairs, though there was no love now to wait for and no bed but his own too many miles away to lie in, and only the approaching day to remember his discovery. All around him the disturbed inhabitants of the house were falling back into sleep. Then he walked out of the house on to the waste space and under the leaning cranes and ladders. The light of one weak lamp in a rusty circle fell across the brickheaps and the broken wood and the dust that had been houses once, where the small and hardly known and never-to-be-forgotten people of the dirty town had lived and loved and died and, always, lost.

QUESTIONS

1. Describe Thomas's attitude toward the protagonist during the course of the narrative. What devices enable him to convey his attitude to the reader?
2. What function does the imagery of light serve in the story? The imagery of enchantment? Of speed? Of eroticism?
3. What effects are produced by moving the setting from the beach to the pub to Lou's apartment?
4. Justify a description of Thomas's style as visual and cinematic. Does the subject of "One Warm Saturday" seem to encourage such a description?
5. Describe the attitudes toward love which Thomas conveys through the tone. What is ironic about the narrator's losing his way at the end of the story?

Truman Capote *(1924–) was born in New Orleans, grew up under the tutelage of aunts in Louisiana and Alabama, and attended private schools in New York. He began writing stories as a boy and when he was nineteen* Mademoiselle *accepted for publication "Miriam," a story that was later included in the O. Henry Memorial Award volume for 1946. Capote's early fiction* Other Voices, Other Rooms *(1948),* A Tree of Night *(1949), and* The Grass Harp *(1951), reflects his boyhood in the South. He has also written the film script for John Huston's production of* Beat the Devil *(1953) and has had two novels,* Breakfast at Tiffany's *(1958) and* In Cold Blood *(1965), adapted to the screen. His more recent works include the short stories in* A Christmas Memory *(1966), a play,* The Thanksgiving Visitor *(1968), and* The Dog's Bark; Public People and Private Places *(1973). He won an Emmy Award for the television script of "A Christmas Memory" in 1967.*

A Christmas Memory

TRUMAN CAPOTE

Imagine a morning in late November. A coming of winter morning more than twenty years ago. Consider the kitchen of a spreading old house in a country town. A great black stove is its main feature; but there is also a big round table and a fireplace with two rocking chairs placed in front of it. Just today the fireplace commenced its seasonal roar.

A woman with shorn white hair is standing at the kitchen window. She is wearing tennis shoes and a shapeless gray sweater over a summery calico dress. She is small and sprightly, like a bantam hen; but, due to a long youthful illness, her shoulders are pitifully hunched. Her face is remarkable—not unlike Lincoln's, craggy like that, and tinted by sun and wind; but it is delicate too, finely boned, and her eyes are sherry-colored and timid. "Oh my," she exclaims, her breath smoking the windowpane, "it's fruitcake weather!"

The person to whom she is speaking is myself. I am seven; she is sixty-something. We are cousins, very distant ones, and we have lived together—well, as long as I can remember. Other people inhabit the house, relatives; and though they have power over us, and frequently make us cry, we are not, on the whole, too much aware of them. We are each other's best friend. She calls me Buddy, in memory of a boy who was formerly her best friend. The other Buddy died in the 1880's, when she was still a child. She is still a child.

"I knew it before I got out of bed," she says, turning away from the window with a purposeful excitement in her eyes. "The courthouse bell sounded so cold and clear. And there were no birds singing; they've gone to warmer country, yes indeed. Oh, Buddy, stop stuffing biscuit and fetch our buggy. Help me find my hat. We've thirty cakes to bake."

It's always the same: a morning arrives in November, and my friend, as though officially inaugurating the Christmas time of year that exhilarates her imagination and fuels the blaze of her heart, announces: "It's fruitcake weather! Fetch our buggy. Help me find my hat."

The hat is found, a straw cartwheel corsaged with velvet roses out-of-doors has faded: it once belonged to a more fashionable relative. Together, we guide our buggy, a dilapidated baby carriage, out to the garden and into a grove of pecan trees. The buggy is mine; that is, it was bought for me when I was born. It is made of wicker, rather unraveled, and the wheels wobble like a drunkard's legs. But it is a faithful object; springtimes, we take it to the woods and fill it with flowers, herbs, wild fern for our porch pots; in the summer, we pile it with picnic paraphernalia and sugar-cane fishing poles and roll it down to the edge of a creek; it has its winter uses, too: as a truck for hauling firewood from the yard to the kitchen, as a warm bed for Queenie, our tough little orange and white rat terrier who has survived distemper and two rattlesnake bites. Queenie is trotting beside it now.

Three hours later we are back in the kitchen hulling a heaping buggyload of windfall pecans. Our backs hurt from gathering them: how hard they were to find (the main crop having been shaken off the trees and sold by the orchard's owners, who are not us) among the concealing leaves, the frosted, deceiving grass. Caarackle! a cheery crunch, scraps of miniature thunder sound as the shells collapse and the golden mound of sweet oily ivory meat mounts in the milk-glass bowl. Queenie begs to taste, and now and again my friend sneaks her a mite, though insisting we deprive ourselves. "We mustn't, Buddy. If we start, we won't stop. And there's scarcely enough as there is. For thirty cakes." The kitchen is growing dark. Dusk turns the window into a mirror: our reflections mingle with the rising moon as we work by the fireside in the firelight. At last, when the moon is quite high, we toss the final hull into the fire and, with joined sighs, watch it catch flame. The buggy is empty, the bowl is brimful.

We eat our supper (cold biscuits, bacon, blackberry jam) and discuss tomorrow. Tomorrow the kind of work I like best begins: buying. Cherries and citron, ginger and vanilla and canned Hawaiian pineapple, rinds and raisins and walnuts and whiskey and oh, so much flour, butter, so many eggs, spices, flavorings: why, we'll need a pony to pull the buggy home.

But before these purchases can be made, there is the question of money. Neither of us has any. Except for skinflint sums persons in the house occasionally provide (a dime is considered very big money); or what we earn ourselves from various activities: holding rummage sales, selling buckets of hand-picked blackberries, jars of homemade jam and apple jelly and peach preserves, rounding up flowers for funerals and weddings. Once we won seventy-ninth prize, five dollars, in a national football contest. Not that we know a fool thing about football. It's just that we enter any contest we hear about: at the moment our hopes are centered on the fifty-thousand-dollar Grand Prize being offered to name a new brand of coffee (we suggested "A.M."; and, after some hesitation, for my friend thought it perhaps sacrilegious, the slogan "A.M.! Amen!"). To tell the truth, our only *really* profitable enterprise was the Fun and Freak Museum we conducted in a back-yard woodshed two summers ago. The Fun was a stereopticon with slide views of Washington and New York lent us by a relative who had been to those places (she was furious when she discovered why we'd borrowed it); the Freak was a three-legged biddy chicken hatched by one of our own hens. Everybody hereabouts wanted to see that biddy: we charged grownups a nickel, kids two cents. And took in a good twenty dollars before the museum shut down due to the decease of the main attraction.

But one way and another we do each year accumulate Christmas savings, a Fruitcake Fund. These moneys we keep hidden in an ancient bead purse under a loose board under the floor under a chamber pot under my friend's bed. The purse is seldom removed from this safe location except to make a deposit, or, as happens every Saturday, a withdrawal; for on Saturdays I am allowed ten cents to go to the picture show. My friend has never been to a picture show, nor does she intend to: "I'd rather hear you tell the story, Buddy. That way I can imagine it more. Besides, a person my age shouldn't squander their eyes. When the Lord comes, let me see him clear." In addition to never having seen a movie, she has never: eaten in a restaurant, traveled more than five miles from home, received or sent a telegram, read anything except funny papers and the Bible, worn cosmetics, cursed, wished someone harm, told a lie on purpose, let a hungry dog go hungry. Here are a few things she has done, does do: killed with a hoe the biggest rattlesnake ever seen in this country (sixteen rattles), dip snuff (secretly), tame hummingbirds (just try it) till they balance on her finger, tell ghost stories (we both believe in ghosts) so tingling they chill you in July, talk to herself, take walks in the rain, grow the prettiest japonicas in town, know the recipe for every sort of old-time Indian cure, including a magical wart-remover.

Now, with supper finished, we retire to the room in a faraway part of the house where my friend sleeps in a scrap-quilt-covered iron bed painted rose pink, her favorite color. Silently, wallowing in the pleasures of conspiracy, we take the bead purse from its secret place and spill its contents on the scrap quilt. Dollar bills, tightly rolled and green as May buds. Somber fifty-cent pieces, heavy enough to weight a dead man's eyes. Lovely dimes, the liveliest coin, the one that really jingles. Nickels and quarters, worn smooth as creek pebbles. But mostly a hateful heap of bitter-odored pennies. Last summer others in the house contracted to pay us a penny for every twenty-five flies we killed. Oh, the carnage of August: the flies flew to heaven! Yet it was not work in which we took pride. And, as we sit counting pennies, it is as though we were back tabulating dead flies. Neither of us has a head for figures; we count slowly, lose track, start again. According to her calculations, we have $12.73. According to mine, exactly $13. "I do hope you're wrong, Buddy. We can't mess around with thirteen. The cakes will fall. Or put somebody in the cemetery. Why, I wouldn't dream of getting out of bed on the thirteenth." This is true: she always spends thirteenths in bed. So, to be on the safe side, we subtract a penny and toss it out the window.

Of the ingredients that go into our fruitcakes, whiskey is the most expensive, as well as the hardest to obtain: State laws forbid its sale. But everybody knows you can buy a bottle from Mr. Haha Jones. And the next day, having completed our more prosaic shopping, we set out for Mr. Haha's business address, a "sinful" (to quote public opinion) fish-fry and dancing café down by the river. We've been there before, and on the same errand; but in previous years our dealings have been with Haha's wife, an iodine-dark Indian woman with brazzy peroxided hair and a dead-tired disposition. Actually, we've never laid eyes on her husband, though we've heard that he's an Indian too. A giant with razor scars across his cheeks. They call him Haha because he's so gloomy, a man who never laughs. As we approach his café (a large log cabin festooned inside and out with chains of garish-gay naked lightbulbs and standing by the river's muddy edge under the shade of river trees where moss drifts through the branches like gray mist) our steps slow down. Even Queenie stops prancing and sticks close by. People have been murdered in Haha's café. Cut to pieces. Hit on the head. There's a case coming up in court next month. Naturally these goings-on happen at night when the colored lights cast crazy patterns and the victrola wails. In the daytime Haha's is shabby and deserted. I knock at the door, Queenie barks, my friend calls: "Mrs. Haha, ma'am? Anyone to home?"

Footsteps. The door opens. Our hearts overturn. It's Mr. Haha Jones himself! And he *is* a giant; he *does* have scars; he *doesn't* smile. No, he glowers at us through Satan-tilted eyes and demands to know: "What you want with Haha?"

For a moment we are too paralyzed to tell. Presently my friend half-finds her voice, a whispery voice at best: "If you please, Mr. Haha, we'd like a quart of your finest whiskey."

His eyes tilt more. Would you believe it? Haha is smiling! Laughing, too. "Which one of you is a drinkin' man?"

"It's for making fruitcakes, Mr. Haha. Cooking."

This sobers him. He frowns. "That's no way to waste good whiskey." Nevertheless, he retreats into the shadowed café and seconds later appears carrying a bottle of daisy yellow unlabeled liquor. He demonstrates its sparkle in the sunlight and says: "Two dollars."

We pay him with nickels and dimes and pennies. Suddenly, jangling the coins in his hand like a fistful of dice, his face softens. "Tell you what," he proposes, pouring the money back into our bead purse, "just send me one of them fruitcakes instead."

"Well," my friend remarks on our way home, "there's a lovely man. We'll put an extra cup of raisins in *his* cake."

The black stove, stoked with coal and firewood, glows like a lighted pumpkin. Eggbeaters whirl, spoons spin round in bowls of butter and sugar, vanilla sweetens the air, ginger spices it; melting, nose-tingling odors saturate the kitchen, suffuse the house, drift out to the world on puffs of chimney smoke. In four days our work is done. Thirty-one cakes, dampened with whiskey, bask on window sills and shelves.

Who are they for?

Friends. Not necessarily neighbor friends: indeed, the larger share are intended for persons we've met maybe once, perhaps not at all. People who've struck our fancy. Like President Roosevelt. Like the Reverend and Mrs. J. C. Lucey, Baptist missionaries to Borneo who lectured here last winter. Or the little knife grinder who comes through town twice a year. Or Abner Packer, the driver of the six o'clock bus from Mobile, who exchanges waves with us every day as he passes in a dust-cloud whoosh. Or the young Wistons, a California couple whose car one afternoon broke down outside the house and who spent a pleasant hour chatting with us on the porch (young Mr. Wiston snapped our picture, the only one we've ever had taken). Is it because my friend is shy with everyone *except* strangers that these strangers, and merest acquaintances, seem to us our truest friends? I think yes. Also, the scrapbooks we keep of thank-you's on White House stationery, time-to-time communications from California and Borneo, the knife grinder's penny postcards, make us feel connected to eventful worlds beyond the kitchen with its view of a sky that stops.

Now a nude December fig branch grates against the window. The kitchen is empty, the cakes are gone; yesterday we carted the last of them to the post office, where the cost of stamps turned our purse inside out. We're broke. That rather depresses me, but my friend insists on celebrating—with two inches of whiskey left in Haha's bottle. Queenie has a spoonful in a bowl of coffee (she likes her coffee chicory-flavored and strong). The rest we divide between a pair of jelly glasses. We're both quite awed at the prospect of drinking straight whiskey; the taste of it brings screwed-up expressions and sour shudders. But by and by we begin to sing, the two of us singing different songs simultaneously. I don't know the words to mine, just *Come on along, come on along, to the dark-town strutters' ball*. But I can dance: that's what I mean to be, a tap dancer in the movies. My dancing shadow rollicks on the walls; our voices rock the chinaware; we giggle: as if unseen hands were tickling us. Queenie rolls on her back, her paws plow the air, something like a grin stretches her black lips. Inside myself, I feel warm and sparky as those crumbling logs, carefree as the wind in the chimney. My friend waltzes round the stove, the hem of her poor calico skirt pinched between her fingers as though it were a party dress: *Show me the way to go home*, she sings, her tennis shoes squeaking on the floor. *Show me the way to go home*.

Enter: two relatives. Very angry. Potent with eyes that scold, tongues that scald. Listen to what they have to say, the words tumbling together into a wrathful tune: "A child of seven! whiskey on his breath! are you out of your mind? feeding a child of seven! must be loony! road to ruination! remember Cousin Kate? Uncle Charlie? Uncle Charlie's brother-in-law? shame! scandal! humiliation! kneel, pray, beg the Lord!"

Queenie sneaks under the stove. My friend gazes at her shoes, her chin quivers, she lifts her skirt and blows her nose and runs to her room. Long after the town has gone to sleep and the house is silent except for the chimings of clocks and the sputter of fading fires, she is weeping into a pillow already as wet as a widow's handkerchief.

"Don't cry," I say, sitting at the bottom of her bed and shivering despite my flannel nightgown that smells of last winter's cough syrup, "don't cry," I beg, teasing her toes, tickling her feet, "you're too old for that."

"It's because," she hiccups, "I *am* too old. Old and funny."

"Not funny. Fun. More fun than anybody. Listen. If you don't stop crying you'll be so tired tomorrow we can't go cut a tree."

She straightens up. Queenie jumps on the bed (where Queenie is not allowed) to lick her cheeks. "I know where we'll find pretty trees, Buddy. And holly, too. With berries big as your eyes. It's way off in the woods. Farther than we've ever been. Papa used to bring us Christmas trees from there: carry them on his shoulder. That's fifty years ago. Well, now: I can't wait for morning."

Morning. Frozen rime lusters the grass; the sun, round as an orange and orange as hot-weather moons, balances on the horizon, burnishes the silvered winter woods. A wild turkey calls. A renegade hog grunts in the undergrowth. Soon, by the edge of knee-deep, rapid-running water, we have to abandon the buggy. Queenie wades the stream first, paddles across barking complaints at the swiftness of the current, the pneumonia-making coldness of it. We follow, holding our shoes and equipment (a hatchet, a burlap sack) above our heads. A mile more: of chastising thorns, burs and briers that catch at our clothes; of rusty pine needles brilliant with gaudy fungus and molted feathers. Here, there, a flash, a flutter, an ecstasy of shrillings remind us that not all the birds have flown south. Always, the path unwinds through lemony sun pools and pitch vine tunnels. Another creek to cross: a disturbed armada of speckled trout froths the water round us, and frogs the size of plates practice belly flops; beaver workmen are building a dam. On the farther shore, Queenie shakes herself and trembles. My friend shivers, too: not with cold but enthusiasm. One of her hat's ragged roses sheds a petal as she lifts her head and inhales the pine-heavy air. "We're almost there; can you smell it, Buddy?" she says, as though we were approaching an ocean.

And, indeed, it is a kind of ocean. Scented acres of holiday trees, prickly-leafed holly. Red berries shiny as Chinese bells: black crows swoop upon them screaming. Having stuffed our burlap sacks with enough greenery and crimson to garland a dozen windows, we set about choosing a tree. "It should be," muses my friend, "twice as tall as a boy. So a boy can't steal the star." The one we pick is twice as tall as me. A brave handsome brute that survives thirty hatchet strokes before it keels with a creaking rending cry. Lugging it like a kill, we commence the long trek out. Every few yards we abandon the struggle, sit down and pant. But we have the strength of triumphant huntsmen; that and the tree's virile, icy perfume revive us, goad us on. Many compliments accompany our sunset return along the red clay road to town; but my friend is sly and noncommittal when passers-by praise the treasure perched on our buggy: what a fine tree and where did it come from? "Yonderways," she murmurs vaguely. Once a car stops and the rich mill owner's lazy wife leans out and whines: "Giveya two-bits cash for that ol tree." Ordinarily my friend is afraid of saying no; but on this occasion she promptly shakes her head: "We wouldn't take a dollar." The mill owner's wife persists. "A dollar, my foot! Fifty cents. That's my last offer. Goodness, woman, you can get another one." In answer, my friend gently reflects: "I doubt it. There's never two of anything."

Home: Queenie slumps by the fire and sleeps till tomorrow, snoring loud as a human.

A trunk in the attic contains: a shoebox of ermine tails (off the opera cape of a curious lady who once rented a room in the house), coils of frazzled tinsel gone gold with age, one silver star, a brief rope of dilapidated, undoubtedly dangerous candy-like light bulbs. Excellent decorations, as far as they go, which isn't far enough: my friend wants our tree to blaze "like a Baptist window," droop with weighty snows of ornament. But we can't afford the made-in-Japan splendors at the five-and-dime. So we do what we've always done: sit for days at the kitchen table with scissors and crayons and stacks of colored paper. I make sketches and my friend cuts them out: lots of cats, fish too (because they're easy to draw), some apples, some watermelons, a few winged angels devised from saved-up sheets of Hershey-bar tin foil. We use safety pins to attach these creations to the tree; as a final touch, we sprinkle the branches with shredded cotton (picked in August for this purpose). My friend, surveying the effect, clasps her hands together. "Now honest, Buddy. Doesn't it look good enough to eat?" Queenie tries to eat an angel.

After weaving and ribboning holly wreaths for all the front windows, our next project is the fashioning of family gifts. Tie-dye scarves for the ladies, for the men a home-brewed lemon and licorice and aspirin syrup to be taken "at the first Symptoms of a Cold and after Hunting." But when it comes time for making each other's gift, my friend and I separate to work secretly. I would like to buy her a pearl-handled knife, a radio, a whole pound of chocolate-covered cherries (we tasted some once, and she always swears: "I could live on them, Buddy, Lord yes I could—and that's not taking His name in vain"). Instead, I am building her a kite. She would like to give me a bicycle (she's said so on several million occasions: "If only I could, Buddy. It's bad enough in life to do without something *you* want; but confound it, what gets my goat is not being able to give somebody something you want *them* to have. Only one of these days I will, Buddy. Locate you a bike. Don't ask how. Steal it, maybe"). Instead, I'm fairly certain that she is building me a kite—the same as last year, and the year before: the year before that we exchanged slingshots. All of which is fine by me. For we are champion kite-fliers who study the wind like sailors; my friend, more accomplished than I, can get a kite aloft when there isn't enough breeze to carry clouds.

Christmas Eve afternoon we scrape together a nickel and go to the butcher's to buy Queenie's traditional gift, a good gnawable beef bone. The bone, wrapped in funny paper, is placed high in the tree near the silver star. Queenie knows it's there. She squats at the foot of the tree staring up in a trance of greed: when bedtime arrives she refuses to budge. Her excitement is equaled by my own. I kick the covers and turn my pillow as though it were a scorching summer's night. Somewhere a rooster crows: falsely, for the sun is still on the other side of the world.

"Buddy, are you awake?" It is my friend, calling from her room, which is next to mine; and an instant later she is sitting on my bed holding a candle. "Well, I can't sleep a hoot," she declares. "My mind's jumping like a jack rabbit. Buddy, do you think Mrs. Roosevelt will serve our cake at dinner?" We huddle in the bed, and she squeezes my hand I-love-you. "Seems like your hand used to be so much smaller. I guess I hate to see you grow up. When you're grown up, will we still be friends?" I say always. "But I feel so bad, Buddy. I wanted so bad to give you a bike. I tried to sell my cameo Papa gave me. Buddy"—she hesitates, as though embarrassed—"I made you another kite." Then I confess that I made her one, too; and we laugh. The candle burns too short to hold. Out it goes, exposing the starlight, the stars spinning at the window like a visible caroling that slowly, slowly daybreak silences. Possibly we doze; but the beginnings of dawn splash us like cold water: we're up, wide-eyed and wandering while we wait for others to waken. Quite deliberately my friend drops a kettle on the kitchen floor. I tap-dance in front of closed doors. One by one the household emerges, looking as though they'd like to kill us both; but it's Christmas, so they can't. First, a gorgeous breakfast: just everything you can imagine—from flapjacks and fried squirrel to hominy grits and honey-in-the-comb. Which puts everyone in a good humor except my friend and I. Frankly, we're so impatient to get at the presents we can't eat a mouthful.

Well, I'm disappointed. Who wouldn't be? With socks, a Sunday school shirt, some handkerchiefs, a hand-me-down sweater and a year's subscription to a religious magazine for children. *The Little Shepherd*. It makes me boil. It really does.

My friend has a better haul. A sack of Satsumas, that's her best present. She is proudest, however, of a white wool shawl knitted by her married sister. But she *says* her favorite gift is the kite I built her. And it *is* very beautiful; though not as beautiful as the one she made me, which is blue and scattered with gold and green Good Conduct stars; moreover, my name is painted on it, "Buddy."

"Buddy, the wind is blowing."

The wind is blowing, and nothing will do till we've run to a pasture below the house where Queenie has scooted to bury her bone (and where, a winter hence, Queenie will be buried, too). There, plunging through the healthy waist-high grass, we unreel our kites, feel them twitching at the string like sky fish as they swim into the wind. Satisfied, sun-warmed, we sprawl in the grass and peel Satsumas and watch our kites cavort. Soon I forget the socks and hand-me-down sweater. I'm as happy as if we'd already won the fifty-thousand-dollar Grand Prize in that coffee-naming contest.

"My, how foolish I am!" my friend cries, suddenly alert, like a woman remembering too late she has biscuits in the oven. "You know what I've always thought?" she asks in a tone of discovery, and not smiling at me but a point beyond. "I've always thought a body would have to be sick and dying before they saw the Lord. And I imagined that when He came it would be like looking at the Baptist window: pretty as colored glass with the sun pouring through, such a shine you don't know it's getting dark. And it's been a comfort: to think of that shine taking away all the spooky feeling. But I'll wager it never happens. I'll wager at the very end a body realizes the Lord has already shown Himself. That things as they are"—her hand circles in a gesture that gathers clouds and kites and grass and Queenie pawing earth over her bone—"just what they've always seen, was seeing Him. As for me, I could leave the world with today in my eyes."

This is our last Christmas together.

Life separates us. Those who Know Best decide that I belong in a military school. And so follows a miserable succession of bugle-blowing prisons, grim reveille-ridden summer camps. I have a new home too. But it doesn't count. Home is where my friend is, and there I never go.

And there she remains, puttering around the kitchen. Alone with Queenie. Then alone. ("Buddy dear," she writes in her wild hard-to-read script, "yesterday Jim Macy's horse kicked Queenie bad. Be thankful she didn't feel much. I wrapped her in a Fine Linen sheet and rode her in the buggy down to Simpson's pasture where she can be with all her Bones . . ."). For a few Novembers she continues to bake her fruitcakes single-handed; not as many, but some: and, of course, she always sends me "the best of the batch." Also, in every letter she encloses a dime wadded in toilet paper: "See a picture show and write me the story." But gradually in her letters she tends to confuse me with her other friend, the Buddy who died in the 1880's; more and more thirteenths are not the only days she stays in bed: a morning arrives in November, a leafless birdless coming of winter morning, when she cannot rouse herself to exclaim: "Oh my, it's fruitcake weather!"

And when that happens, I know it. A message saying so merely confirms a piece of news some secret vein had already received, severing from me an irreplaceable part of myself, letting it loose like a kite on a broken string. That is why, walking across a school campus on this particular December morning, I keep searching the sky. As if I expected to see, rather like hearts, a lost pair of kites hurrying toward heaven.

QUESTIONS

1. What effect does the retrospective point of view have on the tone? What effect is produced by the narrator's shift to the present tense in the last paragraph?
2. Characterize the woman. How does the comedy of her person and habits affect our attitude toward her? What is ironic about her provincial and insular background?
3. "A Christmas Memory" deals with charity, brotherhood, and spiritual plenitude. How are these themes developed through the imagery of nature? Through setting?
4. The climax of the tale comes with the woman's vision of Christ. How does Capote prepare for the climax? What is the significance of the woman's perception?

STORIES FOR FURTHER STUDY

Herman Melville *(1819–1891) was born in New York City. After finishing his formal education at the age of fifteen, he worked for several years and then went to sea, first on a merchant ship bound for Liverpool and later on a whaler bound for the South Seas. After twice jumping ship to live among the Polynesians, he served on a frigate which brought him back to the United States. These experiences formed the basis of all his early novels:* Typee *(1846),* Omoo *(1847),* Mardi *(1849),* Redburn *(1849),* White Jacket *(1850), and his masterpiece,* Moby Dick *(1851).* Moby Dick *was followed by three relatively unsuccessful novels,* Pierre *(1852),* Israel Potter *(1855), and* The Confidence-Man *(1857). He also wrote a collection of short fiction,* Piazza Tales *(1856), and a long poem about the Holy Land,* Clarel *(1876). In his later years Melville was a customs' inspector in New York and a lecturer. He died in relative obscurity in 1891 while he was revising his last novel,* Billy Budd *(1924).*

Bartleby the Scrivener

HERMAN MELVILLE

I am a rather elderly man. The nature of my avocations, for the last thirty years, has brought me into more than ordinary contact with what would seem an interesting and somewhat singular set of men, of whom, as yet, nothing, that I know of, has ever been written—I mean the law-copyists, or scriveners. I have known very many of them, professionally and privately, and, if I pleased, could relate divers histories, at which good-natured gentlemen might smile, and sentimental souls might weep. But I waive the biographies of all other scriveners, for a few passages in the life of Bartleby, who was a scrivener, the strangest I ever saw, or heard of. While, of other law-copyists, I might write the complete life, of Bartleby nothing of that sort can be done. I believe that no materials exist for a full and satisfactory biography of this man. It is an irreparable loss to literature. Bartleby was one of those beings of whom nothing is ascertainable, except from the original sources, and, in his case, those are very small. What my own astonished eyes saw of Bartleby, that is all I know of him, except, indeed, one vague report, which will appear in the sequel.

Ere introducing the scrivener, as he first appeared to me, it is fit I make some mention of myself, my employees, my business, my chambers, and general surroundings, because some such description is indispensable to an adequate understanding of the chief character about to be presented. Imprimis: I am a man who, from his youth upward, has been filled with a profound conviction that the easiest way of life is the best. Hence, though I belong to a profession proverbially energetic and nervous even to turbulence at times, yet nothing of that sort have I ever suffered to invade my peace. I am one of those ambitious lawyers who never address a jury, or in any way draw down public applause; but, in the cool tranquility of a snug retreat, do a snug business among rich men's bonds, and mortgages, and title-deeds. All who know me consider me an eminently safe man. The late John Jacob Astor, a personage little given to poetic enthusiasm, had no hesitation in pronouncing my first grand point to be prudence; my next, method. I do not speak it in vanity, but simply record the fact, that I was not unemployed in my profession by the late John Jacob Astor; a name which, I admit, I love to repeat; for it hath a rounded and orbicular sound to it, and rings like unto bullion. I will freely add that I was not insensible to the late John Jacob Astor's good opinion.

Some time prior to the period at which this little history begins, my avocations had been largely increased. The good old office, now extinct in the State of New York, of a Master in Chancery had been conferred upon me. It was not a very arduous office, but very pleasantly remunerative. I seldom lose my temper; much more seldom indulge in dangerous indignation at wrongs and outrages; but I must be permitted to be rash here and declare that I consider the sudden and violent abrogation of the office of Master in Chancery, by the new Constitution, as a —— premature act; inasmuch as I had counted upon a life-lease of the profits, whereas I only received those of a few short years. But this is by the way.

My chambers were up stairs, at No. — Wall Street. At one end, they looked upon the white wall of the interior of a spacious skylight shaft, penetrating the building from top to bottom.

This view might have been considered rather tame than otherwise, deficient in what landscape painters call "life." But, if so, the view from the other end of my chambers offered, at least, a contrast, if nothing more. In that direction, my windows commanded an unobstructed view of a lofty brick wall, black by age and everlasting shade; which wall required no spy-glass to bring out its lurking beauties, but, for the benefit of all near-sighted spectators, was pushed up to within ten feet of my window-panes. Owing to the great height of the surrounding buildings, and my chambers being on the second floor, the interval between this wall and mine not a little resembled a huge square cistern.

At the period just preceding the advent of Bartleby, I had two persons as copyists in my employment, and a promising lad as an office-boy. First, Turkey; second, Nippers; third, Ginger Nut. These may seem names the like of which are not usually found in the Directory. In truth, they were nicknames, mutually conferred upon each other by my three clerks, and were deemed expressive of their respective persons or characters. Turkey was a short, pursy Englishman, of about my own age—that is, somewhere not far from sixty. In the morning, one might say, his face was of a fine florid hue, but after twelve o'clock, meridian—his dinner hour—it blazed like a grate full of Christmas coals, and continued blazing—but, as it were, with a gradual wane—till six o'clock, P.M., or thereabouts; after which, I saw no more of the proprietor of the face, which, gaining its meridian with the sun, seemed to set with it, to rise, culminate, and decline the following day, with the like regularity and undiminished glory. There are many singular coincidences I have known in the course of my life, not the least among which was the fact, that, exactly when Turkey displayed his fullest beams from his red and radiant countenance, just then, too, at that critical moment, began the daily period when I considered his business capacities as seriously disturbed for the remainder of the twenty-four hours. Not that he was absolutely idle, or averse to business then; far from it. The difficulty was, he was apt to be altogether too energetic. There was a strange, inflamed, flurried, flighty recklessness of activity about him. He would be incautious in dipping his pen into his inkstand. All his blots upon my documents were dropped there after twelve o'clock, meridian. Indeed, not only would he be reckless and sadly given to making blots in the afternoon, but, some days, he went further, and was rather noisy. At such times, too, his face flamed with augmented blazonry, as if cannel coal had been heaped on anthracite. He made an unpleasant racket with his chair, spilled his sand-box; in mending his pens, impatiently split them all to pieces, and threw them on the floor in a sudden passion; stood up, and leaned over his table, boxing his papers about in a most indecorous manner, very sad to behold in an elderly man like him. Nevertheless, as he was in many ways a most valuable person to me, and all the time before twelve o'clock, meridian, was the quickest, steadiest creature, too, accomplishing a great deal of work in a style not easily to be matched—for these reasons, I was willing to overlook his eccentricities, though, indeed, occasionally, I remonstrated with him. I did this very gently, however, because, though the civilest, nay, the blandest and most reverential of men in the morning, yet, in the afternoon, he was disposed, upon provocation, to be slightly rash with his tongue—in fact, insolent. Now, valuing his morning services as I did, and resolved not to lose them—yet, at the same time, made uncomfortable by his inflamed ways after twelve o'clock—and being a man of peace, unwilling by my admonitions to call forth unseemly retorts from him, I took upon me, one Saturday noon (he was always worse on Saturdays) to hint to him, very kindly, that, perhaps, now that he was growing old, it might be well to abridge his labors; in short, he need not come to my chambers after twelve o'clock, but, dinner over, had best go home to his lodgings, and rest himself till tea-time. But no; he insisted upon his afternoon devotions. His countenance became intolerably fervid, as he oratorically assured me—gesticulating with a long ruler at the other end of the room—that if his services in the morning were useful, how indispensable, then, in the afternoon?

"With submission, sir," said Turkey, on this occasion, "I consider myself your right-hand man. In the morning I but marshal and deploy my columns; but in the afternoon I put myself at their head, and gallantly charge the foe, thus"—and he made a violent thrust with the ruler.

"But the blots, Turkey," intimated I.

"True; but, with submission, sir, behold these hairs! I am getting old. Surely, sir, a blot or two of a warm afternoon is not to be severely urged against gray hairs. Old age—even if it blot the page—is honorable. With submission, sir, we both are getting old."

This appeal to my fellow-feeling was hardly to be resisted. At all events, I saw that go he would not. So I made up my mind to let him stay, resolving, nevertheless, to see to it that, during the afternoon, he had to do with my less important papers.

Nippers, the second on my list, was a whiskered, sallow, and, upon the whole, rather piratical-looking young man, of about five-and-twenty. I always deemed him the victim of two evil powers—ambition and indigestion. The ambition was evinced by a certain impatience of the duties of a mere copyist, an unwarrantable usurpation of strictly professional affairs, such as the original drawing up of legal documents. The indigestion seemed betokened in an occasional nervous testiness and grinning irritability, causing the teeth to audibly grind together over mistakes committed in copying; unnecessary maledictions, hissed, rather than spoken, in the heat of business; and especially by a continual discontent with the height of the table where he worked. Though of a very ingenious mechanical turn, Nippers could never get this table to suit him. He put chips under it, blocks of various sorts, bits of pasteboard, and at last went so far as to attempt an exquisite adjustment, by final pieces of folded blotting-paper. But no invention would answer. If, for the sake of easing his back, he brought the table-lid at a sharp angle well up toward his chin, and wrote there like a man using the steep roof of a Dutch house for his desk, then he declared that it stopped the circulation in his arms. If now he lowered the table to his waistbands, and stooped over it in writing, then there was a sore aching in his back. In short, the truth of the matter was, Nippers knew not what he wanted. Or, if he wanted anything, it was to be rid of a scrivener's table altogether. Among the manifestations of his diseased ambition was a fondness he had for receiving visits from certain ambiguous-looking fellows in seedy coats, whom he called his clients. Indeed, I was aware that not only was he, at times, considerable of a ward-politician, but he occasionally did a little business at the Justices' courts, and was not unknown on the steps of the Tombs. I have good reason to believe, however, that one individual who called upon him at my chambers, and who, with a grand air, he insisted was his client, was no other than a dun, and the alleged title-deed, a bill. But, with all his failings, and the annoyances he caused me, Nippers, like his compatriot Turkey, was a very useful man to me; wrote a neat, swift hand; and, when he chose, was not deficient in a gentlemanly sort of deportment. Added to this, he always dressed in a gentlemanly sort of way; and so, incidentally, reflected credit upon my chambers. Whereas, with respect to Turkey, I had much ado to keep him from being a reproach to me. His clothes were apt to look oily, and smell of eating-houses. He wore his pantaloons very loose and baggy in summer. His coats were execrable; his hat not to be handled. But while the hat was a thing of indifference to me, inasmuch as his natural civility and deference, as a dependent Englishman, always led him to doff it the moment he entered the room, yet his coat was another matter. Concerning his coats, I reasoned with him, but with no effect. The truth was, I suppose, that a man with so small an income could not afford to sport such a lustrous face and a lustrous coat at one and the same time. As Nippers once observed, Turkey's money went chiefly for red ink. One winter day, I presented Turkey with a highly respectable-looking coat of my own—a padded gray coat, of a most comfortable warmth, and which buttoned straight up from the knee to the neck. I thought Turkey would appreciate the favor, and abate his rashness and obstreperousness of afternoons. But no; I verily believe that buttoning himself up in so downy and blanket-like a coat had a pernicious effect upon him—upon the same principle that too much oats are bad for horses. In fact, precisely as a rash, restive horse is said to feel his oats, so Turkey felt his coat. It made him insolent. He was a man whom prosperity harmed.

Though, concerning the self-indulgent habits of Turkey, I had my own private surmises, yet, touching Nippers, I was well persuaded that, whatever might be his faults in other respects, he was, at least, a temperate young man. But, indeed, Nature herself seemed to have been his vintner, and, at his birth, charged him so thoroughly with an irritable, brandy-like disposition, that all subsequent potations were needless. When I consider how, amid the stillness of my chambers, Nippers would sometimes impatiently rise from his seat, and stooping over his table, spread his arms wide apart, seize the whole desk, and move it, and jerk it, with a grim, grinding motion on the floor, as if the table were a perverse voluntary agent, intent on thwarting and vexing him, I plainly perceive that, for Nippers, brandy-and-water were altogether superfluous.

It was fortunate for me that, owing to its peculiar cause—indigestion—the irritability and consequent nervousness of Nippers were mainly observable in the morning, while in the afternoon he was comparatively mild. So that, Turkey's paroxysms only coming on about twelve o'clock, I never had to do with their eccentricities at one time. Their fits relieved each other, like guards. When Nippers's was on, Turkey's was off; and vice versa. This was a good natural arrangement, under the circumstances.

Ginger Nut, the third on my list, was a lad, some twelve years old. His father was a car-man, ambitious of seeing his son on the bench instead of a cart, before he died. So he sent him to my office, as student of law, errand-boy, cleaner, and sweeper, at the rate of one dollar a week. He had a little desk to himself, but he did not use it much. Upon inspection, the drawer exhibited a great array of the shells of various sorts of nuts. Indeed, to this quick-witted youth, the whole noble science of law was contained in a nutshell. Not the least among the employments of Ginger Nut, as well as one which he discharged with the most alacrity, was his duty as cake and apple purveyor for Turkey and Nippers. Copying law papers being proverbially a dry, husky sort of business, my two scriveners were fain to moisten their mouths very often with Spitzenbergs, to be had at the numerous stalls nigh the Custom House and Post Office. Also, they sent Ginger Nut very frequently for that peculiar cake—small, flat, round, and very spicy—after which he had been named by them. Of a cold morning, when business was but dull, Turkey would gobble up scores of these cakes, as if they were mere wafers—indeed, they sell them at the rate of six or eight for a penny—the scrape of his pen blending with the crunching of the crisp particles in his mouth. Of all the fiery afternoon blunders and flurried rashnesses of Turkey, the worst was his once moistening a ginger-cake between his lips, and clapping it on to a mortgage, for a seal. I came within an ace of dismissing him then. But he mollified me by making an Oriental bow, and saying—

"With submission, sir, it was generous of me to find you in stationery on my own account."

Now my original business—that of a conveyancer and title hunter, and drawer-up of recondite documents of all sorts—was considerably increased by receiving the Master's office. There was now great work for scriveners. Not only must I push the clerks already with me, but I must have additional help.

In answer to my advertisement, a motionless young man one morning stood upon my office threshold, the door being open, for it was summer. I can see that figure now—pallidly neat, pitiably respectable, incurably forlorn! It was Bartleby.

After a few words touching his qualifications, I engaged him, glad to have among my corps of copyists a man of so singularly sedate an aspect, which I thought might operate beneficially upon the flighty temper of Turkey and the fiery one of Nippers.

I should have stated before that ground glass folding-doors divided my premises into two parts, one of which was occupied by my scriveners, the other by myself. According to my humor, I threw open these doors, or closed them. I resolved to assign Bartleby a corner by the folding-doors, but on my side of them, so as to have this quiet man within easy call, in case any trifling thing was to be done. I placed his desk close up to a small side window in that part of the room, a window which originally had afforded a lateral view of certain grimy backyards and bricks; but which owing to subsequent erections commanded at present no view at all, though it gave some light. Within three feet of the panes was a wall, and the light came down from far above, between two lofty buildings, as from a very small opening in a dome. Still further to a satisfactory arrangement, I procured a high green folding screen, which might entirely isolate Bartleby from my sight, though not remove him from my voice. And thus, in a manner, privacy and society were conjoined.

At first, Bartleby did an extraordinary quantity of writing. As if long famishing for something to copy, he seemed to gorge himself on my documents. There was no pause for digestion. He ran a day and night line, copying by sun-light and by candle-light. I should have been quite delighted with his application, had he been cheerfully industrious. But he wrote on silently, palely, mechanically.

It is, of course, an indispensable part of a scrivener's business to verify the accuracy of his copy, word by word. Where there are two or more scriveners in an office, they assist each other in this examination, one reading from the copy, the other holding the original. It is a very dull, wearisome, and lethargic affair. I can readily imagine that, to some sanguine temperaments, it would be altogether intolerable. For example, I cannot credit that the mettlesome poet, Byron, would have contentedly sat down with Bartleby to examine a law document of, say, five hundred pages, closely written in a crimpy hand.

Now and then, in the haste of business, it had been my habit to assist in comparing some brief document myself, calling Turkey or Nippers for this purpose. One object I had, in placing Bartleby so handy to me behind the screen, was to avail myself of his services on such trivial occasions. It was on the third day, I think, of his being with me, and before any necessity had arisen for having his own writing examined, that, being much hurried to complete a small affair I had in hand, I abruptly called to Bartleby. In my haste and natural expectancy of instant compliance, I sat with my head bent over the original on my desk, and my right hand sideways, and somewhat nervously extended with the copy, so that, immediately upon emerging from his retreat, Bartleby might snatch it and proceed to business without the least delay.

In this very attitude did I sit when I called to him, rapidly stating what it was I wanted him to do—namely, to examine a small paper with me. Imagine my surprise, nay, my consternation, when, without moving from his privacy, Bartleby, in a singularly mild, firm voice, replied, "I would prefer not to."

I sat awhile in perfect silence rallying my stunned faculties. Immediately it occurred to me that my ears had deceived me, or Bartleby had entirely misunderstood my meaning. I repeated my request in the clearest tone I could assume: but in quite as clear a one came the previous reply, "I would prefer not to."

"Prefer not to," echoed I, rising in high excitement, and crossing the room with a stride. "What do you mean? Are you moon-struck? I want you to help me compare this sheet here—take it," and I thrust it towards him.

"I would prefer not to," said he.

I looked at him steadfastly. His face was leanly composed; his gray eye dimly calm. Not a wrinkle of agitation rippled him. Had there been the least uneasiness, anger, impatience, or impertinence in his manner; in other words, had there been anything ordinarily human about him, doubtless I should have violently dismissed him from the premises. But as it was, I should have as soon thought of turning my pale plaster-of-Paris bust of Cicero out of doors. I stood gazing at him awhile, as he went on with his own writing, and then reseated myself at my desk. This is very strange, thought I. What had one best do? But my business hurried me. I concluded to forget the matter for the present, reserving it for my future leisure. So, calling Nippers from the other room, the paper was speedily examined.

A few days after this, Bartleby concluded four lengthy documents, being quadruplicates of a week's testimony taken before me in my High Court of Chancery. It became necessary to examine them. It was an important suit, and great accuracy was imperative. Having all things arranged, I called Turkey, Nippers, and Ginger Nut from the next room, meaning to place the four copies in the hands of my four clerks, while I should read from the original. Accordingly, Turkey, Nippers, and Ginger Nut had taken their seats in a row, each with his document in his hand, when I called to Bartleby to join this interesting group.

"Bartleby! quick, I am waiting."

I heard a slow scrape of his chair legs on the uncarpeted floor, and soon he appeared standing at the entrance of his hermitage.

"What is wanted?" said he mildly.

"The copies, the copies," said I, hurriedly. "We are going to examine them. There"—and I held toward him the fourth quadruplicate.

"I would prefer not to," he said, and gently disappeared behind the screen.

For a few moments I was turned into a pillar of salt, standing at the head of my seated column of clerks. Recovering myself, I advanced toward the screen, and demanded the reason for such extraordinary conduct.

"*Why* do you refuse?"

"I would prefer not to."

With any other man I should have flown outright into a dreadful passion, scorned all further words, and thrust him ignominiously from my presence. But there was something about Bartleby that not only strangely disarmed me, but, in a wonderful manner, touched and disconcerted me. I began to reason with him.

"These are your own copies we are about to examine. It is labor saving to you, because one examination will answer for your four papers. It is common usage. Every copyist is bound to help examine his copy. Is it not so? Will you not speak? Answer!"

"I prefer not to," he replied in a flute-like tone. It seemed to me that, while I had been addressing him, he carefully revolved every statement that I made; fully comprehended the meaning; could not gainsay the irresistible conclusion; but, at the same time, some paramount consideration prevailed with him to reply as he did.

"You are decided, then, not to comply with my request—a request made according to common usage and common sense?"

He briefly gave me to understand that on that point my judgment was sound. Yes: his decision was irreversible.

It is not seldom the case that, when a man is brow-beaten in some unprecedented and violently unreasonable way, he begins to stagger in his own plainest faith. He begins, as it were, vaguely to surmise that, wonderful as it may be, all the justice and all the reason is on the other side. Accordingly, if any disinterested persons are present, he turns to them for some reinforcement for his own faltering mind.

"Turkey," said I, "what do you think of this? Am I not right?"

"With submission, sir," said Turkey, in his blandest tone, "I think that you are."

"Nippers," said I, "what do *you* think of it?"

"I think I should kick him out of the office."

(The reader of nice perceptions will here perceive that, it being morning, Turkey's answer is couched in polite and tranquil terms, but Nippers replies in ill-tempered ones. Or, to repeat a previous sentence, Nippers's ugly mood was on duty, and Turkey's off.)

"Ginger Nut," said I, willing to enlist the smallest suffrage in my behalf, "what do *you* think of it?"

"I think, sir, he's a little *luny*," replied Ginger Nut, with a grin.

"You hear what they say," said I, turning towards the screen. "Come forth and do your duty."

But he vouchsafed no reply. I pondered a moment in sore perplexity. But once more business hurried me. I determined again to postpone the consideration of this dilemma to my future leisure. With a little trouble we made out to examine the papers without Bartleby, though at every page or two Turkey deferentially dropped his opinion, that this proceeding was quite out of the common; while Nippers, twitching in his chair with a dyspeptic nervousness, ground out, between his set teeth, occasional hissing maledictions against the stubborn oaf behind the screen. And for his (Nippers's) part, this was the first and the last time he would do another man's business without pay.

Meanwhile Bartleby sat in his hermitage, oblivious to everything but his own peculiar business there.

Some days passed, the scrivener being employed upon another lengthy work. His late remarkable conduct led me to regard his ways narrowly. I observed that he never went to dinner; indeed, that he never went anywhere. As yet I had never, of my personal knowledge, known him to be outside of my office. He was a perpetual sentry in the corner. At about eleven o'clock though, in the morning, I noticed that Ginger Nut would advance toward the opening in Bartleby's screen, as if silently beckoned thither by a gesture invisible to me where I sat. The boy would then leave the office, jingling a few pence, and reappear with a handful of ginger-nuts, which he delivered in the hermitage, receiving two of the cakes for his trouble.

He lives, then, on ginger-nuts, thought I; never eats a dinner, properly speaking; he must be a vegetarian, then; but no; he never eats even vegetables, he eats nothing but ginger-nuts. My mind then ran on in reveries concerning the probable effects upon the human constitution of living entirely on ginger-nuts. Ginger-nuts are so called, because they contain ginger as one of their peculiar constituents, and the final flavoring one. Now, what was ginger? A hot, spicy thing. Was Bartleby hot and spicy? Not at all. Ginger, then, had no effect upon Bartleby. Probably he preferred it should have none.

Nothing so aggravates an earnest person as a passive resistance. If the individual so resisted be of a not inhumane temper, and the resisting one perfectly harmless in his passivity, then, in the better moods of the former, he will endeavor charitably to construe to his imagination what proves impossible to be solved by his judgment. Even so, for the most part, I regarded Bartleby and his ways. Poor fellow! thought I, he means no mischief; it is plain he intends no insolence; his aspect sufficiently evinces that his eccentricities are involuntary. He is useful to me. I can get along with him. If I turn him away, the chances are he will fall in with some less indulgent employer, and then he will be rudely treated, and perhaps driven forth miserably to starve. Yes. Here I can cheaply purchase a delicious self-approval. To befriend Bartleby; to humor him in his strange willfulness, will cost me little or nothing, while I lay up in my soul what will eventually prove a sweet morsel for my conscience. But this mood was not invariable with me. The passiveness of Bartleby sometimes irritated me. I felt strangely goaded on to encounter him in new opposition—to elicit some angry spark from him answerable to my own. But, indeed, I might as well have essayed to strike fire with my knuckles against a bit of Windsor soap. But one afternoon the evil impulse in me mastered me, and the following little scene ensued:

"Bartleby," said I, "when those papers are all copied, I will compare them with you."

"I would prefer not to."

"How? Surely you do not mean to persist in that mulish vagary?"

No answer.

I threw open the folding-doors near by, and, turning upon Turkey and Nippers, exclaimed: "Bartleby a second time says he won't examine his papers. What do you think of it, Turkey?"

It was afternoon, be it remembered. Turkey sat glowing like a brass boiler, his bald head steaming, his hands reeling among his blotted papers.

"Think of it?" roared Turkey. "I think I'll just step behind his screen, and black his eyes for him!"

So saying, Turkey rose to his feet and threw his arms into a pugilistic position. He was hurrying away to make good his promise, when I detained him, alarmed at the effect of incautiously rousing Turkey's combativeness after dinner.

"Sit down, Turkey," said I, "and hear what Nippers has to say. What do you think of it, Nippers? Would I not be justified in immediately dismissing Bartleby?"

"Excuse me, that is for you to decide, sir. I think his conduct quite unusual, and, indeed, unjust, as regards Turkey and myself. But it may only be a passing whim."

"Ah," exclaimed I, "you have strangely changed your mind, then—you speak very gently of him now."

"All beer," cried Turkey; "gentleness is effects of beer—Nippers and I dined together today. You see how gentle *I* am, sir. Shall I go and black his eyes?"

"You refer to Bartleby, I suppose. No, not today, Turkey," I replied. "Pray, put up your fists."

I closed the doors, and again advanced toward Bartleby. I felt additional incentives tempting me to my fate. I burned to be rebelled against again. I remembered that Bartleby never left the office.

"Bartleby," said I, "Ginger Nut is away; just step around to the postoffice, won't you? (it was but a three minutes' walk) and see if there is anything for me."

"I would prefer not to."

"You *will* not?"

"I *prefer* not."

I staggered to my desk and sat there in a deep study. My blind inveteracy returned. Was there any other thing in which I could procure myself to be ignominiously repulsed by this lean, penniless wight?—my hired clerk? What added thing is there, perfectly reasonable, that he will be sure to refuse to do?

"Bartleby!"

No answer.

"Bartleby," in a louder tone.

No answer.

"Bartleby," I roared.

Like a very ghost, agreeable to the laws of magical invocation, at the third summons, he appeared at the entrance of his hermitage.

"Go to the next room, and tell Nippers to come to me."

"I prefer not to," he respectfully and slowly said, and mildly disappeared.

"Very good, Bartleby," said I, in a quiet sort of serenely severe self-possessed tone, intimating the unalterable purpose of some terrible retribution very close at hand. At the moment I half intended something of the kind. But upon the whole, as it was drawing towards my dinner hour, I thought it best to put on my hat and walk home for the day, suffering much from perplexity and distress of mind.

Shall I acknowledge it? The conclusion of this whole business was that it soon became a fixed fact of my chambers, that a pale young scrivener, by the name of Bartleby, had a desk there; that he copied for me at the usual rate of four cents a folio (one hundred words); but he was permanently exempt from examining the work done by him, the duty being transferred to Turkey and Nippers, out of compliment, doubtless, to their superior acuteness; moreover, said Bartleby was never, on any account, to be dispatched on the most trivial errand of any sort; and that, even if entreated to take upon him such a matter, it was generally understood that he would "prefer not to"—in other words, that he would refuse point-blank.

As days passed on, I became considerably reconciled to Bartleby. His steadiness, his freedom from all dissipation, his incessant industry (except when he chose to throw himself into a standing reverie behind his screen), his great stillness, his unalterableness of demeanor under all circumstances, made him a valuable acquisition. One prime thing was this—he was always there—first in the morning, continually through the day, and the last at night. I had a singular confidence in his honesty. I felt my most precious papers perfectly safe in his hands. Sometimes, to be sure, I could not, for the very soul of me, avoid falling into sudden spasmodic passions with him. For it was exceeding difficult to bear in mind all the time those strange peculiarities, privileges, and unheard-of exemptions, forming the tacit stipulations on Bartleby's part under which he remained in my office. Now and then, in the eagerness of dispatching pressing business, I would inadvertently summon Bartleby, in a short, rapid tone, to put his finger, say, on the incipient tie of a bit of red tape with which I was about compressing some papers. Of course, from behind the screen the usual answer, "I prefer not to," was sure to come; and then how could a human creature, with the common infirmities of our nature, refrain from bitterly exclaiming upon such perverseness—such unreasonableness? However, every added repulse of this sort which I received only tended to lessen the probability of my repeating the inadvertence.

Here it must be said that, according to the custom of most legal gentlemen occupying chambers in densely populated law buildings, there were several keys to my door. One was kept by a woman residing in the attic, which person weekly scrubbed and daily swept and dusted my apartments. Another was kept by Turkey for convenience' sake. The third I sometimes carried in my own pocket. The fourth I knew not who had.

Now, one Sunday morning I happened to go to Trinity Church, to hear a celebrated preacher, and finding myself rather early on the ground I thought I would walk round to my chambers for a while. Luckily I had my key with me; but upon applying it to the lock, I found it resisted by something inserted from the inside. Quite surprised, I called out; when to my consternation a key was turned from within; and thrusting his lean visage at me, and holding the door ajar, the apparition of Bartleby appeared, in his shirt-sleeves, and otherwise in a strangely tattered deshabille, saying quietly that he was sorry, but he was deeply engaged just then, and—preferred not admitting me at present. In a brief word or two, he moreover added, that perhaps I had better walk round the block two or three times, and by that time he would probably have concluded his affairs.

Now, the utterly unsurmised appearance of Bartleby, tenanting my law-chambers of a Sunday morning, with his cadaverously gentlemanly *nonchalance*, yet withal firm and self-possessed, had such a strange effect upon me, that incontinently I slunk away from my own door, and did as desired. But not without sundry twinges of impotent rebellion against the mild effrontery of this unaccountable scrivener. Indeed, it was his wonderful mildness chiefly which not only disarmed me, but unmanned me, as it were. For I consider that one, for the time, is a sort of unmanned when he tranquilly permits his hired clerk to dictate to him, and order him away from his own premises. Furthermore, I was full of uneasiness as to what Bartleby could possibly be doing in my office in his shirt-sleeves, and in an otherwise dismantled condition, of a Sunday morning. Was anything amiss going on? Nay, that was out of the question. It was not to be thought of for a moment that Bartleby was an immoral person. But what could he be doing there?—copying? Nay again, whatever might be his eccentricities, Bartleby was an eminently decorous person. He would be the last man to sit down to his desk in any state approaching to nudity. Besides, it was Sunday; and there was something about Bartleby that forbade the supposition that he would by any secular occupation violate the proprieties of the day.

Nevertheless, my mind was not pacified; and full of a restless curiosity, at last I returned to the door. Without hindrance I inserted my key, opened it, and entered. Bartleby was not to be seen. I looked round anxiously, peeped behind his screen; but it was very plain that he was gone. Upon more closely examining the place, I surmised that for an indefinite period Bartleby must have ate, dressed, and slept in my office, and that too without plate, mirror, or bed. The cushioned seat of a rickety old sofa in one corner bore the faint impress of a lean, reclining form. Rolled away under his desk, I found a blanket; under the empty grate, a blacking box and brush; on a chair, a tin basin, with soap and a ragged towel; in a newspaper a few crumbs of ginger-nuts and a morsel of cheese. Yes, thought I, it is evident enough that Bartleby has been making his home here, keeping Bachelor's Hall all by himself. Immediately then the thought came sweeping across me, what miserable friendlessness and loneliness are here revealed! His poverty is great; but his solitude, how horrible! Think of it. Of a Sunday, Wall Street is deserted as Petra; and every night of every day it is an emptiness. This building, too, which of week-days hums with industry and life, at nightfall echoes with sheer vacancy, and all through Sunday is forlorn. And here Bartleby makes his home; sole spectator of a solitude which he has seen all populous—a sort of innocent and transformed Marius brooding among the ruins of Carthage!

For the first time in my life a feeling of overpowering stinging melancholy seized me. Before, I had never experienced aught but a not unpleasing sadness. The bond of a common humanity now drew me irresistibly to gloom. A fraternal melancholy! For both I and Bartleby were sons of Adam. I remembered the bright silks and sparkling faces I had seen that day, in gala trim, swan-like sailing down the Mississippi of Broadway; and I contrasted them with the pallid copyist, and thought to myself, Ah, happiness courts the light, so we deem the world is gay; but misery hides aloof, so we deem that misery there is none. These sad fancyings—chimeras, doubtless, of a sick and silly brain—led on to other and more special thoughts, concerning the eccentricities of Bartleby. Presentiments of strange discoveries hovered round me. The scrivener's pale form appeared to me laid out, among uncaring strangers, in its shivering winding-sheet.

Suddenly I was attracted by Bartleby's closed desk, the key in open sight left in the lock.

I mean no mischief, seek the gratification of no heartless curiosity, thought I; besides, the desk is mine, and its contents, too, so I will make bold to look within. Everything was methodically arranged, the papers smoothly placed. The pigeon-holes were deep, and removing the files of documents, I groped into their recesses. Presently I felt something there, and dragged it out. It was an old bandanna handkerchief, heavy and knotted. I opened it, and saw it was a savings bank.

I now recalled all the quiet mysteries which I had noted in the man. I remembered that he never spoke but to answer; that, though at intervals he had considerable time to himself, yet I had never seen him reading—no, not even a newspaper; that for long periods he would stand looking out, at his pale window behind the screen, upon the dead brick wall; I was quite sure he never visited any refectory or eating-house; while his pale face clearly indicated that he never drank beer like Turkey, or tea and coffee even, like other men; that he never went anywhere in particular that I could learn; never went out for a walk, unless, indeed, that was the case at present; that he had declined telling who he was, or whence he came, or whether he had any relatives in the world; that though so thin and pale, he never complained of ill-health. And more than all, I remembered a certain unconscious air of pallid—how shall I call it?—of pallid haughtiness, say, or rather an austere reserve about him, which had positively awed me into my tame compliance with his eccentricities, when I had feared to ask him to do the slightest incidental thing for me, even though I might know, from his long-continued motionlessness, that behind his screen he must be standing in one of those dead-wall reveries of his.

Revolving all these things, and coupling them with the recently discovered fact that he made my office his constant abiding place and home, and not forgetful of his morbid moodiness; revolving all these things, a prudential feeling began to steal over me. My first emotions had been those of pure melancholy and sincerest pity; but just in proportion as the forlornness of Bartleby grew and grew to my imagination, did that same melancholy merge into fear, that pity into repulsion. So true it is, and so terrible, too, that up to a certain point the thought or sight of misery enlists our best affections; but, in certain special cases, beyond that point it does not. They err who would assert that invariably this is owing to the inherent selfishness of the human heart. It rather proceeds from a certain hopelessness of remedying excessive and organic ill. To a sensitive being, pity is not seldom pain. And when at last it is perceived that such pity cannot lead to effectual succor, common sense bids the soul be rid of it. What I saw that morning persuaded me that the scrivener was the victim of innate and incurable disorder. I might give alms to his body; but his body did not pain him; it was his soul that suffered, and his soul I could not reach.

I did not accomplish the purpose of going to Trinity Church that morning. Somehow, the things I had seen disqualified me for the time from church-going. I walked homeward, thinking what I would do with Bartleby. Finally, I resolved upon this—I would put certain calm questions to him the next morning, touching his history, etc., and if he declined to answer them openly and unreservedly (and I suppose he would prefer not), then to give him a twenty-dollar bill over and above whatever I might owe him, and tell him his services were no longer required, but that if in any other way I could assist him, I would be happy to do so, especially if he desired to return to his native place, wherever that might be, I would willingly help to defray the expenses. Moreover, if, after reaching home, he found himself at any time in want of aid, a letter from him would be sure of a reply.

The next morning came.

"Bartleby," said I, gently calling to him behind his screen.

No reply.

"Bartleby," said I, in a still gentler tone, "come here; I am not going to ask you to do anything you would prefer not to do—I simply wish to speak to you."

Upon this he noiselessly slid into view.

"Will you tell me, Bartleby, where you were born?"

"I would prefer not to."

"Will you tell me *anything* about yourself?"

"I would prefer not to."

"But what reasonable objection can you have to speak to me? I feel friendly towards you."

He did not look at me while I spoke, but kept his glance fixed upon my bust of Cicero, which, as I then sat, was directly behind me, some six inches above my head.

"What is your answer, Bartleby?" said I, after waiting a considerable time for a reply, during which his countenance remained immovable, only there was the faintest conceivable tremor of the white attenuated mouth.

"At present I prefer to give no answer," he said, and retired into his hermitage.

It was rather weak in me, I confess, but his manner, on this occasion, nettled me. Not only did there seem to lurk in it a certain calm disdain, but his perverseness seemed ungrateful, considering the undeniable good usage and indulgence he had received from me.

Again I sat ruminating what I should do. Mortified as I was at his behavior, and resolved as I had been to dismiss him when I entered my office, nevertheless I strangely felt something superstitious knocking at my heart, and forbidding me to carry out my purpose, and denouncing me for a villain if I dared to breathe one bitter word against this forlornest of mankind. At last, familiarly drawing my chair behind his screen, I sat down and said: "Bartleby, never mind, then, about revealing your history; but let me entreat you, as a friend, to comply as far as may be with the usages of this office. Say now, you will help to examine papers tomorrow or next day: in short, say now, that in a day or two you will begin to be a little reasonable:—say so, Bartleby."

"At present I would prefer not to be a little reasonable," was his mildly cadaverous reply.

Just then the folding-doors opened, and Nippers approached. He seemed suffering from an unusually bad night's rest, induced by severer indigestion than common. He overheard those final words of Bartleby.

"*Prefer not*, eh?" gritted Nippers—"I'd *prefer* him, if I were you, sir," addressing me—"I'd *prefer* him; I'd give him preferences, the stubborn mule! What is it, sir, pray, that he *prefers* not to do now?"

Bartleby moved not a limb.

"Mr. Nippers," said I, "I'd prefer that you would withdraw for the present."

Somehow, of late, I had got into the way of involuntarily using this word "prefer" upon all sorts of not exactly suitable occasions. And I trembled to think that my contact with the scrivener had already and seriously affected me in a mental way. And what further and deeper aberration might it not yet produce? This apprehension had not been without efficacy in determining me to summary measures.

As Nippers, looking very sour and sulky, was departing, Turkey blandly and deferentially approached.

"With submission, sir," said he, "yesterday I was thinking about Bartleby here, and I think that if he would but prefer to take a quart of good ale every day, it would do much towards mending him, and enabling him to assist in examining his papers."

"So you have got the word, too," said I, slightly excited.

"With submission, what word, sir?" asked Turkey, respectfully crowding himself into the contracted space behind the screen, and by so doing, making me jostle the scrivener. "What word, sir?"

"I would prefer to be left alone here," said Bartleby, as if offended at being mobbed in his privacy.

"*That's* the word, Turkey," said I, "*that's* it."

"Oh, *prefer?* Oh yes—queer word. I never use it myself. But, sir, as I was saying, if he would but prefer—"

"Turkey," interrupted I, "you will please withdraw."

"Oh certainly, sir, if you prefer that I should."

As he opened the folding-door to retire, Nippers at his desk caught a glimpse of me, and asked whether I would prefer to have a certain paper copied on blue paper or white. He did not in the least roguishly accent the word "prefer." It was plain that it involuntarily rolled from his tongue. I thought to myself, surely I must get rid of a demented man, who already has in some degree turned the tongues, if not the heads, of myself and clerks. But I thought it prudent not to break the dismission at once.

The next day I noticed that Bartleby did nothing but stand at his window in his dead-wall reverie. Upon asking him why he did not write, he said that he had decided upon doing no more writing.

"Why, how now? what next?" exclaimed I. "Do no more writing?"

"No more."

"And what is the reason?"

"Do you not see the reason for yourself?" he indifferently replied.

I looked steadfastly at him, and perceived that his eyes looked dull and glazed. Instantly it occurred to me, that his unexampled diligence in copying by his dim window for the first few weeks of his stay with me might have temporarily impaired his vision.

I was touched. I said something in condolence with him. I hinted that of course he did wisely in abstaining from writing for a while, and urged him to embrace that opportunity of taking wholesome exercise in the open air. This, however, he did not do. A few days after this, my other clerks being absent, and being in a great hurry to dispatch certain letters by the mail, I thought that, having nothing else earthly to do, Bartleby would surely be less inflexible than usual, and carry these letters to the postoffice. But he blankly declined. So, much to my inconvenience, I went myself.

Still added days went by. Whether Bartleby's eyes improved or not, I could not say. To all appearance, I thought they did. But when I asked him if they did, he vouchsafed no answer. At all events, he would do no copying. At last, in reply to my urgings, he informed me that he had permanently given up copying.

"What!" exclaimed I; "suppose your eyes should get entirely well—better than ever before—would you not copy then?"

"I have given up copying," he answered, and slid aside.

He remained as ever, a fixture in my chamber. Nay—if that were possible—he became still more of a fixture than before. What was to be done? He would do nothing in the office; why should he stay there? In plain fact, he had now become a millstone to me, not only useless as a necklace, but afflictive to bear. Yet I was sorry for him. I speak less than truth when I say that, on his own account, he occasioned me uneasiness. If he would but have named a single relative or friend, I would instantly have written, and urged their taking the poor fellow away to some convenient retreat. But he seemed alone, absolutely alone in the universe. A bit of wreck in the mid-Atlantic. At length, necessities connected with my business tyrannized over all other considerations. Decently as I could, I told Bartleby that in six days' time he must unconditionally leave the office. I warned him to take measures, in the interval, for procuring some other abode. I offered to assist him in this endeavor, if he himself would but take the first step towards a removal. "And when you finally quit me, Bartleby," added I, "I shall see that you go not away entirely unprovided. Six days from this hour, remember."

At the expiration of that period, I peeped behind the screen, and lo! Bartleby was there.

I buttoned up my coat, balanced myself, advanced slowly towards him, touched his shoulder, and said, "The time has come; you must quit this place; I am sorry for you; here is money; but you must go."

"I would prefer not," he replied, with his back still towards me.

"You *must*."

He remained silent.

Now I had an unbounded confidence in this man's common honesty. He had frequently restored to me sixpences and shillings carelessly dropped upon the floor, for I am apt to be very reckless in such shirt-button affairs. The proceeding, then, which followed will not be deemed extraordinary.

"Bartleby," said I, "I owe you twelve dollars on account; here are thirty-two; the odd twenty are yours—Will you take it?" and I handed the bills towards him.

But he made no motion.

"I will leave them here, then," putting them under a weight on the table. Then taking my hat and cane and going to the door, I tranquilly turned and added, "After you have removed your things from these offices, Bartleby, you will of course lock the door—since every eye is now gone for the day but you—and if you please, slip your key underneath the mat, so that I may have it in the morning. I shall not see you again; so good-by to you. If, hereafter, in your new place of abode, I can be of any service to you, do not fail to advise me by letter. Good-by, Bartleby, and fare you well."

But he answered not a word; like the last column of some ruined temple, he remained standing mute and solitary in the middle of the otherwise deserted room.

As I walked home in a pensive mood, my vanity got the better of my pity. I could not but highly plume myself on my masterly management in getting rid of Bartleby. Masterly I call it, and such it must appear to any dispassionate thinker. The beauty of my procedure seemed to consist in its perfect quietness. There was no vulgar bullying, no bravado of any sort, no choleric hectoring, and striding to and fro across the apartment, jerking out vehement commands for Bartleby to bundle himself off with his beggarly traps. Nothing of the kind. Without loudly bidding Bartleby depart—as an inferior genius might have done—I *assumed* the ground that depart he must; and upon that assumption built all I had to say. The more I thought over my procedure, the more I was charmed with it. Nevertheless, next morning, upon awakening, I had my doubts—I had somehow slept off the fumes of vanity. One of the coolest and wisest hours a man has is just after he awakes in the morning. My procedure seemed as sagacious as ever—but only in theory. How it would prove in practice—there was the rub. It was truly a beautiful thought to have assumed Bartleby's departure; but, after all, that assumption was simply my own, and none of Bartleby's. The great point was, not whether I had assumed that he would quit me, but whether he would prefer so to do. He was more a man of preferences than assumptions.

After breakfast, I walked down town, arguing the probabilities *pro* and *con*. One moment I thought it would prove a miserable failure, and Bartleby would be found all alive at my office as usual; the next moment it seemed certain that I should find his chair empty. And so I kept veering about. At the corner of Broadway and Canal Street, I saw quite an excited group of people standing in earnest conversation.

"I'll take odds he doesn't," said a voice as I passed.

"Doesn't go?—done!" said I, "put up your money."

I was instinctively putting my hand in my pocket to produce my own, when I remembered that this was an election day. The words I had overheard bore no reference to Bartleby, but to the success or non-success of some candidate for the mayoralty. In my intent frame of mind, I had, as it were, imagined that all Broadway shared in my excitement, and were debating the same question with me. I passed on, very thankful that the uproar of the street screened my momentary absentmindedness.

As I had intended, I was earlier than usual at my office door. I stood listening for a moment. All was still. He must be gone. I tried the knob. The door was locked. Yes, my procedure had worked to a charm; he indeed must be vanished. Yet a certain melancholy mixed with this: I was almost sorry for my brilliant success. I was fumbling under the door mat for the key, which Bartleby was to have left there for me, when accidentally my knee knocked against a panel, producing a summoning sound, and in response a voice came to me from within—"Not yet; I am occupied."

It was Bartleby.

I was thunderstruck. For an instant I stood like the man who, pipe in mouth, was killed one cloudless afternoon long ago in Virginia, by summer lightning; at his own warm open window he was killed, and remained leaning out there upon the dreamy afternoon, till some one touched him, when he fell.

"Not gone!" I murmured at last. But again obeying that wondrous ascendancy which the inscrutable scrivener had over me, and from which ascendancy, for all my chafing, I could not completely escape, I slowly went down stairs and out into the street, and while walking round the block, considered what I should next do in this unheard-of perplexity. Turn the man out by an actual thrusting I could not; to drive him away by calling him hard names would not do; calling in the police was an unpleasant idea; and yet, permit him to enjoy his cadaverous triumph over me—this, too, I could not think of. What was to be done? or, if nothing could be done, was there anything further that I could *assume* in the matter? Yes, as before I had prospectively assumed that Bartleby would depart, so now I might retrospectively assume that departed he was. In the legitimate carrying out of this assumption, I might enter my office in a great hurry, and pretending not to see Bartleby at all, walk straight against him as if he were air. Such a proceeding would in a singular degree have the appearance of a home-thrust. It was hardly possible that Bartleby could withstand such an application of the doctrine of assumptions. But upon second thoughts the success of the plan seemed rather dubious. I resolved to argue the matter over with him again.

"Bartleby," said I, entering the office, with a quietly severe expression, "I am seriously displeased. I am pained, Bartleby. I had thought better of you. I had imagined you of such a gentlemanly organization that in any delicate dilemma a slight hint would suffice—in short, an assumption. But it appears I am deceived. Why," I added, unaffectedly starting, "you have not even touched that money yet," pointing to it, just where I had left it the evening previous.

He answered nothing.

"Will you, or will you not, quit me?" I now demanded in a sudden passion, advancing close to him.

"I would prefer *not* to quit you," he replied, gently emphasizing the *not*.

"What earthly right have you to stay here? Do you pay any rent? Do you pay my taxes? Or is this property yours?"

He answered nothing.

"Are you ready to go on and write now? Are your eyes recovered? Could you copy a small paper for me this morning? or help examine a few lines? or step round to the postoffice? In a word, will you do anything at all, to give a coloring to your refusal to depart the premises?"

He silently retired into his hermitage.

I was now in such a state of nervous resentment that I thought it but prudent to check myself at present from further demonstrations. Bartleby and I were alone. I remembered the tragedy of the unfortunate Adams and the still more unfortunate Colt in the solitary office of the latter; and how poor Colt, being dreadfully incensed by Adams, and imprudently permitting himself to get wildly excited, was at unawares hurried into his fatal act—an act which certainly no man could possibly deplore more than the actor himself. Often it had occurred to me in my ponderings upon the subject that had that altercation taken place in the public street, or at a private residence, it would not have terminated as it did. It was the circumstance of being alone in a solitary office, up stairs, of a building entirely unhallowed by humanizing domestic associations—an uncarpeted office, doubtless, of a dusty, haggard sort of appearance—this it must have been, which greatly helped to enhance the irritable desperation of the hapless Colt.

But when this old Adam of resentment rose in me and tempted me concerning Bartleby, I grappled him and threw him. How? Why, simply by recalling the divine injunction: "A new commandment give I unto you, that ye love one another." Yes, this it was that saved me. Aside from higher considerations, charity often operates as a vastly wise and prudent principle—a great safeguard to its possessor. Men have committed murder for jealousy's sake, and anger's sake, and hatred's sake, and selfishness' sake, and spiritual pride's sake; but no man that ever I heard of ever committed a diabolical murder for sweet charity's sake. Mere self-interest, then, if no better motive can be enlisted, should, especially with high-tempered men, prompt all beings to charity and philanthropy. At any rate, upon the occasion in question, I strove to drown my exasperated feelings towards the scrivener by benevolently construing his conduct. Poor fellow, poor fellow! thought I, he don't mean anything; and besides, he has seen hard times, and ought to be indulged.

I endeavored, also, immediately to occupy myself, and at the same time to comfort my despondency. I tried to fancy, that in the course of the morning, at such time as might prove agreeable to him, Bartleby, of his own free accord, would emerge from his hermitage and take up some decided line of march in the direction of the door. But no. Half-past twelve o'clock came; Turkey began to glow in the face, overturn his inkstand, and become generally obstreperous; Nippers abated down into quietude and courtesy; Ginger Nut munched his noon apple; and Bartleby remained standing at his window in one of his profoundest dead-wall reveries. Will it be credited? Ought I to acknowledge it? That afternoon I left the office without saying one further word to him.

Some days now passed, during which, at leisure intervals I looked a little into *Edwards on the Will*, and *Priestley on Necessity*. Under the circumstances, those books induced a salutary feeling. Gradually I slid into the persuasion that these troubles of mine, touching the scrivener, had been all predestinated from eternity, and Bartleby was billeted upon me for some mysterious purpose of an all-wise Providence, which it was not for a mere mortal like me to fathom. Yes, Bartleby, stay there behind your screen, thought I; I shall persecute you no more; you are harmless and noiseless as any of these old chairs; in short, I never feel so private as when I know you are here. At last I see it, I feel it; I penetrate to the predestinated purpose of my life. I am content. Others may have loftier parts to enact; but my mission in the world, Bartleby, is to furnish you with office room for such period as you may see fit to remain.

I believe that this wise and blessed frame of mind would have continued with me, had it not been for the unsolicited and uncharitable remarks obtruded upon me by my professional friends who visited the rooms. But thus it often is, that the constant friction of illiberal minds wears out at last the best resolves of the more generous. Though to be sure, when I reflected upon it, it was not strange that people entering my office should be struck by the peculiar aspects of the unaccountable Bartleby, and so be tempted to throw out some sinister observations concerning him. Sometimes an attorney, having business with me, and calling at my office, and finding no one but the scrivener there, would undertake to obtain some sort of precise information from him touching my whereabouts; but without heeding his idle talk, Bartleby would remain standing immovable in the middle of the room. So after contemplating him in that position for a time, the attorney would depart, no wiser than he came.

Also, when a reference was going on, and the room full of lawyers and witnesses, and business driving fast, some deeply occupied legal gentleman present, seeing Bartleby wholly unemployed, would request him to run round to his (the legal gentleman's) office and fetch some papers for him. Thereupon, Bartleby would tranquilly decline, and yet remain idle as before. Then the lawyer would give a great stare, and turn to me. And what could I say? At last I was made aware that all through the circle of my professional acquaintance, a whisper of wonder was running round, having reference to the strange creature I kept at my office. This worried me very much. And as the idea came upon me of his possibly turning out a long-lived man, and keep occupying my chambers, and denying my authority, and perplexing my visitors, and scandalizing my professional reputation, and casting a general gloom over the premises; keeping soul and body together to the last upon his savings (for doubtless he spent but half a dime a day), and in the end perhaps outlive me, and claim possession of my office by right of his perpetual occupancy: as all these dark anticipations crowded upon me more and more, and my friends continually intruded their relentless remarks upon the apparition in my room, a great change was wrought in me. I resolved to gather all my faculties together, and forever rid me of this intolerable incubus.

Ere revolving any complicated project, however, adapted to this end, I first simply suggested to Bartleby the propriety of his permanent departure. In a calm and serious tone, I commended the idea to his careful and mature consideration. But, having taken three days to meditate upon it, he apprised me that his original determination remained the same; in short, that he still preferred to abide with me.

What shall I do? I now said to myself, buttoning up my coat to the last button. What shall I do? what ought I to do? what does conscience say I *should* do with this man, or rather, ghost. Rid myself of him, I must; go, he shall. But how? You will not thrust him, the poor, pale, passive mortal—you will not thrust such a helpless creature out of your door? you will not dishonor yourself by such cruelty? No, I will not, I cannot do that. Rather would I let him live and die here, and then mason up his remains in the wall. What, then, will you do? For all your coaxing, he will not budge. Bribes he leaves under your own paper-weight on your table; in short, it is quite plain that he prefers to cling to you.

Then something severe, something unusual must be done. What!

surely you will not have him collared by a constable, and commit his innocent pallor to the common jail?—a vagrant, is he? What! he a vagrant, a wanderer, who refuses to budge? It is because he will *not* be a vagrant, then, that you seek to count him *as* a vagrant. That is too absurd. No visible means of support: there I have him. Wrong again: for indubitably he *does* support himself, and that is the only unanswerable proof that any man can show of his possessing the means so to do. No more, then. Since he will not quit me, I must quit him. I will change my offices; I will move elsewhere, and give him fair notice that if I find him on my new premises I will then proceed against him as a common trespasser.

Acting accordingly, next day I thus addressed him: "I find these chambers too far from the City Hall; the air is unwholesome. In a word, I propose to remove my offices next week, and shall no longer require your services. I tell you this now, in order that you may seek another place."

He made no reply, and nothing more was said.

On the appointed day I engaged carts and men, proceeded to my chambers, and, having but little furniture, everything was removed in a few hours. Throughout, the scrivener remained standing behind the screen, which I directed to be removed the last thing. It was withdrawn, and, being folded up like a huge folio, left him the motionless occupant of a naked room. I stood in the entry watching him a moment, while something from within me upbraided me.

I re-entered, with my hand in my pocket—and—and my heart in my mouth.

"Good-by, Bartleby; I am going—good-by, and God some way bless you; and take that," slipping something in his hand. But it dropped upon the floor, and then—strange to say—I tore myself from him whom I had so longed to be rid of.

Established in my new quarters, for a day or two I kept the door locked, and started at every footfall in the passages. When I returned to my rooms, after any little absence, I would pause at the threshold for an instant, and attentively listen, ere applying my key. But these fears were needless. Bartleby never came nigh me.

I thought all was going well, when a perturbed-looking stranger visited me, inquiring whether I was the person who had recently occupied rooms at No. — Wall Street.

Full of forebodings, I replied that I was.

"Then, sir," said the stranger, who proved a lawyer, "you are responsible for the man you left there. He refuses to do any copying; he refuses to do anything; he says he prefers not to; and he refuses to quit the premises."

"I am very sorry, sir," said I, with assumed tranquility, but an inward tremor, "but, really, the man you allude to is nothing to me—he is no relation or apprentice of mine, that you should hold me responsible for him."

"In mercy's name, who is he?"

"I certainly cannot inform you. I know nothing about him. Formerly I employed him as a copyist; but he has done nothing for me now for some time past."

"I shall settle him, then—good morning, sir."

Several days passed, and I heard nothing more; and, though I often felt a charitable prompting to call at the place and see poor Bartleby, yet a certain squeamishness, of I know not what, withheld me.

All is over with him, by this time, thought I, at last, when, through another week, no further intelligence reached me. But, coming to my room the day after, I found several persons waiting at my door in a high state of nervous excitement.

"That's the man—here he comes," cried the foremost one, whom I recognized as the lawyer who had previously called upon me alone.

"You must take him away, sir, at once," cried a portly person among them, advancing upon me, and whom I knew to be the landlord of No. — Wall Street. "These gentlemen, my tenants, cannot stand it any longer; Mr. B——," pointing to the lawyer, "has turned him out of his room, and he now persists in haunting the building generally, sitting upon the banisters of the stairs by day, and sleeping in the entry by night. Everybody is concerned; clients are leaving the offices; some fears are entertained of a mob; something you must do, and that without delay."

Aghast at this torrent, I fell back before it, and would fain have locked myself in my new quarters. In vain I persisted that Bartleby was nothing to me—no more than to any one else. In vain—I was the last person known to have anything to do with him, and they held me to the terrible account. Fearful, then, of being exposed in the papers (as one person present obscurely threatened), I considered the matter, and, at length, said, that if the lawyer would give me a confidential interview with the scrivener, in his (the lawyer's) own room, I would, that afternoon, strive my best to rid them of the nuisance they complained of.

Going up stairs to my old haunt, there was Bartleby silently sitting upon the banister at the landing.

"What are you doing here, Bartleby?" said I.

"Sitting upon the banister," he mildly replied.

I motioned him into the lawyer's room, who then left us.

"Bartleby," said I, "are you aware that you are the cause of great tribulation to me, by persisting in occupying the entry after being dismissed from the office?"

No answer.

"Now one of two things must take place. Either you must do something, or something must be done to you. Now what sort of business would you like to engage in? Would you like to re-engage in copying for some one?"

"No; I would prefer not to make any change."

"Would you like a clerkship in a dry-goods store?"

"There is too much confinement about that. No, I would not like a clerkship; but I am not particular."

"Too much confinement," I cried, "why, you keep yourself confined all the time!"

"I would prefer not to take a clerkship," he rejoined, as if to settle that little item at once.

"How would a bar-tender's business suit you? There is no trying of the eyesight in that."

"I would not like it at all; though, as I said before, I am not particular."

His unwonted wordiness inspirited me. I returned to the charge.

"Well, then, would you like to travel through the country collecting bills for the merchants? That would improve your health."

"No, I would prefer to be doing something else."

"How, then, would going as a companion to Europe, to entertain some young gentleman with your conversation—how would that suit you?"

"Not at all. It does not strike me that there is anything definite about that. I like to be stationary. But I am not particular."

"Stationary you shall be, then," I cried, now losing all patience, and, for the first time in all my exasperating connection with him, fairly flying into a passion. "If you do not go away from these premises before night, I shall feel bound—indeed, I *am* bound—to—to—to quit the premises myself!" I rather absurdly concluded, knowing not with what possible threat to try to frighten his immobility into compliance. Despairing of all further efforts, I was precipitately leaving him, when a final thought occurred to me—one which had not been wholly unindulged before.

"Bartleby," said I, in the kindest tone I could assume under such exciting circumstances, "will you go home with me now—not to my office, but my dwelling—and remain there till we can conclude upon some convenient arrangement for you at our leisure? Come, let us start now, right away."

"No, at present I would prefer not to make any change at all."

I answered nothing; but, effectually dodging every one by the suddenness and rapidity of my flight, rushed from the building, ran up Wall Street towards Broadway, and, jumping into the first omnibus, was soon removed from pursuit. As soon as tranquility returned, I distinctly perceived that I had now done all that I possibly could, both in respect to the demands of the landlord and his tenants, and with regard to my own desire and sense of duty, to benefit Bartleby, and shield him from rude persecution. I now strove to be entirely carefree and quiescent; and my conscience justified me in attempt; though, indeed, it was not so successful as I could have wished. So fearful was I of being again hunted out by the incensed landlord and his exasperated tenants, that, surrendering my business to Nippers for a few days, I drove about the upper part of the town and through the suburbs, in my rockaway, crossed over to Jersey City and Hoboken, and paid fugitive visits to Manhattanville and Astoria. In fact, I almost lived in my rockaway for the time.

When again I entered my office, lo, a note from the landlord lay upon my desk. I opened it with trembling hands. It informed me that the writer had sent to the police, and had Bartleby removed to the Tombs as a vagrant. Moreover, since I knew more about him than any one else, he wished me to appear at that place, and make a suitable statement of the facts. These tidings had a conflicting effect upon me. At first I was indignant, but, at last, almost approved. The landlord's energetic, summary disposition had led him to adopt a procedure which I do not think I would have decided upon myself; and yet, as a last resort, under such peculiar circumstances, it seemed the only plan.

As I afterwards learned, the poor scrivener, when told that he must be conducted to the Tombs, offered not the slightest obstacle, but, in his pale, unmoving way, silently acquiesced.

Some of the compassionate and curious bystanders joined the party; and headed by one of the constables arm-in-arm with Bartleby, the silent procession filed its way through all the noise, and heat, and joy of the roaring thoroughfares at noon.

The same day I received the note, I went to the Tombs, or, to speak more properly, the Halls of Justice. Seeking the right officer, I stated the purpose of my call, and was informed that the individual I described was, indeed, within. I then assured the functionary that Bartleby was a perfectly honest man, and greatly to be compassionated, however unaccountably eccentric. I narrated all I knew, and closed by suggesting the idea of letting him remain in as indulgent confinement as possible, till something less harsh might be done—though, indeed, I hardly knew what. At all events, if nothing else could be decided upon, the almshouse must receive him. I then begged to have an interview.

Being under no disgraceful charge, and quite serene and harmless in all his ways, they had permitted him freely to wander about the prison, and, especially, in the inclosed grass-platted yards thereof. And so I found him there, standing all alone in the quietest of the yards, his face towards a high wall, while all around, from the narrow slits of the jail windows, I thought I saw peering out upon him the eyes of murderers and thieves.

"Bartleby!"

"I know you," he said, without looking round, "and I want nothing to say to you."

"It was not I that brought you here, Bartleby," said I, keenly pained at his implied suspicion. "And to you, this should not be so vile a place. Nothing reproachful attaches to you by being here. And see, it is not so sad a place as one might think. Look, there is the sky, and here is the grass."

"I know where I am," he replied, but would say nothing more, and so I left him.

As I entered the corridor again, a broad meat-like man, in an apron, accosted me, and, jerking his thumb over his shoulder, said, "Is that your friend?"

"Yes."

"Does he want to starve? If he does, let him live on the prison fare, that's all."

"Who are you?" asked I, not knowing what to make of such an unofficially speaking person in such a place.

"I am the grub-man. Such gentlemen as have friends here hire me to provide them with something good to eat."

"Is this so?" said I, turning to the turnkey.

He said it was.

"Well, then," said I, slipping some silver into the grub-man's hands (for so they called him), "I want you to give particular attention to my friend there; let him have the best dinner you can get. And you must be as polite to him as possible."

"Introduce me, will you?" said the grub-man, looking at me with an expression which seemed to say he was all impatience for an opportunity to give a specimen of his breeding.

Thinking it would prove of benefit to the scrivener, I acquiesced, and, asking the grub-man his name, went up with him to Bartleby.

"Bartleby, this is a friend; you will find him very useful to you."

"Your sarvant, sir, your sarvant," said the grub-man, making a low salutation behind his apron. "Hope you find it pleasant here, sir; nice grounds—cool apartments—hope you'll stay with us some time—try to make it agreeable. What will you have for dinner today?"

"I prefer not to dine today," said Bartleby, turning away. "It would disagree with me; I am unused to dinners." So saying, he slowly moved to the other side of the inclosure, and took up a position fronting the dead-wall.

"How's this?" said the grub-man, addressing me with a stare of astonishment. "He's odd, ain't he?"

"I think he is a little deranged," said I, sadly.

"Deranged? deranged is it? Well, now, upon my word, I thought that friend of yourn was a gentleman forger; they are always pale and genteel-like, them forgers. I can't help pity 'em—can't help it, sir. Did you know Monroe Edwards?" he added, touchingly, and paused, then, laying his hand piteously on my shoulder, sighed, "He died of consumption at Sing-Sing. So you weren't acquainted with Monroe?"

"No, I was never socially acquainted with any forgers. But I cannot stop longer. Look to my friend yonder. You will not lose by it. I will see you again."

Some few days after this, I again obtained admission to the Tombs, and went through the corridors in quest of Bartleby, but without finding him.

"I saw him coming from his cell not long ago," said a turnkey, "maybe he's gone to loiter in the yards."

So I went in that direction.

"Are you looking for the silent man?" said another turnkey, passing me. "Yonder he lies—sleeping in the yard there. 'Tis not twenty minutes since I saw him lie down."

The yard was entirely quiet. It was not accessible to the common prisoners. The surrounding walls, of amazing thickness, kept off all sounds behind them. The Egyptian character of the masonry weighed upon me with its gloom. But a soft imprisoned turf grew under foot. The heart of the eternal pyramids, it seemed, wherein, by some strange magic, through the clefts, grass seed, dropped by birds, had sprung.

Strangely huddled at the base of the wall, his knees drawn up, and lying on his side, his head touching the cold stones, I saw the wasted Bartleby. But nothing stirred. I paused; then went close up to him; stopped over, and saw that his dim eyes were open; otherwise he seemed profoundly sleeping. Something prompted me to touch him. I felt his hand, when a tingling shiver ran up my arm and down my spine to my feet.

The round face of the grub-man peered upon me now. "His dinner is ready. Won't he dine today, either? Or does he live without dining?"

"Lives without dining," said I, and closed the eyes.

"Eh!—He's asleep, ain't he?"

"With kings and counselors," murmured I.

There would seem little need for proceeding further in this history. Imagination will readily supply the meager recital of poor Bartleby's interment. But, ere parting with the reader, let me say that if this little narrative has sufficiently interested him to awaken curiosity as to who Bartleby was, and what manner of life he led prior to the present narrator's making his acquaintance, I can only reply that in such curiosity I fully share, but am wholly unable to gratify it. Yet here I hardly know whether I should divulge one little item of rumor, which came to my ear a few months after the scrivener's decease. Upon what basis it rested, I could never ascertain, and hence how true it is I cannot tell. But, inasmuch as this vague report has not been without a certain suggestive interest to me, however sad, it may prove the same with some others; and so I will briefly mention it. The report was this: that Bartleby had been a subordinate clerk in the Dead Letter Office at Washington, from which he had been suddenly removed by a change in the administration. When I think over this rumor, hardly can I express the emotions which seize me. Dead letters! does it not sound like dead men? Conceive a man by nature and misfortune prone to a pallid hopelessness, can any business seem more fitted to heighten it than that of continually handling these dead letters, and assorting them for the flames? For by the cart-load they are annually burned. Sometimes from out the folded paper the pale clerk takes a ring—the finger it was meant for, perhaps, molders in the grave; a bank-note sent in swiftest charity—he whom it would relieve nor eats nor hungers any more; pardon for those who died despairing; hope for those who died unhoping; good tidings for those who died stifled by unrelieved calamities. On errands of life, these letters speed to death.

Ah, Bartleby! Ah, humanity!

Anton Pavlovich Chekhov (1860–1904) was born in Taganrog, Russia, and studied medicine at the University of Moscow. As a physician and grandson of a serf, the tubercular Chekhov was active in humanitarian projects, including his work during the cholera epidemic of 1892 and a famous report on the penal island of Sakhalin (1891). While a medical student, he began writing fiction, first collected in Particolored Stories *(1886). Chekhov represented boredom, wasted lives, and the decay of the feudal system in stories and on stage, beginning with one-act plays and the full-length* Ivanov *(1887). After 1898 he worked with Stanislavsky's Moscow Art Theatre in presenting his most famous tragicomic dramas:* Three Sisters *(1899),* Uncle Vanya *(1902), and* The Cherry Orchard *(1904). Chekhov's mastery of understatement and atmosphere became available to the English-speaking world in 1916 when his tales began appearing in translation.*

On the Road

ANTON CHEKHOV

"Upon the breast of a gigantic crag,
A golden cloudlet rested for one night."
Lermontov

In the room which the tavern keeper, the Cossack Semyon Tchistopluy, called the "travellers' room," that is kept exclusively for travellers, a tall, broad-shouldered man of forty was sitting at the big unpainted table. He was asleep with his elbows on the table and his head leaning on his fist. An end of tallow candle, stuck into an old pomatum pot, lighted up his light brown beard, his thick, broad nose, his sunburnt cheeks, and the thick, black eyebrows overhanging his closed eyes. . . . The nose and the cheeks and the eyebrows, all the features, each taken separately, were coarse and heavy, like the furniture and the stove in the "travellers' room," but taken all together they gave the effect of something harmonious and even beautiful.

Such is the lucky star, as it is called, of the Russian face: the coarser and harsher its features the softer and more good-natured it looks. The man was dressed in a gentleman's reefer jacker, shabby, but bound with wide new braid, a plush waistcoat, and full black trousers thrust into big high boots.

On one of the benches, which stood in a continuous row along the wall, a girl of eight, in a brown dress and long black stockings, lay asleep on a coat lined with fox. Her face was pale, her hair was flaxen, her shoulders were narrow, her whole body was thin and frail, but her nose stood out as thick and ugly a lump as the man's. She was sound asleep, and unconscious that her semi-circular comb had fallen off her head and was cutting her cheek.

The "travellers' room" had a festive appearance. The air was full of the smell of freshly scrubbed floors, there were no rags hanging as usual on the line that ran diagonally across the room, and a little lamp was burning in the corner over the table, casting a patch of red light on the ikon of St. George the Victorious. From the ikon stretched on each side of the corner a row of cheap oleographs, which maintained a strict and careful gradation in the transition from the sacred to the profane. In the dim light of the candle end and the red ikon lamp the pictures looked like one continuous stripe, covered with blurs of black. When the tiled stove, trying to sing in unison with the weather, drew in the air with a howl, while the logs, as though waking up, burst into bright flame and hissed angrily, red patches began dancing on the log walls, and over the head of the sleeping man could be seen first the Elder Seraphim, then the Shah Nasir-ed-Din, then a fat, brown baby with goggle eyes, whispering in the ear of a young girl with an extraordinarily blank, and indifferent face. . . .

Outside a storm was raging. Something frantic and wrathful, but profoundly unhappy, seemed to be flinging itself about the tavern with the ferocity of a wild beast and trying to break in. Banging at the doors, knocking at the windows and on the roof, scratching at the walls, it alternately threatened and besought, then subsided for a brief interval, and then with a gleeful, treacherous howl burst into the chimney, but the wood flared up, and the fire, like a chained dog, flew wrathfully to meet its foe, a battle began, and after it—sobs, shrieks, howls of wrath. In all of this there was the sound of angry misery and unsatisfied hate, and the mortified impatience of something accustomed to triumph.

Bewitched by this wild, inhuman music the "travellers' room" seemed spellbound for ever, but all at once the door creaked and the potboy, in a new print shirt, came in. Limping on one leg, and blinking his sleepy eyes, he snuffed the candle with his fingers, put some more wood on the fire and went out. At once from the church, which was three hundred paces from the tavern, the clock struck midnight. The wind played with the chimes as with the snowflakes; chasing the sounds of the clock it whirled them round and round over a vast space, so that some strokes were cut short or drawn out in long, vibrating notes, while others were completely lost in the general uproar. One stroke sounded as distinctly in the room as though it had chimed just under the window. The child, sleeping on the fox-skin, started and raised her head. For a minute she stared blankly at the dark window, at Nasir-ed-Din over whom a crimson glow from the fire flickered at that moment, then she turned her eyes upon the sleeping man.

"Daddy," she said.

But the man did not move. The little girl knitted her brow angrily, lay down, and curled up her legs. Someone in the tavern gave a loud, prolonged yawn. Soon afterwards there was the squeak of the swing door and the sound of indistinct voices. Someone came in, shaking the snow off, and stamping in felt boots which made a muffled thud.

"What is it?" a woman's voice asked languidly.

"Mademoiselle Ilovaisky has come, . . ." answered a bass voice.

Again there was the squeak of the swing door. Then came the roar of the wind rushing in. Someone, probably the lame boy, ran to the door leading to the "travellers' room," coughed deferentially, and lifted the latch.

"This way, lady, please," said a woman's voice in dulcet tones. "It's clean in here, my beauty. . . ."

The door was opened wide and a peasant with a beard appeared in the doorway, in the long coat of a coachman, plastered all over with snow from head to foot, and carrying a big trunk on his shoulder. He was followed into the room by a feminine figure, scarcely half his height, with no face and no arms, muffled and wrapped up like a bundle and also covered with snow. A damp chill, as from a cellar, seemed to come to the child from the coachman and the bundle, and the fire and the candles flickered.

"What nonsense!" said the bundle angrily, "We could go perfectly well. We have only nine more miles to go, mostly by the forest, and we should not get lost. . . ."

"As for getting lost, we shouldn't, but the horses can't go on, lady!" answered the coachman. "And it is Thy Will, O Lord! As though I had done it on purpose!"

"God knows where you have brought me. . . . Well, be quiet. . . . There are people asleep here, it seems. You can go. . . ."

The coachman put the portmanteau on the floor, and as he did so, a great lump of snow fell off his shoulders. He gave a sniff and went out.

Then the little girl saw two little hands come out from the middle of the bundle, stretch upwards and begin angrily disentangling the network of shawls, kerchiefs, and scarves. First a big shawl fell on the ground, then a hood, then a white knitted kerchief. After freeing her head, the traveller took off her pelisse and at once shrank to half the size. Now she was in a long, grey coat with big buttons and bulging pockets. From one pocket she pulled out a paper parcel, from the other a bunch of big, heavy keys, which she put down so carelessly that the sleeping man started and opened his eyes. For some time he looked blankly round him as though he didn't know where he was, then he shook his head, went to the corner and sat down. . . . The newcomer took off her great coat, which made her shrink to half her size again, she took off her big felt boots, and sat down, too.

By now she no longer resembled a bundle: she was a thin little brunette of twenty, as slim as a snake, with a long white face and curly hair. Her nose was long and sharp, her chin, too, was long and sharp, her eyelashes were long, the corners of her mouth were sharp, and, thanks to this general sharpness, the expression of her face was biting. Swathed in a closely fitting black dress with a mass of lace at her neck and sleeves, with sharp elbows and long pink fingers, she recalled the portraits of medieval English ladies. The grave concentration of her face increased this likeness.

The lady looked round at the room, glanced sideways at the man and the little girl, shrugged her shoulders, and moved to the window. The dark windows were shaking from the damp west wind. Big flakes of snow, glistening in their whiteness, lay on the window frame, but at once disappeared, borne away by the wind. The savage music grew louder and louder. . . .

After a long silence the little girl suddenly turned over, and said angrily, emphasizing each word:

"Oh, goodness, goodness, how unhappy I am! Unhappier than anyone!"

The man got up and moved with little steps to the child with a guilty air, which was utterly out of keeping with his huge figure and big beard.

"You are not asleep, dearie?" he said, in an apologetic voice. "What do you want?"

"I don't want anything, my shoulder aches! You are a wicked man, Daddy, and God will punish you! You'll see He will punish you."

"My darling, I know your shoulder aches, but what can I do, dearie?" said the man, in the tone in which men who have been drinking excuse themselves to their stern spouses. "It's the journey has made your shoulder ache, Sasha. Tomorrow we shall get there and rest, and the pain will go away. . . ."

"Tomorrow, tomorrow. . . . Every day you say tomorrow. We shall be going on another twenty days."

"But we shall arrive tomorrow, dearie, on your father's word of honor. I never tell a lie, but if we are detained by the snowstorm it is not *my* fault."

"I can't bear any more, I can't, I can't!"

Sasha jerked her leg abruptly and filled the room with an unpleasant wailing. Her father made a despairing gesture, and looked hopelessly towards the young lady. The latter shrugged her shoulders, and hesitatingly went up to Sasha.

"Listen, my dear," she said, "it is no use crying. It's really naughty; if your shoulder aches it can't be helped."

"You see, Madam," said the man quickly, as though defending himself, "we have not slept for two nights, and have been travelling in a revolting conveyance. Well, of course, it is natural she should be ill and miserable, . . . and then, you know, we had a drunken driver, our portmanteau has been stolen . . . the snowstorm all the time, but what's the use of crying, Madam? I am exhausted, though, by sleeping in a sitting position, and I feel as though I were drunk. Oh, dear! Sasha, and I feel sick as it is, and then you cry!"

The man shook his head, and with a gesture of despair sat down.

"Of course you mustn't cry," said the young lady. "It's only little babies cry. If you are ill, dear, you must undress and go to sleep. . . . Let us take off your things!"

When the child had been undressed and pacified a silence reigned again. The young lady seated herself at the window, and looked round wonderingly at the room of the inn, at the ikon, at the stove. . . . Apparently the room and the little girl with the thick nose, in her short boy's nightgown, and the child's father, all seemed strange to her. This strange man was sitting in a corner; he kept looking about him helplessly, as though he were drunk, and rubbing his face with the palm of his hand. He sat silent, blinking, and judging from his guilty-looking figure it was difficult to imagine that he would soon begin to speak. Yet he was the first to begin. Stroking his knees, he gave a cough, laughed, and said:

"It's a comedy, it really is. . . . I look and I cannot believe my eyes: for what devilry has destiny driven us to this accursed inn? What did she want to show by it? Life sometimes performs such '*salto mortale*,' one can only stare and blink in amazement. Have you come from far, Madam?"

"No, not from far," answered the young lady. "I am going from our estate, fifteen miles from here, to our farm, to my father and brother. My name is Ilovaisky, and the farm is called Ilovaiskoe. It's nine miles away. What unpleasant weather!"

"It couldn't be worse."

The lame boy came in and stuck a new candle in the pomatum pot.

"You might bring us the samovar, boy," said the man, addressing him.

"Who drinks tea now?" laughed the boy. "It is a sin to drink tea before mass. . . ."

"Never mind, boy, you won't burn in hell if we do. . . ."

Over the tea the new acquaintances got into conversation.

Mlle. Ilovaisky learned that her companion was called Grigory Petrovitch Liharev, that he was the brother of the Liharev who was Marshal of Nobility in one of the neighboring districts, and he himself had once been a landowner, but had "run through everything in his time." Liharev learned that her name was Marya Mihailovna, that her father had a huge estate, but that she was the only one to look after it as her father and brother looked at life through their fingers, were irresponsible, and were too fond of harriers.

"My father and brother are all alone at the farm," she told him, brandishing her fingers (she had the habit of moving her fingers before her pointed face as she talked, and after every sentence moistened her lips with her sharp little tongue). "They, I mean men, are an irresponsible lot, and don't stir a finger for themselves. I can fancy there will be no one to give them a meal after the fast! We have no mother, and we have such servants that they can't lay the tablecloth properly when I am away. You can imagine their condition now! They will be left with nothing to break their fast, while I have to stay here all night. How strange it all is."

She shrugged her shoulders, took a sip from her cup, and said:

"There are festivals that have a special fragrance: at Easter, Trinity, and Christmas there is a peculiar scent in the air. Even unbelievers are fond of those festivals. My brother, for instance, argues that there is no God, but he is the first to hurry to Matins at Easter."

Liharev raised his eyes to Mlle. Ilovaisky and laughed.

"They argue that there is no God," she went on, laughing too, "but why is it, tell me, all the celebrated writers, the learned men, clever people generally, in fact, believe towards the end of their life?"

"If a man does not know how to believe when he is young, Madam, he won't believe in his old age if he is ever so much of a writer."

Judging from Liharev's cough he had a bass voice, but, probably from being afraid to speak aloud, or from exaggerated shyness, he spoke in a tenor. After a brief pause he heaved a sigh and said:

"The way I look at it is that faith is a faculty of the spirit. It is just the same as a talent, one must be born with it. So far as I can judge by myself, by the people I have seen in my time, and by all that is done around us, this faculty is present in Russians in its highest degree. Russian life presents us with an uninterrupted succession of convictions and aspirations, and if you care to know, it has not yet the faintest notion of lack of faith or skepticism. If a Russian does not believe in God, it means he believes in something else."

Liharev took a cup of tea from Mlle. Ilovaisky, drank off half in one gulp, and went on:

"I will tell you about myself. Nature has implanted in my breast an extraordinary faculty for belief. Whisper it not to the night, but half my life I was in the ranks of the Atheists and Nihilists, but there was not one hour in my life in which I ceased to believe. All talents, as a rule, show themselves in early childhood, and so my faculty showed itself when I could still walk upright under the table. My mother liked her children to eat a great deal, and when she gave me food she used to say: 'Eat! Soup is the great thing in life!' I believed, and ate the soup ten times a day, ate like a shark, ate till I was disgusted and stupefied. My nurse used to tell me fairy tales, and I believed in house-spirits, in wood-elves, and in goblins of all kinds. I used sometimes to steal corrosive sublimate from my father, sprinkle it on cakes, and carry them up to the attic that the house-spirits, you see, might eat them and be killed. And when I was taught to read and understand what I read, then there was a fine to-do. I ran away to America and went off to join the brigands, and wanted to go into a monastery, and hired boys to torture me for being a Christian. And note that my faith was always active, never dead. If I was running away to America I was not alone, but seduced someone else, as great a fool as I was, to go with me, and was delighted when I was nearly frozen outside the town gates and when I was thrashed; if I went to join the brigands I always came back with my face battered. A most restless childhood, I assure you! And when they sent me to the high school and pelted me with all sorts of truths—that is, that the earth goes round the sun, or that white light is not white, but is made up of seven colors—my poor little head began to go round! Everything was thrown into a whirl in me: Navin who made the sun stand still, and my mother who in the name of the Prophet Elijah disapproved of lightning conductors, and my father who was indifferent to the truths I had learned. My enlightenment inspired me. I wandered about the house and stables like one possessed, preaching my truths, was horrified by ignorance, glowed with hatred for anyone who saw in white light nothing but white light. . . . But all that's nonsense and childishness. Serious, so to speak, manly enthusiasms began only at the university. You have, no doubt, Madam, taken your degree somewhere?"

"I studied at Novotcherkask at the Don Institute."

"Then you have not been to a university? So you don't know what science means. All the sciences in the world have the same passport, without which they regard themselves as meaningless . . . the striving towards truth! Every one of them, even pharmacology, has for its aim not utility, not the alleviation of life, but truth. It's remarkable! When you set to work to study any science, what strikes you first of all is its beginning. I assure you there is nothing more attractive and grander, nothing is so staggering, nothing takes a man's breath away like the beginning of any science. From the first five or six lectures you are soaring on wings of the brightest hopes, you already seem to yourself to be welcoming truth with open arms. And I gave myself up to science, heart and soul, passionately, as to the woman one loves. I was its slave; I found it the sun of my existence, and asked for no other. I studied day and night without rest, ruined myself over books, wept when before my eyes men exploited science for their own personal ends. But my enthusiasm did not last long. The trouble is that every science has a beginning but not an end, like a recurring decimal. Zoology has discovered 35,000 kinds of insects, chemistry reckons 60 elements. If in time tens of noughts can be written after these figures, zoology and chemistry will be just as far from their end as now, and all contemporary scientific work consists in increasing these numbers. I saw through this trick when I discovered the 35,001-st and felt no satisfaction. Well, I had no time to suffer from disillusionment, as I was soon possessed by a new faith. I plunged into Nihilism, with its manifestoes, its 'black divisions,' and all the rest of it. I 'went to the people,' worked in factories, worked as an oiler, as a barge hauler. Afterwards, when wandering over Russia, I had a taste of Russian life, I turned into a fervent devotee of that life. I loved the Russian people with poignant intensity; I loved their God and believed in Him, and in their language, their creative genius. . . . And so on, and so on. . . . I have been a Slavophile in my time, I used to pester Aksakov with letters, and I was a Ukrainophile, and an archeologist, and a collector of specimens of peasant art. . . . I was enthusiastic over ideas, people, events, places . . . my enthusiasm was endless! Five years ago I was working for the abolition of private property; my last creed was non-resistance to evil."

Sasha gave an abrupt sigh and began moving. Liharev got up and went to her.

"Won't you have some tea, dearie?" he asked tenderly.

"Drink it yourself," the child answered rudely.

Liharev was disconcerted, and went back to the table with a guilty step.

"Then you have had a lively time," said Mlle. Ilovaisky; "you have something to remember."

"Well, yes, it's all very lively when one sits over tea and chatters to a kind listener, but you should ask what that liveliness has cost me! What price have I paid for the variety of my life? You see, Madam, I have not held my convictions like a German doctor of philosophy, *zierlichmännerlich*, I have not lived in solitude, but every conviction I have had has bound my back to the yoke, has torn my body to pieces. Judge for yourself. I was wealthy like my brothers, but now I am a beggar. In the delirium of my enthusiasm I smashed up my own fortune and my wife's—a heap of other people's money. Now I am forty-two, old age is close upon me, and I am homeless, like a dog that has dropped behind its wagon at night. All my life I have not known what peace meant, my soul has been in continual agitation, distressed even by its hopes . . . I have been wearied out with heavy irregular work, have endured privation, have five times been in prison, have dragged myself across the provinces of Archangel and of Tobolsk . . . it's painful to think of it! I have lived, but in my fever I have not even been conscious of the process of life itself. Would you believe it, I don't remember a single spring, I never noticed how my wife loved me, how my children were born. What more can I tell you? I have been a misfortune to all who have loved me. . . . My mother has worn mourning for me all these fifteen years, while my proud brothers, who have had to wince, to blush, to bow their heads, to waste their money on my account, have come in the end to hate me like poison."

Liharev got up and sat down again.

"If I were simply unhappy I should thank God," he went on without looking at his listener. "My personal unhappiness sinks into the background when I remember how often in my enthusiasms I have been absurd, far from the truth, unjust, cruel, dangerous! How often I have hated and despised those whom I ought to have loved, and *vice versa*, I have changed a thousand times. One day I believe, fall down and worship, the next I flee like a coward from the gods and friends of yesterday, and swallow in silence the 'scoundrel!' they hurl after me. God alone has seen how often I have wept and bitten my pillow in shame for my enthusiasms. Never once in my life have I intentionally lied or done evil, but my conscience is not clear! I cannot even boast, Madam, that I have no one's life upon my conscience, for my wife died before my eyes, worn out by my reckless activity. Yes, my wife! I tell you they have two ways of treating women nowadays. Some measure women's skulls to prove a woman is inferior to man, pick out her defects to mock at her, to look original in her eyes, and to justify their sensuality. Others do their utmost to raise women to their level, that is, force them to learn by heart the 35,000 species, to speak and write the same foolish things as they speak and write themselves."

Liharev's face darkened.

"I tell you that woman has been and always will be the slave of man," he said in a bass voice, striking his fist on the table. "She is the soft, tender wax which a man always molds into anything he likes. . . . My God! for the sake of some trumpery masculine enthusiasm she will cut off her hair, abandon her family, die among strangers! . . . Among the ideas for which she has sacrificed herself there is not a single feminine one. . . . An unquestioning, devoted slave! I have not measured skulls, but I say this from hard, bitter experience: the proudest, most independent women, if I have succeeded in communicating to them my enthusiasm, have followed me without criticism, without question, and done anything I chose; I have turned a nun into a Nihilist who, as I heard afterwards, shot a gendarme; my wife never left me for a minute in my wanderings, and like a weathercock changed her faith in step with my changing enthusiasms."

Liharev jumped up and walked up and down the room.

"A noble, sublime slavery!" he said, clasping his hands. "It is just in it that the highest meaning of woman's life lies! Of all the fearful medley of thoughts and impressions accumulated in my brain from my association with women my memory, like a filter, has retained no ideas, no clever saying, no philosophy, nothing but that extraordinary resignation to fate, that wonderful mercifulness, forgiveness of everything."

Liharev clenched his fists, stared at a fixed point, and with a sort of passionate intensity, as though he were savoring each word as he uttered it, hissed through his clenched teeth:

"That . . . that great-hearted fortitude, faithfulness unto death, poetry of the heart. . . . The meaning of life lies in just that unrepining martyrdom, in the tears which would soften a stone, in the boundless, all-forgiving love which brings light and warmth into the chaos of life. . . ."

Mlle. Ilovaisky got up slowly, took a step towards Liharev, and fixed her eyes upon his face. From the tears that glittered on his eyelashes, from his quivering, passionate voice, from the flush on his cheeks, it was clear to her that women were not a chance, not a simple subject of conversation. They were the object of his new enthusiasm, or, as he said himself, his new faith! For the first time in her life she saw a man carried away, fervently believing. With his gesticulations, with his flashing eyes he seemed to her mad, frantic, but there was a feeling of such beauty in the fire of his eyes, in his words, in all the movements of his huge body, that without noticing what she was doing she stood facing him as though rooted to the spot, and gazed into his face with delight.

"Take my mother," he said, stretching out his hand to her with an imploring expression on his face, "I poisoned her existence, according to her ideas disgraced the name of Liharev, did her as much harm as the most malignant enemy, and what do you think? My brothers give her little sums for holy bread and church services, and outraging her religious feelings, she saves that money and sends it in secret to her erring Grigory. This trifle alone elevates and ennobles the soul far more than all the theories, all the clever sayings and the 35,000 species. I can give you thousands of instances. Take you, even, for instance! With tempest and darkness outside you are going to your father and your brother to cheer them with your affection in the holiday, though very likely they have forgotten and are not thinking of you. And, wait a bit, and you will love a man and follow him to the North Pole. You would, wouldn't you?"

"Yes, if I loved him."

"There, you see," cried Liharev delighted, and he even stamped with his foot. "Oh dear! How glad I am that I have met you! Fate is kind to me, I am always meeting splendid people. Not a day passes but one makes acquaintance with somebody one would give one's soul for. There are ever so many more good people than bad in this world. Here, see, for instance, how openly and from our hearts we have been talking as though we had known each other a hundred years. Sometimes, I assure you, one restrains oneself for ten years and holds one's tongue, is reserved with one's friends and one's wife, and meets some cadet in a train and babbles one's whole soul out to him. It is the first time I have the honor of seeing you, and yet I have confessed to you as I have never confessed in my life. Why is it?"

Rubbing his hands and smiling good-humoredly Liharev walked up and down the room, and fell to talking about women again. Meanwhile they began ringing for matins.

"Goodness," wailed Sasha. "He won't let me sleep with his talking!"

"Oh, yes!" said Liharev, startled. "I am sorry, darling, sleep, sleep. . . . I have two boys besides her," he whispered. "They are living with their uncle, Madam, but this one can't exist a day without her father. She's wretched, she complains, but she sticks to me like a fly to honey. I have been chattering too much, Madam, and it would do you no harm to sleep. Wouldn't you like me to make up a bed for you?"

Without waiting for permission he shook the wet pelisse, stretched it on a bench, fur side upwards, collected various shawls and scarves, put the overcoat folded up into a roll for a pillow, and all this he did in silence with a look of devout reverence, as though he were not handling a woman's rags, but the fragments of holy vessels. There was something apologetic, embarrassed about his whole figure, as though in the presence of a weak creature he felt ashamed of his height and strength. . . .

When Mlle. Ilovaisky had lain down, he put out the candle and sat down on a stool by the stove.

"So, Madam," he whispered, lighting a fat cigarette and puffing the smoke into the stove. "Nature has put into the Russian an extraordinary faculty for belief, a searching intelligence, and the gift of speculation, but all that is reduced to ashes by irresponsibility, laziness, and dreamy frivolity. . . . Yes. . . ."

She gazed wonderingly into the darkness, and saw only a spot of red on the ikon and the flicker of the light of the stove on Liharev's face. The darkness, the chime of the bells, the roar of the storm, the lame boy, Sasha with her fretfulness, unhappy Liharev and his sayings—all this was mingled together, and seemed to grow into one huge impression, and God's world seemed to her fantastic, full of marvels and magical forces. All that she had heard was ringing in her ears, and human life presented itself to her as a beautiful poetic fairy-tale without an end.

The immense impression grew and grew, clouded consciousness, and turned into a sweet dream. She was asleep, though she saw the little ikon lamp and a big nose with the light playing on it.

She heard the sound of weeping.

"Daddy, darling," a child's voice was tenderly entreating, "let's go back to uncle! There is a Christmas-tree! Styopa and Kolya are there!"

"My darling, what can I do?" a man's bass persuaded softly. "Understand me! Come, understand!"

And the man's weeping blended with the child's. This voice of human sorrow, in the midst of the howling of the storm, touched the girl's ear with such sweet human music that she could not bear the delight of it, and wept too. She was conscious afterwards of a big, black shadow coming softly up to her, picking up a shawl that had dropped onto the floor and carefully wrapping it round her feet.

Mlle. Ilovaisky was awakened by a strange uproar. She jumped up and looked about her in astonishment. The deep blue dawn was looking in at the window half-covered with snow. In the room there was a grey twilight, through which the stove and the sleeping child and Nasir-ed-Din stood out distinctly. The stove and the lamp were both out. Through the wide-open door she could see the big tavern room with a counter and chairs. A man, with a stupid, gypsy face and astonished eyes, was standing in the middle of the room in a puddle of melting snow, holding a big red star on a stick. He was surrounded by a group of boys, motionless as statues, and plastered over with snow. The light shone through the red paper of the star, throwing a glow of red on their wet faces. The crowd was shouting in disorder, and from its uproar Mlle. Ilovaisky could make out only one couplet:

> "Hi, you little Russian lad,
> Bring your sharp knife,
> We will kill the Jew, we will kill him,
> The son of tribulation. . . ."

Liharev was standing near the counter, looking feelingly at the singers and tapping his feet in time. Seeing Mlle. Ilovaisky, he smiled all over his face and came up to her. She smiled too.

"A happy Christmas!" he said. "I saw you slept well."

She looked at him, said nothing, and went on smiling.

After the conversation in the night he seemed to her not tall and broad-shouldered, but little, just as the biggest steamer seems to us a little thing when we hear that it has crossed the ocean.

"Well, it is time for me to set off," she said. "I must put on my things. Tell me where you are going now?"

"I? To the station of Klinushki, from there to Sergievo, and from Sergievo, with horses, thirty miles to the coal mines that belong to a horrid man, a general called Shashkovsky. My brothers have got me the post of superintendent there. . . . I am going to be a coal miner."

"Stay, I know those mines. Shashkovsky is my uncle, you know. But . . . what are you going there for?" asked Mlle. Ilovaisky, looking at Liharev in surprise.

"As superintendent. To superintend the coal mines."

"I don't understand!" she shrugged her shoulders. "You are going to the mines. But you know, it's the bare steppe, a desert, so dreary that you couldn't exist a day there! It's horrible coal, no one will buy it, and my uncle's a maniac, a despot, a bankrupt. . . . You won't get your salary!"

"No matter," said Liharev, unconcernedly, "I am thankful even for coal mines."

"I don't understand, I don't understand," she said, moving her fingers before her face. "It's impossible, and . . . and irrational! You must understand that it's . . . it's worse than exile. It is a living tomb! O Heavens!" she said hotly, going up to Liharev and moving her fingers before his smiling face; her upper lip was quivering, and her sharp face turned pale, "Come, picture it, the bare steppe, solitude. There is no one to say a word to there, and you . . . are enthusiastic over women! Coal mines . . . and women!"

Mlle. Ilovaisky was suddenly ashamed of her heat and, turning away from Liharev, walked to the window.

"No, no, you can't go there," she said, moving her fingers rapidly over the pane.

Not only in her heart, but even in her spine she felt that behind her stood an infinitely unhappy man, lost and outcast, while he, as though he were unaware of his unhappiness, as though he had not shed tears in the night, was looking at her with a kindly smile. Better he should go on weeping! She walked up and down the room several times in agitation, then stopped short in a corner and sank into thought. Liharev was saying something, but she did not hear him. Turning her back on him she took out of her purse a money note, stood for a long time crumpling it in her hand, and looking round at Liharev, blushed and put it in her pocket.

The coachman's voice was heard through the door. With a stern, concentrated face she began putting on her things in silence. Liharev wrapped her up, chatting gaily, but every word he said lay on her heart like a weight. It is not cheering to hear the unhappy or the dying jest.

When the transformation of a live person into a shapeless bundle had been completed, Mlle. Ilovaisky looked for the last time round the "travellers' room," stood a moment in silence, and slowly walked out. Liharev went to see her off. . . .

Outside, God alone knows why, the winter was raging still. Whole clouds of big soft snowflakes were whirling restlessly over the earth, unable to find a resting-place. The horses, the sledge, the trees, a bull tied to a post, all were white and seemed soft and fluffy.

"Well, God help you," muttered Liharev, tucking her into the sledge. "Don't remember evil against me. . . ."

She was silent. When the sledge started, and had to go round a huge snowdrift, she looked back at Liharev with an expression as though she wanted to say something to him. He ran up to her, but she did not say a word to him, she only looked at him through her long eyelashes with little specks of snow on them.

Whether his finely intuitive soul were really able to read that look, or whether his imagination deceived him, it suddenly began to seem to him that with another touch or two that girl would have forgiven him his failures, his age, his desolate position, and would have followed him without question or reasonings. He stood a long while as though rooted to the spot, gazing at the tracks left by the sledge runners. The snowflakes greedily settled on his hair, his beard, his shoulders. . . . Soon the track of the runners had vanished, and he himself covered with snow, began to look like a white rock, but still his eyes kept seeking something in the clouds of snow.

Stephen Crane *(1871–1900) was born in Newark, New Jersey, and was raised in small cities in New Jersey and New York. After a year of college he moved to New York City and began to submit free-lance sketches to the New York Tribune. The Bowery provided the material for his first novel,* Maggie: A Girl of the Streets *(1893), while the Civil War served as subject for* The Red Badge of Courage *(1895). As a syndicated newspaper correspondent Crane toured the western United States and Mexico and covered wars in Greece and Cuba. He settled in England shortly before his death at the age of twenty-nine.*

The Open Boat

STEPHEN CRANE

A Tale Intended to be after the Fact: Being the Experience of Four Men From the Sunk Steamer Commodore.

I

Nonc of them knew the color of the sky. Their eyes glanced level, and were fastened upon the waves that swept toward them. These waves were of the hue of slate, save for the tops, which were of foaming white, and all of the men knew the colors of the sea. The horizon narrowed and widened, and dipped and rose, and at all times its edge was jagged with waves that seemed thrust up in points like rocks.

Many a man ought to have a bath-tub larger than the boat which here rode upon the sea. These waves were most wrongfully and barbarously abrupt and tall, and each froth-top was a problem in small-boat navigation.

The cook squatted in the bottom, and looked with both eyes at the six inches of gunwale which separated him from the ocean. His sleeves were rolled over his fat forearms, and the two flaps of his unbuttoned vest dangled as he bent to bail out the boat. Often he said, "Gawd! that was a narrow clip." As he remarked it he invariably gazed eastward over the broken sea.

The oiler, steering with one of the two oars in the boat, sometimes raised himself suddenly to keep clear of water that swirled in over the stern. It was a thin little oar, and it seemed often ready to snap.

The correspondent, pulling at the other oar, watched the waves and wondered why he was there.

The injured captain, lying in the bow, was at this time buried in that profound dejection and indifference which comes, temporarily at least, to even the bravest and most enduring when, willy-nilly, the firm fails, the army loses, the ship goes down. The mind of the master of a vessel is rooted deep in the timbers of her, though he command for a day or a decade; and this captain had on him the stern impression of a scene in the grays of dawn of seven turned faces, and later a stump of a topmast with a white ball on it, that slashed to and fro at the waves, went low and lower, and down. Thereafter there was something strange in his voice. Although steady, it was deep with mourning, and of a quality beyond oration or tears.

"Keep 'er a little more south, Billie," said he.

"A little more south, sir," said the oiler in the stern.

A seat in this boat was not unlike a seat upon a bucking broncho, and, by the same token, a broncho is not much smaller. The craft pranced and reared and plunged like an animal. As each wave came, and she rose for it, she seemed like a horse making at a fence outrageously high. The manner of her scramble over these walls of water is a mystic thing, and, moreover, at the top of them were ordinarily these problems in white water, the foam racing down from the summit of each wave, requiring a new leap, and a leap from the air. Then, after scornfully bumping a crest, she would slide and race and splash down a long incline, and arrive bobbing and nodding in front of the next menace.

A singular disadvantage of the sea lies in the fact that, after successfully surmounting one wave, you discover that there is another behind it, just as important and just as nervously anxious to do something effective in the way of swamping boats. In a ten-foot dinghy one can get an idea of the resources of the sea in the line of waves that is not probable to the average experience, which is never at sea in a dinghy. As each slaty wall of water approached, it shut all else from the view of the men in the boat, and it was not difficult to imagine that this particular wave was the final outburst of the ocean, the last effort of the grim water. There was a terrible grace in the move of the waves, and they came in silence, save for the snarling of the crests.

In the wan light the faces of the men must have been gray. Their eyes must have glinted in strange ways as they gazed steadily astern. Viewed from a balcony, the whole thing would, doubtless, have been weirdly picturesque. But the men in the boat had no time to see it, and if they had had leisure, there were other things to occupy their minds. The sun swung steadily up the sky, and they knew it was broad day because the color of the sea changed from slate to emerald-green streaked with amber lights, and the foam was like tumbling snow. The process of the breaking day was unknown to them. They were aware only of this effect upon the color of the waves that rolled toward them.

In disjointed sentences the cook and the correspondent argued as to the difference between a life-saving station and a house of refuge. The cook had said: "There's a house of refuge just north of the Mosquito Inlet Light, and as soon as they see us they'll come off in their boat and pick us up."

"As soon as who see us?" said the correspondent.

"The crew," said the cook.

"Houses of refuge don't have crews," said the correspondent. "As I understand them, they are only places where clothes and grub are stored for the benefit of shipwrecked people. They don't carry crews."

"Oh, yes, they do," said the cook.

"No, they don't," said the correspondent.

"Well, we're not there yet, anyhow," said the oiler in the stern.

"Well," said the cook, "perhaps it's not a house of refuge that I'm thinking of as being near Mosquito Inlet Light; perhaps it's a life-saving station."

"We're not there yet," said the oiler in the stern.

II

As the boat bounced from the top of each wave the wind tore through the hair of the hatless men, and as the craft plopped her stern down again the spray splashed past them. The crest of each of these waves was a hill, from the top of which the men surveyed for a moment a broad, tumultuous expanse, shining and wind-riven. It was probably splendid, it was probably glorious, this play of the free sea, wild with lights of emerald and white and amber.

"Bully good thing it's an on-shore wind," said the cook. "If not, where would we be? Wouldn't have a show."

"That's right," said the correspondent.

The busy oiler nodded his assent.

Then the captain, in the bow, chuckled in a way that expressed humor, contempt, tragedy, all in one. "Do you think we've got much of a show now, boys?" said he.

Whereupon the three were silent, save for a trifle of hemming and hawing. To express any particular optimism at this time they felt to be childish and stupid, but they all doubtless possessed this sense of the situation in their minds. A young man thinks doggedly at such times. On the other hand, the ethics of their condition was decidedly against any open suggestion of hopelessness. So they were silent.

"Oh, well," said the captain, soothing his children, "we'll get ashore all right."

But there was that in his tone which made them think; so the oiler quoth, "Yes, if this wind holds."

The cook was bailing. "Yes! If we don't catch hell in the surf."

Canton-flannel gulls flew near and far. Sometimes they sat down on the sea, near patches of brown seaweed that rolled over the waves with a movement like carpets on a line in a gale. The birds sat comfortably in groups, and they were envied by some in the dinghy, for the wrath of the sea was no more to them than it was to a covey of prairie-chickens a thousand miles inland. Often they came very close and stared at the men with black, bead-like eyes. At these times they were uncanny and sinister in their unblinking scrutiny, and the men hooted angrily at them, telling them to be gone. One came, and evidently decided to alight on the top of the captain's head. The bird flew parallel to the boat, and did not circle, but made short sidelong jumps in the air in chicken fashion. His black eyes were wistfully fixed upon the captain's head. "Ugly brute," said the oiler to the bird. "You looks as if you were made with a jack-knife." The cook and the correspondent swore darkly at the creature. The captain naturally wished to knock it away with the end of the heavy painter, but he did not dare do it, because anything resembling an emphatic gesture would have capsized this freighted boat; and so, with his open hand, the captain gently and carefully waved the gull away. After it had been discouraged from the pursuit the captain breathed easier on account of his hair, and others breathed easier because the bird struck their minds at this time as being somehow gruesome and ominous.

In the meantime the oiler and the correspondent rowed; and also they rowed. They sat together in the same seat, and each rowed an oar. Then the oiler took both oars; then the correspondent took both oars; then the oiler; then the correspondent. They rowed and they rowed. The very ticklish part of the business was when the time came for the reclining one in the stern to take his turn at the oars. By the very last star of truth, it is easier to steal eggs from under a hen than it was to change seats in the dinghy. First the man in the stern slid his hand along the thwart and moved with care, as if he were of Sèvres. Then the man in the rowing-seat slid his hand along the other thwart. It was all done with the most extraordinary care. As the two sidled past each other, the whole party kept watchful eyes on the coming wave, and the captain cried: "Look out, now! Steady there!"

The brown mats of seaweed that appeared from time to time were like islands, bits of earth. They were traveling, apparently, neither one way nor the other. They were, to all intents, stationary. They informed the men in the boat that it was making progress slowly toward the land.

The captain, rearing cautiously in the bow after the dinghy soared on a great swell, said that he had seen the lighthouse at Mosquito Inlet. Presently the cook remarked that he had seen it. The correspondent was at the oars then, and for some reason he too wished to look at the lighthouse; but his back was toward the far shore, and the waves were important, and for some time he could not seize an opportunity to turn his head. But at last there came a wave more gentle than the others, and when at the crest of it he swiftly scoured the western horizon.

"See it?" said the captain.

"No," said the correspondent, slowly; "I didn't see anything."

"Look again," said the captain. He pointed. "It's exactly in that direction."

At the top of another wave the correspondent did as he was bid, and this time his eyes chanced on a small, still thing on the edge of the swaying horizon. It was precisely like the point of a pin. It took an anxious eye to find a lighthouse so tiny.

"Think we'll make it, Captain?"

"If this wind holds and the boat don't swamp, we can't do much else," said the captain.

The little boat, lifted by each towering sea and splashed viciously by the crests, made progress that in the absence of seaweed was not apparent to those in her. She seemed just a wee thing wallowing miraculously, top up, at the mercy of five oceans. Occasionally a great spread of water, like white flames, swarmed into her.

"Bail her, cook," said the captain, serenely.

"All right, Captain," said the cheerful cook.

III

It would be difficult to describe the subtle brotherhood of men that was here established on the seas. No one said that it was so. No one mentioned it. But it dwelt in the boat, and each man felt it warm him. They were a captain, an oiler, a cook, and a correspondent, and they were friends—friends in a more curiously iron-bound degree than may be common. The hurt captain, lying against the water-jar in the bow, spoke always in a low voice and calmly; but he could never command a more ready and swiftly obedient crew than the motley three of the dinghy. It was more than a mere recognition of what was best for the common safety. There was surely in it a quality that was personal and heartfelt. And after this devotion to the commander of the boat, there was this comradeship, that the correspondent, for instance, who had been taught to be cynical of men, knew even at the time was the best experience of his life. But no one said that it was so. No one mentioned it.

"I wish we had a sail," remarked the captain. "We might try my overcoat on the end of an oar, and give you two boys a chance to rest." So the cook and the correspondent held the mast and spread wide the overcoat; the oiler steered; and the little boat made good way with her new rig. Sometimes the oiler had to scull sharply to keep a sea from breaking into the boat, but otherwise sailing was a success.

Meanwhile the lighthouse had been growing slowly larger. It had now almost assumed color, and appeared like a little gray shadow on the sky. The man at the oars could not be prevented from turning his head rather often to try for a glimpse of this little gray shadow.

At last, from the top of each wave, the men in the tossing boat could see land. Even as the lighthouse was an upright shadow on the sky, this land seemed but a long black shadow on the sea. It certainly was thinner than paper. "We must be about opposite New Smyrna," said the cook, who had coasted this shore often in schooners. "Captain, by the way, I believe they abandoned that life-saving station there about a year ago."

"Did they?" said the captain.

The wind slowly died away. The cook and the correspondent were not now obliged to slave in order to hold high the oar; but the waves continued their old impetuous swooping at the dinghy, and the little craft, no longer under way, struggled woundily over them. The oiler or the correspondent took the oars again.

Shipwrecks are *apropos* of nothing. If men could only train for them and have them occur when the men had reached pink condition, there would be less drowning at sea. Of the four in the dinghy none had slept any time worth mentioning for two days and two nights previous to embarking in the dinghy, and in the excitement of clambering about the deck of a foundering ship they had also forgotten to eat heartily.

For these reasons, and for others, neither the oiler nor the correspondent was fond of rowing at this time. The correspondent wondered ingenuously how in the name of all that was sane could there be people who thought it amusing to row a boat. It was not an amusement; it was a diabolical punishment, and even a genius of mental aberrations could never conclude that it was anything but a horror to the muscles and a crime against the back. He mentioned to the boat in general how the amusement of rowing struck him, and the weary-faced oiler smiled in full sympathy. Previously to the foundering, by the way, the oiler had worked double watch in the engine-room of the ship.

"Take her easy now, boys," said the captain. "Don't spend yourselves. If we have to run a surf you'll need all your strength, because we'll sure have to swim for it. Take your time."

Slowly the land arose from the sea. From a black line it became a line of black and a line of white trees and sand. Finally the captain said that he could make out a house on the shore. "That's the house of refuge, sure," said the cook. "They'll see us before long, and come out after us."

The distant lighthouse reared high. "The keeper ought to be able to make us out now, if he's looking through a glass," said the captain. "He'll notify the life-saving people."

"None of those other boats could have got ashore to give word of the wreck," said the oiler, in a low voice, "else the lifeboat would be out hunting us."

Slowly and beautifully the land loomed out of the sea. The wind came again. It had veered from the northeast to the southeast. Finally a new sound struck the ears of the men in the boat. It was the low thunder of the surf on the shore. "We'll never be able to make the lighthouse now," said the captain. "Swing her head a little more north, Billie."

"A little more north, sir," said the oiler.

Whereupon the little boat turned her nose once more down the wind, and all but the oarsman watched the shore grow. Under the influence of this expansion doubt and direful apprehension were leaving the minds of the men. The management of the boat was still most absorbing, but it could not prevent a quiet cheerfulness. In an hour, perhaps, they would be ashore.

Their backbones had become thoroughly used to balancing in the boat, and they now rode this wild colt of a dinghy like circus men. The correspondent thought that he had been drenched to the skin, but happening to feel in the top pocket of his coat, he found therein eight cigars. Four of them were soaked with sea-water; four were perfectly scatheless. After a search, somebody produced three dry matches; and thereupon the four waifs rode in their little boat and, with an assurance of an impending rescue shining in their eyes, puffed at the big cigars, and judged well and ill of all men. Everybody took a drink of water.

IV

"Cook," remarked the captain, "there don't seem to be any signs of life about your house of refuge."

"No," replied the cook. "Funny they don't see us!"

A broad stretch of lowly coast lay before the eyes of the men. It was of low dunes topped with dark vegetation. The roar of the surf was plain, and sometimes they could see the white lip of a wave as it spun up the beach. A tiny house was blocked out black upon the sky. Southward, the slim lighthouse lifted its little gray length.

Tide, wind, and waves were swinging the dinghy northward. "Funny they don't see us," said the men.

The surf's roar was here dulled, but its tone was nevertheless thunderous and mighty. As the boat swam over the great rollers the men sat listening to this roar. "We'll swamp sure," said everybody.

It is fair to say here that there was not a life-saving station within twenty miles in either direction, but the men did not know this fact, and in consequence they made dark and opprobrious remarks concerning the eyesight of the nation's life-savers. Four scowling men sat on the dinghy, and surpassed records in the invention of epithets.

"Funny they don't see us."

The light-heartedness of a former time had completely faded. To their sharpened minds it was easy to conjure pictures of all kinds of incompetency and blindness and, indeed, cowardice. There was the shore of the populous land, and it was bitter and bitter to them that from it came no sign.

"Well," said the captain, ultimately, "I suppose we'll have to make a try for ourselves. If we stay out here too long, we'll none of us have strength left to swim after the boat swamps."

And so the oiler, who was at the oars, turned the boat straight for the shore. There was a sudden tightening of muscles. There was some thinking.

"If we don't all get ashore," said the captain—"if we don't all get ashore, I suppose you fellows know where to send news of my finish?"

They then briefly exchanged some addresses and admonitions. As for the reflections of the men there was a great deal of rage in them. Perchance they might be formulated thus: "If I am going to be drowned—if I am going to be drowned—if I am going to be drowned, why, in the name of the seven mad gods who rule the sea, was I allowed to come thus far and contemplate sand and trees? Was I brought here merely to have my nose dragged away as I was about to nibble the sacred cheese of life? It is preposterous! If this old ninny-woman, Fate, cannot do better than this, she should be deprived of the management of men's fortunes. She is an old hen who knows not her intention. If she has decided to drown me, why did she not do it in the beginning, and save me all this trouble? The whole affair is absurd. . . . But no; she cannot mean to drown me. She dare not drown me. She cannot drown me. Not after all this work!" Afterward the man might have had an impulse to shake his fist at the clouds. "Just you drown me, now, and then hear what I call you!"

The billows that came at this time were more formidable. They seemed always just about to break and roll over the little boat in a turmoil of foam. There was a preparatory and long growl in the speech of them. No mind unused to the sea would have concluded that the dinghy could ascend these sheer heights in time. The shore was still afar. The oiler was a wily surfman. "Boys," he said swiftly, "she won't live three minutes more, and we're too far out to swim. Shall I take her to sea again, Captain?"

"Yes; go ahead!" said the captain.

This oiler, by a series of quick miracles and fast and steady oarsmanship, turned the boat in the middle of the surf and took her safely to sea again.

There was a considerable silence as the boat bumped over the furrowed sea to deeper water. Then somebody in gloom spoke: "Well, anyhow, they must have seen us from the shore by now."

The gulls went in high slanting flight up the wind toward the gray, desolate east. A squall, marked by dingy clouds, and clouds brick-red, like smoke from a burning building, appeared from the southeast.

"What do you think of those life-saving people? Ain't they peaches?"

"Funny they haven't seen us."

"Maybe they think we're out here for sport! Maybe they think we're fishin'. Maybe they think we're damned fools."

It was a long afternoon. A changed tide tried to force them southward, but wind and wave said northward. Far ahead, where coastline, sea, and sky formed their mighty angle, there were little dots which seemed to indicate a city on the shore.

"St. Augustine?"

The captain shook his head. "Too near Mosquito Inlet."

And the oiler rowed, and then the correspondent rowed; then the oiler rowed. It was a weary business. The human back can become the seat of more aches and pains than are registered in books for the composite anatomy of a regiment. It is a limited area, but it can become the theater of innumerable muscular conflicts, tangles, wrenches, knots, and other comforts.

"Did you ever like to row, Billie?" asked the correspondent.

"No," said the oiler; "Hang it!"

When one exchanged the towing-seat for a place in the bottom of the boat, he suffered a bodily depression that caused him to be careless of everything save an obligation to wiggle one finger. There was cold sea-water swashing to and fro in the boat, and he lay in it. His head, pillowed on a thwart, was within an inch of the swirl of a wave-crest, and sometimes a particularly obstreperous sea came inboard and drenched him once more. But these matters did not annoy him. It is almost certain that if the boat had capsized he would have tumbled comfortably out upon the ocean as if he felt sure that it was a great, soft mattress.

"Look! There's a man on the shore!"

"Where?"

"There! See 'im? See 'im?"

"Yes, sure! He's walking along."

"Now he's stopped. Look! He's facing us!"

"He's waving at us!"

"So he is! By thunder!"

"Ah, now we're all right! Now we're all right! There'll be a boat out here for us in half an hour."

"He's going on. He's running. He's going up to that house there."

The remote beach seemed lower than the sea, and it required a searching glance to discern the little black figure. The captain saw a floating stick, and they rowed to it. A bath towel was by some weird chance in the boat, and tying this on the stick, the captain waved it. The oarsman did not dare turn his head, so he was obliged to ask questions.

"What's he doing now?"

"He's standing still again. He's looking, I think. . . . There he goes again—toward the house. . . . Now he's stopped again."

"Is he waving at us?"

"No, not now; he was, though."

"Look! There comes another man!"

"He's running."

"Look at him go, would you!"

"Why, he's on a bicycle. Now he's met the other man. They're both waving at us. Look!"

"There comes something up the beach."

"What the devil is that thing?"

"Why, it looks like a boat."

"Why, certainly, it's a boat."

"No; it's on wheels."

"Yes, so it is. Well, that must be the life-boat. They drag them along shore on a wagon."

"That's the life-boat sure."

"No, by—, it's—it's an omnibus."

"I tell you it's a life-boat."

"It is not! It's an omnibus. I can see it plain. See? One of these big hotel omnibuses."

"By thunder, you're right. It's an omnibus, sure as fate. What do you suppose they are doing with an omnibus? Maybe they are going around collecting the life-crew, hey?"

"That's it, likely. Look! There's a fellow waving a little black flag. He's standing on the steps of the omnibus. There come those other two fellows. Now they're all talking together. Look at the fellow with the flag. Maybe he ain't waving it!"

"That ain't a flag, is it? That's his coat: Why, certainly, that's his coat."

"So it is; it's his coat. He's taken it off and is waving it around his head. But would you look at him swing it!"

"Oh, say, there isn't any life-saving station there. That's just a winter-resort hotel omnibus that has brought over some of the boarders to see us drown."

"What's that idiot with the coat mean? What's he signaling, anyhow?"

"It looks as if he were trying to tell us to go north. There must be a life-saving station up there."

"No; he thinks we're fishing. Just giving us a merry hand. See? Ah, there, Willie."

"Well, I wish I could make something out of those signals. What do you suppose he means?"

"He don't mean anything; he's just playing."

"Well, if he'd just signal us to try the surf again, or to go to sea and wait, or go north, or go south, or go to hell, there would be some reason in it. But look at him! He just stands there and keeps his coat revolving like a wheel. The ass!"

"There come more people."

"Now there's quite a mob. Look! Isn't that a boat?"

"Where? Oh, I see where you mean. No, that's no boat."

"That fellow is still waving his coat."

"He must think we like to see him do that. Why don't he quit it? It don't mean anything."

"I don't know. I think he is trying to make us go north. It must be that there's a life-saving station there somewhere."

"Say, he ain't tired yet. Look at 'im wave!"

"Wonder how long he can keep that up. He's been revolving his coat ever since he caught sight of us. He's an idiot. Why aren't they getting men to bring a boat out? A fishing boat—one of those big yawls—could come out here all right. Why don't he do something?"

"Oh, it's all right now."

"They'll have a boat out here for us in less than no time, now that they've seen us."

A faint yellow tone came into the sky over the low land. The shadows on the sea slowly deepened. The wind bore coldness with it, and the men began to shiver.

"Holy smoke!" said one, allowing his voice to express his impious mood, "if we keep on monkeying out here! If we've got to flounder out here all night!"

"Oh, we'll never have to stay here all night! Don't you worry. They've seen us now, and it won't be long before they'll come chasing out after us."

The shore grew dusky. The man waving a coat blended gradually into this gloom, and it swallowed in the same manner the omnibus and the group of people. The spray, when it dashed uproariously over the side, made the voyagers shrink and swear like men who were being branded.

"I'd like to catch the chump who waved the coat. I feel like soaking him one, just for luck."

"Why? What did he do?"

"Oh, nothing, but then he seemed so damned cheerful."

In the meantime the oiler rowed, and then the correspondent rowed, and then the oiler rowed. Gray-faced and bowed forward, they mechanically, turn by turn, plied the leaden oars. The form of the lighthouse had vanished from the southern horizon, but finally a pale star appeared, just lifting from the sea. The streaked saffron in the west passed before the all-merging darkness, and the sea to the east was black. The land had vanished, and was expressed only by the low and drear thunder of the surf.

"If I am going to be drowned—if I am going to be drowned—if I am going to be drowned, why, in the name of the seven mad gods who rule the sea, was I allowed to come thus far and contemplate sand and trees? Was I brought here merely to have my nose dragged away as I was about to nibble the sacred cheese of life?"

The patient captain, drooped over the water-jar, was sometimes obliged to speak to the oarsman.

"Keep her head up! Keep her head up!"

"Keep her head up, sir." The voices were weary and low.

This was surely a quiet evening. All save the oarsman lay heavily and listlessly in the boat's bottom. As for him, his eyes were just capable of noting the tall black waves that swept forward in a most sinister silence, save for an occasional subdued growl of a crest.

The cook's head was on a thwart, and he looked without interest at the water under his nose. He was deep in other scenes. Finally he spoke. "Billie," he murmured dreamfully, "what kind of pie do you like best?"

V

"Pie!" said the oiler and the correspondent, agitatedly. "Don't talk about those things, blast you!"

"Well," said the cook, "I was just thinking about ham sandwiches, and—"

A night on the seas in an open boat is a long night. As darkness settled finally, the shine of the light, lifting from the sea in the south, changed to full gold. On the northern horizon a new light appeared, a small bluish gleam on the edge of the waters. These two lights were the furniture of the world. Otherwise there was nothing but waves.

Two men huddled in the stern, and distances were so magnificent in the dinghy that the rower was enabled to keep his feet partly warm by thrusting them under his companions. Their legs indeed extended far under the rowing-seat until they touched the feet of the captain forward. Sometimes, despite the efforts of the tired oarsman, a wave came piling into the boat, an icy wave of the night, and the chilling water soaked them anew. They would twist their bodies for a moment and groan, and sleep the dead sleep once more, while the water in the boat gurgled about them as the craft rocked.

The plan of the oiler and the correspondent was for one to row until he lost the ability, and then arouse the other from his sea-water couch in the bottom of the boat.

The oiler plied the oars until his head drooped forward and the overpowering sleep blinded him; and he rowed yet afterward. Then he touched a man in the bottom of the boat, and called his name. "Will you spell me for a little while?" he said meekly.

"Sure, Billie," said the correspondent, awaking and dragging himself to a sitting position. They exchanged places carefully, and the oiler, cuddling down in the sea-water at the cook's side, seemed to go to sleep instantly.

The particular violence of the sea had ceased. The waves came without snarling. The obligation of the man at the oars was to keep the boat headed so that the tilt of the rollers would not capsize her, and to preserve her from filling when the crests rushed past. The black waves were silent and hard to be seen in the darkness. Often one was almost upon the boat before the oarsman was aware.

In a low voice the correspondent addressed the captain. He was not sure that the captain was awake, although this iron man seemed to be always awake. "Captain, shall I keep her making for that light north, sir?"

The same steady voice answered him. "Yes. Keep it about two points off the port bow."

The cook had tied a life-belt around himself in order to get even the warmth which this clumsy cork contrivance could donate, and he seemed almost stove-like when a rower, whose teeth invariably chattered wildly as soon as he ceased his labor, dropped down to sleep.

The correspondent, as he rowed, looked down at the two men sleeping underfoot. The cook's arm was around the oiler's shoulders, and, with their fragmentary clothing and haggard faces, they were the babes of the sea—a grotesque rendering of the old babes in the wood.

Later he must have grown stupid at his work, for suddenly there was a growling of water, and a crest came with a roar and a swash into the boat, and it was a wonder that it did not set the cook afloat in his life-belt. The cook continued to sleep, but the oiler sat up, blinking his eyes and shaking with the new cold.

"Oh, I'm awful sorry, Billie," said the correspondent, contritely.

"That's all right, old boy," said the oiler, and lay down again and was asleep.

Presently it seemed that even the captain dozed, and the correspondent thought that he was the one man afloat on all the oceans.

The wind had a voice as it came over the waves, and it was sadder than the end.

There was a long, loud swishing astern of the boat, and a gleaming trail of phosphorescence, like blue flame, was furrowed on the black waters. It might have been made by a monstrous knife.

Then there came a stillness, while the correspondent breathed with the open mouth and looked at the sea.

Suddenly there was another swish and another long flash of bluish light, and this time it was alongside the boat, and might almost have been reached with an oar. The correspondent saw an enormous fin speed like a shadow through the water, hurling the crystalline spray and leaving the long glowing trail.

The correspondent looked over his shoulder at the captain. His face was hidden, and he seemed to be asleep. He looked at the babes of the sea. They certainly were asleep. So, being bereft of sympathy, he leaned a little way to one side and swore softly into the sea.

But the thing did not then leave the vicinity of the boat. Ahead or astern, on one side or the other, at intervals long or short, fled the long sparkling streak, and there was to be heard the whiroo of the dark fin. The speed and power of the thing was greatly to be admired. It cut the water like a gigantic and keen projectile.

The presence of this biding thing did not affect the man with the same horror that it would if he had been a picnicker. He simply looked at the sea dully and swore in an undertone.

Nevertheless, it is true that he did not wish to be alone with the thing. He wished one of his companions to awake by chance and keep him company with it. But the captain hung motionless over the water-jar, and the oiler and the cook in the bottom of the boat were plunged in slumber.

VI

"If I am going to be drowned—if I am going to be drowned—if I am going to be drowned, why, in the name of the seven mad gods who rule the sea, was I allowed to come thus far and contemplate sand and trees?"

During this dismal night, it may be remarked that a man would conclude that it was really the intention of the seven mad gods to drown him, despite the abominable injustice of it. For it was certainly an abominable injustice to drown a man who had worked so hard, so hard. The man felt it would be a crime most unnatural. Other people had drowned at sea since galleys swarmed with painted sails, but still—

When it occurs to a man that nature does not regard him as important, and that she feels she would not maim the universe by disposing of him, he at first wishes to throw bricks at the temple, and he hates deeply the fact that there are no bricks and no temples. Any visible expression of nature would surely be pelleted with his jeers.

Then, if there be no tangible thing to hoot, he feels, perhaps, the desire to confront a personification and indulge in pleas, bowed to one knee, and with hands supplicant, saying, "Yes, but I love myself."

A high cold star on a winter's night is the word he feels that she says to him. Thereafter he knows the pathos of his situation.

The men in the dinghy had not discussed these matters, but each had, no doubt, reflected upon them in silence and according to his mind. There was seldom any expression upon their faces save the general one of complete weariness. Speech was devoted to the business of the boat.

To chime the notes of his emotion, a verse mysteriously entered the correspondent's head. He had even forgotten that he had forgotten this verse, but it suddenly was in his mind.

> A soldier of the Legion lay dying in Algiers;
> There was lack of woman's nursing, there was dearth of woman's tears;
> But a comrade stood beside him, and he took that comrade's hand.
> And he said, "I never more shall see my own, my native land."

In his childhood the correspondent had been made acquainted with the fact that a soldier of the Legion lay dying in Algiers, but he had never regarded it as important. Myriads of his school-fellows had informed him of the soldier's plight, but the dinning had naturally ended by making him perfectly indifferent. He had never considered it his affair that a soldier of the Legion lay dying in Algiers, nor had it appeared to him as a matter for sorrow. It was less to him than the breaking of a pencil's point.

Now, however, it quaintly came to him as a human, living thing. It was no longer merely a picture of a few throes in the breast of a poet, meanwhile drinking tea and warming his feet at the grate; it was an actuality—stern, mournful, and fine.

The correspondent plainly saw the soldier. He lay on the sand with his feet out straight and still. While his pale left hand was upon his chest in an attempt to thwart the going of his life, the blood came between his fingers. In the far Algerian distance, a city of low square forms was set against a sky that was faint with the last sunset hues. The correspondent, plying the oars and dreaming of the slow and slower movements of the lips of the soldier, was moved by a profound and perfectly impersonal comprehension. He was sorry for the soldier of the Legion who lay dying in Algiers.

The thing which had followed the boat and waited had evidently grown bored at the delay. There was no longer to be heard the slash of the cutwater, and there was no longer the flame of the long trail. The light in the north still glimmered, but it was apparently no nearer to the boat. Sometimes the beam of the surf rang in the correspondent's ears, and he turned the craft seaward then and rowed harder. Southward, some one had evidently built a watch-fire on the beach. It was too low and too far to be seen, but it made a shimmering, roseate reflection upon the bluff back of it, and this could be discerned from the boat. The wind came stronger, and sometimes a wave suddenly raged out like a mountain-cat, and there was to be seen the sheen and sparkle of a broken crest.

The captain, in the bow, moved on his water-jar and sat erect. "Pretty long night," he observed to the correspondent. He looked at the shore. "Those life-saving people take their time."

"Did you see that shark playing around?"

"Yes, I saw him. He was a big fellow, all right."

"Wish I had known you were awake."

Later the correspondent spoke into the bottom of the boat.

"Billie!" There was a slow and gradual disentanglement. "Billie, will you spell me?"

"Sure," said the oiler.

As soon as the correspondent touched the cold, comfortable seawater in the bottom of the boat and had huddled close to the cook's life-belt he was deep in sleep, despite the fact that his teeth played all the popular airs. This sleep was so good to him that it was but a moment before he heard a voice call his name in a tone that demonstrated the last stages of exhaustion. "Will you spell me?"

"Sure, Billie."

The light in the north had mysteriously vanished, but the correspondent took his course from the wide-awake captain.

Later in the night they took the boat farther out to sea, and the captain directed the cook to take one oar at the stern and keep the boat facing the seas. He was to call out if he should hear the thunder of the surf. This plan enabled the oiler and the correspondent to get respite together. "We'll give those boys a chance to get into shape again," said the captain. They curled down and, after a few preliminary chatterings and trembles, slept once more the dead sleep. Neither knew they had bequeathed to the cook the company of another shark, or perhaps the same shark.

As the boat caroused on the waves, spray occasionally bumped over the side and gave them a fresh soaking, but this had no power to break their repose. The ominous slash of the wind and the water affected them as it would have affected mummies.

"Boys," said the cook, with the notes of every reluctance in his voice, "she's drifted in pretty close. I guess one of you had better take her to sea again." The correspondent, aroused, heard the crash of the toppled crests.

As he was rowing, the captain gave him some whisky and water, and this steadied the chills out of him. "If I ever get ashore and anybody shows me even a photograph of an oar—"

At last there was a short conversation.

"Billie! . . . Billie, will you spell me?"

"Sure," said the oiler.

VII

When the correspondent again opened his eyes, the sea and the sky were each of the gray hue of the dawning. Later, carmine and gold was painted upon the waters. The morning appeared finally, in its splendor, with a sky of pure blue, and the sunlight flamed on the tips of the waves.

On the distant dunes were set many little black cottages, and a tall white windmill reared above them. No man, nor dog, nor bicycle appeared on the beach. The cottages might have formed a deserted village.

The voyagers scanned the shore. A conference was held in the boat. "Well," said the captain, "if no help is coming, we might better try a run through the surf right away. If we stay out here much longer we will be too weak to do anything for ourselves at all." The others silently acquiesced in this reasoning. The boat was headed for the beach. The correspondent wondered if none ever ascended the tall wind-tower, and if then they never looked seaward. This tower was a giant, standing with its back to the plight of the ants. It represented in a degree, to the correspondent, the serenity of nature amid the struggles of the individual—nature in the wind, and nature in the vision of men. She did not seem cruel to him then, nor beneficent, nor treacherous, nor wise. But she was indifferent, flatly indifferent. It is, perhaps, plausible that a man in this situation, impressed with the unconcern of the universe, should see the innumerable flaws of his life and have them taste wickedly in his mind and wish for another chance. A distinction between right and wrong seems absurdly clear to him, then, in this new ignorance of the grave-edge, and he understands that if he were given another opportunity he would mend his conduct and his words, and be better and brighter during an introduction or at a tea.

"Now, boys," said the captain, "she is going to swamp sure. All we can do is to work her in as far as possible, and then when she swamps, pile out and scramble for the beach. Keep cool now, and don't jump until she swamps sure."

The oiler took the oars. Over his shoulders he scanned the surf. "Captain," he said, "I think I'd better bring her about, and keep her head-on to the seas, and back her in."

"All right, Billie," said the captain. "Back her in." The oiler swung the boat then, and seated in the stern, the cook and the correspondent were obliged to look over their shoulders to contemplate the lonely and indifferent shore.

The monstrous inshore rollers heaved the boat high until the men were again enabled to see the white sheets of water scudding up the slanted beach. "We won't get in very close," said the captain. Each time a man could wrest his attention from the rollers, he turned his glance toward the shore, and in the expression of the eyes during this contemplation there was a singular quality. The correspondent, observing the others, knew that they were not afraid, but the full meaning of their glances was shrouded.

As for himself, he was too tired to grapple fundamentally with the fact. He tried to coerce his mind into thinking of it, but the mind was dominated at this time by the muscles, and the muscles said they did not care. It merely occurred to him that if he should drown it would be a shame.

There were no hurried words, no pallor, no plain agitation. The men simply looked at the shore. "Now, remember to get well clear of the boat when you jump," said the captain.

Seaward the crest of a roller suddenly fell with a thunderous crash, and the long white comber came roaring down upon the boat.

"Steady now," said the captain. The men were silent. They turned their eyes from the shore to the comber and waited. The boat slid up the incline, leaped at the furious top, bounced over it, and swung down the long back of the wave. Some water had been shipped, and the cook bailed it out.

But the next crest crashed also. The tumbling, boiling flood of white water caught the boat and whirled it almost perpendicular. Water swarmed in from all sides. The correspondent had his hands on the gunwale at this time, and when the water entered at that place he swiftly withdrew his fingers, as if he objected to wetting them.

The little boat, drunken with this weight of water, reeled and snuggled deeper into the sea.

"Bail her out, cook! Bail her out!" said the captain.

"All right, Captain," said the cook.

"Now, boys, the next one will do for us sure," said the oiler. "Mind to jump clear of the boat."

The third wave moved forward, huge, furious, implacable. It fairly swallowed the dinghy, and almost simultaneously the men tumbled into the sea. A piece of life-belt had lain in the bottom of the boat, and as the correspondent went overboard he held this to his chest with his left hand.

The January water was icy, and he reflected immediately that it was colder than he had expected to find it off the coast of Florida. This appeared to his dazed mind as a fact important enough to be noted at the time. The coldness of the water was sad; it was tragic. This fact was somehow mixed and confused with his opinion of his own situation so that it seemed almost a proper reason for tears. The water was cold.

When he came to the surface he was conscious of little but the noisy water. Afterward he saw his companions in the sea. The oiler was ahead in the race. He was swimming strongly and rapidly. Off to the correspondent's left, the cook's great white and corked back bulged out of the water; and in the rear the captain was hanging with his one good hand to the keel of the overturned dinghy.

There is a certain immovable quality to a shore, and the correspondent wondered at it amid the confusion of the sea.

It seemed also very attractive; but the correspondent knew that it was a long journey, and he paddled leisurely. The piece of life-preserver lay under him, and sometimes he whirled down the incline of a wave as if he were on a hand-sled.

But finally he arrived at a place in the sea where travel was beset with difficulty. He did not pause swimming to inquire what manner of current had caught him, but there his progress ceased. The shore was set before him like a bit of scenery on a stage, and he looked at it, and understood with his eyes each detail of it.

As the cook passed, much farther to the left, the captain was calling to him, "Turn over on your back, cook! Turn over on your back and use the oar."

"All right, sir." The cook turned on his back, and, paddling with an oar, went ahead as if he were a canoe.

Presently the boat also passed to the left of the correspondent, with the captain clinging with one hand to the keel. He would have appeared like a man raising himself to look over a board fence if it were not for the extraordinary gymnastics of the boat. The correspondent marveled that the captain could still hold to it.

They passed on nearer to shore—the oiler, the cook, the captain—and following them went the water-jar, bouncing gaily over the seas.

The correspondent remained in the grip of this strange new enemy, a current. The shore, with its white slope of sand and its green bluff, topped with little silent cottages, was spread like a picture before him. It was very near to him then, but he was impressed as one who, in a gallery, looks at a scene from Brittany or Algiers.

He thought: "I am going to drown? Can it be possible? Can it be possible? Can it be possible?" Perhaps an individual must consider his own death to be the final phenomenon of nature.

But later a wave perhaps whirled him out of this small deadly current, for he found suddenly that he could again make progress toward the shore. Later still he was aware that the captain, clinging with one hand to the keel of the dinghy, had his face turned away from the shore and toward him, and was calling his name. "Come to the boat! Come to the boat!"

In his struggle to reach the captain and the boat, he reflected that when one gets properly wearied drowning must really be a comfortable arrangement—a cessation of hostilities accompanied by a large degree of relief; and he was glad of it, for the main thing in his mind for some moments had been horror of the temporary agony; he did not wish to be hurt.

Presently he saw a man running along the shore. He was undressing with most remarkable speed. Coat, trousers, shirt, everything flew magically off him.

"Come to the boat!" called the captain.

"All right, Captain." As the correspondent paddled, he saw the captain let himself down to bottom and leave the boat. Then the correspondent performed his one little marvel of the voyage. A large wave caught him and flung him with ease and supreme speed completely over the boat and far beyond it. It struck him even then as an event in gymnastics and a true miracle of the sea. An overturned boat in the surf is not a plaything to a swimming man.

The correspondent arrived in water that reached only to his waist, but his condition did not enable him to stand for more than a moment. Each wave knocked him into a heap, and the undertow pulled at him.

Then he saw the man who had been running and undressing, and undressing and running, come bounding into the water. He dragged ashore the cook, and then waded toward the captain; but the captain waved him away and sent him to the correspondent. He was naked—naked as a tree in winter; but a halo was about his head, and he shone like a saint. He gave a strong pull, and a long drag, and a bully heave at the correspondent's hand. The correspondent, schooled in the minor formulae, said, "Thanks, old man." But suddenly the man cried, "What's that?" He pointed a swift finger. The correspondent said, "Go."

In the shallows, face downward, lay the oiler. His forehead touched sand that was periodically, between each wave, clear of the sea.

The correspondent did not know all that transpired afterward. When he achieved safe ground he fell, striking the sand with each particular part of his body. It was as if he had dropped from a roof, but the thud was grateful to him.

It seems that instantly the beach was populated with men with blankets, clothes, and flasks, and women with coffee-pots and all the remedies sacred to their minds. The welcome of the land to the men from the sea was warm and generous; but a still and dripping shape was carried slowly up the beach, and the land's welcome for it could only be the different and sinister hospitality of the grave.

When it came night, the white waves paced to and fro in the moonlight, and the wind brought the sound of the great sea's voice to the men on shore, and they felt that they could then be interpreters.

Sherwood Anderson *(1876–1941) was born in Camden, Ohio, and raised in Clyde, Ohio. He left school at the age of fourteen, served in the Spanish-American War, wrote advertising copy, and managed his own paint factory in a small Midwestern town. In 1912 he moved to Chicago, joining a circle that included Theodore Dreiser and Carl Sandburg, and there wrote* Winesburg, Ohio *(1919), a collection of stories which revealed the frustration and pathos of small-town life. Anderson spent the 1920's in New York and Paris and New Orleans. Apart from the novels of this period he published two collections of stories*—The Triumph of the Egg *(1921) and* Horses and Men *(1923)—and two autobiographical volumes*—A Story Teller's Story *(1924) and* Tar: A Midwest Childhood *(1926). He moved to Virginia in 1927 and died at Cristobal in the Canal Zone.*

I'm a Fool

SHERWOOD ANDERSON

It was a hard jolt for me, one of the most bitterest I ever had to face. And it all came about through my own foolishness, too. Even yet sometimes, when I think of it I want to cry or swear or kick myself. Perhaps, even now, after all this time, there will be a kind of satisfaction in making myself look cheap by telling of it.

It began at three o'clock one October afternoon as I sat in the grandstand at the fall trotting and pacing meet at Sandusky, Ohio.

To tell the truth, I felt a little foolish that I should be sitting in the grandstand at all. During the summer before, I had left my home town with Harry Whitehead and, with a nigger named Burt, had taken a job as swipe with one of the two horses Harry was campaigning through the fall race meets that year. Mother cried and my sister Mildred, who wanted to get a job as a schoolteacher in our town that fall, stormed and scolded about the house all during the week before I left. They both thought it something disgraceful that one of our family should take a place as a swipe with race horses. I've an idea Mildred thought my taking the place would stand in the way of her getting the job she'd been working so long for.

But after all, I had to work, and there was no other work to be got. A big lumbering fellow of nineteen couldn't just hang around the house and I had got too big to mow people's lawns and sell newspapers. Little chaps who could get next to people's sympathies by their sizes were always getting jobs away from me. There was one fellow who kept saying to everyone who wanted a lawn mowed or a cistern cleaned that he was saving money to work his way through college, and I used to lay awake nights thinking up ways to injure him without being found out. I kept thinking of wagons running over him and bricks falling on his head as he walked along the street. But never mind him.

I got the place with Harry and I liked Burt fine. We got along splendid together. He was a big nigger with a lazy sprawling body and soft, kind eyes, and when it came to a fight he could hit like Jack Johnson. He had Bucephalus, a big black pacing stallion that could do 2:09 or 2:10, if he had to, and I had a little gelding named Doctor Fritz that never lost a race all fall when Harry wanted him to win.

We set out from home late in July in a boxcar with the two horses and after that, until late November, we kept moving along to the race meets and the fairs. It was a peachy time for me, I'll say that. Sometimes now I think that boys who are raised regular in houses, and never have a fine nigger like Burt for best friend, and go to high schools and college, and never steal anything, or get drunk a little, or learn to swear from fellows who know how, or come walking up in front of a grandstand in their shirt sleeves and with dirty horsey pants on when the races are going on and the grandstand is full of people all dressed up—What's the use of talking about it? Such fellows don't know nothing at all. They've never had no opportunity.

But I did. Burt taught me how to rub down a horse and put the bandages on after a race and steam a horse out and a lot of valuable things for any man to know. He could wrap a bandage on a horse's leg so smooth that if it had been the same color you would think it was his skin, and I guess he'd have been a big driver, too, and got to the top like Murphy and Walter Cox and the others if he hadn't been black.

Gee whizz, it was fun. You got to a county seat town, maybe say on a Saturday or Sunday, and the fair began the next Tuesday and lasted until Friday afternoon. Doctor Fritz would be, say in the 2:25 trot on

Tuesday afternoon and on Thursday afternoon Bucephalus would knock 'em cold in the "free-for-all" pace. It left you a lot of time to hang around and listen to horse talk, and see Burt knock some yap cold that got too gay, and you'd find out about horses and men and pick up a lot of stuff you could use all the rest of your life, if you had some sense and salted down what you heard and felt and saw.

And then at the end of the week when the race meet was over, and Harry had run home to tend up to his livery stable business, you and Burt hitched the two horses to carts and drove slow and steady across country, to the place for the next meeting, so as to not overheat the horses, etc., etc., you know.

Gee whizz, Gosh amighty, the nice hickory nut and beechnut and oaks and other kinds of trees along the roads, all brown and red, and the good smells, and Burt singing a song that was called "Deep River," and the country girls at the windows of houses and everything. You can stick your colleges up your nose for all me. I guess I know where I got my education.

Why, one of those little burgs of towns you come to on the way, say now on a Saturday afternoon, and Burt says, "Let's lay up here." And you did.

And you took the horses to a livery stable and fed them, and you got your good clothes out of a box and put them on.

And the town was full of farmers gaping, because they could see you were race horse people, and the kids maybe never see a nigger before and was afraid and run away when the two of us walked down their main street.

And that was before prohibition and all that foolishness, and so you went into a saloon, the two of you, and all the yaps come and stood around, and there was always someone pretended he was horsey and knew things and spoke up and began asking questions, and all you did was to lie and lie all you could about what horses you had, and I said I owned them, and then some fellow said "Will you have a drink of whisky?" and Burt knocked his eye out the way he could say, off-hand like, "Oh, well, all right, I'm agreeable to a little nip. I'll split a quart with you." Gee whizz.

But that isn't what I want to tell my story about. We got home late in November and I promised Mother I'd quit the race horses for good. There's a lot of things you've got to promise a mother because she don't know any better.

And so, there not being any work in our town any more than when I left there to go to the races, I went off to Sandusky and got a pretty good place taking care of horses for a man who owned a teaming and delivery and storage and coal and real estate business there. It was a pretty good place with good eats, and a day off each week, and sleeping on a cot in a big barn, and mostly just shoveling in hay and oats to a lot of big good-enough skates of horses, that couldn't have trotted a race with a toad. I wasn't dissatisfied and I could send money home.

And then, as I started to tell you, the fall races come to Sandusky and I got the day off and I went. I left the job at noon and had on my good clothes and my new brown derby hat I'd just bought the Saturday before, and a stand-up collar.

First of all I went downtown and walked about with the dudes. I've always thought to myself, "put up a good front" and so I did it. I had forty dollars in my pocket and so I went into the West House, a big hotel, and walked up to the cigar stand. "Give me three twenty-five-cent cigars," I said. There was a lot of horsemen and strangers and dressed-up people from other towns standing around in the lobby and in the bar, and I mingled amongst them. In the bar there was a fellow with a cane and a Windsor tie on, that it made me sick to look at him. I like a man to be a man and dress up, but not to go put on that kind of airs. So I pushed him aside, kind of rough, and had me a drink of whisky. And then he looked at me as though he thought maybe he'd get gay, but he changed his mind and didn't say anything. And then I had another drink of whisky, just to show him something, and went out and had a hack out to the races, all to myself, and when I got there I bought myself the best seat I could get up in the grandstand, but didn't go in for any of these boxes. That's putting on too many airs.

And so there I was, sitting up in the grandstand as gay as you please and looking down on the swipes coming out with their horses, and with their dirty horsey pants on and the horse blankets swung over their shoulders, same as I had been doing all the year before. I liked one thing about the same as the other, sitting up there and feeling grand and being down there and looking up at the yaps and feeling grander and more important, too. One thing's about as good as another, if you take it just right. I've often said that.

Well, right in front of me, in the grandstand that day, there was a fellow with a couple of girls and they was about my age. The young fellow was a nice guy all right. He was the kind maybe that goes to college and then comes to be a lawyer or maybe a newspaper editor or something like that, but he wasn't stuck on himself. There are some of that kind are all right and he was one of the ones.

He had his sister with him and another girl, and the sister looked around over his shoulder, accidental at first, not intending to start anything—she wasn't that kind—and her eyes and mine happened to meet.

You know how it is. Gee, she was a peach! She had on a soft dress, kind of a blue stuff and it looked carelessly made, but was well sewed and made and everything. I knew that much. I blushed when she looked right at me and so did she. She was the nicest girl I've ever seen in my life. She wasn't stuck on herself and she could talk proper grammar without being like a schoolteacher or something like that. What I mean is, she was O.K. I think maybe her father was well-to-do, but not rich to make her chesty because she was his daughter, as some are. Maybe he owned a drugstore or a drygoods store in their home town, or something like that. She never told me and I never asked.

My own people are all O.K. too, when you come to that. My grandfather was Welsh and over in the old country, in Wales he was—But never mind that.

The first heat of the first race came off and the young fellow setting there with the two girls left them and went down to make a bet. I knew what he was up to, but he didn't talk big and noisy and let everyone around know he was a sport, as some do. He wasn't that kind. Well, he come back and I heard him tell the two girls what horse he'd bet on, and when the heat was trotted they all half got to their feet and acted in the excited, sweaty way people do when they've got money down on a race, and the horse they bet on is up there pretty close at the end, and they think maybe he'll come on with a rush, but he never does because he hasn't got the old juice in him, come right down to it.

And then, pretty soon, the horses came out for the 2:18 pace and there was a horse in it I knew. He was a horse Bob French had in his string but Bob didn't own him. He was a horse owned by a Mr. Mathers down at Marietta, Ohio.

This Mr. Mathers had a lot of money and owned some coal mines or something, and he had a swell place out in the country, and he was stuck on race horses, but was a Presbyterian or something, and I think more than likely his wife was one, too, maybe a stiffer one than himself. So he never raced his horses hisself, and the story round the Ohio race tracks was that when one of his horses got ready to go to the races he turned him over to Bob French and pretended to his wife he was sold.

So Bob had the horses and he did pretty much as he pleased, and you can't blame Bob, at least I never did. Sometimes he was out to win and sometimes he wasn't. I never cared much about that when I was swiping a horse. What I did want to know was that my horse had the speed and could go out in front, if you wanted him to.

And, as I'm telling you, there was Bob in this race with one of Mr. Mathers' horses, was named "About Ben Ahem" or something like that, and was fast as a streak. He was a gelding and had a mark of 2:21, but could step in :08 or :09.

Because when Burt and I were out, as I've told you, the year before, there was a nigger Burt knew, worked for Mr. Mathers, and we went out there one day when we didn't have no race on at the Marietta Fair and our boss Harry was gone home.

And so everyone was gone to the fair but just this one nigger and he took us all through Mr. Mathers' swell house and he and Burt tapped a bottle of wine Mr. Mathers had hid in his bedroom, back in a closet, without his wife knowing, and he showed us this Ahem horse. Burt was always stuck on being a driver but didn't have much chance to get to the top, being a nigger, and he and the other nigger gulped that whole bottle of wine and Burt got a little lit up.

So the nigger let Burt take this About Ben Ahem and step him a mile in a track Mr. Mathers had all to himself, right there on the farm. And Mr. Mathers had one child, a daughter, kinda sick and not very good-looking, and she came home and we had to hustle and get About Ben Ahem stuck back in the barn.

I'm only telling you to get everything straight. At Sandusky, that afternoon I was at the fair, this young fellow with the two girls was fussed, being with the girls and losing his bet. You know how a fellow is that way. One of them was his girl and the other his sister. I had figured that out.

"Gee whizz," I says to myself, "I'm going to give him the dope."

He was mighty nice when I touched him on the shoulder. He and the girls were nice to me right from the start and clear to the end. I'm not blaming them.

And so he leaned back and I give him the dope on About Ben Ahem. "Don't bet a cent on this first heat because he'll go like an oxen hitched to a plow, but when the first heat is over go right down and lay on your pile." That's what I told him.

Well, I never saw a fellow treat anyone sweller. There was a fat man sitting beside the little girl, that had looked at me twice by this time, and I at her, and both blushing, and what did he do but have the nerve to turn and ask the fat man to get up and change places with me so I could set with his crowd.

Gee whizz, craps amighty. There I was. What a chump I was to go and get gay up there in the West House bar, and just because that dude was standing there with a cane and that kind of a necktie on, to go and get all balled up and drink that whisky, just to show off.

Of course she would know, me setting right beside her and letting her smell of my breath. I could have kicked myself right down out of that grandstand and all around that race track and made a faster record than most of the skates of horses they had there that year.

Because that girl wasn't any mutt of a girl. What wouldn't I have give right then for a stick of chewing gum to chew, or a lozenger, or some liquorice, or most anything. I was glad I had those twenty-five-cent cigars in my pocket and right away I give that fellow one and lit one myself. Then that fat man got up and we changed places and there I was, plunked right down beside her.

They introduced themselves and the fellow's best girl, he had with him, was named Miss Elinor Woodbury, and her father was a manufacturer of barrels from a place called Tiffin, Ohio. And the fellow himself was named Wilbur Wessen and his sister was Miss Lucy Wessen.

I suppose it was their having such swell names got me off my trolley. A fellow, just because he has been a swipe with a race horse, and works taking care of horses for a man in the teaming, delivery, and storage business, isn't any better or worse than anyone else. I've often thought that, and said it too.

But you know how a fellow is. There's something in that kind of nice clothes, and the kind of nice eyes she had, and the way she had looked at me, awhile before, over her brother's shoulder, and me looking back at her, and both of us blushing.

I couldn't show her up for a boob, could I?

I made a fool of myself, that's what I did. I said my name was Walter Mathers from Marietta, Ohio, and then I told all three of them the smashingest lie you ever heard. What I said was that my father owned the horse About Ben Ahem and that he had let him out to this Bob French for racing purposes, because our family was proud and had never gone into racing that way, in our own name, I mean. Then I had got started and they were all leaning over and listening, and Miss Lucy Wessen's eyes were shining, and I went the whole hog.

I told about our place down at Marietta, and about the big stables and the grand brick house we had on a hill, up above the Ohio River, but I knew enough not to do it in no bragging way. What I did was to start things and then let them drag the rest out of me. I acted just as reluctant to tell as I could. Our family hasn't got any barrel factory, and, since I've known us, we've always been pretty poor, but not asking anything of anyone at that, and my grandfather, over in Wales—but never mind that.

We sat there talking like we had known each other for years and years, and I went and told them that my father had been expecting maybe this Bob French wasn't on the square, and had sent me up to Sandusky on the sly to find out what I could.

And I bluffed it through I had found out all about the 2:18 pace, in which About Ben Ahem was to start.

I said he would lose the first heat by pacing like a lame cow and then he would come back and skin 'em alive after that. And to back up what I said I took thirty dollars out of my pocket and handed it to Mr. Wilbur Wessen and asked him, would he mind, after the first heat, to go down and place it on About Ben Ahem for whatever odds he could get. What I said was that I didn't want Bob French to see me and none of the swipes.

Sure enough the first heat come off and About Ben Ahem went off his stride, up the back stretch, and looked like a wooden horse or a sick one, and come in to be last. Then this Wilbur Wessen went down to the betting place under the grandstand and there I was with the two girls, and when that Miss Woodbury was looking the other way once, Lucy Wessen kinda, with her shoulder you know, kinda touched me. Not just tucking down, I don't mean. You know how a woman can do. They get close, but not getting gay either. You know what they do. Gee whizz.

And then they give me a jolt. What they had done, when I didn't know, was to get together, and they had decided Wilbur Wessen would bet fifty dollars, and the two girls had gone and put in ten dollars each, of their own money, too. I was sick then, but I was sicker later.

About the gelding, About Ben Ahem, and their winning their money, I wasn't worried a lot about that. It come out O.K. Ahem stepped the next three heats like a bushel of spoiled eggs going to market before they could be found out, and Wilbur Wessen had got nine to two for the money. There was something else eating at me.

Because Wilbur come back, after he had bet the money, and after that he spent most of his time talking to that Miss Woodbury, and Lucy Wessen and I was left alone together like on a desert island. Gee, if I'd only been on the square or if there had been any way of getting myself on the square. There ain't any Walter Mathers, like I said to her and them, and there hasn't ever been one, but if there was, I bet I'd go to Marietta, Ohio, and shoot him tomorrow.

There I was, big boob that I am. Pretty soon the race was over, and Wilbur had gone down and collected our money, and we had a hack downtown, and he stood us a swell supper at the West House, and a bottle of champagne beside.

And I was with that girl and she wasn't saying much, and I wasn't saying much either. One thing I know. She wasn't stuck on me because of the lie about my father being rich and all that. There's a way you know. . . . Craps amighty. There's a kind of girl, you see just once in your life, and if you don't get busy and make hay, then you're gone for good and all, and might as well go jump off a bridge. They give you a look from inside of them somewhere, and it ain't no vamping, and what it means is—you want that girl to be your wife, and you want nice things around her like flowers and swell clothes, and you want her to have the kids you're going to have, and you want good music played and no ragtime. Gee whizz.

There's a place over near Sandusky, across a kind of bay, and it's called Cedar Point. And after we had supper we went over to it in a launch, all by ourselves. Wilbur and Miss Lucy and that Miss Woodbury had to catch a ten-o'clock train back to Tiffin, Ohio, because, when you're out with girls like that, you can't get careless and miss any trains and stay out all night, like you can with some kinds of Janes.

And Wilbur blowed himself to the launch and it cost him fifteen cold plunks, but I wouldn't never have knew if I hadn't listened. He wasn't no tinhorn kind of a sport.

Over at the Cedar Point place, we didn't stay around where there was a gang of common kind of cattle at all.

There was big dance halls and dining places for yaps, and there was a beach you could walk along and get where it was dark, and we went there.

She didn't talk hardly at all and neither did I, and I was thinking how glad I was my mother was all right, and always made us kids learn to eat with a fork at table, and not swill soup, and not be noisy and rough like a gang you see around a race track that way.

Then Wilbur and his girl went away up the beach and Lucy and I sat down in a dark place, where there was some roots of old trees, the water had washed up, and after that the time, till we had to go back in the launch and they had to catch their trains, wasn't nothing at all. It went like winking your eye.

Here's how it was. The place we were setting in was dark, like I said, and there was the roots from that cold stump sticking up like arms, and there was a watery smell, and the night was like—as if you could put your hand out and feel it—so warm and soft and dark and sweet like an orange.

I most cried and I most swore and I most jumped up and danced, I was so mad and happy and sad.

When Wilbur come back from being alone with his girl, and she saw him coming, Lucy she says, "We got to go to the train now," and she was most crying too, but she never knew nothing I knew, and she couldn't be so all busted up. And then, before Wilbur and Miss Woodbury got up to where we was, she put her face up and kissed me quick and put her head up against me and she was all quivering and—Gee whizz.

Sometimes I hope I have cancer and die. I guess you know what I mean. We went in the launch across the bay to the train like that, and it was dark, too. She whispered and said it was like she and I could get out of the boat and walk on the water, and it sounded foolish, but I knew what she meant.

And then quick we were right at the depot, and there was a big gang of yaps, the kind that goes to the fairs, and crowded and milling around like cattle, and how could I tell her? "It won't be long because you'll write and I'll write to you." That's all she said.

I got a chance like a hay barn afire. A swell chance I got.

And maybe she would write me, down at Marietta that way, and the letter would come back, and stamped on the front of it by the U.S.A. "there ain't any such guy," or something like that, whatever they stamp on a letter that way.

And me trying to pass myself off for a bigbug and a swell—to her, as decent a little body as God ever made. Craps amighty—a swell chance I got!

And then the train come in, and she got on it, and Wilbur Wessen he come and shook hands with me, and that Miss Woodbury was nice too and bowed to me, and I at her, and the train went and I busted out and cried like a kid.

Gee, I could have run after that train and made Dan Patch look like a freight train after a wreck but, socks amighty, what was the use? Did you ever see such a fool?

I'll bet you what—if I had an arm broke right now or a train had run over my foot—I wouldn't go to no doctor at all. I'd go set down and let her hurt and hurt—that's what I'd do.

I'll bet you what—if I hadn't a drunk that booze I'd a never been such a boob as to go tell such a lie—that couldn't never be made straight to a lady like her.

I wish I had that fellow right here that had on a Windsor tie and carried a cane. I'd smash him for fair. Gosh darn his eyes. He's a big fool—that's what he is.

And if I'm not another you just go find me one and I'll quit working and be a bum and give him my job. I don't care nothing for working, and earning money, and saving it for no such boob as myself.

James Joyce *(1882–1941), the eldest son of a witty and improvident government officeholder, was born in Dublin. He was educated at Jesuit schools and graduated from University College in 1902. He left Ireland two years later—returning only for a brief visit in 1912—and settled in Trieste as a language teacher in a Berlitz school. During this period he produced a volume of verse,* Chamber Music *(1907), a collection of short stories,* Dubliners *(1915), and an autobiographical novel,* A Portrait of the Artist as a Young Man *(1916). Joyce moved to Zurich during World War I and there began the writing of* Ulysses. *The novel was published in Paris in 1922, two years after Joyce made that city his permanent home. The following years were devoted to the composition of* Finnegans Wake *(1939). Joyce returned to Zurich at the outbreak of World War II and died there of a perforated ulcer.*

Eveline

JAMES JOYCE

She sat at the window watching the evening invade the avenue. Her head was leaned against the window curtains and in her nostrils was the odor of dusty cretonne. She was tired.

Few people passed. The man out of the last house passed on his way home; she heard his footsteps clacking along the concrete pavement and afterwards crunching on the cinder path before the new red houses. One time there used to be a field there in which they used to play every evening with other people's children. Then a man from Belfast bought the field and built houses in it—not like their little brown houses but bright brick houses with shining roofs. The children of the avenue used to play together in that field—the Devines, the Waters, the Dunns, little Keogh the cripple, she and her brothers and sisters. Ernest, however, never played: he was too grown up. Her father used often to hunt them in out of the field with his blackthorn stick; but usually little Keogh used to keep *nix* and call out when he saw her father coming. Still they seemed to have been rather happy then. Her father was not so bad then; and besides, her mother was alive. That was a long time ago; she and her brothers and sisters were all grown up; her mother was dead. Tizzie Dunn was dead, too, and the Waters had gone back to England. Everything changes. Now she was going to go away like the others, to leave her home.

Home! She looked round the room, reviewing all its familiar objects which she had dusted once a week for so many years, wondering where on earth all the dust came from. Perhaps she would never see again those familiar objects from which she had never dreamed of being divided. And yet during all those years she had never found out the name of the priest whose yellowing photograph hung on the wall above the broken harmonium beside the colored print of the promises made to Blessed Margaret Mary Alacoque. He had been a school friend of her father. Whenever he showed the photograph to a visitor her father used to pass it with a casual word:

—He is in Melbourne now.—

She had consented to go away, to leave her home. Was that wise? She tried to weigh each side of the question. In her home anyway she had shelter and food; she had those whom she had known all her life about her. Of course she had to work hard both in the house and at business. What would they say of her in the Stores when they found out that she had run away with a fellow? Say she was a fool, perhaps; and her place would be filled up by advertisement. Miss Gavan would be glad. She had always had an edge on her, especially whenever there were people listening.

—Miss Hill, don't you see these ladies are waiting?—

—Look lively, Miss Hill, please.—

She would not cry many tears at leaving the Stores.

But in her new home, in a distant unknown country, it would not be like that. Then she would be married—she, Eveline. People would treat her with respect then. She would not be treated as her mother had been. Even now, though she was over nineteen, she sometimes felt herself in danger of her father's violence. She knew it was that that had given her the palpitations. When they were growing up he had never gone for her, like he used to go for Harry and Ernest, because she was a girl; but latterly he had begun to threaten her and say what he would do to her only for her dead mother's sake. And now she had nobody to protect her. Ernest was dead and Harry, who was in the church decorating business, was nearly always down somewhere in the country. Besides, the invariable squabble for money on Saturday nights had begun to weary her unspeakably. She always gave her entire wages—seven shillings—and Harry always sent up what he could but the trouble was to get any money from her father. He said she used to squander the money, that she had no head, that he wasn't going to give her his hard-earned money to throw about the streets, and much more, for he was usually fairly bad of a Saturday night. In the end he would give her the money and ask her had she any intention of buying Sunday's dinner. Then she had to rush out as quickly as she could and do her marketing, holding her black leather purse tightly in her hand as she elbowed her way through the crowds and returning home late under her load of provisions. She had hard work to keep the house together and to see that the two young children who had been left to her charge went to school regularly and got their meals regularly. It was hard work—a hard life—but now that she was about to leave it she did not find it a wholly undesirable life.

She was about to explore another life with Frank. Frank was very kind, manly, open-hearted. She was to go away with him by the night-boat to be his wife and to live with him in Buenos Aires where he had a home waiting for her. How well she remembered the first time she had seen him; he was lodging in a house on the main road where she used to visit. It seemed a few weeks ago. He was standing at the gate, his peaked cap pushed back on his head and his hair tumbled forward over a face of bronze. Then they had come to know each other. He used to meet her outside the Stores every evening and see her home. He took her to see *The Bohemian Girl* and she felt elated as she sat in an unaccustomed part of the theater with him. He was awfully fond of music and sang a little. People knew that they were courting and, when he sang about the lass that loves a sailor, she always felt pleasantly confused. He used to call her Poppens out of fun. First of all it had been an excitement for her to have a fellow and then she had begun to like him. He had tales of distant countries. He had started as a deck boy at a pound a month on a ship of the Allan Line going out to Canada. He told her the names of the ships he had been on and the names of the different services. He had sailed through the Straits of Magellan and he told her stories of the terrible Patagonians. He had fallen on his feet in Buenos Aires, he said, and had come over to the old country just for a holiday. Of course, her father had found out the affair and had forbidden her to have anything to say to him.

—I know these sailor chaps—he said.

One day he had quarrelled with Frank and after that she had to meet her lover secretly.

The evening deepened in the avenue. The white of two letters in her lap grew indistinct. One was to Harry; the other was to her father. Ernest had been her favorite but she liked Harry too. Her father was becoming old lately, she noticed; he would miss her. Sometimes he could be very nice. Not long before, when she had been laid up for a day, he had read her out a ghost story and made toast for her at the fire. Another day, when their mother was alive, they had all gone for a picnic to the Hill of Howth. She remembered her father putting on her mother's bonnet to make the children laugh.

Her time was running out but she continued to sit by the window, leaning her head against the window curtain, inhaling the odor of dusty cretonne. Down far in the avenue she could hear a street organ playing. She knew the air. Strange that it should come that very night to remind her of the promise to her mother, her promise to keep the home together as long as she could. She remembered the last night of her mother's illness; she was again in the close dark room at the other side of the hall and outside she heard a melancholy air of Italy. The organ-player had been ordered to go away and given sixpence. She remembered her father strutting back into the sickroom saying:

—Damned Italians! coming over here!—

As she mused, the pitiful vision of her mother's life laid its spell on the very quick of her being—that life of commonplace sacrifices closing in final craziness. She trembled as she heard again her mother's voice saying constantly with foolish insistence:

—Derevaun Seraun! Derevaun Seraun!—

She stood up in a sudden impulse of terror. Escape! She must escape! Frank would save her. He would give her life, perhaps love, too. But she wanted to live. Why should she be unhappy? She had a right to happiness. Frank would take her in his arms, fold her in his arms. He would save her.

She stood among the swaying crowd in the station at the North Wall. He held her hand and she knew that he was speaking to her, saying something about the passage over and over again. The station was full of soldiers with brown baggages. Through the wide doors of the sheds she caught a glimpse of the black mass of the boat, lying in beside the quay wall, with illumined portholes. She answered nothing. She felt her cheek pale and cold and, out of a maze of distress, she prayed to God to direct her, to show her what was her duty. The boat blew a long mournful whistle into the mist. If she went, tomorrow she would be on the sea with Frank, steaming towards Buenos Aires. Their passage had been booked. Could she still draw back after all he had done for her? Her distress awoke a nausea in her body and she kept moving her lips in silent fervent prayer.

A bell clanged upon her heart. She felt him seize her hand:

—Come!—

All the seas of the world tumbled about her heart. He was drawing her into them: he would drown her. She gripped with both hands at the iron railing.

—Come!—

No! No! No! It was impossible. Her hands clutched the iron in frenzy. Amid the seas she sent a cry of anguish!

—Eveline! Evvy!—

He rushed beyond the barrier and called to her to follow. He was shouted at to go on but he still called to her. She set her white face to him, passive, like a helpless animal. Her eyes gave him no sign of love or farewell or recognition.

D. H. Lawrence *(1885–1930) was born in Eastwood, a coal-mining town in the English Midlands, was educated at nearby* Nottingham, *and taught at an elementary school south of* London. *His poetry appeared in* The English Review, *edited by Ford Madox Ford, and in 1911 he published his first novel*, The White Peacock. *The years following saw the publication of* Sons and Lovers *(1913), the suppression of* The Rainbow *(1915), and the delayed release of* Women in Love *(1920). After World War I Lawrence traveled from Italy to Australia to America, and settled briefly in the dry climate of New Mexico. He returned to Europe in 1925, completed* Lady Chatterley's Lover *in 1928, and—ever in ill-health—died of tuberculosis in southern France.*

The Rocking-Horse Winner

D. H. LAWRENCE

There was a woman who was beautiful, who started with all the advantages, yet she had no luck. She married for love, and the love turned to dust. She had bonny children, yet she felt they had been thrust upon her, and she could not love them. They looked at her coldly, as if they were finding fault with her. And hurriedly she felt she must cover up some fault in herself. Yet what it was that she must cover up she never knew. Nevertheless, when her children were present, she always felt the center of her heart go hard. This troubled her, and in her manner she was all the more gentle and anxious for her children, as if she loved them very much. Only she herself knew that at the center of her heart was a hard little place that could not feel love, no, not for anybody. Everybody else said of her: "She is such a good mother. She adores her children." Only she herself, and her children themselves, knew it was not so. They read it in each other's eyes.

There were a boy and two little girls. They lived in a pleasant house, with a garden, and they had discreet servants, and felt themselves superior to anyone in the neighborhood.

Although they lived in style, they felt always an anxiety in the house. There was never enough money. The mother had a small income, and the father had a small income, but not nearly enough for the social position which they had to keep up. The father went into town to some office. But though he had good prospects, these prospects never materialized. There was always the grinding sense of the shortage of money, though the style was always kept up.

At last the mother said: "I will see if I can't make something." But she did not know where to begin. She racked her brains, and tried this thing and the other, but could not find anything successful. The failure made deep lines come into her face. Her children were growing up, they would have to go to school. There must be more money, there must be more money. The father, who was always very handsome and expensive in his tastes, seemed as if he never would be able to do anything worth doing. And the mother, who had a great belief in herself, did not succeed any better, and her tastes were just as expensive.

And so the house came to be haunted by the unspoken phrase: There must be more money! There must be more money! The children could hear it all the time, though nobody said it aloud. They heard it at Christmas, when the expensive and splendid toys filled the nursery. Behind the shining modern rocking-horse, behind the smart doll's-house, a voice would start whispering: "There must be more money! There must be more money!" And the children would stop playing, to listen for a moment. They would look at each other's eyes, to see if they had all heard. And each one saw in the eyes of the other two that they too had heard. "There must be more money! There must be more money!"

It came whispering from the springs of the still-swaying rocking-horse, and even the horse, bending his wooden, champing head, heard it. The big doll, sitting so pink and smirking in her new pram, could hear it quite plainly, and seemed to be smirking all the more self-consciously because of it. The foolish puppy, too, that took the place of the teddy-bear, he was looking so extraordinarily foolish for no other reason but that he heard the secret whisper all over the house: "There must be more money!"

Yet nobody ever said it aloud. The whisper was everywhere, and therefore no one spoke it. Just as no one ever says: "We are breathing!" in spite of the fact that breath is coming and going all the time.

"Mother," said the boy Paul one day, "why don't we keep a car of our own? Why do we always use uncle's, or else a taxi?"

"Because we're poor members of the family," said the mother.

"But why are we, mother?"

"Well—I suppose," she said slowly and bitterly, "it's because your father has no luck."

The boy was silent for some time.

"Is luck money, mother?" he asked, rather timidly.

"No, Paul. Not quite. It's what causes you to have money."

"Oh!" said Paul vaguely. "I thought when Uncle Oscar said filthy lucker, it meant money."

"Filthy lucre does mean money," said the mother. "But it's lucre, not luck."

"Oh!" said the boy. "Then what is luck, mother?"

"It's what causes you to have money. If you're lucky you have money. That's why it's better to be born lucky than rich. If you're rich, you may lose your money. But if you're lucky, you will always get more money."

"Oh! Will you? And is father not lucky?"

"Very unlucky, I should say," she said bitterly.

The boy watched her with unsure eyes.

"Why?" he asked.

"I don't know. Nobody ever knows why one person is lucky and another unlucky."

"Don't they? Nobody at all? Does nobody know?"

"Perhaps God. But He never tells."

"He ought to, then. And aren't you lucky either, mother?"

"I can't be, if I married an unlucky husband."

"But by yourself, aren't you?"

"I used to think I was, before I married. Now I think I am very unlucky indeed."

"Why?"

"Well—never mind! Perhaps I'm not really," she said.

The child looked at her, to see if she meant it. But he saw, by the lines of her mouth, that she was only trying to hide something from him.

"Well, anyhow," he said stoutly, "I'm a lucky person."

"Why?" said his mother, with a sudden laugh.

He stared at her. He didn't even know why he had said it.

"God told me," he asserted, brazening it out.

"I hope He did, dear!" she said, again with a laugh, but rather bitter.

"He did, mother!"

"Excellent!" said the mother, using one of her husband's exclamations.

The boy saw she did not believe him; or, rather that she paid no attention to his assertion. This angered him somewhat, and made him want to compel her attention.

He went off by himself, vaguely, in a childish way, seeking for the clue to "luck." Absorbed, taking no heed of other people, he went about with a sort of stealth, seeking inwardly for luck. He wanted luck, he wanted it, he wanted it. When the two girls were playing dolls in the nursery, he would sit on his big rocking-horse, charging madly into space, with a frenzy that made the little girls peer at him uneasily. Wildly the horse careered, the waving dark hair of the boy tossed, his eyes had a strange glare in them. The little girls dared not speak to him.

When he had ridden to the end of his mad little journey, he climbed down and stood in front of his rocking-horse, staring fixedly into its lowered face. Its red mouth was slightly open, its big eye was wide and glassy-bright.

"Now!" he would silently command the snorting steed. "Now, take me to where there is luck! Now take me!"

And he would slash the horse on the neck with the little whip he had asked Uncle Oscar for. He knew the horse could take him to where there was luck, if only he forced it. So he would mount again, and start on his furious ride, hoping at last to get there. He knew he could get there.

"You'll break your horse, Paul!" said the nurse.

"He's always riding like that! I wish he'd leave off!" said his elder sister Joan.

But he only glared down on them in silence. Nurse gave him up. She could make nothing of him. Anyhow he was growing beyond her.

One day his mother and his Uncle Oscar came in when he was on one of his furious rides. He did not speak to them.

"Hallo, you young jockey! Riding a winner?" said his uncle.

"Aren't you growing too big for a rocking-horse? You're not a very little boy any longer, you know," said his mother.

But Paul only gave a blue glare from his big, rather close-set eyes. He would speak to nobody when he was in full tilt. His mother watched him with an anxious expression on her face.

At last he suddenly stopped forcing his horse into the mechanical gallop, and slid down.

"Well, I got there!" he announced fiercely, his blue eyes still flaring, and his sturdy long legs straddling apart.

"Where did you get to?" asked his mother.

"Where I wanted to go," he flared back at her.

"That's right, son!" said Uncle Oscar. "Don't you stop till you get there. What's the horse's name?"

"He doesn't have a name," said the boy.

"Gets on without all right?" asked the uncle.

"Well, he has different names. He was called Sansovino last week."

"Sansovino, eh? Won the Ascot. How did you know his name?"

"He always talks about horse-races with Bassett," said Joan.

The uncle was delighted to find that his small nephew was posted with all the racing news. Bassett, the young gardener, who had been wounded in the left foot in the war and had got his present job through Oscar Cresswell, whose batman he had been, was a perfect blade of the "turf." He lived in the racing events, and the small boy lived with him.

Oscar Cresswell got it all from Bassett.

"Master Paul comes and asks me, so I can't do more than tell him, sir," said Bassett, his face terribly serious, as if he were speaking of religious matters.

"And does he ever put anything on a horse he fancies?"

"Well—I don't want to give him away—he's a young sport, a fine sport, sir. Would you mind asking him yourself? He sort of takes a pleasure in it, and perhaps he'd feel I was giving him away, sir, if you don't mind."

Bassett was serious as a church.

The uncle went back to his nephew, and took him off for a ride in the car.

"Say, Paul, old man, do you ever put anything on a horse?" the uncle asked.

The boy watched the handsome man closely.

"Why, do you think I oughtn't to?" he parried.

"Not a bit of it! I thought perhaps you might give me a tip for the Lincoln."

The car sped on into the country, going down to Uncle Oscar's place in Hampshire.

"Honor bright?" said the nephew.

"Honor bright, son!" said the uncle.

"Well, then, Daffodil."

"Daffodil! I doubt it, sonny, What about Mirza?"

"I only know the winner," said the boy. "That's Daffodil."

"Daffodil, eh?"

There was a pause. Daffodil was an obscure horse comparatively.

"Uncle!"

"Yes, son?"

"You won't let it go any further, will you? I promised Bassett."

"Bassett be damned, old man! What's he got to do with it?"

"We're partners. We've been partners from the first. Uncle, he lent me my first five shillings, which I lost. I promised him, honor bright, it was only between me and him; only you gave me that ten-shilling note I started winning with, so I thought you were lucky. You won't let it go any further, will you?"

The boy gazed at his uncle from those big, hot, blue eyes, set rather close together. The uncle stirred and laughed uneasily.

"Right you are, son! I'll keep your tip private. Daffodil, eh? How much are you putting on him?"

"All except twenty pounds," said the boy. "I keep that in reserve."

The uncle thought it a good joke.

"You keep twenty pounds in reserve, do you, you young romancer? What are you betting, then?"

"I'm betting three hundred," said the boy gravely. "But it's between you and me, Uncle Oscar! Honor bright?"

The uncle burst into a roar of laughter.

"It's between you and me all right, you young Nat Gould," he said, laughing. "But where's your three hundred?"

"Bassett keeps it for me. We're partners."

"He won't go quite as high as I do, I expect. Perhaps he'll go a hundred and fifty."

"What, pennies?" laughed the uncle.

"Pounds," said the child, with a surprised look at his uncle. "Bassett keeps a bigger reserve than I do."

Between wonder and amusement Uncle Oscar was silent. He pursued the matter no further, but he determined to take his nephew with him to the Lincoln races.

"Now, son," he said, "I'm putting twenty on Mirza, and I'll put five for you on any horse you fancy. What's your pick?"

"Daffodil, uncle."

"No, not the fiver on Daffodil!"

"I should if it was my own fiver," said the child.

"Good! Good! Right you are! A fiver for me and a fiver for you on Daffodil."

The child had never been to a race-meeting before, and his eyes were blue fire. He pursed his mouth tight, and watched. A Frenchman just in front had put his money on Lancelot. Wild with excitement, he flayed his arms up and down, yelling "Lancelot! Lancelot!" in his French accent.

Daffodil came in first, Lancelot second, Mirza third. The child, flushed and with eyes blazing, was curiously serene. His uncle brought him four five-pound notes, four to one.

"What am I to do with these?" he cried, waving them before the boy's eyes.

"I suppose we'll talk to Bassett," said the boy. "I expect I have fifteen hundred now; and twenty in reserve; and this twenty."

His uncle studied him for some moments.

"Look here, son!" he said. "You're not serious about Bassett and that fifteen hundred, are you?"

"Yes, I am. But it's between you and me, uncle. Honor bright!"

"Honor bright all right, son! But I must talk to Bassett."

"If you'd like to be a partner, uncle, with Bassett and me, we could all be partners. Only, you'd have to promise, honor bright, uncle, not to let it go beyond us three. Bassett and I are lucky, and you must be lucky, because it was your ten shillings I started winning with. . . ."

Uncle Oscar took both Bassett and Paul into Richmond Park for an afternoon, and there they talked.

"It's like this, you see, sir," Bassett said. "Master Paul would get me talking about racing events, spinning yarns, you know, sir. And he was always keen on knowing if I'd made or if I'd lost. It's about a year since, now, that I put five shillings on Blush of Dawn for him—and we lost. Then the luck turned, with that ten shillings he had from you, that we put on Singhalese. And since that time, it's been pretty steady, all things considering. What do you say, Master Paul?"

"We're all right when we're sure," said Paul. "It's when we're not quite sure that we go down."

"Oh, but we're careful then," said Bassett.

"But when are you sure?" smiled Uncle Oscar.

"It's Master Paul, sir," said Bassett, in a secret, religious voice. "It's as if he had it from heaven. Like Daffodil, now, for the Lincoln. That was as sure as eggs."

"Did you put anything on Daffodil?" asked Oscar Cresswell.

"Yes, sir. I made my bit."

"And my nephew?"

Bassett was obstinately silent, looking at Paul.

"I made twelve hundred, didn't I, Bassett? I told uncle I was putting three hundred on Daffodil."

"That's right," said Bassett, nodding.

"But where's the money?" asked the uncle.

"I keep it safe locked up, sir. Master Paul he can have it any minute he likes to ask for it."

"What, fifteen hundred pounds?"

"And twenty! And forty, that is, with the twenty he made on the course."

"It's amazing!" said the uncle.

"If Master Paul offers you to be partners, sir, I would, if I were you; if you'll excuse me," said Bassett.

Oscar Cresswell thought about it.

"I'll see the money," he said.

They drove home again, and sure enough, Bassett came round to the garden-house with fifteen hundred pounds in notes. The twenty pounds reserve was left with Joe Glee, in the Turf Commission deposit.

"You see, it's all right, uncle, when I'm sure! Then we go strong, for all we're worth. Don't we, Bassett?

"We do that, Master Paul."

"And when are you sure?" said the uncle, laughing.

"Oh, well, sometimes I'm absolutely sure, like about Daffodil," said the boy; "and sometimes I have an idea; and sometimes I haven't even an idea, have I, Bassett? Then we're careful, because we mostly go down."

"You do, do you! And when you're sure, like about Daffodil, what makes you sure, sonny?"

"Oh, well, I don't know," said the boy uneasily. "I'm sure, you know, uncle; that's all."

"It's as if he had it from heaven, sir," Bassett reiterated.

"I should say so!" said the uncle.

But he became a partner. And when the Leger was coming on, Paul was "sure" about Lively Spark, which was a quite inconsiderable horse. The boy insisted on putting a thousand on the horse, Bassett went for five hundred, and Oscar Cresswell two hundred. Lively Spark came in first, and the betting had been ten to one against him. Paul had made ten thousand.

"You see," he said. "I was absolutely sure of him."

Even Oscar Cresswell had cleared two thousand.

"Look here, son," he said, "this sort of thing makes me nervous."

"It needn't, uncle! Perhaps I shan't be sure again for a long time."

"But what are you going to do with your money?" asked the uncle.

"Of course," said the boy, "I started it for mother. She said she had no luck, because father is unlucky, so I thought if I was lucky, it might stop whispering."

"What might stop whispering?"

"Our house. I hate our house for whispering."

"What does it whisper?"

"Why—why"—the boy fidgeted—"why, I don't know. But it's always short of money, you know, uncle."

"I know it, son, I know it."

"You know people send mother writs, don't you, uncle?"

"I'm afraid I do," said the uncle.

"And then the house whispers, like people laughing at you behind your back. It's awful, that is! I thought if I was lucky . . ."

"You might stop it," added the uncle.

The boy watched him with big blue eyes that had an uncanny cold fire in them, and he said never a word.

"Well, then!" said the uncle. "What are we doing?"

"I shouldn't like mother to know I was lucky," said the boy.

"Why not, son?"

"She'd stop me."

"I don't think she would."

"Oh!"—and the boy writhed in an odd way—"I don't want her to know, uncle."

"All right, son! We'll manage it without her knowing."

They managed it very easily. Paul, at the other's suggestion, handed over five thousand pounds to his uncle, who deposited it with the family lawyer, who was then to inform Paul's mother that a relative had put five thousand pounds into his hands, which sum was to be paid out a thousand pounds at a time, on the mother's birthday, for the next five years.

"So she'll have a birthday present of a thousand pounds for five successive years," said Uncle Oscar. "I hope it won't make it all the harder for her later."

Paul's mother had her birthday in November. The house had been "whispering" worse than ever lately, and, even in spite of his luck, Paul could not bear up against it. He was very anxious to see the effect of the birthday letter, telling his mother about the thousand pounds.

When there were no visitors, Paul now took his meals with his parents, as he was beyond the nursery control. His mother went into town nearly every day. She had discovered that she had an odd knack of sketching furs and dress materials, so she worked secretly in the studio of a friend who was the chief "artist" for the leading drapers. She drew the figures of ladies in furs and ladies in silk and sequins for the newspaper advertisements. This young woman artist earned several thousand pounds a year, but Paul's mother only made several hundred, and she was again dissatisfied. She so wanted to be first in something, and she did not succeed, even in making sketches for the drapery advertisements.

She was down to breakfast on the morning of her birthday. Paul watched her face as she read her letters. He knew the lawyer's letter. As his mother read it, her face hardened and became more expressionless. Then a cold, determined look came on her mouth. She hid the letter under the pile of others, and said not a word about it.

"Didn't you have anything nice in the post for your birthday, mother?" said Paul.

"Quite moderately nice," she said, her voice cold and absent.

She went away to town without saying more.

But in the afternoon Uncle Oscar appeared. He said Paul's mother had had a long interview with the lawyer, asking if the whole five thousand could be advanced at once, as she was in debt.

"What do you think, uncle?" said the boy.

"I leave it to you, son."

"Oh, let her have it, then! We can get some more with the other," said the boy.

"A bird in the hand is worth two in the bush, laddie!" said Uncle Oscar.

"But I'm sure to know for the Grand National; or the Lincolnshire; or else the Derby. I'm sure to know for one of them," said Paul.

So Uncle Oscar signed the agreement, and Paul's mother touched the whole five thousand. Then something very curious happened. The voices in the house suddenly went mad, like a chorus of frogs on a spring evening. There were certain new furnishings, and Paul had a tutor. He was really going to Eton, his father's school, in the following autumn. There were flowers in the winter, and a blossoming of the luxury Paul's mother had been used to. And yet the voices in the house, behind the sprays of mimosa and almond blossom, and from under the piles of iridescent cushions, simply trilled and screamed in a sort of ecstasy: "There must be more money! Oh-h-h, there must be more money. Oh, now, now-w! Now-w-w—there must be more money!—more than ever! More than ever!"

It frightened Paul terribly. He studied away at his Latin and Greek with his tutors. But his intense hours were spent with Bassett. The Grand National had gone by: he had not "known," and had lost a hundred pounds. Summer was at hand. He was in agony for the Lincoln. But even for the Lincoln he didn't "know" and he lost fifty pounds. He became wild-eyed and strange, as if something were going to explode in him.

"Let it alone, son! Don't you bother about it!" urged Uncle Oscar. But it was as if the boy couldn't really hear what his uncle was saying.

"I've got to know for the Derby! I've got to know for the Derby!" the child reiterated, his big blue eyes blazing with a sort of madness.

His mother noticed how overwrought he was.

"You'd better go to the seaside. Wouldn't you like to go now to the seaside, instead of waiting? I think you'd better," she said, looking down at him anxiously, her heart curiously heavy because of him.

But the child lifted his uncanny blue eyes.

"I couldn't possibly go before the Derby, mother!" he said. "I couldn't possibly!"

"Why not?" she said, her voice becoming heavy when she was opposed. "Why not? You can still go from the seaside to see the Derby with your Uncle Oscar, if that's what you wish. No need for you to wait here. Besides, I think you care too much about these races. It's a bad sign. My family has been a gambling family, and you won't know till you grow up how much damage it has done. But it has done damage. I shall have to send Bassett away, and ask Uncle Oscar not to talk racing to you, unless you promise to be reasonable about it; go away to the seaside and forget it. You're all nerves!"

"I'll do what you like, mother, so long as you don't send me away till after the Derby," the boy said.

"Send you away from where? Just from this house?"

"Yes," he said, gazing at her.

"Why, you curious child, what makes you care about this house so much, suddenly? I never knew you loved it."

He gazed at her without speaking. He had a secret within a secret, something he had not divulged, even to Bassett or to his Uncle Oscar.

But his mother, after standing undecided and a little bit sullen for some moments, said:

"Very well, then! Don't go to the seaside till after the Derby, if you don't wish it. But promise me you won't let your nerves go to pieces. Promise you won't think so much about horse-racing and events, as you call them!"

"Oh, no," said the boy casually. "I won't think much about them, mother. You needn't worry. I wouldn't worry, mother, if I were you."

"If you were me and I were you," said his mother, "I wonder what we should do!"

"But you know you needn't worry, mother, don't you?" the boy repeated.

"I should be awfully glad to know it," she said wearily.

"Oh, well, you can, you know. I mean, you ought to know you needn't worry," he insisted.

"Ought I? Then I'll see about it," she said.

Paul's secret of secrets was his wooden horse, that which had no name. Since he was emancipated from a nurse and a nursery-governess, he had had his rocking-horse removed to his own bedroom at the top of the house.

"Surely, you're too big for a rocking-horse!" his mother had remonstrated.

"Well, you see, mother, till I can have a real horse, I like to have some sort of animal about," had been his quaint answer.

"Do you feel he keeps you company?" she laughed.

"Oh, yes! He's very good, he always keeps me company, when I'm there," said Paul.

So the horse, rather shabby, stood in an arrested prance in the boy's bedroom.

The Derby was drawing near, and the boy grew more and more tense. He hardly heard what was spoken to him, he was very frail, and his eyes were really uncanny. His mother had sudden seizures of uneasiness about him. Sometimes, for half-an-hour, she would feel a sudden anxiety about him that was almost anguish. She wanted to rush to him at once, and know he was safe.

Two nights before the Derby, she was at a big party in town, when one of her rushes of anxiety about her boy, her first-born, gripped her heart till she could hardly speak. She fought with the feeling, might and main, for she believed in common sense. But it was too strong. She had to leave the dance and go downstairs to telephone to the country. The children's nursery-governess was terribly surprised and startled at being rung up in the night.

"Are the children all right, Miss Wilmot?"

"Oh, yes, they are quite all right."

"Master Paul? Is he all right?"

"He went to bed as right as a trivet. Shall I run up and look at him?"

"No," said Paul's mother reluctantly. "No! Don't trouble. It's all right. Don't sit up. We shall be home fairly soon." She did not want her son's privacy intruded upon.

"Very good," said the governess.

It was about one o'clock when Paul's mother and father drove up to their house. All was still. Paul's mother went to her room and slipped off her white fur cloak. She had told her maid not to wait up for her. She heard her husband downstairs, mixing a whisky-and-soda.

And then, because of the strange anxiety at her heart, she stole upstairs to her son's room. Noiselessly she went along the upper corridor. Was there a faint noise? What was it?

She stood, with arrested muscles, outside his door, listening. There was a strange, heavy, and yet not loud noise. Her heart stood still. It was a soundless noise, yet rushing and powerful. Something huge, in violent, hushed motion. What was it? What in God's name was it? She ought to know. She felt that she knew the noise. She knew what it was.

Yet she could not place it. She couldn't say what it was. And on and on it went, like a madness.

Softly, frozen with anxiety and fear, she turned the door-handle.

The room was dark. Yet in the space near the window, she heard and saw something plunging to and fro. She gazed in fear and amazement.

Then suddenly she switched on the light, and saw her son, in his green pajamas, madly surging on the rocking-horse. The blaze of light suddenly lit him up, as he urged the wooden horse, and lit her up, as she stood, blonde, in her dress of pale green and crystal, in the doorway.

"Paul!" she cried. "Whatever are you doing?"

"It's Malabar!" he screamed, in a powerful, strange voice. "It's Malabar."

His eyes blazed at her for one strange and senseless second, as he ceased urging his wooden horse. Then he fell with a crash to the ground, and she, all her tormented motherhood flooding upon her, rushed to gather him up.

But he was unconscious, and unconscious he remained, with some brain-fever. He talked and tossed, and his mother sat stonily by his side.

"Malabar! It's Malabar! Bassett, Bassett, I know! It's Malabar!"

So the child cried, trying to get up and urge the rocking-horse that gave him his inspiration.

"What does he mean by Malabar?" asked the heart-frozen mother.

"I don't know," said the father stonily.

"What does he mean by Malabar?" she asked her brother Oscar.

"It's one of the horses running for the Derby," was the answer.

And, in spite of himself, Oscar Cresswell spoke to Bassett, and himself put a thousand on Malabar: at fourteen to one.

The third day of the illness was critical: they were waiting for a change. The boy, with his rather long, curly hair, was tossing ceaselessly on the pillow. He neither slept nor regained consciousness, and his eyes were like blue stones. His mother sat, feeling her heart had gone, turned actually into a stone.

In the evening, Oscar Cresswell did not come, but Bassett sent a message, saying could he come up for one moment, just one moment? Paul's mother was very angry at the intrusion, but on second thought she agreed. The boy was the same. Perhaps Bassett might bring him to consciousness.

The gardener, a shortish fellow with a little brown mustache, and sharp little brown eyes, tiptoed into the room, touched his imaginary cap to Paul's mother, and stole to the bedside, staring with glittering, smallish eyes, at the tossing, dying child.

"Master Paul!" he whispered. "Master Paul! Malabar came in first all right, a clean win. I did as you told me. You've made over seventy thousand pounds, you have; you've got over eighty thousand. Malabar came in all right, Master Paul!"

"Malabar! Malabar! Did I say Malabar, mother? Did I say Malabar? Do you think I'm lucky, mother? I knew Malabar, didn't I? Over eighty thousand pounds! I call that lucky, don't you, mother? Over eighty thousand pounds! I knew, didn't I know I knew? Malabar came in all right. If I ride my horse till I'm sure, then I tell you, Bassett, you can go as high as you like. Did you go for all you were worth, Bassett?"

"I went a thousand on it, Master Paul."

"I never told you, mother, that if I can ride my horse, and get there, then I'm absolutely sure—oh, absolutely! Mother, did I ever tell you? I am lucky."

"No, you never did," said the mother.

But the boy died in the night.

And even as he lay dead, his mother heard her brother's voice saying to her: "My God, Hester, you're eighty-odd thousand to the good and a poor devil of a son to the bad. But, poor devil, poor devil, he's best gone out of a life where he rides his rocking-horse to find a winner."

William Faulkner *(1897–1962) was born in New Albany, Mississippi. He served as a pilot in the British Royal Air Force and spent much of the 1920's in New Orleans—sharing an apartment with Sherwood Anderson, contributing poems and articles to a local magazine, and writing a newspaper column, "Mirrors of Chartres Street." Faulkner's novels of this period—*Sartoris *(1929),* The Sound and the Fury *(1929),* As I Lay Dying *(1930)—dramatically recreate the history of northern Mississippi. Faulkner settled in the university town of Oxford, Mississippi, and after the publication of the sensational* Sanctuary *(1913) he made several trips to Hollywood for script writing.* Light in August *(1932),* Absalom, Absalom! *(1936), and the volume of stories* Go Down, Moses *(1942), are among his major works of the 1930's and 1940's. He received the Nobel Prize in 1950 and died shortly after the publication of his popular comic novel,* The Reivers.

Pantaloon in Black

WILLIAM FAULKNER

1.

He stood in the worn, faded clean overalls which Mannie herself had washed only a week ago, and heard the first clod stride the pine box. Soon he had one of the shovels himself, which in his hands (he was better than six feet and weighed better than two hundred pounds) resembled the toy shovel a child plays with at the shore, its half cubic foot of flung dirt no more than the light gout of sand the child's shovel would have flung. Another member of his sawmill gang touched his arm and said, "Lemme have hit, Rider." He didn't even falter. He released one hand in midstroke and flung it backward, striking the other across the chest, jolting him back a step, and restored the hand to the moving shovel, flinging the dirt with that effortless fury so that the mound seemed to be rising of its own volition, not built up from above but thrusting visibly upward out of the earth itself, until at last the grave, save for its rawness, resembled any other marked off without order about the barren plot by shards of pottery and broken bottles and old brick and other objects insignificant to sight but actually of a profound meaning and fatal to touch, which no white man could have read. Then he straightened up and with one hand flung the shovel quivering upright in the mound like a javelin and turned and began to walk away, walking on even when an old woman came out of the meager clump of his kin and friends and a few old people who had known him and his dead wife both since they were born, and grasped his forearm. She was his aunt. She had raised him. He could not remember his parents at all.

"Whar you gwine?" she said.

"Ah'm goan home," he said.

"You dont wants ter go back dar by yoself," she said. "You needs to eat. You come on home and eat."

"Ah'm goan home," he repeated, walking out from under her hand, his forearm like iron, as if the weight on it were no more than that of a fly, the other members of the mill gang whose head he was giving way quietly to let him pass. But before he reached the fence one of them overtook him; he did not need to be told it was his aunt's messenger.

"Wait, Rider," the other said. "We gots a jug in de bushes—" Then the other said what he had not intended to say, what he had never conceived of himself saying in circumstances like these, even though everybody knew it—the dead who either will not or cannot quit the earth yet although the flesh they once lived in has been returned to it, let the preachers tell and reiterate and affirm how they left it not only without regret but with joy, mounting toward glory: "You dont wants ter go back dar. She be wawkin yit."

He didn't pause, glancing down at the other, his eyes red at the inner corners in his high, slightly backtilted head. "Lemme lone, Acey," he said. "Doan mess wid me now," and went on, stepping over the three-strand wire fence without even breaking his stride, and crossed the road and entered the woods. It was middle dusk when he emerged from them and crossed the last field, stepping over that fence too in one stride, into the lane. It was empty at this hour of Sunday evening—no family in wagon, no rider, no walkers churchward to speak to him and carefully refrain from looking after him when he had passed—the pale, powder-light, powder-dry dust of August from which the long week's marks of hoof and wheel had been blotted by the strolling and unhurried Sunday shoes, with somewhere beneath them, vanished but not gone, fixed and held in the annealing dust, the narrow, splay-toed prints of his wife's bare feet where on Saturday afternoons she would walk to the commissary to buy their next week's supplies while he took his bath; himself, his own prints, setting the period now as he strode on, moving almost as fast as a smaller man could have trotted, his body breasting the air her body had vacated, his eyes touching the objects—post and tree and field and house and hill—her eyes had lost.

The house was the last one in the lane, not his but rented from Carothers Edmonds, the local white landowner. But the rent was paid promptly in advance, and even in just six months he had refloored the porch and rebuilt and roofed the kitchen, doing the work himself on Saturday afternoon and Sunday with his wife helping him, and bought the stove. Because he made good money: sawmilling ever since he began to get his growth at fifteen and sixteen and now, at twenty-four, head of the timber gang itself because the gang he headed moved a third again as much timber between sunup and sundown as any other moved, handling himself at times out of the vanity of his own strength logs which ordinarily two men would have handled with canthooks; never without work even in the old days when he had not actually needed the money, when a lot of what he wanted, needed perhaps, didn't cost money—the women bright and dark and for all purposes nameless he didn't need to buy and it didn't matter to him what he wore and there was always food for him at any hour of day or night in the house of his aunt who didn't even want to take the two dollars he gave her each Saturday—so there had been only the Saturday and Sunday dice and whiskey that had to be paid for until that day six months ago when he saw Mannie, whom he had known all his life, for the first time and said to himself: "Ah'm thu wid all dat," and they married and he rented the cabin from Carothers Edmonds and built a fire on the hearth on their wedding night as the tale told how Uncle Lucas Beauchamp, Edmonds' oldest tenant, had done on his forty-five years ago and which had burned ever since; and he would rise and dress and eat his breakfast by lamplight to walk the four miles to the mill by sunup, and exactly one hour after sundown he would enter the house again, five days a week, until Saturday.

Then the first hour would not have passed noon when he would mount the steps and knock, not on post or doorframe but on the underside of the gallery roof itself, and enter and ring the bright cascade of silver dollars onto the scrubbed table in the kitchen where his dinner simmered on the stove and the galvanized tub of hot water and the baking powder can of soft soap and the towel made of scalded flour sacks sewn together and his clean overalls and shirt waited, and Mannie would gather up the money and walk the half-mile to the commissary and buy their next week's supplies and bank the rest of the money in Edmonds' safe and return and they would eat once again without haste or hurry after five days—the sidemeat, the greens, the cornbread, the buttermilk from the well-house, the cake which she baked every Saturday now that she had a stove to bake in.

But when he put his hand on the gate it seemed to him suddenly that there was nothing beyond it. The house had never been his anyway, but now even the new planks and sills and shingles, the hearth and stove and bed, were all a part of the memory of somebody else, so that he stopped in the half-open gate and said aloud, as though he had gone to sleep in one place and then waked suddenly to find himself in another: "Whut's Ah doin hyar?" before he went on. Then he saw the dog. He had forgotten it. He remembered neither seeing nor hearing it since it began to howl just before dawn yesterday—a big dog, a hound with a strain of mastiff from somewhere (he had told Mannie a month after they married: "Ah needs a big dawg. You's de onliest least thing whut ever kep up wid me one day, leff alone fo weeks.") coming out from beneath the gallery and approaching, not running but seeming rather to drift across the dusk until it stood lightly against his leg, its head raised until the tips of his fingers just touched it, facing the house and making no sound; whereupon, as if the animal controlled it, had lain guardian before it during his absence and only this instant relinquished, the shell of planks and shingles facing him solidified, filled, and for the moment he believed that he could not possibly enter it. "But Ah needs to eat," he said. "Us bofe needs to eat," he said, moving on though the dog did not follow until he turned and cursed it. "Come on hyar!" he said. "Whut you skeered of? She lacked you too, same as me," and they mounted the steps and crossed the porch and entered the house—the dusk-filled single room where all those six months were now crammed and crowded into one instant of time until there was no space left for air to breathe, crammed and crowded about the hearth where the fire which was to have lasted to the end of them, before which in the days before he was able to buy the stove he would enter after his four-mile walk from the mill and find her, the shape of her narrow back and haunches squatting, one narrow spread hand shielding her face from the blaze over which the other hand held the skillet, had already fallen to a dry, light soilure of dead ashes when the sun rose yesterday—and himself standing there while the last of light died about the strong and indomitable beating of his heart and the deep steady arch and collapse of his chest which walking fast over the rough going of woods and fields had not increased and standing still in the quiet and fading room had not slowed down.

Then the dog left him. The light pressure went off his flank; he heard the click and hiss of its claws on the wooden floor as it surged away and he thought at first that it was fleeing. But it stopped just outside the front door, where he could see it now, and the upfling of its head as the howl began, and then he saw her too. She was standing in the kitchen door, looking at him. He didn't move. He didn't breathe nor speak until he knew his voice would be all right, his face fixed too not to alarm her. "Mannie," he said. "Hit's awright. Ah aint afraid." Then he took a step toward her, slow, not even raising his hand yet, and stopped. Then he took another step. But this time as soon as he moved she began to fade. He stopped at once, not breathing again, motionless, willing his eyes to see that she had stopped too. But she had not stopped. She was fading, going. "Wait," he said, talking as sweet as he had ever heard his voice speak to a woman: "Den lemme go wid you, honey." But she was going. She was going fast now, he could actually feel between them the insuperable barrier of that very strength which could handle alone a log which would have taken any two other men to handle, of the blood and bones and flesh too strong, invincible for life, having learned at least once with his own eyes how tough, even in sudden and violent death, not a young man's bones and flesh perhaps but the will of that bone and flesh to remain alive, actually was.

Then she was gone. He walked through the door where she had been standing, and went to the stove. He did not light the lamp. He needed no light. He had set the stove up himself and built the shelves for the dishes, from among which he took two plates by feel and from the pot sitting cold on the cold stove he ladled onto the plates the food which his aunt had brought yesterday and of which he had eaten yesterday though now he did not remember when he had eaten it nor what it was, and carried the plates to the scrubbed bare table beneath the single small fading window and drew two chairs up and sat down, waiting again until he knew his voice would be what he wanted it to be. "Come on hyar, now," he said roughly. "Come on hyar and eat yo supper. Ah aint gonter have no—" and ceased, looking down at his plate, breathing the strong, deep pants, his chest arching and collapsing until he stopped it presently and held himself motionless for perhaps a half minute, and raised a spoonful of the cold and glutinous peas to his mouth. The congealed and lifeless mass seemed to bounce on contact with his lips. Not even warmed from mouth-heat, peas and spoon spattered and rang upon the plate; his chair crashed backward and he was standing, feeling the muscles of his jaw beginning to drag his mouth open, tugging upward the top half of his head. But he stopped that too before it became sound, holding himself again while he rapidly scraped the food from his plate onto the other and took it up and left the kitchen, crossed the other room and the gallery and set the plate on the bottom step and went on toward the gate.

The dog was not there, but it overtook him within the first half mile. There was a moon then, their two shadows flitting broken and intermittent among the trees or slanted long and intact across the slope of pasture or old abandoned fields upon the hills, the man moving almost as fast as a horse could have moved over that ground, altering his course each time a lighted window came in sight, the dog trotting at heel while their shadows shortened to the moon's curve until at last they trod them and the last far lamp had vanished and the shadows began to lengthen on the other hand, keeping to heel even when a rabbit burst from almost beneath the man's foot, then lying in the gray of dawn beside the man's prone body, beside the labored heave and collapse of the chest, the loud harsh snoring which sounded not like groans of pain but like someone engaged without arms in prolonged single combat.

When he reached the mill there was nobody there but the fireman—an older man just turning from the woodpile, watching quietly as he crossed the clearing, striding as if he were going to walk not only through the boiler shed but through (or over) the boiler too, the overalls which had been clean yesterday now draggled and soiled and drenched to the knees with dew, the cloth cap flung onto the side of his head, hanging peak downward over his ear as he always wore it, the whites of his eyes rimmed with red and with something urgent and strained about them. "Whar yo bucket?" he said. But before the fireman could answer he had stepped past him and lifted the polished lard pail down from a nail in a post. "Ah just wants a biscuit," he said.

"Eat hit all," the fireman said. "Ah'll eat outen de yuthers' buckets at dinner. Den you gawn home and go to bed. You dont looks good."

"Ah aint come hyar to look," he said, sitting on the ground, his back against the post, the open pail between his knees, cramming the food into his mouth with his hands, wolfing it—peas again, also gelid and cold, a fragment of yesterday's Sunday fried chicken, a few rough chunks of this morning's fried sidemeat, a biscuit the size of a child's cap—indiscriminate, tasteless. The rest of the crew was gathering now, with voices and sounds of movement outside the boiler shed; presently the white foreman rode into the clearing on a horse. He did not look up, setting the empty pail aside, rising, looking at no one, and went to the branch and lay on his stomach and lowered his face to the water, drawing the water into himself with the same deep, strong, troubled inhalations that he had snored with, or as when he had stood in the empty house at dusk yesterday, trying to get air.

Then the trucks were rolling. The air pulsed with the rapid beating of the exhaust and the whine and clang of the saw, the trucks rolling one by one up to the skidway, he mounting the trucks in turn, to stand balanced on the load he freed, knocking the chocks out and casting loose the shackle chains and with his cant-hook squaring the sticks of cypress and gum and oak one by one to the incline and holding them until the next two men of his gang were ready to receive and guide them, until the discharge of each truck became one long rumbling roar punctuated by grunting shouts and, as the morning grew and the sweat came, chanted phrases of song tossed back and forth. He did not sing with them. He rarely ever did, and this morning might have been no different from any other—himself man-height again above the heads which carefully refrained from looking at him, stripped to the waist now, the shirt removed and the overalls knotted about his hips by the suspender straps, his upper body bare except for the handkerchief about his neck and the cap clapped and clinging somehow over his right ear, the mounting sun sweat-glinted steel-blue on the midnight-colored bunch and slip of muscles until the whistle blew for noon and he said to the two men at the head of the skidway: "Look out. Git out de way," and rode the log down the incline, balanced erect upon it in short rapid backward-running steps above the headlong thunder.

His aunt's husband was waiting for him—an old man, as tall as he was, but lean, almost frail, carrying a tin pail in one hand and a covered plate in the other; they too sat in the shade beside the branch a short distance from where the others were opening their dinner pails. The bucket contained a fruit jar of buttermilk packed in a clean damp towsack. The covered dish was a peach pie, still warm. "She baked hit fer you dis mawin," the uncle said. "She say fer you to come home." He didn't answer, bent forward a little, his elbows on his knees, holding the pie in both hands, wolfing at it, the syrupy filling smearing and trickling down his chin, blinking rapidly as he chewed, the whites of his eyes covered a little more by the creeping red. "Ah went to yo house last night, but you want dar. She sont me. She wants you to come on home. She kept de lamp burnin all last night fer you."

"Ah'm awright," he said.

"You aint awright. De Lawd guv, and He tuck away. Put yo faith and trust in Him. And she kin help you."

"Whut faith and trust?" he said. "Whut Mannie ever done ter Him? Whut He wanter come messin wid me and——"

"Hush!" the old man said. "Hush!"

Then the trucks were rolling again. Then he could stop needing to invent to himself reasons for his breathing, until after a while he began to believe he had forgot about breathing since now he could not hear it himself above the steady thunder of the rolling logs; whereupon as soon as he found himself believing he had forgotten it, he knew that he had not, so that instead of tipping the final log onto the skidway he stood up and cast his cant-hook away as if it were a burnt match and in the dying reverberation of the last log's rumbling descent he vaulted down between the two slated tracks of the skid, facing the log which still lay on the truck. He had done it before—taken a log from the truck onto his hands, balanced, and turned with it and tossed it onto the skidway, but never with a stick of this size, so that in a complete cessation of all sound save the pulse of the exhaust and the light free-running whine of the disengaged saw since every eye there, even that of the white foreman, was upon him, he nudged the log to the edge of the truckframe and squatted and set his palms against the underside of it. For a time there was no movement at all. It was as if the unrational and inanimate wood had invested, mesmerized the man with some of its own primal inertia. Then a voice said quietly: "He got hit. Hit's off de truck," and they saw the crack and gap of air, watching the infinitesimal straightening of the braced legs until the knees locked, the movement mounting infinitesimally through the belly's insuck, the arch of the chest, the neck cords, lifting the lip from the white clench of teeth in passing, drawing the whole head backward and only the bloodshot fixity of the eyes impervious to it, moving on up the arms and the straightening elbows until the balanced log was higher than his head. "Only he aint gonter turn wid dat un," the same voice said. "And when he try to put hit back on de truck, hit gonter kill him." But none of them moved. Then—there was no gathering of supreme effort—the log seemed to leap suddenly backward over his head of its own volition, spinning, crashing and thundering down the incline; he turned and stepped over the slanting track in one stride and walked through them as they gave way and went on across the clearing toward the woods even though the foreman called after him: "Rider!" and again: "You, Rider!"

At sundown he and the dog were in the river swamp four miles away—another clearing, itself not much larger than a room, a hut, a hovel partly of planks and partly of canvas, an unshaven white man standing in the door beside which a shotgun leaned, watching him as he approached, his hand extended with four silver dollars on the palm. "Ah wants a jug," he said.

"A jug?" the white man said. "You mean a pint. This is Monday. Aint you all running this week?"

"Ah laid off," he said. "Whar's my jug?" waiting, looking at nothing apparently, blinking his bloodshot eyes rapidly in his high, slightly back-tilted head, then turning, the jug hanging from his crooked middle finger against his leg, at which moment the white man looked suddenly and sharply at his eyes as though seeing them for the first time—the eyes which had been strained and urgent this morning and which now seemed to be without vision too and in which no white showed at all—and said,

"Here. Gimme that jug. You dont need no gallon. I'm going to give you that pint, give it to you. Then you get out of here and stay out.

Dont come back until—" Then the white man reached and grasped the jug, whereupon the other swung it behind him, sweeping his other arm up and out so that it struck the white man across the chest.

"Look out, white folks," he said. "Hit's mine. Ah done paid you."

The white man cursed him. "No you aint. Here's your money. Put that jug down, nigger."

"Hit's mine," he said, his voice quiet, gentle even, his face quiet save for the rapid blinking of the red eyes. "Ah done paid for hit," turning on, turning his back on the man and the gun both, and recrossed the clearing to where the dog waited beside the path to come to heel again. They moved rapidly on between the close walls of impenetrable cane-stalks which gave a sort of blondness to the twilight and possessed something of that oppression, that lack of room to breathe in, which the walls of his house had had. But this time, instead of fleeing it, he stopped and raised the jug and drew the cob stopper from the fierce duskreek of uncured alcohol and drank, gulping the liquid solid and cold as ice water, without either taste or heat until he lowered the jug and the air got in. "Hah," he said. "Dat's right. Try me. Try me, big boy. Ah gots something hyar now dat kin whup you."

And, once free of the bottom's unbreathing blackness, there was the moon again, his long shadow and that of the lifted jug slanting away as he drank and then held the jug poised, gulping the silver air into his throat until he could breathe again, speaking to the jug: "Come on now. You always claim you's a better man den me. Come on now. Prove it." He drank again, swallowing the chill liquid tamed of taste or heat either while the swallowing lasted, feeling it flow solid and cold with fire, past then enveloping the strong steady panting of his lungs until they too ran suddenly free as his moving body ran in the silver solid wall of air he breasted. And he was all right, his striding shadow and the trotting one of the dog travelling swift as those of two clouds along the hill; the long cast of his motionless shadow and that of the lifted jug slanting across the slope as he watched the frail figure of his aunt's husband toiling up the hill.

"Dey tole me at de mill you was gone," the old man said. "Ah knowed whar to look. Come home, son. Dat ar cant help you."

"Hit done awready hope me," he said. "Ah'm awready home. Ah'm snakebit now and pizen cant hawm me."

"Den stop and see her. Leff her look at you. Dat's all she axes: just leff her look at you—" But he was already moving. "Wait!" the old man cried. "Wait!"

"You cant keep up," he said, speaking into the silver air, breasting aside the silver solid air which began to flow past him almost as fast as it would have flowed past a moving horse. The faint frail voice was already lost in the night's infinitude, his shadow and that of the dog scudding the free miles, the deep strong panting of his chest running free as air now because he was all right.

Then, drinking, he discovered suddenly that no more of the liquid was entering his mouth. Swallowing, it was no longer passing down his throat, his throat and mouth filled now with a solid and unmoving column which without reflex or revulsion sprang, columnar and intact and still retaining the mold of his gullet, outward glinting in the moonlight, splintering, vanishing into the myriad murmur of the dewed grass. He drank again. Again his throat merely filled solidly until two icy rills ran from his mouth-corners; again the intact column sprang silvering, glinting, shivering, while he panted the chill of air into his throat, the jug poised before his mouth while he spoke to it: "Awright. Ah'm ghy try you again. Soon as you makes up yo mind to stay whar I puts you, Ah'll leff you alone." He drank, filling his gullet for the third time and lowered the jug one instant ahead of the bright intact repetition, panting, indrawing the cool of air until he could breathe. He stoppered the cob carefully back into the jug and stood, panting, blinking, the long cast of his solitary shadow slanting away across the hill and beyond, across the mazy infinitude of all the night-bound earth. "Awright," he said. "Ah just misread de sign wrong. Hit's done done me all de help Ah needs. Ah'm awright now. Ah doan needs no mo of hit."

He could see the lamp in the window as he crossed the pasture, passing the black-and-silver yawn of the sandy ditch where he had played as a boy with empty snuff-tins and rusted harness-buckles and fragments of trace-chains and now and then an actual wheel, passing the garden patch where he had hoed in the spring days while his aunt stood sentry over him from the kitchen window, crossing the grassless yard in whose dust he had sprawled and crept before he learned to walk. He entered the house, the room, the light itself, and stopped in the door, his head back-tilted a little as if he could not see, the jug hanging from his crooked finger, against his leg. "Unc Alec say you wanter see me," he said.

"Not just to see you," his aunt said. "To come home, whar we kin help you."

"Ah'm awright," he said. "Ah doan needs no help."

"No," she said. She rose from the chair and came and grasped his arm as she had grasped it yesterday at the grave. Again, as on yesterday, the forearm was like iron under her hand. "No! When Alec come back and tole me how you had wawked off de mill and de sun not half down, Ah knowed why and whar. And dat cant help you."

"Hit done awready hope me. Ah'm awright now."

"Dont lie to me," she said. "You aint never lied to me. Dont lie to me now."

Then he said it. It was his own voice, without either grief or amazement, speaking quietly out of the tremendous panting of his chest which in a moment now would begin to strain at the walls of this room too. But he would be gone in a moment.

"Nome," he said, "Hit aint done me no good."

"And hit cant! Cant nothing help you but Him! Ax Him! Tole Him about hit! He wants to hyar you and help you!"

"Efn He God, Ah dont needs to tole Him. Efn He God, He awready know hit. Awright. Hyar Ah is. Leff Him come down hyar and do me some good."

"On yo knees!" she cried. "On yo knees and ax Him!" But it was not his knees on the floor, it was his feet. And for a space he could hear her feet too on the planks of the hall behind him and her voice crying after him from the door: "Spoot! Spoot!"—crying after him across the moondappled yard the name he had gone by in his childhood and adolescence, before the men he worked with and the bright dark nameless women he had taken in course and forgotten until he saw Mannie that day and said, "Ah'm thu wid all dat," began to call him Rider.

It was just after midnight when he reached the mill. The dog was gone now. This time he could not remember when nor where. At first he seemed to remember hurling the empty jug at it. But later the jug was still in his hand and it was not empty, although each time he drank now the two icy runnels streamed from his mouth-corners, sopping his shirt and overalls until he walked constantly in the fierce chill of the liquid tamed now of flavor and heat and odor too even when the swallowing ceased. "Sides that," he said, "Ah wouldn't thow nothin at him. Ah mout kick him efn he needed hit and was close enough. But Ah wouldn't ruint no dog chunkin hit."

The jug was still in his hand when he entered the clearing and paused among the mute soaring of the moon-blond lumber-stacks. He stood in the middle now of the unimpeded shadow which he was treading again as he had trod it last night, swaying a little, blinking about at the stacked lumber, the skidway, the piled logs waiting for tomorrow, the boiler-shed all quiet and blanched in the moon. And then it was all right. He was moving again. But he was not moving, he was drinking, the liquid cold and swift and tasteless and requiring no swallowing, so that he could not tell if it were going down inside or outside. But it was all right. And now he was moving, the jug gone now and he didn't know the when or where of that either. He crossed the clearing and entered the boiler shed and went on through it, crossing the junctureless backloop of time's trepan, to the door of the tool-room, the faint glow of the lantern beyond the plank-joints, the surge and fall of living shadow, the mutter of voices, the mute click and scutter of the dice, his hand loud on the barred door, his voice loud too: "Open hit. Hit's me. Ah'm snakebit and bound to die."

Then he was through the door and inside the tool-room. They were the same faces—three members of his timber gang, three or four others of the mill crew, the white night-watchman with the heavy pistol in his hip pocket and the small heap of coins and worn bills on the floor before him, one who was called Rider and was Rider standing above the squatting circle, swaying a little, blinking, the dead muscles of his face shaped into smiling while the white man stared up at him. "Make room, gamblers," he said. "Make room. Ah'm snakebit and de pizen cant hawm me."

"You're drunk," the white man said. "Get out of here. One of you niggers open the door and get him out of here."

"Dass awright, boss-man," he said, his voice equable, his face still fixed in the faint rigid smiling beneath the blinking of the red eyes; "Ah aint drunk. Ah just cant wawk straight fer dis yar money weighin me down."

Now he was kneeling too, the other six dollars of his last week's pay on the floor before him, blinking, still smiling at the face of the white man opposite, then, still smiling, he watched the dice pass from hand to hand around the circle as the white man covered the bets, watching the soiled and palm-worn money in front of the white man gradually and steadily increase, watching the white man cast and win two doubled bets in succession then lose one for twenty-five cents, the dice coming to him at last, the cupped snug clicking of them in his fist. He spun a coin into the center.

"Shoots a dollar," he said, and cast, and watched the white man pick up the dice and flip them back to him. "Ah lets hit lay," he said. "Ah'm snakebit. Ah kin pass wid anything," and cast, and this time one of the Negroes flipped the dice back. "Ah lets hit lay," he said, and cast, and moved as the white man moved, catching the white man's wrist before his hand reached the dice, the two of them squatting, facing each other above the dice and the money, his left hand grasping the white man's wrist, his face still fixed in the rigid and deadened smiling, his voice equable, almost deferential: "Ah kin pass even wid miss-outs. But dese hyar yuther boys—" until the white man's hand sprang open and the second pair of dice clattered onto the floor beside the first two and the white man wrenched free and sprang up and back and reached the hand backward toward the pocket where the pistol was.

The razor hung between his shoulder-blades from a loop of cotton string round his neck inside his shirt. The same motion of the hand which brought the razor forward over his shoulder flipped the blade open and freed it from the cord, the blade opening on until the back edge of it lay across the knuckles of his fist, his thumb pressing the handle into his closing fingers, so that in the second before the half-drawn pistol exploded he actually struck at the white man's throat not with the blade but with a sweeping blow of his fist, following through in the same motion so that not even the first jet of blood touched his hand or arm.

2.

After it was over—it didn't take long; they found the prisoner on the following day, hanging from the bell-rope in a Negro schoolhouse about two miles from the sawmill, and the coroner had pronounced his verdict of death at the hands of a person or persons unknown and surrendered the body to its next of kin all within five minutes—the sheriff's deputy who had been officially in charge of the business was telling his wife about it. They were in the kitchen. His wife was cooking supper. The deputy had been out of bed and in motion ever since the jail delivery shortly before midnight of yesterday and had covered considerable ground since, and he was spent now from lack of sleep and hurried food at hurried and curious hours and, sitting in a chair beside the stove, a little hysterical too.

"Them damn niggers," he said. "I swear to godfrey, it's a wonder we have as little trouble with them as we do. Because why? Because they aint human. They look like a man and they walk on their hind legs like a man, and they can talk and you can understand them and you think they are understanding you, at least now and then. But when it comes to the normal human feelings and sentiments of human beings, they might just as well be a damn herd of wild buffaloes. Now you take this one today——"

"I wish you would," his wife said harshly. She was a stout woman, handsome once, graying now and with a neck definitely too short, who looked not harried at all but composed in fact, only choleric. Also, she had attended a club rook-party that afternoon and had won the first, the fifty-cent, prize until another member had insisted on a recount of the scores and the ultimate throwing out of one entire game. "Take him out of my kitchen, anyway. You sheriffs! Sitting around that courthouse all day long, talking. It's no wonder two or three men can walk in and take prisoners out from under your very noses. They would take your chairs and desks and window sills too if you ever got your feet and backsides off of them that long."

"It's more of them Birdsongs than just two or three," the deputy said. "There's forty-two active votes in that connection. Me and Maydew taken the poll-list and counted them one day. But listen—" The wife turned from the stove, carrying a dish. The deputy snatched his feet rapidly out of the way as she passed him, passed almost over him, and went into the dining room. The deputy raised his voice a little to carry the increased distance: "His wife dies on him. All right. But does he grieve? He's the biggest and busiest man at the funeral. Grabs a shovel before they even got the box into the grave they tell me, and starts throwing dirt onto her faster than a slip scraper could have done it. But that's all right—" His wife came back. He moved his feet again and altered his voice again to the altered range: "—maybe that's how he felt about her. There aint any law against a man rushing his wife into the ground, provided he never had nothing to do with rushing her to the cemetery too. But here the next day he's the first man back at work except the fireman, getting back to the mill before the fireman had his fire going, let alone steam up; five minutes earlier and he could even have helped the fireman wake Birdsong up so Birdsong could go home and go back to bed again, or he could even have cut Birdsong's throat then and saved everybody trouble.

"So he comes to work, the first man on the job, when McAndrews and everybody else expected him to take the day off since even a nigger couldn't want no better excuse for a holiday than he had just buried his wife, when a white man would have took the day off out of pure respect no matter how he felt about his wife, when even a little child would have had sense enough to take a day off when he would still get paid for it too. But not him. The first man there, jumping from one log truck to another before the starting whistle quit blowing even, snatching up ten-foot cypress logs by himself and throwing them around like matches. And then, when everybody had finally decided that that's the way to take him, the way he wants to be took, he walks off the job in the middle of the afternoon without by-your-leave or much obliged or goodbye to McAndrews or nobody else, gets himself a whole gallon of bust-skull white-mule whisky, comes straight back to the mill and to the same crap game where Birdsong has been running crooked dice on them mill niggers for fifteen years, goes straight to the same game where he has been peacefully losing a probably steady average ninety-nine percent of his pay ever since he got big enough to read the spots on them miss-out dice, and cuts Birdsong's throat clean to the neckbone five minutes later." The wife passed him again and went to the dining room. Again he drew his feet back and raised his voice:

"So me and Maydew go out there. Not that we expected to do any good, as he had probably passed Jackson, Tennessee, about daylight; and besides, the simplest way to find him would be just to stay close behind them Birdsong boys. Of course there wouldn't be nothing hardly worth bringing back to town after they did find him, but it would close the case. So it's just by the merest chance that we go by his house; I dont even remember why we went now, but we did; and there he is. Sitting behind the barred front door with a open razor on one knee and a loaded shotgun on the other? No. He was asleep. A big pot of field peas et clean empty on the stove, and him laying in the back yard asleep in the broad sun with just his head under the edge of the porch in the shade and a dog that looked like a cross between a bear and a Polled Angus steer yelling fire and murder from the back door. And we wake him and he sets up and says, 'Awright, white folks. Ah done it. Jest dont lock me up,' and Maydew says, 'Mr. Birdsong's kinfolks aint going to lock you up neither. You'll have plenty of fresh air when they get hold of you," and he says, 'Ah done it. Jest dont lock me up'—advising, instructing the sheriff not to lock him up; he done it all right and it's too bad but it aint convenient for him to be cut off from the fresh air at the moment. So we loaded him into the car, when here come the old woman—his ma or aunt or something—panting up the road at a dog-trot, wanting to come with us too, and Maydew trying to explain to her what would maybe happen to her too if them Birdsong kin catches us before we can get him locked up, only she is coming anyway, and like Maydew says, her being in the car too might be a good thing if the Birdsongs did happen to run into us, because after all interference with the law cant be condoned even if the Birdsong connection did carry that beat for Maydew last summer.

"So we brought her along too and got him to town and into the jail all right and turned him over to Ketcham and Ketcham taken him on upstairs and the old woman coming too, right on up to the cell, telling Ketcham, 'Ah tried to raise him right. He was a good boy. He aint never been in no trouble till now. He will suffer for what he done. But dont let the white folks get him,' until Ketcham says, 'You and him ought to thought of that before he started barbering white men without using no lather first.' So he locked them both up in the cell because he felt like Maydew did, that her being in there with him might be a good influence on the Birdsong boys if anything started if he should happen to be running for sheriff or something when Maydew's term was up. So Ketcham come on back downstairs and pretty soon the chain gang come in and went on up to the bull pen and he thought things had settled down for a while when all of a sudden he begun to hear the yelling, not howling: yelling, though there wasn't no words in it, and he grabbed his pistol and run back upstairs to the bull pen where the chain gang was and Ketcham could see into the cell where the old woman was kind of squinched down in one corner and where that nigger had done tore that iron cot clean out of the floor it was bolted to and was standing in the middle of the cell, holding the cot over his head like it was a baby's cradle, yelling, and says to the old woman, 'Ah aint goan hurt you,' and throws the cot against the wall and comes and grabs holt of that steel barred door and rips it out of the wall, bricks hinges and all, and walks out of the cell toting the door over his head like it was a gauze window-screen, hollering, "It's awright. It's awright. Ah aint trying to git away.'

"Of course Ketcham could have shot him right there, but like he said, if it wasn't going to be the law, then them Birdsong boys ought to have the first lick at him. So Ketcham dont shoot. Instead, he jumps in behind where them chain-gang niggers was kind of backed off from that steel door, hollering, 'Grab him! Throw him down!' except the niggers hung back at first too until Ketcham gets in where he can kick the ones he can reach, batting at the others with the flat of the pistol until they rush him. And Ketcham says that for a full minute that nigger would grab them as they come in and fling them clean across the room like they was rag dolls, saying, 'Ah aint trying to git out. Ah aint tryin to git out,' until at last they pulled him down—a big mass of nigger heads and arms and legs boiling around on the floor and even then Ketcham says every now and then a nigger would come flying out and go sailing through the air across the room, spraddled out like a flying squirrel and with his eyes sticking out like car headlights, until at last they had him down and Ketcham went in and begun peeling away niggers until he could see him laying there under the pile of them, laughing, with tears big as glass marbles running across his face and down past his ears and making a kind of popping sound on the floor like somebody dropping bird eggs, laughing and laughing and saying, 'Hit look lack Ah just cant quit thinking. Look lack Ah just cant quit.' And what do you think of that?"

"I think if you eat any supper in this house you'll do it in the next five minutes," his wife said from the dining room. "I'm going to clear this table then and I'm going to the picture show."

Jorge Luis Borges *(1899–   ), the prolific Argentinian poet, critic, and translator, was born in Buenos Aires and educated abroad in Geneva and at Cambridge University. After frequent travels in Spain, he returned home to collaborate on literary and philosophical journals and to write poetry, first collected in* Fervor de Buenos Aires *(1923). Borges became a librarian in 1938 and, with the fall of Juan Peron's government, was named Director of the National Library in 1955. In 1956 he was appointed professor of English and North American literature at the University of Buenos Aires and has lectured widely since. The multilingual Borges has translated Gide, Kafka, Whitman, Melville, Faulkner, and Virginia Woolf into Spanish. Many of his own works are now available in English, including* Ficciones, *short stories originally published in 1945 which received the grand prize of the Argentine Writers' Association. In 1961 he shared the International Publishers' Prize with Samuel Beckett.*

The Circular Ruins

JORGE LUIS BORGES

And if he left off dreaming about you. . . .
Through the Looking-Glass, IV

Nobody saw him come ashore in the encompassing night, nobody saw the bamboo craft run aground in the sacred mud, but within a few days everyone knew that the quiet man had come from the south and that his home was among the numberless villages upstream on the steep slopes of the mountain, where the Zend language is barely tainted by Greek and where lepers are rare. The fact is that the gray man pressed his lips to the mud, scrambled up the bank without parting (perhaps without feeling) the brushy thorns that tore his flesh, and dragged himself, faint and bleeding, to the circular opening watched over by a stone tiger, or horse, which once was the color of fire and is now the color of ash. This opening is a temple which was destroyed ages ago by flames, which the swampy wilderness later desecrated, and whose god no longer receives the reverence of men. The stranger laid himself down at the foot of the image.

Wakened by the sun high overhead, he noticed—somehow without amazement—that his wounds had healed. He shut his pale eyes and slept again, not because of weariness but because he willed it. He knew that this temple was the place he needed for his unswerving purpose; he knew that downstream the encroaching trees had also failed to choke the ruins of another auspicious temple with its own fire-ravaged, dead gods; he knew that his first duty was to sleep. Along about midnight, he was awakened by the forlorn call of a bird. Footprints, some figs, and a water jug told him that men who lived nearby had looked on his sleep with a kind of awe and either sought his protection or else were in dread of his witchcraft. He felt the chill of fear and searched the crumbling walls for a burial niche, where he covered himself over with leaves he had never seen before.

His guiding purpose, though it was supernatural, was not impossible. He wanted to dream a man; he wanted to dream him down to the last detail and project him into the world of reality. This mystical aim had taxed the whole range of his mind. Had anyone asked him his own name or anything about his life before then, he would not have known what to answer. This forsaken, broken temple suited him because it held few visible things, and also because the neighboring villagers would look after his frugal needs. The rice and fruit of their offerings were nourishment enough for his body, whose one task was to sleep and to dream.

At the outset, his dreams were chaotic; later on, they were of a dialectic nature. The stranger dreamed himself at the center of a circular amphitheater which in some way was also the burnt-out temple. Crowds of silent disciples exhausted the tiers of seats; the faces of the farthest of them hung centuries away from him and at a height of the stars, but their features were clear and exact. The man lectured on anatomy, cosmography, and witchcraft. The faces listened, bright and eager, and did their best to answer sensibly, as if they felt the importance of his questions, which would raise one of them out of an existence as a shadow and place him in the real world. Whether asleep or awake, the man pondered the answers of his phantoms and, not letting himself be misled by imposters, divined in certain of their quandaries a growing intelligence. He was in search of a soul worthy of taking a place in the world.

After nine or ten nights he realized, feeling bitter over it, that nothing could be expected from those pupils who passively accepted his teaching but that he might, however, hold hopes for those who from time to time hazarded reasonable doubts about what he taught. The former, although they deserved love and affection, could never become real; the latter, in their dim way, were already real. One evening (now his evenings were also given over to sleeping, now he was only awake for an hour or two at dawn) he dismissed his vast dream-school forever and kept a single disciple. He was a quiet, sallow, and at times rebellious young man with sharp features akin to those of his dreamer. The sudden disappearance of his fellow pupils did not disturb him for very long, and his progress, at the end of a few private lessons, amazed his teacher. Nonetheless, a catastrophe intervened. One morning, the man emerged from his sleep as from a sticky wasteland, glanced up at the faint evening light, which at first he confused with the dawn, and realized that he had not been dreaming. All that night and the next day, the hideous lucidity of insomnia weighed down on him. To tire himself out he tried to explore the surrounding forest, but all he managed, there in a thicket of hemlocks, were some snatches of broken sleep, fleetingly tinged with visions of a crude and worthless nature. He tried to reassemble his school, and barely had he uttered a few brief words of counsel when the whole class went awry and vanished. In his almost endless wakefulness, tears of anger stung his old eyes.

He realized that, though he may penetrate all the riddles of the higher and lower orders, the task of shaping the senseless and dizzying stuff of dreams is the hardest that a man can attempt—much harder than weaving a rope of sand or of coining the faceless wind. He realized that an initial failure was to be expected. He then swore he would forget the populous vision which in the beginning had led him astray, and he sought another method. Before attempting it, he spent a month rebuilding the strength his fever had consumed. He gave up all thoughts of dreaming and almost at once managed to sleep a reasonable part of the day. The few times he dreamed during this period he did not dwell on his dreams. Before taking up his task again, he waited until the moon was a perfect circle. Then, in the evening, he cleansed himself in the waters of the river, worshiped the gods of the planets, uttered the prescribed syllables of an all-powerful name, and slept. Almost at once, he had a dream of a beating heart.

He dreamed it throbbing, warm, secret. It was the size of a closed fist, a darkish red in the dimness of a human body still without a face or sex. With anxious love he dreamed it for fourteen lucid nights. Each night he perceived it more clearly. He did not touch it, but limited himself to witnessing it, to observing it, to correcting it now and then with a look. He felt it, he lived it from different distances and from many angles. On the fourteenth night he touched the pulmonary artery with a finger and then the whole heart, inside and out. The examination satisfied him. For one night he deliberately did not dream; after that he went back to the heart again, invoked the name of a planet, and set out to envision another of the principal organs. Before a year was over he came to the skeleton, the eyelids. The countless strands of hair were perhaps the hardest task of all. He dreamed a whole man, a young man, but the young man could not stand up or speak, nor could he open his eyes. Night after night, the man dreamed him asleep.

In the cosmogonies of the Gnostics, the demiurges mold a red Adam who is unable to stand on his feet; as clumsy and crude and elementary as that Adam of dust was the Adam of dreams wrought by the nights of the magician. One evening the man was at the point of destroying all his handiwork (it would have been better for him had he done so), but in the end he restrained himself. Having exhausted his prayers to the gods of the earth and river, he threw himself down at the feet of the stone image that may have been a tiger or a stallion, and asked for its blind aid. That same evening he dreamed of the image. He dreamed it alive, quivering; it was no unnatural cross between tiger and stallion but at one and the same time both these violent creatures and also a bull, a rose, a thunderstorm. This manifold god revealed to him that its earthly name was Fire, that there in the circular temple (and in others like it) sacrifices had once been made to it, that it had been worshiped, and that through its magic the phantom of the man's dreams would be awakened to life in such a way that—except for Fire itself and the dreamer—every being in the world would accept him as a man of flesh and blood. The god ordered that, once instructed in the rites, the disciple should be sent downstream to the other ruined temple, whose pyramids still survived, so that in that abandoned place some human voice might exalt him. In the dreamer's dream, the dreamed one awoke.

The magician carried out these orders. He devoted a period of time (which finally spanned two years) to initiating his disciple into the riddles of the universe and the worship of Fire. Deep inside, it pained him to say goodbye to his creature. Under the pretext of teaching him more fully, each day he drew out the hours set aside for sleep. Also, he reshaped the somewhat faulty right shoulder. From time to time, he was troubled by the feeling that all this had already happened, but for the most part his days were happy. On closing his eyes he would think, "Now I will be with my son." Or, less frequently, "The son I have begotten awaits me and he will not exist if I do not go to him."

Little by little, he was training the young man for reality. On one occasion he commanded him to set up a flag on a distant peak. The next day, there on the peak, a fiery pennant shone. He tried other, similar exercises, each bolder than the one before. He realized with a certain bitterness that his son was ready—and perhaps impatient—to be born. That night he kissed him for the first time and sent him down the river to the other temple, whose whitened ruins were still to be glimpsed over miles and miles of impenetrable forest and swamp. At the very end (so that the boy would never know he was a phantom, so that he would think himself a man like all men), the magician imbued with total oblivion his disciple's long years of apprenticeship.

His triumph and his peace were blemished by a touch of weariness. In the morning and evening dusk, he prostrated himself before the stone idol, perhaps imagining that his unreal son was performing the same rites farther down the river in other circular ruins. At night he no longer dreamed, or else he dreamed the way all men dream. He now perceived with a certain vagueness the sounds and shapes of the world, for his absent son was taking nourishment from the magician's decreasing consciousness. His life's purpose was fulfilled; the man lived on in a kind of ecstasy. After a length of time that certain tellers of the story count in years and others in half-decades, he was awakened one midnight by two rowers. He could not see their faces, but they spoke to him about a magic man in a temple up north who walked on fire without being burned. The magician suddenly remembered the god's words. He remembered that of all the creatures in the world, Fire was the only one who knew his son was a phantom. This recollection, comforting at first, ended by tormenting him. He feared that his son might wonder at this strange privilege and in some way discover his condition as a mere appearance. Not to be a man but to be the projection of another man's dreams—what an unparalleled humiliation, how bewildering! Every father cares for the child he has begotten—he has allowed—in some moment of confusion or happiness. It is understandable, then, that the magician should fear for the future of a son thought out organ by organ and feature by feature over the course of a thousand and one secret nights.

The end of these anxieties came suddenly, but certain signs foretold it. First (after a long drought), a far-off cloud on a hilltop, as light as a bird; next, toward the south, the sky, which took on the rosy hue of a leopard's gums; then, the pillars of smoke that turned the metal of the nights to rust; finally, the headlong panic of the forest animals. For what had happened many centuries ago was happening again. The ruins of the fire god's shrine were destroyed by fire. In a birdless dawn the magician saw the circling sheets of flame closing in on him. For a moment, he thought of taking refuge in the river, but then he realized that death was coming to crown his years and to release him from his labors. He walked into the leaping pennants of flame. They did not bite into his flesh, but caressed him and flooded him without heat or burning. In relief, in humiliation, in terror, he understood that he, too, was an appearance, that someone else was dreaming him.

Ezekiel Mphahlele *(1919–) was born in Pretoria and grew up in the urban black ghettoes of South Africa. He taught English and Afrikaans in Johannesburg, and has lectured on African and English literature in Nigeria, Nairobi, Zambia, Kenya, France, and the United States. Although an exile from apartheid policy since 1957, Mphahlele writes stories about South Africa and greater Africa. These were first collected in* Man Must Live *(1947);* In Corner B and Other Stories *appeared in 1967. Mphahlele has also written an autobiography*—Down Second Avenue *(1959)—and a novel dealing with the problems of black African intellectuals called* The Wanderers *(1971). His pioneering study of African literature,* The African Image *(1962), has been followed by* Voices in the Whirlwind and Other Essays *(1972).*

Mrs. Plum

EZEKIEL MPHAHLELE

I

My madam's name was Mrs. Plum. She loved dogs and Africans and said that everyone must follow the law even if it hurt. These were three big things in Madam's life.

I came to work for Mrs. Plum in Greenside, not very far from the center of Johannesburg, after leaving two white families. The first white people I worked for as a cook and laundry woman were a man and his wife in Parktown North. They drank too much and always forgot to pay me. After five months I said to myself No. I am going to leave these drunks. So that was it. That day I was as angry as a red-hot iron when it meets water. The second house I cooked and washed for had five children who were badly brought up. This was in Belgravia. Many times they called me You Black Girl and I kept quiet. Because their mother heard them and said nothing. Also I was only new from Phokeng my home, far away near Rustenburg, I wanted to learn and know the white people before I knew how far to go with the others I would work for afterwards. The thing that drove me mad and made me pack and go was a man who came to visit them often. They said he was cousin or something like that. He came to the kitchen many times and tried to make me laugh. He patted me on the buttocks. I told the master. The man did it again and I asked the madam that very day to give me my money and let me go.

These were the first nine months after I had left Phokeng to work in Johannesburg. There were many of us girls and young women from Phokeng, from Zeerust, from Shuping, from Kosten, and many other places who came to work in the cities. So the suburbs were full of blackness. Most of us had already passed Standard Six and so we learned more English where we worked. None of us likes to work for white farmers, because we know too much about them on the farms near our homes. They do not pay well and they are cruel people.

At Easter time so many of us went home for a long weekend to see our people and to eat chicken and sour milk and *morogo*—wild spinach. We also took home sugar and condensed milk and tea and coffee and sweets and custard powder and tinned foods.

It was a home-girl of mine, Chimane, who called me to take a job in Mrs. Plum's house, just next door to where she worked. This is the third year now. I have been quite happy with Mrs. Plum and her daughter Kate. By this I mean that my place as a servant in Greenside is not as bad as that of many others. Chimane too does not complain too much. We are paid six pounds a month with free food and free servant's room. No one can ever say that they are well paid, so we go on complaining somehow. Whenever we meet on Thursday afternoons, which is time off for all of us black women in the suburbs, we talk and talk and talk: about our people at home and their letters; about their illnesses; about bad crops; about a sister who wanted a school uniform and books and school fees; about some of our madams and masters who are good, or stingy with money or food, or stupid or full of nonsense, or who kill themselves and each other, or who are dirty—and so many things I cannot count them all.

Thursday afternoons we go to town to look at the shops, to attend a woman's club, to see our boy-friends, to go to bioscope some of us. We turn up smart, to show others the clothes we bought from the black men who sell soft goods to servants in the suburbs. We take a number of things and they come round every month for a bit of money until we finish paying. Then we dress the way of many white madams and girls. I think we look really smart. Sometimes we catch the eyes of a white woman looking at us and we laugh and laugh until we nearly drop on the ground because we feel good inside ourselves.

II

What did the girl next door call you, Mrs. Plum asked me the first day I came to her. Jane, I replied. Was there not an African name? I said Yes, Karabo. All right, Madam said. We'll call you Karabo, she said. She spoke as if she knew a name is a big thing. I knew so many whites who did not care what they called black people as long as it was all right for their tongue. This pleased me, I mean Mrs. Plum's use of *Karabo;* because the only time I heard the name was when I was home or when my friends spoke to me. Then she showed me what to do: meals, meal times, washing, and where all the things were that I was going to use.

My daughter will be here in the evening, Madam said. She is at school. When the daughter came, she added, she would tell me some of the things she wanted me to do for her every day.

Chimane, my friend next door, had told me about the daughter Kate, how wild she seemed to be, and about Mr. Plum who had killed himself with a gun in a house down the street. They had left the house and come to this one.

Madam is a tall woman. Not slender, not fat. She moves slowly, and speaks slowly. Her face looks very wise, her forehead seems to tell me she has a strong liver: she is not afraid of anything. Her eyes are always swollen at the lower eyelids like a white person who has not slept for many many nights or like a large frog. Perhaps it is because she smokes too much, like wet wood that will not know whether to go up in flames or stop burning. She looks me straight in the eyes when she talks to me, and I know she does this with other people too. At first this made me fear her, now I am used to her. She is not a lazy woman, and she does many things outside, in the city and in the suburbs.

This was the first thing her daughter Kate told me when she came and we met. Don't mind mother, Kate told me. She said, She is sometimes mad with people for very small things. She will soon be all right and speak nicely to you again.

Kate, I like her very much, and she likes me too. She tells me many things a white woman does not tell a black servant. I mean things about what she likes and does not like, what her mother does or does not do, all these. At first I was unhappy and wanted to stop her, but now I do not mind.

Kate looks very much like her mother in the face. I think her shoulders will be just as round and strong-looking. She moves faster than Madam. I asked her why she was still at school when she was so big. She laughed. Then she tried to tell me that the school where she was was for big people, who had finished with lower school. She was learning big things about cooking and food. She can explain better, me I cannot. She came home on weekends.

Since I came to work for Mrs. Plum Kate has been teaching me plenty of cooking. I first learned from her and Madam the word *recipes*. When Kate was at the big school, Madam taught me how to read cookery books. I went on very slowly at first, slower than an ox-wagon. Now I know more. When Kate came home, she found I had read the recipe she left me. So we just cooked straightaway. Kate thinks I am fit to cook in a hotel. Madam thinks so too. Never never! I thought. Cooking in a hotel is like feeding oxen. No one can say thank you to you. After a few months I could cook the Sunday lunch and later I could cook specials for Madam's or Kate's guests.

Madam did not only teach me cooking. She taught me how to look after guests. She praised me when I did very very well; not like the white people I had worked for before. I do not know what runs crooked in the heads of other people. Madam also had classes in the evenings for servants to teach them how to read and write. She and two other women in Greenside taught in a church hall.

As I say, Kate tells me plenty of things about Madam. She says to me she says, My mother goes to meetings many times. I ask her I say, What for? She says to me she says, For your people. I ask her I say, My people are in Phokeng far away. They have got mouths, I say. Why does she want to say something for them? Does she know what my mother and what my father want to say? They can speak when they want to. Kate raises her shoulders and drops them and says, How can I tell you Karabo? I don't say your people—your family only. I mean all the black people in this country. I say Oh! What do the black people want to say? Again she raises her shoulders and drops them, taking a deep breath.

I ask her I say, With whom is she in the meeting?

She says, With other people who think like her.

I ask her I say, Do you say there are people in the world who think the same things?

She nods her head.

I ask, What things?

So that a few of your people should one day be among those who rule this country, get more money for what they do for the white man, and—what did Kate say again? Yes, that Madam and those who think like her also wanted my people who have been to school to choose those who must speak for them in the—I think she said it looks like a *Kgotla* at home who rule the villages.

I say to Kate I say, Oh I see now. I say, Tell me Kate, why is Madam always writing on the machine, all the time everyday nearly?

She replies she says, Oh my mother is writing books.

I ask, You mean a book like those?—pointing at the books on the shelves.

Yes, Kate says.

And she told me how Madam wrote books and other things for newspapers and she wrote for the newspapers and magazines to say things for the black people who should be treated well, be paid more money, for the black people who can read and write many things to choose those who want to speak for them.

Kate also told me she said, My mother and other women who think like her put on black belts over their shoulders when they are sad and they want to show the white government they do not like the things being done by whites to blacks. My mother and the others go and stand where the people in government are going to enter or go out of a building.

I ask her I say, Does the government and the white people listen and stop their sins? She says No. But my mother is in another group of white people.

I ask, Do the people of the government give the women tea and cakes? Kate says, Karabo! How stupid; oh!

I say to her I say, Among my people if someone comes and stands in front of my house I tell him to come in and I give him food. You white people are wonderful. But they keep standing there and the government people do not give them anything.

She replies, You mean strange. How many times have I taught you not to say *wonderful* when you mean *strange!* Well, Kate says with a short heart and looking cross and she shouts, Well they do not stand there the whole day to ask for tea and cakes stupid. Oh dear!

Always when Madam finished to read her newpapers she gave them to me to read to help me speak and write better English. When I had read she asked me to tell her some of the things in it. In this way, I did better and better and my mind was opening and opening and I was learning and learning many things about the black people inside and outside the towns which I did not know in the least. When I found words that were too difficult or I did not understand some of the things I asked Madam. She always told me You see this, you see that, eh? with a heart that can carry on a long way. Yes, Madam writes many letters to the papers. She is always sore about the way white police beat up black people; about the way black people who work for whites are made to sit at the Zoo Lake with their hearts hanging, because the white people say our people are making noise on Sunday afternoon when they want to rest in their houses and gardens; about many ugly things that happen when some white people meet black man on the pavement or street. So Madam writes to the papers to let others know, to ask the government to be kind to us.

In the first year Mrs. Plum wanted me to eat at table with her. It was very hard, one because I was not used to eating at table with a fork and knife, two because I heard of no other kitchen worker who was handled like this. I was afraid. Afraid of everybody, of Madam's guests if they found me doing this. Madam said I must not be silly. I must show that African servants can also eat at table. Number three, I could not eat some of the things I loved very much: mealie-meal porridge with sour milk or *morogo*, stamped mealies mixed with butter beans, sour porridge for breakfast and other things. Also, except for morning porridge, our food is nice when you eat with the hand. So nice that it does not stop in the mouth or the throat to greet anyone before it passes smoothly down.

We often had lunch together with Chimane next door and our garden boy — Ha! I must remember never to say *boy* again when I talk about a man. This makes me think of a day during the first few weeks in Mrs. Plum's house. I was talking about Dick her garden man and I said "garden boy." And she says to me she says, Stop talking about a "boy," Karabo. Now listen here, she says, You Africans must learn to speak properly about each other. And she says, White people won't talk kindly about you if you look down upon each other.

I say to her I say, Madam, I learned the word from the white people I worked for, and all the kitchen maids say "boy."

She replies she says to me, Those are white people who know nothing, just low-class whites. I say to her I say, I thought white people know everything.

She said, You'll learn, my girl, and you must start in this house, hear? She left me there thinking, my mind mixed up.

I learned. I grew up.

III

If any woman or girl does not know the Black Crow Club in Bree Street, she does not know anything. I think nearly everything takes place inside and outside that house. It is just where the dirty part of the City begins, with factories and the market. After the market is the place where Indians and Colored people live. It is also at the Black Crow that the buses turn round and back to the black townships. Noise, noise, noise all the time. There are woman who sell hot sweet potatoes and fruit and monkey nuts and boiled eggs in the winter, boiled mealies and the other things in the summer, all these on the pavements. The streets are always full of potato and fruit skins and monkey nut shells. There is always a strong smell of roast pork. I think it is because of Piel's cold storage down Bree Street.

Madam said she knew the black people who work in the Black Crow. She was happy that I was spending my afternoon on Thursday in such a club. You will learn sewing, knitting, she said, and other things that you like. Do you like to dance? I told her I said, Yes, I want to learn. She paid the two shillings fee for me each month.

We waited on the first floor, we the ones who were learning sewing; waiting for the teacher. We talked and laughed about madams and masters, and their children and their dogs and birds and whispered about our boy friends.

Sies! My Madam you do not know—*mojuta oa'nete*—a real miser . . .

Jo—jo—jo! you should see our new dog. A big thing like this. People! Big in a foolish way . . .

What! Me, I take a master's bitch by the leg, me, and throw it away so that it keeps howling, *tjwe—tjwe! ngo—wu ngo—wu!* I don't play about with them, me . . .

Shame, poor thing! God sees you, true. . . !

They wanted me to take their dog out for a walk every afternoon and I told them I said, It is not my work in other houses the garden man does it. I just said to myself I said, They can go to the chickens. Let them bite their elbow before I take out a dog, I am not so mad yet . . .

Hei! It is not like the child of my white people who keeps a big white rat and you know what? He puts it on his bed when he goes to school. And let the blankets just begin to smell of urine and all the nonsense and they tell me to wash them. *Hei*, people . . . !

Did you hear about Rebone, people? Her Madam put her out, because her master was always tapping her buttocks with his fingers. And yesterday the madam saw the master press Rebone against himself . . .

Jo—jo—jo! people. . . !

Dirty white man!

No, not dirty. The madam smells too old for him.

Hei! Go and wash your mouth with soap, this girl's mouth is dirty . . .

Jo, Rebone, daughter of the people! We must help her to find a job before she thinks of going back home.

The teacher came. A woman with strong legs, a strong face, and kind eyes. She had short hair and dressed in a simple but lovely floral frock. She stood well on her legs and hips. She had a black mark between the two top front teeth. She smiled as if we were her children. Our group began with games, and then Lilian Ngoyi took us for sewing. After this she gave a brief talk to all of us from the different classes.

I can never forget the things this woman said and how she put them to us. She told us that the time had passed for black girls and women in the suburbs to be satisfied with working, sending money to our people and going to see them once a year. We were to learn, she said, that the world would never be safe for black people until they were in the government with the power to make laws. The power should be given by the Africans who were more than the whites.

We asked her questions and she answered them with wisdom. I shall put some of them down in my own words as I remember them.

Shall we take the place of the white people in the government?

Some yes. But we shall be more than they as we are more in the country. But also the people of all colors will come together and there are good white men we can choose and there are Africans some white people will choose to be in the government.

There are good madams and masters and bad ones. Should we take the good ones for friends?

A master and a servant can never be friends. Never, so put that out of your head, will you! You are not even sure if the ones you say are good are not like that because they cannot breathe or live without the work of your hands. As long as you need their money, face them with respect. But you must know that many sad things are happening in our country and you, all of you, must always be learning, adding to what you already know, and obey us when we ask you to help us.

At other times Lilian Ngoyi told us she said, Remember your poor people at home and the way in which the whites are moving them from place to place like sheep and cattle. And at other times again she told us she said, Remember that a hand cannot wash itself, it needs another to do it.

I always thought of Madam when Lilian Ngoyi spoke. I asked myself, What would she say if she knew that I was listening to such words. Words like: A white man is looked after by his black nanny and his mother when he is a baby. When he grows up the white government looks after him, sends him to school, makes it impossible for him to suffer from the great hunger, keeps a job ready and open for him as soon as he wants to leave school. Now Lilian Ngoyi asked she said, How many white people can be born in a white hospital, grow up in white streets, be clothed in lovely cotton, lie on white cushions; how many whites can live all their lives in a fenced place away from people of other colors and then, as men and women, learn quickly the correct ways of thinking, learn quickly to ask questions in their minds, big questions that will throw over all the nice things of a white man's life? How many? Very very few! For those whites who have not begun to ask, it is too late. For those who have begun and are joining us with both feet in our house, we can only say Welcome!

I was learning. I was growing up. Every time I thought of Madam, she became more and more like a dark forest which one fears to enter, and which one will never know. But there were several times when I thought, This woman is easy to understand, she is like all other white women.

What else are they teaching you at the Black Crow, Karabo?

I tell her I say, Nothing, Madam. I ask her I say, Why does Madam ask?

You are changing.

What does Madam mean?

Well, you are changing.

But we are always changing, Madam.

And she left me standing in the kitchen. This was a few days after I had told her that I did not want to read more than one white paper a day. The only magazines I wanted to read, I said to her, were those from overseas, if she had them. I told her that white papers had pictures of white people and their gardens, dogs, weddings and parties. I asked her if she could buy me a Sunday paper that spoke about my people. Madam bought it for me. I did not think she would do it.

There were mornings when, after hanging the white people's washing on the line Chimane and I stole a little time to stand at the fence and talk. We always stood where we could be hidden by our rooms.

Hei, Karabo, you know what? That was Chimane.

No—what? Before you start, tell me, has Timi come back to you?

Ach, I do not care. He is still angry. But boys are fools they always come back dragging themselves on their empty bellies. *Hei* you know what?

Yes?

The Thursday past I saw Moruti K.K. I laughed until I dropped on the ground. He is standing in front of the Black Crow. I believe his big stomach was crying from hunger. Now he has a small dog in his armpit, and is standing before a woman selling boiled eggs and *hei* home-girl!—tripe and intestines are boiling in a pot—oh—the smell! you could fill a hungry belly with it, the way it was good. I think Moruti K.K. is waiting for the woman to buy a boiled egg. I do not know what the woman was still doing. I am standing nearby. The dog keeps wriggling and pushing out its nose, looking at the boiling tripe. Moruti keeps patting it with his free hand, not so? Again the dog wants to spill out of Moruti's hand and it gives a few sounds through the nose. *Hei* man, home-girl! One two three the dog spills out to catch some of the good meat! It misses falling into the hot gravy in which the tripe is swimming I do not know how. Moruti K.K. tries to chase it. It has tumbled on to the woman's eggs and potatoes and all are in the dust. She stands up and goes after K.K. She is shouting to him to pay, not so? Where am I at that time? I am nearly dead with laughter the tears are coming down so far.

I was myself holding tight on the fence so as not to fall through laughing. I held my stomach to keep back a pain in the side.

I ask her I say, Did Moruti K.K. come back to pay for the wasted food?

Yes, he paid.

The dog?

He caught it. That is a good African dog. A dog must look for its own food when it is not time for meals. Not these stupid spoiled angels the whites keep giving tea and biscuits.

Hmm.

Dick our garden man joined us, as he often did. When the story was repeated to him the man nearly rolled on the ground laughing.

He asks, Who is Reverend K.K.?

I say he is the owner of the Black Crow.

Oh!

We reminded each other, Chimane and I, of the round minister. He would come into the club, look at us with a smooth smile on his smooth round face. He would look at each one of us, with that smile on all the time, as if he had forgotten that it was there. Perhaps he had, because as he looked at us, almost stripping us naked with his watery shining eyes—funny—he could have been a farmer looking at his ripe corn, thinking many things.

K.K. often spoke without shame about what he called ripe girls—*matjitjana*—with good firm breasts. He said such girls were pure without any nonsense in their heads and bodies. Everybody talked a great deal about him and what they thought he must be doing in his office whenever he called in so-and-so.

The Reverend K.K. did not belong to any church. He baptized, married, and buried people for a fee, who had no church to do such things for them. They said he had been driven out of the Presbyterian Church. He had formed his own, but it did not go far. Then he later came and opened the Black Crow. He knew just how far to go with Lilian Ngoyi. She said although she used his club to teach us things that would help us in life, she could not go on if he was doing any wicked things with the girls in his office. Moruti K.K. feared her, and kept his place.

IV

When I began to tell my story I thought I was going to tell you mostly about Mrs. Plum's two dogs. But I have been talking about people. I think Dick is right when he says What is a dog! And there are so many dogs cats and parrots in Greenside and other places that Mrs. Plum's dogs do not look special. But there was something special in the dog business in Madam's house. The way in which she loved them, maybe.

Monty is a tiny animal with long hair and small black eyes and a face nearly like that of an old woman. The other, Malan, is a bit bigger, with brown and white colors. It has small hair and looks naked by the side of the friend. They sleep in two separate baskets which stay in Madam's bedroom. They are to be washed often and brushed and sprayed and they sleep on pink linen. Monty has a pink ribbon which stays on his neck most of the time. They both carry a cover on their backs. They make me fed up when I see them in their baskets, looking fat, and as if they knew all that was going on everywhere.

It was Dick's work to look after Monty and Malan, to feed them, and to do everything for them. He did this together with garden work and cleaning of the house. He came at the beginning of this year. He just came, as if from nowhere, and Madam gave him the job as she had chased away two before him, she told me. In both those cases, she said that they could not look after Monty and Malan.

Dick had a long heart, even although he told me and Chimane that European dogs were stupid, spoiled. He said One day those white people will put ear rings and toe rings and bangles on their dogs. That would be the day he would leave Mrs. Plum. For, he said, he was sure that she would want him to polish the rings and bangles with Brasso.

Although he had a long heart, Madam was still not sure of him. She often went to the dogs after a meal or after a cleaning and said to them, Did Dick give you food sweethearts? Or, Did Dick wash you sweethearts? Let me see. And I could see that Dick was blowing up like a balloon with anger. These things called white people! he said to me. Talking to dogs!

I say to him I say, People talk to oxen at home do I not say so?'

Yes, he says, but at home do you not know that a man speaks to an ox because he wants to make it pull the plow or the wagon or to stop or to stand still for a person to inspan it. No one simply goes to an ox looking at him with eyes far apart and speaks to it. Let me ask you, do you ever see a person where we come from take a cow and press it to his stomach or his cheek? Tell me!

And I say to Dick I say, We were talking about an ox, not a cow.

He laughed with his broad mouth until tears came out of his eyes. At a certain point I laughed aloud too.

One day when you have time, Dick says to me he says, you should look into Madam's bedroom when she has put a notice outside her door.

Dick, what are you saying? I ask.

I do not talk, me. I know deep inside me.

Dick was about our age, I and Chimane. So we always said *moshiman'o* when we spoke about his tricks. Because he was not too big to be a boy to us. He also said to us *Hei, lona banyana kelona*—Hey you girls, you! His large mouth always seemed to be making ready to laugh. I think Madam did not like this. Many times she would say, What is there to make you laugh here? Or in the garden she would say, This is a flower and when it wants water that is not funny! Or again, If you did more work and stopped trying to water my plants with your smile you would be more useful. Even when Dick did not mean to smile. What Madam did not get tired of saying was, If I left you to look after my dogs without anyone to look after you at the same time you would drown the poor things.

Dick smiled at Mrs. Plum. Dick hurt Mrs. Plum's dogs? Then cows can fly. He was really—really afraid of white people, Dick. I think he tried very hard not to feel afraid. For he was always showing me and Chimane in private how Mrs. Plum walked, and spoke. He took two bowls and pressed them against his chest, speaking softly to them as Madam speaks to Monty and Malan. Or he sat at Madam's table and acted the way she sits when writing. Now and again he looked back over his shoulder, pulled his face long like a horse's making as if he were looking over his glasses while telling me something to do. Then he would sit on one of the armchairs, cross his legs and act the way Madam drank her tea; he held the cup he was thinking about between his thumb and the pointing finger, only letting their nails meet. And he laughed after every act. He did these things, of course, when Madam was not home. And where was I at such times? Almost flat on my stomach, laughing.

But oh how Dick trembled when Mrs. Plum scolded him! He did his house-cleaning very well. Whatever mistake he made, it was mostly with the dogs; their linen, their food. One white man came into the house one afternoon to tell Madam that Dick had been very careless when taking the dogs out for a walk. His own dog was waiting on Madam's stoop. He repeated that he had been driving down our street; and Dick had let loose Monty and Malan to cross the street. The white man made plenty of noise about this and I think just to let Madam know how useful he had been. He kept on saying Just one inch, *just* one inch. It was lucky I put on my brakes quick enough. . . . But your boy kept on smiling—Why? Strange. My boy would only do it twice and only twice and then. . . ! His pass. The man moved his hand like one writing, to mean that he would sign his servant's pass for him to go and never come back. When he left, the white man said, Come on Rusty, the boy is waiting to clean you. Dogs with names, men without, I thought.

Madam climbed on top of Dick for this, as we say.

Once one of the dogs, I don't know which—Malan or Monty——took my stocking—brand new, you hear—and tore it with its teeth and paws. When I told Madam about it, my anger as high as my throat, she gave me money to buy another pair. It happened again. This time she said she was not going to give me money because I must also keep my stockings where the two gentlemen would not reach them. Mrs. Plum did not want us ever to say *Voetsek* when we wanted the dogs to go away. Me I said this when they came sniffing at my legs or fingers. I hate it.

In my third year in Mrs. Plum's house, many things happened, most of them all bad for her. There was trouble with Kate; Chimane had big trouble; my heart was twisted by two loves; and Monty and Malan became real dogs for a few days.

Madam had a number of suppers and parties. She invited Africans to some of them. Kate told me the reasons for some of the parties. Like her mother's books when finished, a visitor from across the seas and so on. I did not like the black people who came here to drink and eat. They spoke such difficult English like people who were full of all the books in the world. They looked at me as if I were right down there whom they thought little of—me a black person like them.

One day I heard Kate speak to her mother. She says, I don't know why you ask so many Africans to the house. A few will do at a time. She said something about the government which I could not hear well. Madam replies she says to her, You know some of them do not meet white people often, so far away in their dark houses. And she says to Kate that they do not come because they want her as a friend but they just want a drink for nothing.

I simply felt that I could not be the servant of white people and of blacks at the same time. At my home or in my room I could serve them without a feeling of shame. And now, if they were only coming to drink!

But one of the black men and his sister always came to the kitchen to talk to me. I must have looked unfriendly the first time, for Kate talked to me about it afterwards as she was in the kitchen when they came. I know that at that time I was not easy at all. I was ashamed and I felt that a white person's house was not the place for me to look happy in front of other black people while the white man looked on.

Another time it was easier. The man was alone. I shall never forget that night, as long as I live. He spoke kind words and I felt my heart grow big inside me. It caused me to tremble. There were several other visits. I knew that I loved him, I could never know what he really thought of me, I mean as a woman and he as a man. But I loved him, and I still think of him with a sore heart. Slowly I came to know the pain of it. Because he was a doctor and so full of knowledge and English I could not reach him. So I knew he could not stoop down to see me as someone who wanted him to love me.

Kate turned very wild. Mrs. Plum was very much worried. Suddenly it looked as if she were a new person, with new ways and new everything. I do not know what was wrong or right. She began to play the big gramophone aloud, as if the music were for the whole of Greenside. The music was wild and she twisted her waist all the time, with her mouth half-open. She did the same things in her room. She left the big school and every Saturday night now she went out. When I looked at her face, there was something deep and wild there on it, and when I thought she looked young she looked old, and when I thought she looked old she was young. We were both 22 years of age. I think that I could see the reason why her mother was so worried, why she was suffering.

Worse was to come.

They were now openly screaming at each other. They began in the sitting room and went upstairs together, speaking fast hot biting words, some of which I did not grasp. One day Madam comes to me and says, You know Kate loves an African, you know the doctor who comes to supper here often. She says he loves her too and they will leave the country and marry outside. Tell me, Karabo, what do your people think of this kind of thing between a white woman and a black man? It *cannot* be right is it?

I reply and I say to her, We have never seen it happen before where I come from.

That's right, Karabo, it is just madness.

Madam left. She looked like a hunted person.

These white women, I say to myself I say these white women, why do not they love their own men and leave us to love ours!

From that minute I knew that I would never want to speak to Kate. She appeared to me as a thief, as a fox that falls upon a flock of sheep at night. I hated her. To make it worse, he would never be allowed to come to the house again.

Whenever she was home there was silence between us. I no longer wanted to know anything about what she was doing, where or how.

I lay awake for hours on my bed. Lying like that, I seemed to feel parts of my body beat and throb inside me, the way I have seen big machines doing, pounding and pounding and pushing and pulling and pouring some water into one hole which came out at another end. I stretched myself so many times so as to feel tired and sleepy.

When I did sleep, my dreams were full of painful things.

One evening I made up my mind, after putting it off many times. I told my boy-friend that I did not want him any longer. He looked hurt, and that hurt me too. He left.

The thought of the African doctor was still with me and it pained me to know that I should never see him again; unless I met him in the street on a Thursday afternoon. But he had a car. Even if I did meet him by luck, how could I make him see that I loved him? Ach, I do not believe he would even stop to think what kind of woman I am. Part of that winter was a time of longing and burning for me. I say part because there are always things to keep servants busy whose white people go to the sea for the winter.

To tell the truth, winter was the time for servants; not nannies, because they went with their madams so as to look after the children. Those like me stayed behind to look after the house and dogs. In winter so many families went away that the dogs remained the masters and madams. You could see them walk like white people in the streets. Silent but with plenty of power. And when you saw them you knew that they were full of more nonsense and fancies in the house.

There was so little work to do.

One week word was whispered round that a home-boy of ours was going to hold a party in his room on Saturday. I think we all took it for a joke. How could the man be so bold and stupid? The police were always driving about at night looking for black people; and if the whites next door heard the party noise—*oho!* But still, we were full of joy and wanted to go. As for Dick, he opened his big mouth and nearly fainted when he heard of it and that I was really going.

During the day on the big Saturday Kate came.

She seemed a little less wild. But I was not ready to talk to her. I was surprised to hear myself answer her when she said to me, Mother says you do not like a marriage between a white girl and a black man, Karabo.

Then she was silent.

She says, But I want to help him, Karabo.

I ask her I say, You want to help him to do what?

To go higher and higher, to the top.

I knew I wanted to say so much that was boiling in my chest. I could not say it. I thought of Lilian Ngoyi at the Black Crow, what she said to us. But I was mixed up in my head and in my blood.

You still agree with my mother?

All I could say was, I said to your mother I had never seen a black man and a white woman marrying, you hear me? What I think about it is my business.

I remembered that I wanted to iron my party dress and so I left her. My mind was full of the party again and I was glad because Kate and the doctor would not worry my peace that day. And the next day the sun would shine for all of us, Kate or no Kate, doctor or no doctor.

The house where our home-boy worked was hidden from the main road by a number of trees. But although we asked a number of questions and counted many fingers of bad luck until we had no more hands for fingers, we put on our best pay-while-you-wear dresses and suits and clothes bought from boys who had stolen them, and went to our home-boy's party. We whispered all the way while we climbed up to the house. Someone who knew told us that the white people next door were away for the winter. Oh, so that is the thing! we said.

We poured into the garden through the back and stood in front of his room laughing quietly. He came from the big house behind us, and were we not struck dumb when he told us to go into the white people's house! Was he mad? We walked in with slow footsteps that seemed to be sniffing at the floor, not sure of anything. Soon we were standing and sitting all over on the nice warm cushions and the heaters were on. Our home-boy turned the lights low. I counted fifteen people inside. We saw how we loved one another's evening dress. The boys were smart too.

Our home-boy's girl-friend Naomi was busy in the kitchen preparing food. He took out glasses and cold drinks—fruit juice, tomato juice, ginger beers, and so many other kinds of soft drink. It was just too nice. The tarts, the biscuits, the snacks, the cakes, *woo*, that was a party, I tell you. I think I ate more ginger cake than I had ever done in my life. Naomi had baked some of the things. Our home-boy came to me and said, I do not want the police to come here and have reason to arrest us, so I am not serving hot drinks, not even beer. There is no law that we cannot have parties, is there? So we can feel free. Our use of this house is the master's business. If I had asked him he would have thought me mad.

I say to him I say, You have a strong liver to do such a thing.

He laughed.

He played pennywhistle music on gramophone records—Miriam Makeba, Dorothy Masuka, and other African singers and players. We danced and the party became more and more noisy and more happy. *Hai*, those girls Miriam and Dorothy, they can sing, I tell you! We ate more and laughed more and told more stories. In the middle of the party, our home-boy called us to listen to what he was going to say. Then he told us how he and a friend of his in Orlando collected money to bet on a horse for the July Handicap in Durban. They did this each year but lost. Now they had won two hundred pounds. We all clapped hands and cheered. Two hundred pounds *woo!*

You should go and sit at home and just eat time, I say to him. He laughs and says, You have no understanding not one little bit.

To all of us he says, Now my brothers and sisters enjoy yourselves. At home I should slaughter a goat for us to feast and thank our ancestors. But this is town life and we must thank them with tea and cake and all those sweet things. I know some people think I must be so bold that I could be midwife to a lion that is giving birth, but enjoy yourselves and have no fear.

Madam came back looking strong and fresh.

The very week she arrived the police had begun again to search servants' rooms. They were looking for what they called loafers and men without passes who they said were living with friends in the suburbs against the law. Our dog's-meat boys became scarce because of the police. A boy who had a girl-friend in the kitchens, as we say, always told his friends that he was coming for dog's meat when he meant he was visiting his girl. This was because we gave our boy-friends part of the meat the white people bought for the dogs and us.

One night a white and a black policeman entered Mrs. Plum's yard. They said they had come to search. She says No, they cannot. They say Yes, they must do it. She answers No. They forced their way to the back, to Dick's room and mine. Mrs. Plum took the hose that was running in the front garden and quickly went round to the back. I cut across the floor to see what she was going to say to the men. They were talking to Dick, using dirty words. Mrs. Plum did not wait, she just pointed the hose at the two policemen. This seemed to surprise them. They turned round and she pointed it into their faces. Without their seeing me I went to the tap at the corner of the house and opened it more. I could see Dick, like me, was trying to keep down his laughter. They shouted and tried to wave the water away, but she kept the hose pointing at them, now moving it up and down. They turned and ran through the back gate, swearing the while.

That fixes them, Mrs. Plum said.

The next day the morning paper reported it.

They arrived in the afternoon—the two policemen—with another. They pointed out Mrs. Plum and she was led to the police station. They took her away to answer for stopping the police while they were doing their work.

She came back and said she had paid bail.

At the magistrate's court, Madam was told that she had done a bad thing. She would have to pay a fine or else go to prison for fourteen days. She said she would go to jail to show that she felt she was not in the wrong.

Kate came and tried to tell her that she was doing something silly going to jail for a small thing like that. She tells Madam she says, This is not even a thing to take to the high court. Pay the money. What is 5 pounds?

Madam went to jail.

She looked very sad when she came out. I thought of what Lilian Ngoyi often said to us: You must be ready to go to jail for the things you believe are true and for which you are taken by the police. What did Mrs. Plum really believe about me, Chimane, Dick, and all the other black people? I asked myself. I did not know. But from all those things she was writing for the papers and all those meetings she was going to where white people talked about black people and the way they are treated by the government, from what those white women with black bands over their shoulders were doing standing where a white government man was going to pass, I said to myself I said, This woman, *hai*, I do not know she seems to think very much of us black people. But why was she so sad?

Kate came back home to stay after this. She still played the big gramophone loud-loud-loud and twisted her body at her waist until I thought it was going to break. Then I saw a young white man come often to see her. I watched them through the opening near the hinges of the door between the kitchen and the sitting room where they sat. I saw them kiss each other for a long time. I saw him lift up Kate's dress and her white-white legs begin to tremble, and—oh I am afraid to say more, my heart was beating hard. She called him Jim. I thought it was funny because white people in the shops call black men Jim.

Kate had begun to play with Jim when I met a boy who loved me and I loved. He was much stronger than the one I sent away and I loved him more, much more. The face of the doctor came to my mind often, but it did not hurt me so any more. I stopped looking at Kate and her Jim through openings. We spoke to each other, Kate and I, almost as freely as before but not quite. She and her mother were friends again.

Hallo, Karabo, I heard Chimane call me one morning as I was starching my apron. I answered. I went to the line to hang it. I saw she was standing at the fence, so I knew she had something to tell me. I went to her.

Hallo!

Hallo, Chimane!

O kae?

Ke teng. Wena?

At that moment a woman came out through the back door of the house where Chimane was working.

I have not seen that one before, I say, pointing with my head.

Chimane looked back. Oh, that one. *Hei*, daughter-of-the-people, *hei*, you have not seen miracles. You know this is Madam's mother-in-law as you see her there. Did I never tell you about her?

No, never.

White people, nonsense. You know what? That poor woman is here now for two days. She has to cook for herself and I cook for the family.

On the same stove?

Yes, She comes after me when I have finished.

She has her own food to cook?

Yes, Karabo, White people have no heart no sense.

What will eat them up if they share their food?

Ask me, just ask me. God! She clapped her hands to show that only God knew, and it was His business, not ours.

Chimane asks me she says, Have you heard from home?

I tell her I say, Oh daughter-of-the-people, more and more deaths. Something is finishing the people at home. My mother has written. She says they are all right, my father too and my sisters, except for the people who have died. Malebo, the one who lived alone in the house I showed you last year, a white house, he is gone. Then teacher Sedimo. He was very thin and looked sick all the time. He taught my sisters not me. His mother-in-law you remember I told you died last year—no, the year before. Mother says also there is a woman she does not think I remember because I last saw her when I was a small girl she passed away in Zeerust she was my mother's greatest friend when they were girls. She would have gone to her burial if it was not because she has swollen feet.

How are the feet?

She says they are still giving her trouble. I ask Chimane, How are your people at Nokaneng? They have not written?

She shook her head.

I could see from her eyes that her mind was on another thing and not her people at that moment.

Wait for me Chimane eh, forgive me, I have scones in the oven, eh! I will just take them out and come back, eh!

When I came back to her Chimane was wiping her eyes. They were wet.

Karabo, you know what?

E—e. I shook my head.

I am heavy with child.

Hau!

There was a moment of silence.

Who is it, Chimane?

Timi. He came back only to give me this.

But he loves you. What does he say have you told him?'

I told him yesterday. We met in town.

I remembered I had not seen her at the Black Crow.

Are you sure, Chimane? You have missed a month?

She nodded her head.

Timi himself—he did not use the thing?

I only saw after he finished, that he had not.

Why? What does he say?

He tells me he says I should not worry I can be his wife.

Timi is a good boy, Chimane. How many of these boys with town ways who know too much will even say Yes it is my child?

Hai, Karabo, you are telling me other things now. Do you not see that I have not worked long enough for my people? If I marry now who will look after them when I am the only child?

Hm. I hear your words. It is true. I tried to think of something soothing to say.

Then I say, You can talk it over with Timi. You can go home and when the child is born you look after it for three months and when you are married you come to town to work and can put your money together to help the old people while they are looking after the child.

What shall we be eating all the time I am at home? It is not like those days gone past when we had land and our mother could go to the fields until the child was ready to arrive.

The light goes out in my mind and I cannot think of the right answer. How many times have I feared the same thing! Luck and the mercy of the gods, that is all I live by. That is all we live by—all of us.

Listen, Karabo. I must be going to make tea for Madam. It will soon strike half-past ten.

I went back to the house. As Madam was not in yet, I threw myself on the divan in the sitting-room. Malan came sniffing at my legs. I put my foot under its fat belly and shoved it up and away from me so that it cried *tjunk—tjunk—tjunk* as it went out. I say to it I say, Go and tell your brother what I have done to you and tell him to try it and see what I will do. Tell your grandmother when she comes home too.

When I lifted my eyes he was standing in the kitchen door, Dick. He says to me he says, *Hau!* now you have also begun to speak to dogs!

I did not reply. I just looked at him, his mouth ever stretched out like the mouth of a bag, and I passed to my room.

I sat on my bed and looked at my face in the mirror. Since the morning I had been feeling as if a black cloud were hanging over me, pressing on my head and shoulders. I do not know how long I sat there. Then I smelled Madam. What was it? Where was she? After a few moments I knew what it was. My perfume and scent. I used the same cosmetics as Mrs. Plum's. I should have been used to it by now. But this morning—why did I smell Mrs. Plum like this? Then, without knowing why, I asked myself I said, Why have I been using the same cosmetics as Madam? I wanted to throw them all out. I stopped. And then I took all the things and threw them into the dustbin. I was going to buy other kinds on Thursday; finished!

I could not sit down. I went out and into the white people's house. I walked through and the smell of the house made me sick and seemed to fill up my throat. I went to the bathroom without knowing why. It was full of the smell of Madam. Dick was cleaning the bath. I stood at the door and looked at him cleaning the dirt out of the bath, dirt from Madam's body. *Sies!* I said aloud. To myself I said, Why cannot people wash the dirt of their own bodies out of the bath? Before Dick knew I was near I went out. Ach, I said again to myself, why should I think about it now when I have been doing their washing for so long and cleaned the bath many times when Dick was ill. I had held worse things from her body times without number . . .

I went out and stood midway between the house and my room, looking into the next yard. The three-legged gray cat next door came to the fence and our eyes met. I do not know how long we stood like that looking at each other. I was thinking, Why don't you go and look at your grandmother like that? when it turned away and mewed hopping on the three legs. Just like someone who feels pity for you.

In my room I looked into the mirror on the chest of drawers. I thought Is this Karabo this?

Thursday came, and the afternoon off. At the Black Crow I did not see Chimane. I wondered about her. In the evening I found a note under my door. It told me if Chimane was not back that evening I should know that she was at 660 3rd Avenue, Alexandra Township. I was not to tell the white people.

I asked Dick if he could not go to Alexandra with me after I had washed the dishes. At first he was unwilling. But I said to him I said, Chimane will not believe that you refused to come with me when she sees me alone. He agreed.

On the bus Dick told me much about his younger sister whom he was helping with money to stay at school until she finished; so that she could become a nurse and a midwife. He was very fond of her, as far as I could find out. He said he prayed always that he should not lose his job, as he had done many times before, after staying a few weeks only at each job; because of this he had to borrow monies from people to pay his sister's school fees, to buy her clothes and books. He spoke of her as if she were his sweetheart. She was clever at school, pretty (she was this in the photo Dick had shown me before). She was in Orlando Township. She looked after his old people, although she was only thirteen years of age. He said to me he said, Today I still owe many people because I keep losing my job. You must try to stay with Mrs. Plum, I said.

I cannot say that I had all my mind on what Dick was telling me. I was thinking of Chimane: what could she be doing? Why that note?

We found her in bed. In that terrible township where night and day are full of knives and bicycle chains and guns and the barking of hungry dogs and of people in trouble. I held my heart in my hands. She was in pain and her face, even in the candlelight, was gray. She turned her eyes at me. A fat woman was sitting in a chair. One arm rested on the other and held her chin in its palm. She had hardly opened the door for us after we had shouted our names when she was on her bench again as if there were nothing else to do.

She snorted, as if to let us know that she was going to speak. She said, There is your friend. There she is my own-own niece who comes from the womb of my own sister, my sister who was made to spit out my mother's breast to give way for me. Why does she go and do such an evil thing. *Ao!* you young girls of today you do not know children die so fast these days that you have to thank God for sowing a seed in your womb to grow into a child. If she had let the child be born I should have looked after it or my sister would have been so happy to hold a grandchild on her lap, but what does it help? She has allowed a worm to cut the roots, I don't know.

Then I saw that Chimane's aunt was crying. Not once did she mention her niece by name, so sore her heart must have been. Chimane only moaned.

Her aunt continued to talk, as if she was never going to stop for breath, until her voice seemed to move behind me, not one of the things I was thinking: trying to remember signs, however small, that could tell me more about this moment in a dim little room in a cruel township without street lights, near Chimane. Then I remembered the three-legged cat, its gray-green eyes, its *miau*. What was this shadow that seemed to walk about us but was not coming right in front of us?

I thanked the gods when Chimane came to work at the end of the week. She still looked weak, but that shadow was no longer there. I wondered Chimane had never told me about her aunt before. Even now I did not ask her.

I told her I told her white people that she was ill and had been fetched to Nokaneng by a brother. They would never try to find out. They seldom did, these people. Give them any lie, and it will do. For they seldom believe you whatever you say. And how can a black person work for white people and be afraid to tell them lies. They are always asking the questions, you are always the one to give the answers.

Chimane told me all about it. She had gone to a woman who did these things. Her way was to hold a sharp needle, cover the point with the finger, and guide it into the womb. She then fumbled in the womb until she found the egg and then pierced it. She gave you something to ease the bleeding. But the pain, spirits of our forefathers!

Mrs. Plum and Kate were talking about dogs one evening at dinner. Every time I brought something to table I tried to catch their words. Kate seemed to find it funny, because she laughed aloud. There was a word I could not hear well which began with *sem*—: whatever it was, it was to be for dogs. This I understood by putting a few words together. Mrs. Plum said it was something that was common in the big cities of America, like New York. It was also something Mrs. Plum wanted and Kate laughed at the thought. Then later I was to hear that Monty and Malan could be sure of a nice burial.

Chimane's voice came up to me in my room the next morning, across the fence. When I come out she tells me she says, *Hei*, child-of-my-father, here is something to tickle your ears. You know what?

What? I say. She says, These white people can do things that make the gods angry. More godless people I have not seen. The madam of our house says the people of Greenside want to buy ground where they can bury their dogs. I heard them talk about it in the sitting room when I was giving them coffee last night. *Hei*, people, let our forefathers come and save us!

Yes, I say, I also heard the madam of our house talk about it with her daughter. I just heard it in pieces. By my mother one day these dogs will sit at table and use knife and fork. These things are to be treated like people now, like children who are never going to grow up.

Chimane sighed and she says, *Hela batho*, why do they not give me some of that money they will spend on the ground and on gravestones to buy stockings! I have nothing to put on, by my mother.

Over her shoulder I saw the cat with three legs. I pointed with my head. When Chimane looked back and saw it she said, *Hm*, even *they* live like kings. The mother-in-law found it on a chair and the madam said the woman should not drive it away. And there was no other chair, so the woman went to her room.

Hela!

I was going to leave when I remembered what I wanted to tell Chimane. It was that five of us had collected 1 pound each to lend her so that she could pay the woman of Alexandra for having done that thing for her. When Chimane's time came to receive money we collected each month and which we took in turns, she would pay us back. We were ten women and each gave 2 pounds at a time. So one waited ten months to receive 20 pounds. Chimane thanked us for helping her.

I went to wake up Mrs. Plum as she had asked me. She was sleeping late this morning. I was going to knock at the door when I heard strange noises in the bedroom. What is the matter with Mrs. Plum? I asked myself. Should I call her, in case she is ill? No, the noises were not those of a sick person. They were happy noises but like those a person makes in a dream, the voice full of sleep. I bent a little to peep through the keyhole. What is this? I kept asking myself. Mrs. Plum! Malan! What is she doing this one? Her arm was round Malan's belly and pressing its back against her stomach at the navel, Mrs. Plum's body in a nightdress moving in jerks like someone in fits . . . her leg rising and falling . . . Malan silent like a thing to be owned without any choice it can make to belong to another.

The gods save me! I heard myself saying, the words sounding like wind rushing out of my mouth. So this is what Dick said I would find out for myself!

No one could say where it all started; who talked about it first; whether the police wanted to make a reason for taking people without passes and people living with servants and working in town or not working at all. But the story rushed through Johannesburg that servants were going to poison the white people's dogs. Because they were too much work for us: that was the reason. We heard that letters were sent to the newspapers by white people asking the police to watch over the dogs to stop any wicked things. Some said that we the servants were not really bad, we were being made to think of doing these things by evil people in town and in the locations. Others said the police should watch out lest we poison madams and masters because black people did not know right from wrong when they were angry. We were still children at heart, others said. Mrs. Plum said that she had also written to the papers.

Then it was the police came down on the suburbs like locusts on a cornfield. There were lines and lines of men who were arrested hour by hour in the day. They liked this very much, the police. Everybody they took, everybody who was working was asked, Where's the poison eh? Where did you hide it? Who told you to poison the dogs eh? If you tell us we'll leave you to go free, you hear? and so many other things.

Dick kept saying, It is wrong this thing they want to do to kill poor dogs. What have these things of God done to be killed for? Is it the dogs that make us carry passes? Is it the dogs that make the laws that give us pain? People are just mad they do not know what they want, stupid! But when white policeman spoke to him, Dick trembled and lost his tongue and the things he thought. He just shook his head. A few moments after they had gone through his pockets he still held his arms stretched out, like the man of straw who frightens away birds in a field. Only when I hissed and gave him a sign did he drop his arms. He rushed to a corner of the garden to go on with his work.

Mrs. Plum had put Monty and Malan in the sitting room, next to her. She looked very much worried. She called me. She asked me she said, Karabo, you think Dick is a boy we can trust? I did not know how to answer. I did not know whom she was talking about when she said *we*. Then I said, I do not know, Madam. You know! she said. I looked at her. I said, I do not know what Madam thinks. She said she did not think anything, that was why she asked. I nearly laughed because she was telling a lie this time and not I.

At another time I should have been angry if she lied to me, perhaps. She and I often told each other lies, as Kate and I also did. Like when she came back from jail, after that day when she turned a hosepipe on two policemen. She said life had been good in jail. And yet I could see she was ashamed to have been there. Not like our black people who are always being put in jail and only look at it as the white man's evil game. Lilian Ngoyi often told us this, and Mrs. Plum showed me how true those words are. I am sure that we have kept to each other by lying to each other.

There was something in Mrs. Plum's face as she was speaking which made me fear her and pity her at the same time. I had seen her when she had come from prison; I had seen her when she was shouting at Kate and the girl left the house; now there was this thing about dog poisoning. But never had I seen her face like this before. The eyes, the nostrils, the lips, the teeth seemed to be full of hate, tired, fixed on doing something bad; and yet there was something on that face that told me she wanted me on her side.

Dick is all right Madam, I found myself saying. She took Malan and Monty in her arms and pressed them to herself, running her hands over their heads. They looked so safe, like a child in a mother's arm.

Mrs. Plum said, All right you may go. She said, Do not tell anybody what I have asked about Dick eh?

When I told Dick about it, he seemed worried.

It is nothing, I told him.

I had been thinking before that I did not stand with those who wanted to poison the dogs, Dick said. But the police have come out, I do not care what happens to the dumb things, now.

I asked him I said, Would you poison them if you were told by someone to do it?

No. But I do not care, he replied.

The police came again and again. They were having a good holiday, everyone could see that. A day later Mrs. Plum told Dick to go because she would not need his work any more.

Dick was almost crying when he left. Is Madam so unsure of me?

he asked. I never thought a white person could fear me! And he left.

Chimane shouted from the other yard. She said, *Hei ngoana'rona*, the boers are fire-hot eh!

Mrs. Plum said she would hire a man after the trouble was over.

A letter came from my parents in Phokeng. In it they told me my uncle had passed away. He was my mother's brother. The letter also told me of other deaths. They said I would not remember some, I was sure to know the others. There were also names of sick people.

I went to Mrs. Plum to ask her if I could go home. She asks she says, When did he die? I answer I say, It is three days, Madam. She says, So that they have buried him? I reply, Yes Madam. Why do you want to go home then? Because my uncle loved me very much Madam. But what are you going to do there? To take my tears and words of grief to his grave and to my old aunt, Madam. No you cannot go, Karabo. You are working for me you know? Yes, Madam. I and not your people pay you. I must go Madam, that is how we do it among my people, Madam. She paused. She walked into the kitchen and came out again. If you want to go, Karabo, you must lose the money for the days you will be away. Lose my pay, Madam? Yes, Karabo.

The next day I went to Mrs. Plum and told her I was leaving for Phokeng and was not coming back to her. Could she give me a letter to say that I worked for her. She did, with her lips shut tight. I could feel that something between us was burning like raw chillies. The letter simply said that I had worked for Mrs. Plum for three years. Nothing more. The memory of Dick being sent away was still an open sore in my heart.

The night before the day I left, Chimane came to see me in my room. She had her own story to tell me. Timi, her boy-friend, had left her—for good. Why? Because I killed his baby. Had he not agreed that you should do it? No. Did he show he was worried when you told him you were heavy? He was worried, like me as you saw me, Karabo. Now he says if I kill one I shall eat all his children up when we are married. You think he means what he says? Yes, Karabo. He says his parents would have been very happy to know that the woman he was going to marry can make his seed grow.

Chimane was crying, softly.

I tried to speak to her, to tell her that if Timi left her just like that, he had not wanted to marry her in the first place. But I could not, no, I could not. All I could say was Do not cry, my sister, do not cry. I gave her my handkerchief.

Kate came back the morning I was leaving, from somewhere very far I cannot remember where. Her mother took no notice of what Kate said asking her to keep me, and I was not interested either.

One hour later I was on the Railway bus to Phokeng. During the early part of the journey I did not feel anything about the Greenside house I had worked in. I slept and woke up many times during the bus ride. Right through the ride I seemed to see, sometimes in sleep, sometimes between sleep and waking, a red car passing our bus, then running behind us. Each time I looked out it was not there.

Dreams came and passed. He tells me he says, You have killed my seed I wanted my mother to know you are a woman in whom my seed can grow . . . Before you make the police take you to jail make sure that it is for something big you should go to jail for, otherwise you will come out with a heart and mind that will bleed inside you and poison you . . .

The bus stopped for a short while, which made me wake up.

The Black Crow, the club women . . . *Hei*, listen! I lie to the madam of our house and I say I had a telegram from my mother telling me she is very very sick. I show her a telegram my sister sent me as if mother were writing. So I went home for a nice weekend . . .

The laughter of the women woke me up, just in time for me to stop a line of saliva coming out over my lower lip. The bus was making plenty of dust now as it was running over part of the road they were digging up. I was sure the red car was just behind us, but it was not there when I woke.

Any one of you here who wants to be baptized or has a relative without a church who needs to be can come and see me in the office . . . A round man with a fat tummy and sharp hungry eyes, a smile that goes a long, long way . . .

The bus was going uphill, heavily and noisily.

I kick a white man's dog, me, or throw it there if it has not been told the black people's law . . . This is Mister Monty and this is Mister Malan. Now get up you lazy boys and meet Mister Kate. Hold out your hands and say hallo to him . . . Karabo, bring two glasses there . . . Wait a bit—What will you chew boys while Mister Kate and I have a drink? Nothing? Sure?

We were now going nicely on a straight tarred road and the trees rushed back. Mister Kate. What nonsense, I thought.

Look Karabo, madam's dogs are dead. What? Poison. I killed them. She drove me out of a job did she not? For nothing. Now I want her to feel she drove me out for something. I came back when you were in your room and took the things and poisoned them . . . And you know what? She has buried them in clean pink sheets in the garden. *Ao*, clean clean good sheets. I am going to dig them out and take one sheet do you want the other one? Yes, give me the other one I will send it to my mother . . . *Hei*, Karabo, see here they come. Monty and Malan. The bloody fools they do not want to stay in their hole. Go back you silly fools. Oh you do not want to move eh? Come here, now I am going to throw you in the big pool. No, Dick! No Dick! no, no! Dick! They cannot speak do not kill things that cannot speak. Madam can speak for them she always does. No! Dick . . . !

I woke up with a jump after I had screamed Dick's name, almost hitting the window. My forehead was full of sweat. The red car also shot out of my sleep and was gone. I remembered a friend of ours who told us how she and the garden man had saved two white sheets in which their white master had buried their two dogs. They went to throw the dogs in a dam.

When I told my parents my story Father says to me he says, So long as you are in good health my child, it is good. The worker dies, work does not. There is always work. I know when I was a boy a strong sound body and a good mind were the biggest things in life. Work was always there, and the lazy man could never say there was no work. But today people see work as something bigger than everything else, bigger than health, because of money.

I reply I say, Those days are gone Papa. I must go back to the city after resting a little to look for work. I must look after you. Today people are too poor to be able to help you.

I knew when I left Greenside that I was going to return to Johannesburg to work. Money was little, but life was full and it was better than sitting in Phokeng and watching the sun rise and set. So I told Chimane to keep her eyes and ears open for a job.

I had been at Phokeng for one week when a red car arrived. Somebody was sitting in front with the driver, a white woman. At once I knew it to be that of Mrs. Plum. The man sitting beside her was showing her the way, for he pointed towards our house in front of which I was sitting. My heart missed a few beats. Both came out of the car. The white woman said Thank you to the man after he had spoken a few words to me.

I did not know what to do and how to look at her as she spoke to me. So I looked at the piece of cloth I was sewing pictures on. There was a tired but soft smile on her face. Then I remembered that she might want to sit. I went inside to fetch a low bench for her. When I remembered it afterwards, the thought came to me that there are things I never think white people can want to do at our homes when they visit for the first time: like sitting, drinking water, or entering the house. This is how I thought when the white priest came to see us. One year at Easter Kate drove me home as she was going to the north. In the same way I was at a loss what to do for a few minutes.

Then Mrs. Plum says, I have come to ask you to come back to me, Karabo. Would you like to?

I say I do not know, I must think about it first.

She says, Can you think about it today? I can sleep at the town hotel and come back tomorrow morning, and if you want to you can return with me.

I wanted her to say she was sorry to have sent me away, I did not know how to make her say it because I know white people find it too much for them to say Sorry to a black person. As she was not saying it, I thought of two things to make it hard for her to get me back and maybe even lose me in the end.

I say, You must ask my father first, I do not know, should I call him?

Mrs. Plum says, Yes.

I fetched both Father and Mother. They greeted her while I brought benches. Then I told them what she wanted.

Father asks Mother and Mother asks Father. Father asks me. I say if they agree, I will think about it and tell her the next day.

Father says, It goes by what you feel my child.

I tell Mrs. Plum I say, If you want me to think about it I must know if you will want to put my wages up from 6 pounds because it is too little.

She asks me, How much will you want?

Up by 4 pounds.

She looked down for a few moments.

And then I want two weeks at Easter and not just the weekend. I thought if she really wanted me she would want to pay for it. This would also show how sorry she was to lose me.

Mrs. Plum says, I can give you one week. You see you already have something like a rest when I am in Durban in the winter.

I tell her I say, I shall think about it.

She left.

The next day she found me packed and ready to return with her. She was very much pleased and looked kinder than I had ever known her. And me, I felt sure of myself, more than I had ever done.

Mrs. Plum says to me, You will not find Monty and Malan.

Oh?

Yes, they were stolen the day after you left. The police have not found them yet. I think they are dead myself.

I thought of Dick . . . my dream. Could he? And she . . . did this woman come to ask me to return because she had lost two animals she loved?

Mrs. Plum says to me she says, You know, I like your people, Karabo, the Africans.

And Dick and Me? I wondered.

Nadine Gordimer (1923–   ), a South African, was born in Transvaal and educated in Johannesburg, which serves frequently as the setting for her fiction. Her first collection of stories, Face to Face, *and succeeding volumes have appeared regularly*—The Soft Voice of the Serpent *(1952),* Friday's Footprints *(1960),* Not for Publication *(1965), and* Livingston's Companions *(1971). The latest of her novels is* A Guest of Honor *(1970). Miss Gordimer, who has lectured at a number of American universities, received the Smith Literary Award in 1961 and the Thomas Pringle Award in 1969 for her fiction.*

The Defeated

NADINE GORDIMER

My mother did not want me to go near the Concession stores because they smelled, and were dirty, and the natives spat tuberculosis germs into the dust. She said it was no place for little girls.

But I used to go down there sometimes, in the afternoon, when static four o'clock held the houses of our Mine, and the sun washed over them like the waves of the sea over sand castles. I felt that life was going on down there at the Concession stores: noise, and movement and—yes, bad smells, even—and so I would wander down the naked road, with the hot sun uncomfortably drying the membrane inside my nose, seeing the irregular line of narrow white shops lying away ahead like a jumble of shoe boxes.

The signs of life that I craved were very soon evident: rich and careless of its vitality, it overflowed from the crowded pavement of the stores, and the surrounding veld was littered with sucked-out oranges and tatters of dirty paper, and worn into the shabby barrenness peculiar to earth much trampled upon by the feet of men. A fat, one-legged native, with the patient detachment of the businessman who knows himself indispensable, sat on the bald veld beside the path that led from the Compound, his stock of walking sticks standing up, handles tied together, points splayed out fanwise, his pyramids of bright, thin-skinned oranges waiting. Sometimes he had mealies as well—those big, hard, full-grown ears with rows of yellowish tombstones instead of little pearly teeth—and a brazier made from a paraffin tin to roast them by. Propped against the chipped pillars of the pavement, there were always other vendors, making their small way in lucky beans, herbs, bracelets beaten from copper wire, knitted caps in wonderful colors—blooming like great hairy petunias, or bursting suns, from the needles of old, old native women—and, of course, oranges. Everywhere there were oranges; the pushing, ambling crowds filling the pavement ate them as they stared at the windows, the gossips, sitting with their blankets drawn close and their feet in the gutter, sucked at them, the Concession store cats sniffed at the skins where they lay, hollow-cheeked, discarded in every doorway.

Quite often I had to flick the white pith from where it had landed, on my shoe or even my dress, spat negligently by some absorbed orange-eater contemplating a shirt through breath-smudged plate glass. The wild, wondering dirty men came up from the darkness of the mine and they lay themselves out to the sun on the veld, and to their mouths they put the round fruit of the sun; and it was the expression of their need.

I would saunter along the shopwindows amongst them, and for me there was a quickening of glamor about the place: the air was thicker with their incense-like body smell, and the sudden rank shock of their stronger sweat, as a bare armpit lifted over my head. The clamor of their voices—always shouting, but so merry, so angry!—and the size of their laughter, and the open-mouthed startle with which they greeted every fresh sight: I felt vaguely the spell of the books I had read, returning; markets in Persia, bazaars in Cairo. . . . Nevertheless, I was careful not to let them brush too closely past me, lest some unnamable *something* crawl from their dusty blankets or torn cotton trousers onto my clean self, and I did not like the way they spat, with that terrible gurgle in the throat, into the gutter, or, worse still, blew their noses loudly between finger and thumb, and flung the excrement horribly to the air.

And neither did I like the heavy, sickening, greasy carrion-breath that poured from the mouth of the Hotela la Bantu, where the natives hunched intent at zinc-topped forms, eating steaming no-color chunks of horror that bore no relation to meat as I knew it. The down on my arms prickled in revulsion from the pulpy entrails hanging in dreadful enticement at the window, and the blood-embroidered sawdust spilling out of the doorway.

I know that I wondered how the storekeepers' wives, who sat on soap boxes outside the doorways of the shops on either side of the eating house, could stand the breath of that maw. How could they sit, like lizards in the sun; and all the time they breathed in the breath of the eating house: took it deep into the recesses of their beings, whilst my throat closed against it in disgust.

It was down there one burning afternoon that I met Mrs. Saiyetovitz. She was one of the storekeepers' wives, and I had seen her many times before, sitting before the deep, blanket-hung cave of her husband's store, where a pile of tinsel-covered wooden trunks shimmered and flashed a pink or green eye out of the gloom into the outside—wearing her creased alpaca apron, her fat insteps leaning over her down-at-heel shoes. Sometimes she knitted, and sometimes she just sat. On this day there was a small girl hanging about her, drawing on the shopwindow with a sticky forefinger. When the child turned to look at me, I recognized her as one of the girls from "our school"; a girl from my class, as a matter of fact, called Miriam Saiyetovitz. Yes, that was her name: I remembered it because it was ugly—I was always sorry for girls with ugly names.

Miriam was a tousled, black-haired little girl, who wore a red bow in her hair. Now she recognized me, and we stood looking at one another; all at once the spare line of the name "Miriam Saiyetovitz," that was like the scrolled pattern of an iron gate with only the sky behind it, shifted its perspective in my mind, so that now between the cold curly M's and the implacable A's of that gate's framework, I saw a house, a complication of buildings and flowers and figures walking, where before there was nothing but the sky. Miriam Saiyetovitz—and this: behind her name and her school self, the hot and buzzing world of the stores. And I smiled at her, very friendly.

So she knew we had decided to recognize one another and she

sauntered over to talk to me. I stood with her in the doorway of her father's store, and I, too, wrote my name and drew cats composed of two capital O's and a sausage tail, with the point of my hot and sticky finger on the window. Of course, she did not exactly introduce me to her mother—children never do introduce their mothers; they merely let it be known, by referring to the woman in question offhand, in the course of play, or going up to speak to her in such a way that the relationship becomes obvious. Miriam went up to her mother and said diffidently: "Ma, I know this girl from school—she's in class with me, can we have some red lemonade?"

And the woman lifted her head from where she sat, wide-legged, so that you couldn't help seeing the knee-elastic of her striped pink silk bloomers holding over the cotton tops of her stockings, and said, peering, "Take it! Take it! Go, have it!"

Because I did not then know her, I thought that she was angry, she spoke with such impatience; but soon I knew that it was only her eager generosity that made her fling permission almost fiercely at Miriam whenever the child made some request. Mrs. Saiyetovitz's glance wavered over to me, but she did not seem to be seeing me very clearly: indeed, she could not, for her small, pale, pale eyes narrowed into her big, simple, heavy face were half-blind, and she had always to peer at everything, and never quite see.

I saw that she was very ugly.

Ugly, with the blunt ugliness of a toad; the ugliness of seeming not entirely at home in any element—as if the earth were the wrong place, too heavy and magnetic for a creature already so blunt; and the water would be no better: too subtle and contour-swayed for a creature so graceless. And yet her ugliness was without repellence. When I grew older I often wondered why; she should have been repellent, one should have turned from her, but one did not. She was only ugly. She had the short, stunted yet heavy bones of generations of oppression in the ghettos of Europe; breasts, stomach, hips crowded sadly, no height, wide strong shoulders and a round back. Her head settled right down between her shoulders without even the grace of a neck, and her dun flat hair was cut at the level of her ears. Her features were not essentially Semitic; there was nothing so *definite* as that about her: she had no distinction whatever.

Miriam reappeared from the shades of the store, carrying two bottles of red lemonade. A Shangaan emerged at the same time, clutching a newspaper parcel and puzzling over his handful of change, not looking where he was going. Miriam swept past him, the dusty African with his odd, troglodyte unsureness, and his hair plastered into savage whorls with red clay. With one swift movement she knocked the tin caps off the bottles against the scratched frame of the shop-window, and handed my lemonade to me. "Where did you get it so quickly?" I asked, surprised. She jerked her head back towards the store: "In the kitchen," she said—and applied herself to the bottle.

And so I knew that the Saiyetovitzes lived there, behind the Concession store.

Saturday afternoons were the busiest. Mrs. Saiyetovitz's box stood vacant outside and she helped her husband in the shop. Saturday afternoon was usually my afternoon for going down there, too; my mother and father went out to golf, and I was left with the tick of the clock, the purring monologue of our cat, and the doves gurgling in the empty garden.

On Saturdays every doorway was crowded; a continual shifting stream snaked up and down the pavements; flies tangled overhead, the air smelled hotter, and from the doorway of every store the high, wailing blare and repetition of native songs, played on the gramophone, swung out upon the air and met in discord with the tune of the record being played next door.

Miriam's mother's brother was the proprietor of the Hotela la Bantu, and another uncle had the bicycle shop two doors down. Sometimes she had a message to deliver at the bicycle shop, and I would go in with her. Spare wheels hung across the ceiling, there was a battered wooden counter with a pile of puncture repair outfits, a sewing machine or two for sale, and, in the window, bells and pumps and mascots cut out of tin, painted yellow and red for the adornment of handle bars. We were invariably offered a lemonade by the uncle, and we invariably accepted. At home I was not allowed to drink lemonades unlimited; they might "spoil my dinner"; but Miriam drank them whenever she pleased.

Wriggling in and out amongst the gray-dusty bodies of the natives—their silky brown skin dies in the damp fug underground: after a few months down the mine, it reflects only weariness—Miriam looked with her own calm, quick self-possession upon the setting in which she found herself. Like someone sitting in a swarm of ants; and letting them swarm, letting them crawl all over and about her. Not lifting a hand to flick them off. Not crying out against them in disgust; nor explaining, saying, well, I *like* ants. Just sitting there and letting them swarm, and looking out of herself as if to say: What ants? What ants are you talking about? I giggled and shuddered in excitment at the sight of the dried bats and cobwebby snakeskins rotting in the bleary little window of the medicine shop, but Miriam tugged at my dress and said, "Oh, come on—." I exclaimed at the purple and red shirts lying amongst the dead flies in the wonderful confusion of Saiyetovitz's store window, but Miriam was telling me about her music exam in September, and only frowned at the interruption. I was approaching the confusion of adolescence, and sometimes an uncomfortable, terrible, fascinating curiosity—like a headless worm which lay shamefully hidden in the earth of my soul—crawled out into my consciousness at the sight of the animal obviousness of the natives' male bodies in their scanty covering; but the flash of my guilt at these moments met no answer in Miriam, although she was the same age as I.

If the sight of a boy interrupting his conversation to step out a yard or two onto the veld to relieve himself filled me with embarrassment and real disgust, so that I wanted to go and look at flowers—it seemed that Miriam did not see.

It was quite a long time before she took me into her father's store.

For months it remained a vague, dark, dust-moted world beyond the blanket-hung doorway, into which she was swallowed up and appeared again, whilst I waited outside, with the boys who looked and looked and looked at the windows. Then one day, as she was entering, she paused, and said suddenly and calmly: "Aren't you coming . . . ?" Without a word, I followed her in.

It was cool in the store; and the coolness was a surprise. Out of the sun-naked pavement—and into the store that was cool, like a cellar! Light danced only furtively along the folds of the blankets that hung from the ceiling: crackling silent and secret little fires in the curly woolen furze. The blankets were dark somber hangings, in proud colors, bold and primal. They hung like dark stalactites in the cave, still and heavy, communing only their own colors back to themselves. They brooded over the shop; and over Mr. Saiyetovitz there beneath, treading the worn cement with his disgruntled, dispossessed air of doing his best, but . . . I had glimpsed him before. He lurked within the depths of his store like a beast in its lair, and now and then I had seen the glimmer of his pale, pasty face with the wide upper lip under which the lower closed glumly and puffily.

John Saiyetovitz (his name wasn't John at all, really—it was Yanka, but when he arrived at Capetown, long ago, the Immigration authorities were tired of attempting to understand and spell the unfamiliar names of the immigrants pouring off the boat, and by the time they'd got the "Saiyetovitz" spelt right, they couldn't be bothered puzzling over the "Yanka," so they scrawled "John" on his papers, and John he was)—John Saiyetovitz was a gentle man, with an almost hangdog gentleness, but when he was trading with the natives, strange blasts of power seemed to blow up in his soul. Africans are the slowest buyers in the world; to them, buying is a ritual, a slow and solemn undertaking. They must go carefully; they nervously scent pitfalls on every side. And confronted with a selection of different kinds of the one thing they want, they are as confused as a child before a plate of pastries; fingering, hesitating, this or that . . . ? On a busy Saturday they must be allowed to stand about the shop endlessly, looking up and about, pausing to shake their heads and give a profound "OW!"; sauntering off; going to press their noses against the window again; coming back. And Mr. Saiyetovitz—always the same, unshaven and collarless—lugging a blanket down from the shelves, flinging it upon the counter—and another, and then another, and standing, arms hanging, sullen and smoldering before the blank-faced purchaser. The boy with his helpless stance, and his eyes rolling up in the agony of decision, filling the shop with the sickly odor of his anxious sweat, and clutching his precious guitar.

Waiting, waiting.

And then Mr. Saiyetovitz swooping away in a gesture of rage and denial; don't care, sick-to-death. And the boy anxious, edging forward to feel the cloth again, and the whole business starting up all over again; more blankets, different colors, down from the shelf and hooked from the ceiling—stalactites crumpled to woolen heaps to wonder over. Mr. Saiyetovitz throwing them down, moving in jerks of rage now, and then roughly bullying the boy into a decision. Shouting at him, bundling his purchase into his arms, snatching the money, gesturing him cowed out of the store.

Mr. Saiyetovitz treated the natives honestly, but with bad grace. He forced them to feel their ignorance, their inadequacy, and their submission to the white man's world of money. He spiritually maltreated them, and bitterly drove his nail into the coffin of their confidence.

With me, he was shy, he smiled widely and his hand went to the stud swinging loose at the neck of his half-buttoned shirt, and drew as if in apology over the stubbled landscape of his jaw. He always called me "little girl" and he liked to talk to me in the way that he thought children like to be talked to, but I found it very difficult to make a show of reply, because his English was so broken and fragmentary. So I used to stand there, and say yes, Mr. Saiyetovitz, and smile back and say thank you! to anything that sounded like a question, because the question usually was did I want a lemonade?, and of course, I usually did.

The first time Miriam ever came to my home was the day of my birthday party.

Our relationship at school had continued unchanged, just as before; she had her friends and I had mine, but outside of school there was the curious plane of intimacy on which we had, as it were, surprised one another wandering, and so which was shared peculiarly by us.

I had put Miriam's name down on my guest list; she was invited; and she came. She wore a blue taffeta dress which Mrs. Saiyetovitz had made for her (on the old Singer on the counter in the shop, I guessed) and it was quite nice if a bit too frilly. My home was pretty and well-furnished and full of flowers and personal touches of my mother's hands; there was space, and everything shone. Miriam did not open her eyes at it; I saw her finger a bowl of baby-skinned pink roses in the passing, but all afternoon she looked out indifferently as she did at home.

The following Saturday at the store we were discussing the party. Miriam was telling Mrs. Saiyetovitz about my presents, and I was standing by in pleasurable embarrassment at my own importance.

"Well, please God, Miri," said Mrs. Saiyetovitz at the finish, "you'll also have a party for your birthday in April. . . . Ve'll be in d'house, and everyting'll be nice, just like you want." They were leaving the rooms behind the shop—the mournful green plush curtains glooming the archway between the bedroom and the living room; the tarnished samovar; the black beetles in the little kitchen; Miriam's old black piano with the candlesticks, wheezing in the drafty passage; the damp puddly yard piled with empty packing cases and eggshells and banana skins; the hovering smell of fish frying. They were going to live in a little house in the township nearby.

But when April came, Miriam took ten of her friends to the Saturday afternoon bioscope in celebration of her birthday. "And to Costas Café afterwards for ice cream," she stated to her mother, looking out over her head. I think Mrs. Saiyetovitz was disappointed about the party, but she reasoned then, as always, that as her daughter went to school and was educated and could speak English, whilst she herself knew nothing, wasn't clever at all, the little daughter must know best what was right and what was *nice*.

I know now what of course I did not know then: that Miriam Saiyetovitz and I were intelligent little girls into whose brains there never had, and never would, come the freak and wonderful flash that is brilliance. Ours were alabaster intellects: clear, perfect, light; no streaks of dark, unknown granite splitting to reveal secret veins of brightness, like thin gold, between stratum and stratum. We were fitted to be good schoolteachers, secretaries, organizers; we did everything well, nothing badly, and nothing remarkably. But to the Saiyetovitzes, Miriam's brain blazed like the sun, warming their humbleness.

In the year-by-year passage through school, our classmates thinned out one by one; the way seedlings come up in a bunch to a certain stage in their development, and then by some inexplicable process of natural selection, one or two continue to grow and branch up into the air, whilst the others wither or remain small and weedy. The other girls left to go and learn shorthand-and-typewriting: weeded out by the necessity of earning a living. Or moved, and went to other schools: transplanted to some ground of their own. Miriam and I remained, growing straight and steadily. . . .

During our matriculation year a sense of wonder and impending change came upon us both; the excitement of coming to an end that is also a beginning. We felt this in one another, and so were drawn together in new earnestness. Miriam came to study with me in the garden at my house, and oftener than ever, I slipped down to the Concession stores to exchange a book or discuss work with her. For although they now had a house, the Saiyetovitzes still lived, in the wider sense of the word, at the store. When Miriam and I discussed our schoolwork, the Saiyetovitzes crept about, very quiet, talking to one another only in hoarse, respectful whispers.

It was during this year, when the wonder of our own capacity to learn was reaching out and catching into light like a veld fire within us, that we began to talk of the University. And, all at once, we talked of nothing else. I spoke to my father of it, and he was agreeable, although my mother thought a girl could do better with her time. But so long as my father was willing to send me, I knew I should go. "Ah yes," said Miriam. She liked my father very much; I knew that. In fact she said to me once—it was a strange thing to say, and almost emotionally, she said it, and at a strange time, because we were on the bus going into the town to buy a new winter coat which she had wanted very badly and talked about longingly for days, and her father had just given her the money to get it—she said to me: "You know, I think your father's just right. I mean, if you had to choose somebody, a certain kind of person for a father, well, your father'd be just the kind you'd want."

When she broached the subject of University to her parents, they were agreeable for her to go, too. Indeed, they wanted her to go almost more than she herself did. But they worried a great deal about the money side of it; every time I went down to the store there'd be a discussion of ways and means, Saiyetovitz slowly munching his bread and garlic polony lunch, and worrying. Miriam didn't worry about it; they'll find the money, she said. She was a tall girl, now, with beautiful breasts, and a large, dark-featured face that had a certain capable elegance, although her father's glum mouth was unmistakable and on her upper lip faint dark down foreshadowed a heavy middle-age. Her parents were peasants; but she was the powerful young Jewess. Beside her, I felt pale in my Scotch gingery-fairness: lightly drawn upon the mind's eye, whilst she was painted in oils.

We both matriculated; not so well as we thought we should, but well enough; and we went to the university. And there too, we did well enough. We had both decided upon the same course: teaching. In the end, it had seemed the only thing to do. Neither of us had any particular bent.

It must have been a hard struggle for the Saiyetovitzes to keep Miriam at the University, buy her clothes, and pay for her board and lodging in Johannesburg. There is a great deal of money to be made out of native trade concessions purchased from the government; and it doesn't require education or trained commercial astuteness to make it—in fact, trading of this sort seems to flourish in response to something very different: what is needed is instinctive peasant craftiness such as can only be found in the uneducated, in those who have scratched up their own resources. Storekeepers with this quality of peasant craft made money all about Mr. Saiyetovitz, bought houses and motorcars and banded their wives' retired hands with diamonds in mark of their new idleness. But Mr. Saiyetovitz was a peasant without the peasant's craft; without that flaw in his simplicity that might have given him checks and deeds of transfer to sign, even if he were unable to read the print on the documents. . . . Without this craft, the peasant has only one thing left to him: hard work, dirty work, with the sweet, sickly body-smell of the black men about him all day. Saiyetovitz made no money: only worked hard and long, standing in his damp shirt amidst the clamor of the stores and the death-smell from the eating house always in his nose.

Meanwhile, Miriam fined down into a lady. She developed a half-bored, half-intolerant shrug of the shoulders in place of the childish sharpness that had been filed jagged by the rub-rub of rough life and harsh contrasts. She became soft-voiced, where she had been loud and gay. She watched and conformed; and soon took on the attitude of liberal-mindedness that sets the doors of the mind slackly open, so that any idea may walk in and out again, leaving very little impression: she could appreciate Bach and Stravinsky, and spend a long evening listening to swing music in the dark of somebody's flat.

Race and creed had never meant very much to Miriam and me, but at the University she sifted naturally towards the young Jews who were passing easily and enthusiastically, with their people's extraordinary aptitude for creative and scientific work, through medical school. They liked her; she was invited to their homes for tennis parties, swimming on Sundays, and dances, and she seemed as unimpressed by the luxury of their ten-thousand-pound houses as she had been by the contrast of our clean, pleasant little home, long ago, when she herself was living behind the Concession store.

She usually spent part of the vacations with friends in Johannesburg; I missed her—wandering about the Mine on my own, out of touch, now, with the girls I had left behind in the backwater of the small town. During the second half of one July vacation—she had spent the first two weeks in Johannesburg—she asked me if she could come and spend Sunday at my home, and in the afternoon, one of the medical students arrived at our house in his small car. He had come from Johannesburg; Miriam had evidently told him she would be with us. I gathered her parents did not know of the young man's visit, and I did not speak of it before them.

So the four years of our training passed. Miriam Saiyetovitz and I had dropped like two leaves, side by side into the same current, and been carried downstream together: now the current met a swirl of dead logs, reeds, and the force of other waters, and broke up, divided its drive and its one direction. The leaves floated clear; divergent from one another. Miriam got a teaching post in Johannesburg, but I was sent to a small school in the Northern Transvaal. We met seldom during the first six months of our adult life: Miriam went to Capetown during the vacation, and I flew to Rhodesia with the first profits of my independence. Then came the war, and I, glad to escape so soon the profession I had once anticipated with such enthusiasm, joined the nursing service and went away for the long, strange interlude of four years. Whilst I was with a field hospital in Italy, I heard that Miriam had married—a Doctor Somebody-or-other: my informant wasn't sure of the name. I guessed it must be one of the boys whom she had known as students. I sent a cable of congratulation, to the Saiyetovitzes' address.

And then, one day I came back to the small mining town and found it there, the same; like a face that has been waiting a long time. My Mother, and my Dad, the big wheels of the shaft turning, the trees folding their wings about the Mine houses; and our house, with the green, square lawn and the cat watching the doves. For the first few weeks I faltered about the old life, feeling my way in a dream so like the old reality that it hurt.

There was a feel about an afternoon that made my limbs tingle with familiarity. . . . What . . . ? And then, lying on our lawn under the hot sky, I knew: just the sort of glaring summer afternoon that used to send me down to the Concession stores, feeling isolated in the heat. Instantly, I thought of the Saiyetovitzes, and I wanted to go and see them, see if they were still there; what Miriam was doing; where she was, now.

Down at the stores it was the same as ever, only dirtier, smaller, more chipped and smeared—the way reality often is in contrast with the image carried long in the mind. As I stepped so strangely on that old pocked pavement, with the skeleton cats and the orange peel and the gobs of spit, my heart tightened with the thought of the Saiyetovitzes. I was in a kind of excitement to see the store again. And there it was; the excitement sank out at the evidence of the monotony of "things." Blankets swung a little in the doorway. Flies crawled amongst the shirts and shoes posed in the window, the hot, wet, sickening fatty smell came over from the eating house. I met it with the old revulsion: it was like breathing inside someone's stomach. And in the store, amongst the wicked glitter of the tin trunks, beneath the secret whispering of the blankets, the old Saiyetovitzes sat glumly, with patience, waiting. . . . As animals wait in a cage; for nothing.

In their delight at seeing me again, I saw that they were older, sadder; that they had somehow given themselves into the weight of their own humbleness, they were without a pinnacle on which to fix their eyes. Whatever place it was that they looked upon now, it was flat.

Mr. Saiyetovitz's mouth had creased in further to the dead folds of his chin; his hair straggled to the rims of his ears. As he spoke to me, I noticed that his hands lay, with a curious helpless indifference, curled on the counter. Mrs. Saiyetovitz shuffled off at once to the back of the shop to make a cup of tea for me, and carried it in, slopping over into the saucer. She was uglier than ever, now, her back hunched up to meet her head, her old thick legs spiraled in crêpe bandages because of varicose veins. And blinder too, I could see: that enquiring look of the blind or deaf smiling unsure at you from her face.

The talk turned almost at once to Miriam, and as they answered my questions about her, I saw them go inert. Yes, she was married; had married a doctor—a flicker of pride in the old man at this. She lived in Johannesburg. Her husband was doing very well. There was a photograph of her home, in one of the more expensive suburbs; a large, white modern house, with flower borders and a fishpond. And there was Miri's little boy, sitting on his swing; and a studio portrait of him, taken with his mother.

There was the face of Miriam Saiyetovitz, confident, carefully made-up and framed in a good hairdresser's version of her dark hair, smiling queenly over the face of her child. One hand lay on the child's shoulder, a smooth hand, wearing large, plain, expensive diamond rings. Her bosom was proud and rounded now—a little too heavy, a little overripe in the climate of ease.

I could see in her face that she had forgotten a lot of things.

When his wife had gone into the back of the shop to refill my teacup, old Saiyetovitz went silent, looking at the hand that lay before him on the counter, the fingers twitching a little under the gaze.

It doesn't come out like you think, he said, it doesn't come out like you think.

He looked up at me with a comforting smile.

And then he told me that they had seen Miriam's little boy only three times since he was born. Miriam they saw hardly at all; her husband never. Once or twice a year she came out from Johannesburg to visit them, staying an hour on a Sunday afternoon, and then driving herself back to Town again. She had not invited her parents to her home at any time; they had been there only once, on the occasion of the birth of their grandson.

Mrs. Saiyetovitz came back into the store: she seemed to know of what we had been speaking. She sat down on a shot-purple tin trunk and folded her arms over her breast. Ah yes, she breathed, ah yes. . . .

I stood there in Miriam's guilt before the Saiyetovitzes, and they were silent, in the accusation of the humble.

But in a little while a Swazi in a tobacco-colored blanket sauntered dreamily into the shop, and Mr. Saiyetovitz rose heavy with defeat.

Through the eddy of dust in the lonely interior and the wavering fear round the head of the native and the bright hot dance of the jazz blankets and the dreadful submission of Mrs. Saiyetovitz's conquered voice in my ear, I heard his voice strike like a snake at my faith: angry and browbeating, sullen and final, lashing weakness at the weak.

Mr. Saiyetovitz and the native.

Defeated, and without understanding in their defeat.

Flannery O'Connor *(1925–1964) was born in Savannah and raised on a small farm in Milledgeville, Georgia. She attended a Catholic high school, graduated from Georgia State College for Women in 1945, and studied creative writing under Paul Engle at the University of Iowa. She contributed regularly both to academic journals —*Kenyon Review, Sewanee Review*—and popular magazines—*Harper's Bazaar, Mademoiselle. *In 1950 Miss O'Connor began suffering from disseminated lupus, a disease that forced an invalid's life upon her at the family farm in Milledgeville. During these years she developed an art which joined a casual idiomatic style to a firm Catholic content. She produced two novels—*Wise Blood *(1952) and* The Violent Bear It Away *(1960)—and two collections of stories—*A Good Man Is Hard to Find *(1955) and* Everything That Rises Must Converge *(1965). Two additional volumes,* Mystery and Manners: Occasional Prose *(1969) and* The Complete Stories, *which won the National Book Award for 1972, have appeared since her death.*

Everything That Rises Must Converge

FLANNERY O'CONNOR

Her doctor had told Julian's mother that she must lose twenty pounds on account of her blood pressure, so on Wednesday nights Julian had to take her downtown on the bus for a reducing class at the Y. The reducing class was designed for working girls over fifty, who weighed from 165 to 200 pounds. His mother was one of the slimmer ones, but she said ladies did not tell their age or weight. She would not ride the buses by herself at night since they had been integrated, and because the reducing class was one of her few pleasures, necessary for her health, and *free*, she said Julian could at least put himself out to take her, considering all she did for him. Julian did not like to consider all she did for him, but every Wednesday night he braced himself and took her.

She was almost ready to go, standing before the hall mirror, putting on her hat, while he, his hands behind him, appeared pinned to the door frame, waiting like Saint Sebastian for the arrows to begin piercing him. The hat was new and had cost over seven dollars and a half. She kept saying, "Maybe I shouldn't have paid that for it. No, I shouldn't have. I'll take it off and return it tomorrow. I shouldn't have bought it."

Julian raised his eyes to heaven. "Yes, you should have bought it," he said. "Put it on and let's go." It was a hideous hat. A purple velvet flap came down on one side of it and stood up on the other; the rest of it was green and looked like a cushion with the stuffing out. He decided it was less comical than jaunty and pathetic. Everything that gave her pleasure was small and depressed him.

She lifted the hat one more time and set it down slowly on top of her head. Two wings of gray hair protruded on either side of her florid face, but her eyes, sky-blue, were as innocent and untouched by experience as they must have been when she was ten. Were it not that she was a widow who had struggled fiercely to feed and clothe and put him through school and who was supporting him still, "until he got on his feet," she might have been a little girl that he had to take to town.

"It's all right, it's all right," he said. "Let's go." He opened the door himself and started down the walk to get her going. The sky was a dying violet and the houses stood out darkly against it, bulbous liver-colored monstrosities of a uniform ugliness though no two were alike. Since this had been a fashionable neighborhood forty years ago, his mother persisted in thinking they did well to have an apartment in it. Each house had a narrow collar of dirt around it in which sat, usually, a grubby child. Julian walked with his hands in his pockets, his head down and thrust forward and his eyes glazed with the determination to make himself completely numb during the time he would be sacrificed to her pleasure.

The door closed and he turned to find the dumpy figure, surmounted by the atrocious hat, coming toward him. "Well," she said, "you only live once and paying a little more for it, I at least won't meet myself coming and going."

"Some day I'll start making money," Julian said gloomily—he knew he never would—"and you can have one of those jokes whenever you take the fit." But first they would move. He visualized a place where the nearest neighbors would be three miles away on either side.

"I think you're doing fine," she said, drawing on her gloves. "You've only been out of school a year. Rome wasn't built in a day."

She was one of the few members of the Y reducing class who arrived in hat and gloves and who had a son who had been to college. "It takes time," she said, "and the world is in such a mess. This hat looked better on me than any of the others, though when she brought it out I said, 'Take that thing back. I wouldn't have it on my head,' and she said, 'Now wait till you see it on,' and when she put it on me, I said, 'We-ull,' and she said, 'If you ask me, that hat does something for you and you do something for the hat, and besides,' she said, 'with that hat, you won't meet yourself coming and going.' "

Julian thought he could have stood his lot better if she had been selfish, if she had been an old hag who drank and screamed at him. He walked along, saturated in depression, as if in the midst of his martyrdom he had lost his faith. Catching sight of his long, hopeless, irritated face, she stopped suddenly with a grief-stricken look, and pulled back on his arm. "Wait on me," she said. "I'm going back to the house and take this thing off and tomorrow I'm going to return it. I was out of my head. I can pay the gas bill with that seven-fifty."

He caught her in a vicious grip. "You are not going to take it back," he said. "I like it."

"Well," she said, "I don't think I ought . . ."

"Shut up and enjoy it," he muttered, more depressed than ever.

"With the world in the mess it's in," she said, "it's a wonder we can enjoy anything. I tell you, the bottom rail is on the top."

Julian sighed.

"Of course," she said, "if you know who you are, you can go anywhere." She said this every time he took her to the reducing class. "Most of them in it are not our kind of people," she said, "but I can be gracious to anybody. I know who I am."

"They don't give a damn for your graciousness," Julian said savagely. "Knowing who you are is good for one generation only. You haven't the foggiest idea where you stand now or who you are."

She stopped and allowed her eyes to flash at him. "I most certainly do know who I am," she said, "and if you don't know who you are, I'm ashamed of you."

"Oh hell," Julian said.

"Your great-grandfather was a former governor of this state," she said. "Your grandfather was a prosperous landowner. Your grandmother was a Godhigh."

"Will you look around you," he said tensely, "and see where you are now?" and he swept his arm jerkily out to indicate the neighborhood, which the growing darkness at least made less dingy.

"You remain what you are," she said. "Your great-grandfather had a plantation and two hundred slaves."

"There are no more slaves," he said irritably.

"They were better off when they were," she said. He groaned to see that she was off on that topic. She rolled onto it every few days like a train on an open track. He knew every stop, every junction, every swamp along the way, and knew the exact point at which her conclusion would roll majestically into the station: "It's ridiculous. It's simply not realistic. They should rise, yes, but on their own side of the fence."

"Let's skip it," Julian said.

"The ones I feel sorry for," she said, "are the ones that are half white. They're tragic."

"Will you skip it?"

"Suppose we were half white. We would certainly have mixed feelings."

"I have mixed feelings now," he groaned.

"Well, let's talk about something pleasant," she said. "I remember going to Grandpa's when I was a little girl. Then the house had double stairways that went up to what was really the second floor—all the cooking was done on the first. I used to like to stay down in the kitchen on account of the way the walls smelled. I would sit with my nose pressed against the plaster and take deep breaths. Actually the place belonged to the Godhighs but your grandfather Chestny paid the mortgage and saved it for them. They were in reduced circumstances," she said, "but reduced or not, they never forgot who they were."

"Doubtless that decayed mansion reminded them," Julian muttered. He never spoke of it without contempt or thought of it without longing. He had seen it once when he was a child before it had been sold. The double stairways had rotted and been torn down. Negroes were living in it. But it remained in his mind as his mother had known it. It appeared in his dreams regularly. He would stand on the wide porch, listening to the rustle of oak leaves, then wander through the high-ceilinged hall into the parlor that opened onto it and gaze at the worn rugs and faded draperies. It occurred to him that it was he, not she, who could have appreciated it. He preferred its threadbare elegance to anything he could name and it was because of it that all the neighborhoods they had lived in had been a torment to him—whereas she had hardly known the difference. She called her insensitivity "being adjustable."

"And I remember the old darky who was my nurse, Caroline. There was no better person in the world. I've always had a great respect for my colored friends," she said. "I'd do anything in the world for them and they'd . . ."

"Will you for God's sake get off that subject?" Julian said. When he got on a bus by himself, he made it a point to sit down beside a Negro, in reparation as it were for his mother's sins.

"You're mighty touchy tonight," she said. "Do you feel all right?"

"Yes I feel all right," he said. "Now lay off."

She pursed her lips. "Well, you certainly are in a vile humor," she observed. "I just won't speak to you at all."

They had reached the bus stop. There was no bus in sight and Julian, his hands still jammed in his pockets and his head thrust forward, scowled down the empty street. The frustration of having to wait on the bus as well as ride on it began to creep up his neck like a hot hand. The presence of his mother was borne in upon him as she gave a pained sigh. He looked at her bleakly. She was holding herself very erect under the preposterous hat, wearing it like a banner of her imaginary dignity. There was in him an evil urge to break her spirit. He suddenly unloosened his tie and pulled it off and put it in his pocket.

She stiffened. "Why must you look like *that* when you take me to town?" she said. "Why must you deliberately embarrass me?"

"If you'll never learn where you are," he said, "you can at least learn where I am."

"You look like a—thug," she said.

"Then I must be one," he murmured.

"I'll just go home," she said. "I will not bother you. If you can't do a little thing like that for me . . ."

Rolling his eyes upward, he put his tie back on. "Restored to my class," he muttered. He thrust his face toward her and hissed, "True culture is in the mind, the *mind*," he said, and tapped his head, "the mind."

"It's in the heart," she said, "and in how you do things and how you do things is because of who you *are*."

"Nobody in the damn bus cares who you are."

"I care who I am," she said icily.

The lighted bus appeared on top of the next hill and as it approached, they moved out into the street to meet it. He put his hand under her elbow and hoisted her up on the creaking step. She entered with a little smile, as if she were going into a drawing room where everyone had been waiting for her. While he put in the tokens, she sat down on one of the broad front seats for three which faced the aisle. A thin woman with protruding teeth and long yellow hair was sitting on the end of it. His mother moved up beside her and left room for Julian beside herself. He sat down and looked at the floor across the aisle where a pair of thin feet in red and white canvas sandals were planted.

His mother immediately began a general conversation meant to attract anyone who felt like talking. "Can it get any hotter?" she said and removed from her purse a folding fan, black with a Japanese scene on it, which she began to flutter before her.

"I reckon it might could," the woman with the protruding teeth said, "but I know for a fact my apartment couldn't get no hotter."

"It must get the afternoon sun," his mother said. She sat forward and looked up and down the bus. It was half filled. Everybody was white. "I see we have the bus to ourselves," she said. Julian cringed.

"For a change," said the woman across the aisle, the owner of the red and white canvas sandals. "I come on one the other day and they were thick as fleas—up front and all through."

"The world is in a mess everywhere," his mother said. "I don't know how we've let it get in this fix."

"What gets my goat is all those boys from good families stealing automobile tires," the woman with the protruding teeth said. "I told my boy, I said you may not be rich but you been raised right and if I ever catch you in any such mess, they can send you on to the reformatory. Be exactly where you belong."

"Training tells," his mother said. "Is your boy in high school?"

"Ninth grade," the woman said.

"My son just finished college last year. He wants to write but he's selling typewriters until he gets started," his mother said.

The woman leaned forward and peered at Julian. He threw her such a malevolent look that she subsided against the seat. On the floor across the aisle there was an abandoned newspaper. He got up and got it and opened it out in front of him. His mother discreetly continued the conversation in a lower tone but the woman across the aisle said in a loud voice, "Well that's nice. Selling typewriters is close to writing. He can go right from one to the other."

"I tell him," his mother said, "that Rome wasn't built in a day."

Behind the newspaper Julian was withdrawing into the inner compartment of his mind where he spent most of his time. This was a kind of mental bubble in which he established himself when he could not bear to be a part of what was going on around him. From it he could see out and judge but in it he was safe from any kind of penetration from without. It was the only place where he felt free of the general idiocy of his fellows. His mother had never entered it but from it he could see her with absolute clarity.

The old lady was clever enough and he thought that if she had started from any of the right premises, more might have been expected of her. She lived according to the laws of her own fantasy world, outside of which he had never seen her set foot. The law of it was to sacrifice herself for him after she had first created the necessity to do so by making a mess of things. If he had permitted her sacrifices, it was only because her lack of foresight had made them necessary. All of her life had been a struggle to act like a Chestny without the Chestny goods, and to give him everything she thought a Chestny ought to have; but since, said she, it was fun to struggle, why complain? And when you had won, as she had won, what fun to look back on the hard times! He could not forgive her that she had enjoyed the struggle and that she thought *she* had won.

What she meant when she said she had won was that she had brought him up successfully and had sent him to college and that he had turned out so well—good-looking (her teeth had gone unfilled so that his could be straightened), intelligent (he realized he was too intelligent to be a success), and with a future ahead of him (there was of course no future ahead of him). She excused his gloominess on the grounds that he was still growing up and his radical ideas on his lack of practical experience. She said he didn't yet know a thing about "life," that he hadn't even entered the real world—when already he was as disenchanted with it as a man of fifty.

The further irony of all this was that in spite of her, he had turned out so well. In spite of going to only a third-rate college, he had, on his own initiative, come out with a first-rate education; in spite of growing up dominated by a small mind, he had ended up with a large one; in spite of all her foolish views, he was free of prejudice and unafraid to face facts. Most miraculous of all, instead of being blinded by love for her as she was for him, he had cut himself emotionally free of her and could see her with complete objectivity. He was not dominated by his mother.

The bus stopped with a sudden jerk and shook him from his meditation. A woman from the back lurched forward with little steps and barely escaped falling in his newspaper as she righted herself. She got off and a large Negro got on. Julian kept his paper lowered to watch. It gave him a certain satisfaction to see injustice in daily operation. It confirmed his view that with a few exceptions there was no one worth knowing within a radius of three hundred miles. The Negro was well dressed and carried a briefcase. He looked around and then sat down on the other end of the seat where the woman with the red and white canvas sandals was sitting. He immediately unfolded a newspaper and obscured himself behind it. Julian's mother's elbow at once prodded insistently into his ribs. "Now you see why I won't ride on these buses by myself," she whispered.

The woman with the red and white canvas sandals had risen at the same time the Negro sat down and had gone further back in the bus and taken the seat of the woman who had got off. His mother leaned forward and cast her an approving look.

Julian rose, crossed the aisle, and sat down in the place of the woman with the canvas sandals. From this position, he looked serenely across at his mother. Her face had turned an angry red. He stared at her, making his eyes the eyes of a stranger. He felt his tension suddenly lift as if he had openly declared war on her.

He would have liked to get in conversation with the Negro and to talk with him about art or politics or any subject that would be above the comprehension of those around them, but the man remained entrenched behind his paper. He was either ignoring the change of seating or had never noticed it. There was no way for Julian to convey his sympathy.

His mother kept her eyes fixed reproachfully on his face. The woman with the protruding teeth was looking at him avidly as if he were a type of monster new to her.

"Do you have a light?" he asked the Negro.

Without looking away from his paper, the man reached in his pocket and handed him a packet of matches.

"Thanks," Julian said. For a moment he held the matches foolishly. A NO SMOKING sign looked down upon him from over the door. This alone would not have deterred him; he had no cigarettes. He had quit smoking some months before because he could not afford it. "Sorry," he muttered and handed back the matches. The Negro lowered the paper and gave him an annoyed look. He took the matches and raised the paper again.

His mother continued to gaze at him but she did not take advantage of his momentary discomfort. Her eyes retained their battered look. Her face seemed to be unnaturally red, as if her blood pressure had risen. Julian allowed no glimmer of sympathy to show on his face. Having got the advantage, he wanted desperately to keep it and carry it through. He would have liked to teach her a lesson that would last her a while, but there seemed no way to continue the point. The Negro refused to come out from behind his paper.

Julian folded his arms and looked stolidly before him, facing her but as if he did not see her, as if he had ceased to recognize her existence. He visualized a scene in which, the bus having reached their stop, he would remain in his seat and when she said, "Aren't you going to get off?" he would look at her as at a stranger who had rashly addressed him. The corner they got off on was usually deserted, but it was well lighted and it would not hurt her to walk by herself the four blocks to the Y. He decided to wait until the time came and then decide whether or not he would let her get off by herself. He would have to be at the Y at ten to bring her back, but he could leave her wondering if he was going to show up. There was no reason for her to think she could always depend on him.

He retired again into the high-ceilinged room sparsely settled with large pieces of antique furniture. His soul expanded momentarily but then he became aware of his mother across from him and the vision shriveled. He studied her coldly. Her feet in little pumps dangled like a child's and did not quite reach the floor. She was training on him an exaggerated look of reproach. He felt completely detached from her. At that moment he could with pleasure have slapped her as he would have slapped a particularly obnoxious child in his charge.

He began to imagine various unlikely ways by which he could teach her a lesson. He might make friends with some distinguished Negro professor or lawyer and bring him home to spend the evening. He would be entirely justified but her blood pressure would rise to 300. He could not push her to the extent of making her have a stroke, and moreover, he had never been successful at making any Negro friends. He had tried to strike up an acquaintance on the bus with some of the better types, with ones that looked like professors or ministers or lawyers. One morning he had sat down next to a distinguished-looking dark brown man who had answered his questions with a sonorous solemnity but who had turned out to be an undertaker. Another day he had sat down beside a cigar-smoking Negro with a diamond ring on his finger, but after a few stilted pleasantries, the Negro had rung the buzzer and risen, slipping two lottery tickets into Julian's hand as he climbed over him to leave.

He imagined his mother lying desperately ill and his being able to secure only a Negro doctor for her. He toyed with that idea for a few minutes and then dropped it for a momentary vision of himself participating as a sympathizer in a sit-in demonstration. This was possible but he did not linger with it. Instead, he approached the ultimate horror. He brought home a beautiful suspiciously Negroid woman. Prepare yourself, he said. There is nothing you can do about it. This is the woman I've chosen. She's intelligent, dignified, even good, and she's suffered and she hasn't thought it *fun*.Now persecute us, go ahead and persecute us. Drive her out of here, but remember, you're driving me too. His eyes were narrowed and through the indignation he had generated, he saw his mother across the aisle, purple-faced, shrunken to the dwarf-like proportions of her moral nature, sitting like a mummy beneath the ridiculous banner of her hat.

He was tilted out of his fantasy again as the bus stopped. The door opened with a sucking hiss and out of the dark a large, gaily dressed, sullen-looking colored woman got on with a little boy. The child, who might have been four, had on a short plaid suit and a Tyrolean hat with a blue feather in it. Julian hoped that he would sit down beside him and that the woman would push in beside his mother. He could think of no better arrangement.

As she waited for her tokens, the woman was surveying the seating possibilities—he hoped with the idea of sitting where she was least wanted. There was something familiar-looking about her but Julian could not place what it was. She was a giant of a woman. Her face was set not only to meet opposition but to seek it out. The downward tilt of her large lower lip was like a warning sign: DON'T TAMPER WITH ME. Her bulging figure was encased in a green crepe dress and her feet overflowed in red shoes. She had on a hideous hat. A purple velvet flap came down on one side of it and stood up on the other; the rest of it was green and looked like a cushion with the stuffing out. She carried a mammoth red pocketbook that bulged throughout as if it were stuffed with rocks.

To Julian's disappointment, the little boy climbed up on the empty seat beside his mother. His mother lumped all children, black and white, into the common category "cute," and she thought little Negroes were on the whole cuter than little white children. She smiled at the little boy as he climbed on the seat.

Meanwhile the woman was bearing down upon the empty seat beside Julian. To his annoyance, she squeezed herself into it. He saw his mother's face change as the woman settled herself next to him and he realized with satisfaction that this was more objectionable to her than it was to him. Her face seemed almost gray and there was a look of dull recognition in her eyes, as if suddenly she had sickened at some awful confrontation. Julian saw that it was because she and the woman had, in a sense, swapped sons. Though his mother would not realize the symbolic significance of this, she would feel it. His amusement showed plainly on his face.

The woman next to him muttered something unintelligible to herself. He was conscious of a kind of bristling next to him, a muted growling like that of an angry cat. He could not see anything but the red pocketbook upright on the bulging green thighs. He visualized the woman as she had stood waiting for her tokens—the ponderous figure, rising from the red shoes upward over the solid hips, the mammoth bosom, the haughty face, to the green and purple hat.

His eyes widened.

The vision of the two hats, identical, broke upon him with the radiance of a brilliant sunrise. His face was suddenly lit with joy. He could not believe that Fate had thrust upon his mother such a lesson. He gave a loud chuckle so that she would look at him and see that he saw. She turned her eyes on him slowly. The blue in them seemed to have turned a bruised purple. For a moment he had an uncomfortable sense of her innocence, but it lasted only a second before principle rescued him. Justice entitled him to laugh. His grin hardened until it said to her as plainly as if he were saying aloud: Your punishment exactly fits your pettiness. This should teach you a permanent lesson.

Her eyes shifted to the woman. She seemed unable to bear looking at him and to find the woman preferable. He became conscious again of the bristling presence at his side. The woman was rumbling like a volcano about to become active. His mother's mouth began to twitch slightly at one corner. With a sinking heart, he saw incipient signs of recovery on her face and realized that this was going to strike her suddenly as funny and was going to be no lesson at all. She kept her eyes on the woman and an amused smile came over her face as if the woman were a monkey that had stolen her hat. The little Negro was looking up at her with large fascinated eyes. He had been trying to attract her attention for some time.

"Carver!" the woman said suddenly. "Come heah!"

When he saw that the spotlight was on him at last, Carver drew his feet up and turned himself toward Julian's mother and giggled.

"Carver!" the woman said. "You heah me? Come heah!"

Carver slid down from the seat but remained squatting with his back against the base of it, his head turned slyly around toward Julian's mother, who was smiling at him. The woman reached a hand across the aisle and snatched him to her. He righted himself and hung backwards on her knees, grinning at Julian's mother. "Isn't he cute?" Julian's mother said to the woman with the protruding teeth.

"I reckon he is," the woman said without conviction.

The Negress yanked him upright but he eased out of her grip and shot across the aisle and scrambled, giggling wildly, onto the seat beside his love.

"I think he likes me," Julian's mother said, and smiled at the woman. It was the smile she used when she was being particularly gracious to an inferior. Julian saw everything lost. The lesson had rolled off her like rain on a roof.

The woman stood up and yanked the little boy off the seat as if she were snatching him from contagion. Julian could feel the rage in her at having no weapon like his mother's smile. She gave the child a sharp slap across his leg. He howled once and then thrust his head into her stomach and kicked his feet against her shins. "Be-have," she said vehemently.

The bus stopped and the Negro who had been reading the newspaper got off. The woman moved over and set the little boy down with a thump between herself and Julian. She held him firmly by the knee. In a moment he put his hands in front of his face and peeped at Julian's mother through his fingers.

"I see yoooooooo!" she said and put her hand in front of her face and peeped at him.

The woman slapped his hand down. "Quit yo' foolishness," she said, "before I knock the living Jesus out of you!"

Julian was thankful that the next stop was theirs. He reached up and pulled the cord. The woman reached up and pulled it at the same time. Oh my God, he thought. He had the terrible intuition that when they got off the bus together, his mother would open her purse and give the little boy a nickel. The gesture would be as natural to her as breathing. The bus stopped and the woman got up and lunged to the front, dragging the child, who wished to stay on, after her. Julian and his mother got up and followed. As they neared the door, Julian tried to relieve her of her pocketbook.

"No," she murmured, "I want to give the little boy a nickel."

"No!" Julian hissed. "No!"

She smiled down at the child and opened her bag. The bus door opened and the woman picked him up by the arm and descended with him, hanging at her hip. Once in the street she set him down and shook him.

Julian's mother had to close her purse while she got down the bus step but as soon as her feet were on the ground, she opened it again and began to rummage inside. "I can't find but a penny," she whispered, "but it looks like a new one."

"Don't do it!" Julian said fiercely between his teeth. There was a streetlight on the corner and she hurried to get under it so that she could better see into her pocketbook. The woman was heading off rapidly down the street with the child still hanging backward on her hand.

"Oh little boy!" Julian's mother called and took a few quick steps and caught up with them just beyond the lamppost. "Here's a bright new penny for you," and she held out the coin, which shone bronze in the dim light.

The huge woman turned and for a moment stood, her shoulders

lifted and her face frozen with frustrated rage, and stared at Julian's mother. Then all at once she seemed to explode like a piece of machinery that had been given one ounce of pressure too much. Julian saw the black fist swing out with the red pocketbook. He shut his eyes and cringed as he heard the woman shout, "He don't take nobody's pennies!" When he opened his eyes, the woman was disappearing down the street with the little boy staring wide-eyed over her shoulder. Julian's mother was sitting on the sidewalk.

"I told you not to do that," Julian said angrily. "I told you not to do that!"

He stood over her for a minute, gritting his teeth. Her legs were stretched out in front of her and her hat was on her lap. He squatted down and looked her in the face. It was totally expressionless. "You got exactly what you deserved," he said. "Now get up."

He picked up her pocketbook and put what had fallen out back in it. He picked her hat up off her lap. The penny caught his eye on the sidewalk and he picked that up and let it drop before her eyes into the purse. Then he stood up and leaned over and held his hands out to pull her up. She remained immobile. He sighed. Rising above them on either side were black apartment buildings, marked with irregular rectangles of light. At the end of the block a man came out of a door and walked off in the opposite direction. "All right," he said, "suppose somebody happens by and wants to know why you're sitting on the sidewalk?"

She took the hand and, breathing hard, pulled heavily up on it and then stood for a moment, swaying slightly as if the spots of light in the darkness were circling around her. Her eyes, shadowed and confused, finally settled on his face. He did not try to conceal his irritation. "I hope this teaches you a lesson," he said. She leaned forward and her eyes raked his face. She seemed trying to determine his identity. Then, as if she found nothing familiar about him, she started off with a headlong movement in the wrong direction.

"Aren't you going on to the Y?" he asked.

"Home," she muttered.

"Well, are we walking?"

For answer she kept going. Julian followed along, his hands behind him. He saw no reason to let the lesson she had had go without backing it up with an explanation of its meaning. She might as well be made to understand what had happened to her. "Don't think that was just an uppity Negro woman," he said. "That was the whole colored race which will no longer take your condescending pennies. That was your black double. She can wear the same hat as you, and to be sure," he added gratuitously (because he thought it was funny), "it looked better on her than it did on you. What all this means," he said, "is that the old world is gone. The old manners are obsolete and your graciousness is not worth a damn." He thought bitterly of the house that had been lost for him. "You aren't who you think you are," he said.

She continued to plow ahead, paying no attention to him. Her hair had come undone on one side. She dropped her pocketbook and took no notice. He stooped and picked it up and handed it to her but she did not take it.

"You needn't act as if the world had come to an end," he said, "because it hasn't. From now on you've got to live in a new world and face a few realities for a change. Buck up," he said, "it won't kill you."

She was breathing fast.

"Let's wait on the bus," he said.

"Home," she said thickly.

"I hate to see you behave like this," he said. "Just like a child. I should be able to expect more of you." He decided to stop where he was and make her stop and wait for a bus. "I'm not going any farther," he said, stopping. "We're going on the bus."

She continued to go on as if she had not heard him. He took a few steps and caught her arm and stopped her. He looked into her face and caught his breath. He was looking into a face he had never seen before. "Tell Grandpa to come get me," she said.

He stared, stricken.

"Tell Caroline to come get me," she said.

Stunned, he let her go and she lurched forward again, walking as if one leg were shorter than the other. A tide of darkness seemed to be sweeping her from him. "Mother!" he cried. "Darling, sweetheart, wait!" Crumpling, she fell to the pavement. He dashed forward and fell at her side, crying, "Mamma, Mamma!" He turned her over. Her face was fiercely distorted. One eye, large and staring, moved slightly to the left as if it had become unmoored. The other remained fixed on him, raked his face again, found nothing and closed.

"Wait here, wait here!" he cried and jumped up and began to run for help toward a cluster of lights he saw in the distance ahead of him. "Help, help!" he shouted, but his voice was thin, scarcely a thread of sound. The lights drifted farther away the faster he ran and his feet moved numbly as if they carried him nowhere. The tide of darkness seemed to sweep him back to her, postponing from moment to moment his entry into the world of guilt and sorrow.

Gabriel García-Márquez *(1928–) was born in the village of Aracataca, Colombia. After studying law, at which he was unhappy, he began writing as a journalist and film critic and traveled throughout Colombia, Venezuela, Mexico, Europe, and the United States. Marquez's fiction draws upon his own experiences in Aracataca as well as upon the more general Colombian disturbances of the 1950s. His stories were first collected as* The Funerals of the Grandmother *(1962). He wrote three novels before publishing* One Hundred Years of Solitude *(1967). This mythic saga of the Buendía family has appeared in some eighteen languages and won prizes in Italy and France. His most recent collection of stories is* Leaf Storm and Other Stories.

The Handsomest Drowned Man in the World

GABRIEL GARCÍA-MÁRQUEZ

A Tale for Children

The first children who saw the dark and slinky bulge approaching through the sea let themselves think it was an enemy ship. Then they saw it had no flags or masts and they thought it was a whale. But when it washed up on the beach, they removed the clumps of seaweed, the jellyfish tentacles, and the remains of fish and flotsam, and only then did they see that it was a drowned man.

They had been playing with him all afternoon, burying him in the sand and digging him up again, when someone chanced to see them and spread the alarm in the village. The men who carried him to the nearest house noticed that he weighed more than any dead man they had ever known, almost as much as a horse, and they said to each other that maybe he'd been floating too long and the water had got into his bones. When they laid him on the floor they said he'd been taller than all other men because there was barely enough room for him in the house, but they thought that maybe the ability to keep on growing after death was part of the nature of certain drowned men. He had the smell of the sea about him and only his shape gave one to suppose that it was the corpse of a human being, because the skin was covered with a crust of mud and scales.

They did not even have to clean off his face to know that the dead man was a stranger. The village was made up of only twenty-odd wooden houses that had stone courtyards with no flowers and which were spread about on the end of a desertlike cape. There was so little land that mothers always went about with the fear that the wind would carry off their children and the few dead that the years had caused among them had to be thrown off the cliffs. But the sea was calm and bountiful and all the men fit into seven boats. So when they found the drowned man they simply had to look at one another to see that they were all there.

That night they did not go out to work at sea. While the men went to find out if anyone was missing in neighboring villages, the women stayed behind to care for the drowned man. They took the mud off with grass swabs, they removed the underwater stones entangled in his hair, and they scraped the crust off with tools used for scaling fish. As they were doing that they noticed that the vegetation on him came from faraway oceans and deep water and his clothes were in tatters, as if he had sailed through labyrinths of coral. They noticed too that he bore his death with pride, for he did not have the lonely look of other drowned men who came out of the sea or that haggard, needy look of men who drowned in rivers. But only when they finished cleaning him off did they become aware of the kind of man he was and it left them breathless. Not only was he the tallest, strongest, most virile, and best built man they had ever seen, but even though they were looking at him there was no room for him in their imagination.

They could not find a bed in the village large enough to lay him on nor was there a table solid enough to use for his wake. The tallest men's holiday pants would not fit him, nor the fattest ones' Sunday shirts, nor the shoes of the one with the biggest feet. Fascinated by his huge size and his beauty, the women then decided to make him some pants from a large piece of sail and a shirt from some bridal brabant linen so that he could continue through his death with dignity. As they sewed, sitting in a circle and gazing at the corpse between stitches, it seemed to them that the wind had never been so steady nor the sea so restless as on that night and they supposed that the change had something to do with the dead man. They thought that if that magnificent man had lived in the village, his house would have had the widest doors, the highest ceiling, and the strongest floor, his bedstead would have been made from a midship frame held together by iron bolts, and his wife would have been the happiest woman. They thought that he would have had so much authority that he could have drawn fish out of the sea simply by calling their names and that he would have put so much work into his land that springs would have burst forth from among the rocks so that he would have been able to plant flowers on the cliffs. They secretly compared him to their own men, thinking that for all their lives theirs were incapable of doing what he could do in one night, and they ended up dismissing them deep in their hearts as the weakest, meanest, and most useless creatures on earth. They were wandering through that maze of fantasy when the oldest woman, who as the oldest had looked upon the drowned man with more compassion than passion, sighed:

"He has the face of someone called Esteban."

It was true. Most of them had only to take another look at him to see that he could not have any other name. The more stubborn among them, who were the youngest, still lived for a few hours with the illusion that when they put his clothes on and he lay among the flowers in patent leather shoes his name might be Lautaro. But it was a vain illusion. There had not been enough canvas, the poorly cut and worse sewn pants were too tight, and the hidden strength of his heart popped the buttons on his shirt. After midnight the whistling of the wind died down and the sea fell into its Wednesday drowsiness. The silence put an end to any last doubts: he was Esteban. The women who had dressed him, who had combed his hair, had cut his nails and shaved him were unable to hold back a shudder of pity when they had to resign themselves to his being dragged along the ground. It was then that they understood how unhappy he must have been with that huge body since it bothered him even after death. They could see him in life, condemned to going through doors sideways, cracking his head on crossbeams, remaining on his feet during visits, not knowing what to do with his soft, pink, sea-lion hands while the lady of the house looked for her most resistant chair and begged him, frightened to death, sit here, Esteban, please, and he, leaning against the wall, smiling, don't bother, ma'am, I'm fine where I am, his heels raw and his back roasted from having done the same thing so many times whenever he paid a visit, don't bother, ma'am, I'm fine where I am, just to avoid the embarrassment of breaking up the chair, and never knowing perhaps that the ones who said don't go, Esteban, at least wait till the coffee's ready, were the ones who later on would whisper the big boob finally left, how nice, the handsome fool has gone. That was what the women were thinking beside the body a little before dawn. Later, when they covered his face with a handkerchief so that the light would not bother him, he looked so forever dead, so defenseless, so much like their men that the first furrows of tears opened in their hearts. It was one of the younger ones who began the weeping. The others, coming to, went from sighs to wails, and the more they sobbed the more they felt like weeping, because the drowned man was becoming all the more Esteban for them, and so they wept so much, for he was the most destitute, most peaceful, and most obliging man on earth, poor Esteban. So when the men returned with the news that the drowned man was not from the neighboring villages either, the women felt an opening of jubilation in the midst of their tears.

"Praise the Lord," they sighed, "he's ours!"

The men thought the fuss was only womanish frivolity. Fatigued because of the difficult nighttime inquiries, all they wanted was to get rid of the bother of the newcomer once and for all before the sun grew strong on that arid, windless day. They improvised a litter with the remains of foremasts and gaffs, tying it together with rigging so that it would bear the weight of the body until they reached the cliffs. They wanted to tie the anchor from a cargo ship to him so that he would sink easily into the deepest waves, where fish are blind and divers die of nostalgia, and bad currents would not bring him back to shore, as had happened with other bodies. But the more they hurried, the more the women thought of ways to waste time. They walked about like startled hens, pecking with the sea charms on their breasts, some interfering on one side to put a scapular of the good wind on the drowned man, some on the other side to put a wrist compass on him, and after a great deal of *get away from there, woman, stay out of the way, look, you almost made me fall on top of the dead man,* the men began to feel mistrust in their livers and started grumbling about why so many main-altar decorations for a stranger, because no matter how many nails and holy-water jars he had on him, the sharks would chew him all the same, but the women kept piling on their junk relics, running back and forth, stumbling, while they released in sighs what they did not in tears, so that the men finally exploded with *since when has there ever been such a fuss over a drifting corpse, a drowned nobody, a piece of cold Wednesday meat.* One of the women, mortified by so much lack of care, then removed the handkerchief from the dead man's face and the men were left breathless too.

He was Esteban. It was not necessary to repeat it for them to recognize him. If they had been told Sir Walter Raleigh, even they might have been impressed with his gringo accent, the macaw on his shoulder, his cannibal-killing blunderbuss, but there could be only one Esteban in the world and there he was, stretched out like a sperm whale, shoeless, wearing the pants of an undersized child, and with those stony nails that had to be cut with a knife. They only had to take the handkerchief off his face to see that he was ashamed, that it was not his fault that he was so big or so heavy or so handsome, and if he had known that this was going to happen, he would have looked for a more discreet place to drown in, seriously, I even would have tied the anchor off a galleon around my neck and staggered off a cliff like someone who doesn't like things in order not to be upsetting people now with this Wednesday dead body, as you people say, in order not to be bothering anyone with this filthy piece of cold meat that doesn't have anything to do with me. There was so much truth in his manner that even the most mistrustful men, the ones who felt the bitterness of endless nights at sea fearing that their women would tire of dreaming about them and begin to dream of drowned men, even they and others who were harder still shuddered in the marrow of their bones at Esteban's sincerity.

That was how they came to hold the most splendid funeral they could conceive of for an abandoned drowned man. Some women who had gone to get flowers in the neighboring villages returned with other women who could not believe what they had been told, and those women went back for more flowers when they saw the dead man, and they brought more and more until there were so many flowers and so many people that it was hard to walk about. At the final moment it pained them to return him to the waters as an orphan and they chose a father and mother from among the best people, and aunts and uncles and cousins, so that through him all the inhabitants of the village became kinsmen. Some sailors who heard the weeping from a distance went off course and people heard of one who had himself tied to the mainmast, remembering ancient fables about sirens. While they fought for the privilege of carrying him on their shoulders along the steep escarpment by the cliffs, men and women became aware for the first time of the desolation of their streets, the dryness of their courtyard, the narrowness of their dreams as they faced the splendor and beauty of their drowned man. They let him go without an anchor so that he could come back if he wished and whenever he wished, and they all held their breath for the fraction of centuries the body took to fall into the abyss. They did not need to look at one another to realize that they were no longer all present, that they would never be. But they also knew that everything would be different from then on, that their houses would have wider doors, higher ceilings, and stronger floors so that Esteban's memory could go everywhere without bumping into beams and so that no one in the future would dare whisper the big boob finally died, too bad, the handsome fool has finally died, because they were going to paint their house fronts gay colors to make Esteban's memory eternal and they were going to break their backs digging for springs among the stones and planting flowers on the cliffs so that in future years at dawn the passengers on great liners would awaken, suffocated by the smell of gardens on the high seas, and the captain would have to come down from the bridge in his dress uniform, with his astrolabe, his pole star, and his row of war medals and, pointing to the promontory of roses on the horizon, he would say in fourteen languages, look there, where the wind is so peaceful now that it's gone to sleep beneath the beds, over there, where the sun's so bright that the sunflowers don't know which way to turn, yes, over there, that's Esteban's village.